I0831233

THE OBLIVION SAGA

J.R. MABRY

B.J. WEST

Apocryphile Press

1700 Shattuck Ave #81, Berkeley, CA 94709

www.apocryphilepress.com

Printed in the United States of America

ISBN: 978-1-947826-73-1

BY THE SAME AUTHORS...

BY J.R. MABRY & B.J. WEST

The Oblivion Saga

Oblivion Threshold • Oblivion Flight

Oblivion Quest • Oblivion Gambit

BY J.R. MABRY

The Berkeley Blackfriars Series

The Kingdom • The Power • The Glory

The Temple of All Worlds Series

The Worship of Mystery

BY B.J. WEST

Fog City Nocturne • The Stolen Sky

CONTENTS

AN OBLIVION SAGA PREQUEL

OPERATION CATSKILL

J.R. MABRY & B.J. WEST

OPERATION CATSKILL

"One of you will be Captain. One of you won't be. Are you okay with that?" Admiral Jason Tal waited. He was a patient, largely silent man—a big man, not used to suffering objections. Jeff looked at Danny. Danny looked at him.

"Answer me, dammit."

"Admiral, sir," Commander Jeff Bowers began, "I would be honored to serve under Commander Hightower." It was highly unlikely that would ever happen, but it seemed to Jeff a good way to address the question.

"I feel the same way," Commander Daniel Hightower said. "There wouldn't be any hard feelings at all. I mean…we have time, right? If Jeff makes Captain this year, I'll buy the champagne. And I know he'll do the same for me next year…or whenever."

"You always this chatty, Commander?"

"No sir. I mean, yes sir. I'm just…I'm answering your question. Sir."

The faintest hint of a smile played at the corners of Tal's brown lips. He nodded. "I'm glad to hear this from you, commanders, because I'm going to put you to the test. Captain Bowers, I'm proud to present you with your captain's bars." He leaned over his desk and held a ceremonial presentation box out to Jeff. Jeff's mouth opened, but nothing came out. Instead he simply lifted his hand and received the box. Danny looked down. Then back up at Jeff. He nodded. "Congratulations, man."

Jeff opened the box and stared. Two gold Captain's bars stared back.

"I guess you're wondering why you're finding this out now, instead of at a ceremony."

"Um…I'm proud to receive the bars however they come, sir."

"Good answer. Bullshit, but good. What I'm about to tell you is classified." Tal sat down and steepled his fingers. "Which means, for the moment, Commander Hightower, you are dismissed."

Danny and Jeff met one another's eyes for a brief second, then Hightower stood and saluted. "Yes, sir. Thank you sir." He turned and saluted Jeff. "Sir, thank you sir."

Jeff gulped. He looked down, unable to meet Danny's eyes. He gave a perfunctory salute. A moment later he and the Admiral were alone.

"Captain Bowers, we have a situation."

HE DIDN'T KNOW why they chose him, or why they'd put him in charge of Operation Catskill, but he didn't need to know. He only had one request: that Commander Hightower be his number one. Admiral Tal hadn't been too sure about that, but he granted it. Jeff had been relieved. If they were heading into the field, into the line of fire, with an untested and unfamiliar unit, he needed someone he trusted at his back.

There were lots of things he didn't know and didn't need to know. But he knew this: the captain's chair felt right. He gripped the arms of that chair as the helmsman brought them in for a landing near the Appalachian Colony.

"I've got the handshake from the Colony, Captain," Lieutenant Eliza Todd said.

"Handshake back," Jeff instructed. It was a kind of code. They had to acknowledge that they were on the Colony on official business, but did not officially state what that business was. Handshakes were unusual, but not unheard of. It just meant that a Colonial Defense Fleet maneuver was too classified for the local colonial government to know any details about it. Not that it would be hard for the governor here to guess. But the less people knew anything, the better. They needed the element of surprise.

"Shut 'er down. Lieutenant Todd, I want you here on the bridge. Once we're out, you lock this puppy up tight. Then make sure that every pixel of information from our body cams is transmitted back to Sol Station."

"Aye, sir," Todd nodded, anticipating the order.

"The rest of you, tend to your gear and meet me in the bay in seven minutes."

He turned and charged for his own cabin. He made sure his gear was in order, tended to his toilet, then headed out to the bay.

"Captain on deck!" Danny shouted. Everyone was already in place. They were suited up in combat exoskeletons, their helmets dangling from their left hands. Their right hands rested over the photon canons dangling diagonally from the straps around their necks. None of them made eye contact, but uniformly stared straight ahead at the bay doors.

"At ease," Jeff said. He handed his own rifle to Danny, who received it fluidly without appearing to look. Jeff put his hands on his hips and took a deep breath to calm himself. This was it, the moment when he would either succeed as a captain or fail miserably. His hands were sweating, but he couldn't let the men know he was nervous. He had to be rock solid for them.

"This is a need-to-know operation. And as Captain, I think you need to know what we're up against before I can ask you for your lives. Does that seem fair to you?"

"Sir, yes sir!" they responded in unison. Whoever had drilled this unit had been damned good. They were already in sync. He just needed to make sure *he* was in sync with *them*. "As you have probably heard, there has been a minor rebellion on the Appalachia Colony. The CDF sent a negotiator out to meet with both sides. That negotiator is Desmond Paart, a distinguished member of our diplomatic corps. Negotiator Paart has been kidnapped by the rebels and is being held in a farmhouse three clicks from our current location. If you're wondering why we came in dark…that's it."

He watched the comprehension alighting in their eyes. They kept them facing forward, but he could see their intelligence, their resolve, their will to put right whatever was wrong.

"The locals call the rebels 'Rednecks.' That's what we'll call them too." Jeff gave them a grim smile. "I know, I know, it's ironic, since that's what everyone calls folks on Appalatia. But they don't see themselves that way. They see themselves as loyal members of the Colonial Union, and that they are. All local attempts to communicate with the Rednecks have been unsuccessful. All CDF efforts to communicate have failed…miserably. Which is why we're here. The CDF has tried talking. It got us nowhere. Now it's time for us to act. Our orders are to locate Paart, extract him, and return him to Sol Station for debriefing. It's a simple retrieval. You've prepped for this a thousand times, and I am confident you know what you're doing. So do it."

"Sir, yes sir!" his team responded. Now there was pride in their eyes. Good. They had reason to be proud.

"Any questions?"

One of his team looked over at him.

"Lieutenant Junior Grade Mbeki? What is your question?"

"How do we locate Paart?"

"Excellent question, and a difficult one." He studied Mbeki's face and saw excitement and fear and uncertainty. He also saw that he was just a kid playing soldier. Inwardly Jeff vowed to do everything in his power to make him a real one. "His neural is offline. This could mean it's been deactivated, it could mean he's dead, it could mean it's malfunctioning. We don't know. What we *do* know is that we can't use it to locate him, dead or alive."

The idea that Paart could be dead had not yet occurred to them. He noted the barely perceptible slump in their postures in response to the notion. "We also know that Appalatia colony has picked up an unidentified radiation signature. All Diplomatic Corps members travel with what's called a Radium Pill. Crack it with your teeth and swallow it, and you start emitting a trackable level of radiation."

He saw alarm in their faces, although they tried to hide it. "Yes, it's dangerous. It's fatal if untreated. Which is why we have to extract him quickly. Lieutenant Todd is triangulating on that signature and feeding the result directly to my neural. We'll find him, I promise you that."

They looked confident. Hell, they looked eager. "Nobody messes with the CDF" was an unofficial motto, but it was widely expressed.

"We've got about four hours of dark. Call up night-vision filters for your helmets, and lock in encrypted communication code 17. Make sure your bayonet is fixed and your powder is dry." He actually heard one of the men snort involuntarily. Good. They didn't know him yet, or trust him, and he needed them on his side. "Let's head out."

JEFF'S MEN moved silently through the forest, invisible as shadows on a moonless night. Jeff saw everything around him in crisp detail through his night vision filter. The sound of his own breathing was loud in his helmet. He spoke quietly, almost in a whisper, yet everyone was hearing him fine. Operationally they were on target, but Jeff could not allow himself to relax for a second.

A CDF marine named Charlesworth was on point. He was battle hardened and had clearly put in some time—the kid was nearly thirty. He also looked like he could eat nails for lunch. Just behind him was Lucy Kai, a newbie from Seoul Colony who seemed determined to out-grizzle Charlesworth. It was all an act, but Jeff didn't challenge her. That act would serve her well out here.

Charlesworth held up a hand. Everyone froze. "Got visual confirmation on the structure."

"Show me," Jeff said. Suddenly he was seeing exactly what Charlesworth was seeing through his helmet. It looked like a small farmhouse, in some disrepair. There was farm equipment around. In the distance Jeff could see a barn to one side, looming and dark. Nearer to the house was an old-fashioned well, with rocks built up to encircle it forming a waist high barrier. Stilling his own breath, he heard a cow lowing in the distance, accompanied by the chitter of a tanik.

Accessing his neural, Jeff shrank the incoming feed from Charlesworth's helmet so that he could monitor it yet still see what was in front of him. He created another window and began to stream the radiation locator. It showed the terrain in front of them from a bird's eye perspective. A yellow glow emitted from a rectangle directly in front of their own location—a house. If Paart was alive, he was in that house. If Paart was dead, his fucking corpse was in that house.

Everything was dark. Everything was quiet. It was a good time for a surprise party. "Charlesworth, Kai, Tanner, and Lopez at the front. Tillerson, Hightower, Durand, and Chaiprasit with me at the back. Move it out!"

Holding rifles at the ready, he watched his team diverge into two streams. He followed one to the back of the farmhouse and waited for the signal from Charlesworth. Then he heard the breathy whisper, "All in position, sir."

Jeff could hear his own pulse pounding in his helmet. He took a deep breath and let it out slowly. "Take out those doors on three. One…two…three!"

He heard a percussive crack that came from outside his helmet and he followed as his men rushed up the rickety wooden stairs and into the house.

"Kitchen is clear," he heard Durand say. Jeff saw a large, almost industrial sized sink, a washboard beside it. There was a cook-all unit, but it didn't look functional. A propane stove was set up on the table.

"Captain, we need you in the front room." That was Kai's voice.

Jeff pushed past the rear team, down a short hall, until he saw the flash of CDF helmets. "What do you have?" Jeff asked. But then he stopped.

There was no light, but that didn't stop them. With the aid of the helmets he could see just fine. And what he saw was eight children, five boys and three girls, wide awake, sitting stock still, eyes wide. The youngest looked to be about four, the oldest about thirteen. Between the two eldest was a broken man who could only have been Paart.

He appeared to be unconscious. His hands were tied together and both eyes were blackened. There were cuts on his face and arms. An olfactory notice popped up in his field of vision indicating fecal matter. Paart had shit himself while he was out. Of course the children had done nothing about that, but they had to smell it.

"Medic, check him out," Jeff said. Tillerson slung her rifle to her shoulder and pulled out a diagnostic wand as she knelt beside Paart.

"Captain, what the fuck is going on here?" Danny asked. It was rhetorical. Danny was saying exactly what Jeff was thinking.

The children were spooky. They stared at his team—at him—with defiance. They were silent as stones. He didn't see any fear in their eyes. He did see hate, though, and plenty of it.

Finally, one of them spoke, one of the younger boys. "Ye're the bad men."

"Shut up, Meeker," one of the older ones said.

Jeff ignored them. "How is he?"

Tillerson was just pocketing the wand. "His vitals are strong and stable. He's in shock, though. I need to get him back to the ship as soon as possible."

Jeff nodded. "Our orders are to eliminate the captors and retrieve Paart."

Everyone on his team seemed to freeze, and every eye turned to him. "I know what you're thinking," Jeff said, addressing his whole team. "There's no way we can execute a room full of children."

"You'd be surprised at what you can do," Charlesworth said. He ratcheted his rifle to a different setting, then added, "Sir."

"All right, we're not going to take them out, but we *are* going to take them down. Medic, I want a morphex prick for each of them. Adjust for body weight—just estimate, Tillerson, we don't have much time. Just make sure you give them enough to put them under for a few hours. Do it fast."

"Should we question them first, sir?" Kai asked.

"No time for chasing rabbits, and I wouldn't trust anything they've been coached to say," Jeff said. "So no."

Jeff watched as, one-by-one, Tillerson sized up each child and adjusted the dosage before stabbing them with the morphex prick. Most of them emitted a howl of protest, but that didn't slow her down. The first of them were just nodding off by the time she reached the last of them. Jeff waited until their lids were drooping too before issuing his next orders.

"Charlesworth, I want you to carry Paart," Jeff said. Charlesworth nodded and slung his rifle without protest. He was the strongest and could easily manage by himself, which would help with their speed and mobility.

"I don't like it, sir," Hightower said. "If the children are here, where are the adults?"

Jeff froze. It was such an obvious question. He felt like an idiot.

"Sir, this is a setup."

Danny was right. Jeff's mind raced. He felt a swoon of vertigo, and struggled to master himself.

"Someone among the Appalachian Colony brass sold us out," Danny continued.

Jeff felt sick. Danny should be calling the shots here, not him. Danny was seeing much more clearly. He forced himself to focus.

"Everyone grab a child," Jeff said. "Use it as a human shield. They won't shoot their own kids."

There were more of them than there were children, but soon all but the smallest of them and Jeff himself had a child in one arm and a rifle in the other.

"Okay, I know this is going to slow us down some, but we only need to carry them until we get some shelter. And the ship isn't far away. So let's move out in single file, quickly as we can, going back exactly the same way as we came in. Charlesworth, I want you and Paart in the middle of the line. Go!"

Kai took point. She was physically the most diminutive, so she picked up the smallest child. Jeff was proud to see that she handled her weapon like a seasoned pro, and the child like a mother. The kid had range.

Jeff put every sensor on a hair trigger alert and took up the rear. The only one without a child over his shoulder, he held his own photon rifle ready to pick off any threat to his men. He cleared the stairs and turned around, watching behind the single-file snake they formed as they moved across the farmyard.

"Captain, we got trouble," Kai said.

With a blink, Jeff called up the view from her helmet. Resizing it, he left the line and began jogging toward the front, toward Kai. He understood why she was concerned—a single child had stepped into their path, standing between them and a well. She was barefoot, her hair was greasy and unkempt, dirt or soot smudged her face. She was also carrying an old-fashioned carpet bag.

Jeff arrived at the front of the line and put out a hand, keeping Kai from moving forward. He looked up and blinked, making an adjustment in his sensors. When he looked back down he saw an electronic signature emitting from the carpet bag. He also saw a glint of silver in the child's hand. Adjusting his helmet's zoom, he saw that it was actually a pair of handcuffs, one fixed to the child's wrist, the other to the handle of the carpet bag. The child's eyes were wide, her face slack with fear.

"Bomb," Jeff said.

Before he could move, Jeff caught a blur out of the corner of his eye. He turned his helmet just in time to see Charlesworth snatch the child up in both hands and, in a single, fluid motion, pitch her head first into the well. Jeff was horrified, his mind flashing on the image of the child hitting the side of the well on the way down, then drowning at the bottom. But he needn't have worried about that. The child could not have fallen half the length of the well before the bomb went off.

The blast knocked all of them off their feet. And that was a good thing, too, since no sooner did the reverberations from the blast subside than the shooting began. Photon charges blasted in a random pattern over their heads. "Stay down," Jeff bellowed. Rolling onto his elbows, he looked around, desperate for some sort of shelter. The house was no good—it was wood, soon to be splinters. He saw a low rock wall about fifty paces north of the yard. "Shelter at 12 o'clock. Crawl," he ordered.

It was difficult for them to crawl with unconscious children in tow. They hadn't gone more than six feet when Todd pinged him. A CDF report spilled out over the inside curve of his helmet about a rash of kidnappings in the colony. Jeff's heart sank. These kids weren't going to be much of a shield—they weren't the Rednecks' kids.

He cursed himself. He should have seen it. The kids with them were well fed, they were reasonably clean. Their hair was stylishly cut.

They were not Redneck kids. The girl with the carpet bag—*that* was a Redneck kid. And they had sacrificed her. These kids weren't going to deter the Rednecks for a second. And every moment they continued in the company of his men, they were targets.

"Lose the kids," he ordered. "Just leave them where they are. They're low, and they're not moving. They'll be fine. We need the speed, and we can send the coordinates back for a rescue." None of them had seen the report, so none of them knew what he was talking about. He cursed himself. Sloppy.

"But Captain—"

"Do it. Double time it to that wall."

He wasn't sure how much protection that wall would be—mostly because he didn't know where the photon blasts were coming from. A stone wall would protect them, but which side of it should they be on? He didn't know. And what if they were surrounded? Then the wall wouldn't do a damned bit of good.

Todd pinged his neural, and a trajectory analysis unspooled in his helmet. *God bless her*, he thought. The report clearly showed that none of the blasts they'd witnessed so far had originated from beyond the wall.

It was coming up quickly, and Jeff had point. He would model what he wanted them to do. As he drew near the wall, he rocked back on his haunches and sprang up and over the top of it. A white-hot bolt of pain shot through his calf. *Tagged*, he thought, as he felt the meat of his body drop ungracefully behind the protection of the rock wall.

Others followed, and some of them were hit, too. He was relieved to see Charlesworth drop the meat sack of Paart's body over, followed closely by an expertly executed tuck and roll. Only when the last of them had cleared did Jeff glance down at his own leg—a clean shot through his chamo trousers. The shot had missed his body armor by mere millimeters. *Damn it.* Fortunately, the shot was clean through and hadn't hit bone. It would hurt like hell later, but his endorphins were so high he didn't feel a thing.

"Report, people."

"Mbeki's shot," Tillerson said.

"How bad?"

"Through the hand. Administering the Morphex now."

"Give him a dose of 'phetamine while you're at it. I don't want him in pain, but I don't want him asleep, either."

"Aye, sir."

"Anyone else?"

There were several, but the body armor had stopped the worst of it. Jeff breathed a deep sigh of relief. They were all there, they were all accounted for, they were all mobile.

Jeff detached a sensor probe from his body armor and raised it above the edge of the wall. Instantly, the view from the probe filled his helmet. The shooting had stopped, but he saw the heat signatures of the shooters. They were a couple hundred meters away, some further than others. A couple were sheltered behind the house, but most were in the woods opposite them. He turned and looked for heat signatures in the woods behind them. None. The problem was that their extraction point wasn't behind them, it was across the yard and through the woods filled with hostiles.

Out of the corner of his eye, he saw several heat signatures moving —they were attempting to flank them. Time was running out.

A message pinged in his neural. He looked up and saw an order from CDF command.

—Power through to extraction point. All haste.

Were they crazy? Their weaponry was not superior to the Rednecks'—they all had photon rifles. He had six men—seven counting himself. But he counted nearly thirty among the Rednecks—and that was just what he could see. Who knew how many more were lying in wait in the woods?

He sent a message back.

—Outnumbered. Going to try to lose them in the woods.

Of course, that was a problematic plan. These were the Rednecks' woods. They were on the rebels' home turf. Still, Jeff was from Achorage. He knew the woods, and in his gut he knew it was the best chance they had.

—Negative. Power through.

The signature of the message was the highest rank. It was coming from Admiral Tal, or at least from his immediate team, which was the same as coming from the Admiral himself.

"Shit," Jeff said out loud. If he listened to his gut, he'd be in direct violation of orders. If he obeyed, he'd be lucky to get half of his team home alive.

He looked toward the distance, toward the wall as it stretched out into the woods, saw heat signatures leaping over it about half a kilometer away. No time. There was only one way forward if he wanted to keep his job and his freedom. The problem was he would need to also keep his life.

"New orders to proceed directly toward extraction."

"But—" Kai began, but he cut her off.

"I know, Ensign, but this comes from the top. This is how we're going to do it. There's nothing large enough for us to shelter behind together, but there are lots of smaller possibilities. I want you to scatter. Watch each others' backs if you can, but basically this is going to be a sprint to the finish line. Seek what shelter you can find, and make sure you take at least two of these bastards down with you."

"What about Paart, sir?" Danny asked.

"I'm going to lay down and I want you to fix him to my body armor with plastic ties."

"Sir?"

"I'll adjust my center of gravity in the exoskeleton control panel on the fly."

"That's suicide, sir," Tillerson said. "Besides, you're hit."

"I'll let the frame do the work. I'll be fine. Just do it."

Jeff lay down as if he were letting Paart spoon him. His men pounced on him, four of them fixing ties to his limbs, and another fastening Paart's clothing to his exoskeleton at his midsection via his leather belt. When they were done, Jeff could barely move. But he couldn't let that stop him.

"Okay, soldiers, scatter! Get back to the ship any way you can."

"But, sir—" Kai began.

"Move it, Ensign Kai!"

She did. He opened the battle armor control panel and began wildly making adjustments. When he was done, he barely felt Paart's weight on his back, on his limbs. The armor was powered, intended to compensate for high-gravity situations. It wasn't built for this kind of assist, but it wasn't going to break it, either. Jeff did a quick scan and saw more hostiles jumping the wall on both sides. Enemy control of their flank was almost complete. He looked directly behind him, at the hillside, the forest, the one place his gut told them was the road to safety.

I'm a soldier, dammit, he said to himself. *I follow orders.*

He turned his back on the wooded hill and faced the wall. He scouted beyond it, found what looked like an old-fashioned tractor, and ran to his right along the wall until it was directly in front of him. He scrambled over the wall, and began to run. He felt wildly off balance, the heavy, motionless body of the diplomat pulling him backwards. He could strengthen his muscles with the armor controls, but nothing he adjusted seemed to help with the balance.

He'd only gone a couple steps when a photon blast tore at his left arm. The battle armor absorbed the worst of it, but he felt the sting and smelled burning flesh just the same. He dove for the cover of the tractor and shuddered as a blast hit the metal caging of the engine. A corner of his mind knew that if they hit the fuel source, the machine could explode, but he pushed back at the thought.

He searched for another way forward, but he as he did so, he couldn't help but see the progress of his men. Charlesworth had returned to the well, he was hunkered down, waiting for a break in the fire, probably hoping to bolt toward the barn. But a Redneck sniper on the second floor of the barn got a bead on the top of his head. Jeff saw the glowing red dot on Charlesworth's helmet a split second before it erupted and began raining brain matter and blood.

What the fuck good is that helmet? Jeff wondered. He caught movement out of the corner of his eye and saw Ensign Kai creeping along the corner of the farmhouse. He saw what she was trying to do—once she reached the corner, if it were clear, she could dash into the woods beyond it. Then it was a straight shot toward the shuttle.

He held his breath as she edged to the corner. She held a sensor beyond it, to get a visual read, when the hand that held the sensor exploded in a blast of light. Her armor quickly closed off, torniqueting the blood flow, but the blast had pivoted her out into the open and the hostiles had opened fire. One of the blasts hit her oxygen tank turning her into a human bomb.

Jeff watched the wall of the house buckle and the roof cave in on one side.

He looked to his left and saw Tillerson stepping gingerly over the body of one of the unconscious children. Her foot got caught in mid stride, flipping her onto her back. A sniper did the rest, and quickly, hitting her armor in a score of places. Jeff was sure it stopped most of the blasts, but it couldn't have stopped it all. He watched her struggle to get onto all fours, then she jerked and laid still.

Jeff felt a hand on his back and spun, swinging wildly. The armor overcompensated, and he actually leaped several feet into the air, landing with a thud that shook the tractor.

It was Danny. He'd been hit, and was carrying his rifle in his left hand, his non-dominant hand. His right hand was a bloody tangle of sinew and bone.

"I'm going to cover you," he said, "and you're going to complete this fucking mission."

"Who's calling the shots here, soldier?" Jeff asked.

"You are, sir. Now get moving before I say something insubordinate."

Jeff turned. There was only one route ahead of him: toward the ruin of the house, then *under* the house and out the other side.

"Move it!" Danny called.

Jeff did. He squatted, gathering his strength in his legs, then he released it, dashing for the house in a zig-zag pattern that actually succeeded in dodging a couple photon blasts. Jeff felt a jerk pull at his back. He called up a diagnostic tool and discovered that the weight on his back was no longer breathing. Paart's heart had stopped, too. The diplomat had probably taken a photon blast to the head. Jeff dove for the space under the house's porch, and allowed the hardness of his helmet to smash through the boards. It didn't matter what a move like that would do to Paart's head or body—not now.

Once under the house, Jeff rolled over and waved to Danny to follow. Danny crouched and sprang, then danced like a puppet as his armor was riddled with photon blasts. When his head exploded, Jeff buried his face in the gauntlets of his armor and howled. He loved Danny like a brother, and he would never be able to unsee that. He would always have the vision of his friend's head erupting into gas as his farewell memory.

"God fucking dammit!" he screamed aloud. He twisted around and began to crawl toward the back of the house, over the flinty carcasses of beetles and the brittle bones of rats. He was no longer aware of the body strapped to his back. He fired his rifle at the back of the house, then fired it again. He kept at it until he had nearly depleted his power supply, but had made a hole large enough to crawl through.

He scrambled through it, and without even looking around, made a mad dash for the woods. He heard the pop of photon rifles from what seemed like every direction. He nearly lost his balance as the shots connected, throwing bits of gore from his passenger looping into the air behind him. He could not have asked for better armor, however. Paart's body attracted and absorbed the lion's share of the photon blasts directed at him, and by the time Jeff reached the green sanctuary of the forest, much of the diplomat's body had been pecked from his bones.

The image in Jeff's brain was of himself being ridden by a skeleton —death tied to his heels and close as his shadow—hugging him in a macabre embrace as he ran full tilt and unseeing into a consuming sea of green.

When Jeff opened his eyes, he was surrounded by a sterile white nothingness. A blue-black blur invaded his vision. He struggled to focus. "Go easy, son." It was Admiral Tal's voice. "You've had a concussion. A bad one. It's going to take you a while to recover."

So he was in an infirmary. Admiral Tal was with him. Was anyone else with him? "Who's here?" Jeff asked.

"Just me and the nurse."

"What happened?"

"According to your armor records, you're lucky you made it back to us."

Suddenly Jeff's memory rushed back. He stiffened, overwhelmed by the onslaught.

"Woah, just…take it easy."

"I'm going to need to sedate him," a younger male voice said.

"Not just yet," Tal said.

"My unit—" Jeff began. "What happened to my unit?"

"You don't remember?"

"Of course I remember," Jeff snapped. "I mean…who made it?"

A long silence followed. "Captain, I don't know how to tell you this. You…only you. Only you made it. You and your communications officer—Lieutenant Todd, was it? You left her to mind the shuttle."

"Danny?"

"No, son."

Jeff choked on the phlegm in his throat, then gasped for air.

"Admiral—" the nurse said.

A blurry hand blocked the light—Tal holding the nurse back.

"I'm sorry, son."

"Who gave that order?" Jeff asked. "We could have escaped into the woods, we could have…I could have saved some of them. Who gave that order?"

"Which order, Captain?"

"The order to power through to the shuttle across the yard."

There was another long silence.

"Did *you* give that order?" Jeff demanded. "Did you?"

Jeff heard the Admiral sigh. "Captain, we have no record of that order."

THE OBLIVION SAGA • BOOK 1

OBLIVION THRESHOLD

J.R. MABRY & B.J. WEST

The one principle of hell is “I am my own.”
—George McDonald

PROLOGUE

[STRING 310]

The creature reared back, beholding Stan with its hundred eyes, the hairs around its mandibles quivering. It assumed a fighting stance, but just as Stan stabbed his thumb at it, it retreated into a seam of the navigation control panel.

"Lemme guess—spider lives to torment you another day," Tag teased him, her lips turning up in a mocking smile.

Stan fumed. He never seemed to be quick enough. There were a thousand spiders on this ship, and it seemed they all lived to torment him personally.

"Focus, people. Remember: first contact." Captain Santos' voice was kind but firm, but Stan needed no reminding. Neither did Tag. From the moment they'd detected the alien vessels headed their way, no one talked about anything else.

At first, they'd thought it was just an asteroid, big and fast. But projections showed it would shoot past the Manila Colony without causing any damage—until it changed course and began accelerating. That's when they knew it was a ship, and not a Colonial Defense ship, either. As the object got closer, they realized it was actually a plurality of objects—not a ship, but a *fleet* of ships moving in an almost impossibly tight formation.

At first, people had gone crazy—terrified that it was an attack. But as they got closer, analytics announced that there were no weapons aboard—at least none that they could detect, none that were even remotely like ours. People had relaxed. They became giddy, even. They had outfitted a small passenger liner, *The Avalon*, as a diplomatic vessel and rechristened her the *The Envoy*. And they were on their way to welcome the first sentient species humans had yet encountered. Tag had made party hats out of plastic hygiene sheathing, but one arched eyebrow from the captain had nixed that idea.

Stan checked the flight controls just to be sure he hadn't messed anything up in his arachnidicidal rage. No. They were sitting perfectly still, directly in the path of the oncoming fleet. Stan felt his muscles relax—a bit.

"I keep imagining what they'll be like," Tag whispered.

"Uh-huh. And what are they like?" Stan asked, not really paying attention.

"Oh, you know, all muscly and shit. Green maybe. *Big*. Big parts, too." He shook his head at her erotic fantasies, but in his peripheral vision he saw her do a weapons check.

"Captain!" Science Chief Andrada shouted curtly. "They are dropping out of superluminal."

"On screen, please."

The forward viewer switched to an external view, where several ships snapped into view.

"What the fuck?" Captain Santos rose from his command chair and took a couple steps, squinting at the screen. "Katz, zoom in on the oncoming fleet—maximum power."

The viewscreen refocused, and when it did, Stan gasped.

"Why are these ships…shimmering?"

It was true. Stan hadn't noticed it before they'd zoomed in, but it was obvious now. The surface of the ships reminded him of moonlight on a lake when the winds were high—the choppy surface rippling with light…just exactly as these were doing.

"What are we seeing, Andrada?"

"Checking, sir."

Stan saw the science officer close one eye as his hands flew over his panel, no doubt checking one bank of sensors on his neural while running all manner of remote analyses on his console. Time seemed to stand still as they waited. In the meantime, the rippling surface of the ships became larger, more defined, more turbulent.

"Andrada, I need some answers," the captain barked.

"Sorry, sir, I'm…the hull surfaces aren't like any metal or alloy we know of. But what we're seeing…isn't the surface."

"If it isn't the surface, what the fuck is it?"

Stan felt the hair on the back of his arms and neck rise up. He noticed he was holding his breath. He forced himself to exhale.

"Sir, I can't say with certainty. But I can tell you what it looks like."

"For Christ's sake, spit it out."

"From everything I see here, we aren't actually looking at the ships' *hulls*. We're seeing what looks like beings fixed to the hulls…or *clinging* to the hulls."

"Do you mean to tell me, Andrada, that these aliens travel on the outside of their ships rather than the inside?"

"It would appear so, sir. Yes."

Stan glanced at the captain. His eyebrows bunched in confusion. "How can that possibly—"

"Sir, I've got something else. It's too small to see visually just yet, but sensors show that a number of the…aliens, I guess…have launched themselves from the hull and are…god, they're headed right for us."

"Maybe this is how they say 'hello'?" Stan offered.

"Maybe this is how they say 'Die, bitch,'" the captain answered. "Target weapons."

"Targeting weapons, sir," Tag said. "I've got a lock on the lead alien, and the next five…God, sir—"

"Navigation, get us out of here. Anywhere *except* back to New Manila."

Stan shut his eyes and plotted a course through his neural. He implemented it internally and then opened his eyes again. He watched the star horizon on his panel swing as the ship came about. He tapped out minor course corrections manually as the granular information from stellar cartography began to feed into his brain. *Don't slam into an asteroid while we're making our escape*, he told himself.

"Scans show 759 aliens have now launched themselves toward us," Andrada's voice was pitched much higher than usual and Stan could hear the panic in it. "Oh…make that 15,657."

Someone whistled. Stan couldn't tell who.

"Fire at will, Lieutenant," Captain Santos ordered. "Wide sweep. Get as many of those bastards as you can. Engines to full now! GO! GO! GO!"

"Sir, how can any species survive in the vacuum of space?" Reyes asked.

"I'll be as fascinated as you are to hear how the xenobiologists explain that, Commander."

"Sir, we're accelerating as hard as we can, and rigging for superluminal," Stan said. He could hear the distant whine of the engines climbing in pitch.

"They're gaining on us, Sir." Andrada said. "Our speed is 500K and climbing…nearly 600K now."

"And their speed?"

"Aliens are at 1800K now. They'll be here—"

Stan heard the sound of metal on metal, as if someone had just pounded the outer hull with a sledgehammer. Stan heard its reverberations even above the engine's whine.

Tag whirled in her seat, her eyes rolled up into the back of her head, interfacing with her neural. "Suggest an EM burst on the outer hull."

"That'll take all our electronics down until we can reboot—"

Andrada's voice was drowned out by the sound of a hundred sledgehammers. As if someone were building a railroad on the hull of the ship, metal struck metal all up and down the length of the ship, the blows coming more rapidly by the second. The din grew exponentially louder as thousands of creatures began pounding at the hull.

"Do it!" Santos shouted above the noise. "Full EM burst."

Tag squinted as she initiated the burst—and then Stan heard a pop.

The lights went out. His neural went offline. The whine of the engines disintegrated into silence. Stan felt a panicked vertigo as the artificial gravity cut out, leaving them floating blind and deaf in space.

"At least—" Andrade's voice began, but he was interrupted by the sound of metal pounding on metal once more.

CHAPTER ONE

Summoned. *It's never good news when you're summoned,* Jeff thought. Good news can be handled by neural. Performance reviews can be handled by neural. Mission assignments can be handled by neural. Only bad things have to be handled in person. They'd provided him with a very comfortable apartment, oppressively cheery in décor, specifically designed to offend few and please none. He hated it.

There were those who would say he hated everyone and everything, but they would be wrong. He would be the first to admit that he could be abrasive and anti-social, but he knew it was because he cared too much. He cared too much and had failed.

The call light blinked and the emitter directly below it chirped. "Showtime," he said aloud and permitted himself a groan as he stood and straightened his dress blues.

He touched the pad near the door and it slid open with a quiet pneumatic release. Captain Taylor stood just outside his door, more or less at parade rest.

"Jo," he said.

"Jeff," she said, turning briskly and power walking in the direction of the space station's command center. He forced himself to keep up with her. "You cleaned up good," she said without looking at him.

He grunted. He liked Jo, more than he liked to admit. But they were both captains, and if anything, her ambition far exceeded his. There had been something between them once, but that was a long time ago. A part of him resented the situation, longed for things to be different, but he never blamed her.

It was kind of her to come for him—she could have sent a lackey.

"Where are we going?" he asked.

"Your orders were intentionally vague, so I hope you weren't obsessing over them. You're not in trouble or anything."

Jeff's eyebrows shot up. On the one hand, that was welcome news. On the other, the mystery just got deeper. "In that case, why not just handle this remotely?"

"How should I know? Maybe the admiral just likes to watch introverts squirm. Maybe it's a cruel streak. On the other hand...."

"What?"

"I had an uncle who was a monk, even a supermonk, you might say. A hermit. I don't mean it metaphorically, he was literally a hermit. Took vows and everything. Did you know that hermits are required to come together with their fellow monks once a day?"

"No."

"Neither did I. It avoids morbid isolation."

They walked down a long hall in uncomfortable silence.

"What are you trying to say, Jo?"

She got into an omnilift and only faced him when the door shut. In her own hard, angular way she was still pretty after all these years. "You can't punish yourself forever, Jeff."

He blinked but didn't answer her.

"Your isolation looks a lot like misanthropy, and it's being noticed."

"I thought you said this wasn't a dressing down."

"It isn't. But you're a hair's breadth from it. It's why I wanted to fetch you myself. Give you a heads-up. Warn you off before—"

"Before I cross the invisible line that separates pain-in-the-ass from liability?"

"That's less diplomatic than I would have said it, but sure."

"And this is you…taking me aside…as a friend?"

"As a colleague who respects you and doesn't want to see you wasting your potential." She rolled her eyes as the lift slowed to a stop. "Goddammit, yes! As a friend."

"Can you give me a heads-up what this is all about?"

"Not a chance, soldier."

They exited and Jeff noted they were outside the office of Admiral Paul Jennings.

"Jennings?"

"It's important, Jeff."

He whistled. The station housed a lot of the Colonial Defense Fleet's senior brass, but he hadn't expected to be summoned to the very top. "Why so hush-hush?"

"You'll find out soon enough."

"You sure there's nothing I need to know?"

"Relax. Just be yourself. On second thought, it would be a good idea to make eye contact and speak to people."

"Very funny."

"I *am* trying to help."

He knew that. He knew the complex political reality they both lived in, all too well. He knew exactly in which ways her hands were tied. He knew how closely she could skirt the issue—whatever it was. She wasn't going to compromise herself for a moment, but she was still reaching out. "If I registered human emotion like a normal person, I'd be touched," he told her.

"I'll take that as a thank you."

"You do that." He tightened his jaw. The truth was, he *was* touched. It had been a long time since anyone had gone out on a limb for him. This wasn't exactly limb crawling, but it was *something*. To his surprise, he found he missed such somethings.

The door slid open and he heard Jennings' rough voice call, "Come!"

Jo gave him an "after you" motion with her hand.

"Huh," he said, and entered.

Admiral Jennings was standing at the ready, his hands behind his back, his face betraying nothing, except perhaps avuncular regard. A large round table took up most of the room, surrounded by stylish black chairs.

"Captain Bowers, thank you for coming," Jennings said.

He almost replied *'Didn't really have a choice'*, but thought better of it and simply nodded.

"That will be all, Captain Taylor."

Jo shot Jeff an encouraging glance and took her leave. Once the door had slid closed behind her, Admiral Jennings moved toward the wet bar. "I hear you two have history."

"A very short history," Bowers said. "We're both married to the CDF."

"You're not the only ones." Jennings poured himself a whiskey, and another for Bowers. He handed the glass to the captain.

"I don't really—"

"Yes, you do. You're going to need that, son."

It had been a very long time since Jeff had been called "son." Jeff accepted the glass and took a sip of the whiskey. It wasn't bad, which didn't surprise him, knowing what he did about the Admiral.

"You indicate in your file that you don't believe you are command material. But that's not what Admiral Tal or Colonel Mattocks or Captain Taylor or…God, anyone who has ever worked with you or commanded you says."

"Permission to speak freely, sir?"

Jennings waved his hand, as if batting protocol away like a pesky fly. "Of course."

"A man's own opinion of himself ought to be worth something."

"When you were on the Catskill operation, Captain, you made a judgment call in the field—one that any of us might have made in the same circumstances—*would have made,* most likely. It turned out to be the wrong call. That doesn't make you a bad commander."

"Is there anything else, sir?"

Jennings sighed and pulled up a star chart. It flickered in the air above the round meeting table, but quickly stabilized. Jeff walked toward it and within a few seconds got his bearings. "The Gliese system. That's where New Manila is," he said.

"Was."

Jeff's head jerked toward the Admiral. "Was?"

"We held the news of it back a cycle, but it's going to hit the feed very soon. They were expecting to make first contact."

"Sure. Can't access the feed and hear about anything else."

"As the aliens got closer, the Colony launched a reconnaissance ship. It was destroyed."

"Destroyed? How?"

"This is the only visual footage that we have." Jennings looked up, obviously triggering something in his neural. Jeff's own neural registered that it had received a packet. He accessed it. He closed his eyes in order to enter into the visual feed with as little distraction as possible. When it was over, he opened his eyes and clutched at the table for support.

"Sit down, son," Jennings said. He poured another slug into Jeff's glass. "And for God's sake, drink."

"How many ships?"

"One hundred and eleven verified. Probably more, though."

"And how many of these—"

"We're calling them the Prox."

"Why?"

"Because they were inbound from the general direction of Procyon—"

"Alpha Canis Minoris," Jeff said.

"That's the one. Now, we have no idea whether they're from a planet in the Procyon system or not—possibly they're from a planet *beyond* that system."

Jeff nodded. "How many of these were on each ship?"

"*On* is right. They appear to travel on the outside of the ships, not the inside. It looks like they've stripped the hulls completely off."

"That's not possible," Jeff said.

Jennings brought up a schematic of a CDF ship. “This is *The Envoy*, the ship that went to reconnoiter with the Prox. What you just saw in that file you watched were the Prox launching themselves from their own ship and propelling themselves—somehow—through the vacuum of space to attach themselves to *The Envoy*. The crew’s feed indicates pounding on the hull until they punched through.”

“And then?”

“Then we lost contact.”

Jeff stared into his glass. “What do they want?”

“We don’t know that.”

“Are they intelligent?”

“They’re piloting superluminal ships—or at least riding on them—so we have to assume so.”

“And the colony?”

“They’ve gone completely dark. That’s all we know.”

“How many people are we talking about? I’ve never been to the New Manila Colony.”

“The Filipinas Interplanetary Company says twelve million. Colonial Defense says more like nine.”

Jeff nodded—it was the usual politics muddying the waters. The FIC wanted to maximize public perception of their loss; the CDF wanted to minimize panic.

Jeff looked up at Jennings. “This is above my clearance level.”

“Not anymore. We need information—a lot more information than we have. We need someone to go out there and gather as much intel as possible without being detected.”

“And that’s where I come in.”

“’Fraid so, son.”

“What makes you think I won’t get spotted?”

“Our best guess is that the Prox can detect energy—heat, radiation, electro—”

“I get it.”

Jennings didn’t seem to be put off, but instead took a seat near Jeff and continued without skipping a beat. “So we’ve got every engineer we can spare outfitting a Carson class scout ship with active camouflage, as well as heavy thermal and EM shielding."

"There's no way to completely shield anything," Jeff said.

"We know that," Jennings sighed. "We have no idea how sensitive their sensors—or senses—are. So…it's a risk." He looked up at Jeff apologetically. "We've plotted a course that will use the three suns of the Gliese system to block your approach to the outer system. Then you'll land on a large asteroid with an elliptical orbit that passes pretty close to New Manila Colony."

"How close?"

"127,000 kilometers."

Jeff whistled. "That's pretty close. Gotta seem like an occasional moon."

"The planet has a small moon already. But you're not wrong—they call the asteroid…*called* it *Pangalawang Buwan*—essentially, 'second moon.' We want you to land on the asteroid while it's at the far end of its orbit and let it act as a natural shield. You'll let it carry you toward the colony…and the Prox, of course."

"Why not send a probe?"

"Because we can't shut down a probe and get anything useful. It'll have to be 'on' and they'll see it."

"Got it. So I'm riding a dead ship planted on a careening asteroid hoping not to be eaten by bugs from somewhere beyond Procyon."

"That's the nutshell, yes."

"Do you have a duration estimate for this action?"

"It'll take you three months to get there at C5—"

"Which is the best a scout can do."

"Right. We've got a patch that might get C6 out of her, but it'll be unstable and should only be used in emergencies."

Jeff nodded, pulling up the Carson class schematics in his neural to do a quick check.

"But what's really going to seem like wasted time is hiding out on the asteroid waiting for its orbit to align with New Manila."

"How long?"

"We've worked it out to the second, but roughly six months."

Jeff nodded. "And three months back. We're talking about a year."

"If everything goes as planned, yes."

Jeff blinked and the schematics disappeared. He looked Jennings in the eye. "Is that why you're talking to *me*?"

"Is what why?" Jennings' brow furrowed.

"Admiral, let's not be polite. I know I have a reputation."

"There aren't many men we can send out on solo stretches like this without cracking. You seem to actually like it. Our psychologists say it's because of your own PTSD, and it isn't doing you any favors. But it's one of the things that make you valuable to us. Your battle scars, Captain, have turned out to be an asset."

"I won't let you down, sir." Jeff stood.

Jennings offered his hand. Jeff shook it.

"Admiral, if you don't mind, can I ask you a question?"

Jennings nodded.

"Taylor. She was the last person I was expecting to see. Since when is a captain acting as your errand boy?"

Jennings smiled but glanced away. "We want her close by because…well, she's our best chance of *handling* you."

"Thank you for your candor, but…am I really that difficult?"

"You said it yourself, Captain. You have a reputation."

THE JOURNEY out to New Manila had been uneventful, and he had passed the time studying the history and culture of the Filipino colony. He even had the synthesizer prepare him meals from the Filipino and the Asian fusion cuisine popular on the colony itself. If he was going to investigate something lost, a part of him felt obligated to understand exactly *what* had been lost.

The studying he had considered "work," but in his downtime he read a small stack of paperbacks, their papers yellowed and their covers worn, ripped, and sheathed in protective plastic. He'd picked them up—almost at random—at an antique stall on the Sol Command Station. He'd made a diverse selection: a Western adventure, two romance novels—one of them decidedly spicy—a spy thriller, and a dystopian novel geared for young adults—all from the mid-twenty-first century. He had read them all twice, and the spicy romance novel four times.

He was just at the point where Consuelo had told Geoff off for not respecting her profession and they'd had "angry sex"—one of his favorite parts of the novel—which did kind of disturb him when he stopped to think about it. But as the temperature fell, he pushed such self-examination away.

Despite the gravity of his mission, he enjoyed his time in space. In truth, something in his soul hungered for solitude, and in the nearly nine months since he had launched from Sol Station he had feasted well. His mind flashed back to when he was a teenager and had gotten lost in the woods around Anchorage. He was in the throes of hypothermia when his father had found him, and as he slowly warmed up in the back of the land rover, his father had given him a thorough tongue-lashing. "Why didn't you call for help?" his father had yelled. It was a good question. And the only answer that made sense was a fierce determination to find his way home on his own. *Is that pride?* he wondered. Maybe. But his father had just called it stupid. And when they had finally arrived home and got him into a warm tub, he saw that his father had been crying. Had he been crying the whole time he'd been yelling at him? Jeff didn't know, but he was too shocked to ask. "You've gotta let yourself be helped sometimes, Jeff," his father had said. He remembered thinking at the time, *Not if I can fucking help it.*

He smiled grimly at the memory, but felt a pang of guilt as he did so. His old man hadn't deserved that. Hell, no one had. Not Dad, not Jo, not anyone his obsessive need to do it himself had affected. And that obsession had just gotten worse since the Catskill incident.

As he had approached the Gliese 667 system almost six months ago, Jeff had powered down all engines and glided into a parallel path with the asteroid, then at the far end of its elliptical orbit. Within a few weeks, the paths converged, and using very few short bursts from the nav thrusters, Jeff guided the scout into a ravine on the asteroid that protected it from three of four sides, but left the viewing ports unobstructed. He extended the landing feet, inspired by those of a gecko, which gently reached out and gripped the asteroid, pulling the ship's belly tightly against the rock. Once the ship had "nested," its polymimetic skin changed texture and color to become indistinguishable from the rock it clung to. With a sigh he had switched off the main electricity panel. Only a highly shielded, isolated "box" continued to function, operating only the most basic life support functions.

The asteroid was tumbling slowly, completing a full rotation every twelve hours. While it was pointed away from the star Jeff, endured five hours of bitter cold, followed by an hour of mild, comfortable temperature as it rotated back into sight of Gliese 667. This was followed by five hours of oppressive heat, during which Jeff could do little but lounge, sweat, and read. Then another hour of productive respite, and back into the cold. Jeff wrapped himself in his blanket once more and waited.

After five and a half months of this, he was used to the routine. He made good use of his "spring" and "autumn" periods, as he often thought of them, searching out the remains of the New Manila colony, and watching for signs of Prox activity. Before launching, the station crew had added a high-power optical telescope. It was an archaic bit of technology, but once the scout ship powered down, it alone would allow Jeff to carry out his surveillance without detectable energy or heat signatures. Over the long weeks, as he got closer to the ruins of the colony, there had been much more to see. Jeff squinted into the telescope's eyepiece and turned the primitive knobs, adjusting its attitude.

He sighed and looked in the eyepiece again. As the asteroid drew nearer to the planet, he was beginning to see the devastation wrought by the Prox. He scratched out a few notes on a pad of paper with an old-fashioned lead pencil.

The files he'd reviewed on the colony had shown pristine cities, farms with thriving crops, and suburban areas with tree-lined streets. But all Jeff saw now as he tumbled within sight of the colony was rubble and the active and ongoing raping of the land and infrastructure.

He gritted his teeth as he watched Prox tearing down entire skyscrapers and harvesting the wire and metal.

He had ceased to be angry—that had fueled him for a couple weeks. But now the anger had passed into a grim resolve for revenge. He felt calm as he contemplated it. It would be well planned, utterly devastating, as inevitable as carbon decay, and just as passionless. He knew these things with a certainty that was not rational, not emotional, just gut-solid true.

He adjusted the telescope using light micro-motions, refocusing on the space above the colony. He saw several ships careening stern over bow in their orbits, as lifeless as the castoff elytra of beetles. He ratcheted up the power on the 'scope and zeroed in on what was left of a massive battle cruiser, *The Empyrion*. He watched as Prox swarmed over it, ripping great sheets of metal from the hull. They reminded Jeff of enormous crabs, with squat, flat, armored bodies that moved sideways, and long, articulated tails that looked dangerously barbed at the tip.

As he watched, Jeff began to pick out different kinds of Prox, each of which seemed to have specialized functions. The largest he dubbed *soldiers*, harkening back to the various castes found in ant colonies. Each soldier was at least three meters across and about 1.75 meters high when their jittery legs were fully extended. Like living bulldozers, the soldiers used their huge claws to rip the hull plating off the ship as easily as opening a can of vegetables. Apparently they found it appetizing, as they often nibbled on it, eating the metal itself.

Workers were roughly a meter smaller widthwise than the soldiers. They had no tails, but had smaller, more intricate foreclaws. They flitted between the soldiers, sometimes crawling unnoticed on their flat backs, gathering up the weightless, tumbling sheets of reinforced steel with their numerous legs, all eight of which were moving in circles as if pedaling unseen bicycles. They hustled the plates off the ship, tumbling with them into space.

Every now and then a third class of Prox would approach the ship. They were smaller still, their foreclaws hardly differentiated from their other legs, their swimmeret tendrils extended, spiraling and coiling like a nest of great long snakes gathered in a bunch at their abdominal aprons. These wove around the hulls of the ruined ships, reaching out to touch—compulsively, it seemed to Jeff—every worker and soldier they passed. It looked as though they were delivering instructions, collecting progress reports and coordinating the frenetic activity. Jeff decided to call these *expediters*. "If they are distributing orders, where are they coming from?" Jeff's voiced seemed so loud in the solitude of the cabin that it startled even himself. He paused, scrawled some notes, and then flexed his writing hand against the rapidly accelerating chill. *Wintertime,* he thought. *Time to hang out with Toni.*

Jeff stowed the pad and pencil in a plastic pocket hanging from the telescope. Taking care not to bounce in the almost impossibly low gravity of the asteroid, he propelled himself hand-over-hand toward the stern of the ship, where the heat shield stored just a tiny bit more of the star's warmth than other parts of the hull.

Jeff was aware that this might also just be his imagination. He hadn't bothered to measure it, to see if it was actually true. It was the myth he told himself so that he would have reason to "migrate" to the stern. It was a routine, it kept him active. It was, in its own way, a liturgy of the hours, and he made a procession to his successive seasonal altars. The only thing he didn't do was pray. Instead, at this, his winter altar, he wrapped himself in his blanket and sat with his back against the heat shield. As the temperature cooled, he rocked back and forth to try to generate a little bit of warmth.

"Hey, Toni, did you fix your web?"

The CDF fleet was infested with spiders. It always had been, and although people frequently complained about them, for Jeff it was just a fact of life in space. G-forces, flightplan projections, radiation monitoring…and spiders. When people first went into space, no one had expected spiders to be a problem. No one had given them a second thought—just like they hadn't worried about koala or boa constrictor infestations. But there was something about space that drew them—something that allowed them to flourish here. It didn't matter how many times the maintenance crew fumigated a ship, the spiders would be back in force within just a few months. It was a mystery, but one which by now pretty much everyone accepted.

Jeff was glad of the company, although he didn't consciously admit this to himself. Most of the spiders were small, many were microscopic, but Toni was a rarity—a banded garden spider—large enough to have some personality and objectively beautiful with her brown and green zebra-like stripes running horizontally over her voluptuous abdomen.

During his last winter phase, Jeff had noticed that a couple of the strands of Toni's web had become unmoored, and the upper left section had been left waving in the low gravity. Such disrepair wasn't like Toni at all, who was never derelict about such things, and he expected to see the web once more in good repair. As he drew near he reached a hand out to grab a handle and slow himself down. Then he glanced at the web. The upper left section was still waving. He scowled in concern and moved in closer to the web, careful to stop himself before he plowed into it.

Toni was there, but instead of perching with her legs splayed out, confidently astride her silk, she was curled into a ball, held captive by her own web, as if she were prey. Her legs, once noble and slender, were tucked up under her body, the tips of them jutting out at odd angles, motionless and diminished.

Jeff's mouth was a grim line as he reached out a tentative finger and poked at her. She did not move. She was gone.

A pang of grief stabbed at his chest. Despite how expertly he had suppressed his emotions over the past several years, he still felt the sting of it. It seemed to him that the right thing to do was to simply *be* with her, as if sitting shiva. He stared at the husk of her and felt the prick of an emptiness that, had he allowed it, would have overwhelmed him much of the time.

His thoughts turned to Catskill. Normally, he was on guard against this. But Toni's death prised open a well-guarded door in his memory. He saw himself, as if at a distance, commanding his men. His friend Danny had been his second. They'd known each other since boot camp. They'd had a friendly rivalry since the day they'd met. And when Jeff had been tapped for command ahead of him, Danny had celebrated his promotion without a hint of wounded pride. He'd been a true friend until a hail of blaster fire had filled him with holes...until that day when every single crewmember under his command had been leveled, and Jeff had escaped only by being knocked unconscious and left for dead.

It was this that had led him to seek the solitude of deep space. There was no one to let down out here. There was no one to be responsible for. There was no one who might die should he go left when he should have gone right.

Jeff was so lost in his memories and grief that he didn't notice that his breath had turned frosty, or that his nose had begun to run, or that the blanket he pulled around himself was woefully inadequate. The air was growing warm again when an alarm sounded. It was a quiet alarm, but he heard the dissonant electronic tones as if they were blaring. He leaped up so fast he hit his head on the opposite side of the cabin before he could slow himself down. He cursed his carelessness, but with the help of the handles, found traction again and maneuvered to the shielded display. He tapped on the screen and found the source of it —proximity alert.

Jeff's heart jolted to twice its normal rate as he swung toward the telescope. He fixed his eye to the viewer and swept the sky for evidence of incoming Prox. The asteroid was still rotated away from the planet, so he couldn't see anything just yet. *Did they see me?* he wondered. *Have they detected my energy signature? I've been careful, and the tech crew was meticulous,* he reminded himself.

"Shit," he said aloud and slapped himself in the forehead. "I should have seen this." The asteroid was rich in various metals, but especially iron. Instantly, somehow, he knew. They hadn't seen *him*. They saw the asteroid. And it looked *tasty*. He was just a cherry riding on an irresistible sundae headed straight for the Prox's gaping mandibles.

"Dead meat," he said, because that's what he was. They were on their way toward the asteroid, and once they found *it*, they would inevitably find *him*. And *eat* him.

"Shit shit shit shit shit..." he repeated as he threw himself across the cabin toward the pilot's console. He snatched at an overhead handle and neatly swung into the command chair. If he hadn't been panicking he would have congratulated himself on such a gymnastic move, but all such thoughts were pushed well out of mind. His body automatically went through all the motions of his pre-flight checklist, while his mind raced through multiple aspects of his situation at once.

I can't outrun the fuckers, he thought. *Not in a scout. There's no way I can maintain the steady quantum field needed to go superluminal if I'm doing evasive maneuvers. Colony feed said the Prox were doing 1800K, but I can't do more than that under standard propulsion...* A monad of thought wondering at the impossibility of such a thing flitted into his consciousness, then out again. Despite the cold, he began to sweat as his thoughts flailed, looking for an out.

"Gravity assist," he said out loud. It was a long shot, but it was the only one he had.

He fired up his control panel, blinking as the lights flared on, the cabin filling with the humming of multiple systems stirring from sleep. He released and retracted the landing claws, leaving the scout floating free and beginning to drift from the surface of the asteroid.

His vision sparkled as his neural initialized, filling his field of view with diagnostics and informational displays. He used to take them for granted, but after living without them for so many months, they now felt like magic. He pulled up a virtual model of the system and asked the computer for a course that would give him maximum velocity in the shortest amount of time. Only one possibility resulted in survivable g-forces. He set his head firmly against the headrest and punched the engines for everything they had. The acceleration distorted his face as the scout's engine kicked away from the asteroid with explosive force. Jeff eased back as soon as he was clear, since he still had to be slow enough to maneuver.

He had the advantage of surprise, and he was determined to make the most of it. He could use the gravity of the asteroid—and at first that was his intention. But it would be far less help than the much denser planet beneath him. Surprise was surprise, and it wouldn't last long. He adjusted course and gunned it for the planet.

His slingshot course would use the massive gravity well of the planet to exponentially increase his velocity. By the time he reached the planet he could be doing nearly 700 kps. One orbit around the planet and he should be shooting off and away at nearly 20,000 kph, if he was lucky and the scout didn't shake apart.

Full sensors were up now, and information began pouring in simultaneously on his neural as well as the view pads in front of him. He did a sweep and found that the Prox that had been headed toward the asteroid had stopped and turned. Literally thousands, no, hundreds of thousands of Prox dismantling the colony and the other ships in orbit had also paused, as if momentarily frozen in time. *Probably awaiting orders*, Jeff thought. A moment later, they started moving—fast.

Jeff ran some intercept calculations—he'd have to dodge several of the Prox on the other side of the planet, and at his speed his maneuverability would be severely compromised. He fired up his defensive battery and prepped the particle cannons. If he couldn't go around them he would damn well blast *through* them. And there were a lot of them.

It doesn't matter, he told himself, his inner voice unreasonably calm and encouraging. *You'll make it or you won't. It's your best shot so go full out and fuck 'em 'til they take you down.*

He hit the 700K burst just at the apex of the gravity well. Within seconds he was going upwards of 12,000K and gaining every second. The burst was just icing on the cake.

He made sure his neural was interfacing properly with the weapons system, and, satisfied that it was, he released all the safeties, primed the particle cannons and tuned them to maximum force. Gripping the edges of his console, he closed his eyes and transferred his view to the outside visual array.

The ship was shuddering now under the gravitational grip of New Manila. It was literally being torn in two by tidal forces, twisting between the twin prongs of velocity and gravity. Jeff's mouth opened in a silent scream and his cheeks vibrated from the bodily drag. Jeff could feel his brain pressed painfully against the back of his skull. His speed was 18,000K as the ship began to emerge from the gravity well, hurled like an 80-ton stone from a sling toward the motionless stars.

The Prox were swarming him now. He was leaving thousands behind him in the dust, but those ahead of him were forming a gauntlet to block his escape. Flicking his eyes upward and to the left, he checked the power level on the weapons system and estimated he had about sixty particle blasts, more or less. He held off until he could see the articulated legs of the Prox directly ahead. Mere seconds from colliding with them, he lit them up with the particle cannon and saw their armored bodies explode outward in every direction. He felt the bump and scrape of their scattered parts bouncing off of his shields as their ship dove directly into his beams.

He pumped away at the cannon until he had cleared nine successive waves of Prox bodies, then a tenth. As he cleared the detritus of this final wave, he emerged into a clear field of stars. A sensor reminded him of the planet's moon dead ahead, and for a split second he deliberated. *Just head out into space and hope that it's enough?* he wondered, *Or slingshot off the moon as well?*

The moon as well, he decided. He plotted a second slingshot course, modulating his approach angle so that he'd be slung in the general direction of Sol, and of course, Earth.

He stopped noticing the shaking, until a panel rattled loose from the ceiling and gashed the side of his head. Blood streamed from his temple, and he wiped at it impatiently, trying to keep it out of his eyes. But mixed with the sweat, the blood seeped into his left eye despite his efforts. He squeezed that eye shut, and using a combination of neural and pad controls, braced himself for an acceleration that should exceed 32,000 kps. The ship's shaking became a shuddering again as the gravity began to tear at it. Jeff checked the proximity sensors and was relieved to see that the Prox were still a ways off. He was going to make it.

Hope and elation coursed through him as he prepared for the acceleration. He gripped the console again.

Just then an alarm began sounding. The notification in his neural identified the problem—maneuvering thrusters failure. He watched in horror as his escape trajectory faded and he saw the scout's icon circle the moon again and again and again, trapped now in a very fast orbit. Checking the proximity sensor, he saw the Prox closing in fast. He did a quick diagnostic on the maneuvering thrusters and felt his stomach sink into his boots as he saw the entire starboard array missing.

Is there any point in landing on the moon? His mind raced. *Is it rock or metal? Is it made of anything the Prox would find desirable?* He could do a mineralogical investigation, but he didn't have time for that now. The fact that the Prox were not already consuming it gave him hope. He only had to find a place to hide on the blind side of the moon.

First things first, he told himself. Using his remaining thrusters, he did the one thing they would permit—flip over. He entered his intentions into the neural and let it make the calculations. Then he just held on as the flight action played itself out. He felt the quick jerk of the thrusters, too quick for vertigo, then felt the ship punch forward as the stern thruster array lit up for one more all-out burn. He watched his speed plummet until it was within safety range for a landing—but only just.

Landing with only port thrusters was going to be a challenge. Not impossible, but deep in a crevasse of his brain that he actively suppressed, he knew that it was very, very unlikely. With one eye on his altitude, he searched frantically for a place to hide. His hopes leaped as he saw a canyon about 2,000 kilometers dead ahead. He entered the coordinates as his destination, and the scout spun as he tried to even out its landing.

Descending now, Jeff's eyebrows bunched in confusion as he saw the lunar landscape. It was red. He shook his head and, adjusting the outboard sensor array with his neural, he looked again. It was as if he were looking at Earth's moon through a crimson filter. *Must be damage to the sensor array from the shaking*, he thought. Somehow the green and blue rods must have gotten fried, and he was only receiving input from the red rods. *That must be it,* he thought.

As the ground got closer, Jeff saw that it wasn't just the rocks he was seeing, but some kind of crystalline structure covering every surface. It sparkled in the starlight as the scout hurled past it, but before Jeff could question what it was he was seeing, metal collided with rock and the scout began to tumble end over end. Everything went black as Jeff felt himself spinning in the night for what seemed an eternity. Then with a final screech of tearing metal, the ship lurched to a stop.

Jeff's pinprick of consciousness was snuffed out in the vacuum.

CHAPTER TWO

They're eating my brain, was Jeff's first conscious thought, after…after what? The images cascaded over him in waves. He saw scenes from childhood, the husk of Toni, her legs tucked up beneath her, the night nearly two decades ago when Jo had stumbled into his bed, drunk. He saw his own flight from the Prox, the heat of battle in which he saw the entire platoon under his command obliterated before his eyes in explosive bursts of gore, the lunar surface rushing up under his scout at a lethal velocity.

He opened his eyes—at least he had the impulse to open his eyes, and there was a corresponding visual result. He did not, however, seem to actually have a body. Or, if he did have a body, he was not receiving any sensations from it. He seemed to be floating in deep space, although there were no planets or stars. The only thing he could see looked like…*Like what?* he wondered. *Fireflies*, he decided. *They look just like swarms of fireflies…little blue fireflies.*

I crashed, he thought. No one could have survived an impact with the lunar surface at that speed. The uneven surface would have ripped right through any deflectors or grav-repelling fields the scout had been outfitted with. There was no way…and yet, how was he thinking? How was he conscious? *I'm dead,* he thought.

Yes, dead. It was another voice, not his own. It seemed to be coming from within his own head, though—his own, nonexistent head. *But also, not dead.*

Some of the fireflies seemed to migrate toward one another, hovering before his (impossible but seemingly present) field of vision. Jeff felt a sensation flow over his nonexistent body—as if someone were pouring warm liquid over his head and neck. More of the fireflies flew in from somewhere, until there were millions of them, swarming, bunching, congealing into something larger, denser. The mass of fireflies took on the vague shape of a person—a person of light. He?... she?...shone with an almost impossible luminosity, yet it was not painful to look at it—indeed he did not know how to look away. The person's outline was blurry, but it slowly gained definition, even as the brightness dimmed. It resolved into a solid person of flesh and blood. A person Jeff recognized.

Danny? Jeff thought.

Danny smiled. But Danny was dead. Danny's spine had been ripped out by a particle cannon. *Yes, Danny,* the voice in his head said. Danny's lips moved to form the words, but the sound did not come from his direction. In fact, there was no sound, just...meaning. *But also, not Danny. We perceive that your consciousness is more likely to be receptive to a human form. If we appeared as we are, you would not recognize us as...sentient. We have borrowed this pattern from your memories. We hope it is not unpleasant.* Danny smiled. The look on his face was compassionate and encouraging.

No...just a shock.

We could choose another, Danny said. He became fuzzy around the edges.

No, it's fine. Just...give me a second.

Danny resolved again, his face patient and kind. Danny had been both of those things, but he had also been tough and sardonic. There was no hint of those qualities in this Danny.

Is incorporeality upsetting for you?

It's...unsettling, Jeff responded.

Please forgive our insensitivity, Danny's voice said in his head.

Another constellation of fireflies swarmed into his vision, but instead of coalescing into a form he could see, they seemed to somehow coalesce into a form he inhabited. He looked down—for suddenly there seemed to be a *down*—and saw a body of light forming around his consciousness. A luminescent hand waved before his vision, and he was waving it. Legs spiraled as if he were riding a bicycle, but then found footing as a surface coalesced beneath him.

The light body was now a body of flesh, but it did not feel like his old body. It *teemed*—as if he were amped on the kind of uppers they gave out to rouse slow-run colonists from hybersleep. But it did seem solid, as did the floor, as did Danny. Around them, though, seemed to be a lot of white…nothing. The whiteness just faded into infinity on all sides, creating a ghostly, fog-like effect that was disorienting.

"Um…could we have some walls, please?" Jeff spoke out loud.

"Of course. Forgive us."

Again, he felt warmth flowing down the back of his neck. The whiteness took on color and texture. Patterns emerged and when everything stopped whirling, Jeff instantly recognized his family's hunting lodge near Anchorage. He could think of no more peaceful or pleasant place.

"Will this suffice?"

"This is…wonderful." He was surprised at how much more safe he felt, how much he craved being *bounded.* He would not have guessed it.

"So this is my family's lodge, but where are we *really*?"

Danny's face tightened up into a smile. "We are *inside*."

"Inside what?"

"Inside us." Danny's tone indicated that this was self-evident.

"I'm sorry," Jeff shook his head. "I need more…I don't understand."

"We are the Ulim. We are inside our mind."

"Our mind? As in, yours and mine?"

"There is no yours. Only ours."

"Can you…explain?"

Danny's smile faded into a look of tolerant patience, as one might have with an annoyingly curious child.

"We are the Ulim. We were once as humans are. We had bodies, although they were much different from yours. Over many millennia we learned to create."

"Do you mean that you learned to make art?"

"No, I mean that we learned to create life. We learned how to pull it apart and put it back together. We learned how to rearrange matter at will at the molecular level. We learned to weave it from the dead elements around us. We learned how to make it sentient, and how to transfer sentience."

Jeff cocked his head. "So what happened to you?"

Danny held his hands out, palms up. "We ascended."

"What does that mean, *ascended*?"

"We mapped our patterns. We created a…system…that we could live in. Then we entered it."

"A system?"

"Yes." Danny closed his eyes and seemed to be searching for a word. "I am reviewing your pattern…. A program. We entered the program."

"Like a computer program?"

"Yes, but not mechanical. Biological."

Jeff's eyes snapped open wide. "The red moss on the moon's surface. That's not moss, is it?"

"No. It is a sentient crystalline matrix. It covers the moon. It feeds on starlight. It needs little maintenance. It is our home. It is where our pattern resides. We live…within. We are there now. *You* are there. Here." He smiled, apparently at the awkwardness of language.

"Is there only one…Ulim?" Jeff asked.

"Yes, there is only one Ulim, but we are numerous. We are on this world, and many others. We can choose to separate out patterns—"

"Partition," Jeff suggested.

"Yes, if you like. We can choose to merge as well. You are separated from the main body of the Ulim."

"Why, is…? Oh. Quarantine."

"Just so, yes. There is a lot of pain in your pattern. Pain that would prove…toxic to us."

"That…makes a hell of a lot of sense."

"We are pleased that you do not take offense."

"I crashed on your…on the moon. Did I hurt anyone? I'm sure I damaged the red…the crystal formations."

"All that we are is endlessly redundant. No pattern is destroyed if the host is destroyed. And the host has repaired itself. All is well. Be at peace."

Jeff breathed a deep sigh of relief. He looked down at his hands. They were, in fact, *his* hands. He even saw the scar from the time he had cut his finger as a boy. "So I'm dead. I'm…what? A ghost?"

"No, not a ghost. You are a living pattern, just as we are. We have joined your pattern to ours. You are in us and we are in you. We are one being. And we live forever. As long as you are united to us, *you* will live forever."

"But I *did* die."

"What you once were is gone, that is true. And yet you *are*. This is something to be glad of, yes?" There was a hint of Danny's old buck-up cheerfulness in the voice. Jeff wasn't fooled by it, but he welcomed it.

A fearful thought struck him. "I'm trapped here, aren't I?" The crystalline "moss" might sustain his consciousness, but was it really living or just surviving? He suddenly felt claustrophobic.

"No. You are not. We can delete your pattern. You can *choose* to die."

"I can't stay in this…this *state* forever," he waved at the hunting lodge. As comforting as it was, he knew it was an illusion. It was an emotionally pleasant prison, but… no more. "I would go crazy. I…I don't mean to sound ungrateful, but the truth is that I'd *rather* die."

"We have had much debate over your future—the *if* of your future, to be exact."

"And what did you decide?" If there was one thing Jeff hated more than anything else, it was being at someone's mercy.

"Some have argued that deleting your pattern is best, but this is not our way." He smiled compassionately. "Coercion is not our way. The consensus is that you must be given a choice."

"So…what are my options?" He had the distinct feeling of waiting for the other shoe to drop.

"You can stay here, or we can reconstitute you in your accustomed form. We can return you to your home. It is…what we would want, if the situation were reversed."

"That's very Golden Rule of you," Jeff said, smiling. "But…that's impossible. My ship was destroyed."

"Yes. That is a problem. We did not capture the pattern of your ship in any way that could be understood or retained. Your ship has no pattern remaining, no DNA, no memories. Nothing but a tangle of elements, which we have absorbed."

"And no blueprints."

"Precisely. We do have your memories of the vessel, but they are mere impressions, neither complete nor precise enough to reconstitute the vessel. Nor can we simply coalesce you on the moon."

"I would die instantly."

"Not instantly. Quickly."

"Horribly," Jeff whispered.

"We do not choose this."

"We are in agreement on this." Jeff mimicked Pseudo-Danny's clipped, patient tone. Pseudo-Danny didn't seem to notice. "We are going to return you your planet of origin—to Earth."

Jeff's eyebrows bunched in confusion. "You just said yourself that my ship was destroyed. How do you intend to *get* me to Earth?"

"We will simply reconstitute you on Earth."

"Simply? You make it sound like you're going down to the corner store for the paper."

Jeff watched Danny's eyes move back and forth as he searched for the references. He must have found them, because he smiled. "It is actually easier than that. We don't have to put on our slippers."

"How could it possibly be easy? We're 24 light years from there."

"As I have said, we have Ulim on many worlds. We did not travel there in ships, crossing the distance in-between. We simply *shifted* there."

"Shifted?"

Danny renewed his "patient" smile. At least it seemed genuine. "Space is malleable. Distance is illusory. If you understand that, you can take this point here," Danny held one hand up, as if he were pinching a point in space and holding it between his thumb and forefinger, "and bring it together with this point here." He pinched a different point about two feet away from the first. Then he brought the pinched fingers together, forming for a moment the infinity sign from the two circles made by the fingers of his two hands. He unpinched his fingers, releasing whatever fabric of space they held. "Simple."

"Is this some form of technology?" Jeff asked.

"At first it was. Not now. Now it is merely…knowing how to do it. At first it seemed like a trick. Later we realized it was simply how things worked."

"Didn't you need to know how it worked in order to do it at the beginning?"

"Yes, but we did not have the strength of mind to put it into effect. We needed…technological assistance. Later, we did not."

"So you can…shift…to any point in the universe at will, using the power of your mind?"

"We can."

"And that is how you'll return me to earth?"

"It is. If you choose to go. You may stay here, if you like." He gestured at the hunting lodge again.

"You know the answer to that."

"We do."

Jeff stood up and began pacing, stroking his chin. "You said my body was destroyed."

"It was disassembled, but we recorded its pattern as it did so."

"And you'll reassemble me on Earth?"

"Not from the same matter. We will reassemble your pattern from matter we take from the environment of Earth."

"Then it won't really be me, will it?"

Danny looked confused. “The pattern will be identical.”

“It will look and sound like me. But I’m dead. My body is gone.”

“Your consciousness remains. Your body will be as it was before. All that you were, you will be again. There will be no loss and no change; continuity will be maintained. Any other distinction is meaningless.”

“There are many among my people who would argue that point with you.”

“They will not have the opportunity.”

“So, you’re asking me to return home and to pretend like nothing happened?”

“We are not asking you to pretend at all. Tell them what happened to you. We ask for no secrecy, no allegiance.”

Jeff nodded, taking this in. He had to admit, if they were telling him the truth about everything, then the Ulim were nothing if not honorable. “I don’t mind being dead,” Jeff said, finally. “In a way, it’s what I signed up for. It’s the acceptable risk, you know? And even if you said, ‘We’re going to wipe your pattern now,’ I would have no reason to complain. Having this little chat with you…it’s a form of mercy, even if it was the last thing I ever did. And I would be fine with that. I really would be. I really…*am*.”

Jeff continued to pace as he thought. Danny waited patiently, not at all uncomfortable with the silence. That suited Jeff just fine. He was used to silence.

“Will I feel this…fucking great all the time?” he held his hand up. “Don’t answer that. It doesn’t matter. The thing is, I’ll be different. Myself, and not myself.”

“You are beginning to sound like us,” Danny grinned.

Jeff nodded. “You know, if it meant just my death, I wouldn't complain. But it’s more than that now. I *know* things…things that could save lives.” His head snapped up. “Okay. I don’t know what life in this new body you promise will be like, but I have a duty to perform. So…I accept. I want to live.”

Before he could take another breath the floor disappeared from beneath him, and the walls faded out. Once more Jeff felt himself suspended in space, surrounded by the little blue fireflies. Jeff reached out his hand to touch them, then realized he had no hand. Were these fireflies real, then? He doubted it. He suspected they were being offered to him as a gift—as a symbol or metaphor for something real but incorporeal. But a symbol for what?

For them, he thought to himself. *Each of these fireflies is an Ulim.* He knew it was true. He felt the "rightness" of it. They were nodes of consciousness. Then they began to change. The thrill of wonder rolled over him as he watched each node blossom—opening like a flower, gossamer tendrils reaching out to connect with their neighbors, until all were joined in an immense network. Then, in a single collective motion, each node turned its bloom toward the triple stars of Gliese 667. As they absorbed the power from the suns, a thrumming began. It sounded like an electronic signal, but it also sounded like a tribal rhythm. It pulsed.

What am I seeing? Jeff wondered. The nodes were aligning themselves with the star, capturing as much of its radiation, its energy as they could. They were sending that energy somewhere, for some purpose, but for what?

He realized that he, too, was a node. There were parts of him that were connected, and parts that only he had access to. They knew their "partition" business very well. But he was blossoming. He was collecting energy. He was sending it. He was *them.* He was One and Many. He was conscious of a small "him" and a large "him." The small him was vulnerable, a mixture of hope and aspiration and pain. He pitied it. The large Him was infinite, confident, purposeful.

The large Him reached out, and with unseen hands gripped two very distant corners of space. He began to pull, and he felt the fabric of the distance field give—at first reluctantly, then more easily, until the whole stretch of it was pliable, shapable. He was conscious of every millimeter of that distance field—every asteroid, every star, every planet, every pocket of gas, every particle of dust. It was all known and comprehended.

Then, as if fingers had suddenly set a globe spinning—a globe that he was standing on—Jeff felt a jarring shift in perspective. It was disorienting, but not unpleasant. And he realized that it was no longer Gliese 518 before him, but the familiar yellow glow of Sol. And there, at no distance at all, spun a blue green planet that he knew was Home.

Emotion swelled within him, and he felt a sympathetic echo from the other nodes. They seemed...*happy* for him. No. It was the feeling he had when he finished painting a wall or completing a report. A job well done. It was *satisfaction*.

The earth was rushing toward him now. He saw the familiar continents, then the contours of countries—the verdancy of Greenland, Canada, Russia, and Alaska, the desert wastes of Europe, the States and China...and the radioactive husk of Australia. He saw himself rushing toward Anchorage, toward the tower that housed his apartment.

The partition opened, and Jeff had the distinct and uncomfortable sensation of being fully known. He was being read. An itching began on his scalp—*the scalp I do not have*, he reminded himself—and then spread. Like a wildfire, it raged over his head, down his neck, over his chest, down his arms. Jeff opened his mouth to scream—and actually screamed. And screamed. And screamed.

The pain was like nothing he had ever experienced before. It was as if every cell in his body was being torched simultaneously. He blazed, he swelled, he ground his teeth and wondered that they could be ground. And then the fire cooled. He felt the soft breeze of the air conditioner tingle on his skin, felt the trembling of the hair on his arm.

He had eyes. He opened them. He saw nothing. No, there, a tiny orange light. A node? No, it couldn't be. It wasn't blue, for one thing.

He had ears. He listened. He heard a heartbeat, not his own. Mechanical. A toc-toc-toc sound, almost too loud to be real. *Dad's clock,* he thought. He had fallen asleep to that sound most of his adult life. It was a mantel clock his father had inherited from a distant relative and passed along to Jeff when he graduated from the Academy.

But that wasn't possible. That clock was twenty-four light years away. But the sound was old. Familiar. It sounded like Comfort.

He turned over, feeling the cool fabric of the sheet against his cheek. He had a cheek. He had an arm. He reached it out, the motions familiar from thousands of repetitions over many years. He found the light switch. He turned it on.

He blinked with the force of it. His vision was blurry at first, but it was clear what he was seeing. He was in his bedroom in Anchorage, in his own apartment. He swung his legs out of bed. They looked just like his legs. He stood. They held him.

It was his body, and it was not his body. It looked and acted like his own, but it thrummed with life in a way his old body hadn't since he had been young. He felt the back of the couch. It seemed real. The clock was on the mantel, louder than ever.

It has to be an illusion, he thought, *just like the hunting lodge*. He reached out with his mind to commune with the other nodes, but he found none. He was alone.

Then his ears were assaulted by the sound of a crash. Military police burst through the door, weapons poised and the yelling of many voices. Not comprehending, Jeff stared at them until they tackled him. He laid face down on the floor, felt the intrusion of a blue-uniformed knee pressing painfully into his fresh new spine, did not resist as they cuffed his hands.

CHAPTER THREE

Dr. Emma Stewart sighed as she resumed her seat. First she'd gotten up because the room was too cold. Then she needed "new" tea, because the old tea no longer tasted right. Eventually she realized that she was just procrastinating. There would always be something else that needed doing, anything but what she *needed* to do. And what she *needed* to do was to make a decision.

Two files were open in the air reader before her. Two faces hovering over her desk projecting fresh-faced enthusiasm, straight out of the Colonial Science Corps Academy. One male, one female. Both *summa cum laude*, one year apart. Both had written fascinating dissertations. But she only needed one quantum seismologist for the new team she was building. Debby was a dog person, did watercolor in her spare time, unmarried. Ulrich was a cat person, shot skeet, gay, married with one girl. Debby seemed by-the-book, worked well in an authority structure. She had done a two-year turn in the Colonial Defense Fleet, honorably discharged with commendations. Ulrich was out-of-the-box, arrested twice for protesting CDF military actions. Both were brilliant.

And here she was, about to make a decision that would change the trajectory of their lives forever. She was usually good at decisions, but this was two people's lives she was going to impact—and their families. If one of them were clearly better suited, it would be one thing, but—

An alert in her neural lit up. She looked up, blinked, and read the message.

—Need you for a consult ASAP. C-378.

She scowled. Since when did Admiral Jennings need her input on anything? She closed the air reader and the two faces cascaded into the quartz desktop. The C-300 block was…she stood up. Psychological holding. She shook her head. She could be remembering that wrong. She looked up and consulted her neural. No, that was correct. How could she possibly help with a psych eval? She was a physicist.

In point of fact, she was the CSC's chief physicist and the ranking scientist on Sol Station. Jennings knew her time was valuable, and he had never charged her with anything frivolous before. She fought a wave of resentment. Then the thought emerged: *There is tea to get.* She deflated. Who was she fooling? She wasn't getting anything done here. She rose, put on a sweater, and headed for the hall.

IT TOOK her fifteen minutes to navigate from the main science block to psych services. Something about the distance between them comforted her. *There should be a great distance, after all, between real science and*—she stopped herself before she could complete the unkind thought. She'd dated a psychologist once. Benjamin. That had ended with her kicking him in the teeth. She did *not* like to be pathologized, and his nightly diagnoses of her complex neuroses went from cute to infuriating pretty quickly. She let a wave of rage surge through her, then subside.

She punched the blinking access square just outside of C-378 and the door slid open. Stepping inside, she gave a quick nod to Admiral Jennings, who was seated at a consult table. Another CDF officer was with him. She didn't know her, but she read her rank. Captain. And too pretty by half. Emma hated her already.

"Ah, Dr. Stewart. Thank you for coming so quickly," Jennings said, standing briefly. "Please join us. Do you know Captain Jo Taylor?"

"No. Nice to meet you," Emma offered her hand and a half-smile. Taylor half-rose, shook it, and returned to her seat.

"What's up? You know things are—"

"Hectic, I imagine. How's that new team coming?"

"Almost together. Two more and we'll have a full complement. Then it'll just be support personnel, but I can delegate that."

"I should think so," Jennings' mouth quirked. He wasn't at all interested in her team, but the man had a sense of decorum. He also knew that he wasn't her boss, and he needed to play nice. And Emma knew that nothing on the station happened without his approval. Her world, she mused, was a bureaucratic and diplomatic ball of tangled yarn.

Jennings pointed at the far wall. Emma took a seat to the Admiral's right and looked at the wall. It faded into video feed from an evaluation room. In it was a man dressed in standard CDF casuals. His hair was longer than regulation. He needed a shave. His eyes stared into space as if he were deep in thought. They were eyes that were quick with intelligence, but dark with…what? Guilt? He scratched the back of his neck.

The door slid open and a man walked in, dressed in medical whites. He was tall and lean, with a whisper of a mustache on his upper lip. "Ted," Emma blurted out, "what are—"

"Dr. Osprey is a psychiatrist," Jennings said.

"Yes, I…we know each other," Emma said. Ted had been Benjamin's best friend on the station, and probably still was. His eyes danced knowingly over her, then moved on to Captain Taylor.

Once the introductions had been made, Jennings pointed at the patient. "Captain Jeff Bowers. We sent him out on a reconnaissance mission nine months ago."

"Where?" Osprey asked.

"Now, you all have clearance, and I'm invoking it now," Jennings shifted uncomfortably in his seat. He looked up and blinked, calling up a file on his neural. A 3-D image hovered above the table. "This is where the New Manila colony used to be," he said, "until alien hostiles we're calling the Prox destroyed it. That much is common knowledge. Now we get classified: We didn't get much info on them before the station went dark, so we sent Captain Bowers to gather intelligence. And, unfortunately, his ship was destroyed."

"How?" Emma asked.

"Crashed on New Manila's moon," Captain Taylor said.

"New Manila is how many light years away?" Emma asked.

"Twenty-four," Jennings answered.

"What did the moon base say?" Emma asked.

"What moon base?" Jennings returned.

"The New Manila moon base."

"There is no New Manila moon base."

Emma blinked. "Then his ship can't have been badly damaged."

"According to Captain Bowers, it was completely destroyed," Jo responded.

"This moon has breathable atmosphere, then. How—"

"No. There's no atmosphere to speak of."

"Then…who rescued him?"

"That's why you're here, Doctor," Jennings said. "Just…let's let the man speak for himself."

The far wall shuddered and resolved into feed of what looked like a CDF interrogation. Captain Bowers was there, in the same clothes, looking exactly the same. His voice was reedy and uncertain as he spoke. He told his story, from leaving Sol station to waking up in his apartment in Anchorage. The feed shuddered again and they were once more looking at live feed of the captain staring into space.

"I need to know what really happened," Jennings said. "You're my team. I want you all to put everything aside and give this top priority. Captain Taylor, that's an order. Doctors…this is an urgent request."

Emma nodded. Well, she'd been looking for a distraction. *Careful what you wish for,* she thought to herself.

Jennings rose and started pacing. Emma thought his uniform looked a bit too tight on his boxy, sedentary frame. "The way I see it, we've got three possibilities." He looked up and accessed something on his neural. Then, as he spoke, bullet points appeared on the far wall next to the feed of Jeff. "Option one, he's telling the truth. Option two, he never left in the first place and he somehow tricked all of us with simulated information. Or option three, he's not really Captain Bowers."

"You mean, like an android?" Emma asked. "Surely that's easy to rule out."

"We have." Doctor Osprey pulled up a file and projected it over the table. "He's a completely normal human. He still has every childhood scar, every mole and dimple. His DNA is an exact match, right down to the radiation damage from his duty in the nebula. His neural implants have complete records, going all the way back to when they were first installed. Even the serial numbers are correct."

"And psychologically?" Emma asked.

Osprey's eyebrows rose, acknowledging the question. "Psychologically he's…fragile. But he's *himself*. His personality profile is an exact match to the last time we tested him. He knows things that only Captain Bowers could know."

"And how could *you* know that?" Emma asked.

"How much technical detail do you want me to go into?" He gave her an imperious sneer.

"Do you two have anything going on between you I need to know about?" Jennings asked.

"We know each other." Emma said. "Not well."

"I want professionals on this case. If I see another flash of personal animosity like that one, Doctor Osprey, we'll find ourselves another doctor."

"I understand," Osprey said, looking down.

"Are you finished?" Jennings asked.

"No. There's…one more thing."

"What's that?" Jennings asked.

"He's too young."

"What?" Emma asked. "What do you mean?"

"This guy is in his mid-fifties. His metabolism should be slowing down. His glandulars ought to be congruent with his age, but they aren't. He's running the glandulars of a twenty-year-old. All of his vitals, in fact—they're the vitals of a kid straight out of boot camp. So…I think there's some veracity to your option number three, Admiral. This isn't the same Jeff Bowers that left."

"Which means he could be telling the truth," Captain Taylor said, a note of hope in her voice. "He said that his body was destroyed and he was reconstituted here by the…what did he call them?"

"The Ulim," Jennings offered. "So how do we know he isn't an Ulim plant? Or a Prox plant for that matter? Maybe Captain Bowers is telling us what he thinks is the truth, but he's been duped by the very alien bastards we sent him out there to spy on."

Jo whistled. "When you put it like that, it…well, it doesn't sound implausible. And if the Prox can duplicate people down to that level of detail…"

"There will be no fighting them," Jennings admitted. "Let's pray that is not the case. Doctor Osprey, I want you to head up a medical team that will put Captain Bowers through every test known to humanity—both medical and psychological. Hell, enlist a witch doctor if it will rule anything out. I want to know *exactly* what happened to him."

"What about option number two?" Emma asked. "How sure are you that he actually went out there?"

Jennings pulled up flight plans, with dated transponder signals that were clearly indicated by flashing green lights. "All of our data is here, Doctor Stewart. I hope you'll review it carefully. But…I think you'll find what we found. Every transponder node hit just on the second it should have. No hidden carrier waves, no encrypted virus sequences, no indication of any possible way he could have tripped them remotely. That particular scout hit every one of those destination markers, and I've got a whole operations team who will say the same. What's more, we have medical readings on his vitals for every second of his trip—not a blip, not a dead space, not a single moment that caused us any concern or question. Everything is recorded, right down to his occasional ventricular arrhythmia. The medical team is just as certain—he was *out there*." Jennings leaned on the table, both fists planted solidly on its quartz top. "I want you to prove them wrong, Doctor. If there's a hole in this, I want you to find it."

"I'll do my best, sir."

"Thank you." He rose and rubbed at his eyes.

"And then there's option one," Jo said, her arms crossed over her dress blues.

"And then there's option one," Jennings agreed. "The problem with option one, though, is that it's impossible."

"No. It's improbable," Jo said. "That's not the same thing. I agree that the age hiccup is a problem. But if he's telling the truth, that would account for it, wouldn't it? His…pattern, as he called it, it would have been him through and through, right down to his implants. But when they were re-created—"

"If they were recreated," Jennings corrected.

"If they were recreated, then everything would be new. The stress of age wouldn't apply. Doesn't that speak in *favor* of his story?"

Osprey nodded, looking distantly off into space.

"As for option two, if you find that he really *did* go, then it's impossible that he could be back. Unless, again, he's telling the truth."

It was Emma's turn to nod.

"Or unless he's a Prox plant," Jennings said.

"Didn't he bring back intelligence on the Prox?" Jo asked.

"Yes, but how do we know he's not just telling us what they want us to hear?" Jennings asked.

"He's not lying," Osprey said. "I can tell you that for sure. Even if what he's saying isn't what happened, he is convinced that it is."

"I want to talk to him," Jo said.

"You're the one who…" Osprey began, but then stopped, obviously trying to find a delicate way to put things.

"I'm the one he has an emotional connection to," Jo said. Her face was rigid, but her feelings were betrayed by a flush of red rising into her cheeks.

Osprey looked at Jennings. "It's a good idea. He might open up to her. And psychologically, he needs…well, maybe not her, but he needs some substantial human contact."

Jennings nodded. “All right. We have our work cut out for us. Doctors, I am grateful for your assistance. And spare no expense—the full resources of the CDF are at your disposal for this.” He jerked his head toward the door. “Captain Taylor, with me.”

ADMIRAL JENNINGS WAVED Captain Taylor into the medical exam room. Protocol dictated that he should enter first, but there was a vestige of chivalry in him that overrode even military training. She considered taking offense at the sexist act but decided there were more important things afoot. “Thank you,” she said instead. The door closed behind them, and Jo unconsciously glanced at the place in the wall where the cameras were hidden, through which Doctors Stewart and Osprey were watching them.

And then there was Jeff in front of her. Big, tough Jeff, whom she had loved once upon a time, now looking diminished and haggard. He saw them and rose unsteadily, saluting. Bags hung under his eyes and his color was pale. “As you were,” Jennings said. Jeff sunk back down to his seat.

“You hungry?” Jo asked, taking a seat across the table from him. Jennings took the seat beside her.

“I could eat,” Jeff answered.

“I’ll bet you could eat a horse by now,” she said, and looked back up at the camera. “Can you guys order him some food?” It was silly to pretend no one was watching, after all. Jeff knew the score. “He hates tomatoes.”

Jeff grinned at her sideways. “Thanks.”

“You could have asked for it yourself.”

“I’ve been kinda busy.”

“You get probed and prodded this much, you’ve earned some chow, soldier,” Jennings said.

“Yes, sir,” Jeff said.

“I’m sorry for all the tests and interviews.”

"No need, Admiral. It's protocol. It has to be done. I don't resent it. It's important."

"I'm glad you feel that way," Jennings nodded. He folded his hands on the table in front of him and cocked his head. "Captain Bowers, are you *you*?"

Jo was surprised at the brevity and directness of the question.

"I am," Jeff answered. "And I'm not."

"Can you explain that?"

"I really am me. I'm the same guy who launched nine months ago. I'm the same guy who rode that asteroid in. The same guy who crash-landed on that moon. I have…continuity of consciousness. But this body…" he shook his head. "It's new."

"Son, you have the same scars you've had since you were a boy," Jennings contradicted him.

"It's a good copy, that's for sure," Jeff agreed. "But it's still a copy."

"Son, if that's the case, I'm having a hard time figuring out how I can ask the CDF to trust you."

"If I were them…I *wouldn't* trust me," Jeff shook his head gravely. "Not for a second."

"Should *I* trust you?" Jennings asked.

"As much as you ever did, I guess," Jeff answered. "Different body. Still a prick, though. I can tell you that for certain."

Jennings smiled at that and pulled at his face. "Okay. I want to hear it again. All of it. From the top."

Jeff nodded, knowing the drill, and launched into the story again. This time he added details, thoughts, feelings, intuitions, impressions. Jo saw him grasping at anything new. It was clear to her that he was giving them 110% percent. He was cooperating, and then some. When he was done, Jennings asked him to do it again. He didn't balk, he didn't complain. He just launched right in.

Halfway through the second telling of the session, kitchen staff brought in a hot meal. Jeff fell onto it like a man whose parachute wouldn't open. Jo had never seen anyone demolish a plate of turkey and stuffing that fast. He even seemed a little winded as he forked the last bite into his mouth.

"You could've taken your time with that," Jennings said.

"I could have, but didn't," Jeff said, his mouth still full. "Where was I?"

He didn't pick up mid-sentence, but he might as well have. When he was done, Jennings leaned on his elbows. "Back up to the Ulim. Where are they from?"

Jeff looked up, thinking. "I don't know that, sir. If I sink into the memory of being…connected to them, I can see constellations, but I don't recognize them. And I'm sorry to say that in the moment, I didn't think to ask."

Jennings looked at his hands, nodding thoughtfully. "I don't blame you, son. How many of them are there?"

"They are many…and one." Jeff flinched. "Sorry. That's how they talk. I seem to have picked it up. There are millions of nodes—maybe billions, spread out over more star systems than I could count—but it's kind of a hive mind. There's no individual locus of consciousness, not that I could tell." He leaned back. "They can isolate consciousness. Like, they can wall it off, like they did me at first, for their own protection. But it's not their normal state."

"Do you know anything about their evolution?" Jo asked.

"Only that they used to be like us—not humanoid, maybe, but individual creatures, flesh and blood. Their current form is synthetic, not organic."

"They *made* it? They made *themselves*?" Jennings asked.

"Yes, I suppose they must have. They made it, then they transferred their consciousness into it."

"The Noosphere," Jo whispered.

"What?" Jennings asked.

"A 20th-century theory of the future evolution of humankind. Turned out not to be true for us—at least not yet. But maybe for them…" she bit her finger thoughtfully.

"What do they want with us?" Jennings asked.

Jeff shrugged. "Nothing, so far as I could tell."

"What do you mean, *nothing*?"

"I think they're aware of us. But I don't think we're more than a blip on their radar screen. They don't seem to be concerned about us. They don't seem to want anything from us. They pretty much just ignore us."

"Then why didn't they just ignore you?" Jennings' eyebrows bunched in confusion.

"I think because they took pity on me." Jeff looked the old man in the eye. "That's what happened, sir. They felt sorry for me and they saved me. It was an act of mercy. They don't have any designs on us. There's nothing they want from us. Other than to just be left alone, I guess."

"Then why were they there on that moon?"

Jeff shook his head. "Maybe they were there before we ever landed on New Manila. Maybe *we're* the interlopers. Maybe they only shifted there after the Prox attack—maybe they're worried about the Prox and *they're studying them, too*." Jeff suddenly sat up, and Jo imagined his vitals surging from his excitement.

"But you don't know that," Jennings said.

"No sir." Jeff slumped in his chair again. He yawned.

Jennings' head jerked up and Jo watched as he retrieved something from his neural. "Got a medical report back. No trace of nanotechnology—the kind that would be necessary to reconstruct you."

Jeff shrugged. "I guess they don't use nanobots. What about crystalline structures?"

Jennings shook his head. "It doesn't say."

Jeff tsked.

Jo placed her palms down on the cool surface of the tabletop. "I want to hear how you got back here again."

Jeff nodded. "Okay. I saw this…it was like a cartoon in my head…of alien flowers turning toward the sun."

"A cartoon?" Jo asked.

"Yes."

"What did it mean?"

"I think it was an artistic representation of what was really happening."

"Do you mean like a dream is often a symbolic representation of all that's going on in your life at the moment?" Jo asked.

Jeff moved his head from side to side. "Kind of, I guess. Not so abstract. More…representational. There weren't really flowers, but the Ulim were doing what flowers do, and for the same reason."

"To glean energy?" Jennings asked.

"Yes."

"Then what, son?"

"It's hard to say…I just have flashes…impressions."

Jennings leaned back. "Captain, do you mind if we mine those impressions?"

"What do you mean?"

"I mean, we get a little assistance in here and yank those memories out by the roots."

Jeff nodded. "Be my guest."

"Osprey, you're on," Jennings said to the room. A few minutes later, Doctor Osprey entered with a tray in hand. He stood by the table awkwardly.

Jeff rose, a bit unsteadily, and offered his hand. "Anyone gonna stick a probe in my behind better be on a first-name basis."

Osprey shook it, the corners of a smile turning up on his lips. "No anal probes. I promise."

"What does a guy have to do to get a good anal probe around here?" Jeff sat back down.

Jo snickered and patted his beefy hand, noting how delicate and small her own was in comparison.

Doctor Osprey pulled out the chair next to Jeff and picked a pneumosyringe out of the tray. He checked its settings and then set it against Jeff's throat. "This won't sting."

"Wouldn't matter if it did."

There was a quiet burst of air, and Jeff's eyelids began to flutter. Osprey turned his head and plugged a neural stimulator into his netpiece. It began to blink. "As soon as his eyes close, you can start asking him."

"I didn't want him asleep, goddam it," Jennings barked.

"Don't worry. Ascleperine is a hypnotic, not a narcotic. It won't make him sleepy, just introverted. And the neural stimulator will make sure he stays awake."

Jeff's eyelids finally rested on his sunken cheeks. "Okay. Ask away."

Jennings looked dubious, so Jo took the lead. "Jeff, tell us how you got from the New Manila moon to your bedroom in Anchorage."

"The nodes were winking at me…like fireflies. Then they turned and faced the sun…drinking it up, drinking it up." His words were slurred, but easily understandable. "So many Ulim, all iskondica for the trajj."

"All what for the what?" Jennings asked.

"Then I was with all the trajj, all the way to the top. I could see everything they saw. I could feel it. All of it. Impejaktallic, if you know what I mean."

Jennings looked at Jo and squeezed his hands together, eyes wide. "I'm not sure I do, son."

Then Jeff held his hands out, feeling at the space in front of him as if searching for invisible pull-tabs. "We reached out with our ulnic durr and grabbed the stellak jnar and the stellak ifna." He was talking faster now, clearly excited. A look of fresh wonder broke out over his face. His eyes were still closed, but he held his countenance up toward the light. "And then we pulled." He was hyperventilating now.

Jo looked at Osprey and mouthed, "Is he okay?"

Osprey nodded confidently. Then Jo's hair started to float. So did the doctor's. The cords to the neural stimulator rose as well, as if the gravity generator had gone out and they were suddenly drifting in free space.

"What the fuck?" Jennings asked.

"More tzzen, oppenco tzzen," Jeff said, his mouth starting to foam up. "Ah! There! Yes!" he shouted, a huge smile breaking out on his face. The overhead lights dimmed, as if someone had just turned down a rheostat. "That's it. Afinjjad!"

Jo felt the floor buck beneath her, felt her stomach rise up in protest. She was dizzy with sudden vertigo. Jeff started bleating—not like a goat, but like some unholy mixture of despair and pain and surprise.

Then he stopped. Her hair fell. The lights came back on. Jeff's body was slumped over the table. And on the table—

"Dear God," Jennings said, and clutched at the framed portrait. He dropped the picture just as fast, staring at his hands.

"What is it?" Jo asked reflexively.

"It's burning hot," he said. He held his hands in front of him like a doctor after scrubbing for surgery. But he looked past them to the portrait, lying askew on the table. "That's my wife and son," Jennings nodded. He locked eyes with Jo. "I keep that in my office."

"DID THAT…JUST HAPPEN?" Jo asked no one in particular. Jennings felt paralyzed and said nothing. Osprey, however, didn't suffer from the same paralysis. He jumped up and felt for a pulse at Jeff's neck. Apparently satisfied, Jennings saw him look up and blink, no doubt accessing the captain's vitals.

"Is he okay?" Jo asked.

"He'll live. But let's get him to the infirmary to do a full workup. Whatever he just did here…I don't think the human body was designed to do." Jennings saw Osprey's eyes darting back and forth, navigating menus and no doubt putting in an emergency call.

A red light appeared in the Admiral's peripheral vision. He jerked up and cocked his head, retrieving the message. Then he turned to Jo. "Captain, I…I'm needed elsewhere."

"Something wrong, Admiral?"

"I can't tell you that yet. Stay with him, will you? Send me updates, even if I don't respond."

"Of course."

With stiff movements, Jennings rose and strode out of the interrogation room.

As he walked, the Admiral quickly fired off a message of his own.

—I want the full report. Now.

A moment later, the response pinged in his left eye.

—We're still waiting for it. Sending you everything we've got.

—SAR

Send as received. Jennings had a reputation as a hard ass—fair, but a hard ass just the same. But he knew he didn't hold a candle to his personal secretary, Lieutenant Liu. Adrian was the most no-nonsense person Jennings had ever met, and Jennings trusted him completely. If Adrian got even a scrap of intelligence, Jennings knew he would receive it.

It took five minutes to navigate to his office. As the door slid open Lieutenant Liu snapped to attention. "As you were," Jennings said, striding toward his desk. "What do you have?"

"Incoming signal from the CDF station *Buckland* on the ansible… playable…*now*."

A hologram shimmered in the space just in front of Jennings' desk, showing a star field with a looming planet in the upper right. "That's not *Buckland*," Jennings said.

"I wouldn't know sir."

There was a crackle, and Jennings heard a voice. "CSC station *Buckland* here, Dr. Talon Burton sending. We received this transmission from the merchant vessel *Arcadia*. It wasn't coded to trigger the autorepeater and there's no intended recipient. It's kind of the video equivalent of a scream in the dark. We thought the CDF ought to see it."

"See what?" Jennings said to the room. And then he saw it.

He skirted his desk and came closer to the hologram. He knew if he got too close to it the resolution would deteriorate, so he hovered to find the optimal distance. "Prox," he said. The shape of the ship was unmistakable. A moment later, he saw a second ship emerge from behind the planet. Then a third. "Christ," he swore. "Any way to contact the *Arcadia*?"

"No sir. This is it."

Jennings felt a cold chill spread from his neck down his back as he watched scores of the Prox disengage from their ship and fly directly toward him, toward the camera, toward the *Arcadia*. Jennings expected to feel the impact of the first of the creatures as it lit upon the ship, but the camera didn't even shake. And of course there was no sound. There was just a long shot of enemy creature after enemy creature flying past the camera, until the transmission went black.

"Exactly where was the *Arcadia* located?"

A star chart sprung up in the air where the transmission had been moments before. A red dot indicated the *Arcadia*'s last known location. "Was the *Arcadia* closer to Earth than New Manila or farther away?"

"Closer, sir. If you were to draw a straight line from New Manila to Earth, you'd pass right through that spot."

"I was afraid you'd say that. Lieutenant, what is between *that spot* and Earth?"

"You want a list?"

"Yes, I want a goddam list."

"I'll send it to your neural, sir."

Jennings sighed. "I'm sorry, Adrian. I'm just…"

"I get it sir. No need. You should have the file now."

Jennings pulled it up and whistled. There were about fifty inhabited projects—from colonies to space stations to mining operations to transport and merchant vessels. All were moving targets, of course, but for the moment, all of them fell roughly on a line from the *Arcadia*'s last known position and the Sol system.

"The next sizable colony in its path—"

"Deseret Colony, sir."

"The Mormons."

"Yes sir."

"Distance?"

"Seventeen light years."

"Based on what we know about the cruising speed of the Prox—"

"That's almost nothing, sir."

"Well, how long would it take us at top speed to cross that distance?"

"About fourteen days, sir."

Jennings looked down. "Open a real-time ansible channel to CDF HQ in Regina, as well as our bases on Mars and Europa."

"Yes sir."

"We need every available ship with more than a pop-gun aboard *en route* to Deseret yesterday," he said. "And we need to alert the colony as well, have them muster everything they can."

"They have a formidable defense force, sir."

"Good to hear it. Tell them to get everything they've got in the air."

"Yes sir."

"Oh, and Lieutenant, while we're at it, we might as well remind the Mormons to pray."

EMMA STEWART PAUSED at the door. "Is it okay to come in?" she asked.

Captain Taylor waved her in. "Thanks for coming."

"I'm not a medical doctor, you know," she said.

"No…we're well supplied with those here. That's not why I requested you."

"You think I have some explanation for what happened in there?" Emma took a seat on the other side of Jeff's bed.

"I'm hoping you have a theory," Jo confessed. "Rumor has it you're the best theoretical physicist we have."

"I'm flattered, but they're called 'rumors' for a reason." Captain Taylor was still too pretty, but Emma was warming up to her. Her devotion to Captain Bowers was plain.

Just then Jeff began to stir. He stretched his legs and curled onto his side. Then he must have realized he wasn't alone because he sprung up into a sitting position and looked around wildly.

"Whoa there, soldier," Captain Taylor said with a wry smile. "At ease."

Jeff sank back down on the pillow. Jo hit a button on the bed frame and it rose into a sitting position. "Thanks," Jeff said.

Just then a nurse rushed in, his dreadlocks flailing. "Is he awake?"

"He's awake."

The nurse studied his vitals on the wall display. He keyed in an IV drip adjustment, then turned to Jeff. "How are you feeling?"

"Like I was hit with a landspeeder. I wasn't, right?"

"No landspeeders on the station, no."

"That rules out that theory."

"You were just dehydrated. And exhausted. You need fluids and rest."

"I need to get back to work."

"You *need* a jigsaw puzzle."

Jeff scowled at him. Captain Taylor and Dr. Stewart waited until the nurse finished his business. As soon as he was out of the room, both turned their eyes to Jeff.

"Okay, Captain, how did you do that?" Emma asked.

"Do what?" Jeff asked.

Jo took his hand and smiled encouragingly. "Do you remember… transporting the picture frame from the Admiral's office?"

Jeff cocked his head. Then he found the memory. He brightened a bit. "Oh yeah…that was weird."

Emma tried not to laugh. "That's one way of putting it."

Jeff smiled at her.

"So, tell us how, Jeff," Jo said, squeezing his hand.

"I'm not sure I can explain that, because I don't know."

"We're asking the wrong question, then," Emma said. "Let's try this: Tell us about the *experience* of moving the picture. What do you remember? What were your thoughts and feelings? Physical sensations?"

"Oh, okay. That I can do." Jeff bit his lip, remembering. "It's not like a conscious memory, though. It's more like trying to grasp at a dream. It's…wispy."

"Grab all you can, then," Jo encouraged him.

"I remember how I felt when I was…you know…I was one being, with the Ulim. I remember what it was like to be them, how they reached out—" he closed his eyes and felt at the air with outstretched arms, "how they grabbed it—"

"Grabbed what?" Emma asked.

"Grabbed…space, I guess. So, I just did it again. I was able to find that same place in my head…you know, where they did it…and I was able to do it, too."

"Take us step-by-step," Emma said.

"Okay, sure. I…uh…I closed my eyes, and I felt the big space."

"Big space?" Emma asked.

"Yeah. Oceanic. Infinite. I was able to see…to be…everything. Then I reached out and grabbed it."

"Space?"

"Yes. But it wasn't working. And I realized it was because I have so little power. You know, just what my mitochondria are generating. It's…well, it's not a lot. I needed more—a lot more."

"So what did you do?" Emma asked.

"I did what the Ulim did. I saw myself twisting toward the light, then opening like a flower—"

"You opened like a flower?" Jo asked incredulously.

Emma shot her a warning look. Jo slunk a bit in her seat.

"Yeah, that's what it was like. I felt the power, from the lights—"

"That's not a lot of power, either, those are LQDs."

"It was enough," Jeff said, his eyes still closed. Emma could tell he was concentrating on vividly reliving the experience. "I reached out to the lights and…absorbed the energy. I directed it into my fingers—"

"Your real fingers?" Emma asked.

"Uh…no. The fingers in my mind. Sorry, I know how that sounds."

"Keep going, soldier," Jo said.

"I felt it running through me, the energy," he said, his face brightening, as if he were feeling that energy again. "Then…it was strange. I didn't just feel like I was one with everything. I could actually *see* everything. I could see through the walls. I could see the Ulim on the New Manila moon. I could see every person, every creature on every world…kind of all at once. Distance…there wasn't any distance. You know how it's always *now*? Every *place* was *here*." He opened his eyes and stared at the hands in front of him. "Here," he repeated.

"The picture?" Emma prompted.

"Oh. Yeah. The energy was beginning to…well, the energy wasn't giving out, but I was…I don't know how to put this. My ability to channel it was flagging. I got really tired really fast. So I just grabbed the space around a random object—something nearby, something I knew would have some meaning."

"That's good, Captain," Emma said. "Just stay with the memories a little bit longer. When you grabbed the space around the picture, how did you *move* it?"

"I…uh…" Jeff rubbed his head. Then he closed his eyes again and reached his fingers out as far as they could go. He mimed grabbing at something, pinching the air between his thumbs and forefingers. "I just…*squashed* the space between the photo and the table we were sitting at."

"You *squashed* the space?" Jo asked, frowning.

"Yeah, like pushing the space between them out of the way until the picture and the desk were in the same spot, you know, physically. I gripped the space around the photo, and then I just let go. I guess I released the pressure I'd built up and it snapped back, kind of like a rubber band or a spring being released. And once I did that, all the… distance rushed back in—"

"But the picture remained on this side of the distance gap." Emma looked away as she spoke, thinking.

"Yeah. That's it exactly," Jeff agreed.

Emma nodded. "It sounds like your perception went four-dimensional."

Jeff cocked an eyebrow. "I thought the fourth dimension was time."

She shook her head. "That's different. Space actually has a fourth physical dimension, at right angles to the three we perceive normally—that is, width, height and depth."

"Superluminal travel is only possible because of the fourth dimension," Jo added.

"Yes." Emma pointed at Jo. "A quantum engine warps three-space in the fourth dimension, compressing it in front of a ship, expanding it behind. And the ship surfs that wave in a bubble of normal, unwarped space."

Jeff stared at her, blinking.

"Okay, let's take it down a level," Emma suggested. "There was a book written in 1884 called *Flatland*, and it tried to help people visualize the fourth dimension. A map is flat, right? It's two-dimensional. If your whole world was inside the map, your line of sight would stop at the first object that was in your way. But an observer in three-space would be able to see the entire map at once. You'd be able to see over any two-dimensional obstacles, even *inside* objects."

Jo nodded. "You'd also be able to pick the map up and fold it so that any two points were next to each other."

"Exactly!" Emma said, a broad smile breaking out on her face. "So, what if that's what Jeff was able to do, only in three-dimensional space? What if he tapped into the fourth dimension where he was able to see every point at once?"

"A circle whose center is everywhere and whose circumference is nowhere," Jo recited.

"Huh? What was that?" Emma asked, cocking her head.

"Just...something I read somewhere. I think it's Meister Eckhart."

Jeff nodded. "Well, that's not far off, I think. But the thing about your analogy is that if you're looking down at the map, then you're also outside of the map. I didn't feel like I was outside the universe. Just...present at every point in it."

"It's an analogy," Emma waved his objection away. "You can't drive it to Toledo."

"Where the fuck is Toledo?" Jo asked.

"It used to be in the old sunbelt," Jeff said. "It got scorched, of course."

Jo shifted in her seat. "Jeff, do you think you could do this again? The frame trick, I mean."

Jeff nodded. "Yeah, I don't see why not. I can't do it right now, though. I'm pretty beat."

Emma frowned, staring at a blank space on the wall. "Do you think you could move something...larger?"

Jeff shrugged. "Sure. The only thing I'm not sure about is the energy. I mean, I used the energy from the lights this time, and I think the picture frame was...small. Commensurate, I guess you could say, to the amount of energy I was able to draw. If I wanted to move something larger, then I think I'd need more energy."

"But you don't know," Emma said. It wasn't a question. "So let's find out."

JENNINGS HAD WORKED through the night and had mobilized everything possible. Every ship at his disposal was being prepped and staffed at that very moment. The first of them would launch in just under two hours, and he had only one more appointment to make. He looked around his office and noted for the first time how spare and sterile it was. What was he trying to save, after all, if not life and beauty and art? And yet he had no time for such things in his own life, had devoted no wall space to them. His office had all the charm of an industrial storage room. Becky, if she were still living, would never have permitted this. She would have breezed in one day when he was out and made the place human. Livable. Homey, even. She wouldn't have asked permission. That wasn't her way. She would have just done it. Perhaps that's why he hadn't. There was no way he could have done it as good as she would have.

But he could just hear her clicking her tongue at him, looking at this place. He looked up and made a note on his neural.

—Potted plant. Landscape.

Becky wasn't partial to landscapes, but he liked them. In his mind's eye he saw an oil painting of a windswept Scottish shoreline, perhaps something from the 19th century. He was no great expert on art, but the image in his mind was so vivid he was sure it must exist somewhere. And finding it might make an excellent diversion once he was planetside. For now, though, there were lives to save. He looked up and sent a message to Liu.

—Do you have those time estimates?

A few moments later the answer came.

—Just in. You're not going to like them. If we launch according to schedule, the first of our warships will arrive about eight hours after the Prox do.

"Shit," Jennings said, and punched at the arm of his chair.

—We have to get them there faster.

—Not possible, sir. That estimate is based on a cruising speed of C8.

Dammit, he didn't want those ships there in fifteen days, he wanted them there *now*. He wanted… His eyes rested on the negative space left where the picture of Becky and their kids had been "jumped" from. He usually felt a slight ache when he looked at that picture. He wasn't prepared for a deeper ache now that it was gone.

—Keep me apprised.

He leaped up and began speed walking toward the infirmary. Along the way he sent messages to Captain Taylor and Dr. Stewart, asking them to assemble and give him a full report. Ten minutes later he arrived at the door to Jeff's room. Dr. Stewart arrived a minute later. Jo wasn't far behind. "I don't suggest we go in," Emma said.

"Because?"

"Because he's sleeping. The…squashing…takes a lot out of him. He needs to rest."

"Squashing? Is that what we're calling it?"

"It's what he called it. It's not a technical term, I'll give you that. But until we know what he's actually doing, there *isn't* a technical term for it." Emma waved her arm down the hall. "There's a consult room nearby. Let's go there."

Jennings and Jo followed her down a corridor and into a soft-lit room with a few comfortable chairs gathered around a holodisplay. Jennings sat on the edge of one of the chairs. He turned to Jo. "How do you think he's holding up…I mean, emotionally?"

Jo shrugged. "It's hard to tell with Jeff. He's not exactly a guy who wears his heart on his sleeve. He seems fine to me, though. I mean, I'm not Doctor Osprey, but he seems pretty normal, actually. He's not traumatized or anything. He's certainly cooperating."

Jennings pursed his lips and nodded.

"Admiral, can I ask you something?" Jo asked. "Do you…believe him?"

"Captain Bowers? You mean, do I believe he's telling the truth?" Jennings looked her in the eye. "Hell yes, I believe him. I still have a lot of questions, but my gut knows the truth of it. He's the same man I sent out there. And no one could…no one can do what he did earlier today. No one. He doesn't have any more clue than we do what happened there, I'm sure of that."

He turned to Emma. "I want to find out how he did that. More than that, I want to know how we can *use* it."

"Use it?" Emma frowned.

"Doctor, we have a classified situation going on right now. I can't tell you any details, but what I can say is that people are going to die because we can't get to them in time. If we can figure out how he does…what he does…" he didn't finish the sentence. He stared at the floor, at the worn seam of his boot.

"I get it," Emma said. "We're going to need a lab."

"We're going to need a place where no one will ask any goddam questions," Jennings said. "If word got out about this…let's just say I wouldn't want to…lose control of our asset."

"Jeff's an asset?" Jo asked, a dark note in her voice.

"My God, Captain, I hope so." Jennings made for the door. "And Captain," he paused, "I need to see you in my office in five minutes. You might want to…hell, you might want to say goodbye."

Jo stepped in, looking apprehensive. "What did you want to see me about, sir?" The door slid shut behind her.

Jennings sighed. He called up the cartography holo and waved at it. "The Prox are approaching Deseret Colony. They'll arrive in eleven days."

Jo nodded. She didn't look the slightest bit surprised. Or scared. She just looked *determined*. That was good. "I know you want to be here for Captain Bowers right now, but—"

"Permission to speak freely, sir?"

"Of course."

"I want to be wherever you think I can do the most good. Yes, I have…I care about Captain Bowers. But if I were going to let that get in the way of my duty I would have married him fifteen years ago. I didn't and I don't regret it. You put me where you need me."

"That's what I like about you, Jo. Brassier balls than a monkey. Here's the problem, our fleet can't get there for eleven days, and that's all out at C8."

Jo's eyes moved back and forth as she thought. "What kind of defenses do—"

"Considerable, thank God. More than New Manila had. But will it be enough? I've got scientists from all over the world giving me conflicting opinions about that. The problem is that we know so little about the Prox. If we could capture one of them, we could study it, figure out its limitations. But for now, that's way down on my to-do list."

"What's at the top, sir?"

"Blowing them out of the fucking sky."

"I'm your man, sir," Jo said.

"I hope so, Captain, because I'm giving you the only ship that has a chance of making it there before the Prox do. The *Essex* is the prototype for the Victory class of warships. It's untried in battle, but it's ready to go. It will also get you C8.4."

Jo's eyes widened. She was no dummy. She knew that C-velocity was exponential rather than incremental. She'd be there ahead of the Prox. Not by much, but by God, she'd make it.

"Firepower, sir?" she asked.

"Sixty-eight point-adjustable particle cannons aft and fore, four sear-laser ports with 360-degree targetability, five hundred two cloaked torpedoes, both forty and sixty megaton."

Jo whistled. "I could do some serious damage with that, sir."

"I'm counting on it." Jennings looked up and checked the time on his neural. "Gather your duffle. You launch in twenty minutes."

CHAPTER FOUR

"Welcome to Alberta, Captain." A young enlisted woman moved to hoist Jeff's duffle from the shuttle. Jeff stepped in front of her and lifted it out himself.

"Nobody's entirely welcome in Alberta," he said. "And I'll carry my own bag, thank you."

"Yes sir," the private avoided looking him in the eye.

A moment later Doctor Stewart was beside him. "Why is no one entirely welcome in Alberta?" she asked.

"Oh. Uh…hi." Jeff considered apologizing for his surliness, but thought better of it. He offered his hand, and Emma shook it. He was a little unsettled by her. She wasn't quite his type—a little too overtly feminine. But there was something about her that made him forget his shoe size momentarily whenever he was around her. Instead of looking at her, Jeff deliberately looked around, noting the prairie filled with wild grasses and flowers, underneath the biggest sky he ever remembered seeing.

"Thank you, private," Emma said, dismissing the young woman. "C'mon, Captain, let's get you settled in." With a jerk of her head, she set out for the few structures marring the landscape. "Are you feeling better?"

"It's good to be on terra firma."

"Hmm..." Emma narrowed her eyes at him as he fell into pace beside her. "Nice dodge. I'll have to be careful of that. But I thought you didn't mind being in space?"

"I don't. That doesn't mean I don't like being planetside. Besides, there are fewer spiders here."

Emma laughed. "You got me there. Christ, the spiders."

"So what do we have here?" Jeff gestured at the buildings.

Emma indicated an old farmhouse that looked like it was straight out of a postcard. "The house is HQ here. The longhouses behind are barracks. You get a private room in the house."

"You're shitting me. Why?"

"The gossip is that it's because you're a lucky bastard and for some reason Jennings thinks it's important that you rest."

"No complaints here."

"Next to the longhouses are the mess and rec hall."

"How many stationed here?"

"It's pretty much a skeleton crew," Emma said. "And as I'm sure you've guessed, this is top secret."

"I'm good with that." Jeff gave a quick nod. "What's with the big place?" He indicated with his chin a large, prefabricated box of a building to the left of the barracks.

"Half of that is our lab."

"And the other half?"

"The most powerful electrical generator on the hemisphere."

"What? Why?"

"Because you'll need it." Emma stopped and looked puzzled. "At least, that's what you suggested."

"No, I mean why is there a massive electrical generator out here... in the middle of a cornfield? Why isn't it powering a city?"

"Oh," Emma resumed her pace. "We had limited choices, really. Most generators are...well, *they're near cities*."

"I'm not an idiot," Jeff complained. "My question was about *this* generator and why it's *not* near a city."

"I know you're not, Captain. But the answer to your question is, I'm afraid, above both of our security clearances."

"Like fuck it is."

"So you *are* feeling better," Emma grinned.

"What makes you say that?"

"Everyone says that you're normally a son of a bitch."

Jeff grunted, but couldn't help smiling. "Okay, I can see it. Jennings picked this site because it's nearly deserted. If we blow anything up—"

"Who would know?" Emma finished his sentence. "I mean, besides the mallards?"

Jo LOOKED up and accessed her neural. Reports from all over the ship were coming in like clockwork, exactly as they should. None were marked urgent, but she scanned them anyway. Everything seemed shipshape except for a malfunctioning food synthesizer unit in the aft mess.

She ran her fingers over the arm of the command chair, feeling once again the thrill of being at the helm of such an impressive vessel. Everything about the *Essex* gleamed. The stars on the viewscreen looked immobile, but she knew that was just an illusion, like staring at the hands of an old-fashioned clock. They were moving, just too slowly to see. And yet, she felt she could *almost* see them moving. After all, she had never gone this fast before. No humans ever had. It seemed incredible that she didn't feel like she was moving at all.

She rose and did a lap around the bridge, looking over the shoulders of her bridge crew, as if making sure all was in order. Commander Fin, her navigator, looked over at her as she approached him, and gave her a patient smile. She avoided going too close, not wanting to annoy him.

Her crew was not battle-tested, and that concerned her. They had nearly two weeks in space without much to do, and she wanted to make good use of that time. Starting tomorrow they'd be running emergency drills and battle scenarios.

The lift door hissed open and Commander Tohi entered. He had been assigned to be her number one, her second in command. Captains usually chose their own number ones, but time had not afforded her that luxury. She'd met the Pacific Islander only briefly since their launch, and he seemed a surly fellow. Her gut told her that he had a chip on his shoulder about something, but she would need to have a sit-down with him to figure out what. Well, it wasn't like they didn't have time. "Report, Mr. Tohi?"

The Commander went to the spare duty station without answering, turning his back on her. Jo felt the hair rise on her neck, and she looked around at her bridge crew to gauge their reactions to this unprovoked insubordination. Commander Fin's spine straightened and he studiously kept his eyes fixed on the panel in front of him. To his left, Lieutenant Frey froze, her hands poised over her communications panel. Her eyes darted back and forth, trying not to react to the fact that the captain was looking at her. To Fin's right, Weaponer Raj turned and, unfazed and unafraid, glanced back and forth between the captain and Commander Tohi, a look of puzzlement on his face. Chief Engineer Laru raised one eyebrow but otherwise appeared impassive.

Jo hated confrontations like these. But they were, unfortunately, part of the job. She drew a deep breath and stood, stepping off of the command podium and taking the few steps over to the duty station. "Mr. Tohi," she said.

His face was buried in a monitor and he did not look up. "I'm listening," he said.

"Mr. Tohi, you are in imminent danger of losing your commission if you don't forget about the fascinating object on your viewscreen this moment and face your commanding officer."

Mr. Tohi looked up then, his face a hard mask of resentment and anger.

"Mr. Tohi, do we have a problem?"

"The only problem, sir, is that I have been prepping this ship for the past nine months. I know her inside and out."

"And you think the conn should be yours."

"It should be. And everyone here thinks so."

Jo looked around at the bridge crew again. Everyone was looking at them now. When she met his eye, Fin looked away.

"Weaponer Raj, do you think Commander Tohi ought to be captain?"

Raj looked back and forth between them some more before answering. Finally he spoke, his words careful and deliberate. "I think Commander Tohi has done a fine job preparing this ship. I think he is untested in battle."

"And what is your opinion of me, Weaponer?"

"I do not know you, sir. But your war record is…impressive, sir."

"Will you have any hesitation about following me into battle, Mr. Raj?"

"None whatsoever, Captain."

"You will let me buy you a drink after your bridge shift, Weaponer."

"Yes, sir."

"Mr. Tohi, whose decision was it to put me in charge of the *Essex*?"

"Admiral Jennings."

Jo noted he omitted the "sir" he owed her. He would pay for that.

"And are you in the habit of second-guessing Admiral Jennings?"

Tohi didn't answer, but she could see his quick eyes darting back and forth as he thought about it.

"Commander Fin, please pull up star chart 47392-E and display it on the forward viewscreen."

"Yes sir."

"Commander Tohi, please join me. I want to show you something." She stepped away from the duty station and down two steps to the broad space in front of the viewscreen. She didn't need to look over her shoulder to know what Tohi was doing. He was sitting straight up in his chair, looking at the accusing eyes of the bridge crew. Slowly, he'd rise to his feet, extricate himself from the duty station, and step down.

She heard his foot on the carpeted stair and knew she was right. She continued staring up at the star chart calmly, her hands behind her back. A few moments later, Tohi was standing beside her.

"Yes?" he asked. Not "yes, sir," she noted.

"Being a battle commander requires seeing what's coming, even when it's invisible," she said to him, her voice patient and kind, as if talking to a child. Her tone was perfectly calculated to piss him off.

"If you look there," she pointed at a star cluster in the Horsehead Nebula. "What *can't* you see?"

Tohi squinted at the screen. She glanced over at him with a sad smile on her face. A split second later she dropped to the carpet, rolled, kicked Tohi's legs out from under him, and leaped back into standing position. Before he could even shriek, her boot was on his neck. Just a tiny bit more pressure, and she would crush his windpipe.

"Mr. Tohi, who is captain of this ship?" She released a bit of pressure, to allow him access to his lungs.

"You are, Captain."

"Who is my number one? Who is the person I can count on through thick and thin? Who has my back?"

"I do."

"I don't think you do, Commander. I need to trust my number one. And the only thing I trust you to do is step over my steaming corpse to assume command at the first possible opportunity. Allow me to tell you what you are going to do now. You are going to go to your cabin. You are going to gather your things. Then you are going to head for the escape pods. You're going to get into one of them, and you're going to go back to Sol Station. And you'll do it quickly, because every second you delay will mean a longer trip home for you. Mr. Fin, how long will it take Commander Tohi to return home from our current location at a pod's top speed?"

"Checking, sir," Fin said, his voice shaking. "Four months. Sir."

"If we finish before you get home, we'll give you a lift on our return trip. But for now, I want you off my ship." She turned to Raj. "Weaponer, call a security detail up here to escort Commander Tohi to his cabin, and then to his pod. Oh, and Mr. Raj, until I select a new number one, you'll be acting in that role. Any objections?"

Raj's eyes were full of approval and admiration. "None, sir."

"Good to hear it. I won't tolerate insubordination on this ship. We have a chain of command, and all of our lives depend on it. Attitude gets people killed, Mr. Tohi." She removed her boot from his neck. "I want you to think about that on your long voyage home."

JEFF LOOKED up from his breakfast to see Emma approaching.

"Can't a guy enjoy his eggs?"

"Are you enjoying your eggs?" Emma paused in front of the table and jutted out one hip.

"Not really."

"Then I guess a guy can't. C'mon. We're ready for you."

"I'm gonna finish my fucking eggs," Jeff said. "So have a seat."

Emma smirked, but sat. "The food isn't bad here," she noted.

"Yeah, I got that. Is the cuisine always so good at top-secret joints?"

"I wouldn't know. But my guess is that we just lucked out and got a good cook."

"Who're *we,* by the way?" Jeff asked. He picked up a slice of toast and added some jam to it from a covered jar on the table.

"The *team*. You'll meet them soon enough. How are you doing?"

Jeff chewed and narrowed his eyes. "Define *doing*."

"How are you feeling?"

"Physically?"

"Sure. We can start there."

"I feel great. Better than I have in years. I'm rested. I'm healthy." He shrugged. "Great."

"And emotionally?"

Jeff put the toast back on his plate and ran the napkin across his lips. "Look, Dr. Stewart, I don't really know you, and I don't feel comfortable—"

"I get it, Captain, but let's be clear about something. This project has a chain of command. When Jennings isn't on site, I'm in charge."

"Why isn't Jennings on site?"

"He has…other things to attend to."

"And Jo…Captain Taylor?"

"Her too."

"What things?"

"Need to know, Captain."

He tossed his toast down and licked the jam off his thumb.

"So let's try this again. Because I'm not your mother, I'm not your girlfriend, I'm not your clergyperson, and I'm not your shrink. I'm your commanding officer. How are you doing emotionally?"

Jeff nodded, pursing his lips but not looking at her. "If that's the case, *sir*, I… Look, Doctor, I'm sure I *have* feelings. I just…don't always know what they are. Okay?"

Emma smiled wryly. "So you're basically saying you're male."

Jeff smirked. He dabbed another piece of toast in the egg yolk rampant on his plate. "I'm…different."

"How so?"

"Before, when I was…before I was…before the Ulim deposited me back in Anchorage, let's put it that way—"

"Okay. Before then?" Emma leaned forward on her elbows.

"Before then I was…I just wanted to be as far away from people as possible."

"Captain Taylor told me something about that."

Jeff nodded. He knew Jo had been hurt—that he had hurt her. His eyes moved back and forth as he remembered.

"Go on."

"I wanted to get as far away as possible—not from her—from… everybody. Because—"

"Because of Catskill?"

"Who told you about Catskill?"

"I was read in. I had to be, Captain. Jennings couldn't possibly have left me in command of you without telling me about it."

He couldn't look at her. He swallowed and gave a barely perceptible nod. "I…a lot of people died there…because of me. I figured if I just wasn't around people, they wouldn't be in any danger, you know?"

"If you'll pardon my saying so, Captain, that's bordering on narcissistic."

"Narcissistic?"

Emma leaned back and tapped her fingers on the table. "The danger has nothing to do with you. We both work for the CDF. People will always be in danger."

"It has to do with me when I'm in charge."

"Being in charge doesn't make you omnipotent. I read the reports, Captain. No one—not a single investigation of the Catskill incident—even hinted at an error in judgment on your part."

"I'm still responsible. But…I feel differently now than…before I went out to New Manila."

"Different how?" She looked up and met his eyes.

"I don't need to slink off under a rock now."

"No? What do you need, then?"

"I need revenge."

"Against who?"

"Who do you think?"

"Is this still a Catskill thing?"

"No, it isn't a fucking Catskill thing. It's a Prox thing." Jeff rubbed his fingers over a beard that was beginning to fill in again. "Look, right or wrong, I blamed myself for Catskill. But even though I was there at New Manila, I know I didn't cause it. *They* did. And I want blood."

"It might not be red."

"It better not be."

Emma's lips turned up in the beginning of a smile. In spite of himself, Jeff found he liked her…a little more than he should have.

She stood and straightened her uniform. "So what are we waiting for?"

Jeff picked up his tray and carried it to the bus station. Then he fell into step beside her. "I wish I knew what we were trying to accomplish here."

"We're exploring. Looking for a possible edge. It's R&D."

"I don't see it."

Emma laughed. "Jo said something about you being a meathead."

"Gee, thanks."

"No offense intended. Look, if this is folly, it's Jennings' folly. He's a visionary. It's why he's an Admiral."

"Jennings is a visionary? Are you on morphex?"

"I've worked under Jennings for more than five years now. He has a sixth sense about things. He trusts his gut…and it's usually right. He sees potential in plans that sound crazy. He spots talent in people others dismiss."

"He did pick *me* out of the crowd of cadets," Jeff admitted.

They were nearly at the big, boxy prefabricated building. It loomed over them long before they arrived, much larger than it looked from a distance. Emma held the door for him. Jeff blinked as his eyes adjusted. It seemed no less voluminous inside than it had outside. Instead of being carved up into floors and rooms, the building housed one large, cavernous space. One half of the mammoth building was taken up with machinery that seemed both antiquated and arcane. The other was filled with cubicles and room dividers—all of which felt to him ineffectual, given the enormity of the unbroken space just above their heads.

Emma led him to the bank of cubicles. Standing near a door was a hard mountain of a soldier, a very large laser rifle slung at his side. His uniform-t was pulled tight over his brown neck, and his bulging arm muscles had obviously been modified, probably on a 'roid regimen begun in grade school. "This is Lieutenant Suarez. He'll be providing security for us here." Jeff nodded at Suarez, but the big man's hard, glassy eyes betrayed no response.

Emma then waved her hand toward a middle-aged man who looked like his people might have come from Korea or Japan. He was sitting stock upright, his eyes rolled up into his head, obviously reading something on his neural. He must have sensed motion, because he lowered his eyes and smiled. "Captain, this is Dr. Tan," Emma introduced them. "He's a medical doctor. He's going to make sure we don't kill you while we do…whatever it is we're doing."

Jeff shook hands with the doctor, but withdrew his hand quickly because the man shook with the conviction of a limp toad. Jeff hated that. It made him want to squeeze the man's hand until a bone snapped, but he resisted that temptation. "Dr. Tan is going to be monitoring your vitals and tending to you should there be anything…should…anything unforeseen happen." Jeff nodded and Emma continued. "And I will be monitoring the gravimeter, looking for any unexpected local phenomenon, but most especially for any warping of spacetime."

Jeff nodded. "Let's squash," he said, rolling up his sleeves. "So what is that?" He indicated the massive arcane machinery with a flick of his chin.

Emma turned toward the half of the room filled with the looming machinery. "*That* is your power source. That's primarily why we're here."

"Looks like something out of a Jules Verne novel."

"It does indeed," Emma conceded. "But it was actually built in the mid-twentieth century by Canadian researchers trying to find a limit to the load of a proposed power grid."

"Did they find it?" Jeff asked.

"At about one-one-hundredth of the capacity of that thing."

"So it was a bit of overkill at the time."

"Yes. Lucky for us."

"Surely we have this thing beat by a mile by now?" Jeff said.

"Yes and no," Emma said. "The fact is that most of our electronics use far less power than even your basic toaster did in the mid-twentieth century. We just have no need to generate power on this scale anymore."

"And our propulsion systems—"

"Have electronics, but aren't driven by electricity."

"Right. Of course."

"So sure, we could have rigged up something new and flashy, but why? As Victorian as it looks to you and me, Captain, it will do the job just fine."

"Okay, I'm convinced," Jeff said. "So what's the plan?"

"This way," Emma turned and began walking at a brisk pace toward the east side of the building. Jeff had to nearly trot to keep up with her, but he found he enjoyed the challenge. And the view. The pear-shape of her bottom moved like a ringing bell as she walked, and

Jeff found it impossible not to watch. As he did, he felt his own chemistry changing.

A few moments later, they reached an area a good distance away from the cubicles. In front of them was a horseshoe-shaped structure about nine feet high, made of a dull black material. Jeff reached out and touched it. "Rubber?"

"Close enough," Emma said. "It's a shielded polymer. Nothing gets in, nothing gets out. Not electricity, not radiation, not spiders."

"This is my office, then," Jeff said.

"We hope you like it," Emma smiled briefly. Her short blonde hair bobbed as she jerked her head back to the structure. She keyed in a code and a small door appeared, similar to the kind Jeff was used to seeing on starships between structural sections. In space these could be used as airlocks in case one part of the ship is damaged and depressurizes. "This way."

Jeff followed Emma in. "Will my standard code work on that?"

"Yep," Emma answered ahead of him. The polymer wall seemed to be massive. Jeff estimated it was a solid eight feet. The doorway was, in fact, a short hallway, spilling them into a room that looked like a cross between a hospital room and a starship bridge. Where the captain's chair would be was what looked like an oversized easy chair, ash gray in color, with a matching gray linen headrest. Behind it were IV poles with bags hanging and ready to go. Some kind of medical monitoring device stood to one side. Jeff saw thick rubber cables running into a hole in the floor. A snake's nest of smaller cables lay in a woven basket beside it. "Quaint," Jeff said to no one in particular.

Around the periphery of the room holomonitors were projecting a variety of information. Jeff turned as Dr. Tan entered and watched as he made his way to the chair. He pulled a small metal rolling stool out of some cubbyhole Jeff hadn't noticed and sat down on it, pulling the tangle of cables out of the basket. "We've set you up with a head, right over there, Captain," he said. "Might want to use it before we hook you up."

"I'm fine," Jeff said.

Tan patted the large chair. "Time to get you wired in, then."

Jeff's eyebrows lifted as he caught and held Emma's eyes. She nodded at him encouragingly, and he strode the few paces to the chair and sat down. Tan instantly went to work, first plugging a mercy cord into his neural port, then laying out a series of wires with nodes and suction cups on the ends of them. "Is *everything* from the twentieth century here?" Jeff asked.

"Doctor Tan needs several readings your neural can't give him," Emma explained.

"Doctor Tan is unnecessarily nosy."

Tan harrumphed, but a slight smile escaped him as he pointed to Jeff's shirt. "You need to lose the laundry, Captain. Just your shirt. If you're cold, I can give you a blanket when we're done."

Jeff crunched forward, and removed his CDF jersey with a single motion, tossing it to the floor.

Jeff thought he caught Emma admiring him, and she looked away a little too quickly. He felt pleased about that. Tan applied some kind of gel to the contact sensors from a small tube, and began fixing them to different places on his torso. "I'm going to do a bit of minor surgery now," Tan said. "I need to insert a PICC line so we can run our IV without having to gift you with a new puncture wound every day. It won't be pleasant, but—"

"What's the IV for?"

"To keep your fluids up, keep your electrolytes balanced, supply you with steroids, stimulants, and anxiolytics—"

"I don't need any fucking anxiolytics."

"To be frank, Captain, that's my call, not yours."

"Just do it," Jeff said, closing his eyes in resignation. He was aware that he was less patient with the man simply because the doctor didn't know how to shake his hand properly. He knew there was something wrong with that, but he didn't care enough to do anything about it.

Tan nodded and picked up what looked like a small power tool. He held the narrow end of it just below Jeff's collarbone, and then judged the angle of its descent. Squinting, Tan changed the angle a fraction of a degree, and touched a node on the handle. Jeff heard a puff of air, and then felt a stab in his chest. The pain followed a moment later. "Jesus fucking—"

"Just hold on," Tan said. He fixed a tube connector to the PICC line, and a moment later the pain subsided.

"You could have blocked that with the neural," Jeff said, a note of accusation in his voice.

"Could have," Tan said. "And I was about to suggest it. But you said—"

"Can we just get this done?" Jeff barked.

Tan's face went blank and he continued his work. A minute later he swiveled on his stool and faced Emma. "He's unpleasant, but ready."

Emma walked over, and with a flick of her chin Tan surrendered his stool. She sat on it and rolled close to Jeff. "Captain, the next few days are going to be pretty taxing."

"I'm a soldier, Doctor. Taxing comes with the territory."

"We're also working somewhat at cross-purposes. That's just…full disclosure." She smiled a little sadly. "Admiral Jennings wants to exploit whatever…gift…you seem to have acquired for whatever military applications we might uncover. But I'm…"

"You want to advance science."

"Yes."

"And you don't want it to be abused."

"Right."

"Well, doctor, we're just going to have to trust each other. But the thing about that is…well, you scientists have always been on the losing side of that contest."

She didn't answer. What could she say? It was true.

"If you think we're going to pass up an effective weapon just because it might be…" he fished for the word.

"Immoral?" she asked.

He narrowed his eyes. "I thought you were a physicist. Now you're an ethicist?"

"History holds all of us accountable for our behavior, Captain. You look me in the eye and tell me that you're proud of everything you've ever done as a soldier."

He looked down. He felt suddenly very small. "I…"

"Let's just trust each other," Emma said.

"Okay," Jeff agreed.

"So, here's what we need to do first. I want to see if I can measure how far away you can sense things, and how far away you can affect them."

"How are you going to do that?"

"You're going to tell me what you see, focusing on increasingly distant outposts, and we'll verify your observations by the ansible."

"What if no one answers the ansible?"

"Have you ever known someone not to answer an ansible call?"

"Not if they're alive, no."

"Jeff," Emma placed a tentative hand on his chest. "Don't be difficult."

"Did no one warn you that I had a reputation?"

"You don't need to prove it. Let's have fun with this."

"Fun."

"Yeah. Let's give that a whirl."

Jeff nodded. "All right. Let's have some fun with it."

Emma stood and headed for the exit. "We'll communicate by voice—your chair is fitted with a microphone. Also, when your eyes are open and you're not…under, I suppose…you can see me on the monitors. Also, feel free to use your neural to text."

"And power?" Jeff asked.

"Right over there," Emma pointed beyond the walls of the containment unit toward where the mammoth generator loomed. "We've arranged it to ramp up according to load. So go ahead and draw on it…however you do that…and it *should* keep pace with you. The more you draw, the more it will supply. Its capacity isn't infinite, but I seriously doubt you'll max it out."

"I guess we'll see," Jeff said.

"I guess we will. Good luck, Captain." Steward turned again and, followed by Tan, left him alone in what seemed to him to be a giant rubber donut.

Jo NEEDED a cup of Mayan hot chocolate after her confrontation with Tohi. She felt slightly guilty and wondered if perhaps she'd been too hard on him. As the crew rotation neared she knew exactly what her bridge crew would be talking about in the mess. In twenty-four hours there wouldn't be a single crewmember who hadn't heard the tale—probably wildly exaggerated by that time, which only played in her favor. She didn't know if she'd been too hard on Tohi, but she did know one thing—she wouldn't have any more trouble with her chain of command. She'd have to thank Commander Tohi for that some day. Maybe she'd send flowers.

A blinking red light in her neural alerted her to an incoming message, marked urgent. She looked up and accessed it.

—Engineer Ngoku *en route* to sickbay. Electrical shock while repairing food synthesizer unit in aft mess.

Jo frowned. That should have been a minor repair. She stood and straightened her uniform. "I'm going to supervise a repair. You have the bridge, Mr. Raj."

Raj nodded in acknowledgement and stood to take the con. *I'm going to have to get to know him better,* Jo thought as she headed for the lift. He intrigued her. She also had to admit that she found him attractive. Too young for her, but hot nevertheless.

A few minutes later she entered the aft mess and strode toward the cluster of engineers gathered around a partly disassembled food synthesizer unit. "Captain on deck," one of them shouted when he saw her. The others leaped to their feet and stood at attention.

"As you were," Jo said, clasping her hands behind her back. "Any word on Ensign Ngoku?" she asked.

"They said he was going to be fine, sir." The ranking engineer in this gaggle was only a lieutenant junior grade, and he looked nervous enough to lose his lunch on her shoes if she didn't put him at ease.

"I'm glad to hear it. Thank you for getting him help so quickly."

"Uh…of course, sir." The man was thin and tall, with flaming red hair. He was starting to sweat.

"What happened?"

"A pretty old-fashioned problem, sir. Some wiring wasn't properly shielded when this unit was installed."

"Isn't everything solid state?"

"Yes, sir, but you still have to get power to it. You'll see that the casing is metal—it's a conductor."

"The casing was in contact with the unshielded wiring," Jo reasoned, "and Ensign Ngoku got quite a shock."

"That's what happened, sir."

"Is that the only thing wrong with the unit?"

"Uh…no sir. Its fabrication is…flawed. If you order apple pie, it comes out looking like oatmeal. In fact, everything comes out looking like oatmeal. Still tastes like apple pie, just not that appetizing."

"Is it spiders?"

The lieutenant chuckled, looking at his shoes momentarily. She read the nametape sewed onto his uniform—*Kerr*. "Oh, no sir. No spiders on this ship."

Jo harrumphed. "How long do you think *that* will last, Mr. Kerr?"

"I…uh…oh, probably about three months, sir."

"Tell me the truth. There are spiders aboard now."

"Uh…yes sir. But not many."

"Right. So it's not spiders. Does the fabrication error have anything to do with the wiring problem?"

"No sir. Ensign Ngoku was investigating the fabrication errors when he touched the casing, and…well, *zap*." The lieutenant looked profoundly uncomfortable.

"How much of a charge did he get?"

"Uh…about 240 volts. But the amps were low, thank God."

"Lieutenant, I'm going to eat my dinner from this machine tonight. I don't expect my steak to look like oatmeal."

"No sir."

She turned on her heel and headed back to the bridge, but the idea of the boredom of sitting in that bridge chair—as shiny as it was—depressed her. She made a course correction and headed for stellar cartography. She'd see how the simulations were coming along. And then she'd swing by sickbay. She'd find out for herself how Ensign Ngoku was faring.

JEFF WAS surprised at how comfortable the chair was. *It's like floating,* he thought, as he rested back into it. He stared up through the hole in the big rubber donut at the girders of the pre-fab building, painted a pastel aqua by city workers six generations ago. As he thought about them, the plasticity of time collided with the plasticity of space in his imagination, leaving him with a momentary feeling of vertigo. He wondered if repeated squashing changed more than simply his perceptions. What if, every time he entered *that* space, he was a little less in *this* one? The thought terrified him and he put it out of mind immediately.

He heard Dr. Stewart's voice in his ear. "Okay, Captain, we are ready when you are."

"Roger that," he said, enjoying the archaism. He imagined Dr. Stewart turning to Tan and mouthing, "Who's Roger?"

He smiled involuntarily at the thought and closed his eyes. He reached out intuitively, imagining and perceiving the space around him. In his mind's eye, he saw a great light. Turning toward it, it filled the whole of his field of vision. It was the generator—huge and bright and lovely. He imagined himself drifting toward it instinctively. The closer he got, the more power he sensed. He reached out with his hands and took hold of the power. He felt it enter him, filling him, charging him. *This feels fantastic,* he thought. *I'm unlimited! I'm invincible!*

Whoa, cowboy, he reminded himself. *Feeling and being are not the same thing.* He dimly remembered a similar feeling of invincibility when he was a young cadet. That had lasted until the first of their platoon had gotten their heads blown off by a rebel particle cannon. With effort, he turned his mind from the ecstasy of the moment to his purpose. He experimented with the power, drawing now more, now less. He found it was unpredictable until he imagined a rheostat in front of him. In his mind's eye, he reached out and turned it up. The power swelled within him. He turned it back down and felt the power wane. His brain crackled with electricity. The feeling was intoxicating, even at the lower power levels.

"What are you doing, Captain?" Emma's voice asked.

"Just figuring out how to draw power. I think I've got a handle on it now."

"Good. I want you to reach out with your awareness. Power down and go to the periphery and tell me what you see."

Jeff imagined turning down the rheostat, then reached outward with his mind. He saw every creature for a radius that must have extended hundreds of miles. He heard their thoughts, felt their feelings, faced their dilemmas, experienced their joy, their grief, their orgasms. He read a sign. "Route 135, Fermor," he said.

"That's a transport designation—a highway in Winnipeg. Checking…that's a little over 1000 kilometers, due east. Good. What happens if you go north?"

Jeff saw himself turning and reaching out again, sensing far less activity. Mostly the heavier awareness of animals, even plant life. "Snow! I didn't know there even *was* any snow anymore."

"Some, apparently. Good. West?"

He turned again and saw water as far as the eye could see. He felt the slick, heavy awareness of fish, the quick consciousness of the occasional whale. The strangeness of underwater life surprised him and even shook him. "Yeah. Okay. Fish. Wet. Weird."

"Go south."

He turned again, to complete the points of the compass, and felt repelled by the scorching heat of the Idaho desert. There was life there, but not much of it. His mind filled with the quick, instinctual motion of lizards and buzzards and insects. "Okay, communing with the reptiles. Nice. Next?"

"Draw a little power and see how far you can sense."

Jeff turned and imagined the Great Light of the generator. He saw the power entering him, felt it crackle in his fingertips, as he turned up the rheostat. Then he reached out with his mind again. He felt the circle of his awareness expand. He felt the feelings of a world full of beings

—fear and flight, compassion and caring, violence and love—all of it at once, undifferentiated, cacophonous. He discovered he could pick out individuals, could distance himself from the other voices, could even "enter" into the bodies of random people or animals.

He imagined himself "landing." He looked around, and saw multi-colored flags hanging from twine, strung from one building to the next, from posts to trees to the ground. He saw multi-storied stupas side-by-side with office buildings. *I must be as far as I can go without circling back around. This is Tibet, or Nepal…*then he saw a sign. Ladakh. *Okay, then, India,* he thought. *Yep, that's as far as you can go.*

Because of the heat, there wasn't much left of India. Its few thriving places were in high altitudes like this, where the air was still cool enough to support life. The street was bustling, crowded. Jeff felt assaulted by the color, the multitude, the smells. *The smells.* He followed one particular aroma. It caused his stomach to rumble. He hadn't been aware that he was hungry. Breakfast seemed like mere moments ago, but his perception of time was off—he knew that. He followed the smell to a street vendor, grilling chunks of yak meat on short sticks over a small brazier on a handcart.

He floated toward the vendor, savoring the delicious aroma. He reached out, saw himself grabbing at one of the meat sticks, but his fingers passed through them.

"Captain Bowers, what do you see?" Emma's voice was distant, as if heard in a different room.

Jeff was fixated on the meat skewers and didn't answer. He *had* to have one. He gripped India between the fingers of one hand, and Alberta in the fingers of the other, and he drew them together. He held them side by side until he experienced himself being in both places at once. He reached for a skewer again, grabbed it, and watched as the vendor scrambled back in surprise. He put the skewer to his lips and bit off a huge, steaming chunk of yak flesh. The meat was juicy, filling his mouth with savory goodness. He grinned with pleasure as he felt its grease run down his chin. He also noticed that he was still seated on the couch from the lab, now blocking traffic on the narrow, crowded Ladakhi street.

"WHY ISN'T HE SAYING ANYTHING?" Emma groused. She activated her microphone. "Captain, tell us what you're seeing."

"Uh..." Tan said.

"Uh, what?"

"Uh...you've got to look at this."

Emma scowled at the medical doctor, but rushed over to his side and looked at his viewscreens. "What am I supposed be looking at?"

"You're supposed to be looking at life signs," Tan said. "But there aren't any."

"How could there...oh, Jesus." Emma looked up at the larger viewscreens, expecting to see Bowers, blissed out in his chair—or dead. Instead she saw an empty room. She bolted for the isolation ring, Tan and Suarez on her heels. She opened the outer portal hatch and raced inside. Once through the inner portal, she stopped and gasped. The chair was gone. All the cables running to it seemed to have been neatly and uniformly severed. "What the...?" She moved into the room, her jaw dropping, her head swimming. She felt as though she were viewing the whole scene from afar, somehow. She turned and faced Tan and Suarez. "Where the fuck did he go?"

No one said anything. Emma began to chew on her fingernails. She felt her pulse quicken. She was starting to panic. Just then she saw a red light in her neural. She accessed it.

—I think I goofed.

It was from Jeff. She let out a breath and pointed at her eye. "Bowers."

—Where are you?

—Ladakh, apparently. India.

—What the fuck are you doing in Ladakh?

—Eating yak skewers.

—Yak skewers?

—Yes. They're delicious.

Emma blinked. "He's in India. Eating yak skewers," she said to Tan and Suarez.

—I need a ride.

Emma began to laugh.

"What?" asked Tan.

"Mr. Suarez, I hate to do this to you, but we need to get you to Regina. You're on the next military transport to Asia. We have a captain and a chair to retrieve."

Suarez didn't look very happy about this news. She didn't blame him.

—Suarez is on his way.

—Can't you send someone less threatening?

—Man up, Captain.

Emma leaned against the wall of the donut and crossed her arms. "So we know two things. One, Bowers can indeed move something larger than a picture frame."

"That's good, right?" Tan asked.

"That's very good."

"What's the other thing?"

"We know that in about twelve hours he's going to be as sick as a dog. Doctor, we're going to need a prescription for some altitude sickness meds. And Suarez, get going before the captain passes out on the street."

CHAPTER FIVE

"Deseret Colony within hailing range, Captain," Lieutenant Frey said.

"Thank you, Lieutenant. Open a channel," Jo said. She'd been pacing, but she paused and put her hand on the back of her command chair.

"Yes, sir." Frey paused. Then she nodded. "Channel open and acknowledged."

"Deseret Colony, this is the CDF warship *Essex*, estimating our time of arrival in…" she waved at Fin.

"Ninety minutes, Captain," Fin called over his shoulder.

"Ninety minutes. Request permission to approach?"

"Captain, I have visual," Frey announced.

"On screen," Jo said.

There was a ripple and the sea of stars was replaced by the figure of a middle-aged man in uniform. His hair was beginning to thin, but he made up for it with an impressive beard—although his upper lip was clean-shaven. At first Jo thought it was an odd effect, until she remembered a picture of Abraham Lincoln, who also wore his facial hair in the same curious style.

Men and their hair, she thought.

"This is Captain Joleen Taylor of the CDF warship *Essex*. With whom am I speaking?"

"This is General T.I. Warwick of the Deseret Defense Corps."

Jo wondered if his friends called him "T.I." She also noted that he pronounced his name, "WAR-rick," after the English style.

"General, I bring you greetings from the mother planet and the Colonial Defense Fleet."

"I haven't got time for pleasantries, Captain. In case you didn't know, we're going to be under attack in less than twelve hours."

"I am well aware, General, and that's why we're here. We're the advance guard of a whole fleet of CDF forces. We're just a tiny bit faster than they are."

"We're grateful, Captain, but you won't be needed. We told Admiral Jennings not to send ships. We will have the invaders well in hand." Warwick looked distracted, glancing down as if reading something off of a datapad.

Fin glanced up at the captain, his eyebrows riding high on his head in surprise.

"General, I'm heartened by your confidence. But surely a show of overwhelming strength can't be a bad thing in this case. It may act as a deterrent should the Prox get ideas about attacking other Union colonies."

"We've got overwhelming force already. Maybe you're not familiar with—"

"I assure you, General, I have been fully briefed on your capabilities. I'm concerned that you might be underestimating the enemy."

"Turn around, Captain." Warwick looked back up at the camera now. "We've got this."

"General, the fact that we are here is evidence of your tax dollars at work. You've already paid for our support, now—" The viewscreen went blank.

"I believe he just cut us off in mid-transmission, sir," Frey announced.

"The son-of-a-bitch," Jo said. "Weaponer Raj, what can I blow up around here that won't endanger any Mormons?"

"We've got a dead satellite in geosynchronous orbit around Deseret in our direct line of fire, Captain. No electronic activity at all."

"Perfect. Weaponer, load one of our thermonuclear devices—just a small one ought to do. Fire when ready."

Jo watched Raj's hands fly over his controls. Then he glanced up at the viewscreen in order to see the fruit of his labor. The screen dimmed as the exterior cameras were overwhelmed by the light of the explosion. There was no sound, of course. Once the cameras adjusted, they only saw the emptiness of space where a large rock had been moments before.

"They're hailing us, sir," Frey said, the corner of her mouth turned up in a wry smile.

"On screen." Jo took her seat.

"What in the name of the Prophet's Nanny are you trying to do?" General Warwick spluttered, his eyes wide with alarm.

"Apparently you have a short attention span," Jo said. "I have found that sometimes you have to wave a shiny object in front of people with short attention spans."

"That was a white salamander move, Captain, and it will go in my report."

"Excellent. I'm here to make sure you live long enough to file one."

Warwick looked angry enough to erupt. Jo could see that he was physically shaking. "Put us where we'll do the most good, General. I'm sending over a manifest of the other ships underway, along with their firepower and approximate time of arrival." She nodded at Frey, who began to cull the information into a transmittable datapacket.

Jo was reminded of someone else who had trouble accepting help. She rose and took a couple steps forward toward the viewscreen, trying to create an illusion of intimacy. "Look, General, this is your fight. But we're your friends. It's no shame on you if you let us help. We *want* to help. We value Deseret's role in the Colonial Union. Let your friends be your friends. This is what friends *do* for each other."

Warwick grumbled something inaudible.

"Do you want me to amplify and replay that, Captain?" Frey asked.

Jo held her hand up, fending off Frey's question for the moment. "I'm sorry, General, I didn't catch that."

"I want you with the reserves. I'll call you out only if we need you. As for the other ships on the way—what a colossal waste of resources. We'll have these filthy invaders mopped up before they even get here."

"I hope you're right, General. But if you're not...we've got your back."

JENNINGS SAW the blue light in his neural and checked the message. It was from Liu.

—Dr. Stewart is waiting for you.

—Send her in.

A moment later, the door slid open and Emma Stewart walked in. She strode to his desk and presented herself, hands clasped behind her back.

"Doctor."

"Admiral."

"I hear you have good news. I could use some good news."

"Yes...we've made some real progress."

"Sit down, Doctor," Jennings waved her over to a compact black leather chair. "Whiskey?"

"No, I...why the hell not?" she smiled. "I haven't really let myself celebrate, after all. Too much to do."

"High time, then." Jennings poured two fingers each into crystal glasses and set one of them on his desk in front of the doctor. He sat back in his own seat. "Yes. I've read the report. Hell of a thing. I laughed out loud when I read about India."

"We might have seen that as a setback, but it was actually a breakthrough. And it was his first time out—since we've been monitoring him, that is. In the couple weeks since we've started working together, he's fine-tuned his ability. If we were talking about a merely physical phenomenon, I'd say he has vastly improved his fine motor control."

"Don't want to say he's improved his fine mind control? Same acronym."

"I'd rather avoid it," she smirked. "Since I finished that report, we've made even more progress."

"Do tell."

"Captain Bowers is now able to locate or place objects at precise GPS coordinates."

"How is he gauging those?"

"Neural."

"Ah. I should have guessed that." Jennings took a sip from his glass and made a pleased face.

"And he has succeeded in moving both a Humvee, and then a house."

"Was anyone *in* the house?"

"No, thank God."

"So how did that go?"

"Let's just say there's a cornfield in Saskatchewan that is *very* flat right now."

"Is the house still flattening unsuspecting farms in Saskatchewan?"

"No, he moved it back."

"Um…didn't that—"

"Sever all the power lines? Yes. We're repairing them now."

Jennings shook his head and laughed.

"Is he behaving himself?"

"Captain Bowers? He and Tan don't really get along, but ever since the India trip he and Suarez have been hanging out."

"And how are *you*?"

"Fine."

"Fine? What the hell does that mean, Doctor?"

Emma looked away but didn't answer. "I think we're ready. If what you want to do with this is move troops or warships instantaneously… we're going to need to move our lab to space. And we're going to need a ship."

"A ship?"

"If you want to move a warship, we have to practice on a ship—

some ship, any ship. Preferably something small, at least at first. Then we'll take what we've learned and ramp it up. It's no different from what we've been doing. This is just…it's the next logical step."

"Why can't we just have him move a warship now?"

"Because it's imprudent and unethical and could be potentially disastrous. If you want the brass—"

"I *am* the brass, in case you haven't noticed."

"If you want your *fellow* brass to embrace this project, we don't want any…setbacks."

"You're right. Of course. I just…" Jennings looked at his viewscreen, set to peer into deep space.

"What's happening out there? At Deseret? With Captain Taylor?"

"I wish I knew. The ansible is quiet, which I'm taking as a good sign. I just wish—"

"You wish you could help them *now*."

"Yes."

"We're getting there, Admiral. Think of this as the last time any of our colonies or allies will face anything alone."

—WEAPONER RAJ, please meet me in my consult station.

A moment later, the door whooshed open and the Weaponer saluted.

"Have a seat, number one," Jo said. The consult station was a small office just off the bridge for the captain's private use. She expected Raj to be quick, but his appearance was eerily instantaneous, as if he had been poised by the door, waiting for her call. And what if he had been? Wasn't a senior officer's ability to anticipate the needs of his commanding officer an asset?

Raj sat opposite her, looking uncomfortable. Jo set a cup of Mayan hot chocolate in front of him. He looked at it as if it were a snail.

"Report," she ordered.

Raj's eyebrows rose slightly, but then he started in. "We completed the scenario drills at fourteen hundred hours, sir."

"Did we get that response time up?"

"We did, and we exceeded our goals by twenty-one seconds."

"That's excellent, number one. Truly excellent."

"I must say, Captain, at first I thought that the drilling schedule was excessive, but I can see two benefits. Not only have we exceeded our best response time, but the crew is relaxed rather than nervous."

"Too busy to worry," Jo nodded. She took a sip of her own cocoa.

"It was a shrewd idea."

"Flattery is not a good strategy, Raj."

He smiled. "It was honest, sir. No flattery here."

Weaponer Raj had surprised her. She admired his easy confidence. She also couldn't stop thinking about him. She hated these shipboard crushes. She was far too susceptible to them, and all she could do was wait them out. This one would pass. They always did.

"I've been studying the Deseret defenses," Raj said.

"And?"

"And they've got six times the firepower at their disposal as New Manila had."

"Will it be enough?"

"That is the question, sir."

"Do you have a guess?"

"Based on what I have seen from the New Manila transmissions, I think they're going to get their assess handed to them."

Jo nodded. She'd come to the same conclusion. "You can't tell them that."

"No sir."

"They don't want to hear anything from us."

"No."

Jo dropped her eyes and stared at the gentle rippling on the surface of her cocoa. The silence was long, and Jo was amazed at Raj's comfort with it. He surprised her at every turn. And pleased her.

"I…this might be silly, but Chief Engineer Laru and I have been working on a…a secret project," Jo said.

Raj cocked his head. He still hadn't touched his cocoa.

"What kind of project?" he asked.

"A…a defensive weapon, I suppose."

He scowled, no doubt wondering why, as Weaponer, he was only finding out about this now. Jo held her palm up to ward off his protest, however unspoken. "I know, I know, but I thought it was kind of a silly idea in the first place, and I didn't know if it would even work, in the second."

"I'm listening, Captain."

She heard the note of disappointment in his voice. Disappointment in *her*. It hurt.

"Number one, have you ever heard of an electric fence?"

"Certainly. We had them in Nepal, to deter the goat rustlers."

"Do you mean to tell me that in your own lifetime, you dealt with goat rustlers?"

He shrugged. "You have goats—someone is going to want to rustle them."

She smiled and shook her head slowly. "Okay, so you run a current through the wire. And if someone touches the wire—"

"They get an electric shock."

"And does it have to be wire?"

"It has to be metal, or some kind of conductor."

"What is the hull of our ship made of, Number One?"

"Iconel."

"Is it a conductor?"

"Yes, it's a very good…" he trailed off, his eyes darting back and forth as he grasped her thought.

"We aren't really in any danger until the Prox land on the surface of our ships."

Raj nodded, his face brightening. "We need an electric fence."

"That's just what I was thinking."

Raj's face darkened. "The Envoy fired an EMP burst through the hull—it didn't work."

"EMP is not raw voltage. Anything that lights on our hull is going to be met with 50,000 volts."

"Volts don't really matter. What will the amperage be?"

"Five hundred."

"Will that be enough to knock a Prox on its ass?"

"I think we're about to find out."

AN ALERT LIT up in Jeff's neural.

—Meet me at the starboard docks. I want to show you something.

It was from Emma. Jeff nodded and stood up. *Good. I'm going stir crazy anyway.*

He quickly navigated Sol Station and arrived at the docks in less than five minutes. It was always a busy, bustling area, and he scanned the hurrying crowd. *Maybe I just beat her here?* he wondered. Then he saw her. She broke into a grin and waved, jogging over to him. As she ran he felt a strange, familiar and mostly unwelcome emotion rise from the dead. *I could love this woman,* he thought. *And I shouldn't.*

"Captain," she said, slightly winded. She touched his elbow.

"Doctor," he answered. "What's up?"

"It's here." She tugged at his sleeve and started walking toward the bay windows.

The sleeve-tugging felt a little too playful. *Is she flirting with me?* he wondered. *Or is that just wishful thinking?* He followed her to the window.

It was really a large viewing port out into space, as high as two decks, and twice as wide. The field of stars was brilliant, frenzied, completely unlike the filtered light he experienced when on earth. He thrilled at the sight of it. Large ships in varying stages of approach or departure glided around the docks. Sol Station was the busiest spaceport in the colonies, and that was never so evident as at its docks.

"What am I looking at?" he asked.

"That," Emma pointed.

He followed the direction of her finger. "The *Sahib*?"

"No, to the left of her. The *Bohr*."

It was a small vessel, decked out in the blue and tan of the Colonial Science Corps. It looked to him that a full crew complement might be around ten crewmen. There were no weapons to speak of. The engines were standard propulsion. It was also old—perhaps fifty years old or more, gauging from the design.

"Uh…nice dinosaur."

"True. But it's *our* dinosaur."

"What do you mean?"

"Jennings just assigned her to our project."

"She needs to be assigned to a metals reclamation unit."

"Stop," she slapped his shoulder. "It's a starter ship."

He nodded. "If I can move *that…*"

"*When* you can move that—safely and accurately—we'll move on to bigger things."

"Why not just start with something useful—like a light battle-cruiser?"

"Captain, I know you're impatient. And that might make you a good military commander, but it would make you a lousy scientist. For us it's all about baby steps."

He raised his eyebrows and faced her. "Baby steps."

"Yep. One test at a time. Change one thing, then test again."

"You people drive me nuts. Just fill it with marines and let's fucking head for Deseret."

"Are you always so eager for battle?" She smiled sadly.

The question caught him off guard. He looked away, back to the field of stars. "I'm *never* eager for battle. No sane person who's ever seen it is."

"Then what's your rush?"

"I've seen enough people die in my time, and if I'm in a position to stop it…"

"Then you should."

"Then I should."

She nodded. "I can respect that. But look at it from my perspective. You want to get there with troops and firepower—"

"Damn straight."

"I want to get you there in one piece so you can do some good. Can you respect *that*?"

He looked her in the eye. He saw her sincerity. He nodded.

"Good," she said, turning back to the port window. "And to that end, we're going to spend the next week refurbishing the old girl."

"Are you going to update that engine?"

"Why do we need to?"

"It'll only do..." he trailed off. "Oh. *I'm* the engine."

"Bingo," she said, smiling.

She must think I'm a bigger meathead than Jo does, he thought.

"But we *are* going to rip her guts out and put in a new control matrix. And I'm going to personally supervise outfitting her with a sensor web so we can measure whatever unholy thing you're doing to spacetime."

"Anything I can do?"

"Nothing I can think of. We want you to rest."

"I hate fucking resting."

"You can't do it all yourself, Captain."

"You sound like my father."

"At least I don't sound like your mother. I dated a guy once who... never mind. Look, we want you to rest. The squashing will take it out of you, especially something that big—"

"I'm getting better at that," Jeff insisted.

Emma moved her head back and forth in an equivocating gesture. "Just the same, we want you at 110%."

"Fuck that."

"Captain!" She feigned offense.

"I'm just..."

"Bored?"

He didn't answer. "What's first up?"

"Fumigation, what else? We can't do a damn thing until we clear out all the spider nests."

CAPTAIN TAYLOR GRIPPED the back of her chair as she watched the first of the Prox warships drop out of superluminal space. She was too nervous to sit and tried not to bite her nails—unsuccessfully. She turned to Frey. "Zoom in to wherever the most action is, please, Lieutenant. You're going to have the most work to do."

They were already at priority alert status. She had jiggered the schedules to put her best people in their seats at this moment. The second stringers could grouse—and they probably would—but such is the prerogative and the duty of command. She'd try to make it up to them somehow—if they survived.

The main viewscreen magnified the Prox ship. Scanners recognized it as what was left of the *Envoy,* which had been lost at New Manila. Jo wondered if all of their ships were captured. Two more dropped into normal space behind them, taking flanking positions. Just ahead of them, Jo could see the arrayed forces of the Deseret Defense Corps encircling their planet, their promised land, their Zion. She had no doubt that the Mormons would put up one hell of a fight. They had a reputation in the CDF for being comfortable with authority structures, clean-cut as unholy fuck, and merciless in battle. She expected no less of these Mormons.

They took a defensive tack, which surprised her. None of the DDC ships moved as the Prox dropped out of superlux, but maintained their formation around Deseret. She had expected a more aggressive tactic, but who knew what Warwick had up his sleeve?

She realized she had chewed her thumbnail down to its quick only when it started hurting like hell. She wiped her thumb on her uniform and kept her eyes riveted on the screen. "Weaponer, I want every one of our torpedo tubes full, and every backup in the queue."

"Already done, Captain. We are ready to deploy our full arsenal at your command."

She had expected no less. Raj was one hell of a guy. She was thinking of making him her permanent number one, then realized she didn't have a permanent command. *Ah well,* she thought. *A girl can dream.*

"Prox soldiers detaching, sir," Frey said, and moved to zoom in on the advance alien warship. They were almost invisible, the soldiers. Jo tried to distinguish the different species, but they were too far away to make out. They were just dots, really.

"They don't have any fighters?" Fin asked.

"Oh, they have fighters, Lieutenant, but they're not ships. They're just…aliens. Didn't you read your briefing?" She glanced away from the screen long enough to scowl at her navigator.

"Uh…of course. But reading it in the abstract and seeing it in front of you…"

"They're two different things," she finished his sentence. "I get it. Number one, how long before the first of the CDF support ships arrives?"

"Twelve hours, sir."

She knew that. She just hoped that somehow, when it actually came down to it, it would be different. Better. It wasn't.

"Deseret forces at maximum shields. Long-range sniper cannons on both moons at full power and trained on the enemy, sir."

"We can do a bit of that, can't we?"

"I suggest we send two 30-megaton torpedoes on an elliptical course toward their support ships and take them out now."

"I think that's a splendid call, but unfortunately it's not ours to make. Deseret has nuclear torpedoes, too, and no doubt they've got a strategy. I'm not about to interfere with that. We'll withhold our own assault until ordered to."

Raj scowled at his panel and didn't look at her. "Yes, Captain."

"First of the Prox warriors approaching DDC ships, sir. Contact in fifteen seconds."

Every ship in the fleet with a shot at the alien soldiers had opened fire. She thrilled to see that some of the little black dots disintegrated and disappeared. Jo leaned over the back of her chair, trying to get closer to the screen. "Zoom in, Mr. Frey."

"Okay, but it'll be grainy," she said.

"That's fine. I want to see what we're up against with my own eyes." She'd seen the vids from New Manila, but there was something about seeing it as it was happening that felt qualitatively different to her.

The screen resolved, and she was relieved to see that the image of the defending ship wasn't as distorted as she'd feared.

"Sir, shouldn't we be wary of being hit where we're *not* looking?"

"Stealth does not seem to be in their playbook, number one. And they don't need it."

She held her breath as the first of the Prox soldiers alighted on one of the Deseret ships. A nearby ship fired at the approaching soldier, but, wary of hitting its own side, its shots went wide as the soldier approached. All around the ship, other soldiers landed; some they could see, but others were out of sight. The Prox seemed to take a moment to orient themselves. "What are they waiting for?" Jo asked.

"Perhaps they are fixing a firm grip on the hull," Laru suggested. Jo nodded. It was plausible.

Just then one of the stick-like legs struck downward.

"They're like crabs…" Fin breathed.

"No crab was ever this deadly, Lieutenant," Jo said. Then her jaw dropped as she watched the soldier rip a sheet of metal plating from the hull.

"Holy Christ," Fin breathed.

While its dactyl pulled the metal away from the hull, its pereopods began to scramble inside the hole it had made, ripping out wire and insulation. Jo watched as detritus floated free from the breach. Then there was an explosion as a seal was broken and air rushed into the vacuum of space, carrying with it everything not fastened down, including some Mormon militiamen who jerked and gasped before succumbing to the vacuum of space.

"That's horrible," Frey said, turning her face away from the viewscreen.

"Okay, message received," Jo said. "I want every member of this crew belted in, now." She circled around her command chair and finally sat in it, fastening the restraints. It was obvious that the chair had been built for a bigger body than hers, but she was confident it would hold her. Raj triggered an alert that began sounding all over the ship with a message no one could miss and no one would ignore —belt in.

Jo estimated that over a hundred Prox soldiers had landed on that one ship alone, and all of them were busy ripping up iconel sheeting. It was then that she saw the first of the worker Prox circling around to collect the sheets of hull plating, although some soldiers were pausing to simply eat them. The Prox ignored the shots fired by nearby vessels, none of which came close enough to do any damage. Every now and then a Prox soldier or worker would explode en route to the ship, but there were always more behind. The sheer number of them was staggering, well beyond Jo's ability to estimate.

Fortunately, she didn't need to. "Weaponer Raj, how many of the enemy have been deployed?"

Raj didn't even need to look down. "Six hundred fifty thousand, sir. And counting."

"Pull back, Mr. Frey. I want to see what's happening elsewhere."

The screen zoomed out, and Jo's eyes widened in horror as she saw every visible ship in the Deseret Defense Corps being actively dismantled. Every ship was firing like mad at the approaching Prox, and although they hit a good number of targets, their efforts did not even begin to stop the flood of enemy soldiers.

"This is a slaughter," Fin said.

"It's not a surprise," Jo said. She forced herself to turn away from the screen. "Mr. Frey, contact General Warwick and ask permission to enter the fight."

"Yes sir."

Just then there was a blaze of light as nuclear torpedoes hit their targets. Jo was glad she had not been looking directly at the screen, and she shielded her eyes until the screen adjusted. "What did they hit them with?"

"50-megatons, in a coordinated strike of fifteen torpedoes."

Jo gripped the armrest of her command chair until her fingers were white. "And? And?" she asked, despite her efforts to be a calm presence. It seemed like it took an eternity for the fireball to subside and the screen to adjust. When it did, Jo saw that a corner of a massive triangular ship had been blown off. "Score one for our team," she breathed. But it was clear it would not be enough. The ships capable of firing that kind of power were being dismantled before their very eyes.

"Mr. Frey, open a channel to General Warwick," Jo said.

"I…channel is open, sir, but no one is responding."

"General Warwick, this is Captain Taylor of the CDF *Essex*. Request permission to join the fray."

Jo heard nothing back. "Repeat my request, Mr. Frey."

"Repeating, sir."

Jo watched as worker Prox removed steel plates by the score, by the hundreds, in a fire-brigade operation from their prey back to their ship. There was a flash from one of the Mormon ships and Jo bit the stub of her nail again as she watched equipment, furniture, and crew members float into space as its lost air pressure forced everything into the vacuum.

"Shit," Fin said. He turned and looked at the captain. So did Laru. So did Raj.

"Okay, fuck it," Jo said, pounding the arm of her command chair. "The chain of command here has obviously broken down. Fin, set a course for fly-by stingray attacks on the three Prox carrier vessels. I want us in and out of there in seconds. Weaponer Raj, coordinate with Mr. Fin so that we launch our nukes at our closest proximity to the enemy. Start with the damaged ship, aim straight into the worst of the damage. Hopefully the shields will be damaged in that section, too. Let's go kick a bastard while he's down."

CHAPTER SIX

Jeff poured himself a scotch. He had been drinking a lot of scotch lately. He poured it back into the bottle, spilling a little as he did so. *That was a waste,* he thought. *Should have just drunk it.* He wasn't drinking to relax. He certainly wasn't drinking socially—he was alone in the tiny cabin assigned to him on Sol Station.

"I'm drinking because I'm bored," he said aloud. "Well, so long as you know that." He poured himself another glass. This time, he sipped at it. He sat on the single chair in his cabin and put his feet up on his bunk. He swilled the scotch on his tongue, savoring its acrid smokiness. A song from his childhood kept going through his head. He hated that song. He took another sip and forced himself to think about something else.

But there were too many things he *shouldn't* think about. He had walled off a whole section of his brain relating to Catskill, and he was smart enough not to venture there, even when he was drunk. But there were parallels to the New Manila episode that haunted him. Like Catskill, New Manila had been a slaughter. Like Catskill he had watched it happen—at least, he had watched the enemy feasting on its victory. Like Catskill, he was the only one who walked away.

He knew it wasn't the same. He wasn't in command on New

Manila. He wasn't responsible for the people who died there. New Manila was not his fault. But the similarities pricked at him, opened old wounds, made him want another drink. And since there was no place he needed to be, no one to whom he needed to report, nothing he needed to do…

Jeff opened one bleary eye. He saw the bottle, the bottle he had just opened, saw that it was half empty. He knew that after that much alcohol, he ought to be sick as a dog for a couple days. But his new body handled alcohol like a twenty-year-old. He felt a pocket of sick in his stomach and his head ached a little. He felt slightly fluish, sweaty. But otherwise…fine. He opened the other eye, and jumped, startled.

"Oh shit," he yelled percussively.

"Hello, Jeff."

Danny was sitting on his bed. Jeff sat up, fully awake and alert now. "Water…I need some water." He rose and grabbed a coffee cup and went into the hall. He watched the door slide closed behind him, then turned, passed the communal bathroom, into the break room. It wasn't a mess exactly, just a small kitchen area shared by everyone in his cluster of cabins. He filled the cup with cool water from the dispenser and drank it down. He filled it again and drank that, too. He filled it a third time and then walked back to his cabin.

He paused at the door. Had he really seen Danny on his bed? Or was that the whiskey talking? He pressed the OPEN button. The door slid open and he looked at the bed. Danny was there, smiling patiently. He let the door close again and rested his head on it when it had stopped moving. "Shit shit shit shit shit."

It can't really be Danny, he thought. *It must…*he jerked upright. *It must be the Ulim.*

He punched the button again, and again the door slid open. Jeff stepped inside. "Hello, Danny."

"Hello, Jeff. It is good to see you looking so well."

What's he talking about? I look like hell, Jeff thought. "You are the Ulim."

Danny smiled. "We are the Ulim."

Jeff nodded. "I need to…I…thank you."

Danny cocked his head.

"For saving my life. For sending me home."

"You are welcome."

"But I'm guessing you didn't come here so I could be grateful at you."

"No. We are here because you surprise us."

"I? Surprise you? How?'

"Our…" he seemed to fish for a word, then found it. "Methods. For travel. We thought they were…beyond you. It never occurred to us that just by witnessing our…method…you would be able to do it yourself. Especially since you only saw it happen once."

Jeff nodded and resumed his seat, facing Danny. "I don't think I could explain it to you. I mean, Dr. Stewart has been trying to get me to explain it to her ever since I got back, and I can't. I just can't, because I don't understand it myself. But I remember how it felt…" Jeff paused to consider how ironic that was. He had spent so much of his adult life trying not to feel, and yet it was his capacity for feeling that allowed him to do this. "You know when I remember it best? When I dream."

Danny smiled at this. "That makes a lot of sense to us. Our life is a shared dream, in a way. So much of what we do is shaped by this… dreaming." His smile faded. "But the fact that you have learned to do it is…unfortunate. You are not ready for it."

Jeff scowled. "What do you mean by 'you'? Do you mean me, Jeff Bowers? Or do you mean humanity?"

"We are saying both."

Jeff allowed a little heat into his voice. "Who are you to say I'm not ready for it? Or that humankind isn't ready for it?"

"We are the ones who know about this…method. We are the ones who understand it, who understand what is at stake and what is at risk."

"What are you talking about?" Jeff asked. His head hurt. This was not a conversation he wanted to be having when his head hurt.

"The universe is far more fragile than you suppose it to be. It persists only because of a perfectly balanced set of forces. You are manipulating these forces. It is like…forgive us for saying this, but you are like a child playing with a bomb you found in an abandoned lot."

Jeff wondered where the Ulim had gleaned that analogy. Probably from his own mind. When he was a cadet, he remembered a child who had found a mine in an abandoned lot and had blown himself up trying to take it apart. He'd felt sick about it at the time. If the Ulim needed a disturbing or affecting memory, it would be hard to find a better one. He nodded. He got what they were saying. But… "I think you're overreacting."

Danny cocked his head again. "Are we?"

"Sure. Look, we're being careful. We're starting small. We're scaling up slowly, one thing at a time. You didn't learn this method overnight—you developed it—"

"Over several thousand years, yes."

That stopped Jeff cold. He had only known how to squash for a few weeks. Still… "We're being careful."

Danny looked down, his smile fading. He shook his head. "It does not work that way. Careful is not enough. Small…that is irrelevant. Size is irrelevant. Scale is irrelevant. And scale is everything."

"Now you're sounding like the Ulim again."

Danny allowed himself a smile at that. "We are always the Ulim." He looked Jeff in the eye. "Even the smallest jump, if it is done wrong, can have…catastrophic consequences."

"Not so far. We're doing pretty good."

"You are not hearing me, Jeff."

"What aren't I hearing, *Danny*?"

Danny leaned back. Jeff couldn't tell if he was exasperated or simply searching for another analogy. "The method must be done with attention to many different dimensions. The universe is like a giant, infinitely complex tapestry. If you pull one thread in the wrong direction, you can cause it to unravel."

"I can unravel the universe."

"Yes. You must abandon your attempts at…performing the method."

"Why do you keep saying, 'the method.' Isn't there a word for it?"

"Not in your language. Not in any language mere humans could understand."

"*Mere* humans? What does that mean?"

Danny's lip quirked slightly. "What are you calling it—the method?"

"Squashing."

Danny's brow furrowed, obviously trying to get his head around the implications of the word. "That is most inelegant."

"I agree."

"It is a most inaccurate descriptor of the method."

"Probably. But it's the word that leaped to mind when I was trying to explain it."

"Now we are even more concerned."

Jeff laughed. "Was that a joke? Because your comedic timing was pretty good."

Danny's face became severe. "Please do not think that this is humorous. We are not joking. We are…terrified."

"Terrified? Why?"

"Again, I think you are not hearing us."

"I'm hearing you fine. Don't tug on the carpet. I get it. But you guys do it all the time."

"We do. We understand how to do it properly."

"Okay. If you don't want me to do it wrong, teach me how to do it right."

Danny waved this suggestion away. Jeff wasn't sure whether he should feel insulted or not.

"This cannot happen," Danny said. "The fact that you can do it at all is of grave concern to us. You must cease immediately."

"I *must*?" Jeff asked.

"You must."

Jeff blinked, and Danny was gone.

Jo watched the viewscreen in horror as it panned over the battlefield, randomly zooming in on the Deseret fleet. Every ship she could see was literally swarming with Prox. From their distance, it looked as if each of them were crawling with ants—hungry, metal-eating ants. It was not, she realized, an analogy that was far off the mark.

"Receiving distress calls from fifteen of the Deseret ships, sir," Lieutenant Frey said.

"I don't doubt it," Jo said. She felt momentarily torn between continuing the attack or rescuing what she could of the Deseret crews. And what would she do if she did rescue them? Run? Get them to safety? Where was that? Back to earth? Back to Deseret, a planet on the verge of being picked clean by alien scavengers just as New Manila was? *No no no,* she thought. *I know my job. My job is war.*

"Course locked in, sir," Fin said.

"Take us in, Lieutenant."

The stars blurred for a moment as they sped forward toward the melee. They rushed directly toward the damaged Prox ship, at such velocity Jo was sure they were about to collide. At the last possible moment, however, Fin pulled up and away. The stars on their display careened in their course as the *Essex* banked and blasted away.

"Torpedoes on target," Raj said. "Impact in 2, 1."

Light engulfed the viewscreen again as the nuclear warheads detonated, sending scraps of the invading vessel soaring in all directions. "Raj, what kind of damage did we just do?"

Raj's fingers flew over his controls, and he looked from one display to another. "Their superstructure is losing integrity. It's breaking up, Captain."

"Thank God," Jo said. "At least we know now that they *can* be beat." She swiveled in her seat. "Mr. Frey, send a message to all capable ships to discharge another coordinated round of nukes at the lead ship."

Frey worked her own station, but quickly responded. "There are only three capable ships left, Captain, and one moon base. None of them are answering hails."

"Send the order just the same, firing mark in 45 seconds. Mr. Fin, bring us on a course to add our firepower to theirs without taking on any friendly fire."

"How am I—?"

"I don't care. Just do it."

Fin gulped and nodded, looking up to check a chart. Jo noticed he was sweating. *Well, if ever there were a time,* she thought.

The stars on the viewscreen spun as Fin moved them into position and Raj counted down the attack. At one, he launched the torpedo and Fin piloted them away from the enemy ships again. "How many launched, number one?"

Raj's face fell. "Just ours, sir."

"Damage?"

"Minimal. Their shields absorbed the bulk of it without affect."

"Shit. How many can we launch at once?"

"Three. Which we just…sir, Prox soldiers approaching."

"Laser cannons, Weaponer."

"No good, sir. They're too close. We'd shoot ourselves."

"How many?"

"Thirty-five, with…457 close behind. Make that 650 and counting." Raj's voice was pitched higher than usual, but remained even. "The first of them is going to land on us in five, four, three…"

"I want a visual, Mr. Frey."

"Yes, sir."

The viewscreen changed to an exterior camera. They watched as a massive Prox soldier floated into view. Its six legs spun in free space until it reached out toward the hull. Jo heard the impact above her own head…followed by more, and more, and—it reminded her of popcorn popping, only deeper and more metallic.

She turned toward Laru. "Chief Engineer, deploy the electric fence."

"Deploying the fence, sir."

Jo watched the viewscreen and fought against her own anxiety.

"Fence employed."

Jo expected to hear something—maybe a sound like frying bacon —but there was nothing. She did exhale in pronounced relief to see every one of the Prox clinging onto their hull recoil, their legs lifting off the hull in a quick jerk of pain. A smile broke out over Jo's face. She had to stop herself from jumping up and down. "It worked!" she said in Laru's direction.

"Yes, sir, it—" he stopped when all heard the thumping above them resume.

"Mr. Laru, did you keep it on?"

"No sir. We can only do short bursts."

Jo unconsciously ran her fingers through her hair, caught at it and pulled until it hurt, thinking. "Okay, we don't know how many times that's going to work. Let's make the best of it. Mr. Fin, on my mark, get us out of here. Push the C-drive as fast as she'll go."

"Destination?"

"Away."

"Once more with the fence, Mr. Laru."

Once more she saw the Prox recoil, but not as far this time. "Go! Go! For fuck's sake, get us out of here!"

Fin punched it, and Jo was grateful they were all strapped in as the g-forces slammed them. A moment later, the inertial dampeners kicked in and the pressure eased. Jo looked up at the viewscreen, stifling a wail of relief when she saw that they'd got away without any of the deadly scavengers still holding onto the hull.

Weaponer Raj turned to face her. "Sir, we cannot just run."

"No, we can't. This is a tactical retreat."

Satisfied, he turned back to his controls. "That is all right, then."

Did he just question her authority in front of the crew? She wasn't entirely sure. More likely he was simply saying aloud what everyone was thinking. Fin turned to face her. "We're well away, sir. No sign of being followed."

"Mr. Frey, any sign of pursuit on your end?"

"None sir. All I'm getting is distress calls. But those are…dying out."

"Send a message to the approaching CDF fleet to hold back .5 parsecs from Deseret to await new orders. Send a summary by ansible to CDF HQ. Let them know what's happened here." She turned to Raj. "What were you able to glean about their shields, number one?"

"Almost impenetrable, sir. No obvious openings or vulnerabilities."

"If you had to guess at a weak spot, what would it be?"

"The engines, sir, almost certainly. I noted they were careful to keep them behind them. Their weapons batteries were always facing toward the enemy—toward us, sir. You'd expect that, of course, but there were a lot of us coming at them from all sides. I was trying to decide if they were positioning themselves offensively—bringing the maximum number of weapons to bear, or defensively—keeping the engines out of the line of fire."

"And which is it?" Jo asked.

Raj shook his head. "Impossible to tell, Captain."

Jo raised her fingers toward her lips, but stopped when she noticed blood on them. Only then did they really hurt. "Damn," she said quietly.

"Sir?"

"It's nothing…Listen up, everyone." She waited until all eyes were on her. "We can't win out there today. They beat us." She saw Fin look away. She noted the way that their tense shoulders slumped all around the room at her words. She leaned forward and held her hand up. The motion caught everyone's eye again. "But we're sure as *fuck* going to make a couple of stabs in the dark before we head home."

JEFF WANDERED SOL STATION, not really knowing what he was doing or where he was going. His brain buzzed. He didn't know how he got there, but he found himself staring out the large port glass at where the *Bohr* was docked. Then he heard yelling.

The sound jerked him out of his reverie, and he jogged toward the sound of it. As he got closer he realized it was not the sound of someone in distress, but in considerable frustration. He rounded a corner and continued to follow it down the hall, realizing he recognized the voice—had *dreamed* about the voice. He entered the room from which the voice issued and hovered in the doorway as he assessed the situation.

Dr. Stewart—Emma—was reaming out one of the technicians. Jeff gauged how long it had taken him from the first eruption of her ire to the present moment and was impressed that she had been yelling for nearly thirty seconds. He leaned in the doorway and crossed his arms. She had not yet seen him.

She was looming over a piece of equipment, and over two engineering techs flat on their backs, squirming to find access to the wiring. "The rhonda capillaries connect to the C ports, not the E ports, you idiots!" she tugged at her own hair. "Do you want to fry the terminator board?"

That's when she saw him. He waggled his fingers at her and gave her a sad—hopefully sympathetic—smile. She looked at her shoes and shook her head. Then she sighed and shuffled over to him. She looked like she hadn't slept in a week.

"I was going to ask how it's going," he began, "but…uh…"

"Yeah." She pitched her forehead forward against his shoulder. Jeff blinked. Did she really just do that? It was the most intimate gesture she had ever made toward him. He knew she had been warming up to him during their work together. Her smiles lasted a little longer every time they saw each other, and the small talk had been progressing toward playful banter. He enjoyed that. A little hesitantly, he put one arm around her shoulder and gave it a quick squeeze. "You would not believe the difficulty I've had getting—" she stopped herself mid-sentence, and Jeff realized she was about to say something about the techs in their hearing, but wisely thought better of it.

"Buy you a drink?" he asked.

"No, I…" she made the universal hand swoop indicating way too much work. "Fuck it. It's lunchtime."

"A three-martini lunch?"

"A what?"

"It's…I read old paperbacks. It's a hobby. And a three-martini lunch was…a thing at one time. But you lead the way. I'll follow. I'll even pay."

She grinned at that. No one in the military paid for anything. She turned toward the techs. "I'll be back in an hour—tops." She shot a warning look at Jeff. He raised one eyebrow. "When I get back I want to see that engine up and running." She tugged at his sleeve and almost ran into the hallway.

She held her hand to her mouth until they were out of earshot, then she started in. "Where the fuck does Jennings find these people?"

"What, the techs?"

"And why do we call them 'techs' if they can't tech their way out of a plastic bag? I swear to God, Jeff, I have to watch every fucking moment or they do it wrong."

"They're grunts, Emma. They know how to wire a starship. They don't know what you're trying to do or how to do it. They've never seen the equipment you're installing. Did you even give them the schematics?"

"Oh, sure, take their side."

"I'm not taking anyone's side. I'm just saying they're really good at what they do, and you're asking them to do something else. You might want to cut them some slack. And an even better idea is to give them the tools they need—like the schematics—so that they know enough about what they're doing to do it well."

Emma stopped and faced him. "That sounds like the voice of a man used to leading people and knowing how to get the best out of them."

"They don't call me captain for nothing."

She took his arm and rested her head on his shoulder as they walked. "I'm a bad captain."

He put his right arm around her. It felt good. He instantly felt his pulse rise and his erection stir. "Not *being* a captain, that's not really an indictment."

"Jeff, how do you do it?"

"Do what?"

"Captain." She said it as a verb. *How do you captain?*

"Pretty poorly, actually. I got everyone in my platoon killed. Everyone but me."

"I heard about that. It's why you like solo assignments."

He didn't answer at first. Then he said, "It's not something I like to talk about."

Thinking about Catskill caused his amorous feelings to sour. He dropped his arm. She noticed.

"Jeff, are you all right?"

"I'm...you know what? I'm...I'm pretty...I'm concerned."

She looked up at him and frowned. "About what?"

"You know, I wasn't...I wasn't going to tell anyone about this, but...I'm afraid you'll think I'm crazy."

"Try me."

"I saw Danny again."

"Danny?"

"My friend. He was killed at Catskill."

Emma nodded. "I remember you saying that the Ulim appeared to you...using his form."

"Yeah."

"And did they visit you again?"

He looked down. Then he met her eyes. "Yeah."

She grabbed his hand and jerked him in the opposite direction.

"What are you doing?"

"Taking you to see Jennings. Now."

"But—"

"You can't fuck around with this, Jeff. If you've been visited by the Ulim, it isn't just a private thing between you and them. This concerns all of us, and Jennings needs to know about it."

He didn't protest, because he didn't disagree. She was right. Of course she was. He'd just been in too much shock to see his proper course of action. It *had* seemed private. But it wasn't, not really.

He thought she would lead him to Jennings' office, but she obviously knew more than he did. That wasn't surprising—she was working closely with Jennings while he was playing solitaire and drinking whiskey. He wallowed in the feeling of being a worthless fuck for about thirty seconds. Then he let it go.

Emma had led him to the far side of the dock where the *Bohr* was moored. She approached an airlock and fitted her eye to the retina scanner. It identified her positively; then Jeff did the same. A moment later the lock slid open and she pulled him into it. Once through, she led him to a chamber with high rubber walls just like the one in Alberta, except that one side opened onto a viewing port where he clearly saw the *Bohr*, docked and still undergoing refitting.

In the middle of the chamber was a chair, again much like the one in Alberta, but not exactly the same. Jennings was leaning over it, listening to a tech explain something about its operation. Emma cleared her throat, and Jennings' head swiveled. Catching sight of them he gave a quick nod of acknowledgment, while continuing to listen. He asked a quick question of the tech and listened to the explanation. Then he clapped the tech on the back and said, "You let me know."

The man nodded, and Jennings walked over to greet them, extending his hand to Jeff. Jeff took it and was put at ease by its confident strength. "Admiral."

"Captain. Doctor." Jennings was all business. "Good timing—I was about to call for you. I've got news—just came over my neural. It hasn't hit the feeds yet. HQ is holding it back until we know more, but…"

Jeff's shoulders sagged. "Deseret."

"Yeah."

Jeff felt at his jaw. "It didn't go well?"

Jennings looked down and shook his head. "From all reports—and there were a lot of them—Deseret has been utterly gutted."

Despite thirty years of military training, Jeff reached out and grabbed his superior officer by the forearm. "And Jo?" He instantly regretted it—his failure of protocol, his use of her first name, the wavering note of hysteria in his voice.

To his great relief, Jennings placed both his big beefy hands on Jeff's shoulders and held them firmly, addressing him in the same spirit. "It's hard to say, Jeff. Last we heard from her she was in the thick of the battle. And as of five minutes ago—the last time I checked—we were still receiving ansible transmissions from the *Essex*. I can't say what *will* happen, but I know she's alive now."

Jeff looked over and saw a complicated range of emotions playing out on Emma's face—relief…and a flash of jealousy? Perhaps he had imagined it, or had simply wanted to see it. "But Deseret," Jeff breathed. "How many?"

"Nearly 250 million people." Jennings lowered his hands and turned to include Emma in the conversation. "I've got unqualified support from the civilian authorities for this project now. We're not just getting a trickle of CDF R&D funding now—we've got an unlimited commitment. Dr. Stewart, you order whatever obscure appliances you need to make this work. We're not pinching pennies anymore. Everyone sees this as our best chance to get troops where we need them *when* we need them. They've passed along one request—that you teach someone else how to do…whatever you do."

"I wish I could, Admiral, but—"

"Let me show you your new throne." Jennings cut him off and led him over to the chair. "We're going to upload a patch to your neural that will feed all the vital statistics we need without additional wires sticking out of you. You'll also be able to monitor the *Bohr*'s location and how much power you're drawing—straight through the neural, no control panels. This should give you more control over your jumps."

"That's not why we're here," Emma said.

Jennings jerked up, surprised.

"Jeff's had a…visitation."

"Visitation?"

Jeff took a deep breath and nodded.

Jennings turned to the tech. "Excuse me a minute, Engineer Hsi. We need the room."

The young man's eyebrows rose, but he gave a quick nod and exited without comment. When the door slid shut, Jennings leaned against the massive chair in the center of the room and crossed his arms. "Captain?"

Jeff wasn't sure how to begin. "I was drinking, and—"

"Always a fine start to a story," Jennings tossed to Emma. She pursed her lips and did not smile. "Sorry, son. Continue."

"And the next thing I knew, Danny was in the room."

"Daniel Hightower? *Dead* Daniel Hightower?"

"Yes. If you'll recall, it's how they spoke to me before."

Jennings dropped his arms and stood up. "The Ulim."

"Yes."

"Came here?"

"Yes sir."

"There was an alien invasion of a CDF station and I'm only hearing about it *how long* after the fact?" Jennings looked alarmed, but there was outrage in his voice.

"To be honest, sir, I wasn't sure it was real."

Jennings bunched his eyebrows in confusion. "What do you mean?"

"We had this conversation, and then he just…*disappeared.*"

"Disappeared."

"He was there one minute, warning me, and the next he was gone."

Jennings looked him straight in the eye, and Jeff could tell he was gauging his veracity. "And just what did you talk about?"

"He told me not to squash space, that I didn't know what I was doing. And that I needed to stop doing it—immediately and completely."

"And you said…?"

"I tried to reason with him, sir."

"And?"

"He wasn't having any of it." Jeff looked down, as if he had somehow failed.

"Assuming this wasn't just the whiskey talking—"

"How did you know it was whiskey, sir?"

Jennings gave him an *Are you kidding me?* smirk and continued. "Why do you think they want you to stop…squashing?"

"He said they are afraid, that it was dangerous."

"*They* are afraid?"

"Yes sir."

"What are they afraid of?"

"They said I could…unravel the universe."

Jennings laughed. "Really now? That's a bit dramatic, don't you think?"

"I…I don't know *what* to think, sir." Jeff suddenly felt thirty years younger, as if he were a cadet being called on the carpet.

"I think it's a lot more likely that they just don't want the competition."

"Competition for what?" Emma asked. Jennings looked surprised at the question, as if he had forgotten she was there.

"For trade, for power, for the domination of vast regions of space—for whatever their people might mutually *want*."

"And what do they want?" Emma asked.

Jennings looked to Jeff for an answer, but he didn't have one. "They're so different from us, sir. I couldn't even harbor a guess. My impression was that they just want to be left alone."

"Yes, but for what?" Jennings sighed. "Well…fortunately, this decision is mine, not yours. I'll take this…warning…under advisement. In the meantime, let's step it up. We need this project up and running yesterday now that Deseret has fallen."

"But sir, I—"

Jennings held up his hand. "We can always pull the plug at the last minute. In the meantime, let's get everything operational. Because when we need it, when we *truly* need it, we won't have a choice."

"Navigation, I want you to chart a course to bring us in just behind the supporting Prox vessel—that way we won't be in sight of anyone's guns."

Fin sat up straight, then turned to face her. "But sir, how do we—"

"We come in dark, Mr. Fin. That's how we avoid detection. Get us moving on the exact coordinates we need to get into position to take a shot at their engines. Then, before we're in scanning range, shut down all power, including emergency power. We're a cold, dark, fast piece of driftwood and nothing more. Catch the vision, Mr. Fin?"

"I've got it, sir."

"Mr. Laru, how long will it take us to get back up to power so we can get off a shot at those engines?"

"Too long, sir," Laru said. His wild shock of blue hair was almost incandescent in the emergency lighting. "It will take 7.5 seconds for a complete reboot. I suggest keeping navigation and weapons systems on. We'll still be virtually undetectable. But we'll also be without shields."

"I'm aware of that risk, and I'm prepared to take it." She gave a curt nod. "It's a good idea. Let's do it. Mr. Raj, prepare to launch three thermonuclear devices—the biggest and baddest we've got. Mr. Fin, take us in as fast as we dare. Mr. Frey, complete radio silence, please. Mr. Laru—rig for silent running."

She watched the stars whirl on the main viewscreen as the *Essex* came about, then blur as she found her cruising speed. "Going dark, sir," Laru said. "Navigation and weapons systems blanketed and quiet."

A moment later, the overhead lights went out. The low incandescent glow of the emergency lighting and the flickering control panels provided just enough light to move around the bridge without bumping into anything.

"Course locked in," Fin's voice announced. "We're driftwood, sir."

"Mr. Frey, all decks, please."

"All decks ready, sir."

"This is your captain. From here on out we're running silent. I want all personal communication devices off. I want all neurals in sleep mode. I want nothing above a whisper. Don't drop a wrench, don't shriek if you cut yourself. We are running silent and that means *silent*. We don't know what the Prox can perceive and what they can't, so we're not going to give them anything *to* perceive. I know you are rehearsed, I know you are ready. Everything in your career has led you to this moment. We are either going to survive this run or we aren't. But one thing is clear—we're going to give it the best shot we've got. Captain Taylor, out."

Jo heard the last of the equipment whine into silence. She put her own neural on sleep and raised her upright index finger to her lips and made sure everyone saw her. *Shhhh*. Everyone nodded and glued their eyes to their controls. She was about to chew on a fingernail, but caught herself and stuffed her hand in her pocket.

It felt weird, running without a viewscreen. It was psychological, of course. The viewscreen wasn't a window, it was a monitor. But she still felt cut off from the space around her. She heard a thump on the outside hull, and she turned to Raj. "Prox?" she mouthed.

He shook his head, calm as ice. She nodded, realizing that with the shields down, they'd hear about it every time they hit a piece of rock. It was an extremely dangerous way to fly. If any of those rocks were big enough…

She dug her fingernails into the armrest of her command chair. She checked her straps. She also had to piss. No time for that now.

Fin waved his hand. Then he held up five fingers. Jo suddenly felt claustrophobic, as if the bridge were suddenly very small and very hot. She held her breath as, one by one, Fin withdrew his fingers until there was only one remaining in the air. That one, too, collapsed into his fist and Raj punched at his controls. He turned and whispered. "Torpedoes launched."

"Fin, get us out of here. Engage superlux!" Jo shouted, her voice sounding way too loud in the quiet deck.

It took two seconds for the C-drive to engage and when it did, Jo felt like she'd hit a brick wall. She bore the full impact of the g-forces with gritted teeth and a muffled yowl of pain.

It took five seconds for the dampeners to engage, by which time she was sure she'd sustained a concussion. And if she had, then everyone had. Primary power resumed and the lights came back on. The ambient whine of the equipment resumed its normal levels. "Raj, did we pick up any passengers?" She unbuckled her restraint harness.

"None, sir," Raj said with a note of triumph.

"Frey, viewscreen, please."

The viewscreen flickered, then resolved, but she saw nothing but white. "What's wrong with it?" Jo demanded, swiveling toward her communications officer.

"Nothing's wrong with it, sir," Frey said, her hands flying over her controls. "It's really that bright out there."

"You're seeing the detonation, Captain," Raj said.

"Of our nukes?" Jo asked, confused. "They wouldn't be—"

"Of their engines," Raj interrupted her. And at that moment, she didn't mind his impertinence. Not one bit.

"Hot damn," she said, punching at the arm of her command chair in triumph. A moment later, cheers erupted from her crew. Fin stood up, his arms raised toward the ceiling. He started jumping up and down, making loud whooping noises. Frey crossed and planted a kiss on Raj's cheek. The Weaponer was still emotionless, but Jo noted he was blushing.

It was Chief Engineer Laru that called her back to reality. "Orders, sir?"

She'd been hugging Frey at that moment, but remembering herself, she straightened her uniform and returned to her chair.

"Hell, while our luck is holding, let's hit their other ship," Jo said, turning to Raj. "Weaponer, what's our arsenal looking like?"

"Sir, we're fine on lasers and particle cannons, but we're down to one nuke." Raj's face fell. "I'm sorry, Captain, but we don't have enough firepower to take out the last ship."

Jo nodded. "Okay. There's so much more I wish we could do. But we've done a lot, and we learned a lot. We know at least one way to beat these fuckers, and we have a lot more data that could lead us to other methods once we've analyzed it. We've wreaked enough vengeance and destruction for one day. Mr. Fin, take us home to Sol Station."

"Locking in a course now, sir."

"Mr. Laru, what's the best cruising speed you can give us?"

"We did C8.4 on the way out here, but it wasn't safe," Laru said. She found his long, horsy face compelling in the same way she found zoo animals fascinating. "The Corps of Engineers recommends C7 for this vessel."

"Do it."

"Mr. Frey, prepare a datapacket. Cram everything into it you can—every ounce of data, so that our strategic analysts can get a head start on it."

"On it, Captain."

She stood. "You have the con, Mr. Raj."

"Sir?" he lifted one eyebrow at her.

"I'll be back in five. I have to micturate like a race horse."

THE AIR in front of Admiral Jennings shimmered and a computerized voice broke the silence. "Ansible exchange request from Captain Joleen Taylor."

"Accept," Jennings said, swiveling to face the shimmer. He rubbed at his eyes and tried to force himself to a full state of alertness.

The shimmering resolved into the form of Jo, hovering above his desk. "It's late, isn't it?" she said. "I can never keep the time difference straight. Sorry."

"It's alright, Captain," Jennings said. "I'd want to hear from you no matter what time it was. I'm relieved to be hearing from you at all."

"We got lucky," Jo said. Her features were grim.

"That may be, but I'm guessing good captaining had something to do with it, too," Jennings opined. "Tell me the story—short version first."

Jo brought him up to speed. "The datapacket should arrive at any moment."

As she was saying that, a light pinged in Jennings' neural. "Got it," he said. His impulse was to open it and sift through it while they were talking, but after what she'd just been through, she deserved his full attention. The fact is, he was a little in awe of her. "We'll have our techs pouring over every byte of data you sent, but even just your quick overview gives me hope," he said.

"We learned a lot, and I've got about a hundred ideas I want to try out in a simulator," Jo said.

"Right now I want you to get some sleep," Jennings said, feeling the need himself. "That's an order."

"Calling you was the last thing on my to-do list," she smiled. It was a tired smile.

"Call me again when you've caught eight hours and eaten something and we'll do the longer version."

"Affirmative. Before I sign off…how is Je—Captain Bowers?"

"Ornery, but you knew that," Jennings said. "I've transferred him and his team to Sol Station to begin tests with a spacefaring vessel."

"That must mean the scaling up has been successful?"

"Beyond our wildest dreams," Jennings affirmed. He considered telling her about the visit from the Ulim, but decided it could wait. No need to give her anything that might disturb her sleep.

"Tell me about the ship," Jo requested.

Jennings opened his mouth to complain that it was unimportant, but at the last moment indulged her. "It's a light research vessel, the *Bohr*."

"Compliment?"

"Nine crew members and three science officers."

"When do you begin testing?"

"We should be ready in about…" he did some quick calculations in his head, "…three weeks, if we don't hit any snags."

"Good. That means we'll be back in time."

"You want to watch?"

"I want to do more than that," Jo said. She had that determined look that scared him a little. "You're going to need a captain for that thing."

CHAPTER SEVEN

Jennings had no sooner closed his eyes than he started dreaming. At least, he thought he was dreaming. He heard Becky's voice, so clear, even after all these years. "You can't let him do it, Tom."

This strange dream had no visuals, only audio. Jennings felt someone shaking him. "Wake up, sleepyhead."

He opened his eyes and started. Becky was sitting in the chair near his desk, looking exactly as she had before her illness had diminished her. Her hair shone gold in the dim light of his cabin, and her smile was warm and all for him.

He sat up. *Am I dreaming?* he wondered. He punched his leg. It hurt. *I don't think so.*

"What are you doing, you silly man? Oh, you think you're asleep."

"No, I…"

She gave him that look that said, *You don't fool me for a second.* "You're not dreaming. I'm really here."

"You can't be here. You're dead."

"No, we're really here. We're just not really *her*."

"You're not Becky?"

"No. We borrowed her form to communicate with you. We thought it might get your attention."

"You're successful, then," Jennings said. Not an ounce of weariness remained in his bones. He felt electricity snapping in his brain. "Who are you?"

"We are the Ulim."

"I thought only Captain Bowers could see you."

"Only Captain Bowers has seen us. Until now. We appear to anyone we choose."

"And it's my turn."

"Captain Bowers has chosen not to heed us."

"Ah." Jennings sat upright and swung his feet onto the floor. He was wearing only his shorts, but Becky would not have minded. Weirdly, he didn't feel immodest even knowing that it *wasn't* really Becky beholding him in his glory. "That might have something to do with me."

"So we are appealing to you."

"Moving up the chain of command, eh?"

"It seems expedient."

"What do you expect me to do?" Jennings wondered how he could call for security without alerting the alien—or aliens. There was only one Becky before him, but he was unclear on the actual number of aliens involved in such a visitation. They did speak of themselves in the plural, after all.

"You must cease these experiments."

"Well, the thing is, we *need* these experiments."

"You must cease." The words sounded strangely stiff coming out of Becky's mouth. The real Becky would have said, "Knock it off, you jackass."

"Have you met the Prox?"

She cocked her head, as if searching for the word. She found it. "Ah, the species that destroyed your colony."

"Two of our colonies now, and a whole host of properties in between."

"We know of them."

"They're killing machines. They've murdered millions of our people so far—many, many millions." He looked up at Becky to gauge her response. The real Becky would have put her hand to her mouth, her eyes would have widened, she might even have been sick from the horror of it. But this Becky looked as if he had reported on the weather. "They're moving toward our home world, and we don't know how to stop them."

"And you wish to survive." It was a statement.

"You're goddam right we wish to survive! What do you think?"

"If you wish to survive, you must find another way."

"You got any ideas?"

"We have not applied ourselves to your dilemma," she confessed. "It is not our place."

"You might want to try that before taking away the only chance we've got."

"Jeff Bowers is not the only chance you've got."

Jennings scowled. This was going nowhere. "Do you mind telling me what you have against us defending ourselves?"

"We do not begrudge you defending yourselves. We do not approve of the means."

"And why the hell not?" Jeff had told him about their objections. He just wanted to hear it from them.

"If you do not cease, we fear you will die."

"If we don't use him, I *know* we will die."

"But if you do not cease, we will die, too."

"This is the 'the universe is a carpet' thing, right?"

Becky looked momentarily confused. Then she smiled serenely. Yesterday, Jennings would have given his right nut to see that smile again. "Tapestry, we said. The universe is a tapestry."

"That's a difference of degree, not kind," Jennings smiled.

"You will stop?" Becky asked, giving him that look that promised sexual favors in exchange for a concession.

"No. I'm sorry, but no. We need every weapon in our arsenal."

"That is…unfortunate."

Jennings found her inhuman calm chilling. "So what do you plan to do?"

"You leave us little choice," she said.

ENSIGN ADI PENNER moved her limbs in slow motion as she drifted toward the bow of the *Bohr*. Her space suit was thick and awkward, but she had had enough practice doing repairs in space that she appeared to navigate nimbly into position. Reaching into the pack strapped to her abdomen, she drew forth a bottle of champagne and, with a minuscule puff of nav jets, turned back toward the viewing ports and held it aloft for all to see. In her earphones she heard a cacophony of cheers and whistles. A couple more puffs brought her face-to-face with the *Bohr* again. She concentrated on gripping the neck of the bottle in her thick gloves. It was awkward, but after a moment or two she was confident in her grasp. She drifted toward the bow of the research vessel, raised the bottle above the semi-globe of her helmet, and brought it down on the prow with all the force she could muster.

The bottle exploded, discharging shattered glass and foam in an expanding Rorschach pattern for all to behold and interpret for themselves. She had to turn down the volume in her helmet to save her hearing.

THERE WAS champagne inside as well. Jennings grabbed the elbow of an ensign passing with a tray of flutes and made sure that Jeff, Dr. Stewart, and Captain Taylor all had fresh glasses. “Admiral, I’ve had enough,” Emma complained.

“Nonsense. You can curse me in the morning. Tonight we celebrate.”

She narrowed one eye at him but accepted the champagne.

Looking around, Jeff saw Jason Tan talking with some techs. Tan noticed he was looking and waved. Jeff smiled and raised his glass.

“There’s a lot of brass here,” Jo noted. She pointed with her chin toward a cluster of admirals and captains near the makeshift bar.

“Morale has been pretty low around here since Deseret bit it,” Jennings said, his voice quiet. He kept his smile on for appearances. He raised his glass at one of his fellow Admirals as she passed. "But between the launch of the *Bohr* tomorrow and the intel that you brought back from Deseret, we've got a one-two punch that is making folks feel…well, not just hopeful, but downright elated."

"It was looking pretty grim," Jo affirmed. "When we were watching the Prox dismantling the Deseret forces, I just kept thinking, 'There goes Earth.'"

"You're not the only one, Captain." Jennings took a swig of his champagne.

"How are we explaining this?" Jo asked. Jeff noted the bags under her eyes, and he wondered how long it had been since she'd gotten a full night's sleep.

"What do you mean?" Emma asked.

"I mean the *Bohr* launch. Jeff's…ability is top-secret. What do all these people *think* we're doing here?"

"Ah," Jennings nodded. "Three and four star Admirals are all read in—they've got the clearance. Everyone else thinks that Captain Bowers here discovered a new, alien technology that he brought back from New Manila."

"That's pretty much the truth," Jeff said, his eyebrows raised.

"Hew as close to the truth as you can, and the lies are easier to handle," Jennings agreed.

"A toast!" The cry came out of nowhere, but it was quickly taken up by many others, until the whole bay was chanting in unison, "Toast! Toast! Toast!"

"You're on, Admiral," Emma said, slipping away.

"Hey…" Jennings objected, but within moments he found himself standing alone with all eyes on him.

"Should have been you," Jo leaned over and whispered in Jeff's ear.

While she was speaking, his eyes caught Emma's and held them for a moment until she looked away. She buried her nose in her champagne flute and turned her back. "I'd sooner die," he answered. "This is why he gets paid the big credits."

Jennings raised a thick, red hand and held it up until the noise subsided. When it did, Jeff was amazed at how silent the room was. Everyone seemed to be holding their breath.

"This is a night that history will speak of," Jennings began. "A night when the timid dare to hope, and the brave gird their loins for battle."

A cheer went up. It was a hell of an opening, and not one that Jeff would ever have thought of. He wondered if Jennings had prepared it ahead of time or if he really was as confident and commanding as he seemed to be.

"New Manila caught us by surprise. Deseret dashed our hopes that we might turn back this alien scourge by conventional means. Tonight, however, we find ourselves poised between our recent defeat and our imminent victory."

Cheers again. People hooted and whistled and raised their glasses aloft.

"This is a pause. It is not really a celebration, for as yet we have not triumphed. But consider it a foretaste of that victory celebration we will soon enjoy. Consider it that moment before the trumpet blast when we secure the straps on our shields, draw a full breath into our lungs, revel in the warmth of the sun on our living bodies, take a final draught of sweet wine, and say to our comrades-at-arms, 'this day will bring us glory, it will bring glory to our people, and to our gods.'"

Cheers erupted again from the crowd, more frenzied than before.

"Is he quoting?" Jeff whispered.

"I have no clue," Jo answered.

"So drink up while they're still pouring the good stuff. Because the sack will rot your gullet." Laughs rocked the room. Jeff had no idea what "sack" was, and he wondered if anyone else did, either.

Jennings held his glass aloft and kept it there until quiet once again ruled the room. "A toast to Captain Jeff Bowers, the messenger of the gods, who went in search of wisdom and smuggled a weapon out of Olympus."

Suddenly every eye was on Jeff. They were cheering him. He smiled awkwardly and raised his glass sheepishly.

"And to Dr. Stewart and her team who have prepared the *Bohr* for our test tomorrow." There were more cheers, but they were subdued. The crowd was mostly military, Jeff noted, and there was a long-standing rivalry between the CDF and the CSC. "And finally, to the crew of the *Bohr*, who will be stepping courageously into the void. I give you her captain, Captain Joleen Taylor!"

Jeff's jaw dropped as the cheers exploded around him.

Jo grinned broadly and raised her glass in greeting to the crowd. When she had taken in the room, she lowered her eyes to meet Jeff's.

"I FORBID IT," Jeff said flatly.

"Not your call, Captain," Jennings said. He felt at his head. Too much champagne. He was going to regret this in the morning. Hell, he was beginning to regret it now.

"I won't do it," Jeff said.

"Sit down, Captain."

"I prefer to stand, sir."

"Sit *down*, Captain. That's an order."

Jeff sat. His lips were tight and grim. He blinked.

"You've got a soft spot for Captain Taylor. I get that. And that's exactly why we don't allow romantic entanglements among our officers."

"Yes, sir. But—"

"There ain't a reasonable 'but' on earth to that, so you just keep your mouth shut, son."

Jeff did.

"That ship needs a captain."

All ships did. Jeff did not dispute it.

"Taylor is one of our best."

"So don't risk her."

"Will she be at risk, Jeff? In your hands?"

"This is an experiment."

"So I should just put some greenhorn in the seat, because it doesn't matter if he dies, right?"

Jeff's jaw worked.

"What we need is our bravest." Jennings sighed, ran his fingers through what was left of his hair and leaned forward on his elbows. "Look, Captain, I'm going to level with you. I got you on one side saying, 'Don't you dare send her' and I got Taylor on the other side saying, 'Don't you dare send anyone else.' You ever tried arguing with Captain Taylor?"

Jeff looked down.

"Not a fight you're going to win, is it?"

Jeff shook his head.

"So what do you suggest I do?"

"You're the boss."

"That's right. And I'm putting my best captain in the seat. You're dismissed."

JEFF WASN'T happy about it, but he didn't have a choice. He put on his best game face as he made his way to the docking station, toward his rubber donut, toward the *Bohr*. Emma was there to meet him. "It's about time," she said, looking concerned.

"Let's do this," he said, throwing himself into the chair without ceremony.

Jennings stepped into the donut and scowled. "Everything okay here, Captain?"

"Everything's fine. We'll have him hooked up and ready to go in about two minutes."

"The crew has just finished their checklist. They're ready when you are."

Jeff nodded.

Jennings stepped up onto the riser where the chair was enthroned. He put a hand on Jeff's shoulder. "No hard feelings, son."

Jeff couldn't look at him. "None, sir."

Jennings' eyebrows rose. "I hope that's true." He nodded at Emma. "You take good care of him. Everything we are is riding on this."

"No pressure there, Admiral."

"Sorry about that. Reminding myself, more than anyone else, I guess."

Jeff knew the reminder was meant for him as well.

Dr. Tan entered swiftly and sat in a swivel chair to his right. "Just like old times, eh, Captain?"

"What do you need, Tan?"

"You can keep your shirt on. I just need access to your neural port."

Jeff raised his head a couple inches from the headrest and Tan plugged him in. He always expected to feel something when that happened, but he never did.

"I'm going to run a quick diagnostic, so you'll notice some interior sensations, but nothing uncomfortable. I just need to make sure all our wires are connecting."

Jeff nodded. He was used to this. For the next several minutes, he saw lights flashing in his peripheral vision, felt tingling in his limbs, heard buzzing in his ears, all in rapid succession.

"That's it, then." Tan placed a hand on his arm. "Good luck, Captain."

"Thank you, Doctor." He was surprised to find he meant it. Tan followed Jennings out.

Emma sat on the large chair next to him. He wanted to lean over and touch her lips to his. A part of him knew the gesture would not be unwelcome. But he also knew that he was facing a window facing the *Bohr*. Jo might not be watching, but she could be. He stayed where he was.

"You shut this down at any sign of trouble," she said.

"I know the drill."

"Draw as much energy as you need—"

"Em, I got this."

She nodded and swallowed. She placed her hand on his arm, too, just as Tan had done. But then she leaned down and planted a kiss on his cheek. Without waiting for a reaction, she turned and exited the donut.

"Shit," he said.

"What was that?" Jennings' voice emitted from the speaker next to Jeff's head.

"Nothing. It's just….*shit*, this is on."

"You got that right."

Jeff couldn't let himself be distracted by what Jo might or might not have seen. He didn't do it, after all. Hopefully that was clear. And besides, why should he care? Why didn't he just kiss Emma? What was he afraid of? Jo had made it abundantly clear that she was not girlfriend material. But Emma? Who knew what she wanted or would put up with? *It's worth exploring,* Jeff thought, *even if she's only 80% my type*.

"Focus," he told himself out loud.

He looked through the viewing port at the *Bohr*. There were twelve lives aboard that ship. And one of them was the woman that he had loved for most of his adult life. *How crazy am I?* he wondered. Suddenly the Ulim's warning echoed in his brain, and he marveled at his own hubris, his own foolhardiness.

"Captain, you make those astronauts wait any longer, they're going to want to come back aboard for lunch."

"Sorry, sir. Just…finding my focus."

"Look under the sofa."

"Thank you, sir." The corner of his mouth turned up in a smile and a bit of his anger toward Jennings dissipated.

He closed his eyes and called up a vision of the *Bohr* in his mind's eye. Then he reached out with his mind and took in the whole space station. He drew on the power supply they'd rigged for him. The feed was somehow brighter, crisper than the energy from the generator in Alberta. If anyone had asked him to describe it, he would say it was "quicker," but he'd be hard-pressed to explain what that meant. Instead he just fed from it, and he feasted well. He drew more, then more, reaching out further and further with his consciousness. He took in the earth—all of it, including the thoughts and feelings of all twelve billion sentient creatures there, along with the heavier animal and plant life. All of it was teeming, vibrant, alive.

But not as alive as he felt right now. He reached beyond earth to the

Solar system. He drew more power and reached out toward Alpha Centauri. He embraced the yellow-orange star, feeling its radiation, its pulsing life. It suddenly occurred to him that he didn't need an artificial power source—once in the All, he could tap into any star in the universe. The power at his disposal was infinite.

He hadn't known exactly what he was going to do with the *Bohr* until just that moment, but now it was clear. He would put it into orbit around their neighbor star.

He raised his hands and gripped the space around Sol Station with one thumb and forefinger. With his other hand he grasped at the space surrounding the star. Then he simply ignored the space in between, invalidating it, nulling it, effectively bringing the fingers and thumbs of both hands together.

Then the energy he'd gathered erupted, twisted in on itself, and exploded.

CHAPTER EIGHT

Jeff felt the vertigo of distanceless space rushing back into distance—like a localized big bang, his grasp failed and the elasticity of space exerted itself, resuming its former and natural state. A rubber band snapped with a sound that ended worlds.

He felt like he was falling, the energy no longer buoyant, but ripping through him like shards. He sat up, gasping for breath, clutching at the armrests of the great chair, his eyes wide but unseeing.

A moment later, his vision resolved, as did his hearing. The viewport in front of him was cracked and shock waves continued to roll through the station. The red alert signal was sounding, and emergency crews were rushing toward the cracking glass and spraying adhesive sealant over its surface.

Emma rushed in, followed by Tan and Jennings. She rushed to his side. “Are you all right?” she asked.

Jeff didn’t answer. There was too much to take in. Jennings contented himself with a glance at Jeff, then he stood stock still, his eyes rolled up in his head, reading incoming reports on his neural.

“What happened?” Emma asked.

“I don’t…I don’t know.”

“Oh, shit,” Jennings said.

"What?" Jeff yelled in his direction. "What?"

Tan was by his side, now, unplugging his neural, preparing a dermal spray. Before Jeff could object, his vision dimmed and his panic was replaced by a cold, synthetic peace.

WHEN JEFF AWOKE AGAIN, it was dark. The only lights around him were blinking medical monitors. He raised his arm, feeling the drag of an IV in his arm.

"Look who's awake." The shadow of Dr. Tan leaned in the doorway.

"Tan," Jeff said in greeting. "What happened?"

"You suffered a severe concussion," he answered. "Although we can't figure out how."

"My head hurts," Jeff said.

"It should. Means you're normal and human."

"I feel like shit."

Bits and pieces of memory floated back to him. The grasping of space, bringing his hands together, the collapse of distance, the explosion.

Jeff jerked upright.

"Whoa there, Captain," Tan said. "You're under my orders now. You stay still or I'll sedate you again. That's a promise."

Jeff forced himself to lie back down. It wasn't hard since it hurt like hell to move.

He looked up and to his right, but nothing happened. They'd taken him offline.

"Please call the Admiral," Jeff said.

"It's the middle of the night."

"Call the Admiral or I'll rise up and snap your spine, you weaselly excuse for a man."

Tan blinked, frowning. Then he scowled. Then he looked up and to the right. "It's your funeral, tough guy," the doctor said. It was a perfect exit line, but he didn't leave.

JEFF MUST HAVE DRIFTED off again. He opened his eyes, his vision blurry. When it resolved, Admiral Jennings was sitting beside him, looking a little lost. Jeff smiled. "Reporting for duty, sir."

Jennings looked up and nodded. His face was friendly, but grim.

"What happened?"

"We were hoping you'd be able to tell us that, Captain."

"I don't know. I didn't do anything different. It just…slipped, guess."

"It slipped?"

"I guess."

"I was hoping for a bit more detail than that."

Jeff looked away. The memories were starting to congeal again.

"Jo?"

Jennings looked down. "Captain, there's no easy way to tell you this. And God knows I blame myself. And you're going to blame me too, no doubt. Uh…" he sighed, then met Jeff's eyes. "She's dead, Jeff. I'm so sorry. You can't know how sorry I am."

Jeff felt dizzy. It was a good thing he was already lying down. He clutched at the bedclothes with both hands and struggled to sit up.

"No. Relax, Captain. That's an order. You're pretty beat up yourself."

Jeff eased his aching head back to the pillow. Through gritted teeth, he said, "She can't be…"

Jennings nodded. "But she is."

"And the crew?"

"All dead. And more."

"More?"

"I have no explanation for what happened. I'm just going to lay out what we found, and maybe you can make some sense of it, all right?"

Jeff nodded. He was holding his breath.

"After the explosion, we found that the *Bohr* was wrecked—"

"Where did you find it?"

"Right where it had been, visible from the viewport. It hadn't moved."

"But you say it was wrecked. How?"

"It looked like it collided with another ship. But the thing we can't figure out is…the ship it collided with was also the *Bohr*."

"What? I don't understand."

"Neither do we. What we got down in the dock right now are two ships, both called the *Bohr*, fused together into one massive lump of metal."

Jeff blinked.

"The mass of the wreckage is twice that of the original *Bohr*, before the…the accident. We can see some markings, but it's hard to tell what came from what. The ships appear to be identical, but again… it's just a lump of scrap metal now."

"And the crew? Jo?"

"We've found remains of fifteen people so far—we're collecting DNA."

"But there were only twelve aboard."

"Right. Jeff, it looks to us like whatever you did…it duplicated the *Bohr*, along with everyone inside. Then the original and the duplicate ship…it's like they tried to occupy the same space. And of course, they couldn't."

"But I didn't duplicate them…I mean, I didn't mean to…"

"I know you didn't mean to, son, but whatever you did…that's the effect it had. And there may be other explanations. We're open to any theories you might have."

Jeff tried to speak, but only sounds came out. His throat had swollen up with emotion and his eyes brimmed. "Jo…" was all he could manage.

Jennings placed his hand on Jeff's arm and squeezed it.

"I want you to rest, Captain. Heal. And I want you to go into your memory—into your imagination—and I want you to figure out what you did and why it had that effect. A lot of folks are urging me to give up on this, on you. But I still think what you're doing is one of our best hopes. We just got to figure out how to do it safely. I need you to figure that out, Captain. That's your mission."

Jeff nodded, but his nod was almost imperceptible as he stared straight ahead.

EMMA PAUSED at the door of Jeff's room. She knocked. He didn't look up. She entered anyway and sat on the side of his bed. She took his hand. "Hey, soldier," she said.

Only then did he look up. His head had stopped hurting. They had restored his neural. He'd been ignoring the messages from her.

"You're looking a lot better." She wasn't wrong. His appetite had returned, and so had his strength.

"Jeff, look at me."

He did. His face registered as much emotion as a slab of slate.

"We haven't talked about this, but we need to."

He betrayed nothing.

She pressed on. "I've had some feelings for you. I think that it was mutual."

He didn't deny it. He held her gaze. Slowly, he acknowledged her words with a nod.

"And I know you still had feelings for Jo…for Captain Taylor. At first I was jealous, but I've had some time to think after the accident. I know what it's like to carry a flame for someone that you know…well, that it's never going to be. That doesn't mean you stop loving them. It doesn't mean you should. And it doesn't mean you can't love another."

He nodded again. His eyes became glassy, but he blinked back the water.

"I know you loved her. And it's okay with me that you loved her. Hell…" she allowed herself a brief laugh. "I admit it, I was fond of her. I didn't want to be…but I was. I understand why you would fall so hard, for so long. She was…an amazing woman."

Jeff looked down, his resolve beginning to crumble.

"You need to mourn her. That's good and right and proper. I won't begrudge you that. Not for a second."

He opened his mouth to speak, but only a croak escaped. He closed it again.

"It's okay. You don't need to say anything. I think I understand it all. And…" she touched his chin and guided his eyes back to hers. "…I still have those feelings. I know it's a bad idea." She smiled. "And I don't care."

Jeff cleared his throat. "How can it matter?"

She sat up straight, a little shocked. "What do you mean?"

"The Prox are coming. They're still coming, aren't they?"

Emma nodded. "They're still coming."

"What damage have they done…since I've been here?"

"They took out the Indu Oasis."

"That's not a colony…"

"No, it's a space station. A joint Indian-Nepalese project."

"It's along the path, I take it? The path to earth."

"Yes. In a direct line."

He shook his head. "We're fucked. We're really and truly fucked."

Emma didn't disagree with him. "Jo discovered some strategies—"

"It won't be enough."

"Probably not, no."

"Emma…I like you. A lot. I could see us making a life together, after I retired. Which…wouldn't have been so far away. I didn't dare to hope, but I could see it happening. I *wanted* it to happen."

She squeezed his hand and smiled sadly.

"But I'm going to have a hard time sharing champagne while the world burns around us."

"I didn't ask you to do that."

"I know you didn't. I'm just putting that on the table. The way things are…I need to go down fighting. I can't be in two places at—" he stopped and looked into space.

"What? Jeff, what just happened?"

"Oh. Shit. I know what happened," he breathed.

"What happened to who?"

"What happened to the *Bohr*. To Jo. To everyone in that crew." He sat up straight, felt the screaming protest of his atrophied muscles. He swung his legs over the side and ripped at the IV in his arm.

"Jeff, stop. You're scaring me."

"I know why it did what it did." He stood shakily but steadied himself by putting his hands on her shoulders. He looked in her eyes. "And I know how to make sure it doesn't happen again."

THE PROX SWARMED over the space station. Four fighters made swooping passes near the carrier ships, firing blindly and wildly at every soldier and worker that they passed. The station itself had sixteen gunnery ports, all of them ablaze. Most of their shots connected. Every second, Prox soldiers went down. But their efforts didn't make a dent in the overwhelming numbers of Prox descending on them, dismantling them…eating them.

Admiral Jennings sighed and buried his head in his hands for a moment. Then he opened a different file and watched the entire battle play out from the perspective of a different camera.

He didn't know what he was looking for. He hoped that if he found it, he'd know it. But until then he simply kept replaying the battle over and over, each time hoping a different perspective would show him something—anything—about their enemy that he didn't already know. Something that would give him an idea, a strategy, or some hope.

Captain Taylor had given them much—for one thing, they knew the Prox carrier ships could be destroyed. That was huge. For another, Taylor had hit upon a strategy that worked against them. But the number of battle cruisers they had that could carry the kind of payload needed was limited. It might have worked if they'd been able to move them faster than C8…but that was out of the question now.

He poured himself a scotch and allowed himself to mourn the dream that Jeff Bowers had brought to him. It really had been too much to hope for. And the Ulim had been right—they didn't know what they were doing, and it had ended in tragedy.

He took a sip. It occurred to him that perhaps the Ulim had sabotaged the experiment. Perhaps it was a warning shot, of sorts. After all, they didn't really know what had happened. And he didn't trust the crystalline aliens—why should he?

A message pinged in his neural. He slammed his glass down and swore. Then he looked up and accessed it. It was from Command Intelligence.

—Distress call from Danforth Station. Prox attack.

Jennings blinked. He had an idea where Danforth station was, but he couldn't pinpoint it on a map. Maybe he was wrong. He had to be. He pulled up the stellar cartography interface and did a quick search. Danforth Station, a commercial research and development outpost near Epsilon Indi was… Jennings felt a chill run through him. It was on the other side of the galaxy from New Manila. His hands started shaking and he gripped his scotch and knocked the rest of it back. It could only mean one thing—the Prox were making for Earth from two different directions. "We're fucked," he said out loud. *It's all over but the cyanide capsules*, he thought.

He poured himself another scotch, spilling a little when the door signaled a request for entry. Why hadn't Liu told him? He'd ask later. He put his hands under his desk and said, "Come."

The door slid open, and Captain Bowers limped in, supported by Dr. Stewart.

"Captain, what in hell's—"

"I know what happened."

"What?"

"To the *Bohr*. I know why the…accident…why it happened. And I can prevent it from happening again."

A flicker of hope fluttered in Jennings' breast. He dared not indulge it.

"Sit, damn you, before you fall and break one of my antiques. They're worth more than you are."

Jeff smiled at that, and Emma helped him to a chair directly facing the Admiral's desk.

"Now tell me what you *think* you know."

"When I grabbed the two ends of space—"

"I will never get used to this language."

"It's not scientific, I'll grant you," Jeff acknowledged.

"Just…continue."

"When I grabbed the two ends of space, I saw the *Bohr* where it was, and, in my mind's eye, I saw it where I wanted it to be. I saw it in two different places at once. When I let go—"

"Are you telling me that the mere act of your imagining the *Bohr* in a new space replicated the ship and everything aboard it?"

"I think so, yes. And when I squashed space—"

"The two ships collided," Jennings finished his sentence.

"Exactly."

"That's the steamiest pile of horse shit I've ever heard in my life."

"And yet, I'll bet my life that it's the truth."

"How come this never happened before?"

"Because before, I didn't see the object in two places, I only saw it where it was, and then imagined squashing the space."

"Then why the hell did you do it differently this time?"

Jeff blinked. "I…I don't have an answer for that, Admiral. I just… did. It was bigger, it was…there was more pressure. I was improvising. I thought…"

"And you were wrong."

"I was wrong." Jeff looked down. "This is all on me. Again. It's Catskill all over again."

"Captain, I forbid you to go there."

Jeff ignored him. "And if we don't get back on track, this, and Catskill…it's all going to look like small potatoes compared…" he didn't finish his sentence.

Jennings got it. "Son, you cannot blame yourself for the demise of the human race."

Jeff bit his lip. "Why not?"

"Because it hasn't happened yet. And we're sure as fuck not going down without a fight."

CHAPTER NINE

There were more than 8,000 people on Sol Station, and the hangar would only hold about half that number. Nevertheless, it seemed to Jennings that the whole population had squeezed together to be there. *God help us if there's some kind of incident,* he thought. *The stampede would kill more than the incident itself.* He was confident that whoever wasn't physically there was watching via their neurals or pads or viewscreens. He looked up and connected to the public address system in his own neural.

"We lost some battles. We didn't lose the war. Not yet. Not by a long shot. And God help us, not ever."

There was a murmur of defiant agreement.

"One of those battles was the loss of the *Bohr*. We lost a lot of fine people that day." Jennings stole a glance at Captain Bowers and saw him staring at his shoes. "As with every weapon, you get it wrong before you get it right." He paused and noted the dead, dreadful silence in the hangar. "I just received new intelligence that the Prox are coming at us from another direction as well." He watched their eyes widen, waited for the roar of surprise and dismay to decay. Then he continued. "The need for the ability to move our fleet quickly and efficiently has never been more acute than it is right now. So we need to get this right. We need to try again." He let that sink in a moment. "We're outfitting a new vessel for that test, the *Kepler*. It's structurally identical to the *Bohr*, so we'll know that if we get it right this time, then it's about our technology, not about the ship."

There was a buzz of whispers and commentary. He raised his hands to quiet the crowd. "I know this seems risky. It is. But we need to try again because if we don't, we don't stand a chance against the Prox."

Jennings saw heads nodding at that. No one was blind to the threat that faced them. "But I'm not going to bullshit you. It's dangerous. What happened to Captain Taylor and her crew could happen again… and again." He purposely did not look at Jeff, didn't want to see his protesting glare. "And because of that I can't order anyone onto the *Kepler.* That's not how you make heroes. Heroes aren't made by compulsion, but by self-sacrifice, by brave women and men who don't hesitate to put themselves in harm's way because they're soldiers, and that's what soldiers do. They don't hesitate because they know that there is something at stake that's bigger than themselves." He stopped and listened to the echo of his voice fade. He circled slowly, looking into the eyes of those in the first row.

"Earth needs some heroes today. Who among you has the guts to volunteer for the *Kepler*?"

He kept eye contact with people as he fell silent. He expected a few brave souls to step forward. He wasn't expecting Bowers.

Jeff took three steps forward and stood at attention. "Captain Jeffrey Bowers, reporting for duty, sir. I will command the *Kepler*."

Jennings opened his mouth to swear at him, but closed it again. He understood. Bowers wasn't about to let anyone else go under for his mistake, not unless he was on the line, too. *But he's too great an asset to allow the risk,* he thought. Another voice in his head said, *And if you don't let him take that risk, he'll clam up on you. He'll be no good to you at all*. That was probably right. And a captain stepping forward was a good start. Jennings nodded.

"A captain needs a crew," he shouted.

Dr. Emma Stewart stepped forward to stand with Bowers.

"Oh, Christ," Jennings said, unfortunately out loud. The rest of Stewart's team took a step forward as well.

A pilot stepped up next. Then a weaponer. Within seconds the *Kepler* had a full complement.

"It's good to see the human race still breeds heroes," Jennings said. "Training on board the *Kepler* will begin at 0700 hours. Thank you all for your time, your attention, and your prayers—we're going to need them. Dismissed."

Jennings terminated the neural link to the public address system as he strode over to Bowers and Stewart and the rest of the crew that had assembled. But his words were for Jeff alone. "That was reckless, and you put me on the spot."

Jeff said nothing. Emma cleared her throat. "Looks like we're putting all our eggs in this basket, then."

"It sure the hell looks like it," Jennings barked.

"It's a damn fine basket." Jeff offered a weak smile.

"It damn well better be."

JENNINGS RAISED A GLASS, and the conversation died down. Jeff shifted in his seat, just wishing the evening was over. He'd been hosted in Admirals' dining rooms before, but rarely, and he felt keenly out of place. Emma sat beside him, and despite her best efforts at maintaining professional decorum, tongues were starting to wag.

"This is the best wine on Sol Station," Jennings held his glass up to the dim light, softened for atmosphere. "As for dinner, we flew the head chef at Chez Panisse in Vancouver here to prepare it, and I, for one, cannot wait. Is that extravagant?" He paused for effect. "You're damn right it is. It is, in a way, what we're fighting for. Not wealth or privilege, but something that is as old as our species—conviviality, celebration, the company of friends. I want you all to look around the table tonight," Jennings said, his features growing a bit graver. "This gathering—this *kind* of gathering—is precisely what our enemy seeks to steal from us. Not only existence, but the joy of living, the love of friends, the communion of human souls. Let us enjoy this meal as a symbol for everything we seek to preserve. Let us enjoy it consciously, deliberately, completely." He took a slow sip of his wine, smiled his satisfaction, and returned his glass to the table. "Now who can I pour for?"

There was a general burst of enthusiastic hubbub around the table as people raised their glasses and murmured approvingly.

"He's very good at this sort of thing," Emma whispered.

"Jennings?" Jeff said. "All I heard was, 'Eat, drink, and be merry—for tomorrow we die.'"

"Were you always like this?" Emma asked.

Jeff stared into his glass. After what seemed like minutes, he finally answered. "No. Not always."

Emma sighed and nudged his feet with hers under the table. "Sorry. I don't always think," he confessed.

"That's the human condition."

"Captain Bowers," a voice called across the table. Jeff looked up to see Dr. Osprey, the psychologist. "Do you feel ready for this?"

Jeff shifted in his seat again, but he was writhing inside. "I've never been more ready, Doctor."

"I'm a little out of the loop. How did the tests go? Are you able to move yourself?"

"I have successfully teleported myself to earth and back. I've got the technique down."

"But you had the technique down before—for just moving the ship, didn't you?"

Jeff blinked, his face hard and immovable. *He's fucking with me,* Jeff thought. *He wants to see if I'll crack.* He wondered if Jennings had put him up to this. Probably. "I did. And then I improvised. That was a grave error. It won't happen again."

"Isn't this all improvisation? I mean, there aren't any instruction manuals for what you're doing." Osprey held his gaze. Jeff wanted to rip the man's ridiculous mustache off his face.

"It is, the first time. And then I do it again. And again. Then it's routine, it's protocol."

"But it's only routine when you don't deviate from your protocol."

"I'm not sure what you're fishing for, Doctor," Jeff said, as patiently as he could. "Are you trying to say, 'Don't fuck up tomorrow,' in which case you're being an asshole? Or are you intentionally trying to provoke me in order to gauge my emotional stability, in which case you are also being an asshole?"

Osprey didn't blink, but a humorless smile seeped from one side of his lips to the other. A frosty silence had descended on Jeff's end of the table, and everyone suddenly found their wine glasses profoundly interesting.

"Good luck tomorrow," Osprey said.

Jeff gave him a curt nod and then turned to Emma. "Prick," he whispered. He didn't care who heard.

"He's just doing his job."

Jeff waited until the conversations started up again. "I don't think much of his job."

"Psychologists get that a lot."

Jeff grunted.

"Captain," a woman about Jeff's own age got his attention. He welcomed the change. "How far will you be taking the *Kepler* out tomorrow? Before the test?"

Jeff noted from the woman's uniform that she was from the Colonial Press Corps. Of course they would be here.

"About 500,000 kilometers."

"In which direction?"

"Away from anything with people on it."

She grinned at that. He grinned back.

"Most people think that's for safety," she said, but Jeff heard the implied question.

"Most people would be right. There's no danger, but we're going to get some distance, just so no one worries."

"And by 'no one' you mean the brass?"

"I probably do."

"But you don't think it's necessary?"

He saw what she was trying to do, and he moved to shut her down. "I think it's prudent."

"Prudent..." she said the word as if it were wine, tasting it on her lips. "That's a pretty old-fashioned word."

"I'm an old-fashioned guy."

"What makes you old-fashioned?"

Jeff watched her face. She was looking for some angle, something to make a routine story about an important test pop.

He looked over at Emma and saw her looking at him. She was waiting for his answer, too. He looked across the table. Osprey was watching him like a hawk.

"It's not very popular these days," he began, "but the reptilian brain is still part of who we are. It's territorial. It's aggressive. It doesn't tolerate assholes." He narrowed one eye at the reporter. "And it doesn't like to lose."

JEFF WAS ABOUT to turn in when he heard a knock on his cabin door. *An old-fashioned knock*, he thought. *Quaint*. He touched the button on the wall and the door slid open. "Emma," he said.

She was leaning against the doorframe with a wry smile that betrayed not enough sleep and a bit too much alcohol. "Jeff."

"Come in," he said.

She didn't hesitate. She slunk into his room and sat on his bed. She started taking off her left shoe.

"Um...Emma, what are you doing?"

"Sneaking up on you," she said, dropping her right shoe.

Jeff chuckled and leaned against the wall. "I think you're a little tipsy."

"I feel fucking *great*."

"You need to get some sleep. Tomorrow's a big day."

"We could die tomorrow," she made a face.

"Uh...it's possible."

"And we haven't fucked yet."

Jeff's eyebrows rose. "No…no, we haven't."

"Not gonna die without fucking first."

"Huh." Jeff wasn't sure what to say. Or do.

Emma drew her tunic off. "Help me with this," she said, pointing to her bra.

"Uh…Emma, why don't we, you know, cuddle first?"

Emma pulled up short, as if she hadn't thought of that. "That… that's good. Cuddling is good."

Jeff lay down next to her and spooned with her, drawing her close to him, and savoring the smell of her hair.

"I like you," Emma said.

"I like you too."

"I don't know why I like you. You're not smart."

"Gee…thanks."

"Wait…I didn't mean it that way." She laughed at herself. "Don't take that…I goofed."

Jeff waited.

"What I mean is…I expected I would marry another scientist."

"I *am* a scientist. I have a doctorate in astrophysics. Plus a master's degree in military tactics. Although that's not, strictly speaking, scientific. Still…I'm no slouch in the education department."

"An astrophysicist. I didn't know." She sounded delighted. "Well, poop. You're not nearly as dangerous now."

"It's hard to know how to please you," Jeff confessed.

"I didn't want to die without…telling you how I feel." Emma said.

"And fucking," he added.

"It's all kind of…mixed up together."

"Uh-huh. So…tell me how you feel."

She hesitated. He wondered if it was as difficult for her to speak about her emotions as it was for him. She was a scientist, after all, more comfortable in the world of numbers and empirical facts than in the amorphous, ambiguous world of feelings.

"Emma?" he prompted.

Her breathing had become deep and slow. She started to snore.

It felt good to sit in the captain's chair again. Jeff reveled in the strength and resilience of his "young" body. His mind buzzed with both excitement and information. The bridge was tiny, with just enough room to navigate between the various stations. Whereas larger bridges felt broad and expansive, this one felt stretched and narrow. He'd never commanded a research vessel like the *Kepler* before. His mind briefly flitted on the fact that, just a couple of weeks ago, Jo had been sitting in a chair identical to this one. He shook the thought from his mind and focused on the task before him. Emma covered the science station, looking bleary. She wouldn't admit to being hung-over, but it was hard to imagine she could be feeling otherwise.

"Take us out, Mr. Pho," Jeff said. "Declination minus thirty-eight point six, right ascension twelve hours, nineteen minutes, four seconds."

"Speed?" Martin Pho called over his shoulder. His black hair was cropped short, almost shaved, and his neck was weirdly thin. The kid was…angular.

"Maximum standard propulsion." The ship didn't have a superlux drive, so that was the best they could do. Jeff figured if they got a day out from Sol Station, away from any inhabited human outpost, that would be distance enough. Besides, it would give Emma and her team a chance to finish running their numbers. She'd asked for more time and been denied. The Prox weren't slowing down and every day they delayed…

Jeff shuddered. Just the trip out was a waste, in his opinion, however much of a godsend the extra time might seem to Emma. He didn't need the safety zone between them and other humans. He was confident. Since the accident, every test had gone perfectly. *I know what I'm doing, goddammit.*

But what if he didn't? A niggling voice pricked at the fringes of his soul, of his conscience, of his awareness. He beat it back with logic and a confidence cultivated from a lifetime of military training.

Jeff watched the star field whirl as their vessel banked to head out into uninhabited space. He liked earth. Hell, he even liked Sol Station. But he was never quite so much at home as when he was in a captain's chair.

"Reports," he called, looking up to check his neural for the lists of incoming data from the different stations. There were already three reports waiting for him. Others filed in. He did a cursory check and found everything in order. He silently dictated a message to the ship's medic. Then he rolled his eyes back down and rose, walking over to Emma's station. "The medic wants to see you," he said quietly.

"What?" Emma said, looking confused.

"That's an order," he said, with an amused lilt to his voice. He turned his back and walked back to his chair. She scowled at him but rose and left the bridge. She might be too proud to get some hangover relief, but he wasn't going to let it pass. A steroid, stimulant, and painkiller cocktail was exactly what she needed. He wanted to make sure his chief science officer was at her best.

He'd brought only one shift out, instead of the standard three. It would mean everyone would be on until they got back, but it was a short flight. For all his confidence, Jeff still wanted to minimize the risk for anyone aboard. Jennings had not objected, no doubt thinking the same.

Every day the reports from the colonies were tragic. The casualties were astronomical. Every military planner in the CDF was studying the transmissions and Jo's discoveries. A consensus was emerging on the earth's defensive strategy. Only one piece of the puzzle was missing, and everything was hanging on whether "Bowers' alien technology" (as it was widely referred to) was going to work. Jeff felt the pressure. And despite the risks and the calamity that had already befallen them, Jeff felt a confidence that he could not readily explain or defend.

Emma returned, shooting daggers at him with her eyes. He smiled at her and shot her a message.

—Feeling better?

—Asshole.

—That's "Captain Asshole" to you.

She ignored him and returned to her station.

The rest of the flight was uneventful, as Jeff suspected it would be. The *Kepler* was a sturdy, sound vessel, and the crew was young but capable. When alerted that they were closing in on the arbitrary periphery of the "safe zone" he had proposed, he left the rest of his meal sitting where it was in the mess and returned to the bridge. He nodded at his number one, a swarthy young woman named Camil Nira who was worthy of her own command. If they were successful, her promotion to captain seemed inevitable. He swung into his chair and called for reports. Looking up, he scanned them and found nothing amiss.

"Instructions, Captain?" Pho asked.

Jeff felt the eyes of the bridge crew on him. He met Emma's eyes and saw her smile at him. All was forgiven.

"Battle ready status."

Pho narrowed his eyes. "Battle ready, sir? This is a research vessel."

Jeff laughed. "I'm just…I'm imagining the kind of scenario that would play out if we're successful here. Our ships will need to be ready to leap into the fray the moment we…I…move them. So, let's keep everything up and running. This ship does have weapons—"

"Not enough to warrant a weaponer," Pho noted.

"Fine, but we've got two laser cannons, fore and aft. Or as I like to call them, cigarette lighters."

Pho chuckled and turned back to his station. "Weapons armed and ready, sir."

"Good. Mr. Wall, report on our status to Sol Station. Include a full datapacket with all reports from the last hour."

"Yes sir," the communications officer responded, her voice professional but unsteady. *She's scared,* Jeff thought. *Well, that's not unreasonable.*

"Dr. Stewart, do we have full sensors?"

"All sensors online and responsive," she affirmed. "Sir."

She was clearly not used to serving in a military capacity. He'd have to tease her about that later. *If there* is *a later*, he reminded himself.

"All right then. Let's go someplace…far."

He watched Pho stiffen just before he closed his eyes. He allowed himself to sink into that deep place where he was able to make contact with the All. Then he reached out with his mind toward the nearest neighboring star.

"Captain, an unknown vessel has just materialized off our port bow, range…60,000 kilometers."

Jeff's eyes snapped open. "On screen," he said.

The star field was quickly replaced by an image from a portside sensor. A looming, spherical vessel filled half the screen. "Mr. Wall, get us a better image on that."

The young communications officer adjusted the sensor, bringing the ship into sharper focus, and centering it in the middle of the viewscreen. Jeff rose and took a step and a half toward the viewscreen, all that the cramped bridge would allow. Jeff hadn't ever seen anything like it. It was not perfectly round—it was taller than it was wide, but not by much. At its center there appeared to be a bubble, or at least a smaller sphere set into the vessel that looked like it might be detachable. Radiating out of the bubble were wide flanges that created its circular appearance. It reminded Jeff of the ridges around the eyes of a baboon.

"Mr. Wall, review all ship designs in our database and get me a match. I need to know who this is."

"Aye, sir."

"Dr. Stewart, can you get me some measurements on that thing?"

Emma bit her lip as her fingers flew over her console. "It's…457.2 kilometers across…and deep. 475.8 kilometers high."

"That's a huge fucking ship," Jeff said. "That's almost a space station."

"A space station that moves very fast, I'm willing to bet," Pho added. "I'm getting an energy signal that I don't know how to interpret. It's off the…well, it's beyond the capacity of our sensors to measure."

"Their shields are up," Emma said. "And they're powering weapons."

"What weapons have they got?" Jeff asked. Not that it mattered.

Whatever a ship like that might have, it was far superior to their own firepower. What they had was little more than a glorified can opener.

"Nothing that matches anything in our records," Emma said. "This is an alien vessel."

"Sir, I'm getting a communication on all channels."

"Put it through," Jeff said.

"It's audio only," Wall warned him.

A moment later a booming voice filled the bridge. "You. Must. Stop."

"Who are you?" Jeff asked.

"We. Are. The Ulim." The voice sounded like nothing Jeff had heard before. Then again, he'd never encountered an Ulim ship. Hell, "Danny" had said they didn't use them. Why would a species that can travel anywhere in the universe through the vacuum of space need a ship? And yet, here it was. Almost unbelievably large, possessing weapons and capabilities they could only guess at.

"Mr. Wall, make sure Sol Station is getting this via ansible. All of it."

"Sending them a catch-up datapacket now…and they're in real time." Wall said.

"You don't need a ship to talk to me," Jeff said to the viewscreen.

"It seems we need one for you to listen to us." The voice was softer. Not Danny's but…similar. It sounded human. There were notes of anger, concern, disappointment. *Or,* Jeff thought, *I'm just imagining all of that.* But he wasn't. The Ulim might be as different from humans as a species could be, physically, but their emotional life was rich and morally introspective. Jeff felt a kinship with them—the kinship of sentient species who feel and care.

"I have listened to you. The risk is necessary."

"You have already tasted the risk. It was bitter, we think."

Jeff couldn't deny that. And they were hitting below the belt. "We learn from our mistakes," he said.

"There is no returning from some mistakes," the voice said.

"We are determined to try again," Jeff informed them, defiantly.

"And we are determined to stop you."

"Captain, they are targeting weapons," Emma said.

Oh crap, Jeff thought, but he didn't say it out loud. *Keep them talking.* He knew them. What did he know that would make them hesitate, stop? "Is this what the Ulim desire? To be aggressors?"

"We are not aggressors. Circumstances require us to act. Sentient beings who cause harm to other beings must be stopped."

"We're not trying to hurt anyone. We're just trying to stay alive."

"You will hurt many."

"You don't know that."

"Yes. We do."

"You won't fire on us," Jeff said.

"Yes. We will."

"Weapons locked," Emma said.

Well, shit, Jeff thought. He stroked his chin, mind racing. He remembered his first meeting with them, something their Danny had said. "Coercion is not our way," he said out loud.

Jeff chewed on his lip. He looked around at his bridge crew. He knew what he had to do, but he had been wrong before. The risk was too great. *Or is it...?* Jeff's mind kept returning to that phrase, *Coercion is not our way.*

Like a mantra it shut everything else out of his mind—leaving no room for the self-hatred, the self-recriminations, the doubts and agonizing that had until now tyrannized him. The voices stopped. The self-chatter, the obsessive rumination, the guilt. All of it. Stopped. Hanging in mid-space, just like the Ulim ship, was one solitary thought, one sentence that pinned him like a butterfly to a spreading board.

Coercion is not our way.

"Sir?" Pho asked.

"Mr. Pho," Jeff straightened his uniform and sat on the edge of his captain's chair. "Ahead full speed. Aim for that little bubble in the center of their ship."

"Sir?" Pho's eyes widened.

"You heard me," Jeff said. "Set a collision course and give it everything she's got. Ram them, Mr. Pho."

CHAPTER TEN

Mr. Pho gulped.

"Mr. Pho, you have two choices." Jeff's voice was calm but menacing. "You can obey my order or you can face a court-martial when we get planetside."

Pho's eyes shifted to Mr. Wall, but she kept her eyes glued to her panel. Pho glanced next at Emma, desperate.

"Now, Mr. Pho, or I'll take the wheel myself."

Pho looked at Jeff again, straightened up, and turned back to his panel. "Ramming speed, sir."

Inside, Jeff let out a sigh of relief. Outside, however, he was as impassive as granite. "Take us straight through the pupil of whatever that glass bubble is smack dab in the middle of that ship."

"Course locked, sir. 200,000k…150,000k…100,000k…50,000k…"

The Ulim ship filled the viewscreen now.

"Jeff, this is suicide!" Emma barked.

That's 'Captain,' here, Jeff thought, but he kept his focus squarely on the viewscreen.

"Counting down to impact," Pho said. "Impact in 5…4…3…"

Jeff clutched the arm of his captain's chair and pressed himself as far back in the chair as he could, feeling its solidity, seizing the illusion of safety its sturdiness afforded him.

"2…1…Impact."

But there was no impact. They'd headed straight for the bubble, gone into it…and through it.

Jeff hung his head, resting his chin on his chest, slouching down in his chair.

"We…we're not dead," Pho breathed incredulously.

"No, Mr. Pho. We're not dead. Mr. Wall, aft sensors. Show me the Ulim ship."

The picture on the viewscreen changed, but the scene didn't. Now they were staring at the backside of the Ulim vessel, looking exactly like a mirror image of her front. There were no thrusters, nothing you would expect to see on the underbelly of a ship. Just another front. It was an image, an illusion.

"How did you know, sir?" Pho asked.

"I didn't know, Mr. Pho. I strongly suspected, based on a conversation I had with the Ulim a couple mon—a long time ago."

"Remind me not to question your hunches."

Jeff smiled at that and swiveled in his seat, facing Emma. "Anyone need to go to the little girl's head?"

THE ULIM SHIP—OR at least, the illusion of it—had not moved, but that didn't matter. "Let's stop wasting time," Jeff announced to his bridge crew. "We've got a test to perform. We've got a mission. We've got a lot of people counting on us. So let's get it done."

His bridge crew blinked. "Today, please," he added. Everyone sprung into action.

"Dr. Stewart, with me," he said.

Her eyebrows raised and she followed him off the bridge. Standing in the hallway, she waited until a crewmember scurried by. Then she gave him a half smile. "I thought you didn't need the chair."

"I don't. I just wanted to…" he kissed her.

At first she hesitated. Then she consented. More than consented, she reciprocated, meeting his tongue with hers, searching out the depths of his mouth, his passion, his soul. When he finally drew away, she was panting, eager for him again. "I care about you," he said.

"You can't bring yourself to say it, can you?"

"No….not yet."

She looked into his eyes, and gave him a sad smile. "Neither can I."

"What does this mean?" he asked.

"I think it means that now I can fuck you sober."

"Too bad we have to work," he smiled.

"It is. Too bad," she agreed. "Rain check?"

"Better than that," he said. "It's a date."

Before he could say anything else, she drew him down by his epaulets and kissed him again.

EMMA FITTED the new jack into his neural. "Okay?" she asked.

Jeff moved his head back and forth, feeling for any slack in the connection. There was none. "Okay," he answered. She nodded and returned to her station. Jeff settled back into the captain's chair, finding just the right position for maximum comfort. "Mr. Pho, you will have the con so long as I'm…incapacitated."

"Aye, sir," Pho said.

Jeff glanced over at Emma. She touched a couple of places on her console, then looked up at him and smiled. Then she blushed. Then she nodded. "All good here," she said. Then she added, "Captain. Sir."

His lip turned up slightly and he closed his eyes. "Let's get this done."

Pho sat straight upright in his seat. "We got trouble."

"What now?" Jeff snapped, then internally cursed himself for it.

"Another ship materializing off the portside bow. Er…same ship… I think."

Jeff jerked up, then felt the pain in the back of his neck when the patch to his neural went taught. "Ouch," he said. Emma scrambled to the captain's chair, but he waved her off and began barking orders. "I want a gravitic reading this time," he said.

Emma rushed back to her post. "Can't be in two places at once," she complained. Jeff smiled at that, involuntarily. Inside he was kicking himself for not getting a gravitational reading on the last ship. But then he expected a ship to be a ship—at first, at least.

Emma's fingers flew over her panel. "It has mass," she said. "47 million tons plus change, which is about what you'd expect from a ship that large."

"That's what I wanted to know." He didn't expect them to try the same trick twice. The first one was a feint. This one was for real. Still, deep in his gut, he didn't expect the Ulim to fire on them.

"They're powering weapons, sir," Pho said.

Then again, he could be wrong. Jeff scowled. He'd played chess with people smarter than him…and won. He tried to force himself to think creatively, but it was no good. He felt beaten.

Then he felt his body shift. The air around him became luminous. His surroundings faded and were replaced by an infinite nothingness of white. He was *inside*. He and the Ulim were one.

He caught motion out of the corner of his eye and turned his head. He was surprised to discover that he had a head. Danny was there. He did not look pleased.

"That was a foolhardy move," he said. He looked exactly the way he did before they had shipped out to Catskill, exactly as Jeff liked to remember him.

"Perhaps it was. But I was right."

"What if you hadn't been?"

Jeff shrugged. "At least I wouldn't be around to beat myself up about it."

"You have not healed."

Jeff blinked. "My scars are my armor," he managed.

"Your scars are your undoing."

"Is that a threat?"

"The Ulim do not threaten. The Ulim do not lie. The Ulim do not coerce."

"What do you call this, then? I call kidnapping coercion, don't you?"

"We have not kidnapped you. Your body is still aboard. We just wanted to…to talk."

"In that case, I'm done talking."

"You must see reason."

"I must give in and let the crab bastards eat us? I don't think so."

"You must find another way."

"Then give me another way."

They stared at one another. Danny pulled at his chin in a very human gesture of frustration.

"I'm not hearing a wealth of options," Jeff prompted. When Danny said nothing, Jeff said. "Look, it's been swell catching up. It's time for me to get back to my ship."

He closed his eyes and willed the calm to descend over his mind. He felt the presence of the Ulim, his unity with them, their omniscience and omnipresence. He reached beyond the coziness of their shared mind and found his ship, dwarfed by another. He saw his own body, jacked in, looking peaceful, asleep, maybe dead. He paused to truly "see" Emma. He saw her emotional desperation, her affection for him, her fear. Everything he suspected was true. He widened his focus to take in his crew, saw their confusion, their fear for what might happen next, their pride in serving, their deep desire to save their people. He shared it, all of it.

He drew on the power jacked into his neural. It was a blue-white energy that made everything in him buzz. It was clean—too clean. It was addictive. He widened his awareness in every direction, soon encountering Earth. He took in the lives and fears and feelings of twelve billion souls, suffering with them, triumphing with them, feeling with them. It did not exhaust him.

"Do not do this," Danny said. It was only his voice this time, as Jeff had moved well beyond form. He ignored him and drew on the power again—drew it deeply, sucking at it as if it were a fire hose and he was the thirstiest god on Olympus. When the blue fire turned acid white, obscuring everything but its own terrible power, he reached out toward the wild, compact energy of Alpha Centauri.

He not only saw it, he embraced it, enveloped it, *felt* it. He opened the metaphorical fingers of one hand and grasped it—at precisely the optimal orbit for their position. Then he looked backward and gripped the space surrounding *The Kepler*. Then in his mind, he ignored the space between, negated it, *oned* it with the space held in both of his hands.

The energy cracked with a boom that nearly made him lose his grip, but he held on. Then he released it, feeling the elasticity of space exert itself once again. He felt a moment of vertigo, a disorientation that resolved itself in seconds, leaving him in his chair, surrounded by his crew, orbiting a yellow-orange star.

EPILOGUE

When Jeff opened his eyes, his crew seemed frozen. Their mouths hung open, their eyes were wide as eggs. Jeff reached back and jerked the neural connector out of his port. He stood. Then the crew erupted into applause. "Not now, goddam it," he barked. "Reports."

They each turned back to their stations and he saw their fingers flying. A couple of them looked up, checking stats on their neurals, and then moments later sending reports. The red light in his own peripheral vision indicated they were coming in.

He steadied himself on his command chair as he scanned them. A T-joint needed to be replaced on deck three. It had been registering as needing to be replaced since they began. All was normal. "Mr. Wall, send a datapacket back to Sol Station, give 'em everything we've got. Drown them in data. We don't want anyone saying they don't have the whole story."

"Reports are still coming in, sir. It'll take me about fifteen minutes to send it off."

Jeff waved in her direction. "Just so long as it goes. In the meantime, I think it's time for champagne, don't you?"

He saw a smile break out on Wall's face as she turned back to her panel. He turned to his right and caught Emma's eye. She nodded at him, clearly pleased and proud. It wasn't just pride in him, he knew. There was more to what was shining on her face than that. It was hope. They had a chance against those crab bastards after all.

"Um…sir?"

"Yes, Mr. Pho."

"I just ran a stellar cartographical check to make sure we're… where we think we are."

"I know exactly where we are, Lieutenant."

"Uh…I'm not questioning that, sir. It's just—"

"Just what, Mr. Pho?"

"I think we should hold off on the champagne for a bit. I've found some anomalies."

"What kind of anomalies?" He looked over at Emma, saw the crease in her brow as she began to run some tests of her own. He resented Mr. Pho interrupting his moment of triumph, but hell, it was his job to be thorough.

"Ninety-eight percent of the star field matches our records. Everything is exactly where the star charts say they should be."

"You mean *almost* everything is exactly where it should be?" Jeff clarified.

"Er…yes sir, that's what I mean. The other 2 percent…doesn't match what's on the charts."

"What are you saying, Mr. Pho?"

"One percent of the stars are missing, and one percent are…well, there're stars where there shouldn't be."

THE OBLIVION SAGA • BOOK 2

OBLIVION FLIGHT

“listen:
there's a hell of a good universe next door;
let's go”

—e.e. cummings

CHAPTER ONE

[STRING 311]

"I've found some anomalies." Martin Pho's voice was shaking.

Jeff felt his stomach plummet into a pit from which, he somehow knew in his bones, there would be no return. "What kind of anomalies?" he asked.

He looked over at Dr. Emma Stewart, saw the crease on her brow. She began to run some tests of her own. As he waited, he squeezed the arms of his command chair. He was captain of the *Kepler,* a scientific research vessel specially fitted for…squashing space-time.

Months before, he had crash-landed on a distant moon and been saved by an alien race that had developed the ability to teleport. When they did it, he paid attention, and when he discovered he could do it, too, he didn't hesitate—he put the "talent" at the service of the Colonial Defense Fleet.

They needed all the help they could get, as a deadly race called the Prox was systematically annihilating their colonies on a dread advance straight toward Earth. Jeff had just performed the first successful "jump" of a starship—a small one, granted, but a starship nevertheless.

Mr. Pho's voice continued to waver as he answered. "98 percent of the star field matches our records. Everything is exactly where the star charts say they should be."

"You mean *almost* everything is exactly where it should be," Jeff clarified.

"Er...yes sir, that's what I mean. The other 2 percent...doesn't match what's on the charts."

"What are you saying, Mr. Pho?"

"One percent of the stars are missing, and one percent are...well, there's stars where there shouldn't be."

"How is that possible?"

"It isn't."

"Could there be a corruption in the stellar cartography database?" Jeff asked.

"I checked that, sir, first thing. Backups show the same thing. What we're seeing here," he pointed with his chin toward the view screen, "isn't exactly what's in the computer."

Jeff stood and advanced a step toward the view screen. He couldn't go far—it was a small bridge. "What can that mean?" he asked everyone and no one. He looked at Emma, caught her eye, decided the question was for her.

She nodded, accepting the question. He saw her lips tighten as she thought. *Is she thinking through the problem,* he wondered, *or is she thinking about how to say it?* It didn't matter. He knew the answer already.

"My best guess," she said, "is that we've somehow...relocated...to an adjacent string."

"You mean...we're no longer in the same universe?" There. He'd said it out loud.

She continued to hold his gaze while she gave a curt nod.

Jeff brought one hand to his heart, and with the other, steadied himself on the headrest of Mr. Pho's chair. He glanced at Communicator Susie Wall, saw her eyes widen, then saw her turn to run some tests of her own.

"Jeff, there's more," Emma said. "We've got quantum seismological activity that is...well, it's off the charts."

Jeff blinked. It took a moment, but he found his command voice. He cleared his throat. "On screen."

The stars disappeared and several seismic waveforms looped across the screen in diverse, vibrant colors.

"Tell me what I'm seeing," Jeff said. He wasn't a quantum physics expert, and he wasn't about to start playing at one. Not when he had the best damn scientist in the Fleet on his bridge. It didn't matter that he was sleeping with her—she was still the best.

"The small wave pattern, in blue—"

"That's a wave pattern?" he asked. "It looks like a horizontal line."

"If you blew it up to 1000x you'd notice some slight drifting."

Jeff nodded and waved at her to continue.

"That's steady-state. If we're not adjacent to any gravitational wells or experiencing any significant quantum activity—and you wouldn't expect much out here—this is what it should look like."

Jeff nodded.

"Now see the shallow wave in yellow?" Emma continued. "That's what happens if we initiate a major quantum event."

"Like what?" Jeff asked.

"Like proximity to a black hole, or one of the Balliard experiments."

"You mean something dangerous," he clarified.

"They stopped the Balliard experiments precisely because of the seismic implications."

He didn't remember any details, but he remembered the media going apeshit over the possibility that the experiments would destroy a planet or even a whole a region of space.

"And that last wave, the green one?"

"That's our current reading."

The yellow wave was barely perceptible, extending a few centimeters above the baseline at one end and below it on the other. But the green wave filled the screen. It was not only as far off the baseline as could be contained on the grid, but the wave pattern was "busy" showing at least a hundred fluctuations where the yellow wave showed only one.

"Okay…I'm guessing that's bad."

"I don't know if it's bad," Emma answered. "I just know that it's *big*."

"But what does it mean?" Jeff asked.

"Hold on," Emma said. No one under his command would get away with saying that to him, but she was his equal, a civilian. She probably didn't know better. Besides, protocol would be the last thing on her mind. She was seeing numbers that scientists in her field only dreamed about—or had nightmares about.

Jeff watched as her eyes went wide. Her shoulders slumped, and she leaned back in her chair. Her face was ashen.

"What is it?"

She couldn't tear her eyes away from her screen.

"Dr. Stewart, goddam it, what the hell—" He didn't finish the sentence. He strode over to her workstation and laid a hand on her shoulder. "Emma," he said softly. "Tell me what you're seeing."

She looked up at him, and raised her hand—as if to touch his face—but she stopped midway. She looked back at her screen.

"Emma…" he repeated. "Tell me."

Her voice quavered. "I just…sent a ping to the two adjacent reality strings."

"Is that…a normal thing to do?"

"No," she admitted. "There's no reason to do so…normally. We can't see into them, we can just… It's like sonar. We can tell they're there."

"Go on."

"String 311 didn't ping. Neither did String 309."

"What string is our universe?"

"String 310."

Why didn't I know that? He wondered. *It seems like something I should know.* "So?" he asked, feeling stupid.

"So I pinged 308."

"And?"

"You can't ping 308. You can only ping adjacent strings."

Jeff's head hurt. He'd never been able to twist his brain around quantum mechanics' pretzel logic. He assumed it would only get weirder from here. "But you did. Ping 308."

"Yes."

"And?"

"Nothing. As expected."

Jeff shook his head, not comprehending. Before he could protest, she continued. "So I pinged 312."

"But you can't ping 312, because it's not adjacent," Jeff said, his voice taking on an edge of exasperation.

"Right. But…we got a response."

"*What*?" Jeff asked, his eyebrows bunched in confusion. "What does that even mean?"

"It means that we're no longer on String 310. We could be on String 311."

"Are you saying that we…jumped from our universe to an adjacent universe?"

Emma's lips were a grave, thin line. "Yes," she managed. Then she held her hand up. "There's more."

Jeff blinked again. "Should I be sitting down for this?" he asked.

"It would be best," she answered.

He backed up the few steps to his command chair and sat. "Give it to me," he said.

"I pinged 310."

"You pinged our universe?" Of course she would do that. If they got an affirmative answer it would confirm that they were indeed resident on String 311.

"Yes," she answered.

"And did you get a response?"

"No."

"What…what does that mean?"

"It could mean that we actually jumped several strings, to String 313. So I pinged 314."

"And?"

"Nothing."

"Emma, what the fuck are you saying? Plain English, please."

"I can't say this for sure, and I need to do more tests, but...given everything I'm seeing...I don't think String 310 is *there* anymore."

"What do you mean, it isn't there?" Jeff snapped.

"I mean, it's *gone*."

"STILL RUNNING DARK, SIR," Commander Jo Taylor said.

Captain Jacques Telouse rubbed at his chin, not looking at her. There was no chatter on the bridge, not like there usually was. The air almost crackled with electricity.

The captain nodded. "Telemetry onscreen," Telouse said, his words punctuated in odd places due to his French accent. He was an older man, with wiry gray hair and a scar across his nose. He was a man who had seen his share of battle.

The screen flickered and a map of the region appeared, including the course of their cruiser, the *Talon*.

"Sir, these coordinates—" the weaponer, Lieutenant Greg Shallit began.

Telouse held his hand up to stop him, watching the telemetry closely. "Bring us to a stop, Lieutenant Chi."

Lieutenant Marcia Chi nodded, easing the starship to the precise point she had intended. "We are now in geosynchronous orbit around Avalon II's larger moon, sir."

The Captain checked his report logs, then nodded, finally satisfied. "All right, Mr. Shallit. You had an objection, I believe."

"It's a trap, sir," Shallit said.

"It could be," Telouse agreed. "But it's been cleared by RFC intelligence, and we're in the business of following orders."

"That's what worries me."

The Revolutionary Freedom Coalition had considerable firepower, but shitty coordination, in Jo's estimation. "RFC intelligence" was an oxymoronic joke among the rank and file.

"Coordinated Intelligence is accepting applications, last time I heard," Captain Telouse said. "In case you think you can do it better."

That shut him up.

"Sir, Authority battle carrier approaching. The moon will shield us for another twenty seconds."

That wasn't surprising. Avalon II was in neutral space—a largely uninhabited, disputed area between the regions claimed by the Terran Authority and the Revolutionary Freedom Coalition. The Authority didn't control this space but there was no truce, either. If discovered, they would surely be fired on.

"All out," Telouse said.

The last of the lights were extinguished, and even the computer powered down. Within three seconds, Jo was beginning to feel the vertigo of sensory deprivation. Almost imperceptibly, she could hear the captain counting. She focused on his words, her mind filling in the gaps when he was inaudible. He counted off two minutes, three, four. It seemed like an hour.

"All right, bring us back to operating dark," Telouse said.

Jo blinked as the lights flickered on, seeming impossibly bright. Her computer leaped to life again, stuttered, then was once again displaying their telemetry.

"Status?" the captain barked.

"Carrier is beyond the horizon," Jo said, "but…we're not alone."

Shallit jerked upright, looking straight at her. "What the fu…what do you mean?"

"We've got a messenger bag floating off our port side," Jo said. "Beacon was already pinging when we powered up."

"Excellent, Number One," Telouse stood and straightened the blood-red jacket of his uniform. "Download the contents of that bag and file it under captain's seal. Once that's done meet me in my ready room." He began walking toward the room.

"Aye, sir," Jo began the handshake protocols necessary to retrieve the messenger bag's contents.

"Wait, did that carrier just jettison that bag?" Shallit asked.

"I hope so," Telouse said, nonplussed. "Otherwise, in addition to a war we'd also have a mystery on our hands."

"But—"

"Mr. Chi, you have the conn."

"Aye sir," Chi said, without looking up.

"You sound like you were expecting that bag," Shallit said, his voice accusatory and sharp.

"We certainly were," Telouse said as the door whisked shut behind him.

A slight smile crossed Jo's lips as she completed the download. It was easy to get Shallit spluttering and she'd seen the captain work him into a lather more than once. It was dangerous to egg him on like that, but that wasn't her call, and she was sure that she enjoyed it as much as the captain did. Shallit *was* a bit of a dolt.

She strode to the ready room and waited for it to read the permissions in her ID badge. A moment later it slid open with a whoosh. She stepped in.

"Mayan hot cocoa, am I right?"

"The spicier the better," Jo said. It was a ritual they did every time they had a private chat. Jo was actually a little tired of cocoa, Mayan or otherwise, but she wasn't going to tell the captain that. She enjoyed the ritual too much.

The captain slid a steaming cup of deep brown cocoa toward her. She picked it up and sniffed at it. Glorious. "Care to share?" she asked.

"It's just what we were promised," he said, looking up and scanning the downloaded docs in his neural.

"Which is? I haven't been read in on this, sir," Jo reminded him. The fact was, Telouse was getting old and his memory was not what it used to be. She was very fond of him, however, and she respected him. He might not be able to tell you what he had for supper two days ago, but he was a monster in a firefight. There was no place she'd rather be, and no one she'd rather be serving under.

"Oh? Damn. I thought you had. Right. Well, let's just say we're here to meet some *contacts*."

"Contacts?" She sipped at the cocoa. It was spicier than usual. *That's nice,* she thought.

"There's a certain 'philanthropist' on Avalon II that might or might not have Union security protocols for us."

"Let me guess: the 'might have' is dependent on a sizable donation to a good cause?" Jo offered.

"It is indeed." Telouse sipped at his own tea.

Probably chamomile, she thought, *judging from the dirty-sock aroma.* "And did our messenger bag give you the contact info of this 'philanthropist'?"

"It did, right down to GPS coordinates for the bar in which we'll meet her."

"I'll get an away team ready."

"No. The philanthropist is someone I know. An old…" He smiled sadly. "Let's say an old flame."

"Ah." Jo gave a half nod. She was dying to know more, but she never pushed Telouse. He didn't like it and she cherished the fact that he seemed to really enjoy her company.

"Shallit won't like that," she noted.

"Fortunately, I won't have to listen to Shallit. You will."

Jo scowled.

"I'll take the B team," Telouse smiled.

"Sir, I'm not sure this is a good idea. And Shallit will insist on going along to protect you."

"He can protest all he wants," Telouse said, his accent mangling the normal cadence of his words. "I cannot stand the man. So you must stand him for me." It was an incorrect use of the idiom, but it was clear Telouse didn't care.

"You really shouldn't rile him," Jo warned.

Telouse waved the objection away. "He's an ass."

"He's a well-connected ass."

"That is the most dangerous kind."

"That's exactly what I'm trying to say. It wouldn't hurt you to throw him a bone sometimes, and…well, stop humiliating him in front of the bridge crew."

Telouse moved his head back and forth, from shoulder to shoulder. "You are probably right. Again."

"If I'm right all the time, why don't you listen to me more?"

"Because that would be a betrayal of my muse," Telouse pushed out his bottom lip.

"Has your muse ever been wrong?" Jo asked.

"Not about anything that mattered," Telouse smiled and sipped at his tea again.

She scowled at him. "One day, your gut—"

"Not my gut, my muse," he corrected her. "She's sensitive."

"Fine. One day you're going to wish you had listened to me."

He cocked his head. "One day, commander, you will make a fine captain. Then you can make everyone jump anytime you wish."

"Jacques, I'm not trying to make you jump…" Her voice sounded weary, even to her.

"No, my dear, but you are…overcautious."

"No one has ever said that about me," she protested.

"And you don't want them to," he added. "Not in a war like this one."

JEFF SAT BACK in his command chair as if he'd been punched in the gut. "How could our universe just be *gone*?"

Dr. Stewart shook her head. "I don't know that."

"That may be the least of our troubles," communications officer Susie Wall barked. "We've got an incoming vessel, trajectory 44T mark 811."

"Mr. Pho, set a course in the other direction—as fast as we can manage."

"Aye, sir."

"How fast are they coming at us?" Jeff asked.

"C7, sir. We can't outrun them."

"Shit." Their little vessel could only manage C5 for short distances. "Estimated time until contact?" Jeff asked.

"Six minutes, sir."

Jeff punched at a button on his command chair. "Commander Nira, I need you on the bridge—*now*."

His Number One would be sleeping—it had only been a few hours since he had relieved her of the command chair. He'd need to bring her up to speed—but right now he needed an acting weaponer.

"What kind of a ship are we looking at?"

"It's a design we've never seen before. It's not battle class, but from the readings I'm getting, it's 28.2 times our mass."

Jeff whistled. "Weapons?"

"I'm picking up radiation signatures congruent with particle cannons and nuclear torpedoes. Lasers are a safe bet, but I can't say that definitively."

"Lasers are the least of our troubles." Jeff drummed his fingers on his armrest and chewed on his lip, thinking furiously.

"Prepare to jump," Jeff said.

"Jeff, are you intending to…squash space again?" Emma's voice was grave.

"Do you have a better idea?" he snapped. He instantly regretted it, but she didn't back down.

"Jeff, our universe disappeared after the last jump. It's…I don't think it's a coincidence."

"What are you saying?"

"Can we speak privately?"

"We don't have time for sensitivities. Just say what you need to say."

It was like time was standing still. Every eye on the bridge was on him, then on Emma, then on him. He felt their anxious gazes boring into his skull. He ignored them and remained fixed on Emma's taut mouth.

"Jeff, I need to study this. One possibility is that our last jump… destroyed our universe."

Jeff felt the hair on the back of his neck stand on end. He also felt the pit in his stomach descending into infinity.

"What are you saying?"

"I'm saying…just what I'm saying. The last time you tried to squash space around a starship…well, we know what happened. Something this big…maybe something went wrong again. Maybe we pushed past what the natural elasticity of spacetime could tolerate. I think… maybe we…Jeff, we might have…" she couldn't finish her sentence. It was too, too terrible.

Jeff's throat suddenly felt like a desert. His hands started shaking. His bowels started cramping. "I…I gotta…" His legs felt like rubber bands as he stood and stumbled to the head.

When he emerged again, it was as if no one had moved.

The aft door hissed open and Commander Nira strode in. Her black hair was mussed from sleeping, but her eyes were alert and her mouth grim. "Nira reporting, sir, what's—"

"Incoming alien vessel, Commander. Weaponer's station, *now*."

It was a joke. They had no weapons to speak of. Lasers. Useless. Jeff leaned on the stations he passed on his way back to his chair. He needed to be calm and resolute. But inside his head, the only thing he could hear was a snarling voice saying, "You killed everyone—again," over and over and over.

"Contact in three minutes, sir," Mr. Wall said.

"Can we get a visual?" Jeff managed.

"No, not…sir, we're being hailed—audio only."

"In what language?" Jeff asked.

"In English, sir."

Jeff blinked. "Okay, open a channel."

"Unidentified vessel, this is the Terran Authority vessel *Kepler*. Prepare to be boarded."

"*Kepler*?" Jeff said aloud.

"We're the *Kepler*," Pho stated the obvious.

"We're on an adjacent string to our own universe," Emma said. "Things might be similar…and different."

"What?" Commander Nira said. "What is she talking about?"

Jeff held his hand up. "I'll explain later." He felt his head swimming. His stomach lurched. He was sweating. He stood and straightened his jacket. "This ship is…us…in…in the universe we're in," he said. "We have every reason to believe that we're the good guys in this universe or any other. We can't fight them, and we can't outrun them.

So let's greet them with the same honors we'd greet the esteemed crew of any other ship in our own fleet."

He strode toward the bridge's aft door and paused as it slid open. "Put everything on auto, Mr. Pho. With me, everyone." He didn't look to see if they were behind him. It didn't matter. And if he could get a bit ahead of them, out of sight for a moment, maybe they wouldn't notice the sweat, the shaking of his hands, the jerk of his knees going out from under him. He wanted to curl up in his bunk. He wanted to bury his face in Emma's cleavage. He wanted to be alone.

He stood at attention by the main airlock. He removed his service blaster from its holster and stabbed his finger to open the armory cabinet. It slid open, but a spider had spread its web across most of the opening. He rolled his eyes and scooped the web out, wiping it on the pants of his uniform. When the others came around the corner, looking like scared cats, he held the lid to the armory cabinet open and motioned with his eyes for them to stow their weapons. When Nira approached, she shook her head.

He liked Nira. She was a short, compact ball of fire. Her black hair was bobbed like a boy's, but her eyes were those of a fierce warrior. "It's only going to endanger us, commander. It won't make us safer. Stow it." She hesitated but then obeyed, placing her own blaster in the cabinet beside his. He closed and locked the cabinet with his own code.

A proximity alert was blaring on the bridge, and they could hear it all the way in the aft of the ship. Jeff smoothed what was left of his hair and tugged again at his coat. "Make yourselves presentable," he ordered them. "You represent the Colonial Defense Fleet." The thought struck him that, at that moment, they *were* the Colonial Defense Fleet —sworn to protect colonies that no longer existed.

He couldn't think about that now. He had to stay focused. The feelings that had overwhelmed him after Catskill attacked him with new, vigorous fury, pummeling at him from the inside, coating his guts with a caustic bile that threatened imminent disintegration.

His face twitched as he pulled himself to his full height. "Attention!" he barked.

He could hear the docking rods finding their slots, felt the clamps lock into place.

"Salute!" he ordered. As one, his crew raised their right hands to their brows.

The airlock hissed open and within seconds six black-armored mariners with automatic blasters poured into the hangar, their muzzles trained on Jeff and his crew.

Out of the corner of his eye, he saw Mr. Pho waver. "Salute, Mr. Pho!" Jeff said through clenched teeth.

He saw Pho stiffen, saw his arm straighten into a regulation salute once again.

"Secure," one of the marines called. This was followed a moment later by, "Captain on deck!"

Jeff stood stock still as the captain of the alien *Kepler* stepped through the airlock door and straightened up, adjusting his own jacket.

Jeff's salute faltered, and his hand slid to his side. He didn't need to be introduced. His voice quavered as he spoke. "Hello, Danny."

CHAPTER TWO

Jo spun as the bridge door slid open with a whoosh.

Communicator Tash Liebert darted to his station, avoiding her eyes.

"Your duty shift started at 0100, Mr. Liebert."

"Yes sir," the young man said, still not looking at her. "Sorry sir."

Her eyes darkened and, hands clasped behind her back, she wandered over to his station. He was sitting down, hunkered over his control panel. He stiffened as he realized she was drawing close. Good. He ought to be nervous. "I'm going to let it go, Mr. Liebert. Don't let it happen again."

"No, sir. Thank you, sir."

A smile cracked Jo's command face as she took the captain's chair. "And I want a double check on all comm systems between us and the captain, stat."

"Yes, sir." A moment later, he said, "All systems are transactional. Good signal strength from the surface."

"Good to hear it." There was a lot of waiting on a mission like this one, and among her fears was that a signal would be dropped or a comm path broken when no one was looking. Everything was fine… for the moment. But she reminded herself to be vigilant.

Avalon II wasn't exactly a war zone, but it wasn't a safe place to be, even if there hadn't been a war on. It was in an unregulated part of space, not technically under anyone's jurisdiction, and the locals had lobbied hard on both sides to keep it that way. It was a haven for smugglers, fugitives, runaways, organized crime, deposed monarchs, and anyone who did not want to be found or brought to justice. "It's the fucking Wild West," she whispered.

They'd tucked themselves into the hollow of an asteroid, almost large enough to be a moon by some astronomers' reckoning. This kept them in an appropriate orbit for the time they planned to be there, but shielded them from detection from all sides except directly facing the planet. It had been a real find, and Jo made a mental note to credit Lieutenant Chi in her report for making it.

She studied the map on the view screen, showing the away team's bio signs along the right column, and their location on a street grid covering the larger part of the screen. They were moving again, off a main street, into an alley. Her fingers dug into the leather of the command chair as she imagined what an alley on a place like Avalon II would look like. They were certainly in a more dangerous place away from public view.

"They're meeting up with the enemy," Weaponer Shallit said through clenched teeth.

Jo saw what he meant. Unidentified beings were approaching them—cautiously, it seemed. "They're not enemies until we actually know something about them," she corrected him. "They could be our contacts."

"I should be down there," Shallit pouted.

"But you aren't," Jo said, with a note of finality that warned him away from further whining.

"I should be."

Jo rolled her eyes. "Mr. Shallit, that was the Captain's call."

"It was the wrong one." Shallit didn't look away from his panel. He was on thin ice now, and he knew it.

"You're treading dangerously close to insubordination, Mr. Shallit."

He turned and looked at her now, his eyes small and angry as spent buckshot. "I'm tired of seeing opportunities wasted with weak leadership."

Jo felt her spine stiffen. "And now you're a stone's throw from mutiny."

It was one of the unspeakable words in the military, even among the rebels, or as they preferred to call themselves, the Freedom Fighters. At the sound of it, his shoulders slumped and he looked away. She weighed whether the utterance deserved a note in her report. She hadn't yet decided when Navigator Chi called out, "Authority ship approaching. They'll be passing between us and the planet in forty seconds."

"Power down," Jo called.

"But—" Shallit protested.

"Down!" she repeated. "All the way."

Within seven seconds the lights were out, with only the sound of the crew's breath and the whine of the computers spinning down cutting through the terrible silence of space.

In her head, Jo counted until enough time had passed for them to be clear of the Authority ship's line-of-sight sensors. "Power up," she commanded. A moment later, the lights sprang to life again, and the familiar boot-up figures danced on the main view screen.

"Reestablish contact with the captain, Mr. Liebert," Jo ordered.

"Reestablishing link, sir."

"On screen."

The street map once again filled the main view screen, and Jo could see the dots representing the away team—different colors for their respective ranks. The captain's was red, of course—the most easily recognizable color to the human eye.

"Sir, something's wrong," Liebert said. "I'm not getting bio signs."

"Is there something wrong with the link?" Jo asked.

"Pinging…no, the link is fine."

Jo scowled at the screen. He was right, the bio signs column had no activity, except…

"We are getting body temperature, sir."

"I see that, communicator. What about heartbeat or brain activity?"

"No sir."

Shallit stood up, maybe out of surprise, maybe out of an instinctual effort to get closer to the view screen. "They're not moving," he said, his voice cold and quiet.

Jo blinked and took a couple steps toward the view screen herself. Even if they were standing still, she should still be able to see slight oscillations in their dots as they moved a step here or a step there. But there was nothing. The dots were stock still.

"Holy Christ," Jo whispered.

"They're dead," Shallit said, punching at his station.

"Mr. Liebert, are they dead?" Jo turned to her communicator.

He was shaking his head, his mouth moving, but producing no words.

"I'm gonna fucking kill those Authority motherfuckers!" Shallit swore.

Jo felt an icy waterfall of dread shoot down her spine.

"Mr. Liebert, tell doctor Mbusa to meet me in the shuttle bay, and alert security that I'll need a detail prepped to go planetside. Civilian dress. And have Charlesworth camouflage another shuttle, ASAP."

"When, sir?"

"Now, before someone else finds our people and we can't get them back. Mr. Chi, I want a flight plan plotted and loaded by the time we launch, which should be…" she looked at her display panel, "six minutes from now."

"Sir," Chi gave her a sheepish look. "Pardon the objection, sir, but if something has happened to the captain, that means that you're captain. Do you really think you should be going down there? I mean, obviously, it's dangerous," she said.

"Send me," Shallit said, rising to his full height.

Jo shook her head. "It's the captain's prerogative to lead any away mission. Captain Telouse was well within his rights, and so am I. I'm responsible for what happens down there. I need to be on the ground." She turned and looked at Shallit. "But I need our best bridge crew in position. Let security provide the cannon fodder, I need a trigger finger I can trust up here."

"Then at least give me the conn," Shallit said.

She scowled at him. "Mr. Chi will have the conn. I need you at your weapons panel. Are we going to have trouble, Mr. Shallit?"

He stared at her, his eyes hard, his jaw set like a rock. She held his eyes, keenly aware of every second that was passing. Neither of them blinked.

She didn't have time for this nonsense. Without breaking her gaze she stepped toward him, ignoring the fact that he towered over her. "You will stand down, Mr. Shallit. Now, or I can call a security detail up here for you."

His eyes narrowed, but he turned away and sat back down at his station. Inwardly she sighed her relief. "The ship is yours, Mr. Chi," she said, stepping toward the doors. "Stay out of sight. Stay safe."

JEFF WONDERED why he wasn't more shocked to see Danny. Probably it was because the Ulim—the crystalline aliens who had saved Jeff from certain death on New Manila's moon—had taken Danny's form, as drawn from Jeff's memory. He had recently seen Danny alive and well again...kind of. It was both like and unlike seeing a friend after being a few weeks apart...except that this Danny was twenty years older. He smiled at his friend—for this really was his friend, or closer to it than the Ulim analog had been. This Danny had memories and feelings and ambitions that were truly his own. They just weren't the same as the Danny he had known. *I'll take what I can get,* Jeff thought to himself. "You're looking well. For a dead man."

Captain Daniel Hightower of the Terran Authority stood frozen in place, his mouth open, his eyes wide. His men spread out across the room, leveling weapons at Jeff's crew, then looking back to him expectantly. Danny wasn't barking orders, and Jeff instantly guessed that his paralysis was confusing his men.

For the first time, Jeff wondered about his own fate on this string.

What is the me native to this place doing? He wondered. *Unless...* And then he knew. He knew mostly because of the shock registering on Danny's face. That wasn't the shock of a man thinking, "How did you get from New Delhi to here?" This was a man who was seeing a ghost.

"I'm dead, aren't I?" Jeff asked. The disappointment in his own voice surprised him. "In this universe, I mean."

Danny's mouth moved, but no words came out. Jeff took a step toward his friend, but instantly half of the particle rifles carried by the Authority marines were trained on him, the multi-tonal whine as they powered up filling the air with unmusical urgency. Jeff put his hands up. "No need to die twice," he smiled. He'd need to use words. "It's good to see you. Do you think maybe we could catch up, captain-to-captain? We're not your enemy. Hell, we don't even know who your enemies are. Trust me, we're...not from around here." He chuckled, and his grin was sincere and disarming. "We've already stowed our weapons. Maybe one of your boys can pat me down, show you that we're not dangerous. How about that?"

Danny nodded, still saying nothing.

Jeff put his hands over his head and with a twitch of his jaw invited the marine nearest him to do the honors. The marine looked to Danny. Danny blinked and nodded. The marine began a physical surveillance of Jeff's clothes, starting with his armpits, then his arms, and moving down his torso. He spent extra time with the pockets of his uniform. Finally, though, he stepped back and nodded at his commander. "He's clean, captain."

"Care to pat down my crew, now?" Jeff asked.

Danny looked confused, as much by Jeff's existence as by his cooperation. Danny nodded. His crew looked confused, too. He caught a question in Emma's eye, and there seemed no reason to hold back. He waved over at his friend. "It's Danny. The one I've told you so much about. The one who...the one who died. At Catskill."

Emma's eyes went wide, nodding. He watched as the marines approached his crew. The only person he had any doubts about was Nira. Had she stowed all her weapons? He watched carefully to make sure she wasn't holding anything back. She wasn't. He nodded with satisfaction and, still holding his hands away from his body, turned back to Danny. "I suggest putting them in your brig until you and I have had a chance to debrief," Jeff said. "Just assure me that they'll be treated well."

Danny cocked his head, apparently continuing to be confused by his compliance and cooperation.

Jeff shrugged. "It's what I would do," he said.

Danny only nodded. When the pat-downs were complete, he called out. "Take them to the brig. Split them up. Treat them like they were your bunkmates." He paused for a moment, then said, "Treat them better than your bunkmates. Treat them like your parents. That's an order."

No one protested, from Danny's crew or Jeff's own. One by one, Jeff watched as his crew was marched through the airlock toward the alien *Kepler*. Jeff looked at each of them with grave assurance as they passed. "Hold on. It's going to be fine," he said with a confidence that came only from seeing Danny standing there.

Soon Jeff was the only one left of his crew. Danny hadn't moved since he'd laid eyes on Jeff, but there were still two marines with rifles trained on him. "Shall we?" Jeff asked.

He stepped past Danny into the new *Kepler*. He saw the last of the marines marching his crew aft toward the brig. He halted and called over his shoulder. "Where are we headed?"

"The bar," Danny called.

"Damn straight," Jeff replied. "But one of your men will have to lead the way."

Danny directed one of the two marines to take the lead. The marine was tall and curvaceous and Jeff would have gladly followed her all day. He had difficulty taking his eyes off of her pear-shaped buttocks as they swayed out a cadence, moving deeper into the ship. She was shaped like Jo, and his heart ached with the loss of her. He reminded himself that even if she hadn't died horribly in the *Bohr* accident, she'd be gone now…along with everyone else in their universe.

Then he stopped. If Danny was here, in this universe…maybe Jo was, too. Maybe she hadn't died here. Maybe she was… He almost didn't dare think it. But he couldn't stop the thought. *Maybe she's alive.* His pulse quickened, and his mouth felt like cotton. *Jo, alive.* And he knew—if she was alive, he had to find her.

He realized he was lagging and focused once more on his surroundings. Before long, Danny stepped into a rec area that could have been on any ship Jeff had ever commanded. It was small, which was fitting. This *Kepler* was a small ship—not as small as his own, but modest compared to a lot of battle vessels. "Clear the room," Danny barked. The few shipmen who were there either drinking or playing cards halted, their eyebrows raised in mild surprise. But a moment later they leaped into action, collecting their effects and heading toward the door. A moment later, only Jeff and Danny remained, along with a marine with a rifle undeniably pointed in Jeff's direction.

Danny turned back to Jeff. There was a moment of awkward silence. "Uh, have a seat, I guess."

Jeff smiled, nodded, and sat at one of the gleaming white bar stools. "Okay if I have a drink?" he asked.

"It's a bar," Danny answered, walking behind it to serve. "What'll you have?"

Jeff grinned. "Scotch. Give me every parts-per-million of peat you've got."

Danny's eyebrows raised, then he crouched to look under the bar. No doubt a peaty single-malt was a specialty item, and probably expensive. Jeff smiled at the thought that it would be going on Danny's tab. Just like old times.

A moment later, a rocks glass was in front of him, sans rocks, he was relieved to see.

Danny poured himself two fingers and then walked around the bar to sit next to Jeff.

"Should we toast?" Danny asked.

"What are we toasting?" Jeff asked.

"How about the resurrection of dead friends?" Danny suggested.

"That…is a most appropriate toast," Jeff said. They chinked glasses. Jeff took a swig. It was as smoky as he'd hoped.

"You *are* dead," Danny said. "I watched you die. So you can't be you."

"That is true…and not true," Jeff said, realizing he had picked up an annoying habit of equivocation from the Ulim.

"And you aren't that surprised to see me…and that makes me nervous," Danny confessed. "I want to know what's going on. Now."

Jeff took another sip and nodded. "Sure thing. But…where to start?" He looked down. "When I was tapped to command Project Catskill—"

"*You* were tapped to command Catskill?" Danny interrupted. "Admiral Tal chose *me* to lead that mission."

Jeff nodded. "That would explain a few things." He met Danny's eyes. "So…did I die at Catskill?"

Danny nodded slowly, gravely.

"In my universe, things happened…a little differently," Jeff said.

"What do you mean, 'In my universe'?"

"We're still working out the details, but there's been…an accident." Jeff told him they were experimenting with a new kind of superluminal drive and told him about the failure with the *Bohr*. He omitted the detail about the Ulim, only saying that they'd engaged in an experiment that had shunted them into the next universe on the string.

"That would explain a few things." Danny filled his glass again.

"Like what?" Jeff asked.

"Like the disappearance of the *Bohr*. So they're all dead, huh?"

Jeff looked down. "Yeah. Including Jo. She was captain. But I'm sure you knew that."

Danny looked up sharply. "Jo Taylor?"

Jeff's relationship with Jo had been the only rough patch he and Danny had ever had. They'd both fallen for her, but she'd chosen Jeff, at least at first—until the military became her only real lover. "Yeah. I'm sorry to tell you this, Danny, but she died in that accident."

"Not here she didn't."

"She's alive? Here?" Jeff's heart almost leaped through his chest. The possibility of seeing Jo alive and well pierced him, even if she wasn't technically *his* Jo. Still… "Is she aboard?" That would be hoping for too much. But he couldn't stop the words from leaping to his lips.

"I wish. I'd have her in the brig, of course, until we could transport her to Earth to stand trial."

"Trial? For what?"

"For treason, of course."

"Danny, what are you talking about?"

Danny leaned back. "And just what side are *you* on?"

"What side of what?"

"Of the rebellion."

"What rebellion?" Jeff had noticed that their uniforms were different. Jeff's was midnight blue, while Danny's was black with orange piping. But it didn't occur to him that the political situations would be significantly different.

"It started with New Manila. They refused to pay their taxes, so we refused to send them military aid—or anything else, for that matter. And then it just spread like wildfire—most of the colonies joined forces and seceded from the…what used to be the Colonial Union."

"That didn't happen where I'm from."

Danny's eyes narrowed, as if he wasn't sure whether he believed what Jeff was saying. "Good, because it's been a hell of a war."

"And I take it Jo's on the wrong side of it?" Jeff asked.

"She sure as shit is. She's a commander, number one on a battle cruiser."

"She's a…she was a captain in our world."

"So you said."

They sat together in silence for a few moments.

"Do you know how to get back to your…I'm sorry, but it just sounds too weird to say it, but…to your universe?"

Jeff knocked back the rest of his whisky and looked at the black poly of the bar. "We're pretty sure…Emma…Dr. Stewart is pretty sure that…well, that it isn't there. Anymore."

"Your universe *isn't there*?" Danny's eyebrows bunched up skeptically.

"That's what she...what she's afraid of. Which means...Oh, God." He blew air through his cheeks. "I think...I'm afraid I killed them all."

"I know a thing or two about how that feels," Danny said. "Let me tell you about Catskill..."

Jo looked up to check her neural. Almost there. They'd landed at the same shuttle port the captain had, and had walked into town without arousing any undue suspicion. She was breathing heavy from the exertion, but was trying not to let it show. She'd set a fast clip, and was a little surprised that her away team was keeping pace. Especially Dr. Mbusa, who had a few more pounds on him than the Revolutionary Freedom Coalition preferred. Her three security officers, however, were fit and young.

"What a shithole," one of them said.

What was his name? Jo asked herself. *Oh yeah, Leif. Arnesson. Weird name.* He was solid. Green, but solid.

"How can people live here?" Arnesson continued.

"We live on a grimy starship," another of her security officers said. She couldn't remember his name, but she could hardly forget the weird way his hair hung over his eyes like a wave. She glanced back at him and narrowed her eyes.

"Not...that grimy," he corrected himself.

Jo allowed herself a slight smile that her security detail could not see. Then she checked their position against the map. Straight on. The streets were dusty, and would turn to mud at the first sign of rain—not that there was much of that on Avalon II. *Avalon II, what were they thinking?* she mused. *This place is a dust bowl.* She tried to stay on the pedestrian walkway, mostly constructed of what passed for wood on this world, and was not surprised to find that it was often rotted and soft beneath her boot, and just as often disappeared altogether, only to start up again on the next block.

To her right, across the street, were storefronts with metal, pull-down doors, chains swinging in the slight, dusty breeze. She was grateful for the breeze just now, not that it helped much. It was stinking hot. Without showing too much interest, she noted a tavern, a whorehouse, a vault-for-hire—closest thing to a bank this place could manage—a machine shop, two general stores—each trying to outdo the other with "sale!" signs—a pool hall, six bars, one storefront Taoist temple, and a barber. The offerings to her left were similarly varied, similarly disparate, similarly dusty and decrepit.

She glanced up again and saw that the alley they were shooting for was approaching on the left. She started looking for it, keeping her eyes down, taking care not to be noticed or caught noticing by the rough locals passing them on the street. And they *were* rough, too. Out of the corner of her eye, she saw what must have been pirates—self-consciously styled, but no less dangerous for their scarves, eye-patches, three-cornered hats, and other ridiculous garb. She saw mechanics and street preachers and whores—off work and on. *Who are we supposed to be? Smugglers*, she decided. *Our ship is in for repairs, and we're killing time, seeing the sights.*

The sights repulsed her. The squalor and the petty crime and the macho posing just made her want to punch something. It made her realize just how precious the precision, the regimentation, the obsessive cleanliness of military life was to her, even among the Freedom Coalition. She knew who she was there, where her boundaries were. She knew how to move in that world. Here, she felt like a vulnerable amoeba swimming through a hostile organism, not sure when the next leukocyte was going to swoop in and devour her.

Out of the corner of her left eye, she saw the alley just up ahead. Keeping her hand low, she signaled to her team behind her. Without garnering any more attention than necessary, they turned. The alley was narrow, and she could hear radio jabber in an unfamiliar language coming from the second story window to her right. Music wafted from the building to her left. The alley was paved with trash, apparently thrown from the windows. The smell of rotten food and excrement pricked at her nose.

She strode on, counting doors to the left… Two, three, four… She stopped, facing an expanse of wall, a concrete building with power wires drooping off its roof. A small sign was bolted onto a steel door, "Cajan's Boxing School. Hit or be hit. Cash or barter."

"This would be the place," Jo said. For the first time since they started walking into town, she glanced at her team. Dr. Mbusa's face was grave and determined. If he was still out of breath, he wasn't showing it. Her security boys were alert and serious—even the cute one. She avoided looking at him.

She took a quick glance back the way they had come, but no one was watching them or following them, not that she could tell. She nodded and unholstered her blaster from beneath her jacket. "Let's go." She pushed in on the metal door and it gave without protest.

Inside was a large, mostly empty industrial space. The lights were blazing, hanging from suspended sockets that dotted the cavernous room like motionless, random fireflies, fed by extension cords looped over the metal rafters. They illuminated a cement floor hosting a variety of gym equipment—barbells, medicine balls, weight kits, and platform spotters. Low tech stuff, Jo noted. She smelled the simultaneously repulsive and comforting odor of mildew and stale sweat common to all such places. It was a smell she liked. It smelled like empowerment.

The middle of the room was dominated by a boxing ring, elevated about three feet from the floor, carpeted with impact absorption pads, the kind that you'd throw under a pallet in a cargo bay. Beyond the ring she saw a series of open doors. Wordlessly, she waved for her team to follow. She noted that they had all drawn their weapons, even the doctor. As they approached the open door beyond the ring, Arnesson rushed ahead, putting his hand up as if to say, "Let me take point." He was right. She was acting captain now, and it was stupid to put herself at greater risk than was necessary. It rankled her, though, and she felt the twist of resentment in her gut. But she nodded anyway and let him lead.

Arnesson hugged the side of the wall just beside the doorframe with his back, checking his weapon. Jo could see the light on the grip change from green to red—armed, safety off, ready to fire at the twitch of a nerve. The young man took a deep breath, then turned into the door, swinging his blaster one way, then the other. She saw him lower his weapon. She expected to hear, "All clear," but he didn't say that. Instead, without turning to look at her, he called over his shoulder, "Captain, you need to see this."

"All clear?" the one with the weird hair asked.

"No one is going to shoot us," Arnesson responded.

In a moment, Jo had entered and saw what he meant. "Oh, Christ," she breathed, holstering her weapon.

They were in the mess, or what passed for a mess in that place. An industrial refrigerator stood against one wall, sloping slightly because the wheels were missing on one side of it. A utility sink was on the wall straight ahead of her, with a metal table beside it. Clean dishes were stacked on a gym towel, taking up half of the table. The other half was littered with three-liter jugs of protein powder and supplements, legal and otherwise.

She took all of this in instinctively, but what she really focused on were the bodies. She noticed the Authority cops first—six of them, splayed out over the floor. It seemed they had simply dropped where they stood, black uniforms with orange piping charred and frayed from where the blaster charges had torn them open. The plastic sheet flooring was slick with blood—shining black and crimson, depending on how the buzzing lights of different hues hit it.

She stepped over one of the corpses—a mustachioed sergeant, his eyes wide and still as stone, his mouth frozen in a silent scream. A few steps away were civilians—three men in Bedouin garb and an older woman in a sequined red dress. *Those must be the captain's contacts*, she thought.

There were more bodies on the other side of a stained sectional couch. Her heart fell as she recognized her captain. Telouse was face down, but she would recognize his curly gray locks anywhere. She knelt by him and felt at his neck. There was no pulse, just as she knew there wouldn't be. "Don't touch anything," she said. "Gloves." She pulled a small plastic packet out of her jacket and ripped it open with her teeth. Inside were polyethylene gloves, which she put on quickly. She made a mental note to wipe her prints off the front door. "Don't spit, don't shed, don't blink off an eyelash." It was an impossible order, of course, but she didn't want anything that would tie them to this place. Not with Authority cops involved.

The doctor, his hands already gloved, knelt by the captain to confirm his status, then moved on to their other crewmen. All dead. All by blaster fire. She didn't need him to confirm that. She could see where the particle blasts had ripped through their clothes and spilled their entrails onto the plastic flooring.

"Careful not to step in any blood," she ordered. She stood up and extracted herself from the mass of corpses.

"How are we going to get them back to the ship?" The cute security officer asked. He seemed to be asking no one in particular, but she answered.

"We aren't."

The doctor jerked his head toward her at that. "I need to do full autopsies—"

"But you won't be able to do that. Take good field notes, doctor, because that's all you're going to get."

"That's not how we honor our dead," Arnesson objected, a little sheepishly. He knew he was out of line, but she didn't press it.

"I know, and I'm with you on that. But these are battlefield conditions. Any moment now, Authority detectives could come through that door. Nothing is stopping them. This place is no one's jurisdiction. We've already got six dead Authority cops here. They're not going to make friendly inquiries, especially after they do a retina scan and figure out who we are. We've got to get out of here. The best we can do is offer our dead a dignified disposal." It would also offer the dead the advantage of not being identified by the Authority cops, either, but she didn't say that. She didn't think she needed to.

She pulled another weapon from her jacket, a phase disrupter. She checked to make sure it was fully charged. With luck, she'd have enough juice to send their bodies out of phase and into...*wherever out-of-phase matter goes,* she thought. *Into the Mystery.*

"Doctor, you've got five minutes to finish up. Then we need to get out of this place. If we're not gone before the detectives arrive, we're not getting out of here at all."

"COME." Admiral Jason Tal leaned back in his seat and rubbed the back of his neck.

Captain Daniel Hightower stepped through looking as grim as Tal felt.

"Let's make this brief, can we, captain? I just received some…bad news."

Hightower stood at parade rest in front of the Admiral's desk.

"Sit, son. Bourbon?"

"Don't mind if I do," the captain said. "End of my duty shift, after all."

"Good. It's the start of mine. I don't think this bottle is going to last the shift."

Hightower didn't laugh. Tal poured the whiskey into two antique tin cups. They'd once been part of soldiers' mess kits in the early 20th century. The metallic taste of the tin ruined the bourbon, but Tal didn't care. It wasn't great whiskey to start with.

"Can I ask…?" Hightower started, but couldn't seem to find the words to finish.

"It's classified, but…let's just say someone I was very close to got killed in the line of duty…earlier today…a long way from here. I loved her once."

"I'm sorry sir."

"I want to snap the bastard's neck, whoever it was."

"Read me in," Hightower said.

"What?"

"Read me in. You have the authority. Read me in and I'll snap the bastard's neck for you."

Tal considered this. It was tempting. He glanced at Hightower and suppressed a shudder. He was glad the captain was playing for his team. "Let me think about it."

Hightower nodded. He knocked back his whiskey all at once. He didn't even honor it with a grimace. "Did you see my report?"

"No, I…I guess I was a bit distracted."

"Don't blame you, sir."

"It would be insubordination if you did."

Hightower laughed. It was a harsh laugh, like saw blades on sandpaper. It made Tal's skin crawl.

"Just give me the highlights," the admiral commanded.

"You might need another drink." He put the cup down on Tal's desk. "I do."

Tal raised his eyebrows and poured the captain a double. "This better be good."

"Oh, it is." Hightower took another swig. This time he grimaced, letting the sour mash run between his gums and teeth. "We ran across an unregistered vessel."

"Unregistered? You mean RFC?"

"Nope. Not registered to them, either. Get this: It's called the *Kepler*."

"*Your* ship is the *Kepler*."

"It's another *Kepler*."

Tal blinked. "But *Kepler* is a scientist from Earth."

"Right."

"Why would an alien name its vessel after a scientist from Earth?"

"It's not an alien vessel."

"But it's not one of ours, and it's not RFC."

"Correct."

"Was there a crew?"

"Yes. Human."

Tal blinked. "I don't understand. Your *Kepler* was appropriated from the old Colonial Science Corps for the war effort."

"Correct."

"So…we don't allow more than one ship to have the same name. Just where is this ship registered?"

"As near as I can tell, Admiral, it's a Colonial Science Corps vessel."

"There are no Colonial Science Corps vessels. There's no Colonial Science Corps."

"There's no Colonial Science Corps in *this* universe."

Tal pursed his lips. Was Hightower playing with him? Yes, a little bit. That was clear. He was dancing around something big and was enjoying the guessing game. That was all right. Tal was enjoying it a bit himself. He'd had enough tragedy for one day. The puzzle was a good distraction. He smiled and took another drink of his bourbon. "Okay, Captain, I'll play along. Who is the captain of this unregistered *Kepler*?"

"Captain Jeffrey Bowers."

Tal frowned. "I know that name. Why do I know that name?"

"Twenty years ago, sir, you had to choose between two lieutenants to lead a top secret mission. You chose me, sir."

It all came rushing back. Tal set his cup down, suddenly feeling a little sick. "Catskill." The word dropped off his tongue like an anvil.

"Yes, sir. Jeff Bowers was my best friend. He died on that mission."

"I remember now."

"I saw him die, sir. It's…it's why I snapped. It wasn't in my orders to kill everyone in that village, as you know." Hightower admitted this without a hint of remorse.

It made the hair stand up on Tal's arm. "It earned you a reputation," Tal said, not meeting the captain's eyes.

"One that I hope I've put to good use." Hightower grinned. Actually *grinned.*

Tal knocked back the rest of the whiskey in his cup.

"I'm through playing twenty questions, captain. Tell me what happened. The short version." His mood had soured. Hightower was never company he cared to keep.

"It's Jeff, all right. And several crew members of a contemporaneous Colonial Defense Fleet—as if the war had never happened. They say they were testing a new teleportation technology and ended up in Authority space…on an adjacent reality string."

"What string do they say they're from?"

"String 310. They list us as String 311. I don't know about that, sir—"

Tal nodded. "That's right. 311 is our string. But we've never…it isn't possible…" he trailed off, looking out the large window into space at the stationary stars, burning brighter than seemed natural to someone brought up planetside.

"They seem as surprised as we are. And get this, in their string, you picked him instead of me. In his universe, I died at Catskill."

"And there was no war."

Hightower cocked his head. "What do you mean, sir?"

I picked the wrong man all right, Tal thought. But he didn't say it aloud.

CHAPTER THREE

The chime rang out, indicating someone was at the door of Jeff's cabin. The noise seemed distorted and loopy, bringing him from the depths of oblivion to the surface of consciousness—a place he had absolutely no interest in being. "Go away," he called, not loud enough for anyone to hear. Just the volume he had been able to muster made his head ache. "Jesus Christ," he said, cradling his head and turning over on his bunk.

Then came the knocking. Soft at first, then louder. Then insistent. "Jeff, I know you're in there!" Emma's voice, muffled, higher-pitched than usual, which meant anger or panic. Perhaps both.

"Go away!" Jeff yelled again, bracing himself against the pain.

"I'm not going away," she called through the door. "You've been in there for days."

"Go away," Jeff repeated. She pounded on the door.

"Jesus!" he shouted, sitting up. His stomach leaped from all the whisky, and his face felt like it was on fire. His temples throbbed and a great burning pain the magnitude of the sun burned behind his eyes. "Ahhh!" he moaned.

"Let me in or I'll find a janitor who will let me in anyway."

Jeff continued to moan. This world's *Kepler* had escorted their own

Kepler back to Sol Station. It was, in every way he could discern, an exact replica of their own Sol Station. He knew his way around, and it felt familiar and comforting. His crew had been granted low-security detention status—which means they'd been granted free run of the space station, but their neurals were being closely monitored. It was house arrest…in a really big house.

Jeff glanced at a half-empty glass of whisky and knocked it back, hoping the hair of the dog would take the edge off his torment. He spoke, trying to keep his voice even and normal so the computer would recognize it. "Let her in," he said. The door slid open.

Emma was there, but he didn't look up at her face. He knew what he'd see, and didn't really want to see it.

"You look like hell," she said, stepping in and taking his only chair. The door whisked shut behind her.

He slumped down onto the bed again.

"And you're naked," she pointed out.

He looked down. "Huh," he said. "I hadn't noticed that."

"And there's a pool of vomit by your pants."

"Ugh." *So that's what that smell is,* he thought as he lay back down. The new body given to him by the Ulim was supposed to be resilient. But he had never pushed it like he had been pushing it for the past several days.

"Jeff, you have to stop with the drinking. No amount of alcohol is going to change what happened…what we did."

"What I did," Jeff corrected her.

"What *we* did," she insisted.

"It's Catskill all over again." Jeff rose and poured himself another scotch. He looked up at the small cache of dishes above his sink to see if there was a larger glass. There was. He looked at Emma. He thought better of it and just used the smaller glass he had.

She grabbed the bottle before he could pour her any. "I knew this was going to happen."

"You knew what was going to happen?" Jeff asked.

"This."

"I don't know what you mean."

"Bullshit." Emma wasn't the kind of woman who bandied about profanity. It sounded alien and wrong dropping from her lips. "Jeff, ever since we docked at Sol Station, you've crawled into your hole—just like before, but worse."

Jeff opened his mouth to protest, but she held up her hand. "Don't even try to deny it. You've consumed more whisky in three days than you normally go through in a month. You're sleeping all day. You're irritable and sullen."

"I'm just—" What was he going to say, "drunk"? He certainly was that.

"Shut up or I'll punch you in the head," Emma snapped. "You're not 'just' anything. You're depressed. And I'm not leaving until you accompany me to the infirmary."

"Do you know what will happen if we go to the infirmary?"

"You might get some help? Maybe a dose of Plastaffex to help you manage your emotions—in a *healthy* way?"

"The doctor will want to do some routine scans and will discover that my fifty-year-old-body has the metabolism of a twenty-year-old. And it will be the whole can of shit we went through when I returned from the Ulim, all over again."

Emma nodded, silent now. "You *have* been depressed."

Jeff nodded. "Okay." It was a concession. Of sorts. Sure.

"And it's *not* Catskill."

"Nope. It's a billion times worse. A billion, billion times worse." Jeff eyed the bottle in Emma's hand. He was at the point of diminishing returns for the alcohol, and he knew it. It didn't stop him from wanting it.

"Give me a glass, will you please?" Emma pointed toward the cupboard. "You're scaring me—and you're irritating the shit out of me."

Jeff raised his eyebrows at yet another profanity. He shrugged and passed her a mug. "Always took you for a gin girl."

She poured herself a couple of fingers. "I'm a white wine girl, thank you very much."

Jeff sat on the edge of his bunk and rubbed his hands along his buzz cut hair. "Em, I…if you're right, I just killed every person on Earth—not to mention every creature on every planet there is…was."

"Trying to win a war against creatures that were systematically wiping out the human race. You…*we* didn't do it on purpose. Science is filled with unintended consequences."

"Edison burning his finger and what we did are hardly in the same category of 'Oops.'"

Emma took a sip and made a face. "How can you stand this stuff?"

Jeff felt dizzy. He lay back down, arms spreadeagle. "Puts hair on your chest," he managed.

"You want hair on *my* chest? Really?"

Jeff smiled sadly, but didn't know if she could see it. It didn't matter. They hadn't made love since the accident. He couldn't even summon any desire. *Is that what I'm calling it now?* he wondered. *The accident?*

"Jeff, we're stuck here. There's no home to go to."

"If you're trying to make me feel better—I don't. I feel sick."

"I'm trying to think things through. This is the only universe we've got. You've got to have a physical sometime. They're going to find out you're…altered."

"Yeah. Okay. Sometime."

"You need to get ahead of it."

"What are you…what do you mean?"

"Talk to Admiral Jennings—"

"There is no Admiral Jennings. I checked. The Admiral here is Tal."

Emma looked disturbed. "Do you know him?"

Jeff nodded. "He made me a captain. He sent me to Catskill."

"Oh, Jeff," she moved to his side and put her hand on his chest.

"But in this world, he chose Danny to lead that mission. Which is why I'm…dead here." He swallowed. "So yeah, I know him."

"Then go to him. Tell him…hell, tell him everything."

"He'll just want to use…" he was about to say "me" but after some hesitation, finished with a weak "it."

"He might. And you'll say no. And you'll tell him that *if* you use it you risk destroying this universe too. He won't allow that. He's too smart."

"He might. He's an Admiral. He might try to force my hand."

"What, by tying me to a railroad track and twirling his mustache?"

Despite himself, Jeff laughed. It hurt. "Oh, God, Emma…what have we done?"

She put the glass and the bottle on the counter and laid down next to him on the bed. She rested her head on his chest and hugged him to her. "The best we could, honey."

She'd never used a term of endearment before. He put his arm around her and pulled her in closer. Without knowing where it came from, a sob erupted from his throat.

"That's the best thing," Emma said. "Let it out, baby." She cradled his head into her belly and rocked back and forth as he wet her shirt.

Jo was deep in thought as the shuttle auto-docked with the *Talon*. She felt lost. She felt the gaping hole of loss in her belly. Not just the loss of the Captain and his away team, but personal loss…failure. She wracked her brain replaying the events that had led her to the present moment, every significant decision, every possible way she might have gone in a different direction or pushed things in a different direction. But Captain Telouse was not a man easily pushed, and her own responses had been by the book. She might, conceivably, have done something different, but it wouldn't have made any sense in the moment to do it. She shook her head. She was already frazzled with grief, and now she was making herself crazy with all her second-guessing.

The shuttle set down lightly. She felt a barely perceptible bump as the shuttle's skis kissed the floor of the landing bay. She'd have to make a full report to RFC command, and she'd have to hold it all together until they could rendezvous with a friendly space station and pick up their new captain. She felt unequal to the task. Her hands began to shake, and she squeezed them under her thighs to steady them.

With a whine of servomotors, the shuttle door swung up and clear of the entrance, and their restraints released. Dr. Mbusa avoided her eyes as he rose and headed first for the door. That meant one thing—the doctor was lost in his own thoughts and not really aware of what was happening around him. She decided not to call him on it. The security team followed protocol, however, and waited for her to disembark before them.

She emerged from the door and stepped down to the floor of the bay. Steadying herself against the hull, she turned and began walking across the cavernous bay floor. Then she stopped.

Weaponer Shallit had come to meet her. That was odd. Odder still was the fact that he was accompanied by a double complement of security officers. As her own security detail disembarked, they noted the oddity of it, too, and halted behind her. Dr. Mbusa simply pushed past them and headed for the lift.

"What's up?" Leif Arnesson asked.

"Weaponer Shallit, what's wrong?" Jo asked. "Why aren't you on the bridge?" She felt the tiny black hairs on the back of her neck become stiff and stand upright. A chill ran down her spine.

"This crew is in a state of crisis," Shallit said. "Morale is low—people are scared."

"There's no need for them to—"

Shallit interrupted her. "Confidence in leadership is low. For the good of the crew, for its survival, I am relieving you of your command."

So that was it. Why hadn't she seen this coming? She put her hands on her hips defiantly. "You don't have the authority to relieve me of command."

"I don't need authority, I only need strength and the confidence of the crew."

Jo glanced at the hard faces of the security officers—*her* security officers. "You mean the confidence of Security."

He moved his head back and forth, indicating a flake of agreement. "They do the job."

"This is mutiny. It will never stand."

"Possession is 9/10ths of the law. When we complete this mission and return safely, no one will blink an eye."

That was probably not true, but there was enough truth in it to make Jo nervous. The Revolutionary Freedom Coalition was well funded, but chaotic. There was a command structure, but there was an anarchic streak that made precise coordination of forces difficult at best. If he could gin up a good enough story, he might just get away with it. Or he was planning a career in piracy with a stolen vessel and crew. Jo wouldn't put it past him.

"This is wrong, Greg."

"You're going to appeal to my morality now?" He lowered his head slightly and gave her a smile that said, *Aren't you pathetic?*

Jo felt herself running out of aces. Her mind raced. It was stupid, her appeal to ethics. A man like Shallit only spoke the language of pragmatism. Idealism was an alien tongue.

"Throw down your weapon," Shallit ordered. "You, men, with me." He motioned for the security detail that had returned from the planet to abandon her and join their fellows. Out of the corner of her eye, she could see them wavering. But they could read the score as well as she could. They'd either cross over or surrender their weapons with her. Slowly, reluctantly, they stepped past her. Arnesson glanced over his shoulder and shot her an apologetic grimace.

She took a deep breath and squared her shoulders. If she was going to go down, it was going to be with some dignity.

"Your blaster, commander," Shallit insisted. "Throw it down."

"I'm not going to throw it down," she said. "It'll get damaged. Hell, it might explode. Here." She removed her blaster from its holster and flipped it around. She held it out so that its handgrip was pointed toward Shallit.

He nodded and strode forward to take the weapon.

She held it out to him. Holding it as she was, her thumb was nowhere near the ID pad. Just as he reached out to take the weapon, she pushed the trigger forward with her thumb.

The particle blast erupted from the butt-end of the barrel, and it was close enough to catch Shallit full in the chest. The man went down, howling with pain and rage. Jo flipped the blaster into the air and caught it the right way 'round, placing her thumb on the ID pad as God had intended so that this time the gun would know its owner—would know it was *her*—and would fire properly and at full, hull-melting capacity. She trained the blaster at Shallit's head as he clutched at his chest and writhed. "Nice try, asshole." She glanced up at the assembled security teams. "You've all got two choices. Behave like loyal RFC Security from this moment out and we'll forget any of this ever happened. Continue to back this asshole and you can join him for a tea party in the airlock until your guts explode out the top of your head. Which will it be?"

She watched as, one by one, they holstered their blasters and saluted.

"Grab this asshole and take him to *that* airlock." She pointed to the one across the room.

No one complained. No one objected. They dragged his twisting body across the landing bay floor to the airlock and waited as it slid open, then shoved him in.

She stabbed a button with her finger and stepped back slightly as the inner hatch slid closed and sealed. Jo's demeanor was like steel as she entered the executive code overriding decompression, then watched through the small porthole in the hatch as Shallit's body was blown into the void.

"Come."

Jeff's and Emma's eyes locked. She smiled encouragingly.

He'd slept some and his headache had abated, thanks to a gallon of Elektro and some Morphex. He felt slightly altered—and maybe a tiny bit still drunk—but he was alert and functional. He waited as the door slid open, and motioned for Emma to enter first. He followed her into a wood paneled office adorned with nautical tchotchkes and antique lithographs of jazz musicians.

Admiral Tal looked up from the pad in his hand only when they were halfway across the room. He didn't smile exactly, but gave a satisfied nod. He was older than when Jeff had seen him last. His dark brown skin was more weathered, and his hair had grayed. He seemed to be the same Admiral Tal in every respect, except Jeff knew he wasn't.

"Captain. Doctor. Please have a seat." They did. Jeff felt a fleeting wave of nervousness. He flashed on being in the principal's office as a teenager. He knew it was a silly thought, but knowing that didn't make the feeling go away.

"You've come to us with quite a tale," he said. He sat. "Can I offer you a drink?"

"No thank you," Emma answered for both of them, a little too quickly. "Especially not him."

A slight curl of a smile crossed the Admiral's face, but it disappeared quickly. He leaned back in his chair. "It's been a long time since I've seen you, Captain."

"Since I died twenty years ago, I suppose that's true. I've seen you since…in our universe. But it *has* been a long time."

"Are you still holding a grudge?" Tal asked.

"Why should I? In my universe, you picked me."

"Did I?" Tal nodded slowly. "Well, it was a close thing." He drummed his fingers on his desk. "I have to confess, I find your story almost impossible to believe."

Emma gave no reaction. Jeff nodded. "I understand completely."

"You look like Commander Bowers to me. You're older, but I'd know you anywhere. If I didn't know better, I'd suspect you were haunting me. An admiral has to live with the ghosts of all the men he sent into battle who didn't come back. We just don't often have to confront them in the flesh."

Jeff nodded. He swallowed. He could see the Admiral was struggling with this. There was nothing he could do but let him struggle.

"You could be a plant, a trick. But the fact is that you know things that only Captain Hightower and the original Commander Bowers could know. So that's…convincing." He turned to look at Emma. "And there's the odd fact that there are now two of you. You are teaching particle physics at MIT. Right now." The air over his desk shimmered and a moment later a tiny version of Emma was lecturing on the admiral's desktop. "Specialist in Quantum seismology."

"Guilty as charged," Emma said. "Admiral, can I ask a frivolous question? Am I…single?"

Tal chuckled. "I did not think to ask, my dear."

Emma shrugged.

"Needless to say, we're interested to hear about what you all were working on, when the whole…"

"Accident?" Jeff offered, hating himself for saying it.

"Yes, when the *accident* happened."

"I'd be happy to write up a technical evaluation," Emma offered. "I was the one supervising the technical operation."

Tal nodded. "Good, because we want to know what you were really up to."

Jeff and Emma looked at one another.

"What do you mean, 'really up to'?" Jeff asked.

"I've just received a report from our experts evaluating your voice and vid records ever since you returned—specifically your initial debriefing. Not a single man on your ship was telling the truth—not the whole truth, anyway. And that includes you, Captain."

Jeff nodded. "I guess that's why we asked to see you."

"I can't tell you how glad I am that you asked to see me before I summoned you. It was a close thing." He folded his hands in front of him and leaned over his desk toward Jeff. "Are you gonna come clean with me, Captain, Doctor, or are you going to spin some more gold out of your asses?"

"You want the whole truth?" Jeff asked.

"I do, Captain. Knowing the whole situation is the only way you win a war. It's the only way I can keep these people safe. So you can either give it to me straight or you can continue your depressive funk in a maximum security cell."

Jeff glanced at Emma. She nodded. "Okay. The whole truth, then."

"I'm going to be recording this. So we can *tell* if you're telling the truth."

"That's fine, sir." Jeff launched in. He told the admiral about Catskill, about the mysterious, suicidal commands, and about Danny's death. He told the admiral about New Manila being dismantled by the Prox, about his crash landing on the moon, and about the Ulim.

The admiral blinked as Jeff related all he knew about the crystalline aliens, about how he'd been reconstructed back home in Anchorage. About how he'd seen them squash space and how he'd learned to do it himself. He told Tal about their early experiments, about the facility in Alberta, about the yak meat in Ladakh, about the disaster with the *Bohr*. Finally, he related the surprise attack of the Ulim and the desperate jump Jeff had initiated that had apparently wiped out an entire string of reality and landed them in a familiar but alien universe.

When he finally finished speaking, Tal's eyes were wide. "I…need that drink." He did not ask again whether Jeff or Emma would join him. Tal opened a drawer and poured himself a glass. He knocked it back.

Jeff blinked, waiting. Tal wiped the corner of his mouth on his sleeve. Then he propped one elbow on the desk and rested his chin in his hand. "So you're…actually an alien."

"I don't know what I am. I'm me, though," Jeff answered.

Tal sighed. "You're sure none of these…Prox…made the jump with you?" Jeff knew what he was after. The admiral did not need another enemy to contend with, not with a civil war raging.

"No, sir. We would have picked that up on our sensors. We came through alone."

Tal nodded.

"Good…that's…good." Tal nodded again. "Um…Captain, Doctor, I'm going to need some time to…"

"Process?" Emma offered.

"I was going to say, 'have these recordings evaluated for veracity,' but yes, I'm going to need to…process what you've told me."

"Of course." Jeff rose and straightened his jacket.

"I may have more questions," Tal said.

"Of course, sir."

Emma rose, too. "Are you going to lock us up?"

"If my experts tell me you're telling the truth? No. If they tell me you aren't, you'll wake up in the brig. How's that?"

"That's only fair," Jeff said.

"Are you going to wake up in the brig?" Tal asked.

"We've told you everything, sir," Jeff said. "We might not have gotten it all right…I mean, we're just guessing about the science…but you know everything we know."

"That's what I want to hear. Dismissed, Captain." He nodded at Emma. "Doctor."

Without another word, Jeff and Emma exited the office. The door slid shut behind them. Jeff watched Emma slump.

"Whew," she said. "Do you think he really believes it?"

"Who knows? I'm not sure I believe it," Jeff admitted.

"He seems suspicious."

"Of course he's suspicious. Seems like the old Tal, though. I might not know *him*, but I trust him."

Emma slumped against the wall. "I need…to lie down a bit. Care to come?"

Jeff didn't need a nap, he needed a drink. But he didn't want to say so.

"I can see that you don't. Never mind. See you for dinner?"

"I have an appointment with a depressive funk. I'll see if I can reschedule."

"You'd better."

He watched her walk off, appreciating her figure. His cabin was in the same direction as hers, but he wanted space, so he decided on a more circuitous route. He wandered off toward the docks. There was something about the massive windows into space that soothed him. Whisky might be poison, but the stars were medicine.

About halfway there he started feeling sleepy himself. He heard his mother's voice in his head, telling him that a rest would be healthier than a drink. He started to regret not taking Emma up on her offer. He'd been feeling distant from her. He had some responsibility to be intimate with her, didn't he? Hadn't he made some kind of implied contract when they'd begun to be intimate to continue it, to go deeper? He suspected so, but the question wasn't really in his field. Besides, the large bay windows loomed in front of him, and words failed in the face of awe.

He put his face against the window, felt the biting cold of space against his hot cheek. It felt like bliss. He rolled his forehead along the glass, savoring the coolness. He opened his eyes and saw stars so vivid and bright that he was tempted to reach out and touch them. He reminded himself that he alone, among all the humans in this universe or any other, could actually do it. It also occurred to him that he would roast and die just like any other human. A despairing, cowardly part of him was tempted.

A commotion erupted just out of sight. Reflexively, he turned his head to see the source of the noise. A passenger transport was docking and a couple thousand people were disembarking. Their laughter and conversation reverberated through the docking port, making the room suddenly many times louder than it had been mere seconds ago.

Jeff never considered himself much of a people watcher—he suspected you had to like people more than he did to make a go of it—but he had nothing better to do and no place he needed to be. He saw a gaggle of marines, clamorous and ebullient, followed by two families, clearly on vacation. They were probably on a layover and would leave for one of the resort colonies later today or tomorrow. He saw scientists and lawyers and government suits. He saw the whole spectrum of human life, spilling over from the Earth into the petri dish that was Sol Station.

One man emerged from the docking tube that surprised him. He was short and dark, with small black eyes and severe cheekbones. He wore a brightly colored poncho and a comically tiny bowler hat at an angle. His jet-black hair was shoulder length. Jeff straightened as the man walked directly toward him. Jeff looked around to see if there was anyone else nearby that might be the man's intended destination, but there wasn't. Nor were there any facilities—just him and the long expanse of window. He relaxed. Of course, the window. The man had come to look out into space, just as he had.

Jeff turned and looked out again. A few moments later he felt a presence beside him, heard the man's breathing in spite of the noise that filled the dock.

"There are two kinds of beauty," he said.

Jeff looked down at the little man. What was he, a tribal chief? A shaman? As soon as he had the thought, he felt it was right. He didn't know how he knew it, but he did. The little man was a shaman. And where was he from? Peru? Bolivia? Were those places even habitable now? He didn't know. He didn't bother to check it on his neural, however. Some sort of answer seemed in order.

"Uh…okay. What would those be?"

"Eternal and ephemeral."

"What's eternal beauty?" Jeff asked.

"Those are beauties that do not change—moral beauty, mathematical beauty, the beauty of complexity in nature."

"And what are…what was the other kind?"

"Ephemeral. Ephemeral beauty is the kind we love best. It is the beauty of everything that can be lost. And the most beautiful things of all are those that are already gone." The shaman turned and looked him up and down. "You strike me as a man who knows something about this."

Jeff glanced down and caught the man's eyes. A chill ran through him. It felt like this man was looking through him, into him, maybe even past him toward some greater truth that Jeff was not aware of. Jeff said nothing. He turned back to the stars.

"Ah, I see," the small man said. "You have lost faith in yourself."

"What?" Jeff snapped.

"A wise man once said, 'The only limit to our realization of tomorrow will be our doubts of today.'"

"Who said that?" Jeff asked.

"FDR," the shaman said.

"Who?" Jeff asked.

"Franklin Delano Roosevelt." The little man's brows furrowed. "You are from a place where there was no FDR. You have come a long way indeed."

Jeff was tempted to look up this Roosevelt character but his thoughts were buzzing too fast. Before he could sort through them, the man spoke again. "They're not gone."

"Who's not gone?" Jeff asked. Part of him was anxious for the impossible news that the beings of String 310 might still be alive…somewhere.

"The Ulim," the man said.

Jeff's mouth opened. He stared at the little man—at the shells and teeth dangling around his neck, at his ridiculous little hat. Time froze. "What did you say?"

"They go by another name, too. You will need to discover it. But… you should find them."

"How do you know about the Ulim? And how did you know…"

"That you knew? We're part of a very elite club, you and I." The man didn't look at him, but stared out at the stars.

"Wh-what do you mean? Have you…met…the Ulim?" Jeff asked.

"I have."

"Where?" Jeff asked.

"That is a story that requires…some telling. Perhaps another time." He smiled. "Perhaps not."

"Tell me now," Jeff insisted.

"I cannot. I have a connection to catch." The man turned.

"Wait," Jeff said. "How did you know…about me?"

"You can see it."

"*I* can't see it."

"You can. You are just not looking for it." He leaned in closer and fluttered his fingers. "It's like little blue fireflies." He smiled and patted Jeff's arm. "Adios, mi amigo."

CHAPTER FOUR

Jo stared as Shallit's body tumbled away through the cold vacuum of space. She thought she'd feel satisfaction and triumph as his arms pinwheeled and his legs moved as if riding an invisible bicycle, then stopped. She balled her hand up into a fist to keep it from shaking. With effort, she tore her eyes away from the view port and faced the borderline mutineers that made up her security teams. "We have work to do, people," she said and strode toward the lift.

She wasn't usually conscious of herself as she walked, but as she pushed past her shocked men, she was aware of every muscle as she moved it, every articulated joint in its mobility. She almost stumbled from the alienness of trying to consciously coordinate the simple—or, as she discovered in the moment—extraordinarily complex act of walking.

She felt lightheaded, too, which didn't help. She willed herself to be calm as the lift slowed. She was once more upright and regal as the doors to the bridge slid open and she stepped out.

She arrived to the great surprise—and horror, it seemed—of the bridge crew. The odd thing was that none of them were bridge officers. She vaguely recognized the man sitting at the communications station, and the woman in the weaponer's chair. She knew the navigator, too, from engineering, but none of them were bridge crew. Everyone stopped and stared at her. None of them saluted. Their mouths gaped and she saw fear flame in their eyes. “Captain on the bridge!” Jo shouted, and watched as they scrambled to attention beside their stations.

“At ease,” Jo said, taking the captain’s chair. “Reports. You.” She pointed at the man at navigation. He looked down at his console and stammered, “Um, c-course set for Luyten, Gamma Station, sir.”

“Who gave that order, Mr.—”

“Vale, sir.”

“Mr. Vale, who gave that order?”

“Captain Shall—Mr. Shallit, sir.”

“Why are we headed for Gamma Station, Mr. Vale?”

“Mr. Shallit said something about ‘joining up’ with someone there.”

“With whom?”

“I don’t know, sir. He didn’t say.”

She turned toward communications. “Mr…Fein, is it?”

“Yes, sir.” The young man blinked, and Jo could see him sweating straight through his uniform. She pitied him.

“Did Mr. Shallit send any communications after the away team left?”

“Um, yes, sir. One secure data packet.”

“Send that to my neural now, please.”

The young man looked down and tapped in a few commands. “Should ping you right about…now, sir.”

Indeed, an orange light blinked in her peripheral vision. She looked up to retrieve the message. She read it carefully but quickly. *So it was to be piracy after all. Good to know your true colors, Mr. Shallit.*

She turned and faced the acting weaponer, a bulky young woman with short blonde hair. “Mr.—”

“Hagen.”

“Mr. Hagen, I wonder if you can tell me the location of my primary bridge crew? Or the secondary bridge crew, for that matter?”

The young woman’s eyes grew wide and she gulped.

"They are aboard this ship, are they not?"

"They are," she said. "They're in the…in the brig, sir."

"And what offense landed them there, Mr. Hagen?"

"Insubordination, sir."

"By which you mean they refused to be subordinate to Mr. Shallit when he took over the ship?"

"Yes, sir."

"Which only leaves one question in my mind," Jo tapped on the arm of her command chair. "Why are you here and not there?"

Hagan froze, as did every member of the crew.

"You may be wondering if you can band together to overwhelm me," Jo said with an eerie calm in her voice, so calm that it unsettled even her. "Mr. Fein, I wonder if you can lock onto Mr. Shallit's neural and get us a picture of where he is now?"

Fein turned to his console and tapped in a few instructions. "I have him…kind of."

"Then let us see him. Main viewer, please."

The larger view screen flickered and suddenly Greg Shallit's body was clearly visible, tumbling slowly in space.

"What…happened to him?" Fein asked, his voice uncertain.

Jo let every one of her next words drop with as much ice as she could summon. "I. Happened. To. Him."

She saw Fein's hand start to shake. Good. He ought to be afraid of her. They all should.

"There's a reason mutiny is treated like no other crime in the armed forces," she said. "And it is also the only crime I have license to handle without due process." She waited for that to sink in. "So I handled it."

She stood and began to circumambulate the small bridge. "The problem before me now is discerning the fate of Shallit's accomplices. Which actions among them constitute mutiny, and which are simply survival under mutinous conditions?"

No one moved. She saw Hagen's fist balling. Open, shut, open, shut. She intentionally turned her back to her and measured her steps—slow, steady. She needed to create an inviting enough target. The blur in her peripheral vision told her that she had succeeded. Jo lunged to the left, simultaneously reaching toward the pouncing weaponer and snagging her uniform by the neck, hoisted down with every ounce of strength that was in her. Hagen's head hit the side of the navigation panel with a sickening *thuk*. Her body dropped to the floor. Jo straightened her red uniform jacket and leveled her gaze at Fein and Vale. "Anyone else want a shot?"

Fein looked like he was about to cry.

"Mr. Vale, lay in a new course for Ross 154. Then send me a full report."

He gulped. "Speed, sir?"

"C6."

"Aye, sir."

"Mr. Vale, where did you learn to fly?"

"Mars Academy, sir."

"Are you a Martian, Mr. Vale?"

"I am, sir."

"You're awfully polite for a Martian."

"Enhanced training, sir."

"Obviously." She afforded him a slight smile. Then she turned to Fein. "Mr. Fein, connect me to Security."

"Security here," a voice answered promptly.

"To whom am I speaking?" Jo asked.

"Security chief Dixon, sir." The voice sounded Jamaican.

"That's quite a patois you've got there, Dixon."

"I work on that in my spare time, sir."

"I hear you've got some of my crew members in lockup down there."

"We do, sir, yes."

"I'm going to need those folks on the bridge."

"They're pending charges, sir."

"I'm invoking Captain's Privilege subsequent to regulation 27, subsection F, item 2. I want them back on the bridge in five minutes, sir."

"They're in the middle of dinner, captain."

"Then get them to-go bags and promise them a picnic on the

bridge. I also have one here for you to take back with you. Captain out."

Somehow, Jeff found himself back at his cabin, although he had no memory of what transpired between the docking port and the moment he was standing outside his own door. He felt as if he were floating outside his own body, watching his movements from above. Everything was surreal and slightly out of focus. His arm lifted to hit the button that would open the door, but he didn't know why he was there. *Habit, I guess,* he thought. But there was nothing in his cabin he wanted. He didn't want to sleep, he didn't want to change, he didn't want a drink…

His head snapped up. *That's odd,* he thought. *Why don't I want a drink?* The craving for alcohol, for respite from his guilt and despair, however temporary, however problematic, however many unpleasant side-effects it brought in its wake, was omnipresent. But now it simply…wasn't there. He blinked. He didn't know what to make of it.

He broke the surface of his affect, as if dipping a toe into water of a suspicious temperature, lightly touching the place that housed his shame. It was there, but he felt strangely detached from it. He could see it. If he poked at it, he could feel it, but it was as if he were watching something horrible on display in a museum—it was preserved and observable, but not something he needed to live with.

His eyebrows bunched in confusion, and he decided maybe he needed to lie down after all. The dissociation was not dissipating and brought with it a nauseous and unpleasant vertigo.

He punched at the button, the scanner performed its handshake with his neural, and the door slid open. He cast off his boots and stumbled to the bed. Lying down, he stared at the ceiling, but the only thing filling his vision was the memory of the little man, the shaman.

He wanted to speak to him again—*needed* to speak to him again. But what was his name? Where was he going?

A feeling of urgency sped through Jeff. *I'm not thinking straight,* he thought. *I shouldn't be here, I should be tracking that man down.* He blinked and accessed his neural. He did a search for interstellar launches, and discovered only one for two hours before or after—to Barnard Station—and it had already left. The little man was right—he'd had little time for the transfer.

Jeff sought access to the flight manifest. There would be hundreds, maybe thousands of passengers on that flight, but a part of him hoped for a name that sounded Peruvian. *What the hell does a Peruvian name sound like?* he asked himself. *And how would it be different from a Panamanian or Mexican or Chilean or Argentinian name?* He didn't know. *Goddam it,* he sighed.

Just then there was a ping from the door. "Who is it?" he asked the door. "Neural scan indicates Dr. Emma Stewart," the computer's voice said. It was the same annoyingly calm voice he was used to from his own universe. He hated it.

"Let her in."

A moment later, Emma was hovering over him. He didn't look at her. He could feel her there. "Hi."

"Jeff, you've got to come quickly. They've been arrested."

"Who's been arrested?" He opened his eyes and hoisted himself up on his elbows.

"Members of the crew. Pho and Nira. Not Wall, though."

"Whaaaat?" Jeff sat up. "Why? Neither Pho or Nira is the type to get into a bar fight."

"I don't know. I just know…that you'd want to know."

"Christ. Have you seen them?"

"No. I just heard about it from Wall. I came straight here."

He was glad his head was clear. The dissociation seemed to be dissipating, too. "Guess I have a mission. You along?"

She cocked her head. "I have no other duties." There was a note of sarcasm in her voice.

Jeff stood and straightened his jacket. "Let's find out what's going on."

Leaving his cabin, Jeff accessed his neural and inquired as to the location of the brigs. They were just where he expected them to be—

three of them, in precisely the same places they had been on their own Sol Station.

He sent an inquiry as to the location of his crew, but got nothing back. That decided it—he needed to go to the main security station and beat some heads together. He didn't need a map to find *that*.

Emma seemed to have trouble keeping pace with him, and every few yards she had to scramble to match him. He noticed, but didn't slow down. He could feel the adrenaline bolting into every system in his body—it was the feeling of clarity, of purpose, of indignation. He didn't eschew any of it. Instead, he bathed in it, the polar opposite of the alcohol's effects. It was euphoric and ecstatic in every way that whisky was not. It felt right and good.

It took them ten minutes to traverse the distance. He supposed they could have taken a tube, but that would have meant going the other way straight out of his cabin, and he hadn't been thinking clearly enough for such a non-intuitive move. It didn't matter. The exercise was doing him good, too, and it wouldn't have saved them that much time.

He burst through the doors of security with Emma trailing. She seemed to have given up on keeping pace, but was still following. She caught up to him as he stood at the desk.

Jeff glared at the duty officer, who was talking to someone through his neural. His fingers drummed at the counter impatiently. The officer put his hand out, which Jeff took to mean, *I see you, just a minute*. Jeff studied the man. He seemed to be of African descent, and part of his head was clearly prosthetic. Jeff surmised that he'd been wounded in battle and in exchange for his courage and health had been awarded this lovely desk job. Jeff drummed his fingers some more.

Emma covered Jeff's hand with her own, stilling it. He took a deep breath.

A few moments later the duty officer looked down from his neural and gave them a perfunctory smile. "What do you need?" he asked.

"I need to know where my crew is being held, and I need to see them," Jeff said.

"Names?" The man sighed and looked up to retrieve the records from his neural.

"Lieutenant Martin Pho and Commander Camil Nira, from the crew of the *Kepler*. The…uh…the other *Kepler*."

"Oh yeah, I heard about that," the duty officer said. "Weird thing. Can't wait to get the whole story."

Strangely, the young man did not ply Jeff for any details to the story. That was just fine with him.

"Uh…huh. Okay. I can see where they are…but it's classified."

"What do you mean, it's classified?"

"What do you mean, what do I mean? It's just classified."

Emma put a hand on his arm. "Don't take it out on him, Jeff. We just need to go around."

The duty officer looked down and smiled at Emma. "That's exactly right."

"I'll send a message to Danny," Jeff said to Emma. He turned back to the officer. "Perhaps you can explain to Captain Hightower where they are."

The duty officer recoiled a bit. "The Butcher?"

Jeff blinked. "What do you mean by that?"

"Nothing," the young man said, obviously rattled. "Uh…Captain Hightower does not have sufficient clearance."

"We'll go to Tal, then," Jeff said.

"*Admiral* Tal?" The young man asked. His voice actually cracked.

"Yes, of course, Admiral Tal," Jeff snapped. He looked up and shot off a message to the Admiral. When he looked back down, he narrowed his eyes at the young officer. "Does Admiral Tal have enough fucking clearance to access this information?"

"Uh…yes sir, of course sir."

"Good. We'll wait."

"How about some coffee, Jeff?" Emma asked. She pointed to a compact food synthesizer on the wall and cocked her head at the service officer.

"Oh, sure. You'll find cups right over there. Help yourself. They've got a new cocoa in that's wonderful."

"Fucking cocoa," Jeff said, as Emma handed him a cup. "Jo drank cocoa."

"Don't go there," Emma said.

"You jealous?"

"I am not jealous of Jo. Jo is…" Jeff knew she was about to say "dead," and she must have realized how it would sound out loud. "I have never been jealous of Jo."

"Bullshit," Jeff said.

"I liked Jo."

"Mm-hmm."

"I did."

Jeff gave her a dubious look.

"Okay, if we had met under different circumstances, we would never have hung out together or anything. But I didn't *dislike* her."

"The double-negative speaks volumes."

"And I understand why you did. Like her."

Jeff nodded. It was big of her to concede it. He felt grateful somehow. "Thanks."

Jeff considered telling her about the shaman, but thought better of it. He needed to know more before he said anything.

"Uh…excuse me," the man at the desk waved to them. Jeff leaped up and Emma came to his side a moment later. "Okay, you've got clearance to see them, courtesy of the Admiral." The man looked shocked. "You must have some fucking clout."

"I'm a ghost," Jeff answered, "and that seems to be worth something, at least until the novelty wears off."

"Here are your passes." The man handed a lanyard to each of them. "Now if you'll just hold still so I can get a retina scan, I'll pull up your neural codes and enter your permissions."

Jeff and Emma stood still until the green light flashed and the man nodded, apparently satisfied. He manipulated something on his pad and then gave them a perfunctory smile. "That will do it. Now…no explosives, drugs, weapons, or contraband of any kind. No liquids, fruits, vegetables, or spices while you're inside—"

"I know the drill, sergeant."

"I don't!" Emma slapped him on the arm. "I'm curious. What else can't we bring in?"

"No granulated sweeteners or perfumes or cosmetics. No prosthetics or religious materials."

"Why are those in the same category?" Emma asked Jeff. He shrugged.

"No electronics or bio-drives or disease agents or biological fluids or organs."

"I assume you don't mean those I'm carrying within my body?" Emma clarified.

The man jerked a bit, disturbed at having been interrupted in the middle of his recitation. "Er…that would be correct."

"Good thing I'm not accustomed to carrying around internal organs in a bag," Emma said.

"We get the idea, sergeant. Can you just let us in, now?" Jeff asked, trying not to sound too testy, but failing.

"Sure." The desk sergeant tapped on his console and a loud "clack" sound emitted from a large metal door on the far side of the room. Jeff strode toward it, noting that it looked more like an airlock than a door. As he approached he saw a red light on the keypad switch to green as it caught the handshake from his neural. It flashed green again as Emma came within range.

"I'd rather walk beside you than behind you," Emma said, not sounding too annoyed.

"Sorry," Jeff said. "I'm…" he paused to consider what he was actually feeling. The jumble of emotions was hard to sort out in the moment.

"Anxious? Harried?" Emma offered. "I get it, Jeff. Just…let me be part of it."

He nodded and they passed through the large metal door together.

The hallway on the other side was claustrophobically narrow and gleaming white—a bit too bright for Jeff's eyes. He squinted as they walked. "Why so bright?" he asked.

"You tell me. You're the military expert."

At the end of the hall was another airlock-style door.

"Are they actually holding them off-station?" Emma asked.

"It's a detention pod. Only one way in or out. It's a maximum security tactic," Jeff explained.

"How big is the pod?"

Jeff shrugged. "Could be five cells and a common space, could be a hundred. Hard to say."

"Remind me never to sneak another piece of pie again."

The airlock door opened—it was smaller at this side, so Jeff stepped back and waved Emma in.

Once inside the vestibule, they waited until the inner door read their neural clearances and activated. It swung open and Emma exited first. Stepping over the raised threshold, Jeff looked around. It was still glaringly bright. *Probably so no one can hide,* he thought, but he didn't remember their own holding cells being like that. *You have to account for minor differences here,* he reminded himself.

Inside, an armored and armed guard held a hand up as he read their neural clearances. Apparently satisfied, he nodded wordlessly and waved them to the left. They entered a large common area. Jeff noted white poly tables and chairs, a large view screen set to display a calm forest waterfall. The sound of the waterfall filled the air with white noise. Jeff felt himself relax. *Well, that works*, he thought.

The guard waved them over to another door. He tapped some commands into the pad beside it, and it swung open. Again, it was airlock-style. "It's a double-hatch system," the guard explained. "When this door latches, the next one will open."

Jeff nodded and he and Emma stepped through. He fought back a moment of panic as he considered the possibility that the guards would not allow them back out. *That's not how they do things,* he reminded himself. Once he heard the lock latch, the door in front of them emitted a series of complicated sounding clacks. Eventually, with the sound of hissing air, it swung inward. Jeff met Emma's eyes, wondering if she was having the same thoughts. The fear in her eyes told him all he needed to know. "There's no going back now," he said, waving her in.

She stepped over the airlock threshold, and he did the same. Inside, Nira and Pho were poised to act—although what those actions might be, Jeff couldn't say. Were they ready to attack or run for the back of the pod?

Nira and Pho relaxed when they saw who it was. Nira rushed up and hugged Jeff—a serious breach of protocol, but he didn't reprimand her. "I was afraid they'd capture you, too," she said.

"They didn't capture us…at least, I don't think we're under arrest," Jeff said as she pulled away from him. "We just came to see you."

"You mean they'll let you two back out?" Pho asked.

"I hope so." Jeff said.

"I hope so, too," Pho confessed, but his face was stricken.

Jeff looked around. The blinding light was gone, replaced by a cool blue glow—no doubt engineered to inspire calm. The pod was about fifteen feet square—roomy enough, even for two. Bunkbeds took up one side of the room, with a table and chairs on the other. Exercise equipment was set into one wall, a treadmill stood erect against it, ready to be pulled down for use. The door to a toilet facility was just past the table. It was tidy, if a little dim. *Maybe my eyes will adjust,* he thought.

He sat down on the bottom bunk. "What did you two do?"

Nira and Pho glanced at each other and blinked. "What do you mean?" Nira asked. "We didn't do anything."

"Then why are you here?"

"We don't know. They kept calling us 'rebel spies,' and—" Pho's voice became hard—"they spit on us."

"They…spit on you?"

He nodded. *That can't happen,* Jeff thought. *Not in my universe anyway.* He didn't need to remind himself that he wasn't in his universe.

"Did they hit you?" Jeff asked.

"No," Nira said. "They just…there was a lot of rough language. It…it was like being in high school again."

"That is not the conduct of professional soldiers," Jeff pronounced. No one disagreed with him, but it was hardly a revelation.

"Are you well treated now?" Jeff asked.

"They leave us alone. We're comfortable here. The food is decent —at least lunch was."

"And the other inmates?" Jeff asked, pointing to the door leading to the common space outside.

"There are no other inmates," Pho said. "I mean, we didn't see any at lunch."

Jeff cocked his head. *This is a big facility. Why...* But he couldn't fathom it. Still, there were two other brig facilities. Perhaps this one was just used for suspected rebels.

"When did this happen?" Jeff asked. "I mean, when did they arrest you?" *And why didn't they contact me as your commanding officer?* he wondered, but didn't say it.

"About 10 hundred hours," Nira said. "Security just knocked on my door and told me to come with them."

"Same here," Pho agreed.

"Why you and not Wall?" Jeff wondered aloud.

"They didn't get Wall?" Pho asked. "And they didn't get you. I figured you were all being held in a different pod."

"No. We haven't been arrested…yet." Jeff wracked his brain to understand what sort of charge they might be bringing. But this was not his universe. There was simply too much he didn't know.

He rose and put a hand on Pho's shoulder. "Don't worry, Mr. Pho. I won't rest until I get the two of you out of here."

Nira hugged him again, and in spite of his training, he hugged her back. Emma hugged both of them and then followed Jeff to the door. Jeff waited for the door to read their neural signal. "Now I guess we'll see whether they plan to let us out of here," he said.

To his great relief, the airlock opened and he and Emma stepped into it. Five minutes later they were clear of the brig and were speed-walking toward Tal's office. Emma grabbed at his sleeve. "Whoa, tiger. What's the plan?"

"I'm going to find out why my people were arrested."

"Admiral Tal isn't Jennings. He isn't even your Admiral Tal. He's not going to have a lot of patience for intrusions."

He felt torn. She was making sense—too damned much sense. But he felt driven to resolve the situation. The pull toward Tal's office was almost magnetic. Emma seemed to notice. She put her arms around him and squeezed. "We aren't going to solve this in the next five minutes. And we don't want to do damage we can't undo. We have to be smart about this."

She was right, and he knew it.

"Let's eat and come up with a plan."

It was a good idea. He looked at his shoes. He didn't seem to be able to move them. He fought the urge to sit down right in the middle of the hallway.

People were already looking at them curiously as they passed. Jeff started to sweat.

"This way, baby. Come on," Emma said. She took his hand and pulled him toward the mess.

"I'LL BE in my ready room. Mr. Liebert, when you've established an encrypted channel to Coalition Command, patch me through."

"Aye, sir."

Jo straightened her jacket, narrowed her eyes, and strode to the door of her ready room with the confidence and swagger of a victorious gladiator. The door slid open and then closed behind her. As soon as it was closed, her knees buckled. "Holy Christ," she said out loud. She reached for the back of a chair and steadied herself as she sat. She pitched forward until her forehead rested on the cool poly surface of the table top. She felt like crying, but she didn't. She felt like screaming, but she didn't. She felt like lying on the floor, curling up into the fetal position, and rocking—but she didn't. Instead, she just felt the table grow slowly warm, breathing in, breathing out, willing the shaking in her limbs to cease.

She'd never thought about what Captain Telouse—or any other captain she'd ever served under—was like when they were behind closed doors, with no other company but themselves, their gods, and their conscience. She never suspected they might be like this. It was unthinkable. How could she ever expect to rank among them?

I can't, she thought. *I don't.*

Yet here she was, in command of a war vessel, hurtling through deep space, going…where? She was about to find out.

There was a computerized ping, and Mr. Liebert's voice broke the silence. "I've got an encrypted channel, sir. Patching you through now."

Jo jerked upright and ran her fingers through her hair. *For what good that will do,* she thought. She straightened her red uniform jacket and stared at the monitor. "Thank you, Mr. Liebert."

The screen flickered and a 3D image of Admiral Alinto resolved itself. She was Maori and about fifteen years her senior. Her broad brown face was deadly serious. "Acting Captain Joleen Taylor. I wish we were meeting under better circumstances."

Jo swallowed, then nodded. "Admiral Alinto. Captain Telouse was the best captain I ever served under."

The admiral's mouth quirked. "He was…a complicated man. I could tell you stories, but…now is not the time for stories. But he was a fine captain, as you know. No enemy was safe when he was at the helm of a battle cruiser."

"No sir."

"How are you doing, Commander?"

"Sir?" It wasn't like an admiral to make small talk. Jo felt at a loss.

"I'm not saying 'How do you do?', Commander, or as you Yanks used to say, 'howdy.' No. No. No. It is imperative that I know your state of mind. Are you physically fit? Are you emotionally stable? Are you well rested? I must assess your well-being. So I will ask you again. Commander Taylor, *how are you doing*? Please be aware that if you answer, 'fine,' I'm going to instigate a court-marshal."

Did the Admiral almost smile? It was hard to tell. Jo swallowed. How much should she say? She opened her mouth, then closed it again. Then she said, "I just threw a man out an airlock. He had instigated a mutiny and declared himself captain. He was stealing the ship and going pirate."

The admiral's eyebrows rose. "I look forward to the full report on that one."

"Yes, sir. I retook the ship, liberated my bridge crew from the brig, and put things in order. Then I came…to…talk to you."

"I'm going to make a few guesses and you're going to nod if I'm right." It was not a request. It was an order.

Jo nodded.

"The adrenaline is wearing off and your hands are shaking."

Jo nodded.

"You're extremely thirsty, but you don't really have the energy to do anything about that."

Jo nodded.

"Commander, is everything well and truly under control there? Don't lie to me, *kotiro*."

"Everything is in order. My A crew is on bridge, my B crew is free and sleeping. The mutineers have been offered clemency for returning to their regular posts without complaint, although a note will go in their permanent file. And the leader, as I said, has been dealt with. Everything is f—" She stopped short of saying "fine." "—satisfactory. Sir."

The Admiral's eyes narrowed momentarily. Then her face softened. "Good to hear that. Now let's see if you can follow orders. Can you follow orders, Commander?"

"Sir. Yes, sir."

"We'll see about that. First, I want you to put another pip on your uniform. We've got a fight brewing about fourteen parsecs off your starboard prow, and I need a captain I can trust in your seat. I don't have time to play musical chairs, so you're my man. Effective immediately. Welcome to the chair, Captain Taylor."

Jo swallowed again. She tried to move her lips, but nothing came out.

"We need you in battle as quickly as you can get there—"

"But sir, Captain Telouse and four of our men are dead. Someone needs to find out who killed them and why."

"Yes, they do. That someone will not be you, however. I'm up to my hairy armpits in agents, but what I need are seasoned battle commanders. You can rest assured someone is going to investigate, but you, my dear, you're going to fight. Is that understood?"

Jo didn't agree, but she didn't protest. "Understood, sir."

"Good. Now here's what I want you to do. Turn about and make for the Aken system—I'm sending a data packet with the coordinates now. It will take you about nine hours to get there at C7. Don't delay, we actually need you there sooner, but don't tax your engines. Do you hear me?"

"I hear you, sir."

"Good. Once you get your new course laid in, I want you to go to the infirmary for a cocktail of Paxium, Newzit, and Flush. I'm putting the request in to the doctor myself, so I'll know if you don't. Then I want you to get a massage. There are six registered masseurs among your crew. Pick one. If there's a ship's counselor, go and talk—what you've been through is traumatic, I don't care how tough you want to appear. Then eat something heavy—none of that salad crap—and hit the sack. When you drop into normal space I want you to be rested, relaxed, and invigorated. Do let me know if there's anything you don't understand, Captain."

"I understand, sir."

"Good. Then get moving. Sensors show that we have twenty-six Authority battle cruisers headed our way, and we need every gun in the fight. Alinto out."

CHAPTER FIVE

It was the shaman. He was holding a globe aloft—the globe was spinning on the tip of his finger, like a basketball—but slowly, too slowly to stay in place. Jeff could see the land masses as it turned, but he didn't recognize any of them. The shaman looked up at him and smiled. "Find me." Jeff was certain the little man was speaking to someone else, but when he looked away, the only one he saw was Emma, getting out of the shower. She slipped, and bashed her elbow on the poly sheeting of the shower stall. "Goddam it," she said. He thought he should help her up, but he couldn't move. He could admire her boobs, though, and did.

He looked over at the shaman again, but he was gone. The globe was still spinning, however, hanging in free space...

Jeff's eyes snapped open. He looked up to access his neural and read the time. He relaxed. He had forty-five minutes before he had to meet Danny. Plenty of time.

He flipped the gray blanket aside and headed for the shower. Ten minutes later he was walking toward the mess and his first cup of coffee.

He felt a stab of guilt that he was walking the corridors free when two of his crew were in the brig. He should be storming heaven to free them, but Emma had been right, as she often was. He had to play this smart.

The mess was busy, but not crowded. He snagged a tray and piled up a good breakfast. He placed two cups of coffee on it and found a table in the corner away from everyone. No one seemed to notice him.

He was grateful to Emma for stopping him. He knew his emotions were running the show, and that had never worked out well for him. Somehow knowing that didn't help to quell his impulses. And he had little hope when they'd settled down to eat that they'd come up with much of a plan. The answer had come when they were nearly finished eating. Jeff's neural had pinged and he called down a note from Danny inviting him to join him on inspection of a newly commissioned battle cruiser this morning.

He'd often wondered what would have happened to Danny had he not died. This was probably as close as he was going to get to finding out. He flashed on something the kid guarding the security desk yesterday had said: "The Butcher."

Every drop of taste seeped out of Jeff's tongue at the memory. His toast became a dry, unsavory thing, sawdust in the form of slices. He chewed anyway.

That's me, he thought. *I'm the Butcher. The Butcher of Catskill.*

Only in this world, it was Danny who had to wear that mantle, to carry that weight. His heart went out to his friend in a way he had never allowed himself. Pity was anathema, a gift to be given but never received. The revelation was jarring but there was nothing to be done about it. A person like him didn't deserve pity or forgiveness or love or…

"Anything good," he said out loud. Just then it struck him why he felt so neurotically driven to get Nira and Pho released. He longed for some form of redemption, as if the emancipation of these two might somehow balance the scale of justice—even the tiniest bit—for his crimes. Catskill had been heavy enough. He'd been kicking himself in the gut for twenty years over that one. But now…

I'm the Butcher of String 310, he thought. He stared at his plate, but he did not see it. He reached mechanically for his coffee, but he did not taste it. There was no redemption for someone as damned as he was, as unlikely, as worthy of hatred and scorn.

And if the people of this universe couldn't quite muster that hatred and scorn, he would confect enough of it, all by himself. Hell, he was already overflowing with it—enough bilious self-loathing to power a starship.

It occurred to him that he could just squash space, put himself four parsecs hence, in the middle of deep space—no helmet, no suit, no ship. It would be over in minutes. But Nira and Pho needed him. There would be ample time for suicide once they were released.

He wasn't sure why that made him feel better—and it wasn't very much better—but it did.

"Come find me," the shaman's voice said in his head. Wisps of the dream invaded his memory.

"I thought you'd come find me," Danny said, sliding into the seat across from Jeff.

"Uh…" Jeff said.

"Are you hungover?" Danny asked.

"Uh…no." Jeff lied.

"Your eyes look…lizard-like."

"You're pretty, too," Jeff said.

"I don't look like a lizard."

Jeff rubbed at his eyes. "Sorry."

"You feeling okay?" Danny asked, taking a sip from Jeff's untouched cup of coffee.

"Uh…yes. Fine. Just…worried about my crew."

Danny's head jerked. "What's up with your crew?"

"In the brig. Two of the four of them."

"What for?" Danny asked.

"I don't…no clue. And no one is talking. I was hoping, maybe…"

"Let's find out," he said, looking up and blinking.

Jeff watched as his eyes twitched, making the micro movements necessary to navigate and read what he was seeing. Jeff was just polishing off his coffee when Danny looked back down.

"Damn."

"What?"

"Your crew are rebel spies."

"I was afraid you'd say something like that. What makes them think that?"

"Because one Commander Martin Pho and Sergeant Camil Nira are both registered combatants with the RFC."

"RFC."

"You have some homework to do. Revolutionary Freedom Coalition. It's what the rebels call themselves. We just call them rebels. Or traitors."

"I see." Jeff set his cup down. "But here's the problem with that. Pho isn't a commander, he's a lieutenant. And Nira isn't a sergeant, she's a commander. And these are not the same people—they're different."

"We have DNA on record from before the war—"

"Was Pho even born when that war started?" Jeff asked.

"Look, the action you died in—" Danny began.

"Catskill," Jeff said between gritted teeth.

"Fine. Catskill. It started the snowball rolling that led to the war."

Jeff nodded. "So Pho would have been three."

"And we collect DNA samples from every newborn. They're sequenced and logged in the Authority's organic database."

"What's your point?"

"The point is, your man Pho is a 100% DNA match."

"Of course he is, he's the same person—genetically. But he isn't from here. Our...my Martin Pho isn't in rebellion against the CD...the Authority. He's as loyal a serviceman as you'll ever meet. He's *my* navigator."

"And until we can prove that he isn't the Martin Pho enlisted with the rebels, he'll enjoy the hospitality of *our* brig."

"Danny, I can't allow that."

"Jeff, you can't do anything about it."

Jeff looked at the table top.

"I'm sorry," Danny said. "Look...I don't know what to believe. I think you're lucky not to be in the brig yourself."

Jeff nodded. He wasn't sure it was luck, but he didn't know what it was. "I get it. It's war time. I just want you to know this: as sure as there are spiders in space, my crew is innocent."

Danny cocked his head. "Spiders in space?"

"Sure, you know—" Jeff saw Danny's brow knit together. He stopped. Come to think of it, he hadn't seen a single spider since they'd jumped strings. "Do you mean to say that every ship in the...in the Authority isn't crawling with spiders?"

Danny shook his head slowly, and had a look on his face that could only mean one thing—the man was questioning his sanity. Just then Danny shot up onto his feet. "Crewman!" he shouted.

Jeff looked over his shoulder and saw a young ensign cringe. The young man couldn't have been out of the academy more than a few months, Jeff guessed. He raised his head slowly, saw Danny, and his face crumbled. *Oh, no,* he mouthed.

Danny put his hands on his hips and raised himself to his full height, his chest puffed out unnaturally. He dwarfed the ensign. "Who told you you could eat among people with honor, crewman?"

The ensign said nothing.

"Who told you that you had the right to breathe in my presence?"

The crewman's lips were as tight as an airlock seal.

"Drop and give me a hundred, soldier. Now!"

With everyone watching, the ensign slowly got to the floor.

"Today, ensign, or you'll do pushups in the brig!"

By now the ensign was on the ground, pushing himself up the full length of his arms with efficient jerks. Jeff could hear him counting under his breath.

After about thirty repetitions, the ensign's left arm began to shake.

"That was a poor showing, crewman," Danny said. "Begin again."

The crewman started over from "one."

At around fifty, both arms were shaking, but Danny didn't call him on it. The last twenty were touch-and-go, but the young man struggled through to a hundred. He collapsed to the floor and panted, his cheek kissing the poly.

Danny squatted near his head.

"You either find another mess or you make damn sure I'm not in this one. You won't speak to me, you won't come near me, and you will walk the other way if you ever see me in the corridor. Am I understood, ensign?"

Between pants, the young man said. "Yes…sir…"

Danny stood up abruptly and returned to his table.

Jeff's eyes were wide. "That was quite a display. What did the kid do?"

"Who, him? Nothing, I guess. Don't like his look." He pointed at his face. "Lazy eye. I hate the smell of weakness."

Jeff blinked.

"Listen, Jeff, let me talk to Tal about your crew. Give me a day or so…I'll see what I can do."

Jeff nodded.

Danny grabbed a last piece of bacon off Jeff's plate and tossed it into his own mouth. He grinned and chomped on the bacon with his mouth open.

THERE WAS NOT a ship's counselor on board. Jo had never trusted them, and when she checked, was relieved to see that the one assigned to them was on sick leave and a replacement had not yet been assigned. But she felt obligated to honor the spirit of Admiral Alinto's orders, if not the letter. As captain, who could she talk to that wouldn't be inappropriate or create an ethical breach?

"Palamar," she said out loud.

Cordwainer Palamar was one of her oldest friends—although perhaps "friend" was not the right word. They had been at the academy together, but while Jo rose quickly in the ranks, Palamar had not done much of anything with his commission. He served as senior boatswain, which meant he was a glorified supply clerk.

Still, he was the one person aboard she knew well enough to talk honestly with. And he knew her well enough to know when she was bullshitting. Accessing her neural, she saw that he was off duty. She did a search for him—his neural put him in the bar, which surprised her not at all.

In minutes she entered the bar and spied him at a table, looking over something on a datapad. She slid into the seat across from him.

He looked up and did a double-take. "Jo…er, Captain! Uh…am I dreaming?"

"What the fuck does that mean?"

"It means that you have a lot to do…and I'm confused as to why you'd be bothering with the *hoi polloi.*"

"You are *not* the *hoi polloi.*"

"I'm not?"

"You flatter yourself."

He grinned and swirled his drink in his glass. "You drinking?"

"I'll have whatever you're having."

Palamar raised his glass to the barkeep. A moment later another glass arrived. Jo sipped at it.

"I hear you've had quite a day."

"Ain't that the truth?" she said. "I want to know…if Shallit had succeeded, would you have gone along with it?"

"As opposed to mounting a rescue?"

She didn't answer that.

"Do I look like the heroic type?"

He did not. His hair was thinning, and his middle was just about as thick as it could be without getting him bounced from duty.

"No, sorry to disappoint you, if that shit Shallit had prevailed, I would have kept my head down and waited to see what would happen. Like most people, I assume. Any other response is likely to get you a hole blasted through your chest."

"I suppose…"

"No hard feelings, then?"

She didn't answer him. She did have some hard feelings, if she were honest with herself.

"Look, Jo, you *are* the heroic type. It's one of the things that makes you *you*. It's why you've got the pips. Not everyone can be you. We can't all be captains. The fact that you did what you did…it just means you're in the right place."

Her lower lip trembled. "Do you think so?"

His look softened. "Ah…this is the comedown. The self-doubt is kicking in. All those little voices in your head nattering about how you're not worthy and shit. Am I right?"

Jo looked surprised. "You can hear them?"

Palamar chuckled. "Loud and clear, sunshine. And you've come here because I'm the only person aboard who can keep your secrets."

"And I'm not too sure about that," Jo narrowed one eye at him.

"Well…you know, if the price were right." He winked at her.

There were a few moments of awkward silence. "I am glad you're here," Jo said, not looking at him. "Just knowing that you're aboard…."

"Stop…before you embarrass yourself."

She did stop. She looked down, twitched her nose, and nodded. "Yup, you're right." Then she took a swig from her glass. "Admiral Alinto told me to talk to someone. So I can check that off my list."

"Happy to oblige."

"Next I'm going to get a massage."

"I have just the guy—"

"Do you get a kickback for this referral?" She scowled.

"Something wrong with that?"

"You never change, do you?"

"I don't know, sunshine." He cocked his head. "Do you?"

THE DOOR SLID OPEN. Hightower stepped in.

Tal waved him in, unable to speak for the moment.

"You met him?"

"Yes, I met him."

"Creeped you out?"

Tal nodded. "He's aged, but it's him, isn't it?"

"It sure as shit is....uh, begging the admiral's pardon."

"As you were." Tal motioned to the chair. "Sit."

"I heard you just put his crew in the brig," Hightower said, taking the seat.

"What else could I do? Intelligence was able to trace their neural codes—they belong to rebel soldiers that go by the very same names."

Hightower's eyebrows shot up and he nodded, as if to say, *That's reasonable.* "Can't prove they're rebels," he offered.

"Can't prove they're not," Tal said. "If we're wrong on this, it would mean enemy spies loose in Sol Station. No matter how you slice it, that's grand-scale incompetence on our part."

"On your part," Hightower corrected him, reminding Tal exactly why he hated the captain. He knew exactly where the razor's edge of insubordination was, and he rode this side of it like a surfer on a wave. If only there were a dangerous mission he could send the captain on, something he might not come back from, the entire civilized world would be a safer place. But so long as there was a war on, he needed every killer wearing his colors. Black. "One thing in their favor: Ensign Wall is assigned right here on Sol Station."

"Our Ensign Wall?"

"Right. There are two Susie Walls on board. One from this universe and one from theirs."

"I think their Wall is a lieutenant. Our Wall is the slacker."

"Okay, but it shores up their story."

"It does that. If there are two Walls—"

"And two of Dr. Stewart—she is indeed on earth and very much alive and well."

"—it stands to reason that their Nira and Pho are not rebels."

"You can't let them out of the brig until you can establish that definitively."

"Right. Is that going to create a problem getting Captain Bowers to be cooperative?"

"Cooperative with what?"

"With revealing to us whatever technology he was working on."

Tal had never seen Hightower look alarmed before. This was close to it. "Uh…if they're right, that technology wiped a reality string from the cluster. I don't know about you, but I'm kind of attached to this reality. I mean, if we're not, what are we fighting for?"

"True."

"Begging the Admiral's pardon, but did you really ask me here to give you an update on Bowers? Because you could have—"

"No, goddam it." Tal looked up and triggered a holo display that flickered and then resolved, hovering just above his desk. He could still make out the captain's face through the holo-display's shimmering opacity. "I've decided to read you in. I need a fresh set of eyes on this. Besides…" he didn't finish the sentence.

Hightower cocked an eyebrow, studying the display.

"There's a lot of dead people there."

"There sure are." The admiral pointed, not sure that the captain would be able to pick out who he meant because of Hightower's angle of vision. "You see that woman? The one with the red dress."

Hightower nodded gravely. "Was that your girl? The one who got killed?"

Tal nodded. "She was an operative for the Authority. Under cover. There was a supply pipeline running through Avalon II—do you know it?"

"I know it. Hotbed of thugs, from what I've heard."

Just your type of folks, Tal thought. Aloud, he said, "Gunned down along with her bodyguards and a whole shitload of local cops. Authority cops, too. And a handful of rebels. You ever hear of a Captain Telouse?"

"Yeah," Hightower nodded. "Decorated son-of-a-bitch, before the war. Shame we lost him to the other side."

"He was my friend, too, at one time." Tal looked down.

"Who did it?" Hightower asked.

"That *is* the question," Tal said. "If it wasn't us and it wasn't the rebels—"

"How do we know it wasn't the rebels?"

"Because the goddam rebels would not want to lose a war hero like Telouse. He might be an old man—same age as me, so no snide quips—but his record is golden. He's taken out more of our boys than any other rebel commander. That's a fact."

"Who did it?" Hightower asked again.

"Intelligence has a couple of theories. Their best one is that a registered rebel has seized control of their battle cruiser and is headed for unclaimed space."

"Who?"

"Her."

The admiral blinked and the face of Commander Jo Taylor floated above his desk.

"Oh shit," Hightower said. "You're kidding me."

"I am not. It's why I'm reading you in. Intelligence says you have history with rebel Commander Taylor."

"Yeah. We used to date. She fell in love with me. It wasn't mutual." Hightower shrugged, cold as a salamander. Tal shuddered.

"What can you tell me about her?"

Hightower looked down and away. His shoulders deflated. "She…" he sighed. "She's hard as nails. Pretty, in a butch kind of way, but she'll rip your guts out soon as look at you."

"Really?"

"No, not really. She's got it in her, but she's strictly by the book."

"You seem to know her pretty well."

"Look, we *were* lovers, but only briefly. We were kind-of-friends for a while though—at the academy. So yeah, I know her pretty well."

"The civilian authorities want her."

Hightower laughed, met his eyes again. "Good luck catching her! And she's in unclaimed space?"

"I want you to go after her. Find her." Tal swallowed. "Take her out."

Hightower narrowed his eyes. "You don't want to question her?"

"Triage. Intelligence thinks we can kill her, but can't spare the resources to capture her."

Hightower nodded. “I have a better idea. Let’s let Bowers do our work for us.”

“Finding her?”

Hightower’s lip curled as he held the admiral’s eye. “Destroying her.”

CHAPTER SIX

Jo arrived on the bridge feeling better than she had in weeks. She hated to admit that the admiral had been right about the self-care.

"Captain on the bridge," Communicator Liebert announced.

Everyone started to stand.

"As you were," she said, watching them sink back to their seats. No one actually expected to stand all the way up, but the navy had always had its traditions.

Jo sat in the command chair and glanced toward the ceiling, accessing her neural. She read the various duty reports and, satisfied that the ship was battle-worthy, she looked down again, focusing on the main view screen as stars streamed past them.

"ETA to target?" she asked.

Navigator Chi didn't need to consult anything. "We're set to drop into normal space in twenty minutes, sir."

Good. She'd timed that well. She turned to her new weaponer, a thin-limbed young woman with a severe countenance which took some getting used to. "Weaponer Ditka, welcome to the bridge crew."

The young woman's eyes were sharp and wide-set, and her hair was a blonde buzz cut. "Thank you, sir. It's an honor, sir."

"This is going to be your first battle situation, I understand."

"Yes sir."

"I'll be honest with you—if there were another weaponer aboard with any experience at all, they'd be in that seat right now."

"Yes, sir."

"But your simulations reveal that you're the meanest gun-toting bitch on this vessel."

"I am, sir." One lip curled back, showing Jo more crooked teeth than she cared to see.

"What's our situation?"

"I've got sixteen gunners, all first class, and three with first-class honors. They're prepping every cannon port we've got. The torpedo crew has been drilling for the past four days. I told them to get some rest last night, but they're in place and they've run one simulation—we're at 104% efficiency, according to RFC goal standards, sir."

Jo nodded. "Good. Get to work."

"Yes sir." Ditka's head snapped down to look at her console and her fingers flew over it. Every now and then she looked up to reference something on her neural.

Jo swung about to face the view screen again. A calm came over her that only materialized in the heat of battle. It was how she knew she was destined to be a soldier. Every woman she grew up with would have been scared shitless—that was true of most of the men as well. But she welcomed it, like an old friend, the feeling of ecstasy mixed with centered, focused attention. Let others opt for whisky or morphex. *This* was her drug of choice.

She punched at the arm of her command chair. "Dr. Mbusa, everything battle ready in sickbay?"

It took a moment, but seconds later she heard the doctor's sonorous voice. "We're ready, sir. Fully staffed, with first aid teams located throughout the ship. I've got stasis tubes powered up and ready to hold the worst injuries until we can get them proper treatment."

"Excellent. Bridge out."

They were as ready as they were going to be.

"Mr. Chi, I want you to adjust our course."

"Sir?"

"Aim wide of the battle and overshoot. In fact, I don't want to drop into normal space until we're past the thick of it. As soon as we're running on conventional thrusters, I want you to bring us about on an arc, approximately 750k from the epicenter of the conflict, and keep us there."

"Adjusting course settings, sir."

Captain Felix of the *Fang* had mission authority, but until she got a direct order she was going to trust her gut. It had never steered her wrong before.

A few minutes later, Jo heard the telltale whine of the thrusters, and felt the momentary, gut-lurching transition as the ship dropped out of its C-register and into normal space. She watched the star wheel turn on the main viewer as they came about.

"Full tactical display," she called over her shoulder to Liebert.

A moment later the main view screen was segmented, and she was able to sort through what they faced. At the top was a bird's-eye view of the conflict. She saw the moving red dot that was the *Talon* near the periphery, just as she'd hoped. Other colored circles identified friendly and enemy ships, fifty-two of them all told.

There didn't appear to be anything just ahead of them, and indeed, the portion of the screen reserved for the prow camera showed her nothing but distant stars.

She began to sort through the specs of the ships they had and those they were facing. She made mental notes and occasionally looked up to check a fact on her neural. She rubbed at her jaw. Finally she spoke.

"Here's what we're going to do. Mr. Chi, set a spiral course working our way into the center of the conflict, adjusting only to intercept enemy ships within 100,000 kilometers of that course. Instead of joining the thick of the battle, we're going to clean up the field of every single ship not engaging. Try to come up behind these ships if you can. Use your head.

"Mr. Ditka, I want you to be smart about how we attack. I don't care about destroying these ships, I only care about their ability to fight. Don't waste firepower making big explosions. Target smart and take out their weapons and drives. Do the most you can as fast as you can. We've got a lot of ships to cripple."

"Yes, sir."

Jo spun in her chair. "Mr. Liebert, I have a special assignment for you. I want you to catalog every enemy ship within hailing range. Find me the one that isn't doing anything."

Tash Liebert scowled. "Not doing anything?"

Jo spun back toward the main viewer. "Look at that—they're kicking our asses, and they're doing it smart. Someone is calling an organized game—more than we're doing. We need to find them."

Chi and Ditka looked at each other, then back down at their consoles.

Liebert spoke, his voice much higher than usual. "Sir, I have an Authority vessel coming up on our starboard bow—distance 498 kilometers."

"On screen."

There was a flicker, but the ship soon came into view. It was facing the main battle, and looked like it was aligning itself for a run at one of the RFC battle cruisers.

"Swing wide, Mr. Chi. Try to get us in his exhaust chute."

"No good, Captain. He's seen us. He's coming about."

Jo's eyes narrowed. "Mr. Ditka, take out those guns and seal those torpedo ports. Fire at will."

The Authority ship had fired first, however, and the bridge lurched as Navigator Chi tried to evade the fire. Jo felt the metal bones of the ship shake as the torpedo connected.

She punched at the arm of her chair, calling up engineering. "Status?"

"Direct hit to our port bow," Chief Engineer Avery's voice was quick and distracted. "Shields at 95% and holding. No structural damage."

"That's what I want to hear," Jo said.

Shell Ditka's fingers were flying, and Jo watched as a barrage of particle bursts erupted across the hull of the enemy ship. Then, a surprise—two thin laser lines converged on a point she could not make out. There was an orange flare.

"The enemy's aft cannons are offline," Ditka called out.

Two torpedo bursts shot from beneath them and arced toward the enemy cruiser, one following the other along a slightly divergent route. A swarm of laser fire caught the first one and lit it up—the explosion filled the screen for a few seconds, but a larger explosion followed as the second torpedo found its mark and the ship's exhaust cones transformed into a blinding fireball that soon consumed the whole ship.

"That's one way to do it," Jo said. "Good work, Mr. Ditka. Only next time, let's just disable the ship, if we can. Ships are cheaper to appropriate than they are to build." She tapped at her temple, "Long range vision."

"Captain," Liebert called, "I've got RFC Mission Command for you—Captain Felix."

"On screen."

There was a flicker, and then Jo was staring at a bridge much like her own. In the command chair was a slight, Indian-looking man of about her age with a large nose and a wispy mustache. There was a lot of noise on his bridge, but his own voice cut through. "Captain, welcome to the fight. I see what you're doing there, and it's a good idea, but I need you in the thick of it. I'm sending coordinates. I want you in place ASAP. Good to have you alongside. Good hunting." The screen flickered and was quickly replaced by tactical schematics.

"Damn," Jo said under her breath. "That's no way to survive a firefight." She spoke up. "Do you have those coordinates, navigator?"

"Just coming through now, sir."

"Set a new course once you've unpacked them. Weaponer, remember: disable, don't destroy. Communicator," she turned to face Liebert again. "That ship that's not doing anything? Keep looking for it. That's your number one assignment."

The ship lurched, then a moment later the motion dampers kicked in. "Easy, Mr. Chi," she said, leaning forward in her chair. "Get us to the fight in one piece."

"Sorry, sir," Marcia Chi's shoulders rose above her ears as she hunkered sheepishly over her console.

Jo watched the whirling stars in the view screen as they came about and punched at the comm buttons on her armrest. "Battle stations, everyone. This is the big one."

HE WAS STARING at the stars when he felt a presence behind him. He knew it was her before he looked, although he didn't know how. Was it her scent, or the way her foot fell on the poly flooring? It was hard to say. "Hey," he said without turning.

She slipped her arm around his waist and joined him at the window. "I expected to find you in a bottle," she said. "This is better."

"Yeah, strangely…" He shook his head, not finishing the thought.

"I was on my way to your cabin. I was hoping we could catch dinner."

Jeff nodded. "Yeah. That sounds fine." He backed up from the window and caught her eye. He smiled. She took his arm, and they began to stroll toward the mess.

"I just came from Wall," Emma said. "She's…a little freaked out."

"That seems appropriate."

"She's freaked out because she ran into herself."

"That would freak me out too," Jeff admitted.

"Then…they had sex," Emma said, watching Jeff for his reaction.

"That's…just weird," he said, eyes wide. "I didn't know…I mean, I'm not surprised…but still…with *herself*?"

"Yep. It's a little narcissistic—"

"By definition."

"Now she's holed up in her cabin with the covers over her head."

"Huh."

"Plus, she's got survivor's guilt."

"Who doesn't?" Jeff almost spat.

"Oh…well, that's not what I mean. She's feeling guilty that Pho and Nira are in the brig and she isn't."

"She's feeling so guilty she's on a sex binge, you mean."

"People react to stress in odd ways," Emma said.

"Isn't that technically masturbation, though?"

"Does that make it better if it is?"

"No. It's still weird."

A moment later they were standing outside the mess. "After you," Jeff said.

After loading up their trays, Jeff followed her to a seat near the rear of the galley, as far away from anyone else as she could manage.

"Are you sure we don't want to find a storage closet or something?" Jeff said. "Cause we could probably do that."

Emma sat. "I don't want to be overheard," she explained.

"Fair enough." Jeff's nostrils twitched as the aroma of his dinner filled them. "This looks surprisingly good."

"The food aboard Sol Station was always good."

"Our Sol Station. I think this Sol Station slips a bit."

"Just eat."

"Yes, sir." Jeff said, picking up his cutlery. "I had breakfast with Danny this morning."

"Any help?"

"He said he'd talk to Tal. You never know. I have no idea how much pull he has. But…"

"But?"

Jeff put down his fork before he'd tasted anything. "I watched him humiliate an ensign for absolutely no reason at all. He did it in front of the entire mess. It was cruel and abusive, and…completely unlike him." He stared at his plate, aware that it was cooling. "I don't know what to think about it."

Emma pursed her lips. "You want to know what I think?"

"Sure."

"I think this is not your Danny, in two senses."

"Okay…"

"First, the obvious—this is a different world, and this Danny is just a different guy. Maybe he has a cruel streak that the Danny of String 310 didn't have."

Jeff nodded. "And the non-obvious?"

"Let's say that, twenty years ago, this Danny and your Danny were exactly the same—not just physically, but psychologically. He lived through Catskill, you didn't. So let me ask you, did Catskill change you?"

Jeff froze. He didn't respond.

She continued. "And did it change you for the better?"

Jeff shook his head slowly.

"People deal with stress in odd ways," she repeated. "You became an extreme introvert."

"Morbid isolation," he intoned.

"That is as good a term for it as I have heard," she smiled. "Where did you hear that?"

"It was something Jo said once," he said. "She had an uncle who was a monk, an actual hermit."

"Ah…" She took a sip of her tea. "How did you sleep?"

"Fine, but…I had some very weird dreams."

"Tell me about them," she began to cut into her steak.

"I dreamt about—" he realized he hadn't told her about the shaman. "I met this shaman, at the docks."

"Shaman?"

"Yeah, he was from Peru or something."

"How do you know he was a shaman?"

"I…" Jeff stopped. "I guess I don't. It was just a…I guess I just knew."

"Okay. That's weird. So what happened?"

"He knows about the Ulim."

She dropped her knife. "He what?"

"So I dreamed about him. And in the dream, he was saying, 'Come find me.'"

"That was all?"

"No, then I dreamt about you in the shower—"

"Jeff, don't tease—"

"No, I'm serious. I saw you getting out of the shower, and you slipped and hit your elbow. You swore." He smiled. "I like it when you swear." He stopped when he saw her eyes were wide.

"Jeff, that wasn't a dream." She pulled back her sleeve and showed him her elbow—an angry purple welt graced her skin. "That really happened."

"Shit," he said, taking her arm gingerly in his hands. "I'm so sorry."

She pushed her sleeve back down. "It's okay, it doesn't hurt—not anymore."

Jeff blinked.

Emma's brows bunched as she thought. Attacking her steak once more, she said, "Jeff, what if your shaman dream wasn't a dream either?"

Jeff hadn't even considered it.

"How could it not be a dream? It was a dream."

"You seeing me in the shower—that was not a dream. That happened."

"I don't know what to say about that." Jeff realized that he still hadn't touched his food.

"You know what I think?" Emma asked.

"What?"

"I think it's like the early stages of squashing—how you scope things out before you squash. I think maybe you were doing that in your sleep."

"I was squashing in my sleep?" Jeff's voice rose several pitches.

"Don't panic." She put her hand on his arm. "You *didn't* squash, you just…looked."

"But if I tried to squash in my sleep, I could—"

"Destroy another universe?" she asked. "Yes. But you didn't squash in your sleep. Just…relax and examine the theory. Be a scientist for a moment and not an emotional soldier."

"I'm—" He started to protest that he wasn't the emotional one, except that it wasn't true and he knew it. "Fine," he said.

"Nothing bad happened until we tried to move a space ship," she said.

"What are you saying?"

"I'm saying I think we're overlooking another aspect of your… talent. You might not be able to move starships without wrecking the place, but there's nothing saying you can't *spy*."

Just then a light pinged in Jeff's neural. He glanced up and opened the message.

"I'm being summoned," he said. "Admiral Tal."

"BRING us about wide and then loop us in," Jo said, her eyes glued to the tactical screen above her.

"Coordinating with the *Fang* for real-time deployment," Liebert called.

"You do that," Jo nearly spat. Reflexively, she tried to stand, to pace, but her restraints kept her locked into her chair. She chafed at the limitation, but kept her gaze riveted. "Mr. Chi, here's what we're *not* going to do—we're not going to give these Authority fucks an easy target. We're not going to float in like a barge with weapons flashing."

"We're not a Carson scout, sir," Chi called over her shoulder and then cringed, realizing what she'd said.

Jo took note of her tone, knew that it was an honest reaction, not an insubordinate one. "No, we're not. We're a big lumbering brick, so we're going to make inertia work for us rather than against us. Get us into a Möbius loop—"

Marcia Chi looked away from her controls, her forehead bunched in confusion. "Möbius loop?"

"Get us locked into an infinity sign pattern so that we change our horizontal orientation by 180 degrees every 1.5 repetitions. Is that clear enough?"

Jo could see her eyes darting back and forth.

"You want us to lock into a figure eight pattern, but every time we hit the middle you want us to turn over a little bit, so that every third loop 'up' is pointing a different direction?"

"Make it happen before we hit that cluster. Deviate only to avoid collisions—and if we're going to collide with anything that won't destroy us, don't worry about it. Let's push our weight around a little."

"Yes sir. Where did you learn this, sir?"

"I didn't learn it anywhere, lieutenant. I made it up on the spot."

"Fuck..." Chi said under her breath.

"Weaponer—"

"Shooting to disable, sir. We learn fast."

Jo couldn't suppress a smile. Weaponer Ditka learned fast indeed.

"I don't want us to come within 2000 kilometers of a gun we don't take out."

"Aye sir. You can count on us, sir." The oddness of the woman's long face added severity to her tone. Jo instinctively felt they were in good hands.

"Mr. Liebert—"

"Looking, Captain."

"That's my boy. Hold on, everybody."

Chi had done her work quickly. The star field on the main view in front of them began to spin slowly and relentlessly, causing Jo's stomach to lurch. She forced herself to look away from the star field and focus on the tacticals.

"Incoming—torpedoes, bearing 294.6," Ditka announced.

"Hold us steady," Jo said, watching the tacticals as a barrage of torpedoes drew near—too near. Jo felt a lurch as Chi dodged and the torpedoes zipped past them into deep space.

"They're going to clue in to this pattern before long," Chi predicted.

"They are..." Jo agreed. "So let's give them another target. Launch both shuttle craft, fix them in synchronous orbit around the ship at equidistant diametric poles. Do it."

Chi's fingers flew, making the calculations and launching the shuttles. "This is the craziest thing I've ever heard..." she sang under her breath, her lips not moving.

Jo didn't mind. It *was* crazy. And that was exactly why it was going to work.

"Slide us into the heat of the battle, Mr. Chi," Jo said. She glanced up at the tactical screens and assessed the field. They were a barge—so be it. They were now a barge that was not going to sit still long enough for any Authority weaponer to lock onto. They were also moving in a tight enough pattern to give them a host of access angles relative to any ship they approached. They wouldn't have to wait long.

Jo saw fourteen RFC ships, all of various battle castes, spread out in a random assortment against the field of stars. Dotted in between them were twelve Authority ships. Jo noted that while there were fewer of them, they were generally of higher castes, and their collective firepower was greater.

Nearest to them now was the *Claw*, nearly nose to nose with an Authority battle cruiser of similar caste. Just off the *Claw*'s portside prow was a fighter carrier, spilling out nimble fighters faster than the computer could count them. The *Talon* was closing in on this carrier—an excellent test of their battle readiness.

"Weaponer, I want to shut down every fighter spilling out of that carrier."

"Can't do it, but we'll die trying," Ditka said through clenched teeth. She didn't look up, but her fingers were a blur on her console.

"Put the other half of your gunners on the cruiser. Shut those bay doors, fry them out—I don't care what you do. Shut that motherfucker down."

"With lilting joy, sir," Ditka still didn't look up, but she was smiling.

"Do we have gunners for every port?"

"No sir—we have more ports than trainees, I'm afraid. We have three unmanned guns."

"Give me one of them," Jo said.

A moment later a blue light pinged in her neural, and looking up, Jo saw a targeting interface—a familiar sight from her days as a cadet. Keeping one eye on the tacticals, she primed her weapon and went through her mental checklist reflexively. She was surprised at how quickly it all came back.

"Coming within range now, sir," Ditka called, more loudly than she needed to.

"Fire at will," Jo growled.

An explosion lit up the spinning star field, and Jo chanced the vertigo to assess it. Her fingers gripped the arms of her command chair as she leaned forward, hoping to catch view of the Authority cruiser, disintegrating into lumbering sections, but instead she saw that it was the *Claw* that was crippled. "Damn," she swore, tearing her eyes away before she became dizzy.

The first of the fighters buzzed by them and lit up their starboard iconel sheeting. A volley of laser fire converged on the zipping fighter, and Jo was relieved to see it spin off, crazily trying to regain control. She thrilled inside, but reminded herself they had just swatted a gnat, nothing more. The dragons were still in front of them.

They were reaching targeting proximity to the nearest of the Authority ships—the *Nathan Hale*, she noted with a glance at the tactical display. Another squadron of fighters strafed their port side this time, and Jo got off at least three good shots before they passed, although she hadn't disabled any of them. Her marksmen, however, were more successful. Of the twelve fighters in formation, five of them ended their run drifting and dark.

"That's exactly what I want to see," she said under her breath.

"Sir, the Authority ship is readying torpedoes," Liebert noted.

"Mr. Chi, are those shuttlecraft in position?"

"They are, sir, orbiting us at a steady range of five kilometers."

"Excellent. Now, Mr. Chi, as soon as they've fired, dodge—"

"Sir, we're too big to dodge anything."

"It doesn't have to be far or fast, just move so that one of those shuttles is in the direct line of fire and will draw the targeting system of that torpedo. Better an unmanned shuttle than us."

"Aye sir."

Jo had no idea if that would work—it was a labor-intensive way to fight. It was also defensive. *That's all right,* she told herself, *we've got plenty of offense going.*

Jo ignored the next wave of fighters as she watched her tacticals. Her fingers tightened on her command chair as the lines that represented the torpedoes grew closer. The main viewer exploded with light.

"Direct hit, sir," Ditka noted. "We have lost shuttlecraft B."

Jo saw that the other torpedo had gone wide of its mark and was executing a wide turn. It would be back, and soon.

"Mr. Ditka, I want you to target that torpedo and make sure it explodes before it gets another shot at us."

"Aye, sir," Ditka glanced up at the tactical display, then down at her console.

"Sir, I've got an explosion off our starboard stern—the *Nathan Hale* has been hit."

"On screen."

The main viewer switched to a view from their stern camera. A fireball erupted on the *Nathan Hale*'s port side, amidships.

Jo looked up to see the *Claw* drawing closer to the *Nathan Hale*—too close.

"He's ramming it," she said aloud. "That crazy motherfucker. Mr. Ditka, get every gun you've got on the *Hale*. Don't worry about saving it, target everything that could possibly go 'boom.' If the *Claw* is going down, let's make sure those bastards go down with them."

No one said, "Aye"—no one had the time. Jo wiped the sweat from her forehead with her sleeve and watched as her own gunners pounded at the *Nathan Hale*'s shields.

"Their shields are at 20%, Captain," Liebert said.

"Keep at it, boys," Jo said.

"Sir, that torpedo is headed back, and we have not hit it," Ditka informed her.

That was *not* good news. She glanced up at the tactical to gauge its trajectory.

"Impact in five…" Liebert's voice from behind her began to count it off.

"Dodge, Mr. Chi."

"Diving, sir."

Jo scowled to see that their remaining shuttlecraft was not aligned to draw the torpedo's fire. She cursed under her breath. "Brace for impact!" she shouted just before the torpedo hit.

The motion hit before the sound did. With a great heaving lurch the bridge seemed to tumble in free space before the motion dampers caught up with it. The hull screamed as it was torqued out of true. Mr. Ditka's console sparked and caught fire, and several ceiling panels crashed to the floor. Explosions echoed up from the lift chamber.

Jo realized that had she not been strapped in, she would have been plastered against the port wall. Ditka lost no time in racing to a spare station and transferring her controls.

Jo punched at the comm button on her command chair. "Engineering, give me the damage!"

"Shields down to 40%," a voice came back. "Major structural damage starboard amidships, levels C through F."

"Casualties?"

"I don't know that, Captain." Of course he didn't, and she was stupid to ask. They weren't going to have a body count until this whole shindig was over. *Focus*, she told herself.

"Captain!"

She looked up just in time to see the *Claw* ram the *Nathan Hale*. The impact created an explosion that made the entire view screen fade to white.

"Get us out of here, Mr. Chi," Jo said. "Captain Felix is toast, so until whoever assumes command gives us orders to the contrary, we're going back to our previous strategy of picking off the outliers as we work our way inward."

"Strafe coming on our port side, Captain," Liebert called.

"Motherfuckers," Jo said, raising her eyes to her targeting display and firing a volley of laser bolts at the oncoming spray of fighters. This time she set three of them adrift before they pulled even with the *Talon*. *I'm good when I'm mad,* she thought, turning and catching two of them in the tailpipe as they buzzed past.

Turning back to tactical, she saw that they'd moved away from the thick of the battle, and she was grateful that the Möbius pattern had ended. She suspected it was responsible for the headache she felt at the back of her eyeballs.

"Enemy ship in our direct path, Captain, distance 4,200 kilometers."

Jo looked up and located it on the tactical display—it was engaged in battle with the *Fang*, a short-snouted battle puncher favored by the brass recently. They were quick, deadly, and ugly as sin.

"Let's give the *Fang* every assist we can," Jo said. "Come up behind the—" she glanced at the tactical readout for the enemy ship, "—the *Douglas MacArthur* and let's deposit two torpedoes in its exhaust chute before they know we're here."

"Having trouble—" Ditka's fingers kept punching at her borrowed console. "Ah! Got it. Firing now, Captain."

The *Douglas MacArthur* saw them and dodged—or as close to a dodge as a ship of her weight and size could manage—but their torpedoes corrected. Ditka had spaced them once again so that the first disrupted their shields and the second broke through to slide up its ass. The screen erupted with green flame and Jo watched with satisfaction as the great beast of a ship began to break up.

"We need more like that."

"I thought we were wounding," Ditka called without looking up.

"Wound where you can, kill where you have to. That kill was a must," she said with a note of finality, to which Ditka responded with a smile—but she still didn't look up.

Jo checked to see where their trajectory would take them, and saw that Chi had plotted a spiral course that would take them in a direct line to seven battles already underway in quick succession. "Let's pick the motherfuckers off," Jo said. She leaned forward in her seat and began to study the tacticals, already making plans for their next attack.

"Uh...Captain?" Mr. Liebert's voice was hesitant.

"What is it, Mr. Liebert?" Jo didn't look away. She already had an idea and she was teasing it out in her imagination.

"I think I found your sleeper."

CHAPTER SEVEN

Jeff set his jaw and headed for the corridor. Emma jumped up. "Don't think I'm not coming with you."

"You weren't summoned."

"I don't care. We're in this together."

Jeff grunted but he didn't complain. He'd begun to chafe recently at how closely she stuck to him. He caught himself stealing odd moments alone and savoring them. As much as he cared for her, there was a part of him that craved the isolation he'd spent the last twenty years pursuing. It wasn't an exile, he was discovering, but a hunger. Not an aberration, but a fulfillment. That would take some sorting out. There were times when he could see how a ship's counselor might be helpful. Those times were fleeting and few, but he had them.

"Any hint in your summons?"

"As to what this is about?" Jeff rubbed at his jaw. "Danny said he would speak to Tal about the crew—"

"About their being in jail?"

"We call it 'the brig,' but yeah."

"Sorry. 'The brig.' Do you think he's going to release them?"

"Or put me in it."

"Great. It was really that vague?"

"It was just a summons. Here look at it yourself." He looked up and blinked, forwarding it to her.

She was silent for several paces, obviously reading. "That…is pretty minimalist."

"Like I said."

"It's…ominous."

"Now you're just reading into it."

"Maybe. Jeff, I don't think you should worry. They know you have a…talent. They're not going to want to alienate you. They will want to exploit this. They're the military, after all."

He scowled at her. "*I'm* the military," he said.

"So you know exactly how they think," she affirmed. "It's going to be fine."

Her forced optimism was beginning to annoy him. He once again felt the urge toward solitude. *I may get more of that than I want in the brig*, he thought to himself.

"Captain!" A voice came out of nowhere. Jeff stopped. It was Danny's voice, he was sure of it. But he saw no one. Emma rushed ahead a few paces before she realized he'd frozen in place. She turned to look back at Jeff, a confused look on her face. Then she brightened, walking back and snagging Jeff's sleeve. "C'mon, it's Danny."

Jeff turned and saw Danny standing at the corner of a side corridor intersection looking tense. Jeff looked up and down the main corridor, at the hundreds of people coming and going. Something wasn't right, here. Why was Danny hiding? Who was he hiding from? Security cameras? *Danny has a neural,* he thought. *It doesn't make any sense.*

He followed Emma over to his friend nevertheless. "Captain," he said cautiously.

"This way," Danny said, looking around. He strode into the side corridor, and they followed.

"I've been summoned," Jeff said.

"I know," Danny answered. "You can't go to Tal's office."

"Why not?"

"Because there's a security detail there waiting to take you into custody."

"Thanks for the heads up," Jeff deadpanned.

"I can't let that happen."

"Why not?"

Danny didn't answer. As they approached another intersection, he held his hand up. Jeff and Emma froze. Danny looked around the corner, then waved them on. Apparently it was clear.

"I'm not liking this," Jeff said.

"You'll like what Tal has in mind for you a lot less."

"It's what *you* have in mind that worries me."

"Shut up and follow me."

Jeff clenched his jaw and did just that. Even Emma got quiet. They followed Danny through a series of service corridors, then through a crawlspace onto a catwalk over a hangar. Looking down, Jeff saw the *Kepler*. His *Kepler*, although he noted that the seal of the Colonial Science Corps had been covered over with a generic merchant ID.

"Danny, what's going on here?"

Danny had begun to descend a ladder set into the far wall of the hangar. He didn't answer. Jeff climbed down after him. Looking up, he saw that Emma was following.

Once at floor level, Danny waited for them both to finish their descent. Once on the floor, Jeff turned to Danny. "I want to know what's going on, right now."

"What's going on is that you're getting out of here."

"I'm not leaving without my crew."

"Your crew are on board," Danny said, waving them over to the ship. He continued to look around nervously, but there didn't seem to be anyone else in the hangar.

"Are you offline?" Jeff asked.

Danny didn't answer. Jeff sent him a message. Danny didn't answer, and there was no acknowledgment of receipt. Jeff scowled.

When they reached the ship, Danny handed Emma a data chip holder shaped like a koala bear.

"Cute," Emma said.

"Those are launch codes for a class F merchant vessel, the *Silver Goose*. If anyone asks, you specialize in smoked waterfowl."

"Smoked duck, got it." Jeff said. "Where are we going?"

"Anywhere that isn't Authority space."

"When will they come looking for us?"

"As soon as they discover you're gone."

"We can't outrun a cruiser," Jeff said.

"We've got bigger fish to fry," Danny said. "I've just been deployed to neutral space myself—every Authority ship with guns is being dredged up for this one."

"Battle?"

Danny nodded. "A big one. The rebels are putting everything they've got in it. It looks like we're doing the same."

"Looks like you're not happy about that."

"I'd prefer something a little more...strategic. As it is, we're simply throwing every gun we've got into the fight and…" Danny shifted to his left leg, looking down. "I guess we'll see who's left."

"You're taking a huge chance, here, buddy," Jeff gripped his friend's arm. He didn't understand everything that was going on, but he understood enough. Danny was putting his career on the line to keep him out of the brig.

"Look, I let you down once," Danny looked at his feet. "You didn't survive it. Now that I've got another shot…I'm not going to let it happen again." Then he looked into Jeff's eyes, and Jeff saw his friend's sincerity. For the moment, it was enough.

"It was an honor to serve with you, Captain," Danny saluted him.

Jeff saluted back. Then with the crisp, jerky movements the military loved so well, Danny turned and strode from the hangar.

"SEND ME THE COORDINATES," Jo said, feeling the hair rise on the back of her neck. She suddenly felt thirsty, and she felt her pulse rate jump. The thrill of the hunt was upon her, and she crouched in her command chair like a cat on the prowl.

Jo checked the coordinates against the tactical display—saw where they were, and where they needed to go. Liebert was right—there she was: a small ship, barely noticeable amid the fighting, just hovering in space like a drifting asteroid. "I see you," she said under her breath. "And I am going to eat you for lunch."

"Sir?" Mr. Chi looked over her shoulder. Jo wasn't sure whether she was questioning her sanity or asking for their next destination. She discovered she enjoyed that ambiguity.

Jo punched at the comm button on the arm of her chair. "Engineering, this is the captain."

"Ocampo here, Captain."

"Commander. Can a science probe deliver a nuke?"

"Huh…a probe is plenty maneuverable, and it has power. In space, it wouldn't be hard. Problem is just attaching the two so that the probe could get free—"

"Never mind salvaging the probe."

"Oh. Then, no problem, sir."

"How quickly can you rig one up for me?"

"Uh…how about fifteen minutes?"

"How about seven?"

"I'll meet you at ten."

"Make it seven. Hail me when it's ready to launch. Captain out."

"Mr. Chi, set coordinates for 297.21 by 592.6. Take us in so we come up behind the Authority vessel."

"Aye, sir. Laying in course now. We'll be there in…seven minutes, sir."

"Perfect."

The coordinates were for the nearest Authority vessel adjacent to the dark ship—which looked like the…the *Dwight Eisenhower*. She scowled, studying the tactical panels. That ship looked like it was putting up a hell of a fight. She saw the flaming remains of two RFC battle cruisers already drifting off into space, and a third was engaged in active fire. "Hold on, brother," she said through her teeth, "we have got your fucking back."

It seemed like seconds rather than minutes. Jo gripped the arms of her command chair as they slid into firing range of the *Eisenhower*.

"Sir, we're being fired upon," Ditka shouted. "Their aft gunners are opening up—looks like strategic lasers and particle cannons. They've got one aft torpedo bay as well."

"Shields?" Jo asked.

"Back up and holding at 95%."

"Mr. Ditka, you've got one thing at the top of your to-do list—plug that torpedo bay."

"Yes sir."

Jo's eyes moved back and forth between the tactical display and the image sent by the forward camera. She knew she needed to bring her ship about to get as many guns into the fight as possible, but there was a tactical advantage to being a small target as well, and she clung to it as long as possible. Torpedoes could maneuver, however, and she noted that Mr. Ditka lost no time getting off two, four, then six rounds.

"Captain, this is engineering," Ocampo's voice broke through her concentration. "Your…nuclear probe is ready. I call it the *Little Shit*."

Jo allowed herself a smile. "Get ready to launch the *Little Shit*, then, Mr. Ocampo. On my signal." She turned in her seat. "Mr. Chi, I want you to program and load a course for that thing ASAP."

"But I'm—"

"I know you've got your hands full. Multitask, navigator. Send it back the way we came, then dip in whichever direction is down for our sleeper. Navigate back on stealth mode, and come up beneath her as quiet as a fucking mouse. Got it?"

"Got it, sir."

"Then let's show the *Eisenhower* our starboard broadside, Mr. Chi. Let's open this girl up."

The stars swung on the viewer as the *Talon* pivoted, bringing a full complement of her guns to bear. "This is not how I like to fight," Jo whispered to herself. It wasn't nearly sneaky enough. *But it sometimes has to be done*, the voice in her head reasoned, and she knew it was right.

"How are we doing on that torpedo bay?" she called.

"Six direct hits, but their shields are holding—although they're down to 50%."

"Keep pounding them until we get something through."

Jo glanced to see how their sister ship—the *Claw*—was faring. Their shields were down to 30%, and nine of their seventeen guns had been taken out. Jo saw that the *Eisenhower* was holding the *Talon* off with one hand, but her full attention was on the *Claw*.

The *Claw*'s captain seemed to be pummeling away at a structure that Jo guessed must house a reactor—it was the only explanation that made sense given the ship design. "Swing us around to her starboard side, Mr. Chi. Let's give the *Claw* a hand."

"Aye, sir. By the way, sir, course is laid in for *Little Shit*."

"Excellent, Mr. Chi." She punched at the arm of her chair. "Mr. Ocampo, launch that probe when ready."

"Ready and…launched, sir."

Jo watched as they approached the *Claw*. Jo looked up and blinked, performing a handshake with the ship's captain. He no doubt knew she was there, but now they had an open comm link. Jo used it.

—Reactor?

—Main reactor.

"Mr. Ditka, give that reactor housing everything we've got—" Before she could finish, her screen erupted with blinding white energy, and she felt the *Talon* lurch and rumble beneath her. Her eyes darted over to tactical, and she saw the last thing she expected or hoped for—the *Eisenhower* was still intact. It was the *Claw* that had gone up in a spray of atoms.

"Shit," Jo said out loud. That would mean one thing—the *Eisenhower* would now be turning the full barrage of their firepower on the *Talon*, and they were not in a strategically advantageous position. Far from it.

"Keep plugging at that reactor housing!" Jo yelled.

"Sir, debris from the *Claw* took out three of our guns."

She jabbed at the arm of her chair. "Damage, Mr. Ocampo?"

"Still awaiting reports, sir. Looks like we need to seal off deck two —we've got hull breaches in two places. My men are on their way now. We'll get patches in place as soon as I can get them into suits."

"Damn damn damn…" Jo realized she was chewing on her nails, but she didn't stop. "Think think think…" she told herself.

A patterned burst of laser fire sprayed out from the *Eisenhower*, pinpointing targets along the *Talon's* hull.

"They're targeting our guns, sir," Ditka was yelling, though there was no reason for it. "Shields holding."

Just then Jo heard a boom that reverberated along the *Talon's* hull.

"What the fuck is that?" she asked.

"That…is an e-disruptor mine, set to go off in five…"

An electrical disruptor mine would take out their power—temporarily, but that didn't matter. They only needed to get through their shields for a few seconds to polish them off. "All power to C-drive. Gun it, Mr. Chi, get us out of here!"

Chi's eyes were wide as she punched away at her console. Jo heard the standard propulsion engines' whine rise to a high-pitched whistle as they strained against physics to move them faster than was actually possible. Before the C-drive kicked in, however, there was the sound of metal striking metal that shook their hull, creating an ominous, metallic echo.

Then everything went dark.

"DON'T ENGAGE C-drive until we're well clear of the station," Jeff ordered. "We don't want to look like we're running." Danny had risked a lot to orchestrate their escape. He sure as hell didn't want to mess it up.

"How soon would a merchant ship actually move to their C-drive?" Emma asked.

"I don't know anything about merchant ships. But with military vessels, you want 500,000 kilometers out, just for safety. C-forces can buckle the hull of a ship or a station. I've seen it happen."

"Begging your pardon, sir, my uncle had a transport business," Commander Nira offered. "The designated safety margins are the same."

"Okay, then. Light 'em up at 500,000K," Jeff said.

Martin Pho worked at his console and nodded. "Aye, sir." He turned to look at him. "And then where?"

"They didn't really give us a choice. Head for neutral space. Mr. Wall, give me a list of options—space stations, planets, casinos, any possible port in the storm. Ideally, we want a place we can refuel and get some supplies."

"With what funds?" Emma asked.

That caught Jeff up short. He was a military man; he didn't think about *paying* for things. "I…I have no idea." He stood up. "But we've got some time. Commander Nira, you and Dr. Stewart are with me. Until further notice, the mess is off limits. Let me know if we hit any trouble. Mr. Pho, you have the conn."

Jeff felt a little wobbly as he rose from his chair and made his way to the door. It slid open and he crossed the short distance to the mess. It was a very small ship, and he didn't have far to go. He could hear that Nira and Emma were behind him. He stopped at one of the wall units and got a cup of coffee before sitting down.

Emma did the same, but Nira seemed to have no interest. She moved directly to the table, her brow bunched and her jaw tight. "Out with it, Commander," Jeff said.

"I don't understand why they just let us go."

"I don't think they did. Danny risked a lot—"

She interrupted him. "And you trust him?"

Jeff blinked as Emma took her seat. It was a very good question, and if he was honest… He squirmed in his seat. "No, I don't trust him. But having you *out* of that heightened-security pod, in our own ship, under our own power certainly seems preferable to—"

She looked at his coffee and nodded. "I just don't trust them."

"This," Emma said softly, "is *not* our home. I don't think we should let our guard down for a second."

"This war is not our war, either," Jeff said, agreeing. "I don't know much about the other side, but the Authority is *not* the CDF. I'm not sure where our loyalties should lie."

"I don't think we have any," Emma said.

"I don't think we have any choice but to take sides eventually," Jeff said. "After all, we're here. We can't be anywhere *but* here."

"We could jump to another string," Emma said.

"And destroy—or even risk destroying—every creature on *this* string? Not a chance."

"What if we could figure out a way to jump the ship without endangering the string?"

"Too risky," Jeff shook his head resolutely. *I already have too much blood on my hands*, he thought. "Besides, from what I've read, the theory is that the further out we go from our own string, the more... different...the universes become. We're not going to find a world more like our own than this one."

"We could try String 309," Emma said.

"No," Jeff said, with an edge in his voice that brooked no further discussion. He softened, adding, "Like it or not, this is our new home." Neither of the women looked at him. They didn't like the sound of it—hell, *he* didn't like the sound of it—but it was true. It had to be said.

"If you don't mind me saying so," Nira said, "you look like hell. Sir."

Jeff didn't doubt it. He hadn't been sleeping well, with his crew in the brig and the dreams.

"Why don't you let me take this shift?" Nira asked. "All Pho and I have been doing is lying around and sleeping anyway. I'll let you know at the first whiff of trouble."

Jeff saw the corners of Emma's mouth turn up in compassionate agreement. She reached over and placed her hand on top of his. "It's a good idea, Jeff. Get some rest."

Now that he stopped to notice, he felt an aching weariness in his bones. It would feel good to lie down. It was not unreasonable. "Okay, I'll take four. But wake me if we hit a dust mite out there."

"Of course, sir."

"Go," Emma said.

He stood and straightened his jacket, crossing the mess toward the cabins. They weren't really cabins—that was too generous a term. There was barely room to stand up straight or walk three paces in them. When first entering, it looked like an empty 1x3 meter room, save for a chair at the far end, along with a sink and some bookshelves set into the wall. He pulled the little table top out from the wall and placed his coffee on it. Then he folded the bed down and eased himself onto it with a great, groaning sigh.

He didn't remember falling asleep. One moment he was looking at the ceiling of his cabin, and the next, he was by a campfire. The shaman was there, smiling enigmatically.

"You found me," he said. "That's good." The fire crackled and the night sky blazed with stars. The ridiculous little hat sat cock-eyed on the man's jet-black hair. "I have much to tell you. But we need time."

"Tell me now," Jeff said.

"No. You must be here in body, not just in spirit. The body is as important as spirit. But you know that. You remember what it was like to lose one."

He did. It had been terrifying, awkward. Not physically uncomfortable, but psychologically…

"Look at these stars," the little man said. "When you see them again, you'll know where I am."

Jeff found himself looking at constellations he had never seen before. It took him a while, but he was able to identify a couple of clusters. They were different, of course, because his perspective had changed, but they were undeniably stars he knew. The others…there were just too many of them. His eyes grew wide as a serpent slithered across the night sky, twisted into an unnatural shape, and froze. Then it faded, leaving only blazing balls of light where the various bends and folds of its articulated body had been.

Jeff was conscious that he was no longer dreaming. He was more in control of this…vision…than he would be in a normal dream. He looked down and saw the shaman sitting alone by his fire, on a world that seemed untouched by technology. That couldn't be true, but it seemed true. Perhaps the vision showed him something more or less than actual geography. Perhaps it was more…interpretive. He didn't know.

He felt his consciousness gather to a point in his own brain, and then expand, filling the All. A question nagged at him, invading the ecstasy of the moment. Was he experiencing the true All, the All across all strings of reality, or was he just experiencing the All of this string?

The string was infinite, but he knew the answer to it instinctively. He could sense a barrier, the intangible separation between worlds, the limits of his Allness. *That's fine,* he thought. *I don't care one way or the other, I just wanted to know.* He allowed his awareness to fill the All, every square kilometer, every millimeter of it, every beating heart and excreting organ in every creature on every world. He experienced it all. Every topographical feature of every landscape. Every meteorological event on every continent on every planet. He didn't try to hold on to it, or even to comprehend it. He simply entered into it, felt it. Then he rested in it.

And he felt her—felt her panic, her danger, her spiking pulse rate, the quickening adrenaline shooting into her blood stream.

Jo was in trouble.

CHAPTER EIGHT

They were sitting ducks, and Jo knew it.

"Mr. Chi, you have one job and one job only. As soon as power is restored—no matter what condition we're in, your job is to hail our probe out there and plot a new course for it. Bring it back here and put it right up their main exhaust chute. *Little Shit* is fully cloaked, so they won't notice it navigating until it's sitting on top of their reactor. Got it?"

She couldn't see Chi nod. The blackness was total. The only sound was the sound of her crew breathing, the fabric of her uniform squeaking against the imitation leather of her chair, and the rushing of blood in her own head.

Then, a moment later, the emergency lighting came on. She saw Chi poised to pounce as soon as her console had rebooted. Nothing yet.

Jo gripped the arms of her chair. "What are they waiting for?"

Then it came—an explosion that made the bridge buck and lurch as if it were made of some poly material, as if it were being shaken. She wanted to yell, "Damage report!" but she bit her tongue. There would be no damage reports, not until power was restored—*if* power was restored.

She saw raw terror in the eyes of her crew. She pounded on the arm of her chair, desperate to *do* something. She'd never felt so helpless in all of her life.

Another explosion sent them reeling. Jo felt the straps of her restraints bite into her shoulder, into her sides. She tasted a warm coppery fluid that filled her mouth and realized, in the midst of the unwelcome g-forces, that she'd bit her tongue.

I've failed. The thought invaded and tried to take over, tried to shut down all other thought. She shoved it down and insisted her brain be open, unencumbered, nimble.

Just then she heard a familiar whine of computers rebooting, of power coming online. It had never sounded so welcome or so good. "Shields up!" she roared and watched as Ditka's fingers flew the moment power was available to her console. Chi leaped into action at exactly the same time.

"Shields at 22% and holding."

"Target their engines, Mr. Ditka," Jo said. "Make sure they don't go anywhere before our little friend arrives."

"Yes, sir." She saw the cruel smile creep unconsciously onto Ditka's face. She decided she liked Ditka—so long as Ditka was fighting for her.

She punched at the comm buttons on her chair. "Damage reports, Mr. Ocampo."

It took a few moments for Ocampo to respond. When he did, he was yelling over the engine room noise. "Massive damage, sir. We're still trying to get a handle on the extent of it. We're getting no reads from decks A through C. My guess is that they're just gone. The good thing about this ship's design is that all the essential functions are tucked up into its interior."

"Get to work. Send me updates by neural as soon as you get anything. Do we have C-drive?"

"No sir, and standard propulsion is down to 40%. We can achieve maybe 600 kilometers per hour right now."

"Let me know when we've got C-drive capability again. In the meantime, direct all available power to our shields. Let's see if we can bump them to 75%."

"Yes sir."

She felt the bridge rock from another missile assault. This time the shields absorbed the brunt of it.

"Mr. Chi—"

Chi didn't wait for the question. "New course laid in, sir. *Little Shit* can do almost T1, but carrying the nuke…I'm putting it at 20 minutes."

Jo relaxed. She hoped they could hang on for another 20 minutes, but they didn't need to. As long as the *Eisenhower* didn't engage its C-drive, *Little Shit* would find it. And end it. Her mission was accomplished. The enemy would be destroyed. The only question for her now was, could she save her crew?

There were 127 souls aboard the *Talon*. She had to do everything in her power…

"Why wait?" Chi asked.

"Wait for what?" Jo asked.

"Chief engineer Ocampo put *Little Shit* together in under twenty minutes. Why not do another one? It will cut our time in half."

Jo leaned forward, thinking about it. Maneuvering under standard power, they could block its launch from the *Eisenhower*. And once launched and cloaked…it could work.

But it gave Jo another idea. She punched at the arm of her chair again. "Mr. Ocampo, can you put a nuke in an escape pod?"

Again, it took a moment for the engineer to answer. *Well, he is busy,* Jo thought. Soon, however, his voice came through, sounding harried and rough. "Uh…yeah."

"How quickly?"

"Remote detonation or timer?"

"Remote."

"Seven minutes."

"Do it. Put it in the captain's pod. Send the detonation codes directly to me for neural activation."

"Also, can you fake a C-drive core breach?"

"We routinely ramp it up to test it. We could prolong that without any permanent damage to the core—but it would certainly look like trouble at a distance."

"Perfect. Do it."

"Aye sir."

She punched the comm button on her chair. "Security Chief Dixon."

"Dixon here."

"I want twenty volunteers from security to make their way quickly and calmly to the escape pods. Arm them with regular blasters, but make sure they've got silicone disruptors hidden on their persons—we're going to need them."

Dixon didn't respond for a moment. "Uh…yes sir."

Jo knew they didn't trust her. She was green. This was her first time in the chair. And she was doing crazy shit. The fact that they were even going along with her amazed her.

Jo turned to her navigator. "Mr. Chi, thank you for the brilliant idea. And by the way, turn *Little Shit* around and reload its original flight plan. We may not survive this battle, but that sleeper ship calling the shots sure as hell won't, either."

JEFF REACHED out with his mind. He found her. He felt the sticky elasticity of space as he willed himself onto her bridge. He saw the tactical screen, the tense determination on her face. At the same time he was aware of every aspect of the battle taking place all around her. He felt her rising pulse, could almost taste the sweat on her upper lip—and wanted to.

Something in his chest twisted at the sight of her. Something precious to him, something lost forever, had suddenly been found. It wasn't his Jo, he knew that. And if Danny had taught him anything, it was that the versions of the people he knew in this world could be vastly different than those he knew in his own.

Was that fair? he asked himself. After all, Danny had risked everything to help them escape. But he had a knot in his stomach when he thought about it, one that he couldn't quite figure out.

Why not check it out? he wondered. He reached out in the other direction and found Danny. His friend was in a dark room, licking the breasts of a woman—a prostitute?

He moved toward Jo again, just staring at her. He could hear the things going on around her, but he wasn't really paying attention. It was enough to see the way her black hair swooped over her shoulders, the crow's feet at the corners of her eyes, the angularity of her jaw. He noted how the red rebel uniform hid her breasts, making her look flat-chested, even masculine. That only made her hotter. He wanted her so badly his soul ached. He realized that his body, so far away, actually had an erection, but it was an academic fact, like the rules of calculus or the tendencies of particle physics.

I have to go to her, he thought.

And that was all. He knew it was a bad idea. He knew nothing about the rebels or the details of this conflict. He had studied the events out of sheer curiosity, certainly, but he hadn't lived them—they were just more academics.

But here was the one thing that wasn't academic or theoretical. Here was Jo, in the flesh, giving orders—orders that his own body would kill to obey.

I need a drink, he thought. But he didn't. He was just conflicted, and didn't know how to sort it out in the moment.

He watched her until the ache simply became too great for him, and he allowed his consciousness to return to the cramped confines of his cabin. *Okay. Shit. What am I going to do now?* he asked himself. He'd never needed guidance before—or never felt like he'd needed it. Not once. But now… But there was no one to ask. He wished he could speak to the shaman, although a part of him also realized how absurd that was. What did a traditional healer from Peru know about his troubles? And why should he care?

Jeff sat up. He felt guilty. How would Emma feel if she knew the feelings he was having for Jo? It would crush her. He couldn't bear to think about it, but he couldn't stop thinking about it, and the thought created a desperate ache in his stomach.

He took a quick sonic, savoring the feeling of the pulses on his skin. Then he dressed and headed for the bridge.

As he walked on, Nira shouted, "Captain on the bridge!"

They all began to rise, but he gave the almost liturgical response, "As you were."

Jeff noted the crew members were all present—all except for Emma. He nodded at Nira. "Anything to report?"

"Nothing sir. Quiet flight."

He'd expected to be pursued. Maybe they still would be. "How far to neutral space?"

"Eighteen hours, sir," Mr. Pho said.

"Are you just dropping by, sir, or are you taking the helm?" Nira asked.

"I can't sleep anymore," he said. "But you all need to. Let's start rotating off, four hours each. Mr. Nira, you're first. When you return, you can fill in for Mr. Pho."

"Yes, sir. Thank you sir." Nira surrendered the chair and padded off the bridge, no doubt to grab a bite and a nap in her own, even smaller, quarters.

Jeff took the chair and wondered where Emma was. Probably sleeping. He should have let Nira stay, should have gone to lie down next to Emma—maybe make love to her. The thought made him feel even more conflicted than he already was. He wondered if it would feel like a lie. He decided he already knew the answer to that.

He needed to distract himself. He read through the hourly crew reports. Everything seemed to be ship-shape. He was considering how awful it would be to work a puzzle in his neural where no one could see it when Mr. Pho looked over his shoulder.

"Uh…Captain, I'm getting some trajectory predictions I can't reconcile."

Jeff cocked his head. Finally, something to solve, something *solvable*.

Mr. Pho put their course on the main viewer. "When we set out, I plotted this course, sir. The blinking red light should be our position."

"What do you mean, should be?"

"I just ran a stellar cartographical check using the neutrino sextant program—"

That was standard procedure, Jeff knew. "And what did you find?"

Another course appeared, superimposed over the original one on the display.

"That is our *actual* location," Pho said, pointing to a green blinking light.

Jeff saw an elliptical trajectory that seemed identical for the first three-quarters of its arc, but began to diverge very slightly as the arc reached its end. The blinking lights were almost on top of each other. Almost.

"Have you run a diagnostic, Mr. Pho?"

"Waiting for the results now, sir—wait, here they are. Uh…" He studied them, then sat up and looked at Jeff. "Nothing, sir. Everything is working normally."

"Well, something's off." Jeff said.

"Yes sir."

"So what is it?"

"I…I don't know, sir."

"Well, let's start testing. I'll get Dr. Stewart up here to work with you." He leaned back and shot a glance at Mr. Wall. "Mr. Wall, will you please summon Dr. Stewart to the bridge? Tell her we have a mystery to solve."

CHAPTER NINE

"The Captain needs twenty volunteers for a tactical launch of our escape pods." Security Chief Dixon's thick Jamaican accent was musical but staccato. Leif Arnesson heard the order through his neural, but chose to ignore it. He had always been the kind of guy who needed to finish one job before he could move on to something else, and he was only halfway through his weapons check. They were in the middle of a firefight, after all, and weapons systems required constant attention. He had gotten good at running three diagnostics simultaneously, but it required focus. Dixon could wait.

Except that, apparently, he couldn't. Leif brushed his almost silver-white hair from his eyes and studied the three panels he was monitoring. All good, except for a power fluctuation in one of the starboard particle cannon arrays. He was about to chase that down when he felt a tap on the shoulder.

"Too good to volunteer for the captain?" Security Chief Dixon asked, his lips tight, his perpetually bloodshot eyes drilling Leif to his place.

Leif looked around. There were a few engineers in the bay, who immediately looked away and pretended nothing was going on.

"Your captain has asked for volunteers," Dixon asked. "But I demand compliance."

"But sir, I've got three diagnostics going, and—"

"Mr. Arnesson, is there a reason you're not leaping for this assignment?"

"Sir?"

"Perhaps a bullshit psychological reason?" Dixon raised one eyebrow, his hands behind his back.

Leif looked down. "I let her down."

Dixon inclined his head slightly. "We all let her down. We let a usurper take her place, and because none of us thought she was strong enough to stop him…we didn't stop him, either."

Leif looked up and saw the sincerity in his superior's eyes.

"I want to help, but…I don't want to see her. I'm…I feel…"

"I think the word you're looking for is shame, Mr. Arnesson. It's a tragically underused word in the military. Embrace it. Learn from it. It is telling you something true. But I want you to hear the next thing I'm going to say." He leaned in so that his head was almost touching Leif's. "Failure in the past does not justify failure in the future."

Leif looked down again. "No sir."

"Do you want to advance in this man's army, ensign?"

"I do, sir."

"Then plant your ass in an escape pod within the next thirty seconds or you'll be cleaning lint out of blaster hardware for the next fifteen years."

"Yes sir. But…there's a power fluctuation in one of the starboard—"

Dixon raised one eyebrow, his lips pursed in a look that said, *Do not fuck with me*.

"Yes, sir," Leif said. He stepped away from the panel and began to jog toward the nearest pod launch deck.

"Run, you sorry excuse for a security officer!" Dixon shouted.

Leif ran.

Ten minutes later, Jo was staring out the port of her escape pod, designated as the captain's pod with an eagle ornament over the door. She saw flashes in the distance, evidence of the extended battle going on all around them. Jo had never seen this many ships engaged at one time. If the RFC's full complement of battle cruisers wasn't present, it would soon be. The Authority fleet outnumbered them, of course, and always had. They'd survived this long by fighting sneaky, fighting dirty. She hoped she was faithfully carrying on that tradition.

Just before launching, engineering had instigated a sustained burn of the C-drive core. She knew what it would look like to the captain of the *Eisenhower*—a core breach, especially when the pods started launching. If the *Eisenhower* was smart, it would turn tail and put as much distance between itself and the *Talon* as possible.

And it looked like that was exactly what was happening. The great lumbering beast of a ship was turning about, showing the giant cones of her exhaust ports to the *Talon* as it prepared to run. Jo opened a channel to the bridge on her neural. "Release pods," she said. Then she pressed the manual release on her own pod, and was pushed back against her restraints as the g-force of its acceleration pushed her away from the *Talon*—directly past the massive exhaust cones of the *Eisenhower*.

She was the bait. She knew the captain's pod would be irresistible. A captured captain was prestige, a round of drinks on Sol Station, a step toward a significant reputation as a battle-seasoned hard-ass—which was every captain's aspiration.

But she was also the hook. The sheer irresistibility of her would be their undoing. It would be she that wins the reputation. She felt a swelling in her chest, and let a smile slip onto her angular lips.

Sure enough, just as she was slipping past their midships, a tractor beam arrested her flight. There was a jarring jolt as her inertia was interrupted and reversed. The pod began moving backward toward the aft docking bay. She glanced at the nuclear device, hastily disguised as a thermal duct. A glance wouldn't betray its presence, but a detailed search of the pod would. She felt her pulse quicken at the thought, but chose to trust the arrogance of the Authority not to investigate too carefully.

Her neural contained a short-range transmitter, standard with all neural models, capable of reaching a transceiver anywhere on board a ship. Her neural wouldn't be able to reach the *Talon*, nor would she be able to interface with the Authority computer without the proper clearance protocols. She glanced up and blinked, completing a test handshake between her neural and the nuke's detonator. Online and operational. She grinned as the pod touched down in the bay.

She could just see the bay doors closing through her viewing port. She had expected them to retrieve a few more of the pods, and her anxiety rose as she realized she would have no backup here. Her security men would be safe—as safe as people in escape pods could be in the middle of a firefight—but they wouldn't be here. Apparently capturing the captain was the only thing the *Eisenhower* cared about. That was good information.

And maybe that was a good thing. If she needed to detonate while she was still aboard, she wouldn't put any of the rest of them in danger. Of course there was always the possibility that they were bringing the others in through a different bay. She pushed the thought aside.

She heard a banging on the outside of her pod hatch. She took a deep breath and set her face to something approximating crestfallen defeat. Then she pushed the button and waited for the hatch to swing wide.

Climbing to the floor of the deck, she saw herself surrounded by a security team, blasters pointed directly at her. *I think I'm getting used to this*, she thought. She marveled at how calm she was. She had a plan, after all, and so far most of it was going as she'd hoped.

"Put any weapons on the ground," the security chief barked.

She had brought a blaster, just for show. She unholstered it and let it drop onto her boot. She kicked it away.

"Any others?"

She didn't meet his eyes, but shook her head.

"Get moving, through those doors." He motioned with the muzzle of his blaster toward a set of insulated doors at the back of the bay.

They marched through the bowels of the ship directly to the brig. Several of the security force stepped aside, guarding each side of the sliding metal door. When the door opened, she stepped inside.

She was being handed off to the gaolers. They processed her, forced her to strip and shower. She was glad to see that they allowed her privacy for this, or that at least there was the semblance of privacy. In place of her own uniform she was given a white paper jumpsuit. She put it on without complaint.

Along the way she'd felt the dampened lurch of the C-drive kick in, but it had been a short burst. They'd gotten some distance from the *Talon*, but not much. They wouldn't want to be seen leaving the battlefield before it was over. Indeed, she expected they would simply jump to the aid of another ship—at least, that was what she would do.

A subordinate gaoler with pretty, bobbed red hair led her to a cell, and waved her in. A security officer stood behind her, blaster at the ready. Jo didn't give them any trouble. She stepped into the cell and sat on the poly stool to one side of the bunk. The cell wasn't palatial by any means, but it was bigger than an ensign's cabin aboard her own ship. The door to the cell slid shut, affording Jo a view of frosted white security glass.

She blinked at the brightness, the antiseptic white of the cell. Moments passed, but they seemed elongated. She felt a heaviness in her chest she didn't understand. Other than her breathing, nothing moved or changed in the cell. There was no indication of anything going on outside of it. Time seemed to be standing still.

She knew she might have to wait until a lull in the battle to be summoned. She hadn't thought of that, and it was a major flaw in her plan. She weighed the damage she'd be able to do as part of this ruse against what she'd be able to do at the helm. She felt a sinking feeling in her gut, realizing her error. She had expected her confrontation to be quick, but of course there was no way to guarantee that. She was a gnat, an annoyance, a prize of war now, nothing more. They would not bother with her until the fighting was over for the day.

Which left the *Talon* adrift without firm leadership, without even a Shallit to command her. Sure, she'd given Chi the helm, but Chi was a navigator, not a commander. She'd keep things safe, keep things together, but the girl wasn't built for war.

"I just fucked everything up," she said out loud. *They are listening,* she thought, and then internally kicked herself. Her mind raced, trying to think through all the ways they might possibly interpret what she'd just said. But the most obvious meaning was the one that her ruse rested upon. She relaxed.

Then the door slid open, and the pretty gaoler was there. She stepped aside and waved Jo out. "The Captain wants to see you."

JEFF WATCHED as Mr. Pho studied his test results. The kid's head seemed unusually oblong and pointed. It had never bothered Jeff before this moment. Hovering over the navigator's shoulder, Emma glanced back and forth between her own data pad and the navigator's console. "Anything?" Jeff asked.

"Sir, I've got that list you asked for," Susie Wall said.

"Good. Post it, please." Jeff blinked and called up the document. *It's a good list, though,* Jeff thought. *Thorough.* Every possible place for them to refuel and restock was here, it seemed. But where would they be least likely to be noticed? They could head for some little moon or outpost where the smallest number of people would see them. The problem with that was that they were likely to make a bigger impression on those few folks. Plus, there would be limited choices when it came to supplies. They could go for a crowded place, get lost in the masses. The advantage of that was they'd be able to get everything they needed in one stop. More chance of being noticed, though. And Jeff did not know what he was up against.

He wanted to trust Danny, but his gut was off whenever he thought about it. He was glad to be rid of Sol Station, but he wasn't sure who knew about them, who might be looking for them, or lying in wait for them. He didn't know whom to trust. *Sometimes the Devil you know...* he thought. He was flying blind, and he did not like it.

"Epworth Station," he said out loud. It was a good two parsecs into the neutral zone, and seemed to be huge. He'd also never heard of it—obviously it was one of the many things in this universe that did not have an analog in his own.

"What was that?" Emma said looking over.

"Uh…nothing. Just looking for a destination to restock."

She nodded and returned her attention to her work. Jeff got up and walked over to Pho's station. He put a hand on the young man's shoulder. "What have you found?"

"Running one more test, sir," Pho said without looking up. "Just… here's the results now."

Jeff saw a string of numbers that were as mysterious to him as the whole flight trajectory anomaly.

"Huh," Pho said.

"Huh, what?" Jeff asked.

"Okay, these numbers here"—Pho pointed to the first column—"are the expected weight distribution inventories for this class vessel."

"Okay," Jeff said, his brows knitting.

"This second column are the adjustments we make because of stocking or…furniture or storage or whatever."

"I follow you."

"See the third column? Those are the actual weights."

"How did you achieve the actual weight? We're nowhere near a space dock."

"Uh…Dr. Stewart figured those out with a…" He fished for a word.

Emma interrupted. "It's complicated, but basically we factored the distortion in the space-time fabric against our speed and the nearest gravity well for each section of the ship."

Jeff's eyes moved back and forth as he thought. "Those…would be some pretty precise measurements."

"What do you think has been taking us so long?" Emma asked, with a note of mock exasperation. She followed this up with a smile.

He nodded. "And what did you find?"

"We found that there are four tons of mass in the fore cargo hold that are not accounted for, distributed on both port and starboard sides —the distribution is not precisely even, however."

"What the fuck is down there?" Jeff wondered. "Mr. Wall, bring up security cams in the hold."

They all looked at the main view screen as the picture switched. Jeff saw only a dim, quiet hold. Nothing out of the ordinary. "Mr. Wall, summon commander Nira. Have her meet me in the armory ASAP."

"Aye, sir," Wall said, fingers playing over her console.

"Everyone else…stay put," Jeff said. He straightened his jacket and strode to the door. *I should have looked back at Emma. I should have kissed her,* he thought. The bridge door slid shut behind him. He walked through the mess to the armory, and sighed when he saw it empty. "Great," he sighed. "I should have guessed." He rummaged through each of the metal cabinets, to no avail. They were empty. No weapons.

"Reporting, Captain," Nira stepped into the tiny alcove that housed the armory.

"We're cleaned out, I'm afraid," Jeff said.

"Damn," Nira said. Her mouth stayed open in alarm. "What's…" It seemed to Jeff that she was about to say, "What's up?" but caught herself. She closed her mouth and tried again. "What are we up against, sir?"

"We don't know. We've got unexpected weight in the fore cargo hold."

He saw her head jerk and her eyes dart back and forth, thinking. "How much weight?"

"Four tons."

"Not a stowaway, then."

"Not unless it's a very, very large stowaway. Whatever it is, it doesn't seem to be moving."

"Stay here, sir."

"What?"

"Uh…please…just for a moment. I'll be right back."

She darted out of the armory. Jeff checked a few more drawers. He was not surprised to find them empty. Danny had wanted them gone, but he had not wanted them armed. Jeff shook his head. He didn't understand it.

Just then Nira reappeared, handing him a hunting knife. He took it with a nod, and noticed a set of nunchucks in her other hand. "You know how to use those things?"

"Manila champion two years running," she said. There was not a hint of pride or braggadocio in her voice. It was just a fact, like the Telluride quantum field equation or the fact that earth's sky is blue. "I'm deadly." Now he saw a smile curve onto her lip. He smiled back.

"Let's go find our stowaway," he said.

LEIF CLUTCHED his poly neural disruptor, and for the fifth time made sure it was charged and loaded. Looking out the window, he saw the *Talon* drifting away as his pod was ejected from her port side. He didn't understand the captain's plan, but a part of him wanted to do something—anything—to make things even with her. For the thousandth time in the past couple of days, he berated himself for supporting that asshole Shallit. He knew what was right, he knew the chain of command, but he also didn't know how—when they'd stepped off that shuttle—he could have done anything differently without getting his head shot off or getting thrown into the brig.

"Maybe getting thrown into the brig wouldn't have been the worst thing in the world," he said out loud to the empty pod, "especially given how things worked out." If he had done that, he'd be out of the brig now, and he'd be in full possession of his pride and the captain's favor. *If, that is, I didn't have my head shot off,* he thought. Then he shuddered.

The pod was a standard ensign's escape pod. It was built for two, yet there was only about five feet of space to walk in, and about seven feet of clearance. If you needed to sleep in one of these, you had to turn off the artificial gravity, since there was no way to lie down. There was a kneeling toilet, which he hated, and four months' supply of cold rations in a cabinet.

The idea of drifting in space for four months, hoping someone would find your signal before you ran out of food and oxygen, terrified him. The only comfort was the fact that there were two doses of Happy Ending in the medicine cabinet. Within seconds of taking one, you would be flooded with euphoric feelings—no pain, no worries, just delightful giddiness. Then you'd get sleepy. Happy, dopey, and sleepy. And then you'd be dead.

That is definitely how I want to go, Leif thought. *Not a blaster to the head.*

But he'd have little control over that, and he knew it. He checked the poly disruptor again. It was still charged and loaded.

He looked out the tiny circular window and saw several other pods drifting off into space near him. He had friends in those pods. He sighed.

Just then he felt a jarring change of direction. It didn't feel like he'd collided with anything, more like a quick acceleration.

"Oh shit," he thought as he saw the great metal underbelly of the *Eisenhower* drift into view as his pod turned. *Tractor beam,* he thought. *Was this what the captain intended?* Why else had they been armed with the poly disruptors? He would have felt better if he'd known the details of her plan.

Mine is not to wonder why. Mine is just to do...

He didn't finish the thought.

CHAPTER TEN

Jo controlled her breathing as she followed the security officer. She had no choice about following—she was flanked by a full security detail on all sides. The only choice before her was panic or control.

The fact that she was being summoned quickly was good—they might still be in the game. She still wondered about where her men might be, but she couldn't let it distract her.

The layout of the ship was unfamiliar—it wasn't a class she had boarded before. But the various parts of the ship they walked through were all familiar enough. There would be no mysteries here—a warship was a warship, and she knew warships.

A few minutes later the young woman ahead of her held up her hand as she requested permission to board the bridge. It must have been given, as the door slid open and she was waved through.

Jo went to straighten her red jacket, but realized she was only wearing the white paper jumpsuit. She raised her head with a note of exaggerated pride to compensate for the indignity and stepped onto the bridge.

Jo's eyes darted back and forth, assessing the scene before her. The bridge was massive, and it looked like every station was manned.

Women and men in black uniforms with orange piping huddling over their panels, fingers flying, eyes wide with the electricity of battle. No one took much notice of her. A captain was on deck, but no one rose.

She followed the blonde security officer with the bobbed hair directly to the command chair. The captain was about ten years her senior, his buzz cut shining with a faint orange tint—a common Authority affectation. It matched their uniforms.

He didn't even glance at them—his eyes were riveted to the tactical screen. On the main viewer, Jo could see another RFC vessel. It wasn't the *Talon*, but she couldn't make out the name. But her shields were holding and her guns were giving as good as they got. She nodded her approval.

After a moment, the captain barked. "Take the helm, number one."

The XO assumed command seamlessly, studying the tactical and calling out orders.

The captain turned to face her now, looking her up and down for the first time. His cheeks puffed into jowls, and his eyes darkened. He did not look impressed by the sight of her.

"I am Captain Johann Federer. And you are?"

"Captain Jo Taylor of the Revolutionary Freedom Coalition ship *Talon*. Sir."

"You had a core breach."

"We did."

"But our scans show your ship is still intact."

"Lucky us."

His eyes narrowed. "Are there still crew aboard your ship?"

"I ordered everyone out. I don't know if there is anyone aboard now or not." She held his gaze. She was a damn good liar, and she knew it. "Of course, if they're still there, then it sounds like engineering got a handle on the problem. Crack engineers, my guys."

Now was the time. Jo looked up, accessed the interface with the nuke, started the countdown. Four minutes until detonation. She had four minutes to bluster her way to mastery of the situation. *Piece of cake*, she thought, but she made a fist to stop her hand from shaking.

"Captain, I regret to inform you that there is a fifty-megaton nuclear explosive on board your ship, and unless I disarm it, your ship and everything on it will be a husk of smoking carbon in a little less than four minutes." She swallowed, and narrowed her eyes as they looked into his. "I'll be taking over as captain now, and you will hand your security codes over to me. You will also prepare to be boarded. This will be a peaceful transition of ownership. You and your crew are free to leave via your escape pods." She smirked. "Never let it be said that the RFC is inhumane."

"The RFC is humane? Is that why you gunned down a businesswoman and six cops back on Avalon II?"

Jo cocked her head. "We did no such thing. Where did you get such an idea?"

"It is established fact. You have a price on your head—not just for being a enemy combatant, but for espionage and mass murder."

"It can't be an 'established fact' if it isn't, in fact, true," Jo said. "And it isn't."

"You can tell it to the Authority. And your threats are useless. We found your nuke as soon as you came aboard. We disarmed it. Thank you for the plutonium." He hadn't yet blinked, but his lips curled into a cruel grin that made her squirm. "As soon as we're finished here, we'll be heading back to your ship—the *Talon*, is it? You may have the honor of contacting what's left of your crew and informing them that it is you who will prepare to be boarded."

Jo felt like she had been punched in the gut. An old childhood voice began to shout, *Stupid, you are so stupid*, over and over in her head. Despite her best efforts to keep her eyes fixed and her chin up, her shoulders sagged noticeably. She thought about the last time a cruel asshole had tried to steal her ship from her. *Goddam Shallit,* she thought. And this guy's just like him.

Until Shallit, she never thought she'd be capable of killing someone—not outside of a battle situation, anyway. She had learned a lot about herself that day—who she was, what she could do when pressed into a corner. Her mind flashed on how she'd shot him in the very act of handing over her gun.

Her head jerked. *That…is an idea,* she thought. "Put me through to my crew," she said through gritted teeth.

Captain Federer looked up at his communicator, who was, it seemed, listening in and standing by. He nodded. The communicator pressed a few nodes on his panel, and turned back to them. "We have the *Talon*."

"On screen."

A moment later, Jo was looking at Marcia Chi, looking grave and scared. The command chair seemed to dwarf her. "This is the RFC battle cruiser *Talon*," she said, her voice high and tentative.

"Navigator Chi, this is your captain," Jo said, forcing her voice to be strong and steady. It did not fail her.

"Captain, are you all right?" Chi's eyes were wide as she recognized her captain out of uniform.

"I am unharmed. Unfortunately, our plan is in shreds. I'm afraid they caught us with our boots off. I want you to surrender the ship with as little disruption as possible. Surrender protocol Zed 8593."

Chi blinked. Her mouth opened, but no sounds came out.

"Mr. Chi?"

"I…need to…I'll get right back to you…"

Jo's heart sank. She had counted on Chi to be clever, to pick up on her clues and signals. She hung her head. She had no ideas left.

JEFF LOWERED himself down the ladder into the fore cargo hold. His feet hit the sloped deck and he grabbed at a handrail to steady himself as he watched Nira lower herself down. She was a good deal shorter than he was, but he didn't for a second doubt her ferocity. The nunchucks stuck awkwardly out of a long pocket on the leg of her flight suit, ready at hand should she need them.

He remembered the knife in his own pocket and carefully withdrew it. Nira's boots hit the deck, and she turned to him for instructions. For some reason, it didn't seem necessary to speak. He just nodded at her and began to climb up the sloping curve of the deck.

The floor was covered with poly restraint belts, cables, and buckles. Strangely, this made it easier to navigate, since one could find purchase on them where the sloping deck alone would have been slippery. The hold was small, maybe five meters square. It also appeared to be empty. Jeff circumambulated the hold once, looking carefully at the floor, hoping, under the tangle of straps, to find some unexpected cargo or passenger.

Nothing. No one.

Finishing his circuit, he steadied himself near the ladder and looked to his number one with a brooding eye. Finally he spoke. "Did you see anything?"

"Not a thing."

"Did you notice anything unusual?"

"I don't understand why the military can't come up with a more orderly way of storing hold restraints."

Jeff grunted. It was a mild joke, but he was grateful for it. Nor did he disagree with it—it was a mess down there.

"Okay, then…we look again. Only we look closer this time."

"Aye, sir."

Jeff began another clockwise examination of the hold, only this time, he did it on his knees. He crawled along the edge of the wall, while Nira was on her hands and knees directly to his right, pouring over every inch of the regions closer to the center of the hold.

Aside from the proliferation of straps, the floor appeared to him almost antiseptic in its cleanliness. Sure, there were spider nests here and there, but strangely, the spiders seemed to be gone. Where had they gone? He had no idea. Maybe the Authority mechanics had sucked them up. But why remove the spiders but not the nests? Maybe they simply hadn't had time yet? He couldn't fathom it.

He completed the circle and sat back on his haunches, shaking his head. Nira looked as puzzled as he did.

"We need an imager," she said.

He nodded—the handheld device could detect light not visible to the human eye, as well as radiation and mass. "I'll run up," she said, and a moment later she was crawling up the ladder to the deck above.

Jeff used the time for another pass, looking for something, anything, that he might have missed.

Then he found it. A white splash on one of the straps. Jeff fished a small flashlight out of his flight suit and trained it on the spot. It looked as if someone had spilled—or wiped—some kind of liquid epoxy on the strap. Teasing the end of the splash with his fingernail, he peeled it off the strap, enclosing it in his fist. Then he tied a knot in the strap he had found it on.

The strap was directly at the intersection of the floor and the wall—hell, the floor almost *was* the wall, it was so steep at that point. Jeff examined the wall from where it joined the floor, moving toward the ceiling. He didn't see anything out of the ordinary—joist plates at the intersection with the deck, then an unbroken expanse of white, until—

A hole.

A single hole, about five millimeters in diameter, nearly invisible, as it was sealed off with some kind of poly epoxy that had dried almost an identical shade of white as the rest of the wall.

He knew he was looking at what ship engineers called the tertiary hull. There would be a gap of about twelve millimeters between that and the secondary hull. It was a poly lining to insure a zero aeropermeability status. Basically, it was the plastic bag that kept the air in and the great cold void of space out.

Beyond the secondary hull would be the outer or primary hull—20 millimeters of solid iconel. Had someone put something in between the secondary and tertiary hulls? Jeff scowled. He began to run his fingers across the tertiary hull, in a straight line to his right. He stumbled once over a strap, but caught himself before he fell. He kept looking.

There. Another hole.

He heard the rustle of Nira's flight suit behind him as she descended. She came up beside him and he pointed at the holes. Her eyes grew wide and she nodded. He held out his hand and opened his fist. A tiny scrap of some kind of poly material lay crumpled in his palm, its wispy ends quivering under the force of their breathing.

Nira's eyes looked up to his, filled with questions. Unfortunately, he had no answers for her. He motioned for her to follow him to the rear wall.

"Let's see what that thing can show us," he said.

Nira turned the tiny device on, and Jeff looked up, interfacing with it using his neural. A few moments later the diagnostic screen materialized in front of him, superimposed over the cargo hold. "Fire it up," Jeff said.

Nira nodded, and began the first of a series of scans. The infrared showed them nothing. The ultraviolet, however, showed several specks along the wall, and some on the deck, where whatever had been pumped into those holes had spilled out.

"We're not wrong," Jeff growled. "Some kind of polymer has been pumped in between the hulls."

Nira nodded again, but said nothing. She selected another scan and gasped.

So did Jeff—he could clearly see what looked like the silhouette of a range of mountains. He scowled, trying to make sense of the image.

"They poured the epoxy in there," Nira said, pointing to one of the holes in the wall. It appeared on the readout as the peak of one of the mountains. Then Jeff saw that all the holes showed up as mountain peaks. And the mountains descending from those peaks were simply where the epoxy had flowed down from the holes, filling up the space between the secondary and tertiary hulls. The mountain range descended to ground level gradually, roughly on equal sides of the port and starboard hulls. At least it was more-or-less balanced, and thus had a greater chance of avoiding detection.

But not today.

"Do you think there could be four tons of epoxy in between those walls?" Jeff asked.

"Easily," Nira answered.

Jeff opened his fist again and stared at the quivering scrap of epoxy in his hand. "Okay, then. Let's go to the lab and find out what the fuck this stuff is."

THE POD HIT the docking bay floor with a jarring clank. A moment later, the door swung open and Leif Arnesson was staring down the barrels of four blasters trained on him by Authority security. "Hands where we can see them," barked one of them, a short man with a ridiculous handlebar mustache.

Leif put his hands up and followed orders, stepping over the gunwale and onto the deck.

"Pat him down," the mustache ordered. His eye never left his scope.

One of his men slung his blaster over his back and started feeling at Leif's clothes—his arms, under his arms, his torso and waist, then down his legs.

"He's clean."

"These other bastards had disruptors."

"No disruptors here," the man said.

"You sure?"

"I'm fucking sure. You want to feel him up yourself?"

The man winced at the barb. "Where's your disruptor?" he asked Leif, still not removing his eye from his scope.

"We ran out of disruptors. I have a blaster in the pod—" Leif started to turn back, but the mustache barked at him again.

"Don't! Move!"

"Okay, okay, I thought you wanted the blaster."

"We'll get your fucking blaster when we strip your pods for parts." He motioned toward the other RFC security personnel, huddled together in the middle of the bay. They were surrounded by Authority soldiers, weapons trained and eager for an excuse to shoot.

Hands still in the air, Leif joined his fellows, and tried to keep his face neutral.

"What's going to happen to us?" his friend Alison asked.

Before he could say anything, Ernesto answered her. "We'll be taken to Earth and tried for treason. Then we'll be executed."

Alison's eyes narrowed.

Alison may not believe it, but Leif did. He wished he'd snagged the doses of Happy Ending from the pod before he'd left it. One for him, one for her. They could fall asleep together.

But it was too late for that now.

"Move out!" the mustache ordered, and the Authority security team shifted, opening a way for them to move—in only one direction.

Leif knew what direction that would be—toward the brig. *So I'm not going to escape the brig after all,* he thought. *It's really not my week.*

CAPTAIN FEDERER OFFERED a smug smile that Jo wanted to rip from his face—preferably with a blaster.

"Security," he said, with an imperial air. "You can return the rebel captain to her—"

Jo lifted her hand, "Please, Captain Federer, if you don't mind, there's a matter of honor at stake." She looked down at her feet. "I mean, captain-to-captain…we're supposed to go down with our ships. If I can't do that…I should at least have to watch it." She looked up at him again, her jaw jutted out bravely.

He seemed to take her measure and approve. He nodded slowly. "That…is fitting. You may watch." He nodded at the security guard standing a little too close to her. The guard took a step back but did not remove her hand from her holstered blaster.

"Hail the *Talon*, Mr. Barrow," the captain said to his communicator.

"I have the acting captain," the young man at the communications station said.

"On screen."

Once again, Jo saw Marcia Chi's worried face.

"Prepare to be boarded."

She saw Chi nod. "The crew have been informed. They will be docile and compliant."

"Either that or they'll be dead," Federer pronounced.

"I understand sir," Chi said with a quick nod. The screen was quickly replaced by a field of stars. Jo watched the *Talon* slowly float into view as the *Eisenhower* moved into position.

"Ready the boarding tubes," the captain said.

Several moments passed when silence reigned on the *Eisenhower* bridge, broken only by the occasional electronic alert from one of the dozen stations that surrounded them. Jo dug her nails into the meat of her palm, the pain focusing and calming her.

"Boarding tubes in place, sir," the weaponer called. She was a stocky woman with fiery red hair. It occurred to Jo how much she'd like to fight her. But it wouldn't be today.

"Begin boarding," the captain said with a wave of his hand.

He turned to Jo. "I have two hundred men pouring through those tubes into your cargo and shuttle bays. How many people do you have aboard?"

Jo shook her head. "Who knows? Our full complement is one hundred and twenty-seven, but I don't know how many got away in the pods."

He sneered. "So it will be over quickly."

Jo said nothing. Instead, she felt bile at the back of her throat. Inwardly, she cursed Chi for being so thick, so scared, so stupid. She needed an XO she could trust, someone who could complete her sentences. Her mind flashed on a distant memory of Jeff. It had been a long time since she'd thought of him. She felt an unfamiliar wave of grief ripple through her. She shook her head to clear it. She didn't have Jeff, or even Danny. She didn't have a competent XO. She only had her wits, and those, it seemed, were in short supply.

"What is going to happen to me?" she heard herself ask. She was shocked at the words—her people were dying, and she was concerned with herself? Obviously, some deep part of her was.

The captain narrowed his eyes at her, disapproving. *As well he should,* she thought, feeling the heat of shame on her neck.

"You? You'll be delivered to the Terran Authority War Crimes Division for trial and execution."

"Execution how?" She couldn't look at him.

"Live public disembowelment is the current penalty. It's live-streamed, of course. Your admirals could watch, if they like, if only to get a glimpse of their own fate." He smiled.

Jo felt a wave of vertigo wash over her. She clutched at a nearby chair, willing her knees to hold. She stood straight, she felt her knees lock into place. Like a winch hoisting a girder, she willed her chin to rise, forced herself to look him in the eyes. She locked onto them, and willed her lips to slide back into a sneer. It was all force of will, a show, a charade. But at the moment it was the only thing in her power she could draw on.

Captain Federer met her eyes and gave her a look that was one part sneer and two parts pity.

"Bring it on, motherfucker," she said.

CHAPTER ELEVEN

Jeff dropped the scrap of epoxy into a plastic dish filled with solution. He fixed the lid to it and slid it into the electron analyzer. As the machine began its work, he saw multicolored lights dancing across its display. Soon, strings of numbers began to organize themselves into groups. He felt hot breath on his ear. He didn't have to turn to know it was Emma. He could smell her. Instead, he leaned ever-so-slightly, touching his ear to her cheek. She squeezed his shoulder.

Looking past the machine, he saw Nira standing at the other end of the small lab, staring at an auxiliary display, no doubt studying the same information he was. He admired her—she was a compact tornado of cunning and will, and he did not doubt her loyalty. She was as good an XO as he had ever worked with. Her eyes widened suddenly, and she looked up. Then she pointed down at the display.

He looked at it himself, but didn't understand at first what he was looking at. Chemistry was not his best subject—but it didn't matter. Apparently, there was nothing that Nira didn't excel at, and she didn't mind translating.

"It's a poly explosive," she said. "R-29."

"R-29? Who uses R-29 anymore?" he asked. "It's not quite as powerful as the R-30s."

"It's still plenty powerful, though," Nira said. "And apparently the Authority still uses it. Maybe they haven't developed the R-30s."

"Maybe," Jeff said, staring at the molecule on his display. There were three molecules, actually, but he could see that one was a simple poly base, another a standard explosive stabilizer. It was the third one that was exotic, sporting connections to nucleotides that reminded him of bed hair or an upside-down waterfall.

"How stable is it?" Jeff asked. Emma squeezed his arm. He gave her a quick, grim smile.

"It's as stable as R-29 ever is. Which is to say that as long as we don't hit an asteroid or discharge a bunch of electricity between those hulls, it's going to stay inert."

"They must have put it there for a reason."

"There's no question they put it there for a reason."

"It wasn't there before," Jeff said.

"No."

Jeff chewed on his lip. "Do you think they intended us to discover it?"

Nira blinked, her black eyes a little too large for her head. "To what end?"

"Who can say?" Jeff asked.

"So what's your theory?" Emma asked.

Jeff sighed. "I think they hid it pretty carefully. They tried to even it out so that there wouldn't be any flight anomalies—"

"Except that there was one," Emma reminded him.

"Yeah…"

"I think we should come back to that," Nira said. "Buddha's arrow."

"What?" Jeff made a face.

"Buddha's arrow. A follower of the Buddha was asking all kinds of impossible-to-answer questions—like 'Is the world eternal,' and 'What happens to us when we die?'—and to shut him up, the Buddha told him a story."

"What's the story?" Jeff asked.

"A man is shot with an arrow, and his friends need to pull it out in order to save his life. But the man won't let them pull it out until he gets all his questions asked. 'The man who shot me, was he short or tall? What color was his skin? Is the fletching done with vulture feathers or hawk feathers?' Shit like that."

Jeff scowled. "What difference could any of those things possibly make?"

"None. That's the Buddha's point. He's saying, 'Unanswerable questions are a distraction. Deal with the danger that's in front of you.'"

"And the danger that's in front of us?"

"We have four tons of poly explosive sealed into the hull of our ship, and no idea how it's rigged to detonate."

Jeff felt his stomach sink. She was absolutely right. Obviously, the explosive was not cargo. Someone wanted them dead, or something destroyed, or someone—

He felt like an idiot. He shook his head to clear it. "Okay, then, let's find that detonator. Preferably before it goes off…"

THE GOOD NEWS was that the cell was much larger than the escape pod. The bad news was that Leif was crammed into it with all twenty of his fellow RFC security personnel. Leif shifted, trying to worm his way into a space on the floor where he would not be touching one of his fellows. It was pretty much impossible, and he resigned himself to the fact that he was going to have to lean on someone, or someone else's leg was going to be draped over his. He sighed.

The cell was built to accommodate four comfortably. There were four beds, and each of them had three people seated on them, side-by-side. There were two chairs, both occupied. Someone else was even sitting on the toilet, although not using it, thankfully. But that would come.

Svoboda was pacing, picking his way around and over people. It was annoying and Leif wished he would just light somewhere.

"We're fucked," Cheodon said. His black hair and swarthy skin revealed his Tibetan ancestry, and he wore a dark wooden wrist mala. It wasn't regulation, but no one gave him any shit about it.

Leif glanced over at Alison. He liked her because she was funny, smart, and real. She also didn't take shit from anyone. After trying to squeeze into a number of places, she finally gave up on trying to find a spot on one of the beds, and instead, climbed over the bodies of her shipmates toward him. She kicked him with her boot. "Scooch," she said.

"Scooch where?" he asked.

"Don't care," she said, sitting down almost on top of him. Everyone around them shifted resentfully, but they made space. Leif was beginning to feel claustrophobic.

"What was the plan, anyway?" asked Teeley. Leif hated Teeley. He was a back-stabbing opportunist who would sooner sell his mother to the wolves than do an honest day's work. Leif kept expecting his superiors to catch on, but if there was one thing Teeley worked hard on, it was making himself seem indispensable. The man had a mane of bright red hair that made Leif hate red hair no matter who it was on. And that, he knew, was irrational. He didn't care.

"I think we were supposed to infer the plan," Leif said.

"Infer? What the fuck does 'infer' mean?" Teeley's eyes narrowed.

Leif wanted to say, *It means you're an ignorant donkey's ass,* but he kept his mouth closed and just stared.

"Whatever." Teeley was, thankfully, sitting on the bed furthest from Leif. "But fat lot of good the poly weapons did."

Leif looked around, trying to detect a camera. Surely there was one. But all he saw was the frosted white walls of the cell. And there had to be a microphone. He didn't dare speak his secret aloud. Instead, he took Alison's hand and guided it to the small of his back.

"What the fuck are you doing?" She snatched her hand back. "Pervert."

He looked her in the eye, and lowered his head slightly, nodding slowly. He saw her expression change, saw that she knew he was serious. He held his hand out to her. She bunched her eyebrows, but put her hand back into his, and this time allowed him to guide her to his back. And then she felt it. The disruptor.

"Fuck," she said.

"What?" asked James, next to her. His people were from South Africa, and Leif had heard plenty of stories of his rough-and-tumble childhood in Soweto.

She leaned in and whispered. His eyes widened and a grin broke out on his face.

"What the fuck, Frank?" Teeley asked.

James leaned over and whispered to the woman next to him, who passed the message along. But long before the message had gotten to Teeley, he blurted out. "What? Do you have a piece?"

It was the last thing Leif heard for a while. There was a flash of light, and he found himself instantly immobilized—able to think, but not able to move. He was not even able to twitch his finger. And although he could not move his eyes, he discovered he had been frozen at a good time. His eyes were wide open—they could have been at mid-blink, he realized—and they were looking out into the room. He watched as the frosted cell door slid open, and he heard the whine of a small electrical engine.

A moment later, a lab robot with an extended grip rolled in, but found its way blocked by the mass of bodies. It tried several paths, and Leif realized it was trying to move in his direction.

Fucking Teeley, he thought. Of course they were watching. Of course they were listening. And no doubt there was an automatic security monitor system in place listening and looking for contraband—especially weapons. This was probably all automated, but Leif was certain somewhere in the deeper bowels of the security unit, alarms were blasting and Authority security personnel were scrambling. *First chance I get I'm going to punch the teeth out of that fire-headed fuck.*

Leif's feeling of claustrophobia was magnified every second he was frozen. To not be able to move, to not be able to wipe a bead of sweat, to not be able to speak…or scream. He strained against his immobility and an irrational panic began to rise. He felt his heart rate increase, heard the driving *thub, thub, thub* drumbeat in his ears.

He was struggling so hard, he barely noticed when the robot backed out and the door slid shut again.

Like someone letting go of one end of a stretched elastic band, he felt his body lurch as the immobilization beam was shut off.

He met Alison's eyes, and an understanding passed between them. The robot had failed, but people were coming. They were coming for his disruptor and they would not be gentle or kind or pleasant. Alison pivoted so that she faced him, sitting on his lap. Her eyes stayed locked on his as she removed his disruptor from its hiding place in the small of his back. Blocking as much of a view as she could between their two bodies, she passed it around to his groin, then up, under her shirt, moving it into place just above her breasts.

He nodded. He had no idea what she was up to, but he trusted her. If she had any ideas at all, it was more than he had. She climbed off of him and began to roll and crawl her way toward the door.

She is one badass motherfucker, he thought. *And that's just sexy as hell.*

MARCIA CHI FELT PARALYZED. The comm link with the *Eisenhower* had just broken off, leaving her looking at the exterior hull of the great Authority war ship. They were outgunned, outmanned, and whatever plan their captain might have had was disintegrating like an unshielded probe on re-entry. That was when she realized that every eye on the bridge was staring at her, demanding something of her—something she did not have.

Tash was moving his hands furiously over his console.

"Uh, Captain Chi, I looked up protocol Zed 8593."

Marcia's head jerked around to see Tash Liebert's hopeful expression. She realized just how thirsty she was for that hope. "And?"

"It's not a surrender protocol at all, sir. It's an emergency docking protocol."

"Is that a mistake?" The last thing they needed was for their untried captain to be mixing up her protocols. But with everything else going wrong, it wouldn't surprise her for a moment.

Then she saw Liebert smile. "Oh, no sir, it's no mistake. It's…kind of fucking brilliant."

"EPWORTH STATION IN FOUR HOURS, SIR."

"Thank you, Mr. Pho." Jeff felt paralyzed in his command chair. He was keenly aware that he was in the saddle of what was essentially a superluminal bomb. And they were riding that bomb right into a densely populated area. If Danny…or Tal…wanted to effect a terrorist strike against a target in the neutral zone, a strike that would not reflect back on them, this would be the perfect setup. Blame it on the strangers from another galaxy—if there were anything left of the *Kepler*, it wouldn't be traceable to anything from Authority space.

It was almost too perfect, and Jeff admired it…if that indeed had been the plan. There were too many unknowns, however. How did they intend to detonate it? And exactly what was the target—what would trigger the detonation? Proximity to…what? Or did they simply intend to blow the *Kepler* to hell after they cleared Authority space? The epoxy could, he knew, blow at any moment. It made the hair on his arms stand on end.

"Mr. Pho, bring us to a stop."

"Sir?" Pho turned around, his youthful face long with surprise.

"Just…stop."

Pho's eyes darted back and forth. "Stopping sir." He turned back to his station and a moment later, Jeff felt the dampened lurch of a starship exiting C-space.

"Stopped, sir. Drifting."

"Anything we should be concerned about around here?"

"No sir, nothing but open space for a couple hundred thousand kilometers."

"Good." He knew Pho wanted an explanation. But he didn't need to explain everything.

A moment later, Nira stepped aboard the bridge, followed by Emma. Emma flashed him a warm smile and went to her science station. Nira paused by his chair. “Permission to speak in private, sir.”

Jeff rose and gestured toward his ready room.

Nira walked ahead of him, and as soon as the door slid shut behind them, she held her palm out. “Found it.”

In her palm was a poly patch, approximately four centimeters square, no bigger than a mouse. Four wires hung from one side of it like a tail. “It has a flexible bio-chip embedded in it.”

The whole patch was easily bendable. Jeff could even have rolled it, had he wanted to. “Where was it?”

“Fastened to the interior wall of the tertiary hull. Since there’s no metal, it wasn’t detectable by the imager. I inserted a worm-cam into the holes and looked around—found this just above the middle-most hole. I figure they rolled it up, stuck it through the hole, and then, using tweezers or something, stuck it to the near wall inside the tertiary hull. It wasn’t perfectly flattened out, which supports my theory—but it was stuck there pretty good. And the leads were embedded in the explosive.”

Jeff examined the leads. They weren’t wire, but a superconducting polymer they called fibrex in his universe—who knows what it was called here?

Jeff nodded, sighing his relief. “Have you had a chance to scan the bio-chip?”

“Yes. It’s set to trigger in proximity to a neural code.”

“What code?” Jeff’s face looked haggard, drawn, haunted.

“TDP3079317.” She glanced up to check her neural. “It belongs to a Captain Joleen Taylor.”

Jeff felt his legs buckle under him. He reached to steady himself against the table.

“You knew her, didn’t you, Captain? In our world, I mean?”

“I did know her, number one. She was…a close friend.”

“I’m sorry, sir.”

Jeff pulled back a chair and eased himself into it. His hands were shaking.

"Are you all right, captain? Do you need anything?"

Jeff didn't answer. A moment later Nira set a glass of water in front of him. He didn't want it. He took it up and downed it. He couldn't look at her. The heat of shame rose from his neck. He didn't want his XO to see him like this.

Danny had mentioned Jo, had mentioned that she was one of the rebels, that he'd love to see her in the brig. Apparently he also wanted to see her dead, and his old friend didn't mind sacrificing Jeff and his crew to accomplish that. *With friends like these...* he thought.

"They'd been lovers," he said.

"Permission to sit, sir?" Nira asked.

Jeff nodded and she pulled back a chair.

"Who had been lovers, sir?"

"Danny—Captain Hightower and Captain Taylor. Just out of the academy. For a short time—"

"Begging the captain's pardon, but I'd heard a rumor that you and Captain Taylor…." She didn't actually say it.

"That's not a rumor, that's true." He didn't smile at her. He didn't even look at her. He simply stared into space. "I love…loved her." He couldn't believe he'd said that out loud.

"I understand," Nira said, although she couldn't possibly understand. Could she?

"I fell in love with someone. A couple of years ago. She was…she wasn't perfect, but she was perfect for me. I had to make a choice—"

"Between your career and your sweetheart," Jeff said.

"Yes."

"Maybe you do understand."

Jeff felt numb. He stared at his hands. "I know what betrayal feels like. Whoever sent those commands…" he stopped himself. Catskill was classified. He didn't need to say more. "Danny…my Danny… couldn't have done this."

"Were you in love with Captain Hightower, too? I mean, in our world?"

Jeff blinked and looked up. "Huh? Oh, no. I mean…I loved him.

But not…not like that. We were both interested in Jo, though. She picked me, and then she picked the CDF."

"Did your friendship with Captain Hightower survive it?" Nira asked.

"Yes…we had some rocky patches. We had a fistfight. We ended it laughing our fucking heads off."

"I would have liked to have seen that fight, sir."

"It was probably still floating around on some of the file-sharing sites before—" *Before our universe was destroyed. Before we destroyed it.*

Jeff opened his fist and let the poly patch tumble onto the table. "Find the rest of them."

Nira pulled something out of her pocket and held it out to him. "Already done, sir."

He put his hand out and received the square, the detonator mouse, this one's tail curled into a tight circle. He looked at Nira and cocked his head.

"Only two? Are you sure this is the last of them?" he asked.

"Absolutely, sir. I'd say I'd stake my life on it, but I actually am."

"Heh," Jeff chuckled, despite the gravity of the moment.

Nira waited for him to say something, but then broke the silence. "Sir, I don't know how to say this…"

"Say what, commander?"

"This one…it's wired different."

"Different how?"

"This one isn't a proximity trigger. It's live, keyed to another neural."

"Meaning whoever it's keyed to could just access their neural and detonate it?"

"Right."

Jeff felt a chill run through his bones. "Whose?"

Nira swallowed and held his gaze. "It's one of us."

CHAPTER TWELVE

Alison crawled toward the door, then positioned herself beneath the "A" formed by Tyson's knees, drawn up nearly to his chin. Alison's head was beneath one knee, the disruptor beneath the one nearest the door. She checked the safety and made sure it was powered up. She checked the battery—80%. That would give her about five minutes of steady fire—more time than she'd actually get.

A disruptor was a poor excuse for a weapon when compared to a blaster. It was more of a neural disruptor than anything else. Its power was low, and it wasn't instantaneous. Victims didn't even necessarily feel anything when fired upon until their nerves started shorting out. But they couldn't kill anyone—not unless they caused a heart attack. The only thing they had going for them was that they worked through any non-conducting material. If someone was wearing a metallic exoskeleton, they were useless, unless you could directly target some skin, or an area of clothing not covered by the exoskeleton.

"Disruptors are a good tool to have in your kit," Alison remembered her drill sergeant saying, "But they are a sorry excuse for a primary weapon."

But it's all I've got now, she thought, fitting finger to trigger and willing herself to relax.

Two minutes went by…three. Sweat dripped from her eyebrow into her eye. She wiped it with her left hand, then returned it to steady her right. She was grateful to have the floor to rest them on—if she'd been standing up, her arms would be screaming with anaerobic exertion.

Then the white-frosted door slid open, and she was staring down the barrels of a dozen blasters held by Authority pricks in riot gear. She flattened herself as much as possible and, aiming as low as she could, squeezed the trigger on the disruptor.

She was relieved to see they weren't wearing space boots, but the same leatherette service boots they all wore aboard ship. She aimed for the ankles of the men on her far right and, keeping up a steady beam, she slowly panned to the left. She had set the beam to be as horizontally wide as possible, but also as vertically narrow as possible—a setting she knew would tax her unit's charge much more quickly than a simple spot-beam. But it was what it was. It took about twenty seconds to achieve neural disruption, so she panned slowly.

"Back up from the door!" one of the guards in the back barked—probably the one in charge. Of course, no one moved—no one could. "One by one, you're going to come into the hall to be searched. You! Out here now!"

He pointed at Mussorgsky, who put his hands up and stood. A couple of the security guards backed up, giving him space to step into the hall. He hesitated.

As Alison had hoped, none of the security personnel noticed the beam. None of them noticed a tickling on their ankles. None of them noticed anything amiss until it was too late.

The first of the guards fell to the floor and began to jerk about as his nervous system collapsed into involuntary epileptic shudders. Alison kept the disruptor steady and continued panning—it would take them a few seconds to figure out what was happening to them, seconds she would put to good use.

When half of them had collapsed, she shouted, "Now!" and was relieved to see her shipmates launch themselves into the hallway. They were careful to stay to her right, trying to avoid the beam. But by then it was moot, as the power failed and the disruptor became nothing more than a useless gun-shaped pile of poly.

But it was enough. Mussorgsky was the first into the hall, the first to grab a blaster. He threw himself on the ground next to the gun's owner, and forcing the owner's twitching thumb to cover the ID pad, began to fire upon the last few guards still standing. Others mimicked his strategy, and before long every one of the Authority guards were either twitching on the ground or dead.

Without anyone needing to call the shots, they began to turn the blasters on the twitching men. Then, working together, they narrowed the blasters' beams and shot off the hands or thumbs of the fallen security personnel, holding or even binding their grisly trophies to the ID pads of their stolen blasters. It could have been quite a production, but adrenaline and the urgency of their situation made them both ruthless and efficient.

Alison estimated that their coup took all of three minutes to execute, from the sliding back of the door to the jerry-rigging of the last of the blasters. She caught Leif's eye and winked at him.

Good job, he mouthed at her. She smiled.

Once everyone was able to stand and move and had retrieved all the working blasters, the first thing they did was to locate the cameras—or where they suspected cameras might be—and shoot them out. Leif pointed to one of them—he knew they would still be listening—and waved them down the hall. Alison understood. Their first stop—central security. She hoisted her blaster, pressing the severed thumb tight to the ID pad with her own, toggling off the safety, and making sure it was cocked and ready to fire. They needed to light the place up and kill every fucking officer monitoring security on that ship. *Yep,* she thought, *I'm fucking ready for that.*

Aboard the *Talon*, Shell Ditka kicked her boots aside and stared at her toes as she waited. All around her were what was left of the security personnel aboard and every other crew member capable of picking up a blaster. But they didn't have blasters now—they had poly disruptors. She made sure hers was primed, the plastic shells aligned in the transport bridge. To tell the truth, she hated these things—they were flimsy and she was always afraid they would blow up in her face. But there was no time to question it.

She heard the access alarm go off and fixed her eyes on the viewer set into the wall near the door to the docking bay. She held her hand up, and everyone around her went silent. She glanced down the corridor, at nearly forty women and men, all of them readying their weapons, all of them barefoot.

She returned her gaze to the viewer as the docking bay doors slid open. Shell saw fiberglass pallets and scraps of packing material whisked into the vacuum of space. A boarding tube hovered just outside, waiting. When the door widened enough, the tube snaked in, coiling slightly on the floor of the docking bay. Inside, Shell knew, Authority forces were checking their blasters and saying their prayers. Who knew how many there were? The outer tube detached and withdrew, leaving a windowless segmented snake behind.

Shell saw one soldier emerge wearing a space suit. He marched to the manual controls, overrode the security protocols, and closed the space doors. He glanced at the gauge built into his sleeve until the pressurization was complete. He looked around. *Is he disappointed?* she wondered. He had probably been expecting a fight.

The pressurized door on the deposited section of the boarding tube twisted open, and men began pouring out, weapons brandished, primed, and at the ready. Just as the last of them hit the docking floor, the man in the space suit removed his helmet and readied his own rifle, nodding—probably at his team captain.

The man who seemed to be the team captain motioned for them to fall into line behind him as he made for the interior dock doors.

"Now," Shell said. She grinned as she saw the Authority team captain freeze. The entire boarding party froze as their boots stuck fast to the surface of the dock.

Their forward momentum caused some of them to pitch forward, falling amid screams of pain as ankles and tibias snapped. Others issued howls of frustration as they tried to lift their feet.

Shell entered the access codes into the keypad, then looked into the eyes of her warriors. "Let's kick some Authority ass," she said. She flipped the safety off her poly weapon, flimsy as it was, and heard the whine as it charged to full power. Then the door slid open and she rushed through, raising her voice in a ululating whoop of challenge and victory.

Her bare feet pounded the magnetized steel floor of the bay. She shot four of the Authority soldiers before she reached them and took out another with an elbow to the teeth. Those soldiers that were still upright were shooting now, but there was no way to duck their shots. She just kept going, a blonde berserker firing and striking at everything clad in black metal. She didn't need to go for the kill, she only needed them down—the gravity assist, turned up to three times its normal magnetic power, would keep them down and render their weapons unusable as well.

She chanced a glance over her shoulder and saw her team, streaming over the bodies, their weapons ablaze, their eyes filled with bloodlust and triumph. "HAAAAA!!" she screamed, plunging her weapon into the eye of one of the few remaining upright soldiers, drunk on ecstasy as she watched the blood spray from his face, watched him flail, watched him fall.

Jo NOTED how deadly quiet it was on the bridge. The security guard stood two steps behind her, weapon at the ready. A full bridge complement of five were sweating into their panels. The captain presided over it all imperiously. For a moment, it seemed as if time were standing still.

She stole a glance at his puffy face. She had spent her entire career being pushed around by assholes like this one. She had been passed over for jobs, seen her record ignored as less-qualified men were raised to ranks above her, and been nearly gang-raped twice by military mooks with too much testosterone and time on their hands. *They didn't win then,* she thought. *They sure as hell aren't going to get the best of me today.*

Anger flooded her, filling her veins with something more powerful and volatile than hope or despair. She relished the feeling of it and seized onto it like a shipwrecked sailor seizes a piece of flotsam in a storm. She fastened her hands behind her back and stood at parade rest. She dug her nails into her palms again. She fed on the fire of her hate, reveled in its ecstasy, stoked its flame.

Captain Federer was staring at the tactical and seemed to have lost interest in her. That was just fine with her.

"Boarding party, report," he barked.

"No report, sir," the communicator said.

"Tell the team leader I want a report."

The communicator's face went slack. "Uh…sir, team leader appears to be offline."

"What?" the captain bellowed. "Put me through to the team leader immediately."

"I…I would if I could, sir."

Captain Federer blustered.

Jo blinked. *What is this?* she thought. A shudder of hope nearly undid her.

"Uh…Captain, we're being hailed by the *Talon*."

"On screen!" The captain's face was red. Jo could tell he was a man unaccustomed to not getting his way.

Suddenly navigator Chi was on the main viewer, nearly twice her actual size, her face contorting with some unknown effort that Jo could not discern. "Captain Federer, you gave us just enough time to take our boots off, which was very kind," Chi said. She gave up the fight not to reveal her feelings, and a smile broke out across her face. The mousy girl that Jo had been commanding just yesterday was nowhere in sight. "Thing is, no one goes into battle without their boots on, and when we tripled the magnetic gravity assist in the bays, your troops were pretty much glued in place. We disarmed them before any of them thought of taking their boots off. Some of them lost their weapons right away to the magnetized floor. There was a lot of *clanking* going on." She waited a beat for that to sink in.

Jo blinked. Her anger mixed with hope to create something much more volatile, much more dangerous, something utterly unpredictable.

"Your men are enjoying the hospitality of our brig now—your commanders, anyway. The others are safely contained in one of our cargo bays, harmless as kittens."

"Security, prepare another detail—" Federer barked.

Chi interrupted him. "Oh, if you have any more men for us to eat, we're hungry, so you just send them right on over."

Jo's mouth gaped in disbelief.

"Oh, and Captain," Chi said, her face taking on a note of mock sobriety. "I regret to inform you that a fifty-megaton nuclear device is gliding up your exhaust ports toward your main power generator—don't bother trying to find it, it's cloaked. It should be moving into place right about…." she looked off screen, her index finger raised, "…now."

CHAPTER THIRTEEN

The ship was drifting. Jeff always imagined he could feel a bit of weightlessness when they were drifting. It was all in his mind, of course. The artificial gravity worked the same whether they were moving or still. But it still felt different to him.

Before him were his crew, each seated at the large mess table, with Emma directly to his right. There didn't need to be anyone navigating. The ship would alert them if any danger presented itself.

"I called you here to let you know what Commander Nira and I found when we began to investigate Mr. Pho's trajectory anomaly." A couple of them had grabbed coffee or tea, but no one was drinking. All four sets of eyes were on him. He licked his lips.

"We found this," he said. He tossed one of the detonator patches onto the table. He picked it up again and ran one hand along the wires trailing from it.

"What is that?" Mr. Pho asked.

"It's a detonator."

Mr. Pho's eyes were wide.

"A detonator for…what?"

"Four tons of a poly explosive pumped between our secondary and tertiary hulls."

Susie Wall shrank, her eyes darting from side to side.

"Uh…why is there four tons of poly explosive between our hulls?" Pho asked.

"That's a very good question, Mr. Pho, and I'm eager to hear any theories you might have—that anyone might have. That's why I've called you together. Together, the five of us are smarter than any one of us is alone."

Pho nodded, as did Wall. Nira gave him an affirming nod as well. He looked over at Emma, who seemed lost in thought.

"Here's what we've been able to figure out about this," Jeff held up the detonator patch. "It's wired to detonate in proximity to a particular neural serial number."

"Whose?" Pho asked.

"We don't know," Jeff answered. It was a lie, but it was a strategic lie.

"Was there only one detonator patch?" Wall asked.

"Yes, we only found the one," Jeff answered. "Do you think there are more?" He looked at Wall, feigning curiosity.

"No…I mean, I don't know. It's a scary thing. So I'm just…asking questions." Wall looked scared.

"And it's a good question. Commander Nira thought of that, too. These patches are poly, so they're hard to detect—they have no metal and no mass to speak of, so they don't show up on the imager. So we did a physical surveillance of every one of the holes they drilled into the tertiary hull, looking for detonators. This is the only one we found. We looked hard," Jeff gave her a grave nod. "Don't worry, we're sure we got them all."

"That's a relief," she said.

I'll bet it is, Jeff thought.

"Who would do this?" Emma asked. She was pretending to be more out of the loop than she was.

Jeff played along. "As near as we can figure, Captain Daniel Hightower did it."

They all blinked at him.

"Isn't that…your friend?" Pho asked, his Vietnamese face seeming even longer as it registered his surprise.

"Yes. He was my friend. In our universe, he was my best friend… until he was killed." Jeff swallowed. He wished he had gotten himself some coffee. Emma seemed to intuit what was going on and passed him her cup. He accepted it gratefully and drained the lukewarm tea from it. *Shit,* he thought. *I fucking hate tea.* "In this universe, we were friends, too, apparently, until I was killed. But the me from our universe and the Captain Hightower from this universe were *never* friends. I thought I knew who he was. I thought he'd be just like the Danny I…" He looked down at the empty cup in his hands. He put it down. "I was wrong."

He nodded his head a few times. The silence in the mess was almost stifling.

Pho broke it. "Why…why do you think he wants you…us…dead?"

Jeff shook his head, slow and sad. "Son, I have absolutely no idea. The best guess we've got is that whomever this neural serial number belongs to is the real target. Who it belongs to, or how they knew we would ever find her…that's a mystery."

Emma leaned back and stared at him. "How do you know it's a *her*?"

"What?" Jeff asked, blinking.

"You just said, 'how they knew we would ever find her'—how do you know that neural code belongs to a her?"

Jeff's breath caught and his mind raced. He hadn't told Emma about Jo. It would only upset her. "Uh…I—"

Nira's voice interrupted him. "Distribution protocol," she said. "Odd numbered units go to males, even numbered units are assigned to females."

Emma didn't look like she was buying it. "What about transgendered people?"

Nira didn't blink. "You only get the one neural. Its number is assigned with whatever gender you have at the time of implantation."

"Uh-huh…" Emma shot him a look that he took to mean, *We'll talk.*

He didn't look forward to that talk.

"But we're safe now," Pho said, more of a question than a statement.

"Yes, we're safe now," Jeff said. "Unless…"

"Unless?" Wall asked.

"Unless Captain Hightower set some other booby traps for us," Jeff said. No one said anything to that. Once more the ominous silence descended over the table. Jeff glanced at Wall. She was staring at her fingers.

Finally, Emma spoke up. "If we're running around terrified all the time, we're going to mess up. We've got to relax. There was a trap—we found it. We have to trust that we're safe unless and until we find something else. Otherwise we'll be jumping at shadows and second-guessing ourselves all the time. We'll be miserable."

Jeff nodded. That sounded like wisdom. "As FDR said, 'The only thing we have to fear…'" He let the phrase hang in the air.

"…is fear itself," Wall concluded.

Jeff looked around at the confused expressions.

"Who's FDR?" Emma asked.

"President Franklin Delano Roosevelt," Jeff answered.

"There was a President Teddy Roosevelt, but never a Franklin."

"No," Jeff said. "Not in our universe there wasn't." He stared across the table at Susie Wall. "Mr. Wall, perhaps you can explain your familiarity with the quotations of a President we never had?"

Wall's eyes were wide. She sat ramrod straight. Instantly, her eyes rolled up. Jeff didn't know whether she was intending to send a warning message to Sol Station or whether she was intending to detonate the explosive, but it didn't matter—they were ready. Instantly, Commander Nira was behind her. A silver blade flashed in the cold, bright lighting of the mess as Nira drew it across Wall's neck. Blood spewed forth onto the table in front of her. Nira held Wall's head up by the hair for a few seconds, then pitched it forward. Wall's head hit the table with a sickening thud.

"My god," Emma breathed.

Pho leaped back, as much in horror as to avoid the growing pool of blood.

"Mr. Nira, check the communicator's log and make sure you got her before she was able to send any messages," Jeff said.

"Aye, sir," Nira said, wiping her blade on a handkerchief.

"Mr. Pho—" Jeff began. Mr. Pho looked like he was going to be sick. "Resume our course to Epworth Station."

THE SCREEN WENT BLANK, and it seemed that everyone on the bridge began shouting at once. Captain Federer stabbed at the comm unit on his command chair. Over the din, Jo heard him shout, "Find that nuke, goddam it!"

What's chaos and confusion for if you don't make good use of it? Jo asked herself. She lined up her gaoler out of the corner of her eye. Then she took one extra-large step backwards, placing her boot squarely on both of the woman's feet. She swung her elbow back and around as hard as she possibly could, catching the young woman in the ribs, sending her flying backwards. As her elbow completed its follow through, Jo extended her arm and snatched up the blaster as it tumbled backward too.

It was useless without an ID of course, but Jo could certainly use it as a club, and did. The other two security guards flanking both sides of the bridge were only now taking notice of her acrobatics. As if in slow motion she watched their eyes widen and their shoulders slouch as they reached for their guns.

They would be too late. Swinging the blaster by its strap, she aimed the whole of its weight and fury at the captain's chair, catching Federer in the head, and lifting him out of his seat. He fell back into it, but he slouched forward, head gushing, before toppling to the floor.

Once finished with her arc, Jo remained in motion, leaping to the floor and rolling behind a science console. She didn't stop until she was on top of the blonde gaoler. Without even pausing to think or consider or shudder, she took the woman's thumb into her mouth and bit as hard as she could, grinding through muscle, gristle, and bone. The warm, coppery taste of blood filled her mouth, gushing through either side of her lips. She gagged, but kept at it, employing her elbow again to spear the screaming woman's throat to the floor. The gaoler thrashed and hit, but Jo's jaws held fast, grinding, grinding until she felt the last morsel of cartilage snap, and the final shred of soft tissue rip free.

She spat the thumb out, rubbed it on the carpet, and held it on the ID pad, pressing it down with her own. The gun lit up like a navigator's panel. She couldn't hear the whine as it powered up, but she could read the gauge. Out of the corner of her eye she saw one of the security men come into view, and reflexively she shot his legs out from under him. She shot again, more carefully, aiming for his falling head. She felt the kick of the blaster as the man's brains sprayed across the far wall.

As far as she knew there was only one other armed person on the bridge, though surely more security would be on the way. She pushed the thought aside and rose, eyes darting, lighting on the final security officer.

She must be quite a sight, she knew. She rose slowly from behind the console, blood streaming from both sides of her mouth, covering her chin, creating a crimson beard on her white paper jumpsuit. Her eyes shone with berserk brilliance as her lips turned up into the dreadful grin of ecstatic battle. The bloodlust raced through her veins. She reveled in it. She loved it. It was better than Morphex. And she knew without a moment's reflection or regret that she would be chasing this high again and again for the rest of her days.

Jo squeezed the trigger and watched the young man's eyes widen. Saw him quail, saw him fall as his abdomen exploded, saw his guts tumble out of him onto the immaculate charcoal carpet beneath him.

There was no one to oppose her now, and no time to waste. She jumped onto the captain's chair and squatted there, with her feet on the cushion, poised like a cat ready to pounce. The blaster hung between her legs, one thumb on her grisly trigger.

Nearly every crew member was standing, their backs to their consoles, staring at her in open-mouthed horror…all except for one man, who kept pressing a square on his console and shouting for security. Jo aimed for his legs and grinned again as he screamed and writhed on the floor.

When the bridge door swung open, she wasn't surprised. If it was to be her end, she was content with that. She had mastered her enemy. She had exacted her revenge, no matter how fleeting. But from the corner of her eye she saw not the black uniforms of the Authority, but red. Blood red.

There is a God, she thought, as her own security men fanned out around her, their own stolen blasters at the ready. Jo wiped the blood from her chin onto the back of her hand as she looked every member of the Authority crew in the eyes, feeding on their disgust but gorging on their terror.

She met the eyes of the communicator. He gulped. "Communicator, what is your name?"

"Prescott, sir."

"Mr. Prescott, open a ship-wide channel."

"Y-y-yes, sir." He fumbled at his panel, then turned back to her and nodded. "Channel opened, sir."

"Greetings to the crew of the *Eisenhower.* This is RFC Captain Joleen Taylor. Your captain is dead and your bridge is under my command. This ship…is *my* ship. You will not underestimate me or my people. I am a tiger. I fucking *eat* people."

She watched the eyes of the Authority bridge crew as she said it. *These people,* she thought, *these people, at least, know that I am telling the literal truth.*

"But I am not a monster," she continued. She cocked her head compassionately, not losing eye contact, not ceasing for a second her maniacal grin. "I am going to spare your lives. You have exactly four minutes to get to an escape pod. Anyone not launched in a pod four minutes from now will be shot on sight. I suggest you not test me on this, because I will fucking hunt you down and shoot you myself. And I will enjoy it. Captain out."

She watched the light on the comm button wink out. The bridge crew remained frozen in front of her. "That means you, assholes," she said. "Run—before I pounce on you and rip the arteries from your neck with my own teeth."

EPILOGUE

There were probably nicer restaurants on Epworth Station, but Jeff doubted he would feel comfortable at any of them. The one he picked was already two stars above his standard fare, and they had accommodated his request for a private room without hesitation.

Despite his crew's shock over Wall's betrayal—and execution—they seemed to be bouncing back. Nira was laughing—an unnatural sight that would take some getting used to—and Pho seemed downright gregarious. Emma was cautiously upbeat. She met his eyes, but her smile was tentative. She knew something was up, and it seemed like she sensed she wasn't going to like it.

She was right, and Jeff felt his stomach tighten. He had good news and bad news, and he didn't really know where to start.

A few minutes after they'd been seated, a waiter came by to fill their glasses. He wore a scarlet suit, from foot to head, and was so poised Jeff wanted to give him a push just to see how he'd cope with being off balance. Instead, he chose to respect the man's dignity, however affected it might be.

Just beyond their table was a large window, running floor to ceiling. Beyond was the Epworth space dock. It was an impressive view.

"What are those?" Pho asked, pointing to a stack of yellowed, ancient paperbacks at Jeff's right hand.

"Books," Jeff smiled. "It's…a bit of a hobby."

"Do you collect antiques?" Nira asked.

"Uh…not really. More like I consume them."

"You actually *read* those old things?" Nira looked shocked. "Can't you find those on the Lookup?"

"I probably could," Jeff said. "But the medium is…novel." He grinned at the pun. No one else seemed to get it. It didn't matter. "I like the feel of the book in my hand. I like the smell of the paper. I like coming across the printing flaws and errors. It's…I guess it makes me feel connected to the past. It makes me feel…human."

"Is there any doubt that you're human?" Nira asked, picking up a butter knife and holding it out defensively in front of her. "Anything you need to tell us, Captain?"

Pho laughed, and Nira couldn't stop the smile from breaking out across her face.

Jeff sighed. It was good to see them like this. They were letting off some steam, enjoying themselves, feeling safe and hopeful for the first time since…since their world had ended. It was good for them, and Jeff was glad of it.

But there was business to attend to. He bided his time until they had ordered. Jeff wondered if he could anticipate their selections, but he was mostly wrong. He'd expected Emma to order a salad, but instead, she'd selected BBQ ribs and slaw. He hadn't seen that coming. Nira chose a Thai dish he'd never heard of, while Pho chose a Brazilian Paella. Jeff shook his head and ordered steak and potatoes. He was not an imaginative eater and he made no apologies for it.

Once the waiter exited the room, Jeff put his elbows on the table and cleared his throat. "I guess you're all wondering what the plan is."

"I'm hoping there is one," Emma said. She was not quite smiling, hovering on the lip of approval and its opposite, waiting him out.

"We're in a new world," Jeff said. That was obvious to all of them. He looked down at the silver in front of him. "And it's not our world. I…I can't tell you where your allegiances should lie here. And you need to be free to choose them. Our old…obligations are moot. You don't owe anything further to me or to the CDF…because there is no CDF. Not here, not any more."

When his words stopped, there was dead silence. Six eyes were on him, Pho's mouth was open. He wished the young man would close it, but there was always something about the kid that unsettled him—his elfin appearance, or the awkwardness of his movements…it was always something.

"We all need to make a new start. You can go to Authority space, you can join up with the rebellion. You can…hell, get a plot of land and be a farmer. Teach. Start a family. Do…whatever you want to do. I release you. There's a whole new world here," he waved at the space dock outside their window. "Go and explore it."

"With what cash?" Emma asked. She crossed her arms and her brow was furrowed. She wasn't liking this one bit, and that made Jeff uncomfortable. Not that he'd expected her to like it. It was, in fact, what he was dreading most.

Jeff took three chit cards from his pocket and put them in the middle of the table. "We've all been exploring the station—and I hope you've enjoyed it. I haven't just been buying paperbacks, though. I've been busy…arranging some business."

Emma raised one eyebrow, which Jeff took to mean, *What business?*

"As you might expect, four tons of poly explosive is worth a good deal of money. Even if the buyer has to extract it, it's worth more than any of us would make in our lifetimes. And then the ship…that's worth a good deal, too. I have…I've sold both."

There was an eruption of protest and alarm. Jeff held his hand up for silence. When he got it, he continued, "The ship is still at our dock and you have twenty-four hours of access to collect your effects."

They all visibly relaxed. He should have led with that…but then how would he…never mind. He got there. They're fine. So far. Jeff took a deep breath. He waved toward the chit cards. "I opened bank accounts for all of you in your legal names—you can change those if you want, of course, but it was expedient. These cards will give you access until you can square your neural registrations with the networks here. And if you lose them, don't worry—they're cross-registered with your neural serial numbers at the bank, the…" he looked up, remembering, "Dogstar Credit System. There are two or three major banks here, but Dogstar seems to be the biggest and most reliable—I checked it out. There's a Dogstar portal on every level of this place, and I even remember seeing the name on Sol Station, so it's not even confined to neutral space or the rebellion, or…wherever. Your money will be secure."

"How much money are we talking about?" Nira asked.

Jeff smiled for the first time. Finally, some good news. "You'll never need to work again, unless you want to."

"Take me to a planet with beaches," Pho said, his face breaking out into something that looked a lot like joy.

"Some of you will have family here," Jeff said. "You can find them."

"Some of us have doppelgängers here," Emma said. "Which makes family complicated."

"True," Jeff said.

"What about Wall?" Nira asked.

"What about Wall?" Jeff asked.

"The Wall you killed wasn't our Wall," she said. "Our Wall is still being held by the Authority."

Jeff nodded. "I opened an account for her, too, and sent her a secure message. She'll be able to access it with her neural serial number."

"If she ever gets out of jail."

"They'll let her out, if they haven't already. They have no use for her now." Jeff sounded more sure than he felt. But it did make sense. Besides, there was little he could do about it at the moment.

"What's she going to do?" Nira asked.

Jeff shrugged. "I sent her a message saying…pretty much what I'm saying to you now. She'll do…anything she wants."

"And what are *you* going to do?" Emma asked.

She still had her arms crossed. Her lips were tight. She didn't look angry, exactly…not yet, anyway.

Jeff looked away.

"I see." Now she looked angry. He could feel her eyes drilling him. "Could we have a moment alone, Captain?"

Pho was looking at the ceiling. Nira was studying the lines in her palm. The tension in the room was so thick Jeff felt like he was going to suffocate on it. Jeff rolled his eyes but scooted back from the table.

As soon as they were out of earshot, Emma whirled on him. "You're going to *her,* aren't you?"

She wasn't wrong. He knew he had to find Jo, but he didn't know why.

"It's not her, you know. You do know that, right?" Emma asked. "She's no more your Jo than Captain Hightower was your Danny."

Jeff knew it. She was right. And still, it didn't matter.

"Jeff, I'm right here. And it's me. It's really me. I'm *your* Emma."

There was so much packed into that word *your*. It was possessive in every sense.

Emma waited, her eyes fixed on him. He looked back at the table, then back at her. He met her eyes and held them. His face softened into an apologetic frown. He was sorry, really and truly sorry. But the fact was the fact. He had been struggling with it since they'd arrived in this universe. He *had* to go to her.

But not yet. "I'm not going to deny it, Emma. Yes, I need to seek Jo out…sometime. Sometime…yes, yes, I will. But first…first I need to find someone else."

Emma cocked her head.

"WELL, THAT WAS A CLASS A CRAP-EFFORT," Tal said.

Captain Daniel Hightower stood at attention before the admiral's desk. He did not deny it. He did not say anything.

"What happened?"

"They must have detected the explosive, sir—"

"You idiot, I know *what* happened." Tal pounded his desk with one balled brown fist. "I want to know *why*."

"I can't say why, sir. We got an encoded message from Wall saying that they discovered a flight path anomaly—probably from uneven weight distribution of the explosive."

"Or maybe someone forgot to change the payload weight defaults."

"That's unlikely, but…it's possible."

"It's more than possible," Tal looked up and blinked, sending Hightower a report. "It's what fucking happened."

"So…if you know *why*…?" Hightower began.

"Because, Captain, I want to fucking hear you say it!"

Danny bit down on his tongue to hold it. Sweat began to bead on his forehead.

"Have you recovered your man?"

"Wall, sir?"

"Yes, fucking Wall."

Danny shook his head.

"What was that, Captain?"

"No, sir, Admiral sir!" Danny shouted.

"That's better." Tal swiveled in his chair and rubbed at his eyes. "And why haven't you recovered Ensign Wall?"

"We don't know what happened to her, sir. One minute her signal was there, and the next…well, it just wasn't."

"And that tells you what?"

"That she's either offline or she's dead, sir."

"So what's your best guess?"

"She could be offline. Maybe they're holding her in the brig."

"But we know they've reached Epworth Station. And our eyes and ears there report no sign of Wall."

"True." Danny blinked. "In all likelihood, she's dead."

"So what are we going to do with *their* Wall?"

"Kill her, sir?"

Tal blinked. "You really are a sociopathic monster, aren't you? The only thing standing between you and galactic genocide is your rank. God help us." Tal looked away.

Danny felt heat rising on his neck. He said nothing.

"She's not a spy. She's not even a fucking threat." He sighed. "Give her a ticket to Epworth Station and let's wash our hands of this whole affair."

Danny said nothing.

"Is that understood, Captain?"

"Sir, yes sir."

"No tricks, no underhanded passive-aggressive schemes. Just release her, give her a ticket and wave bye-bye."

"Yes sir."

"That's an order."

"I understand, sir."

"Don't test me, Captain."

"No, sir." Danny waited a few moments. The time seemed to crawl by. "Will that be all, sir?"

"No, that will not be all."

Tal was angry about something else, it seemed. Danny took a deep breath, fortifying himself against the next onslaught.

"Have you read about the defeat at Aken?"

"It's all over the news, sir. I've read the classified reports, too." Danny chanced a glance directly at the admiral. Finally, something that wasn't his fault. "Hell of a thing, sir."

"Your ex, rebel captain Jo Taylor—"

"She's captain, now? I mean, not acting-captain?"

"Our sources say it was a field promotion, but that it came from the top, from Alinto herself."

Danny nodded. *Good for Jo*, he thought, but didn't say it.

"As I was saying," Tal said, an edge returning to his voice.

"Sorry, sir."

"Your ex, Captain Jo Taylor, has won herself the distinction of becoming public enemy number one."

Danny nodded. Those were the admiral's words, but the news of her victory over the *Eisenhower*—and the subsequent turning of the battle into a humiliating defeat for Authority forces—was all that the news feeds could talk about.

"Have you seen this?" Tal tripped a switch on his desk console and a display lit up, hovering over the desk in the space between them. It was a holographic political cartoon showing Jo—looking bustier and sexier than he ever remembered her—as a giant, astride two starships, rodeo-style, with one foot planted on each ship. She held the reins taut in her left hand, while her right waved a nautical captain's cap behind her. Her mouth was open in a howl of victory, and blood smeared her mouth like an explosion of mashed lipstick, covering her chin.

"No, sir. I haven't seen that…not until now."

"My fellow admirals are not happy about this. She caught us with our pants around our ankles. We look like idiots."

"Yes, sir."

"She needs to pay."

"Yes, sir."

"*You* need to *make* her pay." Tal stood and leaned over his desk, his head jutting through the cartoon, his eyes dark and mean.

"Yes sir." So that was it. Well, he didn't know what to do with shame, but he certainly knew what to do with an order. That such an order entailed killing a woman he had once been intimate with bothered him not at all. There was a sweetness to the notion that he had never felt before. He savored it. It made his heart rate jump. It made him hard. He grinned. "With pleasure, sir."

THE OBLIVION SAGA • BOOK 3

OBLIVION QUEST

J.R. MABRY & B.J. WEST

Love is the enemy of efficiency.
—*Gerald May*

CHAPTER ONE

We were wrong to suffer them to exist for so long.
They are dangerous. They must be controlled.
We have been controlling them. It has not worked well.
But they are as we were. They have potential.
They must be destroyed.
No, he must be destroyed. Kill the one who learned.
How? There is nothing we can do that he cannot.
We must act.
We must not act.

[STRING 311]

"This just arrived for you, sir."

Captain Jo Taylor had been on her way to the bridge. She stopped and faced the ensign who had called out to her. The young woman didn't meet her eyes—didn't dare—which Jo understood but didn't like. The ensign held out a small package which Jo received, head cocked. She looked at the tracking code, and her eyebrows raised.

Central Command on Devonshire Base to Shams Outpost, then by courier drone to the *Talon*. Jo looked at the young ensign and nodded her thanks. "Duly delivered, Ensign. On your way."

"Yes sir," the ensign smiled her relief and almost ran down the cramped corridor of the battle cruiser.

Jo tucked the package under her arm and continued her journey. Stepping onto the bridge, she hesitated as everyone stood. "Captain on deck," Shell Ditka shouted.

"As you were," Jo said. Her B-team commander vacated the captain's chair and stood by at parade rest.

"You are relieved for the day, Mr. Bourgeois," Jo said.

"Thank you, sir." Bourgeois' face was unreadable.

Jo scowled at him. Sometimes she hated military formality. "Got any plans?"

"I plan to continue my study of the logs of the *Eisenhower* sir. I hope to have a report for you by this time tomorrow."

"Excellent," Jo said. "But I also need you rested. By all means, spend an hour on your report, but…don't spend more than that. Do something fun. That's an order."

"Yes sir."

"Get out of here." She waved toward the door.

"Yes sir."

She surveyed her prime crew, all of them in their places, all of them rested and ready. A vast starfield filled the main viewer, motion detectable only at the outer edges of the screen. A sense of order and rightness washed over her and she stood a little straighter. She was about to sit down, but then remembered the package under her arm. "I'll be in my ready room, Mr. Liebert. You have the conn."

"Aye sir," Liebert said, smiling but not looking at her.

Jo stepped into the small room that was her on-duty sanctuary. She pulled at a red poly tab and peeled the lid off the package. Then she cocked her head again as a furry green plush toy fell out of it, landing with a slight bounce on the table.

Jo picked it up and turned it over. *A stuffed animal? Who in the world would send me a stuffed animal?* Then she saw that actually it was a stuffed vegetable. Jo raised one eyebrow as she held it aloft by one tiny arm. It was, in fact, a peapod, about twenty-five centimeters long, forest green, with large goofy eyes and a sewn-in smile. There were also two biologically incorrect arms with white-gloved hands emerging from the middle of the pod.

A note had also fallen out. She picked it up and read it.

Sweet Pea,

Don't forget to do something out of the ordinary on your birthday.

Love,

Grandma Taylor

Jo smiled. Her paternal grandmother had called her "sweet pea" since she was a little girl, and never stopped, even after she joined the military, after graduating from officer's academy with honors, after rising up through the ranks. To Granny Taylor, Jo would always be a little girl in pigtails, her *sweet pea.* In a life that required her to constantly be so hard, having that touch of softness was a welcome respite.

She tucked the poly tab in the box and set it aside. She sat in one of the chairs and tried to make the plush toy sit up. Surprisingly, she found it had a little pocket of beads sewn into its veggie derriere, and it sat up quite handily. Jo glanced at the plushy peapod. Her grandmother was the only family she had left, and practically the only family she'd ever had. Keeping her safe had been a large part of why Jo had joined the military in the first place, putting herself on the line to stand between her and the Authority, keeping the wolves far away from hearth and home.

As she was discovering, there was no shortage of wolves. She strode back onto the bridge. "Reports, Mr. Liebert?"

"All in, sir."

"Can you give me a summary?"

"Nothing out of the ordinary, sir."

Now it was the waiting. Since the Battle of Aken, the Authority had withdrawn—presumably to lick their wounds. That was fine with Jo, but she knew it would be a temporary reprieve. The Authority was not going to back off just because some rookie female captain had handed them their asses. They would regroup and be back with a vengeance. Jo had no doubt of that.

In the meantime, she was not sorry to be given a more pedestrian assignment. There had been a slew of pirate attacks on merchant vessels near neutral space, and they had been assigned a caravan to escort. Jo knew very well she was no slouch in battle, but she didn't relish the danger. She could get used to assignments like this.

She went to the wall dispensary and punched in the code for Mayan hot chocolate, adding the rider for extra cayenne pepper. She carried it back to her command chair and set it in the shallow well that would keep it from spilling should they hit any minor turbulence.

She looked up and accessed her neural, calling down the reports, and began to go through them methodically. They were routine, and all seemed in good shape, and her mind quickly wandered.

She thought about Captain Telouse. He had been kind to her. She flashed on the image of his corpse lying side-by-side with dead Authority police, and a knot twisted up in her gut.

She'd been pressed into command duty before she'd gotten a chance to figure out who killed him or why. The Captain had said they were there to meet a contact—an old flame of his, as she understood it. And they were there on RFC orders…or at least with permission. Well, which was it?

I'm the captain now, she thought. *Jacques is dead. His records are no longer privileged.*

She looked up and blinked, navigating on her neural to the captain's command communications. She'd start there and then move on to his personal log. No one on the bridge would know she was doing anything but reading reports, if they cared. The only one who might discover what she was accessing was Liebert, and she didn't need to explain herself to him. And even if she did…her crew would understand. Everyone had been fond of Captain Telouse—everyone but Shallit, and Shallit was nothing but an icy-cold gas bag floating somewhere in deep space thirty-two parsecs away.

She saw a blinking blue light in her peripheral vision, and looked up to access the new message. It was another birthday greeting—this one from Palamar. She had known Palamar since her academy days. On the one hand, he was a creepy old man who kept his formidable secrets a little too close to his vest. On the other hand, he was funny, avuncular, and one of her oldest friends.

"I have an errand to run," Jo said. "Mr. Chi, you have the conn."

Jo made her way to supply, where Palamar served as senior boatswain in charge of supplies. As soon as she stepped through the door of his office, the old man brightened, and whatever dark cloud had been hovering over him disappeared. "Out, everyone, out. The birthday girl is here."

There were two ensigns standing in front of his desk with datapads. Both were hesitant to leave—Jo surmised that it was because they had not yet gotten what they needed from Supply. She hated to interrupt them—they were, after all, working for her.

"Please take five," she assured them, looking them each in the eye in turn and touching their shoulders. "You'll still get what you need."

Both uttered some form of "Yes sir" and scuttled from the room.

"To what do I owe this pleasure, Sunshine?" Palamar stretched his arms to their full length and then put them behind his head.

"I hear you have a surprise for me," she said.

"Surprising you is one of my chief joys in life."

"Got that right," she sat and rocked side to side in the swiveling chair.

Palamar opened a drawer in his desk and took out a box. There was no ornamental wrapping, just a loosely-tied tangle of red poly, obviously left over from some kind of packaging.

"You suck at the gift-wrapping thing. You know that, right?"

"Just open it."

She tugged at the poly, but it pretty much just fell off of its own accord. Jo opened the box and pulled forth an old-fashioned bottle.

"What is this?"

"Whisky. Single malt scotch. Glenfiddich Albert Miser Reserve, 2137. This baby trades for about 14,000 chits."

"What the fuck, Palamar? How did you get this?"

"Ah..." he scratched at his head. "Let's say it was tangled up in another deal and there's no way I can ever move it without getting in legal trouble. More than that you don't need to know."

"Uh-huh. So basically, you just want me to drink your evidence."

"It's the best damn contraband you'll ever put to your lips, I can promise you that."

Jo cocked her head. "Hey, Palamar, what do you know about Admiral Alinto?"

"Ah...your new boss. Trying to figure her out?"

"Something like that, yeah."

"Well, let's see." He looked up, as if he were accessing his neural, but he seemed to just be thinking. "The word is, she's an eccentric. When she warms up to you, she gets kind of *familiar*—but don't let it fool you. She's tough as nails and sharp as a diamond. But she does go out of her way for the human touch, especially when she's giving orders. At least...that's what I've heard." He leaned in. "But I hear a lot. Most of it's right."

"Thanks," she said.

"Hey, the whiskey was a gift, the intel is going to cost you."

"Like hell." She laughed. "I don't know what to do with you, Palamar. I don't know whether to kiss you or throw you into the brig."

He smiled at her and reached for the bottle. He cracked the wax seal and pulled two glasses from his desk. "I prefer the kiss, in case you're wondering."

"Will you ever fucking grow up?"

He poured two fingers and slid it to her. Then he poured one for himself. "There are two things about me that are immutable," he said.

She sipped from her glass and her eyes went wide. Her mouth exploded with smoky complexity and water came to her eyes. She wiped her mouth on the back of her sleeve and set the glass down as if it were an explosive device. "Oh, yeah?" she asked, trying not to cough. "What are those?"

"I will do *anything* for a chit, and I am *always* on your side."

JEFF ROUNDED THE CORNER, then hugged the wall of the mall corridor. *That*, he told himself, *was hard*.

He and his crew had escaped Sol Station, only to be nearly killed on their way to neutral space. *Murdered*, he corrected himself. But none of that seemed as difficult as what he had just done. He had told his crew—and his girlfriend, Emma—that he was going his own way. Temporarily, he had said, but that hadn't made it any easier. None of them had been happy about it. And Emma—

Emma stepped around the corner and crossed her arms. "Thought you'd just slip away between courses, did you?" She leveled a gaze at him that could atomize planets.

Jeff looked around for an escape route. There were plenty, but unless he wanted to be seen being chased by a woman scorned… He looked at his shoes. "I thought it would be easiest."

"It's certainly the most cowardly." She was rock-solid, her gaze unwavering. Jeff could almost feel the heat radiating from her angry core.

"I'm trying to protect you," he said, but couldn't bring himself to meet her eyes as he said it.

"Uh-huh. By leaving us alone and vulnerable in an unfamiliar universe. The logic of that is impeccable."

Jeff could feel himself about to sweat. A trio of young people—engineers, from the look of their uniforms—approached and passed, talking to one another in gregarious, animated tones. Jeff waited until they were past earshot. "I'm…I have to—"

"You have to go to *her*. I know."

"I have to find the shaman."

Emma jerked back slightly. He had surprised her. He'd almost confessed it to the whole crew but didn't want to try to explain. But

Emma knew about the little man from Peru. He saw that he'd caught her off guard, so he pressed his point. "I can't explain why it's important…I just know that it is."

"So, let me get this straight: You're suddenly feeling your metaphysical oats, so chasing after some guru is more important than making sure your crew—whom you brought from another universe, remember—is safe and gainfully employed?"

Well, since you put it like that, Jeff thought. He didn't know how to answer her. "Emma, I know how it looks. This isn't about personal fulfillment. My gut tells me he knows something. Something…vital. Something we need to know."

"Then why is he playing cat-and-mouse? Why not just come to you and tell you?"

Jeff looked away again. "I don't know that." A thought struck him. "Maybe seeking is part of the finding."

"See there? That's what I hate about metaphysics. Nonsense."

"Emma, I have to go. You have to…let me go." He finally looked up at her.

Fire flashed in her eyes. "I can't stop you. I know that. Even Nira can't stop you, and she would if she could. Did you see her, by the way? She's crushed. Not just at your abandonment, but by the weight of responsibility. It's all falling on her shoulders now. She's a stormy little raincloud back there. On the surface she's studying the dessert menu, but on the inside she's about ready to kick someone's throat in. Preferably yours."

"You'd like that, wouldn't you?"

"It would provide a great deal of momentary satisfaction, yes it would," she agreed. Her arms were still crossed over her breasts, like battle armor.

"I'm sorry," Jeff said, looking her in the eye. He hoped she would see his sincerity.

"No, you're not," she said, speaking the truth of it. Her eye pierced him, deep, pinning him to his place like a butterfly on a spreading board. "But I'll tell you what you are…"

Here it comes, he steeled himself.

"You don't trust anyone but yourself. Hell, I don't know if you even trust yourself, but you sure as hell don't trust anyone else."

"That's not true. I don't want to endanger them any further—"

"That's such utter bullshit. Listen to yourself. Sticking together is the safest thing we can do. Throwing us to the four winds—"

"I'm not throwing you—"

"Shut the fuck up, I'm not finished."

Jeff shut up.

"Throwing us to the four winds is the most selfish, irresponsible act I can imagine right now. You want to go see your shaman? Fine. Let's all go. Maybe we can all benefit from a bit of his ego-transcending enlightenment crap. I'm game! But you can't handle that, because you have to be the tough guy who goes it alone—"

"That's not fair—"

"You're damn right it's not fair!"

Emma was yelling now, and other pedestrians were starting to stare at them as they passed in the hall. She looked at the floor, hugged herself and waited for her passion to die down a bit. Then she resumed, at a lower decibel. "We are not expendable," she said. "We're your team. You need us as much as we need you."

Jeff couldn't hear any more. Inside, he fought back against her reasoning. He felt himself starting to panic. He was sweating now. His own anger was rising, and he knew if he endured any more, he'd lash out. That would be bad. He breathed deeply a few times, stilling his mind, willing himself to be calm. He met her eyes and gave her a sad smile. Then he kissed her cheek. Then he walked away.

"Asshole!" she shouted after him.

He kept walking.

"You coward!" she yelled. People were staring again.

He kept walking, ignoring the eyes following him from all sides of the mall corridor.

"Fuck you! Fuck fuck fuck—fuck you!" she shouted again. He cringed. He'd rather face a battlefield filled with alien hostiles than an angry woman of Emma's caliber. He couldn't dismiss her—she was smarter than he was. He couldn't argue with her—she was more articulate than he was. The only thing he could do was escape her.

"Goodbye, Emma," he said out loud, although no one could hear it. His gut churned with the incompleteness of it all, the accusations, the betrayal. "What a royal fucking mess," he said out loud, but whether he was referring to the situation or himself he wasn't completely sure.

DANNY PERCHED on a stool at a small and awkwardly tall table in the back of the bar, sipping unenthusiastically on the worst sazerac he had ever tasted. That it was terrible didn't surprise him; what did was that a sleazy dive like this one had absinthe at all. It didn't really matter though, as he wasn't there to drink.

The bartender had directed him to the table in back, saying that his contact would meet him there when she arrived. This also surprised Danny. Flynn hadn't said anything about his contact being a woman. It seemed unlikely, considering the nature of the business he was soliciting. He kept watch on the door, taking stock of each new customer who wandered in. They were typical clientele for a dive bar in the grimy lower decks—cargo handlers, mechanics, and other laborer types—probably just off a shift on the docks.

Then she walked in, at first just a silhouette against the smoky glow of the promenade outside. She couldn't have been more out of place if she had three heads. Easily the tallest woman Danny had ever seen, ducking slightly as she came through the doorway, long slender legs gliding beneath a calf length sack dress. Her long blonde hair shimmered in the few lights that hung from the ceiling as she walked with the elegance of a runway model toward the bar. Her small but perky breasts jiggled freely under her dress.

It couldn't be, I'm not that lucky, Danny thought. But the day was full of surprises. She inclined her head slightly as she talked to the bartender, then he pointed directly at Danny. She turned to follow his finger, then began striding directly toward him. Danny smiled.

She paused at the table, towering over Danny. She had to be at least seven feet tall. The height of the table suddenly made sense. He could also now see that she wasn't human. Her skin looked smooth, hard like a shell, and was a pale mint green. Her eyes were almost comically oversized, like a cartoon version of a sexy woman, white saucers with a black dot like an iris, but which appeared to be painted on the surface. Below that, her lower face, with a tiny nose and full red lips, appeared to be some kind of a mask.

"Well aren't you a tall drink of water…" Danny said, leering.

She stared back at him a moment, showing no emotion, then the mouth on the mask began to move. "No, I am quite solid," she said in a clear, almost musical voice with just a hint of smoky raspiness that Danny found very nice. "I am Amberline, and I was told you wish to discuss business."

Danny watched the plump lips move, mesmerized. He didn't care if they weren't real, he was already imagining them wrapped around his cock. "I can think of many kinds of business we should discuss." Was she ignoring the innuendo, or did she not get it? Either way, she gave no response, simply standing motionless. He gestured to the stool next to her. "Have a seat."

"I prefer to stand."

Danny shrugged. He didn't really care either way, and with her standing, her protruding nipples were right at his eye level, which was just fine with him. "Are you sure you are the, uh, person I'm supposed to meet? I'm looking for someone to do some work for me, and it could be a bit…rough."

She nodded slightly. "Yes, I am here to arrange contract services. I was told you need someone who is not concerned with the legality of the work done."

"That's a good way to put it." He tore his eyes away from her tits and stared into her unblinking eyes. It seemed unlikely she was working for the cops, local or otherwise. He usually had a pretty good sense of whether someone was square or not, and he decided to go for it. "I need two people tailed. I want someone watching them at all times, and I want updates as to where they are. They are currently in Authority custody, but should be released any minute now."

Amberline nodded. "Understood. That doesn't sound as challenging as you implied."

Danny smiled. "That's not all there is. I also need something retrieved and put into secure storage until I call for it again."

"That can be arranged. What is the nature of the item?"

"A woman."

"Human?"

"Yes."

Amberline inclined her head slightly, reminding Danny of a confused dog. "Yes. Kidnapping is most definitely illegal."

Danny laughed. "Yes, yes it is. That won't be a problem, will it?"

The corner of her mouth turned up in a slight smile. "No, it will not. But it will not be inexpensive."

He nodded. "Yeah, I figured as much."

"Is she also in custody?"

"No, she's free, on Epworth station. I can give you her neural ID; she should be easy to track."

Amberline brushed a lock of hair out of her eye. "When would you prefer that she be obtained?"

"As soon as possible, but at your discretion, of course."

She nodded. "Do you have a preference where she will be held?"

"No, just stash her somewhere nobody else can find her and keep her there till I call for her."

She stood motionless for a moment. Danny watched her breasts rise and fall with her breath while he waited. After a moment, she stirred, and the artificial mouth began to move again.

"Very well. The surveillance will cost you 1,000 per person, per day, plus expenses. "

Danny nodded agreement. "And the... uh, the other thing?"

"100,000 for the initial acquisition, plus 1,000 per day for her care."

Danny winced. He knew it was going to hurt, but not that much. He considered the leverage this was going to provide him, how much it would hurt Jeff, and it suddenly didn't feel pricey at all. He smiled savagely, nodded, and pulled a datachip from his pocket. It was an antique, a relic from before the advent of the neural, and the de facto currency of criminals, since it was untraceable.

"This is linked to an anonymous account with more than enough funds to cover your needs for at least a month. The relevant neural codes are on there too."

Amberline produced an equally old reader from somewhere inside her dress and inserted the chip. She waited patiently for the green light that indicated the transaction had cleared, then smiled.

"Is there anything else you need?"

Danny grinned. "Funny you should mention that. What exactly are you?"

Amberline frowned slightly. "I don't understand."

"Your, uh, your species?"

"Ah. Humans call my people Alverians."

"And you *are* female, yes?"

"Yes."

He leered at her. "You've got a nice rack for a bug. How much for a go?"

"A go?"

"Yeah, you and me in a quiet room somewhere, some music, some drinks, and I get you out of that dress and see what's going on underneath…"

Amberline stared. "You want to mate with me?"

Danny was practically drooling. "Yeah. How much?"

She threw her head back and laughed loudly, mockingly. Then with a wicked smile she shook her head. "Our parts would not be… *compatible*."

"I bet we could make it work. How incompatible could it be?"

Still smiling, she gestured her long arm towards her crotch. "It has teeth."

CHAPTER TWO

Jeff lifted his hand and discovered that if he pressed hard enough, he could erase parts of the room. He pressed and wiped upwards, and the keypad blurred into the wall. He wiped a few more times, and all trace of it disappeared.

That's amazing, *he thought and turned his attention to the window. It was as if he were sweeping a number of items off of a counter. With the motion of his hand and a little pressure, the window was gone. First it was just a blurry smudge, then it blended into the white expanse of the wall.*

Fascinated, he kept at it, working his way around the room, wiping away all traces of the vents, the doorframe, the door, the wall monitor, until his gaze was an uninterrupted field of peaceful, blessed white.

"The color of death," he heard a voice say from over his left shoulder.

He turned to look, but no one was there.

Nothing was there. He turned and turned again. Then he felt his pulse quicken. He had wiped away every feature in this room. He had wiped away every exit from this room—he couldn't get out and no one else could get in.

Frantically, he began to search for any cracks, any omissions in his suicidal art project. Just a line would be enough—he'd find a way to widen it, he'd find a way to fit through the cracks...

JEFF AWOKE WITH A START. Hovering over him was a puffy, elderly man with sagging jowls and a sneer. His nose was drinker's red, and Jeff could see the veins clinging to its surface like spiders. His eyebrows were six months out from their last reasonable trim, and flakes of skin clung to his forehead. Clearly, this was not a well man.

But he was a familiar man. "Admiral Jennings," he said reflexively.

"Ha!" the man snorted, "In what universe?"

"Mine, actually," Jeff said. He sat up and leaned against the wall behind him. He reflexively pulled the bedclothes around himself. Was he dressed? He felt around under the blanket. No, dammit.

"You been following me," Jennings said.

"How did you get in here?" Jeff asked, beginning to collect his wits.

Jennings ignored the question. "I don't much like being followed."

"I don't blame you."

"So why are you following me?"

"That's a long story."

"I got twenty-four hours before the *Annabel Lee* is ready to leave space dock and no money to spend on Nancy Boys or the holo." He grinned. "So entertain me. Especially if you're buying the whiskey."

"I think I can manage that," Jeff said. "Um...do you mind giving me a bit of privacy?"

"I do, actually. I'd like to see you naked."

"And I'd like to clock you so hard you'll see red until Wednesday." Jeff narrowed his eyes.

Jennings' billowy eyebrows rose and his puffy lips pursed. "That's the way it is, is it?"

"Wait in the hall and don't be an asshole, and I'll buy you all the whiskey you can stomach."

"And what do I got to do for you?" he sneered. "Since you won't do for me?"

"I'll talk and you'll listen."

"That's it?"

"Maybe."

Jennings scowled. "I'll be in the hall," he said, and turned toward the door.

The door. It was there. The blessed door. Jeff felt something in his gut relax. As soon as Jennings was clear of the room, Jeff leaped up and threw on his clothes, slightly sour from the day before. He sniffed at his shirt before he put it on. He'd need to grab the rest of his gear from the *Kepler* before the clock ran out.

Jeff snatched up the rest of his effects from the nightstand. He wondered if perhaps Jennings might have snatched something before he woke, but everything was there. He splashed some water on his face and looked at his own eyes in the mirror. *I'm looking at a traitor,* he thought.

He reached for a towel and wiped his face.

Not a traitor. Not a traitor, he told himself. *Decisive, maybe. Expedient.*

But that's not what his eyes said. It's not what Emma's eyes would say, either. He pushed the thought aside. He couldn't afford to second-guess himself. Not now.

He exited his hotel pod, hearing the door slide shut behind him.

Jennings sized him up. "You're taller than I thought you were," he said.

"Meaner, too," Jeff said, starting off down the hall.

"I'm not mean," Jennings said. "I'm thirsty."

"It's eight o'clock in the morning," Jeff said.

"There's no sunrise or sunset in space," Jennings countered. "It's always happy hour."

"It's weird," Emma said. "This was our ship. And now it's not." She had never felt any fondness for the place before. It was all military grays, with a utilitarian design that yielded not an inch to aesthetics. She supposed it did have an aesthetic of a sort, but not any kind that spoke to her. It was cold, efficient, but also inhuman. "I'm having a hard time sorting out how I feel about this," she said out loud, although to no one in particular. "I am indifferent toward the ship, you know, as a ship. But now I feel the loss of it. And it certainly does feel like loss."

An ache tore at her breast. It was like a large black hole in the center of her gut, swallowing all other feelings and concerns. She supposed it was better than anger, though, and her anger at Jeff over the past twenty-four hours had been intense.

She hated herself for being so much at the mercy of her emotions. At times they felt overwhelming, even abusive. This was one of those times. As much as she hated Jeff's detachment from his emotions, she also envied it. She could see how important it could be on the battlefield. She wished she could just turn them off, as he did—or at least turn them down.

Nira didn't respond to her comment about loss. *She's like Jeff,* Emma thought, *under total control.* Pho nodded, though. Emma realized she liked the kid. He was eager and sensitive. He didn't always show the best judgment, but he seemed to mean well.

"Collect your effects and meet back here in five minutes," Nira commanded.

Emma bristled. She didn't like being told what to do. She hadn't had any trouble acknowledging Jeff as captain, but since she wasn't, strictly speaking, military, she wasn't sure how much authority Nira actually had over her.

Emma went to her cabin—more of a pod, really—and stuffed her clothes into a poly duffle bag. It only took a minute or two. She didn't have much to pack because they hadn't intended to stay on the ship for long. They had only been there to make a jump, an experiment. They had expected to sleep aboard Sol Station that same night. *Their* Sol Station.

But no one in their universe had survived that experiment—no one but them. The thought made her shudder. They'd been in this universe for weeks now, but she couldn't get used to the thought.

She slung the duffle over her shoulder and made her way back to the airlock. The others weren't much longer. As they stepped through to the boarding catwalk, Pho asked, "Does anyone else think the captain seems…a little off?"

Nira said nothing. Emma felt the discomfort of silence growing as they walked back toward the spaceport. "He *is* off," she said finally. "He's crazy with guilt and grief. He's struggling with a hundred conflicting emotions, and he is barely conscious of any of them. They're like invisible strings pulling at him, every one in a different direction."

"You're awfully forgiving," Pho ventured, "since he's basically leaving you…us…to see *her*."

He meant Jo. Captain Jo Taylor. Emma hadn't been surprised to hear he was going to seek out her analog here on String 311, but she was hurt. How could she not be? But she felt like she ought to be a good soldier, to buck up, to take it on the chin. *Why?* she asked herself. *I'm* not *a soldier. I'm a jilted woman. Why shouldn't I have my feelings, cry, make a scene? Why shouldn't I scream at him, punch him, beat him until he's purple and bruised? That's what any normal woman would do, isn't it? Why do I need to be on my best behavior?*

She hated the situation. She hated Jeff. She hated herself for allowing it. But what could she have possibly done to stop it? Love him more? Could she have been more doting somehow? And why the hell should she have to do that? She fumed as they walked, her feelings of loss about the ship subsumed now in a sea of hurt feelings.

"I'm sorry," Pho said, when she didn't answer. "I didn't mean to—"

She put a hand on his arm and gave him a sad smile. He stopped talking. That was good. She turned to Nira. "So, what is this rendezvous point? And how are we going to get there?"

They were in the main spaceport now. Above them, arrival and departure information were displayed, names and numbers hovering in the air. Hundreds of people rushed by them, everyone in a different direction.

“The captain only gave me coordinates,” Nira answered. “But I looked them up last night. It’s a rebel outpost at the edge of neutral space. Just a fueling station, really. There’s a hostel there where we can find accommodations, but we’ll need a cover story.”

“Why?” Emma asked. “What’s the purpose of all the cloak-and-dagger?”

“It’s appropriate caution. We possess secrets. Secrets that can… destroy universes. As we’ve seen, people will do a lot to get their hands on those kinds of secrets. Even decent people like the Authority brass.”

“I don’t know if I’d go that far,” Emma crossed her arms. “I haven’t met anyone here I’d consider actually friendly.” She wasn’t too sure about some of her crew members either. Especially Nira, whom she couldn’t read.

“There are two freighters heading in that direction. One of them is carrying supplies for the outpost,” Nira said. “I’ve made reservations for us.”

“How much is that going to cost?” Emma asked.

Nira narrowed her eyes at her but didn’t answer.

“I mean, I’m asking because we have only so much money,” Emma explained. Pho’s eyebrows raised as he listened. “It’s all we have in this world. I’m not under your authority. Why should I go to some god-forsaken outpost to wait for…who knows what? I mean, why shouldn’t I go and just make a meaningful life here? I have skills.”

Nira cocked her head. Emma watched a range of emotions cycling just below the surface. Was the little bitch going to punch her? Yell at her? Or perhaps try some more skillful means of coercion?

Emma deflated a little when the commander simply turned her back on her. “The freighter leaves at 2200 hours,” she said to Pho. “We need to be aboard at 2100. Purchase whatever supplies you need. We don’t know what will be available at the outpost, and we don’t know how long we’ll be there.”

“Yes sir,” Pho said, glancing up at Emma.

Without another word, Nira walked off in the direction of the commercial zone.

Pho clutched his duffle to his chest and gave Emma a pained expression. "You're…not coming?"

Emma fought back tears. "I don't know…what the hell I'm doing."

"I'll be sad if you don't come," he said, managing a weak smile.

Emma felt a twisting in her heart. Just this tiny amount of candor and affection nearly undid her. She could survive on this kind of food. She was ravenous for it. And it had been way too long since she'd had it.

She planted a kiss on his cheek and turned away.

She didn't know where she would go or what she would do. She needed to think. She needed to be touched, heard, understood.

She stopped. Was there a somatic counselor on this station? It was a sizable station—there had to be. She looked up and accessed her neural. There were precisely four, three of them in private practice and one employed by the station itself, available to anyone with Telestock insurance.

She didn't know what Telestock was, but she chose randomly from the other three.

"Karin Zeufladt," she said out loud. "I need to talk. I need a massage and a good cry." She put in a reservation for 1900 hours. Two hours from now.

"Tampons, underwear, and comfortable shoes," she said, and turned toward the commercial zone herself.

Jeff found a table at the back, reasonably far from eavesdropping ears. He waved Jennings over and was not at all surprised to see that the transport captain had already procured an unopened bottle of whiskey.

"Got my breakfast," Jennings said, slamming the bottle on the table so loudly that the other patrons stopped their talking or reading to look. "What are you having?"

Jeff tried not to look uncomfortable with all the staring eyes on him. He ignored them and pulled back a chair. He picked up a menu and entered his payment ID. Then he made a selection—whipped eggs, sausage, toast, and lila. He closed the menu, then shook his head at his own stupidity and selected coffee. Large. Then he bumped it to two.

He handed the menu to Jennings. "The solid food is on me."

"The liquid food is, too. I told them your room number." Jennings sat with a groan. "Had my knees replaced last year, thank god. Now it's my hips." He picked up the whiskey and cracked the seal. "Medicine."

Jeff ignored him. *Where the hell do I start?* he wondered.

Jennings took a deep pull from the bottle. He made a face that was somewhere between pain and ecstasy. He blew air through his pursed lips and color rushed to his face. "Okay. Now I'm fortified. The day can begin." He put his elbows on the table and steepled his fingers in front of him. "So, if you don't want to fuck me, why are you following me?"

"Because I recognize you."

"From where?" Jennings reared back in his seat, as if ready to bolt.

"From another universe." Jeff looked him straight in the eye so he could see he was serious.

Jennings' eyebrows bunched up and he leaned forward again.

"I'm listening."

"You know about the strings?"

"Everybody knows about the goddam strings. Everybody knows they're theoretical. Religious folks say they're a hoax."

"Are you religious?"

"Sure. I piss on beads of any denomination." Jennings cracked a smile and sipped at his whiskey.

Just then a meal pod lowered from the ceiling and hovered just above Jeff's head. Careful not to tip it, he snatched at it until he felt the magnetic grip release. He put it on the table in front of him and released the lid, setting it aside. The eggs were steaming and the sausages were still sizzling. A holder to the right bore two cups of coffee. He snapped open the lid on one of them.

"You want some cream in that?" Jennings held his bottle up.

Jeff hesitated. He shrugged. “What the hell?” he said, and let Jennings pour a finger in, almost making it spill.

“Strings,” Jennings repeated.

“You know what string this is, right?”

“Every schoolkid knows that.”

“Tell me.”

“*Allegedly*…we’re on String 311.”

“I’m from String 310.”

“No shit.” Jennings had said this too fast, without a hint of wonder. He didn’t believe him.

“Let me tell you about it,” Jeff said. Taking his time, he ate a mouthful of eggs. Fluffy. Good. “A lot is the same. A lot is different, too.”

“Like what?”

“Like the fact that every ship in the galaxy is infested with spiders.”

Now Jennings looked surprised. He hadn’t expected that. “Spiders? Why the fuck…?”

“No one knows. We fumigate, we set traps, we try sonic and electronic arachnid deterrents. Nothing works. You can build a perfectly clean, new ship, and within six months it will be crawling with spiders.”

“They’d get into the electronics and the mechanics—”

“They do.”

“That’s fucking weird.” Jennings narrowed one eye at him. “That’s not something someone would just make up.”

“There’s no war there. There’s no Authority or rebels. There’s the Colonial Defense Fleet.”

“Used to be a CDF…”

“Until Catskill happened.”

Jennings sat bolt upright. He looked around. He looked back at Jeff and his shoulders hunched as he whispered, “Where the *fuck* did you hear that name?”

“I was there. In my universe, the same thing happened. Only…only there…*I* was the only survivor.”

Jennings ran his fingers through his gray, thinning hair. He fidgeted in his seat, his eyes darting back and forth.

"I'm Captain Jeff Bowers."

Jennings' eyes widened and his mouth hung open. "Bowers?" he said finally. Recognition dawned on his face. "I thought you looked… but you're older." The wonder on his face blackened into suspicion. "You're dead."

"No, the Jeff Bowers you know—the Jeff Bowers of String 311—is dead. I'm from String 310, remember? I'm alive."

Jennings stared, his eyebrows raised, his face frozen.

"Let me tell you about the Jennings of String 310. You're…he's… well, he's the finest goddam soldier I know. He's also among the top brass in the CDF."

"Shit me. I must be rich." He took another swallow of whiskey.

"I don't know about that. You…he made more than I did, that's for sure. But what's more important is that he was loved, respected, admired…" Jeff took a bite of sausage. "…by pretty much everyone I ever met."

"I must be quite a disappointment," Jennings mumbled.

"You're…definitely not what I expected," Jeff agreed. "I was hoping to find an ally. I was hoping there was something of him in you."

"Sounds like he got some breaks I didn't. It's been a hard life," Jennings admitted.

"I can see that." Jeff downed the rest of one of the coffees and picked up the other. He held it out to Jennings for a little "cream." Jennings obliged. "Tell me about what you do."

"I'm a cargo man."

"You mean you're a smuggler?"

"You can call me what you want. The fact is that I have a ship and people pay me to take shit from here to there. End of story."

"How are you registered?"

"Import/Export."

Jeff grunted and turned his attention to his toast. He squeezed lila out of a tube and spread it over the crispy gold surface of the bread. "Now you know why I was following you."

"I guess so. You need a friend in this place."

Jeff nodded.

"And we used to know each other."

Jeff shook his head. "I used to know a Jennings in another universe…but not you. You used to know a Jeff Bowers, but not me. I'm getting pretty clear on that. But me and him…we're *related*. Just as you and Admiral Jennings are. Like cousins, maybe. Consider me a distant relative." Jeff smiled sadly.

"So how can I help you, cousin?" Jennings lowered his head and pierced Jeff with one steely eye.

"I've got some cargo, and I need to move it from here to there," Jeff said.

"And that cargo is?"

Jeff shrugged. "Just me."

"What's the catch?" Jennings cocked his head.

"No catch. Just…discretion. What's your fee?"

Jennings pursed his lips and considered for a long moment. "10,000 a parsec."

"5,000 a parsec."

Jennings drank. "6,000."

"Deal. When do we leave?"

"Where are we going?"

"I need to find…another friend."

Jennings nodded. "Another…analog?"

"Yeah. But the fact is, I don't really have connections here. Do you know how I can locate someone?"

"Oh, I can find anyone you want." Jennings gave him a sly smile. "But it'll cost you extra."

COMMUNICATOR SUSIE WALL's eyes teared up as she touched the frayed edge of her CDF uniform. It was in a poly bag with the rest of her effects. Time seemed to stand still as she explored the artifacts of her former life.

"All there?" asked the young man behind the security desk. He seemed to be of African descent. Part of his organic head was missing. The prosthetics were well-designed, though, and Wall almost didn't notice the seams. Not that she was really paying attention.

I thought I would die in prison, she thought to herself as she played with a button. She was still wearing the yellow jumpsuit issued to all prisoners. She felt an urgency to put her uniform on. When she did, she would be putting on her dignity, her identity, her hope. She almost began to strip right then and there, but modesty and a sense of military decorum prevented her.

"All there?" the guard asked again, this time with a note of annoyance in his voice. He sighed. "Sign here."

Wall realized her reactions were slow because of trauma. Knowing that didn't make her any faster, but it occurred to her that the guard must be used to this and might make some allowance for it. After all, people were people, and she couldn't be the first person to find herself overwhelmed with relief.

She signed. "Where are my people?" she asked.

The young man's brow furrowed—just the organic one. "Uh…how should I know? What's your ethnicity?"

Wall cocked her head. It took a moment. "No, I mean, where is Captain Bowers? Where is the rest of the crew of the *Kepler*?"

A slight grin broke out on the young man's face. "Oh yeah…I remember that guy. Had a woman with him. Older, pretty. Emma?"

"Yes!" Wall said, her face brightening.

"Long gone. Admiral Tal let them go. Everyone's talking about it."

Wall's shoulders slumped. Her face felt frozen. She might just as well have been stranded on a desert planet with no supplies.

"Your neural should be coming back online in a minute or two," the man said. "Aaaaand…you're free to go." He gave her a perfunctory smile. "You have a good day now."

"But…where do I go?"

"Wherever the hell you want."

"How will I live?"

"You'll need to get a job, same way the rest of us do." His smile faded, and his face changed. She realized that a moment ago he had been looking at a released prisoner. Now he was looking at a homeless person. The difference in his demeanor was palpable. Then he softened. "Look…in the meantime, the Sufis run a hospice on Deck 117. You can get a bed there and a meal. You can take some time to figure things out. They even have a counselor that comes by now and then, I think."

"Uh…okay…thanks," Wall said. She looked around. The room seemed sterile and cold. People bustled by in the corridor just outside the glass door. She shrank inside.

"Move along then," the young man said, making a shooing motion with his hand.

"Is…is there a place where I can change?" she asked.

"Out the door, turn right. A hundred meters down you'll see a family head. You can change there."

Wall nodded and turned toward the door and her freedom.

EMMA PAUSED BY THE KIOSK, checking the address. The somatic counselor was listed. But when she scanned the line of shops again, their addresses seemed to skip right over that number. She scowled and went to the shop with the closest number, L48. It was a gift shop filled with inexpensive knick-knacks, some from local indigenous species, but most cheap knockoffs. As the saleslady was finishing up with another customer, she paused by a display of plush animals, recognizing most of them. A moment later, the clerk turned to her with a tired smile. "How can I help you?"

"I'm so sorry," Emma began. "I'm looking for L50, but the next number is L54."

The woman nodded and pointed to a small door just inside the shop. Above the lintel was a hand-written sign, "L50."

"I don't know why I didn't see that," Emma said, shaking her head.

"No one does. Go on in. Aspy does good work. I rent to her, and part of it is barter. I get a session a week."

"Isn't that..." she was going to say, "a breach of ethics," but she stopped herself. "It's good to hear," she said. "Thanks."

Emma walked quickly to the little door and opened it. It swung open easily, and she was met with a steep set of stairs. "The somatic therapy begins now," she said out loud as she began to climb the stairs. At the top was a small but stylishly appointed waiting room, complete with a magazine download kiosk advertising the latest. She fixed her eye on the code and blinked and within seconds the magazine had loaded to her neural. She took a seat and began browsing through it, blinking to access the links from section to section.

Before long, a curtain parted, and a much younger woman than she emerged. Much shorter, too, she noted. The woman had short-cropped dark hair and was dressed in a flowery kimono. She seemed to be rubbing lotion into her hands. "You must be Emma." She flashed her a professional smile.

"I am. Are you...Aspy?"

"The very same. Come in. Have you had somatic therapy before?"

"Oh, sure. I saw one regularly back on Earth when I—"

Aspy jerked her head. "You're from Earth?"

Emma realized her mistake at once. "Yes...a long time ago," she tried to cover.

"I wouldn't be too vocal about that if I were you." Aspy eyed her suspiciously.

"Um...thanks for the advice. I'm new here."

"I guess you are. Well, hop up." She led her through the curtain into an even smaller room and patted a firm, blocky table that dominated the space.

"Clothes on or off?" Emma asked.

"As you like. My work is easier without them. Why don't you just strip down to your bra and panties until we get to know each other?" Her professional smile was back, and she began to rub more of the lotion into her hands.

Emma complied and hung her clothes on the hooks just to one side of the table. She lay face down, grateful to find that the surface of the table was not too cold. Aspy pulled a warm blanket over her legs, up to her waist.

Emma was tingling with anticipation. She had come to rely on massages as a basic element of her own self-care, and it had been far too long. She knew her body, how it held on to unresolved feelings and unprocessed events. She felt the accumulated knots of anger and grief and loss contorting her body every time she moved, and she could not wait to have them kneaded out of her.

"I'm going to direct a scent generator toward us. It will help you relax."

"I like that," Emma assured her.

Aspy laid one hand on her back and held it there. The moment of connection, one of the most sacred elements of somatic therapy. Emma savored it as Aspy paused.

"A burden shared…" Aspy intoned.

"…is a burden borne." Emma completed the aphorism, relieved that the ritual was the same in this universe as in hers.

Aspy's hands dug into her back with languid strokes, and Emma emitted a low moan of pleasure. She could smell the therapeutic aroma now. Lavender and telia.

"Tell me a story from your childhood," Aspy inquired. This too was standard.

Emma began to relate the time her father had ditched her at an amusement park just to see how she would react. But halfway through, she lost her train of thought, wispy snatches of memory fading into a fog of numb oblivion.

CHAPTER THREE

They won't try it again.
Yes, the one who learned from us
—he is chastened and afraid.
He has destroyed a universe.
We were wrong to help him.
Agreed. We were wrong. We must kill him.
Not just him. If he can do it, he can teach others to do it.
The time for managing them is over.
We must kill them all.
All? Surely not.
All. Before another reality string is severed.

Emma dreamed of voices in the darkness;

"Who is she?"

"Dunno, but she must have done something serious to piss off the Butcher this much."

"You'll be next if you don't get moving."

"Fuck off."

Emma opened her eyes but she couldn't make them focus, She tried to sit up, but couldn't move. She was lying on a hard surface covered in some rough fabric like burlap, scratchy on her face. The room was spinning, and her thoughts felt lost in fog.

Drugs... she thought. *I've been drugged.*

She reached back, searching for the last thing she could remember. Aspy's office, getting somatic therapy. She had often fallen asleep as she relaxed, but this was something else.

She forced herself to breathe normally. She could access her neural, it was working, but it wasn't finding a network to connect to. The clock read 9:00 pm. It had been more than twenty-four hours since her appointment. Suddenly her heart was racing. She still couldn't move much, but she was able to slide her hand under the coarse fabric and press her palm flat on the cold metal surface underneath. She felt a familiar vibration, the subsonic rumble of a starship cruising at superluminal speed.

Panic swelled in her and she began to tremble, her breath becoming quick and shallow. The only thing that made sense was that she had been drugged and abducted, and her mind began to spin with possible fates that might be waiting for her.

Get ahold of yourself, girl, she thought. *You'll be more vulnerable if you hyperventilate and pass out again.* She took a long, slow breath through her nose, then let it out slowly through her mouth. *That's it, be cool. Don't get caught up in imaginary threats. Be logical. Take stock of your situation. Stick to facts.*

She still couldn't raise her head, but she could look around. She surveyed her environment, which appeared to be a dimly lit cargo hold. A pile of crates was secured to the wall with a cargo net. A long work table ran down the opposite wall. A hatch opened to a corridor on the far wall, and she flinched as someone emerged from it.

It was a tall, almost impossibly slender woman. There was something surreal about her proportions, her limbs too long, her eyes too big. Emma wondered if the drugs weren't causing her to see things strangely. The tall woman walked to the work table, arranged a mirror, and pulled her hair off. The blonde hair was a wig; underneath, her head was smooth—and pale green. Two delicate antennae had been folded flat under the wig, and they flexed and extended upward. She laid the wig delicately on the table, then removed her face. Her nose and mouth were some kind of mask, and she laid it down on top of the wig. In the mirror, Emma could see intricate mandibles wiggling where the mask had been, not unlike the mouth of a grasshopper. She shuddered.

The macabre striptease continued. The woman—if that's what she was—gently tugged off her gloves, which came away with a fake finger on each one. She then pulled her floral muumuu-like dress up over her head and tossed it to the floor. Underneath, she was more like a praying mantis than a human. Her knees bent the wrong way, and she crouched into a more insect-like posture, taking several feet off her height.

In Emma's universe, back in String 310, there were very few extraterrestrial civilizations, and this was definitely not one of them. She wondered why she had seen so many more alien cultures in this universe. Maybe humans had just made different exploratory choices, paying off in more alien contacts.

The alien removed a belt made of some kind of foam material, which seemed to be intended to disguise her articulated hips, making them appear more human-like through the dress. She also wore a bib of the same material over her breasts, only when she took it off, she revealed they weren't breasts at all, but rather a second set of arms, smaller than the primary arms, which had been held crossed underneath the padding. Lastly, she picked at a corner of her enormous eye and peeled away a thin coating like a layer of white paint. It revealed the green pebbled surface of her compound eye.

As she began to peel the other eye, the mask on the counter said, "I know you're awake."

Emma held her breath, slamming her eyes closed. Adrenaline surged through her, breaking the pharmaceutical paralysis. Her transformation complete, the alien turned around to face Emma where she lay.

"The drugs you were given were very precise. You may feel a bit unsteady, but the effects will pass quickly."

Emma opened her eyes, flinching at the insectoid hovering over her. "Please don't hurt me," she stammered.

"I will not harm you. You are safe," said the mask on the table.

Emma lifted her head slightly, which set it pounding with pain. She gritted her teeth. "Safe? You've kidnapped me! Where are you taking me? What do you want?"

The alien gestured dismissively, then turned back to the work table. The mask said, "I do not want anything." She attached a cord to the corners of the mouth and hung it around her neck, a surreal medallion. The pouty lips on the mask moved, speaking in a soft melodic voice. "I have been contracted to transport you to a remote location and keep you safe."

Emma carefully rose to a seated position. "Contracted? By whom?"

The alien made a strange circular gesture. "I am not at liberty to disclose that at this time."

"And where are you taking me?"

"I am also not able to disclose that."

"If you are hoping to collect ransom, I have some bad news for you. I don't know anyone in this entire universe." She chuckled nervously, desperately.

If the alien was amused, she didn't show it. "There is no ransom sought."

She began to protest again, but stopped. *What exactly is happening here?* It was not a basic kidnapping as she understood it. "How long are you going to keep me?"

"I do not know. Until you are sent for."

Emma shook her head, trying to clear the confusion. Her head was swimming. "What did you give me anyway?"

"Morphex, in the dose indicated for a human of your mass."

She rubbed her eyes. "I think you gave me too much. I'm really out of it. Would it be possible to get a cup of coffee?"

The alien crossed its small arms. "What is coffee?"

Emma sighed. *This is gonna be a long ordeal.* "It's a beverage that humans drink. It contains the stimulant caffeine."

"I do not have coffee. I can provide you with a mild stimulant if you would like."

Her eyes brightened. "What do you have?"

The alien stepped over to a cabinet, punched a code into the keypad next to it and opened the door. She brought out a small box and examined the contents. "I have L-lysine-dextroamphetamine in 20 milligram capsules."

Emma shook her head. "Too strong."

"Nyarlathotine, 35 milligrams."

She coughed. "Holy shit, I want a little pick-me-up, not for my heart to explode!"

"Methylphenidate, 12 milligrams."

Emma nodded. "Yeah, that should do."

The alien plucked a tiny gleaming pearl from the box with her delicate pincer-like fingers and handed it to Emma, who dry-swallowed it. She could instantly feel the mental fog beginning to recede.

"Thank you. That will help a lot."

Her captor merely nodded and put the box back in the cabinet and closed it.

"OK," Emma began, mustering some courage, "it sounds like we're going to be together for some time. Can you at least tell me your name?"

The mask smiled slightly. "You can call me Amberline."

SUSIE WALL FINISHED BUTTONING her uniform and looked at herself in the mirror. The midnight blue cloth was a little rumpled from having been stuffed in the effects bag, but she felt like a new person. For one thing, it fit her properly, unlike the one-size-fits-all yellow prisoner's jumpsuit that hung on her like a bag. But more importantly, it connected her to her past, her purpose, and her people.

My people, she thought. *Where the hell are my people, and how could they have just left me behind?*

As if in answer, a light appeared in her peripheral vision. Her neural had come online.

Reflexively, she looked up and blinked. There were two messages, both from Captain Bowers. Her shoulders relaxed and she almost burst into tears from sheer relief. They hadn't abandoned her after all. She opened the first of them—the earliest of them—and read quickly, her eyes darting back and forth.

It was short and to the point: They had an opportunity for escape. They were taking it. He thinks they're holding her for future leverage. She shouldn't worry. They wouldn't forget her. They would come back for her…somehow.

Okay, she thought. She blinked and opened the second message.

Captain Bowers had opened a bank account in her number. It had more money in it than she could ever hope to earn in her career. They were at Epworth Station, in neutral space. There were coordinates for a rendezvous point.

She lowered her eyes and looked at herself in the mirror again. Her fingers trembled as she straightened her epaulets and smoothed out the creases in her jacket.

Fuck the Sufi hospice, she thought. *I'm renting a pod. With a hot tub. Then I'm buying a ticket for the next ship out to Epworth Station.* She'd had enough of the Authority's hospitality, after all. She needed to be with her people.

"Approaching Gamela Three." Lieutenant Marcia Chi's voice broke through her reverie.

"Being hailed by the *Baronet,*" Mr. Liebert added.

"On screen," Jo said.

A small, mousy man appeared. He sported a wispy blond mustache that made Jo want to retch. The little man's smile looked like it caused him pain in some minor abdominal organ. "Captain, I can't tell you how grateful I am for your escort."

"It was our pleasure, Captain." Jo forced a warmish smile. "It gave us a chance to play catch-up aboard ship."

"Well, with the war on, I wouldn't think you'd have time for... well, for protecting merchant vessels."

"The Revolutionary Freedom Coalition isn't here just to protect us all from the Authority, but from any danger—including pirates," Jo assured him.

"That is reassuring, certainly." The man's smile now looked very genuine. "Well, thank you again."

"Good enough. Smooth sailing, Captain." Jo nodded at Liebert, and the view screen once again showed only stars.

"Course, Captain?" Chi asked.

"I'm still waiting on our next assignment." Jo shrugged. "Let's dock. Mr. Liebert, inform Mr. Palamar that he needs to get his ass in gear. I want requisition orders in an hour. Gamela is a major hub, and there's little we need that we can't get here. I want us fully stocked by 2100 hours. We've got time for a few shuttle loads to go to the main station for R&R. So...let's start a lottery. Inform the lucky bastards that they need to be back aboard by...hell, by noon tomorrow. If orders come through for anything urgent, I'll recall them. Let's get as many of our folks down for a couple of hours of playtime as we can."

"Yes sir," Liebert said with a wide smile. He probably wouldn't make the lottery, but he was happy to see that someone would. And that was what made Liebert a man she trusted.

She stood and stretched. "Inform Mr. Bourgeois that I'm going to my quarters. No need to call him in early. And call me if you need me."

"Aye sir." Liebert gave her a quick nod.

She picked up the plushy peapod and headed for the door.

Jo didn't need to go stationside for R&R. She just needed a little time alone. She craved it, but duty compelled her to stay on bridge, to constantly be "on." She was exhausted. No sooner had her door slid shut behind her than her shoulders slumped and she sighed. She set the peapod, seated upright, on the small table that hugged one wall of her cabin. "It's rough being Kali," she said to it. It grinned back at her, almost maniacally. "You're going to have to work on that smile," she told it. "It's unsettling."

She turned toward her private bath—one of the few luxuries afforded a captain on a war vessel—and quickly undressed, getting into the sonic. She relished the exfoliation, and when she stepped out, her skin was red and she felt mildly exhilarated. She put on a thin robe, grabbed half a bar of chocolate, and fell onto the bed.

ADMIRAL TAL LOOKED up to see the door to his office slide open. Captain Daniel Hightower stepped in and saluted.

"As you were," Tal said. "Take a seat."

"Aye sir," Hightower said. "Thank you, sir."

Tal glowered at the captain, uncertain what to make of him. On the one hand, he was the fiercest fighting machine the Authority had. If you wanted killing done, Hightower was your man. On the other hand, he was reasonably certain the captain was a sociopath. His only comfort was that he was *his* sociopath. *God forbid he ever changes sides,* he thought, and shuddered.

"What are your plans regarding Jo Taylor?" Tal asked.

"I've got some feelers out." Hightower gave him a confident nod. "I'll have a bead on her soon."

"We just received some intelligence that will help you with that," Tal said. "We've heard from one of our contacts in the RFC that Captain Taylor and the *Talon* are currently in proximity to Teegarden's Star. I'll send you the exact coordinates." He looked up to access his neural and sent them to the captain. He watched Hightower look up and retrieve them.

The captain looked down again. "Teegarden's Star. What's there?"

"It's in neutral space, which means it's disputed territory."

"The entire colonial fuckmess is disputed territory," Hightower objected.

Tal didn't disagree, but he ignored the ejaculation. "Right now the *TAV Horatio Nelson* is nearby on active guard. Our intelligence says that Taylor is on her way to engage the *Nelson*."

"ETA?"

"Faster than we can get support there at C8."

Hightower whistled, looking down at the desk. He looked up. "Why are you telling me?"

Tal leaned on his desk, steepling his fingers. "We've got a new prototype that can do C9. As you know, speed is exponential."

Hightower grinned. "How much firepower will I be bringing?"

"None, unfortunately. The prototype is a research vessel."

Danny blinked. "So…?"

"I want you to assume command of the *Nelson* in time to engage the *Talon* when she drops into normal space." Tal's voice was icy as he spoke. "I want you to shoot the shit out of every bolt on her ship. I want vids of her clutching her throat as she succumbs to the icy void, pinwheeling off into space."

"You should have been a poet, sir."

"I mean it. I don't just want you to blow up the *Talon*. I want to see her die with my own eyes. Not only that, we need to broadcast it. It's the only way to undo the damage she's done. Morale is low throughout the Authority. The civilian authorities on Earth are thinking about reshuffling the admiralty. We need results, and we need them quickly."

"I'm your man, sir." Hightower stood, saluting.

Tal didn't return it. He looked down at his desk. "And Captain, if you don't succeed…" He looked up and pierced the captain with one steely eye, "…don't come back until you do."

CHAPTER FOUR

Jo hadn't even taken a bite of her chocolate when a hailing signal woke her. "Nuuuhhhh," she moaned. She raised her head wearily. "Computer, what time is it?" she asked.

"2017 hours," came the response.

"Who the fuck is hailing me?"

"Lieutenant Tash Liebert."

"Oh Christ. Okay." She rose, snatched at the chocolate and bit off an enormous bite.

Chewing, she said, "Answer hail."

Jo slid out of her robe and snatched her trousers off the hook at the foot of her bunk. She heard a connecting beep. "Captain here," she said. "What's wrong?"

"Nothing wrong, Captain. The computer selected the lottery, and we currently have thirty-six lucky people enjoying the station."

"Stocking?"

"Almost complete, sir."

"And you woke me because…"

"Incoming hail from an unknown vessel, the *Annabel Lee*. Their captain asked for you by name."

"What sort of vessel?" Jo fastened the buttons on the flap of her red, double-breasted jacket.

"Merchant class."

"What does he want?"

"He's asked for permission to come aboard."

Jo scowled. She didn't know any merchants. Nor did she care to. Most freelance merchant captains were little better than pirates, in her opinion. "What's his name?"

"Uh…" Liebert was obviously checking. "Captain…Carl Jennings."

Jo stopped short. "Christ," she said.

"Something wrong, sir?"

It had been twenty years since she'd heard that name. Old ghosts tugged at her, raising her pulse and making her heart shrink in trepidation.

"Nothing wrong, Lieutenant. I'm…" She didn't finish the sentence. She wasn't fine. "What does he want?" she asked again, senselessly expecting a different answer this time.

"I don't know, sir. He said he had a private delivery to make. Should I call security?"

Jo blinked, thinking this over. From the far depths of her memory, she latched onto the slim wisps surrounding Jennings and hauled them to the surface. She remembered him as an able captain, about ten years ahead of her and Jeff and Danny. Jeff and Danny had both served under him, briefly, before…

She felt momentarily dizzy. She sat, steadying herself with one hand on the small table. The peapod grinned at her.

She hadn't thought of any of them for a long time. The memories weren't so much painful after all these years as they were tender to the touch. She looked up and accessed her neural, calling up Jennings' file. She pursed her lips and scowled as she read. "You've been a busy little beaver since we met last," she said out loud.

"What's that, sir?" She could hear the lilt of surprise in Liebert's voice.

"Uh...nothing. Tell Captain Jennings permission is granted. Have security meet me at the shuttle bay."

"Aye sir. Expect him in ten minutes, sir."

A sudden rush of memories flooded over her, released now from the vault of what seemed to her ancient and irrelevant history. She remembered Jennings' ribald jokes, Danny's incessant teasing, and the sweat and smell of making love to Jeff. She remembered the sting of his beard stubble against her cheek, her thighs. She remembered the night her roommate woke her when the notice guard and chaplain had arrived with the news that Jeff was missing in action. Later, they had pronounced him dead, and she remembered the agonizing time between the first notice and the second, the torture of not knowing, the cruelty of hope.

She shook her head to clear it. The air was thick with ghosts. Too thick. She felt sick to her stomach. She went to the wall dispenser and pressed her thumb against the activator tab. "Vodka, two shots, ice cold," she said. A moment later, she reached in and withdrew a glass. It was freezing. She took a large swig and then stared at the glass, at the slenderness of her hand. It was shaking.

Commander Nira glanced up, checking the chronometer on her neural. It was time. Looking down, she scanned the crowd again. She could see thousands of people, from as many planets and cultures and races, all of them hurrying somewhere. The noise was overwhelming, as was the chaos in the spaceport.

"Where is she?" Pho asked, for about the seventh time.

Nira saw no need to answer him again. She didn't have the authority to do a neural search, not here. She could go to security and request one, explaining their situation, giving them Emma's neural serial number, waiting for clearance... Their ship would be long gone by then, and the local authorities would know way too much about them. She scowled and tapped her foot.

"She said she might go her own way," Pho offered.

"She was just talking," Nira said.

"Maybe she wasn't. Maybe she was serious. Send her another message."

"I've sent her twelve messages. Thirteen isn't going to change things."

"If she were going to go her own way, she'd answer," Pho reasoned. He was pacing, his impossibly thin limbs slicing through the air with nervous energy. "Which means something must be wrong."

No shit, Nira thought, although she maintained her command demeanor. "I'm guessing that even if we did request a search, and even if they did it, and even if they told us the results…"

"There wouldn't be any results," Pho finished.

"There might be results, if she's dead." Nira countered her own thoughts.

"Don't say that," Pho said, his voice rising and starting to quail. "I liked…*like*…Doctor Stewart."

Nira didn't disagree. The doctor wasn't the kind of woman Nira was into, or would even hang out with, but she admired the scientist's grit—not to mention the way she handled Captain Bowers. *The woman has balls of steel,* she acknowledged to herself. And it was for that reason, and probably that reason alone, that she couldn't just let it go.

"If she's off grid, we need to know that," Nira said. "And if she's dead, we need to know that too."

"So should we go to security?"

Nira chewed on her lip, her hard, pretty face a mask of tension as she thought. "First things first," she said, looking up. "I need to cancel our flight while I can still get a refund. We're going to need every chit we've got." Her eyes flashed back and forth, blinking occasionally as she navigated to the merchant site and called up their purchase order. A moment later, she looked back down and nodded. "We lost our deposit," she said, "but got most of it back."

Pho nodded, his elfin face looking uncharacteristically sad. "Where do we start?"

"With a neural search, obviously," Nira said. "Just not an *official* neural search."

"Uh…how do we get an unofficial neural search?" Pho asked.

"We need to find people who will work…unofficially," Nira said. She started to walk. She looked up, calling down a map of the station, searching it.

"Uh…okay," Pho said, obviously trying not to sound too stupid. "How do we find those people?"

Nira stopped and faced him. "Just where do you *think* you'd find disreputable people who know things?"

Pho's eyes moved back and forth as he thought. "Uh…I have no idea, sir. I've never really been around…disreputable people."

Nira's eyes narrowed. She wanted to say, *What good are you?* But it occurred to her that Pho's usefulness in the situation was not a measure of his worth. His worth was not at issue. Hers was. It was her job to keep him safe—and Dr. Stewart, too. She had no idea what Captain Bowers was up to, but she was determined to deliver his crew to him intact, or she would die in the effort. She started walking again. "We're not going to meet the people we're after right off," she explained patiently. "We're going to find people who know people who know the right people—people who can make an introduction."

"Uh…and where do we find *those* people?"

"Where do you think? Where the grease monkeys drink."

JO STOOD at parade rest as the airlock pressurized. Her face betrayed nothing. It was an impassive landscape of hills and valleys with dried, cracked riverbeds forming deltas at the corners of her eyes. She heard the sound of air rushing in, then the deep-bones click of heavy, moving metal. Then the door slid open.

Captain Jennings stepped through, squinting in the bright light, attempting to take in his surroundings. He appeared to be alone. His face brightened as his eyes adjusted and he recognized her. "Jo Taylor," his skeevy lips drew back in a smile.

"That would be *Captain* Taylor," Jo corrected him.

"You look like a million," he said, running his eyes up and down her slender form, his eyebrows raised in appreciation of how her uniform clung to the contours of her body.

"You look like a tired old goat," she said.

He laughed. "That is an entirely fair assessment." He put his hand out. She didn't take it. "Ensign," she said over her shoulder at her security detail, "take Captain Jennings into custody. Captain Carl Jennings, you are under arrest on six outstanding warrants—three counts of smuggling, one count of suspected piracy, one count of indecent exposure, one count of fraud."

"Not guilty," Jennings said as the security men turned him around roughly and placed his hand in poly secure-cuffs.

"Not interested," Jo said. "Save it for your arraignment."

"Surely you didn't come all the way down from your perch in the catbird seat just to oversee my arrest," Jennings sneered.

"No, my security team is more than competent. I just wanted to see the look on your face while they did it."

SUSIE WALL FELT ALMOST human again after a good night's sleep as a free woman. She had drunk champagne and lounged in her private bath —the first since her incarceration—and it had felt wonderful. She flipped her hair back as she boarded the ship bound for neutral space. She met the purser and was directed to her pod. It was the third from the floor, but that didn't bother her. She climbed the ladder, opened the door, and climbed in.

The pod was about 1.25 meters across and a meter high. It was about three meters deep. One couldn't stand in it, obviously, but crawled. The bed took up most of the pod, with a small silver sink to one side. Beside that was a place to hang clothes, with fixed hangers already in place. She saw that they were covered with foam so that they wouldn't keep you awake clinking together when the ship experienced turbulence. And, blessedly, the foam was still in place—they weren't new, but nearly so. Stretching out, she looked up and saw the view screen on the ceiling. All the usual entertainment streams were there. She poked at the screen and called up the flight plan, noting the countdown. That was the last thing she remembered before the engine's whine woke her. Then the red alert siren.

She punched at the view screen—it showed there was a red alert, but not why. She scooted to the end of the pod and hit the release handle with her foot. The door swung open and she crawled down the ladder, jumping the last couple of feet. She hadn't even bothered to take off her boots, so she was ready to go. She swung the door to the pod closed and began to jog to the common area. Every passenger on the ship seemed to be there, all of them staring at the massive view screen taking up one wall. Some were looking out the port window, but Wall couldn't see anything there. The action was all on the view screen, it seemed.

She pushed past the other passengers, trying to get a look. She was short, so she didn't feel bad about it. Besides, now was not the time for—

She froze. Ice poured down her spine like water. Her lip began to quiver.

"What is it?" people around her were calling.

"What kind of ship is that?"

"What kind of creature is that?"

She'd seen that kind of ship before. She'd seen those kinds of creatures before.

"Prox," she breathed.

CHAPTER FIVE

"Bonus score," Jo said, turning on her heel and returning to the bridge. Jennings had been objecting, shouting something about a package, but she didn't need to bother herself with his nonsense. He wasn't much of a prize, but the RFC regional authorities would be pleased. The door to the bridge slid open and Tash Liebert called, "Captain on the bridge!" Everyone began to stand until she said, "As you were."

She sat in her command chair and sighed. Reports. There were always reports. *I'm so fucking tired of reports.* Still, it was the job. And god forbid she should miss anything. She looked up and accessed her neural.

"We're being hailed, sir," Mr. Liebert said. "Text only."

"That's medieval," Jo scowled, relieved to have a distraction from the reports. "Display."

—Can we get a status update on Captain Jennings?

Jo pursed her lips. "Computer, reply with text. Captain Jennings is under arrest. Please articulate new command structure." *Maybe there's more than one criminal in this nest,* she thought, and wondered why she hadn't thought of that before.

There seemed to be a long several minutes before a reply manifested on the screen.

—Permission to come aboard. One man. Unarmed. Request meeting with Captain Taylor.

"Oh sweet Christ on a donkey!" Jo said. But she was intrigued. Something was going on here, and the mystery sure beat the hell out of reports. "Mr. Liebert, inform security chief Dixon I'll need yet another detail at the main airlock in five minutes."

"Yes sir."

"Computer, reply with text. Permission granted. Access in five minutes."

She stood. Marcia Chi looked back at her, one eyebrow raised.

"I'm getting my exercise," Jo said to her.

Chi raised the other eyebrow and looked back to her console without comment.

Jo turned and headed for the door.

She retraced her steps through the ship, muttering to herself, but it was a routine. She wasn't as annoyed as she played at being. The corners of her lips even turned up a bit as she passed the mess, the gym, the common lounge.

She arrived at the airlock first. The security team scuttled in a few seconds later, their heads lowered sheepishly for not having arrived first. She narrowed one eye at them. "Did you have to finish your game level?" she asked.

One of the team members' eyes opened wider.

Nailed it, Jo thought. *Well, he won't do that again.*

She bounced a few times on the balls of her feet, waiting. Whoever it was, she'd take them into custody first, then she'd run their neural code for offenses. If they were clean, she'd apologize and plead appropriate caution.

The airlock pressurized and the door slid open.

Jo gasped.

"Hello, Jo."

Her mouth opened, but nothing came out. Her hand moved in slow motion, but her feet were rooted in place.

His mouth turned up in a slight, patient smile. He was older…as old as she was. It was wrong. He had scars and lines on his face from battles and stresses that he could not have had. *Corpses don't age, they rot,* she thought.

"What kind of trick is this?" she finally managed, feeling for the wall behind her. She found it. She leaned against it.

"It's the cruelest fucking trick the universe can manage," he said.

"You're dead," she said.

"That's true," he agreed.

"So…what the fuck is going on?"

He didn't answer that. Instead, he said, "I'm not the person you loved. But I'm…I'm like him."

She shook her head. Comprehension did not seem possible.

"Why…why are you here?" she asked. She couldn't think of another question.

"That's…complex," he smiled. She knew that smile. She *loved* that smile. She bit her lip, she wrestled within herself as her throat swelled and tears rose up behind her eyes, threatening to flood her, to drown her in grief and memory and a million fantasies of a life unlived.

"I'm here mostly because I loved you…or someone very much like you. And I had to see her…you…again. I wish that were the whole of it." His shoulders sagged and he looked at his feet, sighing audibly. "I'm also here because I need help…although I'm not entirely sure what it is I'm up against." It wasn't much of an explanation, and he seemed to sense it, because he looked up and smiled grimly. "More immediately, though, I suppose I'm here to get my captain out of jail before his indiscretions completely derail any chance I have of… finding what I need to find."

She could see the intensity in his eyes even as she fought against the raging storm in herself. "Are you Jeff?" she asked.

"I am. But not the Jeff you loved." He grimaced. "I could try to deceive you…but I can't do that to you. It's…we've both been through enough."

She nodded, still frozen to her spot.

"Can we talk?" he asked.

She nodded.

"Can we drink?" he added, his grin widening.

"It really *is* you," she said, her face betraying her wonder.

"No. No it isn't. But strangely…we can still catch up."

CAPTAIN DANIEL HIGHTOWER called down the summary report on his neural. Right on target, right on schedule. He smoothed the blanket over the bunk in the tiny ship's even tinier cabin, pulling it tight so that a medal tossed on its surface would bounce, as if it were the head of a drum. He quickly surveyed the room. *Shipshape,* he thought. He turned to his toiletries and ran his fingers over the stubble of his beard.

It was the style in the Authority these days to shave every third day, so as to let the stubble grow. It was considered sexy, tough. Danny just considered it sloppy. He shaved daily, and he did it the old-fashioned way. Eschewing folljacks, the grooming neutralizers that were ubiquitous in every bath and hotel room, he pulled forth a straight razor and lathering soap from his toiletries kit.

He didn't mind using a laser-based sharpener on the razor—one must make some concessions to modernity, after all—but he relished the feel of the warm soap on his face, and the surgical precision of the blade at his throat.

He imagined holding it to Jo Taylor's throat. For a moment, he was twenty years old again, holding a knife to her temple as he drooled on her face, his mouth hovering above hers, his cock pounding into her, hard enough that they both had welts afterwards. He remembered her angry protests, how she had struggled…but not much. *Good times,* he thought. There were moments when he missed her, moments when he thought he might have gone in a different direction.

"Family man," he said to himself, looking at his soapy face in the mirror. He laughed out loud at the absurdity of it. Besides, this was Jo he was talking about. Did he honestly think he could have broken her, domesticated her, even if he had wanted to?

"That would have been a challenge to sink my teeth into," he confessed to his reflection.

But holding a knife to her temple again? That was the opportunity of a lifetime. A career-making opportunity, given what Jo had become, or at least, had come to represent. He felt the thrill of it rise within him. It made him hard.

He wiped the last of the soap from his face and inspected his work. One tiny nick. Good. It confused people. He liked keeping people off their balance. He quickly donned a crisp uniform and buttoned the black double-breasted coat. Starships were always cold, after all. He didn't know why. But he liked his uniform, and he liked the cool air on his cheek, so he wasn't complaining.

He grabbed a cup of coffee and a muffin from the synthesizer and settled into his command chair. There was no one to command, of course, and he might have sat anywhere, but the ship was small, and it really was the most comfortable place to settle in, probably by design.

"Detail reports," he called out to the computer. He could have pulled them down on his neural, but the damn thing made him feel claustrophobic. If he wanted to live in his head, he'd have become a scientist. He was a warrior, and he relished his kinetic attachment to the world. Computers left him cold. He craved flesh and steel and sweat, the satisfying crack of bone, the primordial machinery of hard muscle lifting humanity from ignorance and chaos into the serene beauty of domination and order.

The reports contained no revelations. He had a single starboard engine manifold pushing an acceptable fluctuation limit, but there were thirteen others. Even if he had to take that one offline, it wouldn't cripple him. It would slow him down, but it had done its job. Arrival in twenty minutes.

He swiveled the chair and opened the small safe used to house sensitive documents and withdrew the hand-written letter from Admiral Tal and folded it once, creating a neat crease. He placed it in the upper left-hand inside pocket of his jacket and buttoned it closed.

"I could get used to this little ship," he said out loud. "It would make me the fastest man in the universe." But as soon as he said it, he knew it wasn't true.

If everything Jeff Bowers had told him was true—the *other* Jeff Bowers, he reminded himself—he was faster. Jeff couldn't use that speed, so he had said, without destroying the fabric of space-time, but the fact that he had it, that he could if he wanted to… Danny felt the heat rise in his face. He didn't mind being a captain. He didn't mind taking orders or making the admiralty feel like they had some authority or control over him. That was, after all, the game. But to have one man out there who could actually best him? Danny's teeth ground together at the thought of it. A man he had already mastered, dominated, eliminated…

"Why couldn't you just stay dead?" he said out loud, though he was barely aware of it.

He had his orders, but those orders didn't limit his agenda. There was more than one name on his hit list, and he already had plenty of feelers out there. What was it Jeff had said about spiders in space? Danny was the spider-master. He had an army of spiders, all spinning silk threads that would lead him to his prey.

"THIS PLACE…IS NOT MY PLACE," Pho said, his voice rising with anxiety. They'd gone down fourteen levels and emerged from the lift in what felt like another world entirely. Instead of the gleaming frosted white poly surfaces they were used to on Epworth Station's promenade, the walls here were slate gray and often stained with something Pho could not identify. Instead of the opalescent poly flooring, there was metal grillwork beneath their feet, and every now and then moisture of mysterious provenance dropped from above. It was only a matter of time before some of it fell in his hair, and Pho was not looking forward to that.

"Below your pay grade, huh?" Nira asked, not looking at him. She was glancing around, taking stock of everything and everyone who moved. Pho didn't know what she was looking for, but he trusted her completely. Whatever they were there to find, he knew Nira would find it. He'd known her long enough to know that you did not stand in her way if you expected to see tomorrow.

"I'm not saying that," he answered. "I don't think that what we do is more noble than what these people do."

"Uh-huh," she said. "Very egalitarian. Just try not to get a neck ache from holding your nose at that angle."

Pho's shoulder was bumped by a passing gaggle of people in blue-gray coveralls. Some had smudges of grease on their faces, none of them seemed clean. The hallway was swarming with people, none of whom paid any attention to them at all.

"I'm not—" he didn't bother to finish. She was right, and there didn't seem to be any reason to deny it.

"They can smell condescension and patronization a mile a way," she said. "So let me do the talking." She paused at an intersection—two wide hallways at right angles to each other. One seemed to head into an industrial area, the other into a rough commercial zone. Nira followed the neon.

"My dad was a grease monkey," she explained. "He was a better man than half of those I've ever met in uniform. In fact, I'm the first person in my family to trade the coveralls for the uniform. It doesn't make me better, just…angrier."

Pho's lips pursed. *Nira needs more anger like a starship needs a crack in the hull*, he thought.

She held her hand out, palm down, facing backwards, next to her thigh. He took the signal to mean *wait*, and slowed, letting her take point. It turned out to be sheer expedience, as the hallway was jammed with people either scrambling to grab a meal or rushing back to their shifts.

Nira's head jerked back and forth, and Pho realized she was tracking where people were headed, and probably what kind of people were headed where. The dim corridors were lit by multicolored signs promising "hot grub," "cheap eats," and "quick fucks" all jumbled on top of one another. Pho felt a drop of mysterious liquid light on the top of his head and grimaced.

"This way," Nira said, grabbing the front of his uniform and pulling.

She ducked into what looked like an ancient airlock door—the kind you might have seen on ships built seventy-five years ago or more. Pho had to duck to clear it, stepping over a gunwale that seemed inordinately high. *If there were a fire,* he thought, *every single person would trip on this trying to get out.*

Inside, he found his senses assaulted by light and sound and not unpleasant smells. It took a couple of minutes to take it in, but it appeared to be a bustling tavern. Grease monkeys of every species were sitting at large, family-style tables seating twenty people or more. They ordered from kiosks and meal pods descended from the ceiling. Most of them seemed to be drinking something, and from the level of gregarity, Pho guessed it was probably alcohol or some other intoxicant. A live band was playing—the start-stop jerky rhythm of Stomp, a genre of music popular among workers that involved harpsichord and tympani samples in 11/8 time and the trumpeting wail of a dragon sax. Pho liked the music when he heard it, but wouldn't be caught dead seeking it out. He wondered, for the first time, if he considered it beneath him. He realized he did. He frowned.

Nira tugged at him and pulled him toward a press of bodies that began to part before them as they approached. *No doubt due to Nira's scariness,* he thought. But then he realized it was probably also the uniform. It occurred to him that a change of clothes might have been a good idea.

Once through the crowd, he saw a bar, and Nira was making a beeline toward two seats, improbably empty. *Someone is watching out for us,* he thought, hopping up into one of them beside her. He swiveled in it, taking in the overwhelming chaos of the place. Near the band—a trio consisting of a keyboardist, percussionist, and dragon sax player, as he expected—several people were dancing. Many more were joking or arguing or fighting. Pho could barely hear himself think over the din.

Pho looked at Nira for her next signal, but she was too busy to give him one. She was studying the crowd. He had no idea what she was looking for, but he could see she was looking hard.

"What'll you have?" the barkeep asked. He was about Pho's own height, his head shaved, his bicep about twice as big around as Pho's own.

"Uh, nothing for me," Pho said.

"You don't order, you don't stay," the barkeep said flatly.

"Oh…well, then…a water, please."

The barkeep narrowed one eye. "I'm going to pull a beer for you, and one for your friend, and you're going to pay for it, or you're going to vacate those seats before I turn around again."

"That…that sounds perfect," Pho said. "Uh…but in that case, please make mine an IPA, the hoppier the better."

"That's more like it." The barman grinned for the first time, and Pho felt his shoulders relax a bit.

"Stay here," Nira commanded, and without waiting for his response, waded out into the crowd.

A moment later, the barman placed two beers on the counter, one slightly darker than the other. "This here is the IPA." The barman slid the slightly darker brew in front of Pho.

"Thank you," Pho said, and took a tentative sip. He brightened. "That's excellent."

"It is," the barman agreed. He seemed to be warming up to him. "Grimy down here, isn't it?"

Pho could tell the man was watching him carefully, as if gauging his response. He steeled himself for caution. "What…uh…what do you mean?"

"You're uniform people. Lieutenant, am I right? Never could get the hang of insignia. Besides, I've never seen yours before."

"Yes, lieutenant."

"Well, we don't get many lieutenants down here. Must seem pretty grimy to you."

"Uh…" It was true, but Pho didn't want to offend. It occurred to him that the man had as much prejudice against him as he did against the grease monkeys that frequented the place. *At least we're talking,* he thought.

"Up top, that's your place, where it's all white frosted poly and crisp, clean uniforms. Am I right?"

Pho had known some engineers in his day, and had even had some friends in engineering, but that wasn't the same. He blinked noncommittally. That didn't seem to stop the man.

"Every station is like this," the barman continued. "The top floors are gleaming, not a stray hair or dust speck allowed. That's where the people with money are, and the military folk, like yourself. Underneath, it's messy, dirty. We're the folks that keep everything working up there. You make as much in a month as we do in a year. You wanna know why?"

Pho could hear the resentment in the man's voice. He didn't want the conversation to go south, but he didn't want to lose track of Nira either. His eyes scanned frantically and finally found her, leaning her head down to talk to a large, fleshy man in coveralls sitting at a booth.

Pho glanced back at the barman and opened his mouth, but before he could say anything the barman plunged ahead.

"I'll tell you why." He leaned over and said in a slightly lower voice, still audible above the din. "Neo-Platonism."

He leaned back and nodded, giving Pho a satisfied look of arcane knowledge successfully transmitted.

Pho shook his head. "Come again?"

"Neo-Platonism," the man said again. "Spirit is good, clean, pristine—it resides at the top. Matter is bad, grimy, dirty—it sinks to the bottom. Everything in between is a mixture—purer at the top and fouler the further down you go."

"Uh-huh," Pho said. He had no idea what the man was talking about.

"It's hard-wired into the human psyche. So we build our stations to reflect it—top levels are clean, bottom levels are covered with shit. You look at stations built by other races—are they like this? Not a chance. Their designs are built on other metaphysical assumptions. They make no goddam sense to us. But to humans, this just seems right and proper. Virtue rises to the top. Shit gathers at the bottom. Same as it ever was. Excuse me." The man turned away, apparently needing to fill a drink order.

That was fine with Pho, who didn't really know how to respond to the man's philosophical monologue. It was finally starting to make some sense, but Pho didn't find that comforting. What he was saying was actually pretty disturbing, and it was exactly the kind of thing Pho would rather not think about if he could help it.

Pho's eyes sought out Nira again and found her. Now she was huddled up with two of the mechanics—or whatever they were. She was talking in an animated way, smiling broadly, as if joking. *This is not a Nira I know,* he thought, and realized it was an act. He saw her shake hands.

Pho turned back to the bar and noted a light blinking in his peripheral vision. He looked up, and located a new message—a bar tab. He authorized payment, along with what he hoped was a generous tip for the philosopher-barman.

Nira was walking back toward him now, one lip curled in satisfaction. She resumed her seat with only a bit of difficulty due to her height.

"Well?" Pho asked.

"Just gotta ask the right people," she said.

"And did you find the right people?" Pho asked.

"I have an address and a name," Nira said.

"That's…that's good, isn't it?" Pho asked.

"It's exactly what we came for," she assured him.

"And we have beer," he said, pointing to hers. "Consider it a celebratory indulgence—for a job well done. It's on me."

She raised an eyebrow, but lifted the beer to her lips anyway.

"So where do we go now?"

"To the one place where no one asks questions about neural code searches, and no one wants to know more than they have to."

"And…where is that?"

"The morgue."

SHE KNEW she shouldn't be excited. She knew she should be afraid. She was being kidnapped after all, but as kidnappings went, this one didn't seem as bad as it could have been. And Emma was a scientist after all, and here she was, meeting an extraterrestrial for the first time. Since there didn't seem to be anything she could do about the whole abduction thing at the moment, she decided to make the most of it.

"Amberline, what are your people called?"

The insect-like alien made a series of intricate gestures with all four arms, while also clicking its mouthparts. The mask hanging around her neck remained silent.

Emma waited, then realized what had happened. "Oh! That's your language?"

"Correct," said the mask.

She shook her head. "Wow, that's…" she held her arms up like a mantis, then smiled. "I don't have enough arms."

"Correct again. Human scientists have chosen to call us Alverians. That will serve for you."

"So *Amberline* isn't your actual name then."

"Correct. That is a label I use when dealing with humans, because they can't say this." She made a swooping gesture with only her primary arms, punctuated with a single sharp mouth click at the end.

"That's beautiful!" Emma repeated the gesture and mimicked the final click with her teeth.

Amberline suddenly stood taller. After a moment the mask spoke again. "That was fairly close. I have never seen a human even attempt our language before. They have always been very willing to allow us to conform to their needs."

Emma nodded. "Yes, I believe that. We can be very self-centered. Do you deal with humans often?"

"That is my primary function."

"Like, an envoy?"

Amberline shrugged. "I do not know that word. My people do not choose to interact with others often, so when they do, they send one of us to represent the hive. I have been trained to represent the hive when dealing with humans."

Emma's mind was racing. "Oh! That explains your… the uh, the outfit you were wearing when you came in!"

Amberline nodded. "Correct." Emma was getting used to her voice coming from the artificial mouth hanging from her neck. "When I first began interacting with humans, I encountered resistance or discomfort. I learned that humans fear or distrust beings different from themselves. I began wearing garments that would minimize my differences, make me appear more human. It seems to be effective, especially with the males of your species."

Emma giggled, then quickly covered her mouth with her hand. "Yes, our males are, well, *extremely* susceptible to manipulation, especially where sex is concerned. We do a lot of similar things ourselves —makeup, high heel shoes, corsets, padded bras…" She noticed that Amberline merely stared at her without response. She probably had no idea what she was talking about. "What about your males? Are they easy to manipulate as well?"

"Our males are not like us. They are not sentient. They are creatures of instinct alone."

Emma gasped. "How unusual."

Amberline shook her head. "It is you who are unusual. As with most species throughout the galaxy, females and males are distinct and dissimilar. Even the animals of your Earth have clear sexual dimorphism. With humans, males and females are nearly identical, and what few traits do distinguish you are largely superficial. I can barely discern one from the other. Even so, that seems to cause you… great confusion."

"What do you mean?"

"You do not appear to know how to behave toward each other. You are uncomfortable in each other's presence and become entangled in meaningless rituals and dominance struggles."

Emma suddenly remembered Jeff, the way he smelled, the sound of his voice, the way he abandoned her at the mention of Jo Taylor's name. Her face grew flush with pain and anger; the corners of her eyes grew damp. She frowned and shoved him out of her mind. “Yeah, you got that right.”

“Our way is easier, less ambiguous.” Amberline shrugged again. “But I suppose you are locked to your own biology, as are we. And as I’ve said, that confusion is easy to take advantage of for my own purposes.”

Emma nodded. It made perfect sense. “Ah, and your, uh, mask, thingy…” She made a circle over her sternum, approximating where Amberline wore her false face.

“It is a communication device, converting my thoughts to human speech via neural link.”

“Yeah, I get that. But it could have looked like anything. You made it look like a woman’s face, and a very kissable one at that.”

Amberline gently touched the mask. “I did not design it, but I was informed that humans find our mouth parts disturbing and would find this configuration more pleasing. Many purposes are served at once. It is highly efficient, and that is something my people value.”

“We would call it an *elegant solution.*”

“Yes. I can see the rightness of that phrasing.” The false mouth smiled, revealing tiny, perfectly even teeth.

WALL FELT PARALYZED. Her mouth dropped open as she saw the soldier Prox detach from their ship and float off in formation—directly toward them.

“No no no no no…” she repeated, until other passengers started to look at her.

They noted her uniform, and someone asked about it. No one recognized it, of course.

“I’m not from around here,” she explained, tearing her eyes away from the view screen. “But I’ve seen those before…where I’m from.”

A babble of voices began lobbing questions at her. She suddenly felt claustrophobic. She backed up, but ran into more people. They were shouting questions, too.

"They're Prox!" she shouted above the din of their questions, above their confused, frightened babble. The blaring of the red alert siren didn't help.

"What's Prox?" she heard distinctly, although she couldn't make out who asked it. It didn't matter.

"They're death," she said simply.

So they exist in this universe too, she thought. *Of course they do. Most things are the same here. They just found us a little bit later on this string. But they found us. Of course they found us. And of course, they want to kill us. That's what they do.*

She wasn't actually sure of that. She was sure that they wanted to eat their ships, they wanted to feast on the metal. She wasn't sure that the species had any animosity toward humans at all, or that they were even aware of the existence of human beings. *We have metal, so we're just a ready supply of food,* she thought. It was how it seemed to her, anyway. *We're pesky when we fight back, but otherwise, they seem perfectly content to ignore us... as they eat the ships that surround us and protect us.* That seemed to be as good a warning as any.

"They don't want to hurt us," she said. Amazingly, everyone became quickly quiet so as to hear her. They didn't know if what she was saying had any veracity, but it was the only information coming at them. Truth be told, Wall didn't know if what she was saying had any veracity. But it was her best guess, based on what she had seen. She raised her voice and said again, "They don't want to hurt us...because they don't care about us. They would completely ignore us if..."

"If what?" someone asked.

"They just want the metal," she said. "They eat it."

People looked confused. A buzz arose as they started to whisper and discuss.

"But the ship is *made* of metal," one of them protested.

"Right," Wall affirmed. She'd never thought of herself as a leader, but she was an officer of the CDF. It was time to step up. "We have about five minutes to live. If there are people you love on board, you need to tell them so."

People started shouting at her, but she moved through the crowd as if parting the Red Sea. She couldn't take her eyes off the main view screen, and she had to get closer. She watched as the ship's meager defense batteries opened up on the advance guard Prox, thousands of their fellows in a swarm just behind them, nothing but a blurry cloud. The first of the Prox were clearly visible now, their metal, crablike legs extended, pointed toward the hull. The ship got off a couple of lucky shots—she saw two of them in quick succession spinning away from the blast force. But more were coming, and quickly.

Wall was arm's length from the view screen now. She reached out and touched it. As she did so, the first of the Prox landed with a metallic thud on the outside hull. The sound of it reverberated throughout the room, even over the hubbub of voices. The hull screamed as great sheets of it were torn off, rivets popping, seams shorn open, until there was a great rushing of wind and Wall felt the air sucked from her lungs by an irresistible force.

CHAPTER SIX

Jeff poured himself a scotch and held the bottle out to Jo. She nodded. He poured two fingers into another glass and pushed it across the table to her. They were in a small lounge, alone. The lights were dimmed, and soft piano music played in the background.

Jo picked up the glass and knocked it back, slamming it onto the table in front of her. "Hit me," she said, pointing to the bottle.

Jeff laughed and filled her glass again. He was putting a good face on things, but inside he was awash with emotions that threatened to undo him. *I'm barely holding it together*, he admitted to himself. He kept his hands under the table. They were shaking. Then he noticed that Jo's hands were shaking too, and his heart nearly melted.

Here we are, he thought. *We've traveled through hell and back to find each other, and we don't know what to say.*

She was beautiful. He couldn't stop looking at her. He forced himself to look at the table. He bit his lip.

Jo was not beautiful by the standards of conventional attractiveness, he knew that. Not that he cared. She was thin, certainly, but her nose was a little too large, her cheeks a little too hollow. She had a hard look to her that put many people off. But it was precisely such imperfections that fascinated him. He loved her severity—loved it so much that he felt nearly paralyzed.

Jo knocked back another glass. Jeff sipped at his, relishing the acrid smokiness of it. The silence between them became long, turned awkward.

"Out with it," Jo said finally. "Tell me how it is that you're…alive. Goddammit."

"What?" Jeff asked. He had heard her. He just didn't understand where the edginess of her final words had come from.

"You were dead. I had to…" She looked away. "Okay, it's not fair to go into how *I* suffered because *you* died. But…" She rocked back and forth a little. She was fishing for words and not finding them. Jeff wished he could help her, wished he could do *anything* for her. "I never thought…" she started again but got no further.

Jeff sipped his whisky again. He held up his hand to stop her from struggling on. "First, I want to say I'm sorry," he began. "In my universe, I did something that…that resulted in your death."

He found he couldn't meet her eyes. He stumbled forward. "I didn't mean to. I would do anything to go back and…" He forced himself to look up. He held her eyes with his. "I'm sorry."

"So here, you were dead and I'm alive," she clarified. "And there, you're alive and I'm dead?"

"Yes."

"And just where is *there*?"

"You know about the string universes?"

"Of course."

"Right now, we're on String 311. My world, where I was born, is String 310." He looked away again. "But String 310…isn't there anymore. I…I destroyed it."

"You destroyed the entire universe?"

He nodded. To hear it said out loud like that, it sounded grandiose, megalomaniacal even. He had trouble believing it himself. But it was true. "Every creature, every person, every world in every galaxy… gone. Including you. And it's my fault."

Jo pointed to the bottle again. "Hit me."

He obliged.

"That's a lot of guilt," she said, picking up the glass. She didn't knock it back this time. "How come you're not crazy with guilt? How come you haven't slit your wrists…or overdosed on Morphex?"

"That's a good question. I did…I went through a tough time on Sol Station."

"You were on Sol Station?"

He nodded. Her eyes narrowed. He sighed. "Perhaps I should… begin at the beginning."

"Perhaps you should."

So he did, beginning with Operation Catskill. After all, what did a classified designation mean in a universe that was no more? And maybe it was still classified in the Authority, but what did that matter to Jo, the Authority's sworn enemy? Besides…this was Jo. Not his Jo, but still Jo. And she was more like his Jo than he had expected. In fact, he had yet to divine a way to prove that this Jo was not identical to his own.

He held back little. He told her about Danny's death. He told her about Admiral Jennings, the Prox, the Ulim, and his miraculous resurrection. He told her about Emma and their experiments, his teleportation, and the attempted teleportation of the *Bohr*. As he related the death of Captain Jo Taylor, he forced himself to look up, to watch her eyes. They were wide, searching, haunted. Her lips pursed into a grim circle, her cheeks growing even more hollow than usual.

He told her about the final experiment, the quantum seismological readings, their being boarded by Danny. He told her about Admiral Tal and the arrest of his crew, as well as their escape and near destruction by Danny's treachery. He told her about how he had abandoned his crew.

Throughout it all, she sat rigid, leaning forward, wanting more, straining for every flake of detail. He did not disappoint her. When he finished, he polished off his glass of whiskey and poured another. "And then I found Jennings…the Jennings of your world," he said, shaking his head. "And hired him to bring me here…to you."

They sat in silence for what seemed like an hour, but must have only been a minute or two.

"That's quite a story," she said.

He nodded.

"Tell me why I shouldn't throw you into a cell with Jennings, as a spy?"

He shrugged. "You could do that." He narrowed one eye at her. He watched her shoulders sag, watched her look away. *But she's not going to do that,* he said to himself.

"Why did you come here?" she asked. "Why did you come to me?"

Jeff felt a wave of panic roll through him. Wasn't that obvious? Yet…maybe she just needed to hear it.

"Because I…uh…I love you," he said. It could have sounded facile or manipulative, but it didn't. His voice caught as he said it, and he met her eyes. If she couldn't see the truth of it, there was no more he could say. "I always have. And I lost you once, and now…"

Incredibly, he felt himself tearing up. Instantly, he hated himself for it. He bit his lip and nodded, waiting, pleading inside for the water to recede. It took a few moments of hard mastery, but the pressure eased. His throat unclenched. His breath slowed. He looked up at her again. "I'm sorry," was all he could say.

It was a very general apology. It could have meant that he was sorry for killing her, for ending a universe, for the momentary awkwardness, or for allowing his control to slip for a fraction of a second. And in truth, it was for all of these things.

She reached across the table and placed her right hand down, palm up. He lifted his own right hand from beneath the table and clutched at hers. They held onto one another for dear life.

"I'm glad you're not dead," she said.

"I'm glad *you're* not dead," he repeated.

"So that makes two of us then," she said. Then they both laughed. The awkwardness was almost unbearable.

"What now?" she asked.

"There's one part of the story I didn't tell you," he admitted. "Aboard Sol Station, I met someone. He was from Earth, from Peru.

He…knew." Jeff was nodding, but it was a compulsive motion, not a response to anything. He continued to squeeze her hand.

"What do you mean?" she asked. "Knew what?"

"I don't know," he said. "But he seemed to know about me, about what I can do, about where I came from. It was all very…mysterious and evasive. It was like he was telling me he knew all about me, but didn't want to say it in case anyone else was listening. It was…I don't know…it was like spies talking."

She nodded slowly, thinking. "If he knows…he might know a lot more."

"Right," he nodded, relieved that she seemed to get it. "I have to find him."

"He could be anywhere."

"I have…talents, remember?" he said. "When I'm ready to find him…I can find him. I can find anyone." He fixed her eye and held it. "I found you, didn't I?"

She nodded. "Okay. I get that. I believe you, too. Just…how do you know you won't destroy this universe, too, if you…you know…use your talent?"

"I don't," he admitted.

"Oh." she said. "So that's bad."

"It is," he agreed.

"Hey Jeff," she said.

"What?"

"Don't kill me again."

He felt like someone punched him in the chest. That was Jo, all right—straight for the jugular.

"I'm going to do everything in my power…" he started, but it sounded feeble. He shut up.

"Don't. Kill me. Again," she repeated, slower and lower this time.

He nodded. He couldn't look at her. He poured himself another drink. He picked it up and looked at it. He set it back down. He needed to ask something but didn't know how. Finally, he just blurted it out. "I have a favor to ask." There, he'd said it. He'd forced it from his throat like rocks on a cheese grater.

"It's a little soon, don't you think?" she asked. Until that moment, he hadn't given any indication that he had an agenda, other than finding her. Now he felt slimy, as if he was playing her and had just been found out. He hated himself.

"You can say no," he said. "And it kills me to ask. But…if you can…well…I need your help." He cringed at his own words. Every one of them hit him like the stab of a hunting knife in naked flesh.

She crossed her arms. "What?"

"I have to find this shaman…or whatever he is. I have to find out what he knows. I know I don't…I don't know anything. But my gut says it's the right move, and my gut…"

"Your gut was always right," Jo said.

"Yes."

"Okay, you need to find him. You need transport…because we don't want you destroying the universe trying to teleport," she reasoned it out. "Which means you need a ship, which means you need Jennings." She sighed. "You want me to release Jennings."

"Uh…actually, Jennings is a disaster. He's nothing like Jennings… the Jennings I know."

"Thank God." Jo rolled her eyes.

"You take him off my hands, I can fly his damned ship and won't have to deal with his bullshit."

"That's cold." She smiled.

"Yeah, but…fuck him. He's a pain in the ass." He smiled back.

"So that's not the favor?" She cocked her head and waited. Finally, she seemed to get tired of waiting and said, "So what's the goddam favor?"

He leaned forward. "I've got a crew—the finest XO I've ever served with, a better-than-average navigator, and one of the most brilliant quantum seismologists in known space. They need jobs."

"Jobs?"

"I left them floating with some lame plan about a rendezvous. A rendezvous I can't make. I want to make sure they have a place to land, so that I don't have to…"

"So you don't have to worry about them," she finished his sentence.

"Yes."

"You're a good captain."

"I just suck at the whole human being thing," he countered.

She laughed. It wasn't a big laugh. It was more of a chuckle. She played with her glass but didn't ask him to refill it. "You've made some shit moves," she said, "but this…this isn't one of them."

"It sure feels like it, though. But…thank you for saying that. It would…it would mean a lot to me, and it would be a great relief."

"The RFC is always looking for good recruits," she said.

"You won't find better."

"You realize you're asking me to rescue your girlfriend, right?"

He said nothing.

"That part is fucked up."

He pursed his lips and nodded.

She teased him further, adding in a sing-song voice, "'If you love me you'll rescue my girlfriend.' That's what you're saying. You know that, right?"

He tried to stop the smile. He couldn't. And when she leaned across the table and kissed him, he grinned like an idiot.

"I'VE NEVER BEEN TO A MORGUE," Pho admitted. They stepped into a lift, but it was nothing like the gleaming elevators they were used to. Nira could see Pho react to the griminess of it. For one thing, it wasn't completely enclosed. If you weren't careful, a girl could lose a limb if she stuck it through the grillwork. Nira kept her hands behind her back, standing at parade rest as the elevator descended.

"I didn't think there was any further down to go," Pho said, his voice almost despairing.

"It's a big station," Nira said.

"Not compared to Sol," Pho said. Nira didn't find the comment worthy of answer. She stared at the floors passing by rapidly through the grillwork. Out of the corner of her eye she saw Pho notice and react to the mess on the floor of the lift. It looked like raw sewage but wasn't. It didn't smell for one thing. It was the typical mixture of water, grease, and grime that collected in the bowels of any ship or station.

"At least there aren't any spiders," Nira said.

"I never thought I would miss the spiders," Pho said. For a moment, they shared a smile. She could tell it helped him.

Eventually the elevator found its level, and the cage door rattled open. Nira pushed past it and stepped out on to an equally grimy bit of grillwork scaffolding.

"This seems precarious," Pho said.

She was beginning to tire of his trepidation. She looked up and consulted the map on her neural. "This way," she said, heading through a low metal door to their left. Pho followed.

The hallway was almost deserted, but every now and then they passed someone wearing the light blue coveralls of a mechanic. A couple of people passed them, arguing excitedly in a language Nira didn't understand, dressed in street clothes that had seen better days. "Do people live down here?" Pho asked.

"Of course they do."

"That's grim."

Nira ignored him. She paused, checking the number stenciled above a wide metal door. "This must be it." The door, she noted, hung from thick metal tracks. It was made to slide open along the wall—she could see the tracks end about 2.5 meters from the door's edge.

She looked around for an entry pad. She would have settled for an old-fashioned door knocker, but there was nothing.

"Aw, hell," she said. She kicked at the door repeatedly with the steel toe of her boot, trying to make as much noise as possible.

Pho's eyebrows rose.

A moment later they heard movement. The door swung open a crack. "What do you want?" came a voice that sounded like it had been sleeping moments before.

Nira put her face to the crack. "I need to find someone. Elba Jannar recommended your services. Under the table."

"You Authority pricks?"

"No."

"You station dicks?"

"No."

"Legally, you have to say if you are," he insisted.

"We don't represent any law enforcement agency or…existing government."

"You represent a non-existing government?" She saw a milky eye widen.

"I guess we do."

"You get points for novelty," he said.

"We can pay," she said.

"Well, then, that's the magic word." He slid the door open far enough to admit them. Nira slipped past him and motioned for Pho to follow. The man scowled at the hallway outside and looked quickly one way, then the other, then slid the door to. He turned, and Nira caught her first complete glimpse of him.

He was middle-aged, overweight, with wispy strands of hair clinging to the top of his balding head. He wore a stained surgical apron. His eyebrows were feral and his nose was bright red and bulbous. *This is not a man who eats well,* she thought, but didn't say it.

The room was large, industrial, well lit. Several gurneys were lined up in one corner—she counted six—empty, silver surfaces gleaming. On one of them there was a pile of light blue sheets, roughly folded.

"Okay, explain," he said, walking past them and waving them through a swinging door into a further room. Nira caught the door as it was about to close and followed him in. It was cold inside, and she noted that the gurneys in this room were not empty. Most of them held what she assumed to be cadavers, most of them covered head to toe in light blue sheets. One gray wall was made entirely of what looked like meter-square refrigerator doors. Nira could guess what those were for. She felt Pho behind her and wondered how freaked out he was becoming. *I need to trust him to be professional,* she told herself. *Focus.*

She had always prided herself on reading a situation right and acting with speed and precision. It hadn't failed her yet. The fact that no one expected such efficiency from her challenged her to even greater heights of meticulousness. Her family lacked a gene for ambition, and she had no idea how she had acquired one. And some others assumed she was lazy because she was Latina. It was a racist stereotype which had persisted far too long yet was still prevalent. *Had been prevalent,* she thought, *before our universe was destroyed.* She had no idea whether Latinos in this universe suffered the same injustice. Probably.

"I am an officer of the Colonial Defense Fleet," she said.

"The Colonial Defense Fleet splintered into the RFC and the Authority twenty years ago," the man scowled, his flaky eyebrows knitting.

"Not in our universe."

"Huh," he scanned their uniforms. "I haven't seen a uniform like that since I was at school," he admitted. "So you're either some weird, alien CDF or you just picked those up at a thrift shop. The latter is more likely."

"It probably is," Nira admitted. "It's just not what's true."

Something in her voice seemed to make him pause. "Well, your provenance is none of my concern, so long as you're not security."

"We're not. I promise you that."

"Give me access to your neural."

"What?" Nira's eyes went wide.

"If you're not security—of one kind or another—prove it. Give me access to your neural."

Nira knew that if she did that, the man would have full access to her life. Not memories—neurals weren't that deeply embedded in the brain—but certainly all the details of her life, including her bank account. "Sorry. I can't give you that."

"Eh, it was worth a shot." The man shrugged and pulled the sheet back, revealing the corpse of a species Nira had never seen before. There certainly seemed to be more aliens in this universe. The creature was humanoid, but obviously not human. It had gills, for one thing.

The man leaned over it and pried open one of its eyes. The pupils were bright gold but very dead.

Nira panicked inwardly. It seemed like they'd been on the brink of losing their opportunity when she refused him, but the man hadn't kicked them out yet. She tried to establish a new connection with him. "What's your name?"

"No names. You can call me Goat. I'll call you Mouse."

Nira didn't like being called Mouse. She certainly didn't like being reminded that she was small. She made a decision to ignore it. "What about him?" She pointed at Pho.

Pho looked around as if he were suddenly on stage.

"Him? I haven't seen the need to call him anything. The only thing I can see that he's good at is listening. Let's call him Ear." Goat shot a half smile, half sneer in Pho's direction. "What are you, Chinese?"

"Vietnamese," Pho said.

"Huh. Catholic?"

Pho's brows knotted. "Buddhist."

"Huh." He turned back to the corpse and began flaring one of the gills with a silver instrument. "So out with it," Goat said. "What do you need?"

"We need to find a friend of ours," Nira said.

"You need a neural scan of the station," Goat inferred.

"Yes."

"And you can't go to security for that." It wasn't a question, but Nira answered it as if it were.

"No."

"This 'friend' of yours. Why do you want to kill him?"

"What?" Nira asked. "No! We don't want to kill anyone! And it's a her."

Goat stood up straight and leveled one narrowed eye at Nira. He didn't bother looking at Pho at all.

"Huh," he said. "So if you don't want to kill…*her*…why do you need to find her?"

"She's a member of our crew, and we were supposed to meet up at a rendezvous point yesterday. She didn't show."

"Maybe she decided you weren't her type."

Nira ignored the jab. "She isn't answering any messages. We parted on good terms. There's no reason she shouldn't answer a message."

"Unless she's offline," the man said.

"Or dead," Nira admitted, looking down at the corpse.

"She could be here," the man said.

"She could be," Nira admitted. She looked around at the other covered corpses.

"Well, let's find out." Goat began a circuit of the room, uncovering each of the bodies in turn.

Nira followed behind him—not too closely—and shook her head after each.

"Huh," the man said when they were finished.

"How about those?" Nira pointed to the refrigerator cells in the wall.

"Too old," Goat said. "She died…disappeared…yesterday?"

"Yes."

"Too old."

Nira breathed a sigh that was part depression and part relief. "About that neural scan…"

"Okay, okay." Goat raised the sheet on the last of the cadavers. "You know this is illegal, right?"

"Of course. That's why we're here and not at the security office."

"So you know it's going to cost you."

"Yes. We're prepared. How much?"

"20,000."

Nira put her hands on her hips. Her face screwed up in a mask of instant indignation. "20,000 for thirty seconds of effort?"

"Hey, I've been talking to you for ten minutes now, haven't I?" Goat spread his hands as if to say *I got nothing to hide*.

Nira sincerely doubted that. "10,000."

"Fifteen."

"10,000." Nira held firm.

"15,000 and that's final."

Nira nodded sadly. She looked at Pho and jerked her head toward the door. “C’mon. We’ll find someone else.”

Pho’s eyebrows shot up, but he followed her as she headed for the exit.

“Okay, okay. Jeez!” the man said. “10,000. Christ.”

Nira turned around, almost bumping into Pho.

Goat didn’t seem to notice. He went to a work station and tapped out a few lines. Then he handed her a black datapad. “Enter her neural number.”

Nira did. She handed it back to him, but he ignored her. He scowled at his panel, and his fingers flashed as he ran the number. His seborrheic eyebrows bunched as he read the answer.

“What?” Nira asked. “What did you find?”

Goat looked up at her and crossed his arms. “Pay me first. Then I’ll tell you.”

Nira scowled, but she nodded.

Goat touched several nodes on his panel, then pointed to the datapad again.

“Enter your payment ID.”

She looked at him uncertainly. “I’m not going to give you my account number.”

He shook his head. “You really aren’t from around here, are you?” He blew air through his cheeks. “Okay, in your neural, navigate to your account…”

“Uh…Nira,” Pho said. “On your account page, in the upper left corner, there’s a code. It’s your payment code. You enter that whenever you want to pay for something.”

Nira looked up and found it. She looked back down. “How did you know that?”

“I…it’s different from how we do it in our world…but not very different. It’s just kanji rather than numeric. I had to find it to pay for the beer.”

She nodded. Then she looked at the pad. She switched to the kanji interface and entered the code.

“That wasn’t so hard, was it?” Goat asked.

Nira ignored him. Goat continued doing something on his panel, then he looked up. Probably checking to make sure the money was transferred, she thought. He looked down again and gave them a professional smile. "Nice doing business with you."

"The results?" There was a sharp edge in Nira's voice, and she moved her body into an attack position.

Goat must have noticed because he put his hands up defensively. "All right. Sheesh. She's not here."

"What do you mean, 'She's not here'?"

"If she were dead, I'd still be able to ping her neural. No ping. Even if her power was depleted, there's a backup cell for just these kinds of situations. All it does is ping the transponder. No ping," he repeated.

"What if she's just offline?" Pho asked.

"Same thing. She wouldn't be able to access the Net, but we'd still be able to ping the hardware. No ping."

"Which means?"

"Which means she's off-station," Goat said.

"Where did she go?" Nira asked.

"You'll need to find another criminal to tell you that," Goat said, standing and heading for the door. Nira realized he was showing them out. "Now if you'll excuse me, I have dead people to desecrate."

"CAPTAIN ON DECK!" a crewman shouted. The bridge crew of the *Horatio Nelson* began to stand. They expected him to say, "As you were." But he didn't. He let them stand. One of them even faltered, off balance for having expected to sit right back down. Captain Daniel Hightower narrowed one eye at the offender. He then looked around, meeting the eyes of every member of the crew, making sure they knew where their respective roles were in the Authority pecking order. Finally, the captain rose from his seat, a middle-aged man with a healthy head of brown hair and graying temples. He didn't need to stand for him, but Danny took it as a sign of courtesy, respect, and just plain friendliness. He shook the captain's hand. "Captain Oswald." He gave the captain a professional smile. Dropping his hand, he surveyed the room again, waiting—keeping every woman and man on the bridge standing, subject to his whim. "As you were," he said finally, as if it were a gift.

The air was tense. He could feel it. It was exactly what he had intended to create. No one doubted his command, not even Oswald.

"We weren't expecting you, Captain," Oswald said, cocking his head.

"Is your ready room available?" Danny jerked his head toward the door at the side of the bridge, the traditional place for such rooms.

"Of course." Oswald turned. "Kasweki, you have the conn."

A young woman with a blonde ponytail and a scar across her cheek rose without comment and occupied the command chair. Oswald gestured toward the ready room. Danny led the way, pausing only to wait for the door to slide open. A moment later they were alone, seated across from one another at the small table that filled most of the space.

"This is highly unusual," Captain Oswald began. "Of course, I'm always glad to see you." He smiled.

Liar, Danny thought. He and Oswald had known each other at the academy…briefly. Devin Oswald had been two years ahead and moved in different circles. But they knew each other well enough to recognize one another, even to make small talk as they had on a handful of occasions since graduation. "You won't be glad of this." He withdrew Tal's note from his pocket and tossed it at him.

It almost slid off the table, but Oswald caught it. "What is this?" he asked.

Danny said nothing, but watched as Oswald broke the seal on the envelope. "Pretty arcane technology." He grinned in Danny's direction, but it was a complicated grin, as it should be. In it Danny saw trepidation, fear, dread. Oswald unfolded a cream-colored sheet and moved his eyes over it.

He wasn't smiling now. He threw the paper on the desk.

"You're relieving me of my command?"

"Not me. I'm just here to take over."

"Why is Admiral Tal relieving me of my command? Has there been an ethics inquiry that I don't know about?"

"Should there be?"

Oswald scowled. His eyes flashed sheer venom. It was a side of Oswald he hadn't seen before. He discovered he suddenly liked the man more than he had mere moments ago. Danny didn't know what to do with "nice," but he certainly knew where he stood with hate.

"You're to collect your effects immediately and board the *Faraday*. It will take you back to Sol Station for reassignment."

"How do I know this is really from Tal?"

"You have an ansible. Send a confirmation text." Danny's face was impassive, calm, in control.

Oswald was a tense knot of suspicion and hurt. His hands clenched into fists and released unconsciously. He looked up, blinked a few times, and looked back down again.

Danny knew exactly what he had done. He had connected to the ansible and had sent a vague but pointed inquiry to Admiral Tal directly. Not everyone could contact the admiral without going through his office staff, but captains could.

Danny counted twenty-seven breaths before Oswald looked up and blinked again. He looked down, and his eyes were smoky but resigned. "I'll get my things."

"Don't take it personally, Devin," Danny smiled. "It's nothing you did. You'll get an even better ship, I'm sure."

Oswald blinked.

"I'll take your command spindle now. Are all the codes on it?"

Oswald fished in his pocket and withdrew a datachip in its holder. "All. At least the codes to the codes. As per regulations." He placed it on the table between them. Danny noted that the label on the holder was written by hand. *How quaint,* he thought.

Oswald leaned over the table, his voice lowered. "What I don't understand is why *you* are replacing me."

Danny stood, straightening his coat. "Devin, nobody doubts that you are a solid captain. You run a tight ship. Your crew likes you and respects you."

Oswald's eyebrows rose.

"I've read your files." He smirked. "There was a lot of dead time in transit. Even at C9."

"C9? Really?"

"Enjoy it," Danny said and headed for the door.

"Wait, you didn't answer my question," Oswald objected. "Why you?"

"Because everyone generally agrees that you are a good man. This mission requires something less…or more. This mission requires ruthlessness." He waited for the door to slide open. It was *his* ready room now. But before going through, he looked over his shoulder at Oswald, still sitting motionless, probably in shock. "We need someone who isn't afraid of blood."

Danny grinned, aware that his teeth were showing. He was a handsome devil when he smiled. It was something he liked about himself. He also knew that it was a smile that scared people. He liked that; in fact, he cultivated it. It was one more weapon in his arsenal. "And that person is me. I'm *dying* for blood."

THEIR LOVEMAKING WAS FIERCE. Every regret he'd ever felt over the past twenty years around how things had ended between them poured out of him. He wanted to make it up to her, wanted to make it right. All of his grief at losing her made him clutch at her all the more tightly—an improbable but precious second chance to express all of the passion he felt for her that he hadn't spoken, hadn't admitted, even to himself. Her ferocity had matched his, snarl for snarl, moan for moan. As he entered her from behind, she ground against him with a fury he didn't remember her having, and he realized she was making up for lost time and lost opportunity as well. He clutched at her breasts and heaved himself into her, edging nearer the point of no return until the white-hot explosion in his brain obliterated all knowledge, all sensation, all concern…until it subsided, leaving him panting, jerking with the last spasmodic remnants of passion.

He withdrew and collapsed beside her, feeling heavy and blissful until his worries rushed in again like oxygen filling an airlock. He groaned and rolled toward her until their foreheads were touching.

"All my bones have dissolved," Jo said. "That's awkward."

Jeff laughed and pulled her closer.

Jo nuzzled his neck. "That…was not like old times."

"No. That was different."

"I could do that again."

"Uh…give me a few minutes," Jeff said, chuckling. He had no doubt that his newish body was up to a repeat performance, but even he needed a bit of reset time.

They lay in silence for a time. At first, it was delicious. The sound of Jo's breathing was like music. The feel of her beside him was like the best dream he could imagine—and far better than anything he let himself fantasize about. After a while, though, Jeff began to feel anxious as the quiet continued. Did he really have nothing to say to her? Or her to him? Or was he just too chickenshit to say it?

He sensed the rightness of that. But just what was the "it" that he needed to say?

"I've missed you," he said.

Her arm was thrown across his chest, and she pulled him closer to her. "I missed you too. Kind of…crazily."

He smiled. "I never even let myself hope…"

"No," she agreed.

"You know, the Danny you got here is a real piece of work."

"He's an assbag maniac."

"No kidding."

"Was he like that in…where you come from?"

"No. Nothing like. He was…he was a good friend."

"They call him the Butcher here."

"I know."

"Did they call you that…in the other universe?"

"No."

"At least there's that."

"But I felt like it."

She hugged him close.

"What are you going to do about Jennings?"

"Turn him over to the authorities. I told you. You can fly his ship, right?"

He could. But her question brought them to the uncomfortable subject of his intentions. After a long moment, he said, "I have to go."

"I know."

"I don't want to."

"Yes, you do."

She was right. Deep down, he knew he had to go, even wanted to go. But he felt torn, too. "I'll come back," he promised.

She kissed his stubbled cheek. "You better."

CHAPTER SEVEN

Emma was relieved by Amberline's openness. She'd always associated kidnappings with cruel, violent men who tortured their captive for sport, at least until the ransom was paid and the victim was returned alive—if she was lucky. But Amberline was a gentle, almost gracious host, and she wondered what that said about the character of her own species.

Emma's offline neural indicated that they had been flying for nine hours at some unknown speed, when an alarm from the control room drifted back through the open hatch. Amberline stood from her crouch and walked towards it.

"May I come with you?" Emma asked. Amberline beckoned her to follow and walked away.

The control cabin was tiny compared to the spacious bridges of the military ships she was used to, two beefy flight seats arranged in front of a complicated control panel, nestled into the transparent bubble at the front of the ship. Amberline folded herself into the left seat, Emma clambered into the right. She glanced at the controls and found that all the labeling was in an unknown script that looked a bit like cuneiform, which Emma assumed was the Alverian alphabet.

Amberline's claws danced lightly on the controls, and the ship shuddered and dropped out of superluminal space. The stars, which had been irregular smeared squiggles, again became clear bright points of light, and ahead of them was a small asteroid that must be their destination. It was mostly a naked rock with no atmosphere. There were no visible structures that would give Emma a sense of scale. Without knowing how big it was, she couldn't even guess how far away it was. She decided it didn't really matter, they'd be there soon enough.

"Is this your homeworld?" Emma asked.

"No," she replied. "This is the hive."

Emma had heard Amberline mention 'the hive' before, it still held little meaning to her even as she was seeing it grow larger and nearer by the minute. Her captor was no doubt communicating with the asteroid via neural, providing authorization codes and receiving approach vectors. On the surface, a ring of landing lights blazed to life in the shadows of a small crater, and Amberline guided the ship toward them with expert precision. Before long they had landed, and a boarding tube extended and docked with the ship.

Amberline rose out of the seat. "Come with me."

Emma winced at the formality of the command, but stood, following her captor to the airlock. Amberline clawed at a keypad, and the hatch unlocked and slid aside. The air that rushed in from outside was hot, humid, and had a strange, metallic aroma.

Four Alverians waited in the chamber outside, varying slightly in height and coloring from Amberline. One of them wore a bright red sash tied around her waist. Amberline bowed deeply to them, and then, suddenly, the group all began waving their arms wildly and making ratcheting sounds with their mandibles. Was it a formal greeting or an argument? Emma had nothing to compare it to, no context to provide meaning. Every few seconds, one of them would reach out and tap herself or another sharply on the shoulder or thorax, making a hollow-sounding clack. As aggressive as it looked, Emma surmised it was just another part of their vocabulary. More than once, one of them would point at Emma, and they would all look over. Clearly she was at least one of the topics being discussed. She stood respectfully still until they finished. The four nodded and broke away, scrabbling off down the corridor. Amberline watched them walk away, then turned back toward the ship.

Emma followed her. "So, how'd that go?"

Amberline continued back into the cargo bay and began unlashing the crates from the wall. "Not exactly as I had hoped."

That surprised Emma. "Did they know you kidnapped me?"

"Of course," said the mask, "the contract was sanctioned. But since the decision was made, they have begun reconsidering the wisdom of bringing a human inside the hive."

"Why? What happened the last time?"

Amberline waved horizontally at shoulder height.

"What does that mean?"

"It means there was no last time."

"Wait, are you saying I'd be the first? Ever?"

"That is correct."

Emma whistled. "Well, I wouldn't want to cause you any trouble. You can just let me go if it makes things easier…"

Amberline paused as if she was actually considering it, then shook her head. "No. The plan is already set in motion. You will remain here, in the hive. Would you please carry this case?"

Once again, Emma knew consciously she shouldn't be anywhere near as excited about this as she was.

"SIR, I have an incoming message from RFC Command…text," Lieutenant Tash Liebert's voice was urgent.

"Display it," Jo said. She didn't want to be on the bridge. She wanted to fuck Jeff's lights out. Again. She sighed. At least the message was a welcome distraction.

"It's classified, sir. Your eyes only."

"Port it to my neural, then."

In a few hours, Jeff would be fully stocked and be on his way. She would lose him again. Everything in her screamed against it, everything but the military decorum that kept the rest of her intact and restrained.

Jo looked up and blinked, seeing the flashing red dot attached to the message. She blinked with her right eye and the message opened.

—AA to JT, classified. JT, proceed immediately to co. 47920-95138. Engage Authority warship *Horatio Nelson*. Destroy it.

Jo looked down. Everyone was looking at her. She sighed. So much for the quiet of their R&R time at Gamela station.

"Mr. Chi, recall all personnel. And plot a course for…" she glanced up again to retrieve the coordinates and read the message again. Then she stopped.

She chewed on her lip. This was an official order. Everything seemed proper and in place. But it was cold, formal… Jo paused, an intuition unfolding in her guts. *No human touch*, she thought.

She rose and headed for her ready room. "Mr. Chi, belay that. Mr. Liebert, I need a direct, secure ansible connection to Admiral Alinto. Now, priority one."

"Yes sir," she heard Liebert say, his voice high and loaded with questions. Then the door slid shut behind her. She sat down at the table and summoned a holo viewer.

It took longer than she had expected, but finally an image flickered and materialized. Admiral Alinto was there, but there were bags under her eyes, and she was wearing a teal muumuu. In the distance she could see mussed bedclothes and a giant lump beneath them—a lump she assumed to be Alinto's spouse. It didn't occur to her to question the gender of that spouse until just this moment. It looked like a male lump.

Alinto rubbed at her eyes. "Captain Taylor? What's the emergency?"

"Admiral sir, I'm sorry to disturb you, sir. I just received a classified text from you." She must have scheduled its sending for a time when she was in bed—but why would she do that? Jo's eyebrows knotted in confusion.

"You did?" It was Alinto's turn to look confused. Her broad Maori forehead pushed her flattened nose downward. "Naw, that was not from me."

"I'm supposed to proceed to 47920-95138 to engage with Authority warship *Horatio Nelson.*"

"You will ignore that…spurious order, Captain." Alinto looked disturbed. And worried. And awake. "And forward that message to me immediately. I want to find out who sent it. And why."

"Yes sir."

"And if you get any other messages that are supposed to be from me—"

"I know how to tell."

"Do you now?" Alinto narrowed one sleepy eye. "You're a sharp one, I'll give you that. "You know, some folks are starting to call you the Kali of Aken."

"I have…no idea what that means, sir."

"Look it up in the morning." She yawned, then the holo winked out.

Jo turned, swiveling in her seat and chewing on her lip. She vaguely remembered something that Jeff had said about Catskill. She rose, straightened her uniform jacket and strode back onto the bridge.

Tash Liebert looked at her expectantly. "Mr. Chi, you have the conn."

"Sir?" Liebert asked without asking.

"I need to…check something out," she explained without explaining.

He raised one eyebrow but didn't pursue it. "Aye sir."

Marcia Chi rose and settled into Jo's command chair without a word.

Jo left the bridge and made directly for the docking tube leading to the space dock of Gamela station. She glanced up to retrieve the docking manifest available to all ships in port, and a few minutes later she was standing in front of what she assumed to be Jennings' ship.

She sent Jeff a message and waited until the airlock on the connecting tube opened. Boarding the cargo vessel, she wasn't surprised to see Jeff meet her at the airlock door.

"Did I forget my underwear or something?" he asked. He leaned in to kiss her, but her arms were crossed. She was in business mode. He straightened up. "What's wrong?"

"I just got a message," she said. "From Admiral Alinto. Except it wasn't from Admiral Alinto."

"It was a fake," Jeff said, a feeling of dread running through him. "What did it say?"

"New orders. To leave off here and proceed directly to engage Authority vessel *Horatio Nelson*."

Jeff's brows knitted and he crossed his own arms. He waved her toward the nearby mess and sat at one of the small tables. She joined him, her lips set in a tight grimace.

"That's what happened to me," Jeff said.

"That's what…I thought you said something about a false order at Catskill."

"Yes." He drummed his fingers. "Were all the proper protocols in place?" he asked.

"Yes."

"How do you know it's a fake?"

"Because I called Alinto on the ansible to verify."

"And?"

"And she didn't send it. She told me to forward it to her immediately, so she can have intelligence investigate."

Jeff whistled.

"Jeff," Jo said. "Do you think…that whoever sent your message to you at Catskill is the same person…or persons…who sent this message?"

Jeff blinked. A long silent moment passed. Finally, he said, "No. I don't think there's even the smallest chance of that being true."

"Except that you know it is." She nodded slowly.

He held her eyes. He did not contradict her.

"WHAT NOW?" Pho asked.

"Lunch," Nira said. "C'mon."

She waved him toward a busy hub.

"Can't we go topside to eat?" he asked.

"What are you worried about?" she scowled up at him.

"Food poisoning?"

"Look at all these people." She gestured at everyone before them. "Do you think they eat topside?"

"Uh…no. They can't afford it."

"Many of them, no. But that's not the point."

"What's the point?"

"Are they sick?"

"Uh…they look okay."

"They eat down here every day, at the little corridor vendors, at the hole-in-the-wall noodle places. They don't get food poisoning."

"Some of them must. We get it topside every now and then."

"Some of them must," she conceded, rolling her eyes. "But what are the odds of you getting it in your odd meal down here?"

"Better than getting it topside."

"Don't…." she shook her head. "Just don't."

"Don't what?" he asked.

"Don't make me crazy," she grumbled. His neurotic babbling had gotten the best of her, and she hated it. She paddled hard to keep Pho's nebbishness at bay with strict military decorum.

She was tired and stressed, she knew that, and she could see no straight line between where they were and getting Emma back. Until she saw that straight line, she'd be rattled. *One thing at a time,* she told herself. *Just do the thing in front of you.*

"Can we at least pick a place that doesn't look botulistic?"

"Botulistic isn't a word. Botulism isn't an adjective."

"Botulistic is the adjectival form of botulism."

"You just made that up."

He grinned, proud of himself. She was pretty close to punching him. But then he'd win. Again.

"Or at least can we eat in a place that doesn't look like it's held together with rat poop."

Nira halted in her tracks. "Will you *stop*?"

Pho looked genuinely surprised. "Stop…what?"

"Stop being so goddam…" she faltered, searching for the right word. *So goddam Pho?* It wasn't fair to ask that of him, any more than she could stop being Nira. She straightened her uniform. "Are all Vietnamese people this annoying?"

Pho scowled. "Are all Hispanic people so irritable?"

It was a fair question, and it answered hers. Her shoulders relaxed and she shook her head. "I'm sorry." She put her hand on his arm. "I'm just…"

"Stressed to the gills," Pho answered. "I get it. You're in command, and things aren't…going as planned. If I were in your place I'd be running in circles making loud 'Whoop! Whoop!' noises. I think you're doing great."

Her mouth tightened into a thin attempt at a smile. "Thanks," she said.

"And we'll find her," he continued. "I know we will. I believe in you, Commander."

It was a little too much, but Nira let it pass. He was trying to comfort her, after all.

They were on the periphery of a mid-sized hub. She could see four main corridors going in different directions, all emptying out into a massive, if grimy, shopping district. The smell of grease and body odor battled for primacy with diverse cooking aromas. It was a pungent punch in the nose.

"What are you in the mood for?" Nira asked.

"Pho," he said.

"You're Pho," she said, her eyebrows bunching in confusion.

"Pho is the Vietnamese word for 'noodle soup,'" he said.

"Wait…your last name means 'noodle soup'?" She put her hands on her hips.

"Not exactly. It's pronounced a little differently."

"Still…didn't you get teased about that?"

"Not in Vietnam. It's a very common name."

"Huh. Well, let's find you some goddam Pho, Pho."

He brightened. "Right over there." Apparently he could read the stylized Vietnamese script, because she didn't see "pho" written on any of the signs in either Latin letters or kanji.

She let him lead for the moment, freezing only when Pho nearly fell over after bumping shoulders with a tall, meaty alien of a species Nira did not recognize. Pho tottered and righted himself. "Sorry," he said. It wasn't at all clear to Nira that Pho was in the wrong, but he wasn't the kind to let his ego get the best of him. Better to just apologize and move on. Nira approved. Unfortunately, the same could not be said for the alien.

He—at least Nira assumed it was a he—was half again as tall as Pho and twice his girth. He was humanoid, but his head was thick, elephantine, though without a trunk. There was an elongated snout, however, that rose in indignation. The creature raised his head and looked down on Pho through baggy, thickly-lidded eyes.

"Watch where you're going," he commanded.

"Of course," Pho said. He apologized again.

"What kind of uniform is that?" the alien asked.

"Colonial Defense Fleet," Pho said proudly, although Nira knew he knew there was no such thing here. Not anymore.

"CDF," the alien said and snorted.

"Yes!" Pho's face brightened. "You've heard of it!"

"Heard of it?" The alien's mouth twitched and one side of it rose up into a sneer, revealing his pointed fangs. "The CDF conquered my planet forty-five years ago. You killed my father and my uncles. You threw my entire family into poverty. My mother became a prostitute to support us." The alien's snout began to twitch.

Nira felt the hair on her neck rise to attention. A voice in her head began to shout *Intervene! Intervene!* and she moved to insert herself in between the two. But before she could get there, the alien had pulled his blaster and pumped two rounds into the thick of Pho's chest.

Pho went down like someone had cut the strings of a marionette, his gangly limbs folding up on one another as he sank to the floor in a tangle. Nira didn't hesitate. She pounced, throwing the whole of her weight into a horizontal kick that took out the alien's left leg. She heard the clunk of bones separating from their rightful sockets and rolled away before the giant creature came down on top of her.

There was no question in her mind that he *would* go down—and when he did, she was poised with her next attack. His shoulders hit the grillwork with a meaty *thuk* and a surprised yowl erupted from his snout that was not, she realized, terribly dissimilar from an elephant's trumpeting. She positioned her elbow like the point of a spear and launched herself at the fleshy part of his throat, catching the meat of it and crushing it instantly. She felt the cartilage give way and saw his enormous eyes bulging almost beyond their baggy lids.

She kicked at his blaster, watching it skitter off into the crowd in her peripheral vision.

Satisfied that her enemy was subdued, she leaped over his body to her fallen comrade. She knelt by Pho and felt at his neck, hoping against hope for a pulse. But the two gaping, dripping cavities of gore adorning his chest told her all she needed to know. There was no pulse. There was no way there could be a pulse. Pho's eyes stared at the ceiling, void of life. His mouth was open, as if ready to form one more aggravating observation. But it never came.

A crowd had gathered, but she was oblivious to them. It was all too much. The stress and the strain of command welled up and a scream of rage exploded from her. It wasn't Pho himself she was grieving—a part of her wasn't even conscious of him. It was the death of her self-image as a commander, as a person who could lead, who could keep her people safe. She'd had only one job, and she had failed. Miserably. She howled until security arrived and dragged her away.

ADMIRAL TAL LOWERED himself into the hot pool at Sol Station's one and only sento. Instantly he felt the stress melt out of him. He felt his muscles relax. He almost felt human again. The lights were low and the only sound was the soothing white noise spray of a waterfall in the near corner. "Ahhhhhh…"

He couldn't let down his guard completely, of course. There were about twenty other bathers in the sento, of various genders and species. He didn't dare do or say anything undignified, so he moderated the volume of his moan, even as he succumbed to it.

The sento was a public place, of course, but it was also his oasis. It was the place where he could escape from the duty and the detail and the constant vigilance of his role. He couldn't visit every day, but he relished the times he could.

But even as the hot water leeched his stress from him, his mind couldn't let go. He thought about Hightower, about sending him to take over the *Horatio Nelson* without warning Captain Oswald. In a week or so, he'd have to face Oswald and would need to give him an explanation. Tal did not look forward to that.

Conflict was the business of the military, and Tal had no trouble firing on an enemy. But he had little stomach for conflict with his inferiors, those with whom he would have to work on a day-to-day basis. Killing people wasn't a problem. Getting along with them was.

It was the one thing about leadership that he hated—making the hard choices and setting boundaries for those under his command. It didn't matter how battle-hardened his captains or lieutenants were, their egos were always as tender as snails, and there was nothing Tal hated more than stepping on a shell.

Let it go, he told himself. *Feel the water. Deal with this another day...*

He heard someone clearing a throat. That wasn't good. He opened one dark eye a tiny slit. Adrian Liu stood before him in full uniform, the only person in the sento not naked.

"This better be good, Lieutenant."

"Bad news, sir. You're needed in Ops immediately."

"How bad can it be?" he asked rhetorically. Then again, there was a war on.

"I can't say here, sir. This is...well, will be...classified."

Tal scowled and rose, reaching for his towel.

He climbed from the pool, wrapped the towel around his ample midsection, and without another glance at Liu, made his way to his locker. Five minutes later, he was fully dressed and walking crisply beside the lieutenant toward Operations.

"What are we dealing with?"

"I'd…rather not say, sir. Not where someone might hear."

Tal grunted. It was the right answer, of course, but Tal expected people to bend the rules when instructed. But he didn't press. Instead, he bided his time until the door to Ops had slid closed behind him. Then he turned and faced Liu.

"Now, Lieutenant, what the fuck was so important that I couldn't be left alone for a half-hour soak?"

Liu glanced around, taking note of others in the room. Everyone he could see had clearance, and many of them were looking at Tal expectantly.

"We just received a transmission. You need to see it, sir."

Liu strode toward where a small gaggle of brass was gathered around a viewing table. As Tal approached, they parted to allow him the prime spot. Then the air flickered and Tal scowled, trying to orient himself to what he was seeing.

Liu noticed and narrated. "This is the exterior feed from a civilian transport ship, the *Jackrabbit Sage*."

"*Jackrabbit Sage*? What the hell does that even mean?" Tal asked no one in particular. The feed was sexto-directional, showing a steady field of stars he assumed to be from the transport ship's bow, stern, starboard, port, topside and keel cameras. "I mean, does it mean a rabbit flavored with the herb *sage* or does it mean a wise rabbit?"

No one answered. No one else knew either, obviously. Tal scowled. Just what the fuck was he supposed to be looking at, anyway?

Liu indicated the stern view. Tal leaned over, placing his hands on the table, getting as close to the view as possible without losing resolution. Then he saw it. A creature, looking a bit like a cross between a jellyfish and a crustacean sped past the camera at lighting speed. If Tal had blinked he would have missed it. But he didn't miss it. Long, spinning tendrils extended behind its cigar-shaped body.

"What the *fuck* was that?"

"We don't know, sir. There's nothing in the database that's a match for that particular xenobiology," Liu said, his face taut and grim.

"So...we have an interesting new species for the scientists to..." he cut off midsentence. He saw something else emerge from the inky blackness of space on the viewer. "What the fuck..." his eyes widened.

There were thousands of them. Maybe tens of thousands. They were coming in a great swarm, blocking out the stars. Now they were filling the screen. Their metallic bodies shone silver, dappled with shadow as their fellows blocked the feeble light emitted by the *Jackrabbit Sage*.

"What are they?" Tal breathed. It didn't matter that no one answered him. His jaw hung open as he watched the first of them heading straight for the camera, spindly silver crab-like legs extended. He saw the legs disappear as the thorax of the alien filled the camera's view. He saw the slight shudder of impact, or at least he thought he did. A moment later the camera cut out, its picture replaced with a buzzing distortion pattern.

Tal looked to the other cameras, until one by one, they too went blank.

He straightened, looking around at his fellows. There were three admirals in attendance, but he was senior. There was also a captain and Liu. All of them looked grave. No one knew what to say.

"Was there any report from the *Jackrabbit*?" Tal asked.

"Yes sir," Liu said. "A text message. It said simply, 'We are under attack.' That's it."

"That's it," Tal repeated, leaning back down on the table. He shook his head slowly.

"There's nothing on this species...these species...in the database?"

"No sir, except..."

Tal's eyebrows bunched. "Except?"

Liu pulled up a sworn statement and blew it up large enough for Tal to read it without transferring it to his neural or grabbing a pad.

"Captain Bowers?"

Liu nodded. "These creatures exactly match the description he gave of what attacked the Colonial Defense Fleet in…well, in the other universe. String 310 to be precise."

Tal blinked, reading the description. "Three subspecies. We only saw two, but…they sound like the same creatures."

"Yes sir. He called them 'Prox.'"

Tal straightened up, his eyes still flitting over the text. "They're unstoppable, he says."

"They were…for them."

Tal shook his head. "Have there been other sightings?"

"Yes sir. We've got this."

A blurry, distant image hovered over the table.

"What is this?" Tal asked.

"It looks like a ship."

"Does that—?"

Liu anticipated his question. "It matches Bowers' description too. Yes sir."

"And where is it headed?" Tal asked. All the hair on his neck and arms rose to attention. He did not want to hear the answer he knew was coming.

"They're headed directly for us, sir. And if they get through us, they'll be on course—"

"For Earth," Tal completed the sentence.

CHAPTER EIGHT

Aboard the *Talon* again, Jeff steeled himself as he prepared to say his goodbyes. He paused as a frosted white door slid open. Inside, Jennings was waiting, alert, upright, and unnaturally sober.

"This was a bad idea," Jennings said.

"Why didn't you tell me about your outstanding warrants?" Jeff stepped inside and heard the door swoosh shut behind him.

"Figured they were kind of common knowledge." Jennings gave a pained smile. "Now I got a question for you: Why didn't you stay dead?"

Jeff smirked. He sat on a white poly seat and fought back a feeling of claustrophobia. If he were Jennings, he'd be angry too, but… "Why did you take the risk?" he asked.

"You take risks for friends. Especially old ones."

Jeff could not deny the simple truth of that statement. For a minute the two men sat in silence. "I tried to get Jo to release you." He shook his head. "Her hands are tied."

"That woman gets exactly what she wants 100% of the time, so that's not exactly an argument that's gonna hold any water for me."

Jeff shrugged. "Whatever. I tried. She didn't budge."

"That sounds like a more honest assessment." He nodded. "I hate spin."

"You hate spin when it's other people spinning, I think," Jeff commented.

Jennings grunted. "What's going to happen to my ship?"

"Jo wanted to confiscate it."

"Booty." Jennings raised his eyebrows.

"I talked her into...well, letting me keep it in trust for you. I promise to take good care of her so that when you get out—"

"If I get out."

"—*when* you get out," Jeff insisted, "you'll still have a living."

"So you're here to very kindly explain to me how you're stealing my ship," Jennings deadpanned. Jeff opened his mouth to protest, but Jennings waved it off. "Don't bother. It's okay. It's not okay, but it's okay."

More silence stretched out between them. "Look, Carl, I never intended for this to happen," Jeff said. "I'm sorry it happened this way."

"Despite it being such an outrageously convenient outcome for you, yes, I'm sure you are." Jennings ran his hand over his balding head. "You don't have any whiskey, do you?"

Jeff glanced up at the camera, then down again at his friend. He pulled a bottle out of the double breast of his uniform jacket and set it on the floor. There was no way the camera didn't see it, and he knew they were being monitored. He also knew it was technically illegal, but he didn't care. Jo wasn't going to throw him into the brig for a class five infraction, and he owed his friend at least this much.

Jennings seemed mollified. A genuine grin lit up his face. He leaned back against the wall, calm and satisfied. "You gonna go find that shaman of yours?"

"Yes."

"When?"

"Right now."

"Huh." Jennings' eyes travelled from Jeff's face down to his belt, then back up again in a way that made Jeff feel a little slimy. "Suck your cock before you go?"

"I'm going to pretend I didn't hear that."

"Last chance…I could show you some tricks."

Jeff stood, wishing his final meeting with his old friend could have ended differently. He reminded himself that this Jennings was not his old friend and that his behavior was entirely in line with everything he had observed about this particular Jennings. He sighed, but he wasn't surprised.

"Goodbye Carl."

"Goodbye Jeff."

CAPTAIN DANIEL HIGHTOWER LOOKED DOWN, once more entering the bridge. He'd spent the better part of an hour reading detailed reports on all aspects of the *Horatio Nelson*. Most of it was routine. With the exception of a couple of maintenance projects underway in Engineering, the ship appeared to be in good shape, so that didn't worry him. Weapons were at 100%, he was glad to see. Crew morale was good, although the real-time psyche barometer—in which he had never placed any credence whatsoever—was registering troubling fluctuations starting from the moment he had relieved Captain Oswald. It was an annoying distraction.

What had troubled him more was the crew profile, specifically his bridge crew. Mr. Anderson was a faggot. He hated faggots. Tess Maruka was Tongan. The Tongans had a sub-colony on New Manila and had originally declared for the rebellion. Cooler heads had prevailed—that and the threat of sanctions against the tiny island nation—and all of the colonial Tongans had been recalled. Some of them returned, some of them didn't. But in his mind, all Tongans were suspect.

Worse was Oswald's XO. She certainly wouldn't be *his* XO. She was Mauro, a religious sect made up of humans who followed the alien Mauroxilian religion. The Mauroxils had managed one monolithic faith for their entire planet. Danny admired the ruthlessness that must have been necessary to root out dissent in their history. He didn't even necessarily object to the basic tenets of the faith. It was a form of strict moralism handed down from a largely absent deity, so far as he could tell. And that was the problem. The Mauro were not only traitors to their indigenous, human religions, but they were inflexible when it came to what they called "the Moral Law," which, of course, people jokingly referred to as "the Mauro Law."

Doing a few quick searches, he pulled up files of crew members he thought would make good replacements. Especially appealing was his candidate for XO. Commander Foulon had numerous infractions against him—most of them derived from field duty, where his decisions had been deemed too violent, and one where he had been disciplined for questioning the decision of a superior. Looking into the incident further, Danny discovered he agreed with Foulon. Some idiot commander had ordered him to be "easy" on the enemy civilians during a skirmish. Foulon had blown away anyone who got in his way, and he accomplished his mission objective. He was a man after Danny's own heart. He summoned the man to the bridge.

Might as well get the unpleasantness over with, Danny thought. Although in truth, he enjoyed conflict, and he would enjoy this. He stood and straightened his black jacket, the orange piping popping to the fore. He cleared his throat and addressed the bridge crew. "We're going into battle, men, and I need an A team I can trust. Mr. Anderson, Mr. Maruka, Mr. Cashan, you are dismissed. Please report to HR Command for reassignment."

He waited for that to sink in. No one moved. Danny counted to ten. Still no one stirred. He touched a node on the arm of his command chair. "Security, please send an armed escort team to the bridge." That got them moving.

Maruka rose first, incomprehension and anger clouding her eyes. She was a bulky, fleshy woman, having inherited the solidity of many Pacific Islanders. She didn't directly challenge him, however. She didn't even look at him. She just marched toward the lift. *Good soldier,* Danny thought.

Mr. Anderson was next. He, too, kept his eyes averted. He seemed masculine enough as he walked, and for a brief moment Danny wondered if he had been wrong about him. *Nah*, he thought. *Doesn't matter what he looks like. I'll always know what he is.* Queers had been fully integrated into society for centuries, but that didn't mean there weren't dissenters. And Danny had always dissented from this particular point of sociological dogma.

Cashan, however, did not go quietly. She stood and faced him, standing at parade rest, her arms fixed behind her back, her chest full and proud. Her black hair was tied tightly behind her head in a bun. She was about thirty, he guessed. Her face betrayed not a hint of nonsense.

"Captain Hightower, I have held this position for three years, with distinction. If I am to be dismissed, I respectfully request to know your rationale."

"You have no right to my rationale, Commander. You are dismissed."

"Respectfully, sir, I will go willingly and without complaint—just as soon as I hear your rationale."

Hightower sighed. A pissing contest, then? She could not hope to win that. "Mr. Cashan, if I told you to execute a prisoner, would you obey my order?"

Cashan's eyes darted back and forth. "That would be a violation of both Terran Authority policy and my personal moral code."

"Then I can't trust you, can I?"

"Begging your pardon, sir, but obedience to one's superiors is not absolute. It can't be. Terran Authority regulations state—"

"I know Terran Authority regulations inside and out, Commander. But out here, *I* am the Terran Authority. And I interpret the code. Do you have a problem with that, Commander?"

"I do, sir."

"Then I have a problem with *you*. You are dismissed."

Cashan did not move. "I suspect, Captain, that my dismissal is due to the fact that I am Mauro. The Terran Authority Code enshrines the complete freedom of religious expression within the armed services—"

"Don't make me kill you, Commander. Disobeying a direct order is mutiny under the Terran Authority Code, section 26, subsection C. I will drop you where you fucking stand."

He saw her shoulders wilt. Then he saw her eyes search for some internal connection. She found it. He saw her shoulders straighten, her chest puff out again. She continued in her defiance. "I would like you to point out to me, from my previous record, where I have ever been disloyal or lacking in my service. Sir."

You poor, stubborn fool, Danny thought. Just then the bridge doors slid open and the security detail poured onto the bridge.

"Security, please escort Mr. Cashan to the brig to await my further orders."

He saw Cashan's eyes narrow, her chin harden. She did not protest as she was led away.

No sooner had security cleared the bridge than Mr. Foulon stepped aboard.

"XO on deck," Danny announced, grinning as everyone stood. He let them stand up all the way and watched them turn to face his new XO. Mr. Foulon saluted. A nasty red scar violated his face, stretching from one cheek, across his nose, and to the corner of his mouth, creating a disturbing effect. Danny returned the salute.

IN THE HALL ONCE MORE, Jeff headed for the airlock. He bounced on his toes in the lift, once again considering going to the bridge to see Jo one last time, but he knew he couldn't risk embarrassing her in front of her crew. The lift slowed gently to a stop and the doors opened, revealing Jo leaning against the opposite wall of the corridor like a magic trick. She looked up and smiled slyly.

"You don't get away that easy."

Jeff stepped out of the lift sheepishly. "You didn't have to see me off."

She wrapped her arms around him. "You know better." She kissed him deeply. After what seemed like an eternity, she loosened her grip. "You keep yourself alive. I won't lose you again."

"No ma'am," he agreed. "You'll..." He wanted to make sure she'd rescue his crew, but didn't know how much she wanted her own crew to know about it.

But she caught his eye and nodded. "You leave it to me."

He smiled gratefully. Then he clicked his heels and saluted. "Captain," he said.

"Captain," she saluted back. He turned on his heel and began down the boarding ramp to the *Annabel Lee*, his throat swelling up. He was grateful she could only see his back, couldn't see him struggle with his feelings.

WHEN THE ELEVATOR door slid open, Emma gasped. It opened to a gigantic cave, its rough ceiling arching in a jagged dome above them. Brilliant spotlights shone against the darkness, shining down on the multitude of Alverians spread out across the floor below.

Emma stopped and bent down to feel the rock floor with her fingers, noting the fine dust, the larger grains of sand on its surface. Amberline was not slowing down and she rose, doubling her pace to keep up.

A loud hum of activity filled the chamber, reverberating off the ceiling high above. The workers were grouped in wedges by activity, though much of it was baffling to Emma. In one section, hundreds of workers were wrapping a band of fabric around what appeared to be a paper wrapped ball. In another, they were boiling some kind of grain in huge vats, clouds of steam roiling upward. *No wonder it's so humid in here,* she thought. In another section, she saw huge machines that looked like giant mechanical spiders, clacking as they wriggled their legs. Alverians darted between them, trailing cords that unrolled off the large spools they carried.

Broad pathways separated each occupation, converging on a central courtyard like the spokes of a wagon wheel. The Alverians milling about the center wore brightly colored bands of fabric on their limb segments or tied around their waist, like the ones worn by the welcoming committee Amberline spoke to previously. They huddled in groups, gesticulating frenetically, then quickly darting to another group for more interaction. Occasionally they would run into the apex of the work group they were probably managing, communicate further, and quickly return to the fray in the middle. It reminded Emma of historical videos she'd seen of the old stock markets back on Earth.

Amberline strode directly into the middle of the melee, Emma scurrying close behind, suddenly terrified of the hard limbs and sharp elbows being flung all around her. She ducked, raising her arms to protect her face; several Alverians stopped and turned toward her expectantly, shrugged, then went back to whatever they were doing. *They though I was going to speak!* she thought, amazed. In her surprise, she nearly crashed into Amberline, who had stopped without warning in front of her. She gesticulated wildly, talking with several others. Then one of them pointed off down one of the wagon wheel lanes radiating back out toward the walls of the chamber. Amberline glanced back at Emma, gestured for her to follow, then started off in the indicated direction.

The section they walked through next could only be described as a ranch. Low walled pens made of some kind of mud teemed with animals, thousands of them. They looked like a cross between a pig, a dog, and a cockroach, but colored a vivid blue-green, some with bright yellow stripes or spots. Ahead of them, down the road, a team of Alverians had opened a gate in the wall and were prodding a group of the creatures out of the pen with long poles. Once twenty of them were out, they closed the gate and began herding them toward the nearest arched portal in the chamber wall. Amberline followed them through the portal into a low, poorly lit tunnel. The shepherds steered their flock through an opening on the right, while Amberline continued straight on.

Emma peeked through every doorway they passed. Some of them were sleeping chambers, containing long rows of Alverians sleeping on thin mats on the floor. She realized that Amberline hadn't discussed the nature of her captivity here, whether she'd be sleeping with the others or kept somewhere with more privacy. Would they even understand privacy? Would they value it as humans do? She hoped Amberline's expertise in humans included what they ate.

"So," Emma said, trotting up along side Amberline once they were alone in the corridor, "Where are you taking me?"

"That's the question we are going to answer."

"What do you mean?"

"We all serve the hive. We will need to determine how you will serve the hive while you are here."

"You mean you're going to put me to work?"

"Of course."

"So now I'm not just a hostage, I'm a slave."

Amberline stopped abruptly. "I do not understand. What is a 'slave'?"

"Slave is the word humans use to describe someone who is forced to perform labor against their will."

"I still do not understand. Humans... refuse to work? To serve?"

Emma shook her head. "Uh, not exactly. We reserve the right to choose for ourselves what we do for a living. We call it *self-determination.*"

Amberline began walking again. "It sounds... unorganized."

"Well, it is," Emma agreed, falling in step. "But we take freedom *very* seriously. That's why we severely frown on things like, say, kidnapping." She glared pointedly.

After a moment of walking silently, Amberline's mask said, "Interesting. Yes, we have a very different set of values. We all serve the hive. It isn't a choice, it is merely the way we are. The specifics of our service are determined by our strongest abilities and the greatest needs of the hive."

"What happens to someone who can't serve the hive?"

Amberline shrugged. "They die."

Emma's mouth dropped open. "They die? Or they are killed?

Amberline shrugged again. "Either. None of us could survive the shame of a useless existence, a life without value or purpose."

Emma thought a moment. It made sense, but she wasn't sure how it applied to her specifically. "I will be required to serve the hive."

"Of course."

"And if I can't, you'll kill me."

Amberline's mask smiled. It wasn't comforting. "Of course not. You are not of the hive. But you don't have to worry about that. I have no doubt we have work that even a human can do."

TAL STARED out the window of his study at the stars. He knew they were violent, flaming bags of radiation, but from a distance they seemed peaceful, serene. "Everything seems better at a distance," he said out loud.

The Prox were still at a distance. But they were coming. He knew that the panic he felt now would steadily rise as their proximity increased. He was only at the beginning of this ramp. It was a familiar feeling, being on the cusp of an inevitable battle, yet there seemed to be something more ominous about this one.

He couldn't get the images of the *Jackrabbit Sage* out of his head. He had never seen destruction like that. He had never seen an enemy like that.

He glanced up and accessed his neural, sending a call for Liu. A moment later the door slid open and his secretary entered. "Yes sir?"

Tal motioned toward the window with a jerk of his head.

Liu came near, standing at parade rest at about arm's length.

"Do you ever just look at the stars, Adrian?"

Liu looked out the window, then back at the Admiral. "Um…sometimes. Yes sir."

"How do they make you feel?"

"Feel, sir?"

"Feel," Tal said.

Liu bit his lip and hesitated.

"C'mon, it's not a trick question."

"They make me feel scared, sir."

Tal reared back. “Scared?”

“Yes sir.”

“You’re telling me that when you gaze out at the stars you don’t feel peace or wonder?”

“No, sir. When I look at the stars I see everything we don’t know. I see the space we haven’t conquered...the enemy lying in wait. I see the unseen threat.”

Tal grunted. “I read a psychologist once who said that when some people encounter mystery, they find it enticing. Other people find it threatening.” He looked away from the window and narrowed one eye at his secretary. “I never took you for the glass-half-empty sort.”

“Sorry to disappoint you, sir.”

“No apology needed. It’s…good to know.”

Liu stood there. Tal could feel the tension rise in his secretary. The man had work to do, after all. “Will…that be all, sir?”

“Adrian, do I often call you in here to stargaze?”

“No, sir.”

“I’m not going soft in the head yet. I want you to recall every ship we’ve got. And I don’t just mean military ships. I want you to requisition and commandeer every civilian ship with anything greater than a grade-two laser attached.”

“Sir?”

Tal waved. “Oh, I know we’re not going to get 100% compliance, but we’ll get a lot. Just call them. Top speed that they can safely get here. Those that can get here quick we can refit for greater firepower.”

“How far out, sir?”

“When I said ‘every ship,’ I meant ‘every ship.’ Our ships in neutral space, our spy ships in RFC territory, those doing deep space exploration. Ships that are doing security work on our colonies, all of them. We’re going to need every gun we can summon to meet these fuckers.”

“Now sir?”

“Put out the call right now. All possible speed.”

“And…reason given, sir?”

Tal nodded. “You’re afraid of creating panic?”

"Aren't you?"

"The panic is coming, no matter what we do."

Liu didn't disagree. He only nodded.

"Oh, I don't know, Lieutenant. I've gone round and round about this in my head. Truth is, I can't think of any reason that won't sound fishy. So…let's give them no reason."

"No…reason, sir?"

"Here's what I'm thinking. We make it a top-priority, mandatory rule, but don't say why. What will the feeds be talking about?"

"They'll be falling all over themselves with speculations."

"Will they be crying foul at the conscription of civilian property?"

"Sure…but probably not as much."

"My thoughts exactly. Instead of freaking out about civil rights, or even about the Prox, they'll be fascinated with the 'why' of it all." Tal clapped his hand on Liu's shoulder. "You see, Adrian? Sometimes mystery is our friend."

CHAPTER NINE

Once more aboard the *Annabel Lee*, Jeff dropped his duffel in the tiny compartment that had been his cabin. He imagined he'd eventually move into the slightly larger captain's cabin, but he'd need to clear Jennings' stuff out of it. That would be a good way to pass the empty hours of interstellar travel time, but he imagined it would also require hazardous waste disposal and multiple showers in the sonic.

First things first—disengage from the *Talon* and find a quiet stretch of space where he could simply put the ship on autopilot and move into his mind for a bit.

He perched himself on the edge of the command chair and swung his analog interface into place. He opened the communications panel and tapped out a few quick commands. "*Annabel Lee* requesting decoupling protocols at O-nine-hundred-twenty-three hours," he said.

"You have clearance for undocking *Annabel Lee*," came the reply.

A moment later, a tiny green light illuminated his screen, and he heard the metallic jolt of the boarding tube detaching.

Four minutes later, he engaged the conventional drive and backed the *Annabelle Lee* away from the *Talon*. Once he was at a safe distance, he switched to the aft thrusters and began the acceleration protocol needed to make a successful jump to C-space.

The acceleration was uneventful, and he glanced up to call up the stellar cartography charts for this region in his neural. There was a 4,000-parsec region of empty space less than 0.5 parsecs away. He made the slight course adjustments necessary and rose. "Unpack," he told himself. It would be about twenty minutes until the ship entered the dead region. He wanted the ship at a full stop before he ventured beyond.

Most of his effects were still aboard, still in place. It only took a few minutes to empty the duffel and do some minor housecleaning. As he did so, he struggled with his feelings about Jo. Did they reawaken old passion? They had. Was that wise? Probably not. Was it fair to Emma? Decidedly no. He felt like a heel. And at the same time, he felt like an elated teenager. He wondered how much of his euphoria was due to the newish body the Ulim had bestowed upon him. Would his old, middle-aged body have been buffeted to the same degree by the inner storms that tore at him now? He didn't know. He realized he also didn't care.

I love her, he admitted to himself. *I always have. I lost her. Then I killed her. And now I have her back.* There was no arguing with that. There was no shaming him for that. He felt a mass of roiling emotion that included guilt and infatuation and lust and elation and confusion and pity for Emma and he didn't fucking care. *I love her.* That was the truth of it. No more needed to be said.

He had just gotten a cup of coffee from the tiny mess station when he felt the conventional thrusters kick in. The jolt was minor but noticeable, and he had expected no less. He positioned himself in his command chair and set the coffee down beside him. He closed his eyes. He knew the coffee would be cold when he opened them again. That was all right. There was always more coffee.

NIRA'S EYES OPENED, but she didn't know where she was. She felt a pinch in her arm, and looked down. An IV was feeding some kind of light aqua liquid into her vein. She looked around. She didn't seem to be in a hospital. She was sitting in a comfortable recliner, the kind you might see in someone's living room. But it was clearly a clinical place she was in. It didn't make sense.

If not a hospital, then…what?

A door slid open and a young man entered. He seemed almost impossibly young to her. What did that say about her? She blinked.

"Ah. You're awake. Good. How are you feeling?"

"Who the fuck are you?" Nira asked.

"I'm Doctor Chujan. My first name is Ram. You can call me whatever you like." He gave her a smile that was warm, genuine, and professional. She noted his straight black hair, cropped short and stiff. His eyes were slightly almond-shaped and his skin was bronze.

"Are you Chinese?" she asked. Instantly she felt stupid. Why had she asked that? "Sorry," she said.

"Don't worry. You're on a sedative, and it decreases inhibitions. It's easy to say the first thing that comes into your head and harder to filter things. I'm not offended. My people are Thai. Although I have an Irish grandfather. Word has it he was a bit of a rogue."

Did he just wink at her? Maybe she was seeing things. "Why am I…" questions flooded her brain. She didn't know which one to ask first. They came out in a rush. "Where am I? Why am I here? Why am I on a sedative?"

He smiled at her patiently. *He's very kind,* she thought. *He's also just a kid.*

"I'll take those in order. You are aboard Epworth Station. You are in the Wesleyan Psychiatric Clinic for observation. You are here because you have experienced a very traumatic event—"

"I did?" Nira's eyes grew wide. It was a strange feeling, the mixture of adrenaline and deep peace. It reminded her of the focused, heightened state of calm she experienced in the heat of battle. Except that she felt scattered now, not focused.

"The authorities will also want to question you about what you saw, and what you…well, what you did. Don't worry. They just want to ask you some questions."

Nira realized she wasn't wearing her uniform. She was wearing a flannel jumper. It was nice. Comfortable. Utilitarian. She liked it. But it made her feel naked, as if her identity had been taken away. "Where's my uniform?"

Dr. Chujan cocked his head. "Your uniform was…soiled. It's also evidence. We gave you some clean clothes. You can choose a different style if it will make you more comfortable."

Nira felt confused, but not frightened. A part of her mind realized that whatever was being pumped into her vein was making her feel very good indeed. A part of her objected to that. A part of her wanted it to go on forever.

"Can I talk to you about your uniform?" Dr. Chujan asked.

"Sure."

"It appears to be the uniform of the Colonial Defense Fleet, a military coalition that doesn't exist any more."

"Yes," Nira agreed. "Well, it does in my world. Except that it doesn't."

"Why don't you back up and tell me about that from the beginning?"

Nira nodded.

"Oh, and legally, I must inform you that we'll be making a holo of this conversation and anything you say may be used as testimony either for or against you." He smiled reassuringly. "Is that all right?"

Nira felt wonderful. Everything was all right.

She started to talk. For the better part of an hour, she told her story. It simply flooded out of her. She could see that he was trying not to look surprised, but failing. When she got to the point in her story when they were looking for noodle soup, she stopped short. Her eyes grew wide. She sat up, and despite whatever drugs they were pumping into her, she felt panic. "Where is Pho?"

"I'm so sorry, Nira. Martin Pho is dead."

She remembered now. Her lower lip began to tremble and she felt agitated. "I've got to…" She reached for the IV needle with her left hand.

"You just leave that there," the doctor said. He reached for the interface on the IV drip and tapped at it a couple of times. In a few moments, Nira felt calmer and a little cloudier.

Dr. Chujan once more gave her his full attention and a very compassionate look. "I'm sorry about your friend."

"That alien shot him."

"That would be Charjath Vlat, a Numer centurion. You crushed his windpipe."

"Is he dead?" Nira asked.

"Yes."

"Good." Nira felt satisfied. She had avenged her friend. Her score was settled. She could die now. It would be fine.

"Did you know Centurion Vlat previous to your encounter in the food court?"

"No. He just…attacked Lieutenant Pho. I just…defended him."

"Mr. Pho had already sustained fatal injury when you attacked Centurion Vlat."

Nira shook her head. "I was…it seemed…I just…" Her words trailed away.

"You know what?" Dr. Chujan said. "This has been a lot to take in." He patted her arm, the one with the IV drip in it. "We are going to keep you here for a little while, in this safe place. The detectives are going to come and talk to you. And of course, I will be here. Anytime you want to talk, you let me know. Every now and then, I will come and ask you questions. Will that be all right?"

She liked him. That would be fine. She nodded.

"All right. You just sit there and relax and try to remember as much as you can. That's your job right now. You don't need to think about the future or about work or about your captain. Just…try to remember as much detail as you can about the incident. The more you can tell us, the better we can help you, and the better we'll be able to discern the best way forward for everyone."

"Everyone?"

He smiled, but didn't explain further. "Well, for you mostly, but also for Centurion Vlat's family. But no need to think about that right now. What happened to your friend and to Centurion Vlat was very sad and very complicated. Together, we're going to tease out what really happened and what should happen now. Doesn't that sound like a good plan?"

It did. It sounded like an excellent plan.

"All right then. I'm going to do some rounds—"

"Rounds?"

"I have some other patients to see. There are other people who are hurting just as much as you are, and this is what I do. I help them." He rose and placed a reassuring hand on her shoulder. "I'll be back soon and we can talk some more."

With another encouraging smile, he rose and left the room.

When he left, it seemed all of the life and warmth left with him. The office suddenly felt small and cold and clinical. Although, she had to admit, it was a nice chair.

There was something nagging at her, something on the tip of her consciousness. She wanted to think more about the chair, but she…

Pho. Now she remembered. In her mind's eye she watched the centurion's blaster go off in slow motion. She saw the flesh ripped from Pho's chest, saw him go down. Again.

"Oh shit," she said. Through the sedative haze she caught a glimmer of where she was, of the situation she was in, of the dangerous chemical dripping into her, sapping her of caution, propriety, of her capacity for critical thinking. "You fucking prick," she said, meaning the nice doctor, and eyeing the IV needle as the enemy it was.

"Feels good though," she said. Then she ripped it out of her arm and stifled a howl as the jagged stab of pain rooted her once more in reality.

"Approaching neutral space, Captain," Navigator Galli said. Her short black hair reflected the blue light coming from the communicator's station, and her nose was unconventionally large. She would have been pretty except for that. Still, it made her unique. Her voice was brisk, efficient, all business. *She will do well,* Danny thought.

According to the daily reports, they would need supplies soon. And Danny had no clue where to start his search for Jo Taylor. A space station or a trading post or a planet with a sizable population would allow them to restock, and would afford him an opportunity to seek out some intelligence. "Mr. Galli, find us a place to restock. Preferably a place that gets a good deal of traffic."

"Aye sir."

"Mr. Foulon, in my ready room." Danny rose and headed for the door to the side of the bridge.

Ernst Foulon's eyebrows rose, but he got up and followed the Captain. When the door slid shut behind them, Danny waved him toward a chair and put two glasses on the table. He reached for the scotch.

"On duty, sir?"

"We're going to drink, not get drunk."

Foulon smiled. "I've heard you bend the rules a bit."

"But I never break them." Danny returned the smile. Foulon's scar was unsettling. It would take some getting used to. It made him appear angry even when he wasn't. "I bet you're wondering what we're up to."

"The thought has crossed my mind. I want to support our mission, of course, but…"

"But it would help if you knew what that mission was."

"Er…yes sir."

Danny poured two fingers in each glass. "What do you think of Mr. Lo?"

Foulon cocked his head. "He's a good communicator. Intuitive, quick, creative."

"He used to be a she."

Foulon shrugged. "I saw a duty report from…before. No loss. She wasn't much of a looker."

Danny laughed. Oh yes, he was going to like this guy. "It doesn't bother you?"

"Lots of trans people in the service. It never bothered me any. Have you never served with a trans?"

"They give me the willies. Always had them transferred out."

"Well, if you are interested in my counsel—"

"I am."

"Well then, sir, I'd give Lo a chance. He's loyal and he'll work hard for you."

Danny nodded. He sipped at his whiskey. Then he set the glass down and tapped at the display interface. An image of Jo came up. The one from the news site—riding the two spaceships like a rodeo cowgirl, her long black hair trailing behind her in the wind, wild triumph in her eyes.

"See this woman?"

"Yeah. Crazy bitch. Read all about Aken."

"I used to fuck her."

Foulon's eyes grew wide. "No shit," he said. "What was she like?"

Danny smiled at his informality. They'd be pals, then. Good. He needed a right-hand man he could really trust. "She liked it rough."

"I'll bet she did." Ernst sipped at his whiskey. He cocked his head. "How'd she end up on the wrong side of the war?"

"Uh…we were involved in a bit of a love triangle. My best friend, Jeff."

"Uh, you and Jeff didn't….?" He left the sentence unfinished.

"No. It wasn't like that. But we both liked Jo. She picked him."

"Damn."

"Yeah. Then he got killed under my command. Jo blamed me."

"Damn," Ernst said again.

"She was convinced there was some kind of conspiracy. A cover-up. Didn't help that the mission was top secret."

"Ah…I see it coming."

"Yeah."

They sat in silence for a few moments. "It's a pity," Ernst said finally. "She'd have been an asset to our side."

"She's a fucking monster," Danny agreed. "But…she's not on our side. In fact, she's a thorn in our side. We've got one mission and one mission alone."

"What's that?"

"Find her. Stop her. And send her back to Earth in a jar."

"That's a shame. She's pretty. Fuckable thing like that..." Ernst said.

"She'd eat you alive, Commander." Danny narrowed one eye. "And then she'd shit you into space."

A hailing signal pierced the air. Danny jerked his head toward the sound. "Speak."

"Begging your pardon, Captain," Mr. Lo's voice was high-pitched, agitated. "I have level one orders from Admiral Tal."

Danny scowled. "Thank you for the alert, Mr. Lo. I'll take it in here."

He looked up at Foulon's scarred face, noted the concern.

"Do you want some privacy, sir?" Foulon made to rise.

"No, sit. Whatever it is, I need my XO on board."

"Yes sir." He sat again.

Danny punched at the panel, and the static image of Jo was replaced by a moving holo of Admiral Tal. "Attention all Authority vessels. We have a Code Red alert. Alien hostiles are converging on Earth. We need every gun we have. Whatever your mission, whatever your orders, break off and return to Sol Station. Your planet needs you." The holo flicked off.

"That was dramatic," Danny said. His face was impassive.

"Sir?" Foulon began. "Should I give the order to set a course?"

Danny tapped his fingers on the glass. "There are over five hundred vessels sailing under Authority colors—more than three hundred of them are battle-class. This is not a battle-class ship."

"What are you saying, sir?"

"I'm saying that whether we're there isn't going to alter the outcome one way or another." He finished off his whiskey. "I'm saying we never got that order. I have an...well, I have an old flame to snuff out. And I mean to do it, aliens or no aliens."

He looked up and studied his XO. For such a hard man, he was amazingly easy to read. Danny saw the uncertainty, followed by confusion, followed by a moment of panic. Then he saw the resolve settle in. Danny raised an eyebrow. Was he going to like this resolve, or was there a bug that needed squashing? The truth was, he didn't care either way. Either way, there was fun to be had.

"I'm your man, Captain," Foulon said. "If you say we didn't get this, we didn't get this."

Danny grinned. "Tell Mr. Lo that due to the sensitive nature of the message we just received, we will no longer be sending or receiving messages from Sol or any other command station. We'll be running dark from here on out."

JEFF SETTLED into his command chair and looked at the expanse of stars before him on the view screen. The *Annabel Lee* was at a complete standstill. The space around him was dead quiet. Except for his own breathing and the occasional blinking of lights, all was still.

He knew it was an illusion. He knew that every point of light he saw, every star in the universe was a roiling furnace of unimaginable violence and fury. But here, all seemed serene. He sank into that serenity and closed his eyes.

For a moment, it felt like he was falling. There was a bottom, a ground within himself, and he found it. He rooted himself in it. But he was tempted to stay there.

It was, after all, peaceful there. It was safe. It was even pleasurable. He had never been much of a meditator—hadn't seen the point. But he understood this. There was a peace in silence, in stillness, in the depths of his own being that he had not given its proper due. He regretted that now. But at least he had discovered it.

He hesitated to step away from that center. He remembered what had happened the last time he had willingly done so. He had become an unwitting avatar of Shiva, the destroyer of worlds. He, personally, had been responsible for snuffing out the light of every being on every world in an entire universe. Truly, he was the Lord of Death.

He shuddered at the thought of it. Back on Sol Station he had struggled with the guilt and shame of it like he had never struggled before. He coped now mostly by not thinking about it, by drowning it in a single-minded drive for…for what? *For what he was about to do.*

For this, he had betrayed his friends. For this, he had sold Jennings to the justice system, such as it was. For this mystery he was abandoning his duty. And for what? What was it really? He didn't know. A hunch.

He breathed, feeling the air fill his lungs, then letting it go. He was about to step off of the brink again, fully aware of the consequences of his actions, the potential for even greater destruction. He hated himself for it, yet he felt compelled. He hated himself for that, too.

He gripped at the arms of his command chair. What would Emma tell him if she were here? He felt another wave of regret at the thought of her, yet she more than anyone—perhaps in this world or any other—understood the risks. She would say, "You're not trying to move a starship. You're not trying to move anything. You're just…looking."

There was a name for what he was doing. Remote viewing. He remembered, in some dusty corner of his military training, hearing of spies in earlier centuries using their alleged psychic abilities to remotely see what the enemy was doing. *But the difference between what I'm doing and what they're doing,* he thought, *is that I can fucking do it.*

He snapped his eyes closed and once again found his center of peace. Then he reached out with his mind.

He reached far. It was easier now than it had been. He thought perhaps he would be out of practice, but no. It was like muscle memory. It was almost too easy. He felt his consciousness reach out to the furthest limits of this universe, saw the outermost stars surging toward the void in every direction, toward No Thing, toward space that is not space, that doesn't conceptually exist until something, anything, is there.

He knew it all, with himself at the lopsided center of it. He felt every creature's existence, their joy, their struggle, their sorrow, their births and deaths, all of it at once. He could disentangle the mass of emotions and experience of each one individually if he wanted to, but he kept his focus diffuse, general, a massive soup of sensation.

Then, as if his mind were a bullet fired into the sky, it reached as far as it could go, froze in midair as gravity overwhelmed velocity, and began its descent. He shifted from the general to the particular.

He was tempted to check in on Jo, on Emma, on Nira, even on Danny—but he dismissed the thought. Yes, he could spend all day spying on his friends and enemies. It would be a satisfying, if slimy way to pass his time. But he needed to maintain his objective, and he did so with military precision. He felt for the presence of the shaman…

…and he found the Prox. A shudder ran through him.

Holy shit, he thought. *Where the fuck did they come from?* As far as he knew, there weren't any Prox in this universe. On the other hand, he hadn't experimented with his…talent…since the accident. If they were in his own late, dearly departed universe, why shouldn't they be in this one? He focused in, saw their entire horde, the hundreds of thousands of them clinging to the surface of their ships. He saw the three subspecies: the crablike soldiers, the relentless, bulky workers, the spinning, squid-like expediters. And they were headed for Sol Station.

And once they had consumed that, he knew, it was only a short hop to Earth.

He felt his pulse leap, heard the pounding in his ears, felt the rush of blood in his head. The danger in the phenomenal world matched the panic in his interior. The medieval axiom "as above, so below" had never made sense in the way it did now. With this awareness, this unity, he finally understood how all things were connected. It wasn't academic, nor was it theory. It was experiential fact.

And the experiential fact of Earth's imminent destruction caught him up in a tornado of cosmic urgency. He flailed inwardly, paralyzed by panic. A thousand action plans unreeled before him in his mind's eye. And in his sinking heart he knew that not one of them was worth a damn. Every idea he could think of involved moving something large, and that, he suspected, would put an end to this reality string just as it had his own. If he tried to save this universe, he would destroy it. He wasn't certain of much, but he was certain of that.

In the midst of his panic, he felt a pinpoint of calm. Instinctively, he moved toward it.

"There you are," the little man said. Jeff recognized him instantly. The poncho, the weird little hat, the wise eyes, blacker than space.

He watched the shaman smile, but it was a grim smile. *It was a smile that said, I'm glad to see you. You are almost too late*. "Come," he said. "Come now."

As if holding a finger on a map and backing up, Jeff noted the position of the shaman's consciousness in space, and with a god's eye view, took note of what surrounded him.

He recognized the galaxy as the one he was in, the star system as not adjacent, but not far as interstellar distances were reckoned. He noted the planet, the continent, the forest, the mountain, the cave.

He knew where the shaman *was*.

And he knew he had a choice. He could abandon this ship and just *go there*. He could be there in the next heartbeat. Or he could spend the next few days getting there by starship.

He knew what he wanted to do, but he also knew the risks, and he wasn't willing to take them. He might be the destroyer of worlds, but it was not a mantle he would assume intentionally or even willingly. No, he would go against every impulse that was relentlessly driving his gut. He would take the time. He would play it safe.

"On my way," Jeff said aloud. His eyes snapped open. He set a course and steeled himself as the *Annabelle Lee* punched into superluminal space.

CHAPTER TEN

Jo sipped at her hot chocolate, savoring the bitter, spicy aftertaste. She looked up and called forth the image of Kali from her neural. The ancient Hindu goddess glared at her—no, she seemed to be looking past her, or maybe *into* her, which was unsettling. She was blue, her naked breasts full and firm. Her only clothing seemed to be a necklace made of severed heads and arms strung together, all of them dripping blood. Her right foot was crushing the corpse of a dead man—also blue, with an impressive mustache. She had four arms, each hand holding a grisly trophy—a bowl of blood, a scimitar (also dripping with blood), a severed head, and the last hand raised in greeting, or maybe blessing. *Talk about a mixed message,* Jo thought. But what really drew her attention was the goddess' face—round and hard, her tongue unnaturally long, almost prehensile, hanging down past her blood-soaked chin. And on her forehead, a third eye—sideways, staring…elsewhere.

They're calling you the Kali of Aken, Admiral Alinto had said. Jo could understand the blood on the chin part—she had noted she had blood on her chin when she took over the *Eisenhower*. *It tends to happen when you bite off people's thumbs,* she thought. A wave of vertigo washed through her. *Oh my god, I* am *her.*

"Sir, incoming orders from Central Command."

Jo looked up to retrieve the message. This one wasn't from Alinto, personally, but was a more standard directive. All the protocols were in place. Still, the bogus orders had made her gun-shy and suspicious.

The order was routine—accompany a caravan of ships from New Avignon to Deseret. She looked down and tapped her fingers on her command chair, thinking. Then she rose and walked over to the communications panel. She leaned over Tash Liebert's shoulder and noticed him stiffen. "Relax," she said quietly in his ear. "I don't want to alarm the others. But I want you to run two level C redundant confirmations on that order, and every other order we receive from now on. I don't even want to see it until you have two independent confirmations from real, live beings that the order is legit. Understand?"

"So, three independent information points for each communication?" Liebert whispered.

"I know…that's a lot of work. And if anything's urgent, go ahead and loop me in earlier. But if it's standard stuff…run your checks before passing it on."

"The more classified it is, the harder—"

"I know. The classified stuff is…I'll be able to tell. It's the routine stuff that I'm worried about."

"Got it, sir."

She patted his shoulder and turned back to her command chair. As she did so, he caught the scent of the communicator. The sharp, spicy male body odor that wasn't offensive, so much, as…she straightened her jacket and sat. It reminded her of Jeff. That connection made her flash on another. He had asked her to rescue his crew. She looked up and accessed stellar cartography. Jeff's crew was aboard Epworth Station. She located that first and put an electronic pin in it. Then she located New Avignon and Deseret. Finally, she added a pin for their current location. She zoomed out and studied the resulting constellation.

Epworth wasn't along any direct line, she was sorry to see. However, if they took an elliptical path to Deseret they could, conceivably make a stop there first. But why would they need to?

She stood. "I'm...going to take my break," she announced. "Mr. Chi, you have the conn."

"Aye sir," Chi said, rising to take her place at command.

Jo strode to the lift and chewed on her lip as she traversed to Deck 11. She nodded as she passed crewmen, acknowledging their deference and smiling encouragingly. She loved this part of her job—and hated it. She had to be "on" at all times when about the ship, and if there was anything bothering her, she couldn't let it show, for the sake of morale. It was often exhausting.

Fortunately there were people she could be real with. She entered the boatswain's office and noted everyone snapping to attention at the sight of her. Her presence here was unusual, and the supply crew was not prepared. "As you were," she commanded them. She stepped to the counter, behind which a young ensign almost cowered, his eyes growing huge at her approach.

"Ensign, is there a problem?"

"N-n-no sir."

"Is he in?"

"He, sir?"

"Palamar. Is he in?"

"Uh...yeah, he's in. He might be..." He didn't want to say.

"Asleep?" Jo asked.

"Uh...napping, sir."

"Do you mind?" She indicated the counter with her chin.

The young ensign's hands shook as he swung the counter up, allowing her to pass through. She didn't say another word to him, but strode to the door of Palamar's office. She entered her master code and it slid open.

Palamar was inside, snoring on a cot. She stepped in and went to the wall synthesizer. Ordering up a cup of water, she grabbed it and stepped to the sleeping old man. She poured it over his head.

Palamar woke with a start. He spluttered and wiped his face, emitting a howl of protest. Then he recognized her. "Jo. Shit. You scared the hell out of me."

"You're supposed to call me Captain."

"Fuck that. Uh…it's always good to see you…but I usually don't end up wet. So what's up, Sunshine?"

"I need some advice," she said. "I need privacy."

He shrugged. "You got it." He rose and went to a wall panel. He opened it up and located a grouped plug with his thick fingers. He tugged it out and left it hanging from its wires. He pointed to the camera in the corner. The omnipresent red light beside the lens was gone.

Given the ease with which he had performed this maneuver, she wondered just how many "private" conversations he had had over the years, how many times he had removed that particular plug, and what kind of deals had been made with no one the wiser. She decided not to think about it.

"No microphones?"

"I had them all routed into this one plug. It's out, so we're completely offline."

Jo jerked at the thought. "Disconnect," she said. She looked up to access her neural.

"No, don't," he said. "It's suspicious. Run a diagnostic instead. Nothing goes in or out for a diagnostic, nothing is recorded, and it takes three minutes to reboot. So talk fast."

It was a great hack, and not one she had thought of. She instigated the diagnostic, and noted he had done the same. She waited for him to look back down, then lost no time. "I don't need advice."

"You never do."

"That's not true—never mind. Listen, I need a favor. We need supplies that will take us to Epworth Station." She winked at him.

"We do?" His eyebrows rose. "Oh. We do. Of course we do. I'll put together a requisition. It will be marked urgent. Sorry I didn't notice we were getting low on all these things."

"Don't let it happen again, Boatswain Palamar."

"No sir. Sorry sir." He winked at her.

COMMANDER FOULON CHECKED his neural to make sure he had the number right. He did. He scowled. *This doesn't look like a shop,* he thought. He pushed the button on the service plate. The light flashed. Foulon bounced a couple of times on the balls of his feet. Patience was *not* one of his virtues.

Foulon disliked space stations. He had spent several years of his life aboard them, but their immobility grated on him. *If you're going to be in space, you want to be moving,* he had said more than once. It wasn't much of a life axiom, but it was his.

Still, for short periods of time, they were all right. They were, at least, a necessary evil. Not everyone liked the peripatetic life, he realized. Some folks liked to be rooted in a place. Planet dwellers, for instance. Some people, like him, preferred to be on the move. And folks who lived on space stations? He supposed they were somewhere in between.

He'd never considered it before, but it was a liminal kind of life—in between planet and ship, in between here and there, in between coming and going. He rarely thought this deeply, however. It made his head hurt. He blinked and focused on the door.

A voice came from the speaker on the service plate. "Who is it?"

"Terran Authority Commander Ernst Foulon. I'm here on business."

"What sort of business?"

"Whatever…the sort of business you…do…here." Foulon faltered. Really, he had no idea. He would feel like he was on more solid ground if it was an actual shop.

"Are you here for yourself or on Authority business?"

"I'm here on behalf of the Terran Authority Ship *Horatio Nelson* and her captain, Daniel Hightower."

"Fuck…" he heard the man mutter. "The Butcher of Catskill Daniel Hightower?"

"*That's* supposed to be classified."

"Fuck me. People tell that story to their kids. It's like Mother Fucking Goose around here."

Foulon grinned and rocked back on his heels. He could almost smell the gears burning in the man's head as they churned. He leaned in to the service plate and whispered. "You don't want to keep the Butcher waiting, do you?"

"How do I know you are—"

"I'm sending my creds now." Foulon looked up, accessed his neural, and forwarded his credentials to the address he was standing at.

A moment later he heard, "Fuck me."

"It's easier to talk without a door between us," Foulon suggested. "Easier to do business, too."

"Oh, Christ."

A moment later the door slid open. Foulon stepped in. It took a moment to get his bearings. He wasn't sure what he was expecting. He supposed, if it wasn't a shop, it would be an industrial space. But it wasn't. It was a domicile. It was a rough domicile, short on aesthetics, but it was roomy. It was also strange. There were ramps here and there, leading to different levels, some of them non-permanent, like risers. He blinked, unsure of what he was seeing. There was also a large hoisting robot, the kind you saw in warehouses, dormant in a corner.

A whine pierced the air, and Foulon jerked his head toward the sound. A hover chair glided into view. "Sorry, I was in the loo."

The man who lives here is an invalid, he thought. He purposely used the out-of-date, disrespectful term for the differently-abled. It was closer to how he felt. Nevertheless, the notion that he needed something useful that such a man could provide did not strike him as odd. Unfair perhaps, unjust, but not odd.

"Shit. You *are* from the Authority."

"Are you Tavin Neeks?"

"At your service."

"What is this place?"

"You mean the space station? Drona Station. You didn't notice the constant stink of curry?"

"No, I mean *this* place?" Foulon waved around.

"What happened to your face?"

"I usually answer that question with a demonstration," Foulon sneered. "Care to participate?"

Neeks visibly gulped. If the man had been able to stand, he would have come up to Foulon's shoulder. As it was, however, there was no way he was leaving that chair. His body was twisted, his muscles thin and atrophied. His hands waved in front of him, but his fingers were misshapen, and they looked as if they were no longer prehensile, if they ever had been. A tube was permanently fixed to the man's throat, the other end attached to the inner workings of the chair, no doubt. Foulon couldn't guess what it was for.

The little twisted man chose to answer the original question. "This is my home. It's also where I work."

"What do you sell here?" Foulon was determined to sort out his confusion.

"I don't sell anything here, you—" the man caught himself. What was he about to say, *—you dolt?* Probably, or something very like it. Foulon let it pass. He believed he was a generous man at heart. "I'm an accountant."

"Oh." Foulon blinked. Well, that made sense. It was a good job for a man of…limited mobility. He didn't need a shop, it was all data anyway. Foulon nodded. It made sense. He could proceed. "We need some information."

"What kind of information? And why me?"

"You work for Aerospace Partners Limited?"

"Nobody has called it that for a century. APL, it's just APL."

"The articles of incorporation—"

Neeks waved his objection away. "Yes, I work for them. Jesus."

As in, *Jesus what an idiot?* Probably.

"We know that," Foulon said. "We're not idiots."

The two men held each others' eyes for a tense moment. Foulon's eyes narrowed, as much as his scar would allow.

"Why don't you get that fixed?" Neeks pointed to his own face.

"Why don't you get that fixed?" Foulon pointed to him, to his chair, to his condition.

They both stared at one another until Neeks looked away. "What the fuck do you want to know?"

"All starships burn thorium—"

"All C-drives burn thorium," Neeks corrected him. "Not all starships have C-drives."

"All starships that hope to travel anywhere in the lifetime of their crew burn thorium," Foulon said, an edge creeping into his voice.

Neeks waved his assent with a gnarled hand.

"Commercial-grade thorium is only produced in the neutral zone by APL."

"That's not a law or anything—"

"It's just a fact," Foulon said. Neeks waved his assent again. Foulon was getting tired of the cripple's bullshit.

"I want to know who bought thorium and where."

"What? In the whole neutral zone?"

"Yes."

Foulon watched Neeks' eyes roll. "Do you have a time frame?"

"In the past month."

"Oh, well thank God you have some parameters."

Foulon was not fond of sarcasm. In the past, before he had achieved his rank, he had often been the object of it, and just as often missed it while it was happening. People rarely insulted him twice. He clued in to the sarcasm this time, however.

"Some sales will be under the table, you know."

"The one I'm looking for won't be."

"And which one are you looking for?"

Foulon grinned. It was an ugly, wicked-looking grin. He knew that and used it to good effect. "That is classified."

"Ah." Neeks chewed on his lip. "You know it's illegal for me to give you information like that, don't you?"

"No, it isn't."

"Well, it's against company regulation."

Foulon shook his head. "Not my concern."

"I could lose my job."

Foulon shrugged. "Not my concern."

Foulon noticed a normal chair. He retrieved it and sat it down near the hover chair. He rested his elbows on his knees. Even sitting, he towered over the invalid. "Besides, who needs to know? We're not going to tell anyone. We just want to know what we want to know, and we'll delete the file after we get what we need. We promise."

He could see Neeks wrestling internally. He knew what was going through the little twisted man's mind. He was wondering what would happen if he said "no." Foulon decided to show him. He rose and strode the short steps to the man's chair. He saw the cripple's eyes widen, and his squeaky voice begin to protest.

Foulon ignored him, and took the tube running from the man's throat to the bowels of his chair between his thumb and forefinger. He pressed the tube together, collapsing it momentarily. "Just out of curiosity," Foulon said, "What happens if I do this?" He pressed it again, and held it there.

The squeaking emitting from the little man rose in pitch. The twisted body began to squirm. Foulon's face was unreadable, as if he were shaving or scanning a news feed. The chair began to rock as the little body bucked against it. *Must be oxygen*, Foulon thought. *Good to know*.

He released the tube, and the twisted little man gulped greedily at the air, now restored to his use. His eyes remained huge, however, as was his air of disdain. Foulon appreciated that. "Where were we?" he asked. Then he answered himself. "Ah yes, we want a comma-delimited-file. Every thorium fuel sale in neutral space in the past thirty days. From every vendor that stocks your product." Foulon smiled patiently.

Neeks was still hyperventilating. His eyes narrowed in hate. "It will cost you."

Foulon sighed. He picked up the tube again. Then he put it down again and patted the twisted man on his chest. "How much?"

Neeks' eyes flitted back and forth. "Fifty thousand."

Foulon had been authorized to offer twice that, but the little man didn't need to know. "Done. Would you like that transferred to your commercial account, personal account, or perhaps…a private account?"

"I'll give you a number."

Foulon looked up to access his neural. "I'm ready."

Neeks rattled off a string of numbers. Foulon entered them, then engaged the transfer. He looked down and watched the little man's eyes roll up into his head as he checked his own account. He looked back down. "Okay, this will take some time."

"How much time?"

"I don't…okay, I do know. Thorium is a Schedule B substance in most jurisdictions—even in most micro-jurisdictions in neutral space—and all sales are tracked as a matter of course. I run a report every seven days. It takes two hours to compile. It'll be a big file."

Foulon looked up at his neural to note the time. Two hours was enough time for a drink and a fuck at the local cathouse. He felt his pulse quicken at the thought of it. But he also smelled foul play. He would leave and come back and there would be no sign of the little man. "That'll be fine. I'll sit right here while you work. But I'll take some whiskey, if you don't mind."

"I don't have whiskey."

"You can order out. And Neeks," Foulon leaned in so that his scarred nose was almost touching the cripple's own. "Don't fuck with me—or there isn't a hover chair in the universe that can spoon you up and carry you around. Got it?"

EMMA PACED IN THE CORRIDOR. The door to the council chamber was closed. In the entire time she had spent in the hive, it was the only door she had seen, so the fact that it was closed seemed especially significant. Inside, Amberline was addressing the Alverian rulers—she did not understand how the Alverian government was organized, but anyone watching Amberline bow and defer to them could tell which ones were in charge—and the topic of conversation was how Emma could best serve the hive.

She thought back on the tasks she had seen the Alverians working on as she passed through the main chamber. There had been groups of Alverians washing fabric, though Emma was unsure what it was for since, except for Amberline, she hadn't seen anyone wearing much that counted as clothing. She'd seen food being prepared—her stomach gurgled at the thought. It had been hours since she'd last eaten, and she was apprehensive both about how long it was going to be before she was offered food, and what that food was going to be. Clearly, she was going to be unsuitable for most of the work the Alverians needed done. She didn't know the language, anything about the culture, and she was missing a pair of limbs. Even the "chair" they had provided for her to sit on while she waited was a bad fit, something more like a stationary bicycle with no wheels than anything a human would sit on. But then, it wasn't made for a human.

She was suddenly annoyed that the Alverian language was primarily gestural. If it were a meeting of humans on the other side of the door, she'd at least be able to tell if someone was shouting. Even the cuneiform-like markings on the door mocked her. She hated not understanding what was going on around her. It was a big part of why she became a scientist in the first place.

She checked her neural. It was still offline, but it wasn't because she was locked out; there wasn't even an indication that there was any network to connect to. The greatest miracle of human technology, the ability to link the brain directly to computer networks, allowing effortless access to the sum total of knowledge or any other person anywhere in the galaxy, all reduced to a very expensive surgically implanted clock. And the clock told her that she had been waiting in the hallway for more than an hour.

Emma was standing directly in front of the door when it swung open, startling her. She leapt to the side as Amberline stepped out, closing the door behind her.

"Has the jury reached a verdict?" She expected Amberline to miss the reference.

Much to her surprise, the mask replied, "We have, your honor," as Amberline started down the corridor.

Emma trotted alongside. "So what's it to be? Garbage collector? Fish skinner?"

"First things first." Amberline said nothing more, merely leading Emma though a confusing network of tunnels.

Emma tried to makes sense of the signs at each junction, but the symbols remained as alien to her as the Alverians themselves. After what felt like a hundred random turns, she began to wonder if Amberline was lost, but just before she could say anything, the alien stopped and entered a room. Emma followed her into what appeared to be some kind of equipment locker, with floor-to-ceiling shelves stacked with arcane devices of unknown function. No! There was a device she recognized—a false human face mask, nearly identical to the one Amberline wore.

Amberline searched the shelves until she found what she was looking for and picked it up, carrying it over to Emma. “I believe this will be compatible…” She held it up to Emma’s chest. It was a prosthesis, a fake set of the Alverian’s smaller arms. “Please hold this here.” Emma held the base plate of the arms while Amberline fastened and adjusted the straps around the back of her neck and around her waist. When she was done, she pressed a button on the base, and a small red light came on. She stood back and watched as the arms activated and assumed a neutral posture.

“Wow,” Emma said. “How do they work?”

“You should find a device on your neural now.”

And she did. Her neural indicated a device ready for pairing. She activated it, but nothing happened. “Nothing’s happening.”

Amberline nodded. “It may take a while for you to gain control of them. It would be instinctive for an Alverian. We have these sub-arms from the day we hatch. These are made for one of us who has lost their sub-arms in an accident.”

“I thought someone who couldn’t serve the hive was put to death.”

Emma was surprised by the level of offense the fake mouth was able to muster. “Not if there is a way to overcome the reasons someone cannot serve. We aren’t monsters.”

Emma smiled and resisted the urge to tell her that they certainly looked like monsters. “No, of course, I apologize.”

Amberline bowed and made a pose with all four arms that Emma interpreted as acceptance of the apology. Emma returned the bow and made the same gesture, the sub-arms moving in a sloppy semblance of what she imagined.

"Good!" Amberline shouted. "But the right sub-arm should be higher, with the hand pointed more to the right." She gently guided the artificial hand to the correct posture. "The way you had it implies that the acceptance is insincere, and that you are mocking the one apologizing."

Emma laughed. "We call that *sarcasm.*"

The mask smiled. "Of course humans would have a word for that."

Amberline gestured for Emma to follow and left the room.

"Hey," Emma said, "I've been meaning to ask you—where is the neural network?"

"There is no neural network in the hive."

"Really? But you have a neural…"

"I have to have a neural as part of my function. I need to use this prosthesis," she gestured at the mask, "and I need to interact with the humans in their own world. A neural was absolutely necessary."

"Nobody else has them?"

"Very few. Our brain is not well suited to the surgery. More often than not, the subject does not survive the surgery."

Emma's mouth dropped open. "You took that risk?"

Amberline shrugged. "The hive required a... what was your word? An envoy? The hive needed an envoy to interact with humans."

"And you answered the call."

"We *always* answer the call of the hive."

Emma shook her head. "Even though you might die?"

"I was the fourth to attempt the surgery. I was the first to survive. That is how I came to my function."

Emma fell silent, flexing the false arms as they walked. They moved, but not reliably, and with no coordination. "It's going to take a while for me to get the hang of these."

"Yes. It will take you a lot of practice to develop enough competency with the prosthesis to speak our language."

"Oh, for sure. Wait, what?" Emma followed Amberline through an archway into a room crawling with miniature Alverians, some not much more than a foot tall, their chitinous shells nearly translucent. Two adult Alverians stood in front of a large video screen at the front of the room. Emma looked around and instantly realized what she was looking at. *Kindergarten.* "Oh, no, wait a minute... Amberline, can I have a word with you outside?" Emma stormed out into the tunnel.

Amberline followed momentarily. "Is there a problem?"

"You're sending me to primary school? I'm a scientist! I have three master's degrees in physics, two in advanced trans-dimensional theory, and one in quantum seismology! I'm published, for god's sake…"

Amberline shook her head slowly. "And none of that is of any use if you cannot tell anyone about it."

"I can tell you about it!"

"I cannot serve as your translator. I have other work to do, and the hive requires that I return to it."

Emma worked her mouth, but she couldn't find a rebuttal.

Amberline continued, "As I said, if someone cannot serve the hive, we do whatever is needed to overcome the difficulty."

"Right," Emma said, smiling and nodding. "You're not monsters."

NIRA STOOD and discovered her legs were rubbery and unreliable. She stumbled toward the door and fell, hitting her right elbow on the floor. Bolts of pain lit up her brain, clearing it of much of its fogginess. She rolled on the ground, cradling her elbow with her left hand, stifling a groan of pain. *Fine. I'll crawl,* she thought. Blocking out the throbbing from her arm, she turned onto all fours and scuttled toward the door. *This might actually be a good thing. They won't be looking down,* she thought, then realized this was ridiculous. The only thing more glaringly obvious than a person stumbling around in pajamas was a person crawling in pajamas.

This is not a good plan, she told herself. *Fuck. This isn't even a plan.*

She scuttled to the door and hugged the wall, thinking. *I need a place to recover, to wait until my head clears. What was wrong with the chair?* It was exactly where people expected her to be—she wouldn't arouse any suspicion. She'd need to fix up the IV so that it looked like it was still attached. She could do that. She'd give it a half hour or so, and then she'd try again. *Play the long game*, she instructed herself. *Don't be impulsive*. Easier said than done. Still…it was the beginnings of a plan.

She crawled back to the chair, climbed into it, and was relieved to see the tape that held the catheter was still sticky enough to adhere to her skin. She pressed it, smoothed it, and then sat back and clawed through the cobwebs still sticking to bits of her brain. Once she got up, then what? She'd go to the door. *I'll be seen,* she thought. She didn't know the layout of the clinic. She didn't know where the exit was. *I'm wearing pajamas,* she reminded herself.

The doctor had said she could choose other clothes. Surely he wouldn't be the one helping her with that, would he? No. He was a doctor. So who would? Patient Services. *Was that even a thing?* she wondered. One way to find out.

"Computer," she said with a voice of command. "I want to pick out new clothes. Can you connect me with…Patient Services?"

It took a moment. Then she heard a soothing voice, speaking in an accent she couldn't quite identify. "The duties of Patient Services were assigned to Patient Care three years ago. Shall I put you in touch with Patient Care?"

"Yes, please," Nira said, her eyebrows rising.

"Patient Care," said another computerized voice. "Please tell me about your need. Use complete sentences and spell your name."

"Commander Camil Nira," she said. She spelled her name. She might not, technically, be a commander in any military branch recognized by this universe, but she sure as hell was not going to surrender her rank or her identity.

"Do you know what kind of clothes you want?"

"Uh…no. Is there a catalog?"

"Of course."

The air in front of her shimmered, and beautiful models wearing bland hospital gear began to circle in front of her eyes.

"Uh…you know what? It's hard to get a good sense of what these really look like—"

"Shall I adjust the resolution?"

"No, no, I…could you just send someone with a few of the most popular for me to choose from. I…well, I prefer people to computers. No offense."

"None taken!" The computer chirped. "I'll send someone by in about fifteen minutes."

"That would be perfect. Thank you."

"You just sit tight, Camil. Would you like to enjoy some relaxing music while you wait?"

"Sure. What the hell?"

"Would you like to hear 'What the Hell' by the medulla trance group Apnia Collective or the 'What the Hell Suite' by minimalist composer Hishashito Stewart?"

"Uh…neither. How about Mozart's Requiem?"

"I have that right here. Enjoy."

"Thank you. You're…very pleasant to talk to."

"Would you like me to keep you company until your Care Specialist arrives?"

"Uh…no, that's okay. Thank you, though."

"I'll just be standing by. You let me know."

"Will do."

Nira had met friendly AI's before, but this one seemed special. She genuinely liked it. Of course she knew that there was no one to like. But the experience had been pleasant. She shook her head to clear it of distractions. *Focus*, she told herself. The cobwebs were receding, and she needed to take advantage of that.

She thought furiously, making plans and contingency plans. She'd only have one shot, and since she didn't really know her circumstances… It was a long shot, she knew.

The swish of the door sliding open broke her reverie. *Can I stand now?* she wondered. *I fucking better*.

"Hi there!" A chipper young woman in her early twenties crossed the room and stood in front of Nira's chair. Her long dark hair hung behind her in a pony tail, and her uniform fit her in a baggy way that did her no favors. “I’m Tish. I’ll be your Care Specialist today. I understand you wanted to see some clinic wear options.”

“Yes,” Nira said, forcing a smile. *She’s too damn perky,* Nira thought. *I will have to kill her.*

“I brought five”—she held up one hand so Nira could see five fingers, and she spoke loudly, just in case Nira was deaf, apparently—“so you’ll have the best selection of our best designs. Sound okay?”

“Sounds…great.”

Tish placed a tote bag with a navy blue Epworth Wesleyan Clinic logo on it on the counter near where the doctor had been sitting. From it she pulled a short stack of options, each individually wrapped in poly. She pulled the poly off the top one and allowed it to cascade dramatically before her. It was a sand-colored set of scrubs. Tish held the shirt up against her own torso, holding it at the shoulders, which she moved back and forth in a silly approximation of a model on a catwalk.

She held up the trousers briefly, did a weird little curtsy, and then opened the second bag.

And so it went, for five bags. By the end of it, Nira found that she hated Tish’s ponytailed guts.

“I like the first one,” Nira said.

“The sand scrubs?”

“Yeah.”

“A lot of people do. It feels the most ‘normal,’ and then there’s the whole ‘When in Rome,’ thing.”

“When in Rome?”

“You *are* in a clinic, so why not dress like the staff?” She indicated her own scrubs—light blue string-tie trousers and a white top.

“Right, that’s what I was thinking.” Nira smiled. “I’m a little woozy, so can you help me out of this?”

“Uh…I’m not sure you should stand.”

“I’ll be okay. The drip ended a while ago.”

She brightened. “Okay. Let me just get this for you.” She disconnected the IV line from a port close to Nira's wrist so she could get her arms out of her shirt.

Nira stood. *I am still a little wobbly*, she thought. *But it'll have to do.* She rested one hand on the arm of the chair and gave Tish a smile that said *please be patient with me.*

Tish nodded encouragingly, raising her arms, ready to snag Nira's shirt as soon as she was ready.

"Uh…could I have a little privacy, please?"

"Oh, I thought you wanted help," Tish said, her voice rising in surprise.

"You're fine, but…the computer. I don't want some assholes in Security or Patient Care jerking off to my boobs."

"Ha!" Tish covered her mouth with her hand and gave Nira a look that said *we could be girlfriends!* "I love what that stuff makes people say!" She pointed to the IV.

"Sorry."

"No, it's totally okay. Computer, privacy mode, please."

"Privacy mode engaged. Please say 'Computer' again to reengage."

Tish cocked her head and readied her hands to pull Nira's shirt over her head again. "Ready?"

"Ready," Nira said, lifting her arms. Then she twirled and struck Tish at the base of the neck. The girl crumpled and collapsed in a heap at Nira's feet. Nira was ready and squatted quickly, making sure the girl's head didn't hit the floor. "Prissy bitch," Nira said. Then Nira started to undress her.

CHAPTER ELEVEN

It was an accident of orbit. Sol Station kept an orbit around the sun midway between Mars and Jupiter. It was the jumping off-point between the home planet and the rest of space. It just so happened that the Prox's approach would encounter Sol Station first—thirteen months from now, at the other end of their elliptical orbit, that would not have been the case.

But it was the case, and Admiral Tal was grateful. It was not as if Earth had no defenses. They had plenty. But if they could stop these bastards here, there would be no reason to test those defenses. And those defenses paled beside the staggering might now amassing for battle.

Tal leaned over and put his hands on his desk, his broad nose almost touching the edge of the holo display. He had adjusted the display to be as wide as possible, and indeed, the projection ran the whole length of his formidable desk, hovering and shimmering above it.

His eyes darted back and forth, checking the position and readiness of each ship under his command.

He had seen his share of battles before, but even the largest of them had paled in comparison to this. Every ship in the fleet had been recalled. And they had all come…except for one. Tal tried to put it out of his mind, but he felt a painful stab in his gut every time he thought about Hightower. The man wasn't a traitor, exactly. He just wasn't obedient, and that was a fatal flaw in a military man. As fatal flaws went, Hightower had a whole complement.

He looked to the right to check the summaries—a column of tabulations collating the sum of the many statistics being displayed. He had a total of 314 ships, 65 of them battle-class, with over 150,000 personnel on board. All of them were armed to the teeth with a total of 6,441 repeating particle cannons and 12,679 nuclear torpedoes. They all had lasers as well, over 6,000 of them, but Tal wasn't putting much stock in those.

They had laid mines, out among the asteroid belt, with photogenaic trip-wires between them. They'd be harmless to any Authority—or hell, any human or allied ship with the proper code. But if anything didn't send the proper handshake, it'd be in for a rough ride. Tal didn't know of a single ship in existence that could weather the beating those mines could dish out. *Thank God we had enough time to lay them,* he thought. If they held, he wouldn't need to lose a single ship, even a single man.

He straightened up. He turned toward Lieutenant Liu and gave him a grave smile. "Now it's just the waiting."

"We've done everything we could do, sir." He didn't say, *Let's hope it's enough*, but it was implied.

"No, we didn't." Tal looked at his shoes. They were real leather, made by hand. He knew that was eccentric, but he didn't care. Every other pair of shoes he'd ever had on his feet hurt. But he could stand in these shoes all goddam day and he felt like a million chits. They were imported from Argentina and cost enough to make a midshipman gasp. Tal wasn't married. He didn't have a life apart from the service, not really. His shoes were one of the only indulgences he allowed himself.

"What do you mean, sir?" Liu cocked his head.

"I mean we could have asked for a truce with the rebels. We could have asked them to stand alongside us. We could have doubled our numbers here, if we…" he trailed off.

"If the civilian leadership would have allowed it."

"Hell, I'm not sure I could have rammed it through the military authorities. But we should have tried. It might have…I don't know, shifted things."

"'Enemies who fight shoulder to shoulder emerge from battle friends,'" Liu quoted.

"Mauro?"

"Indeed."

"You dabble in that religion?"

"No sir. But I've read pretty widely on it. It's…pretty wise, I think."

"You and half a million human converts."

"There's a lot more people who admire their philosophy that aren't believers."

Tal grunted. "Your quote is apt. I think there was an opening there. We didn't take it."

"Did you try?"

Tal looked up at his assistant. It wasn't an accusation; it was a sincere question.

"I floated the idea. Burned a lot of good will, I'm sure. It was shot down. As I knew it would be."

"A part of me thinks that's a shame."

"And the other part?"

"Understands why it was shot down."

Tal grimaced, but nodded sadly.

Liu looked up suddenly, and Tal knew the moment had arrived. "Estimated time of contact with the enemy is less than an hour away, Admiral. They're calling for you in Battle Command."

Tal straightened up and adjusted his uniform jacket over his sizable midsection, the orange piping popping into place. He gave a curt nod and headed for the door.

It slid open and he strode down the frosted white corridor toward the command center. Liu fell into step just behind him. He held his head high and squared his shoulders, projecting more confidence than he felt. They'd need every bit of it, he feared, feigned or real.

The door to Battle Command slid open, revealing a buzzing room filled with people—hundreds of people. The noise was deafening, and he looked up and switched the dampeners on in his neural. The noise level plummeted to where he could focus comfortably. Anyone speaking to him normally would come through fine, but the ambient noise was screened out. It had been an expensive feature, and he had almost passed on it, considering it a concession to old age, but now he was grateful for it.

Massive holo displays mirrored the one he had been studying in his office, but with much greater detail. Most folks were working at small stations and everyone seemed to be talking to someone not present. Fingers flew, eyes rolled, and everyone he could see was getting ready for battle.

Some of his fellow Admirals were poo-pooing the preparations, calling it overkill. Tal had kept the vids from the *Jackrabbit Sage* classified, but what the Prox were capable of was no secret to his peers. Maybe it was denial, maybe it was wishful thinking, maybe it was sheer stupidity. But Tal saw anyone not taking this threat seriously as a problem to be dealt with every bit as much as the approaching enemy.

Tal's eyes flitted to a task list hovering over one of the doors, feeling a rising sense of satisfaction as the items disappeared. There were only two items left when he heard a voice from behind him.

"Sir, the Prox have just entered visual scanning range."

"On screen."

The air above them shimmered, and Tal looked up to get his first live glimpse of their enemy. In the back of his mind, Tal reminded himself that if they survived this, his neck was going to hurt like a motherfucker by the end of this day. He'd be craning it up for hours to see the holo displays and he could already feel the tightening muscles in his neck and shoulders. There was Morphex and a muscle relaxant in his future. *If I survive*, he reminded himself.

The ships looked just as they had on the *Jackrabbit*'s vid, only there were three of them. If each ship carried 500,000 enemy soldiers, as they had estimated based on the vid…he did the math. He had never loved numbers, but he actively hated these.

"Enemy ships are approaching the first mine field," Liu called from behind him. Tal clutched at the faux-leather back of the chair in front of him. Every eye in the command center was glued to the displays. Tal held his breath as the first of the mines erupted, sending a billowing flash of nuclear energy across the display. "Come on, baby," he breathed, not conscious of his own words.

As the resolution on the display adjusted to the brightness, Tal's stomach sank into a hard knot of dread. The Prox ship had sailed right through the line of the mines. He watched the explosions, biting his cheek, and then saw the Prox ships emerge whole from the fireballs. If there had been any damage it wasn't evident. "Holy shit," Tal breathed. Then, with a voice of command, full of courage he did not feel, he announced, "Battle stations, all personnel. This is going to be the fight of your lives."

NIRA LOOKED IN THE MIRROR. Tish's uniform—the white scrubs with the light blue bottoms—hung on her. Nira was shorter than Tish. Nira was shorter than most people. She took one knee and rolled the pant legs up. *They're not going to stay up*, she noted to herself; the cloth was too thin and light.

It was the best she could do. She smoothed out the top, and then noticed the blood and puncture marks from where she had ripped the IV from her arm. She spat on her hand and rubbed at it, ignoring the pain. Most of the blood came off—enough of it, anyway.

Time to get out of here, she thought. Standing as straight as she could, she forced her face into a mask of professionality. She needed to look like she belonged here. She held her head as high as she could and waved Tish's badge in front of the doorplate. It slid open, and she stepped out into the hall.

First, she thought, *I'll circumambulate the floor to get my bearings.*

The corridor was nearly deserted. Every now and then she passed a doctor or nurse, even the occasional worker. *Are they visiting friends or loved ones, or are they here for outpatient treatment?* she wondered.

Without talking to someone, it was impossible to tell. And she was determined not to talk to anyone.

Turning a corner, she saw an elevator straight ahead. She made a beeline for it and waited for it to arrive. She looked at no one. She looked at nothing. She stared at the doors until they slid open, then she stepped on.

She was distressed to find she was not alone. There were two people already on the lift, and another stepped in behind her. She turned and faced the doors, studiously avoiding any of the faces.

Where do I go once I get out of here? she wondered. No doubt they would be monitoring her accounts. If she tried to make any purchases... Her neural. They'd be able to find her, no matter where she went. Her neural signal, so long as it was connected, would be traceable anywhere in known space.

Shit, she thought, and felt a rising spike of panic. *I've got to get offline.*

She could do it, if she had the tools—the right interface, the right computer programs. Surely, she could find others who could do it quickly and easily. *Can I get to the underdecks before they notice I'm gone?* She gritted her teeth. The elevator door slid open.

And there, on the ground floor, was Doctor Ram Chujan, looking impossibly young, with a full complement of security officers standing behind him. Her brain kicked into high gear. *Can I take them all?* she wondered. She would try. She had to try. She crouched for a spring and got hit with a poly disruptor that left her twitching and prone on the clinic floor.

Doctor Chujan knelt beside her and placed a compassionate hand on her arm. She could break that arm, if 53,000 volts of electricity hadn't just completely derailed her nervous system. "Commander Nira, this is too much excitement for you. We need you calm for sentencing."

Sentencing? Nira's brain churned, stumbling and stuttering over the word. *Sentencing? Shouldn't there be a trial?*

Doctor Chujan seemed to be on the same wavelength. "The security cams captured your whole...event. Security has been able to construct a complete 3D rendering of your actions. And now there is, it seems, another event—the assault of our Care Specialist, Ms. Patricia Lyon. Let us hope she is all right, or there will be more cards added to your stack."

Doctor Chujan's head jerked, and he looked up, accessing his neural. "Ah, sentencing is complete. Civil ritual code aboard Epworth Station requires that you be standing to receive your sentence, as you are able. Are you able?"

Nira's thoughts raced and her pulse pounded. It was all happening so fast. Was there no due process here? Were there no lawyers? Would she not be able to present a defense? Could she not tell her side of the story? It appeared she could not. She was still twitching as two of the security guards shoved their gloved hands roughly into her armpits and yanked upwards.

They held her upright and steady, even as her knees were buckling beneath her. Doctor Chujan stepped back as a uniformed security officer stepped up, standing formally at attention, and looked up, accessing his neural and blinking as he navigated to the document he needed. His voice, when he spoke, was thin and high and reedy, completely inappropriate for the gravity of his words.

There was so much about this that was wrong, but there was no opportunity or means for her to protest any of it. "Commander Camil Nira, in the incident labeled Nira vs. Vlat, you have been judged guilty of criminal assault in the first degree and manslaughter in the first degree with extenuating circumstances. In the incident labeled Nira vs. Lyon, you have been judged guilty of criminal assault in the second degree. For these crimes you are hereby sentenced to VRE Rehab, beginning with level one, effective immediately."

"Shit no," she breathed. "No no no no." But her protests meant nothing. She was not in command of her limbs, let alone her powers of persuasion, not that it would have mattered. She knew what the sentence meant, and what it entailed, and what was about to happen to her. And she would not wish it on her worst enemies. She let out a flailing attempt to break free from the officers who held her arms, her voice rising in an inarticulate siren of protest, but to no avail.

She felt the momentary sting of the hyper spray, heard the puff of air that accompanied it, and felt what little strength and will and resolve and consciousness she still possessed melt into oblivion.

AFTER FIFTY-SIX HOURS of superluminal travel, *The Annabelle Lee* reentered normal space. Jeff had spent that time sweating over his decision, his insides grinding away in an intestinal infestation of doubt and self-recrimination. He had left off showering, and he knew he was rank, even to himself. A part of him felt he was not worth cleaning.

But he was here. He would soon be in the company of the shaman. The answers were so close he could taste them. He checked the course and the time. It would take forty minutes to reach the planet under standard propulsion. For the shaman's sake, he would shower. He jerked upright and headed for the sonic.

As the silent sound waves beat at him, stripping away bacteria and dead skin, whipping his flesh into red, fresh wakefulness, he leaned against the wall with one hand and wished there were some analogous process for his interior scuzziness. *I need a soul shower,* he thought. *Something that can pound away guilt.*

But wishing does not make it so. He knew that. He wasn't fine with it. He would live with it. He dressed and shaved and emerged from the head looking like a human being, even if inside he felt like something less.

He prepared for landing, and made sure the entry trajectory seemed plausible. It did. The computers were rarely wrong, but it was always worth a glance. As the landing sequence unfolded, the computer's soothing voice kept him apprised of the various stages as they were initiated, most of which bounced off his conscious awareness. If anything had been out of the ordinary, he would have caught it, but the routine was almost unconscious by now. The computer's voice registered about as much as his autonomic system's commands. It was like breathing—when he tuned into it, it was somehow comforting to see that it was still happening.

He looked up and blinked, accessing whatever files he could find about this particular system and this particular planet. There wasn't much. There were a host of indigenous species, some of them sentient, none of them self-reflective. But it was lush and wild and, from all reports, beautiful.

He set down about a click from the cave he had seen. He waited for the atmosphere check to run. The air on this planet was a little higher in argon than Earth-normal, but breathable. He scowled as he read the results. The particulate matter was far higher than the files he had read indicated. *Perhaps there's a forest fire nearby,* he thought. After all, fires were natural occurrences. A lightning strike can cause one. The meteorological conditions were such that lightning was possible. It hadn't been observed, so far as he could see, but it was possible.

He readied his weapon and inserted it in his holster. He checked the exterior temperature and adjusted the temperature setting on his field jacket—instructing it to maintain a steady 21 degrees centigrade. Satisfied that all was ready, he pushed the access button on the airlock.

As he descended the ramp, his jaw dropped.

The soil was black. He could see no living tree or bush. Turning in a full circle, he beheld an utterly desecrated landscape, charred and stinking of ash, as if it had been firebombed.

Jeff's nostrils twitched and he scowled. The sky looked nothing like it had in the files. It was hazy and a deep, murky red. He knew that was from all the burnt particulate matter in the air. It seemed apocalyptic. It was the perfect mirror for how he had been feeling ever since he had glimpsed the Prox.

He reached into his field jacket and pulled up a face mask. The flexible fabric settled comfortably over his mouth and rested on the bridge of his nose. In seconds, the air was cleaner and he was able to breathe more easily—the tiny scrubbers in the field jacket were doing their job.

Scowling, he checked his direction on his neural and set out for the cave. There was still smoke rising from several clumps of what had no doubt recently been organic matter—trees, probably. So whatever had caused the destruction was recent. It had happened in the last twenty-four hours, he guessed. It had happened since he had seen the shaman during his last…exploration.

A vague suspicion arose within him, but he chose not to speculate. It was too easy for his imagination to run away with him, and that way led to conspiracy theories and madness. He wasn't the scientist Emma was, but he was still a man of science. He'd speculate when he had the facts.

The terrain was crumbling and silty, and more than once he stumbled. Every now and then he passed a rock jutting out of the hellish terrain large enough to lean on and push against.

Then he saw it—as he approached a dark, ashen hill, he saw the gaping mouth of the cave. He made a beeline toward it—there was nothing left of the landscape to impede him, after all. Without hesitating, he ducked and entered the cave, switching on the electric torch set into the chest panel of his field jacket.

The place was empty. He saw bones in one corner, however, and an arrangement of what looked like straw or some other fibrous plant matter heaped together to make a rough mattress. Someone had been here, and recently.

"Goddammit," he said out loud. The shaman was not here. Of course he wasn't here. If he were here, he'd be dead. Was he dead? Had Jeff unwittingly just climbed over the charred remains of the little man? Who could know?

"Who did this?" Jeff asked the smoky air. "Who the fuck…"

There was no use spending any more time in the cave. Jeff walked back into its recesses, and confirmed that it did not go far back. It was empty of life, as far as he could see.

Grinding his teeth, he set out again toward the ship. The knot in his stomach tightened. *It's always something*, he thought. There was always something keeping him from finding this motherfucker. One obstacle after another. If it wasn't duty, it was distance. If it wasn't friendship, it was fear. He wanted to scream. He stopped. Then he let it come. He squatted, and allowed the pressurized rage that had been building up in him explode, hearing himself roar like an animal for the first time. Ever. He did it again, feeling the raw power of his own voice, his own creaturely passion, his aggression toward the universe, toward fate, toward God, toward whatever cosmic powers were at play.

Spent, he stumbled to his knees. He rested for a moment, panting on all fours.

He plunged his hand into the ash, trying to find purchase to push himself up, and connected with something solid. It was curved, it had a lip, like the shell of a giant tortoise. Puzzled, Jeff lifted it from the ash. Then he dropped it in horror, leaping to his feet, struggling backward, away from the object.

It was indeed a shell—an exoskeleton, to be exact. And he knew the shape of that shell. It was shaped exactly like one of the apron plates of a soldier Prox. *It could be a coincidence,* his brain rattled off. *Perhaps the indigenous life here is also a giant, crablike...* he let the thought die. There was nothing in the files even remotely like that.

He turned in a circle, taking in the landscape anew. This wasn't just a lightning strike. He knew that now. This was a hit. This was a gut-punch aimed directly at the shaman by…by the Prox or whomever commanded them. Snarling, he picked up the carapace and balanced it on his back. Setting his feet with resolve, he marched back toward the ship, a tiny voice in his brain still screaming with alarm.

THE OBLIVION SAGA • BOOK 4

OBLIVION GAMBIT

You can survive on your own;
You can grow on your own,
You can prevail on your own;
But you cannot become human on your own.

—Frederick Buechner

CHAPTER ONE

[STRING 311]

Is the shaman dead? Jeff wondered.

On the bridge of the *Annabel Lee*, Jeff stared at a scan of the carapace on the main view screen. It was covered with soot, like a gigantic, slate-gray fingernail, torn from its host and discarded. He stood and examined it from various angles, wondering about the life of the being who had grown it, worn it, died in it. A flash of inspiration—he trotted to the command chair and pulled up a panel. He did a planet-wide search for human life forms. There had been two frontier towns, one on this continent, another on an adjacent one. Was it possible that the shaman was there? As possible as anywhere, he supposed. It was much more likely, however, that Jeff had been grinding the little man's ashes into the dust as he carried the carapace back to the ship.

There's one way to find out, Jeff thought to himself, feeling an instant curl of dread in his gut. A part of his brain began screaming at him, *Going into the All cannot be your first response whenever something happens. That way lies danger and destruction. One day you're going to push it too far again, and you'll have another whole universe of souls to bury.*

He heard the voice. He felt the twist in his intestines. But still, he took his command seat, gripped the handsets, and closed his eyes.

He sent his consciousness out into the void, as he had done so many times. It had become easier with practice. Once again, he saw the Prox approaching Sol Station.

There's nothing I can do about that, he thought. He knew that wasn't true. He felt torn. He could teleport there. If the universe survived, he could ask to captain a ship. In his heart, he knew it wouldn't stop the Prox, but he might die trying…if he didn't kill everything and everyone else.

No…he let his awareness widen, searching out the energy matrix that was the shaman. He gritted his teeth, hoping against hope that the little man was still among the living.

He found him.

Jeff felt almost giddy with relief. He surrounded the shaman's energy with his own, willed his consciousness to descend to where the man was.

A cluster of yurts, a ring of trees, a sky bursting with stars. "Thought you'd lost me, huh?" the little man said. There was no one else around.

Is he talking to me? Jeff wondered.

He backed up, finding the position, the constellation, the star system, the planet. It was…far. Jeff's body whistled. He did a quick calculation. Doing an equation in his head while holding presence in the All felt a bit like juggling, but he managed it. He figured it would take him three weeks to reach the shaman's location. *How the fuck…?* But he knew. Jeff was not the only person playing with fire. Prometheus had a twin.

"Come," the little man said. "Come now."

"It will take me three weeks to reach you," Jeff said.

"It will take less than a heartbeat to reach me. Come."

Jeff struggled. He could do it. He knew how to do it. He was just… afraid to do it. "I've already destroyed one universe."

"You won't destroy the universe. I'm here."

Jeff's brows knitted over his closed eyes. What the fuck did that mean?

"Come," the shaman's voice was insistent. "We're running out of time."

Jeff knew it was true. Even now the Prox were closing in on Sol Station. He opened his eyes and made some adjustments to the autopilot. Then he closed them again. Then he simply wasn't there.

"I HAVE BAD NEWS," Mr. Liebert whispered. He had approached her captain's chair, which was unusual to start with.

"Nobody likes to hear that, Mr. Liebert."

"No sir. I've found Camil Nira."

"Surely that's good news."

"She's in prison, sir."

"Good god." Jo buried her head in her hand. "What for?"

"It seems that another of the crew members we're looking for, Martin Pho, was shot in a food court. Near as I could figure, Nira acted to neutralize the threat, but too late. Did a real number on the attacker, though."

"Dead?"

Liebert nodded.

"Shit," Jo swore. "Now what?"

"There's one more crew member we were searching for, Dr. Emma Stewart."

Of course. Jeff's girlfriend. Jo felt black clouds gathering above her. She ignored them. *Duty*, she reminded herself.

"She does not appear to be aboard."

"Also dead?"

Liebert shook his head. "I have no idea. There's no record of it, if that's the case. She's just...gone."

She could have just gotten so pissed at Jeff that she took off, Jo thought. Jeff did have that effect on people. "Okay, we can't do anything about Pho, and Stewart needs more investigation. What can we do about Nira?" Jo realized they were speaking in low, conspiratorial voices, but that in fact, everyone on the bridge could hear them. She felt momentarily ridiculous.

"I don't know, sir," Liebert says. "Her sentence is ten years in the Interworld."

"My god, she'll atrophy away to nothing. She'll never get that muscle tone back. That's practically a death sentence for a military person," Jo said, thinking out loud.

Liebert did not disagree.

"What kind of pull do we have?" Jo asked.

"Pull, sir?"

"Yes. What kind of jurisdictional authority do we have at Epworth Station?"

"Uh, none, sir. It's an autonomous microjurisdiction."

"With whom we have a protection pact, do we not?"

Liebert blinked. "I…I don't know, sir."

"Well, someone is guaranteeing their security. If it's not the RFC it's the Authority."

Liebert was apparently speechless.

"Don't just stand there, Liebert, pull up everything we have on any agreements between the RFC and Epworth Station."

"Do you have an idea, sir?" Liebert asked.

Of course I do, she thought, but she just gave him a hard stare.

"Right away, sir."

"HEY, BABE. WANNA PLAY?" The guy was handsome, a little too handsome. He twirled his pool stick and posed with it at a suggestive angle.

Nira shook her head and turned back to her drink. *I wonder what he really looks like?* she wondered. *He's probably a little troll, ugly as a pug, with BO and long wisps of single hairs combed over his bald pate.* But he'd picked out a nice avatar, that was for sure.

She didn't get to pick her avatar. It was assigned to her. And it looked like her—kind of. She still had long black hair, now permanently hanging behind her in a pony tail. She was still lithe and athletic. But she was taller, which she didn't mind at all. What did bug her was that her avatar wasn't very Latina, it was more *generically ethnic*. Her skin was a soft brown, which she quite liked—darker than her real skin, and it suited her. But her facial features were just off enough to make looking in the mirror difficult.

Another guy sat down next to her and ordered a beer. He placed his elbows on the bar and glanced over at her. She caught his eye and gave a quick nod. He nodded back. Once more she wondered what he really looked like. Like everyone else here, his avatar was nondescript—handsome, 20s-normative, completely lacking in dandruff or body odor or bed hair.

She took a sip. She knew that every time she did, a tiny amount of ethanol was released into her IV. She could try to get drunk, but at a certain point, the drip would cease. She could drink all fucking night, but she'd get a little tipsy and no more. In some ways that was a relief. In others it was a pain in the ass.

Her own body, she knew, was in a hibernator, hooked up to a snake's nest of tubing. Tubes to feed air to her lungs, tubes to carry nutrients to her stomach, tubes to carry her piss and shit off to where it could do someone some good. Her mind could amuse itself to death—within limits—while her body atrophied a little bit more every day. She imagined she could even feel it, but it was probably her imagination. There was a mild ghosting effect between her actual body and her avatar, and it was unsettling at first. It was a bit like riding a bicycle—you got the hang of it, and then you just didn't think about it. Unless you did.

"You're new," the guy said.

"You live here?" She narrowed one eye at him.

"Nah. I keep a condo, though."

She nodded. A lot of folks did. Aboard a space station like Epworth, where real estate was valuable, it was cheaper to rent a coffin pod in the real world and rent a spacious Interworld apartment for your off-hours. It wasn't a thing that military people did, but she knew lots of folks made their meager paychecks go a little further that way.

"You live here?" he asked her.

She knew what he meant. Was she a cripple, a prisoner, or a freak? She held up her right hand so he could see the red band around her wrist.

"Wow, okay. Now I *am* intrigued." He grinned. "I like dangerous girls. What did you do?"

"A hulking Numerian put a blaster hole through the chest of… someone in my care." She swirled the beer in her glass and took a sip. "So I tripped him. Then I crushed his windpipe with my elbow." She glanced up. Even his avatar's eyes were wide. She leaned in so that their noses were almost touching. "Boo!" she said with a sudden jerk.

If he had been there in the flesh, she hoped he would have jumped a bit. But as it was, he turned back to the bar and downed his beer. "I… uh…gotta be somewhere," he said.

She pursed what passed for lips as she watched him walk away. She turned back to her beer and caught the bartender's eye. She raised her glass and he nodded.

It wasn't the end of the world, being in the Interworld. She wasn't in pain. She could move about freely—mostly. There were premium areas off limits to her, but she could go anywhere the standard package allowed, compliments of Epworth Security. Meanwhile, her every move was monitored, studied, quantified. Most importantly, she couldn't get into any real trouble here. Her neural worked, but it was firewalled—she could only access information pertinent to the Interworld. She could access the feeds. She could find out about the real world, but she couldn't manipulate anything there.

They'd started housing criminals in the Interworld about fifty years ago. It was cheaper, it was safer, and it was deemed more humane. The ratio of criminals to the general public was about the same, except that here nothing was truly private and you couldn't actually hurt anyone—not physically, anyway. You could still break someone's heart. It was, she realized, an enticing pastime.

She had to admit, being able to roam freely in the Interworld beat the hell out of being locked in a prison cell, but the torture was the same—the inability to get to anyone or do anything you cared about. Sure, lots of people got jobs. She could do that. She could make money, too. And maybe, after enough time, when despair had softened her will into a desperate pool of resignation, she would.

She knocked back the rest of her beer and signaled for a new one. Before it arrived the pool player took the stool next to her and leaned in a little too close. "Wanna get a room?" he asked.

She scowled at him. "You're barking up the wrong sexual orientation."

She scooted her stool back, re-establishing a comfortable amount of personal space.

He scooted over, closing the distance again. "I don't think you'll be disappoint—"

Grabbing his right arm in her left hand, she swung it like a lever behind his back. With her right hand, she guided his head to the bar—forcefully. The VR provided a very satisfying "cracking" sound as his head hit the virtual wood. She knew she couldn't actually hurt him, but she could surprise him, and that was almost as good. "Sorry to disappoint *you*, asshole. But you're going to back off, or I'm going to kick your ass from here to Sol Station." It was the only real landmark she could be sure of, but the threat seemed to do the trick.

"Okay, okay."

"I'm going to let you go now, and you're going to slink off into whatever sleazy hole you like to call your nest—and let me be very clear about this—you're going to go there alone."

"Okay, jeez."

She released him, but she was ready. He lunged at her and she punched him in the gut. He doubled over, winded and writhing on the ground. Nira wondered how much of that reaction was VR simulation and how much pain he was actually feeling.

Whichever it was, he slunk away as ordered. She turned back to the bar where a new beer was waiting for her.

"On the house," the barkeep said.

She'd lost her interest in it. She felt disgust—for the moron who'd tried to come onto her and for herself. She accessed her neural and paid. The barman looked up and back down again, nodding his acknowledgement. She stepped out onto the street.

The problem was knowing what to do with herself. She loved her job. More than confinement, more than the shame of her conviction, the thing that ate away at her night and day was the emptiness of her time—as empty of meaning as of content.

She stuffed her hands into her pockets and set off walking.

The Interworld was huge. Many of the wonders of myriad worlds were recreated there, and tourism was huge. Did it matter that the sites were simulations? Surely it did, but not as much as you'd think. She loved walking until she was lost, then stumbling upon something like the Parthenon. It was the one thing that really kept her going.

Passing an alley, she caught movement out of the corner of her eye.

"That's her," she heard.

She didn't think, she just reacted. With skill honed over many years of martial arts training, countless simulations, and real-life battle conditions, her reflexes were fine-tuned and exact. She wasn't sure how the idiot from the bar had caught up to her so quickly, or how he had amassed a posse, but distance meant less in the Interworld and with a neural you could call almost anyone.

Besides, she didn't have time to think about how, only to assess the fact of it, the threat, and the parameters of that threat.

She dove into an adjacent alley across the street. Then she positioned herself with her back to one wall, and edged to where the ladder of a fire escape provided an additional out. She was at a disadvantage in that, while free people could "wake up" and exit the Interworld anytime they chose, she was stuck there. However virtual the danger might be, for her it was real since this was the only reality she had.

There were four of them, stepping from the relative brightness of the street into the shadowy confines of the alley. There was the guy who had come onto her, but he wasn't in the lead—his friends were taking point. "Fucking coward," she hissed. She assumed the *jigotai* position, widening the stance of her feet and lowering her torso into a crouch, gathering energy for a possible spring in one direction or another. She raised her hands in the *jigotai* defensive mudra, but this was deceptive. It was defensive until it wasn't. They might be in position to deflect and protect, but they were also in the perfect position to strike when the opportunity was ripe.

She didn't want to hurt any of them, but unless they were prisoners like her, only she was in any real danger.

The two in front both grinned like jackasses, but wore very different expressions. One was tall, with a cool affectation, wearing shades and holding a cricket bat over his shoulders. He swaggered as if he didn't have a care in the world and was walking toward his next pitch. She named him Batter Up.

Next to him was a hulking ox of a man—an exaggerated avatar, surely, originally intended for fantasy play. But he was decked out not in medieval garb, but in contemporary dress, which she thought odd but didn't have time to wonder at. He slouched, and his forehead slouched as well, like a landslide of flesh over a scowling countenance. He even seemed to have an overbite. He had a baseball bat—nails stuck out of it at odd angles in a thick, wiry, unruly mass. She named him Menace.

Just behind him was an odd sight, an older avatar. It was a custom job that wouldn't have come cheap. His hair was thin, and his coat was thick and straight. His eyes were heavy-lidded, like a lizard's, and his face was void of emotion. She could read nothing about him, other than the fact that he was coming. She named him the Fixer.

And then there was Horn Dog from the bar—coming for his pound of ass, any way he could get it.

Nira seemed frozen, motionless, yet her fingertips quivered microscopically with gathered tension, like the string of a drawn bow. She knew how she looked—small, defenseless, easy prey for goons like this. But she knew something that they did not—her *jigotai* position was no ruse.

She meditated on her extended fingertips, willed her breath to slow, felt her heart rate lower. She felt time slow down as she watched Batter Up raise his bat over his shoulder, saw Menace draw back his own, ready to take the second blow.

When they were about 2.5 meters away, she launched herself from the wall with a kick, jumped, and caught Batter Up in the face with her boot. She employed an *ukemi* maneuver, using her arm to absorb the shock of her fall, then rolling. She rolled toward Menace, placing her other boot in his groin with sufficient force to knock him off his feet, howling with pain and clutching at his genitals.

Rolling into a crouched position, she assumed *migi-jigo-tai* and froze, turning her attention to the other two. Horn Dog was backing away now, finally, perhaps, seeing the error of his ways. The Fixer froze in place, contemplating her with dead eyes. She couldn't read what was going on in his head, but she imagined he, too, was surprised by her prowess. His eyes narrowed, boring into hers. She imagined that meant, *We'll resume this at another time. But I'll be watching you.* Then he turned and seemed to almost float toward the street—at least, she couldn't detect any motion from his walking.

"Any more, asshole?" she asked Horn Dog. She started marching toward him, stepping on Batter Up's head along the way. Horn Dog was still backing up. He tripped over a discarded pallet, and Nira found herself improbably towering over him. She knelt and grabbed the front of his shirt, pulling his face up to hers. "Because I'm ready anytime you are. You just bring. It. Fucking. On."

In her peripheral vision she saw something swinging toward her. She launched herself into a sideways roll to the left, and had to stifle a laugh when Menace's nail-studded bat connected with the side of Horn Dog's face.

She gathered herself up to her full, diminutive height and assumed *jigotai* again. She slowly raised her right foot in anticipation of a kick, but this time it really was for show. Balanced on one leg, she knew how she appeared: regal, otherworldly, dangerous. She might have looked ridiculous if she hadn't earned it, but she had. She was poised like a tantric goddess, her pose suggesting more limbs than she actually possessed, all of them seen and unseen dangers.

Running or hobbling, they all cleared out now, leaving her alone in the alley. She lowered her leg and sighed. A blinking light in her peripheral vision alerted her to an incoming message.

"Oh, Jesus," she muttered. Violence of any kind was a violation of her terms of incarceration. She resigned herself to her fate and looked up to retrieve the message.

AND THERE WAS THE BEACH. And there was Jeff. And there were two moons in a hazy, purple sky.

Jeff flexed his knees. The gravity was slightly less than earth-standard, maybe .83. That would be nice, until he had to get aboard another ship. The air was cool, and thank god, breathable.

"Hungry?" asked a voice from behind him.

Jeff turned and saw a campfire on the beach. Sitting on a fallen log was the man he had crossed the galaxy for, betrayed his friends for, the man whose name he did not know.

His eyes were kind but tired. On the fire was a pot. "It's just beans and rice. No meat."

Jeff walked over to the fire and sat down cross-legged on the beach. Now he wished he'd put on his field jacket before transporting. *That was stupid,* he thought.

"I thought you were dead," he said.

"Are you cold?" the man asked, as if reading his mind. He looked behind him and grabbed a colorful blanket. He passed it to Jeff, who noted how the man was wearing his, and draped it around his own shoulders in a similar fashion. It felt like wool, and it didn't take long for him to feel comfortable.

"There are lots of people who wish I were dead," the man answered the question at last. "But I persist."

"It was hard to find you," Jeff said.

"It was easy to find me," the man countered. "You were scared to come."

That was both succinct and true. Jeff conceded as much with a nod. "I destroyed a universe…"

"Maybe."

Jeff scowled. "What do you mean, *maybe*?"

"Destroy is a harsh word. There's a lot of distance between harm and destroy."

"I didn't destroy it?"

The little man started humming.

Okay, he's going to play games with me. Great, Jeff thought. "If something is just harmed, it can be fixed. Right?"

No answer. The little man scooped some beans and rice out of his pot onto a metal plate and passed it to Jeff. He picked up a colorful woven bag and fished in it. He pulled out a spoon and wiped it on his sleeve. He passed it over.

Jeff took it hesitantly and tried the beans. Then he tucked in. He was hungrier than he thought.

"I didn't destroy a universe?" he said again, his mouth full.

"There was damage. Whether it can be repaired…I do not know."

"Is everyone dead or not?" Jeff asked.

"I do not know…because I cannot get there."

Jeff nodded. "So one of the things that was damaged was the connection…to the other strings."

The man nodded. *Okay, we're getting somewhere now,* Jeff thought. His breast filled with hope.

"I've come a long way to find you," Jeff said, trying the rice. "I should at least know your name."

"Tomás. Diaz." He smiled, chewing slowly. "Nice to meet you. Again."

"I've just been thinking of you as 'the shaman.'"

Tomás laughed out loud, and a few grains of rice shot from his mouth. "Ha! Shaman." He shook his head. "No. I am no *curandero*." But he didn't say what he was.

Jeff discovered he didn't know what to say. He'd waited a long time for this. He'd put a lot of hope into it, too. But now that it was here... "Um…where are you from?" he tried. It sounded lame.

"The way you number the strings, I'm originally from 308. There, I lived in Peru. *Mi familia*...they are still there." His English was good, but Jeff detected a Latin American accent. He found it kind of charming.

"So you've crossed over from other strings, too."

The man nodded.

"Did you destroy…or harm your universe?"

He shook his head.

"Why not?"

"You have to know how."

"And I don't know how." Jeff said. It wasn't a question.

"You know how to see. You know how to move. But you do not know how to move *safely*."

"Will you show me how to move safely?"

The man smiled again. "I'll show you."

"Will you show me now?"

"I'm going to finish my dinner. Then I'm going to sleep."

"Okay…" Jeff felt foolish.

"Tomorrow I'll show you."

That seemed reasonable. There was a lot of information Jeff wanted from him, anyway, even before any teleportation lessons. Jeff ate another couple of bites, and as he did so a frivolous question occurred to him. He was about to dismiss it, but it occurred to him that one of the things he needed to do was just to get to know Tomás.

"Uh…did you ever look for your double? You know, on the other strings?"

Tomás broke out into a grin, and it seemed to Jeff like he might lose some of what was in his mouth. His teeth did not look perfect.

"Yes, I did," his head bobbed.

"And did you find him?" Jeff asked.

The man kept bobbing, an affirmative bob, it seemed to Jeff. When he had swallowed his mouthful, Tomás elaborated. "I found him. At Sol Station."

"At Sol Station?" Jeff sat up straighter in surprise.

"Yes, just a few weeks ago."

"When you were there…when we met?"

"That was it." The man narrowed one eye at Jeff, so he would know that what Tomás was saying was significant. "When we met."

Jeff blinked. "Are you saying that you…and I…that we're…?"

"Not the same person, no. Our strings diverge too much. Three hundred years ago, your ancestor Captain Algernon Caldwell was sent to the British colonies. In my string, he was sent to Argentina, initially. Your family settled in what became America. My family eventually settled in what became Peru. One decision can alter a lot."

Jeff nodded. "It's like we're cousins, then."

The man laughed. He did it with his mouth open, showing Jeff all his chewed food. "*Mi primo. Exactamente.*"

"So how did you..." Jeff didn't even know how to finish the sentence. "Are you...reconstructed, too?"

"You mean the Ulim?"

"Yes."

"We call them *los durmientes*."

"What does that mean?"

"It means 'the sleepers.'"

Jeff blinked. "I don't understand."

"I am not rebuilt. Whatever talent we have isn't because of any reconstruction."

"It's not?"

"Humans are...what is the word?" He cocked his head. He seemed to find it. "We are *mimetic* by nature. We see and imitate. I saw *los durmientes* move through space." He shrugged. "Then I did it too."

"But how—?" Jeff began, but Tomás waved him away.

"That is a long story, for another time. But you—I am guessing you saw them move too. And you imitated them."

"Yes."

Tomás gave a curt twist of his head that Jeff took to mean, *So there you have it.*

"They took pity on me," Jeff said. "I would have died. What I don't understand is *why* they took pity on me. I mean, beings die all the time. I was on their doorstep but...it's not like they're human."

Tomás set his plate aside. "Actually, they are."

Jeff scowled. "They are what?"

"They are human."

CHAPTER TWO

Commander Foulon squinted in the dim light of the bar. It was hot, crowded, and just rowdy enough for his liking. He jumped back to avoid two brawling species he'd heard about but never met. One of them swung a short, elephantine trunk at the other, who warded it off with his pincers. Both were weaving and barely upright.

Foulon hopped to the left and skirted the skirmish. His emotions were mixed. On the one hand, he felt a great deal of satisfaction. They had found the ship they'd been looking for. Jo Taylor was here at Epworth Station, at dock just a couple of kilometers away. They had caught up with their prey, and he knew that his work had been essential to that success. His captain was pleased with him.

He just wished he were pleased with his captain. He had come to the conclusion that Hightower was a gasbag who was a little too full of himself. That was okay, Foulon was used to egomaniacal captains. It was, he figured, part of the skillset necessary to *be* a captain. He looked forward to the day when he was granted his own command and could be more overtly narcissistic himself. But there was something else about Hightower that didn't sit right with him.

They called him "the Butcher" behind his back. Foulon had liked that when he had first heard it. He'd enjoyed ferreting out the mythology around the captain. He'd even been honored to serve with him, especially as his XO. It was the fast track to greatness, he thought.

But now his stomach turned sour whenever he thought of the captain. He glanced at one of the monitors. There was a news report about the recall of all Authority ships to Sol Station. The talking heads were speculating as to why. He wanted to hear what they were saying. Truth was, he was almost desperate for news. Hightower had cut the ship off from any communication with the Authority. They were running dark—no messages in, no messages out—which meant no news. Whatever Sol Station was facing, whatever Earth was facing, whatever the Authority was facing, they were facing it without *them.*

Foulon suspected that their entire mission was less strategic than it was personal. At first he'd assumed that Captain Hightower had classified orders to chase down the Kali of Aken and grind her into dust and to use every means necessary in pursuit of that goal. He could get behind that. But…but…but… "Something is not right," he said out loud, although there was too much noise around him for anyone to hear.

"What are you doing here?" a voice said. An older man sidled up to Foulon and winked at him.

"What do you mean?" Foulon asked. *Is this the contact?* he wondered.

"I mean every Authority ship in known space is heading back to Sol Station at maximum C. What are *you* doing *here*?"

There was no way Foulon could actually answer that question. It was, in fact, the question he had been worrying about himself ever since they'd arrived and he began seeing snatches of news.

"C'mon, I got a table in back. It's quieter…kind of." The older man waved him toward the rear of the bar.

Foulon looked around and reasoned that he had no better leads. His contact was supposed to find him, after all. And he knew he wasn't hard to spot. There weren't many Authority uniforms aboard station right now. He shrugged and followed the old man.

He almost bumped into him. The man had stopped at a table, where another patron now sat. He watched the man lean forward, put both hands on the table, and press his grizzled face close to the new patron. "This is my table, friend," he said, with more menace than Foulon thought possible. It was enough, apparently, because the interloper—a small, furry mechanic of a species Foulon didn't recognize—apologized profusely and wiggled off the bench and onto the floor. He walked straight out from under the table without having to stoop.

"Those little guys, Eppets. I hate 'em," the old man said, taking his seat. He waved toward the other side of the table. Foulon sat.

"Drink?"

"I don't have time."

"Sure you do." The old man pulled a flask from an interior pocket of his RFC uniform jacket and twisted off the lid. He took a swig and handed it to Foulon. Foulon accepted and knocked back a good slug. It was better than he'd expected.

"Authority asshole drinking with a rebel asshole," the old man said, his face dusty with beard growth and his lips curled up in a smile. "People are gonna talk."

"Are you my contact?" Foulon asked. It was a stupid question and he felt stupid asking it.

"Are you shitting me?"

Foulon looked at the table, embarrassed. He was used to being in command in situations like this. He glanced at the screen, hoping for some inkling of news from home. But the report was about crop fungus on New Manila.

"Danny said you were a spitfire," the old man said. "But you don't seem like a spitfire to me."

Foulon blinked. A random act of violence might convince the old man of his true nature, but before he could concoct one, the old man leaned forward and said conspiratorially, "What's eating at you, son?"

It was an opening, one that Foulon hadn't expected. There was something about the stranger that he trusted, that he wanted to trust. "What's happening back home?"

The old man cocked his head. "Are you shitting me?" he said again. "Is Danny running you dark?"

Foulon nodded.

The old man scratched at his whiskers and narrowed his eyes. "Now why on *Earth* would he do that?"

"I just want to know why all our ships are being recalled…and we're not, you know, going."

"Danny's not letting you in on the secret and it's eating at you," he said, not as a question, but as an astute reading of the situation.

Still, Foulon nodded.

"Let me tell you a little story about your captain," the old man said. "He and I were stationed at a little moon near…well, near what they call Deseret now. We had this excellent scam running, where we were sucking about half a million chits out of the indigenous species there. Let's call it…protection. Mostly Danny's idea. He was in charge. I got him what he needed to pull it off. That's kind of what I do." He showed Foulon his teeth. Then he took another pull at the flask. "Then we get this meteorological report—storm coming. Bad one. And suddenly we got a dilemma. Do we pass along the information to the locals? Or do we hold back a bit until we've completed our collection for the cycle?"

Foulon's eyes moved back and forth as he thought. "It makes sense to warn them so that they'll be around next cycle to collect from."

"Yeah, that was my advice," the old man's eyebrows rose. "But Danny is an impulsive fuck. Maybe you've noticed that? If not, watch out for it. He wants what he wants, and he wants it *now*. Doesn't matter who it hurts." His eyes rose to meet Foulon's. "You hear what I'm saying to you?"

Foulon nodded.

"Me, though? I'm grateful every day I'm not in command. I got my own little business, and I like that just fine. I like to find the ways to play the system, but it's small stuff, you know? Let other people decide the fate of millions. I'm just here to make a chit." He drubbed his fingers on the table. An uncomfortable silence fell between them, despite the noise from the bar. He leaned closer. "Uh…you *do* have a chit for me, don't you?"

"Oh, yeah, sure." Foulon felt like an idiot. Why couldn't he just fight or torture someone? He knew where he stood then. But this espionage bullshit made him feel off his center. The guilt about not being wherever the rest of their ships were going was not helping. Foulon suspected that Captain Hightower's interests and the Authority's were no longer in sync. And this old guy had all but confirmed it.

Foulon passed an unmarked chit caddy under the table. He felt the old man's stubby fingers, felt him take it. The old guy rummaged in his trouser pocket. "And for you..." he said.

Foulon felt a small box, about five centimeters square. He pocketed it. "What is it?"

"An encrypted communications device. No real-time messages, but it'll send and receive texts, undetectable to your people or mine."

"And you'll let us know where the *Talon* is at all times?"

"I'll send a daily update. No more. No less."

Foulon nodded.

"Have another sip." The old man banged the flask down on Foulon's side of the table.

Foulon didn't mind if he did. He swigged and returned the flask to the center of the table.

"I guess our work is done here," the old man said. "I better get back to my post, and you better get back to yours."

Foulon scooted to the edge of the seat and stood.

"Listen son, tell Danny that Palamar sends his best, okay?"

JEFF WOKE, the rough blanket scratching at his cheek. His neck hurt from the odd angle. He had slept on the ground before, but it had been a long time ago and he'd had a pack to use as a pillow. Last night he'd just used his arm, and his arm had moved.

He sat up, clutching the blanket more tightly around himself, and tried to loosen up his neck. He smelled coffee. He could see Tomás pouring the steaming black liquid into two metal cups. *Camp coffee,* he thought. *It's been a long time since I've had that, too.*

He stood and walked over to the fire, holding his hands out to it.

"I've been thinking about what you said last night," Tomás said, handing Jeff a cup. It was warm in his hands. It was, for that moment, the gravitational center of all things pleasurable and good. "About me being a *curandero*."

Jeff cocked his head.

"I think you might be more correct than I thought originally."

"How so?"

"A *curandero*…a shaman…is someone who goes into another world to find medicine, and brings it back for the healing of his people."

Jeff blinked, but the smell of the strong brew distracted him. He took a sip, but it was too hot.

"Is that what a shaman does? I thought a shaman was…I don't know, kind of like a witch doctor."

Tomás shrugged. "That is what it would look like to someone ignorant of the traditions, I'm sure."

Jeff nodded. He could cop to ignorance. Especially about a subject like this.

"So you are a *curandero* too." Tomás grinned at him.

Jeff shook his head.

"It is what we do. We go into another world…into the place of all-seeing, into other strings. We retrieve medicine…information, knowledge…wisdom, and we bring it back to save our people from destruction." He nodded, liking the sound of his own words. "*Curanderos*."

Jeff truly had no idea what he was talking about. An uncomfortable silence emerged between them, alleviated only by the crackling of the fire.

"I saw them," Jeff said.

"Who did you see?" Tomás asked.

"The Prox."

Tomás narrowed his black eyes at him. "Prox?"

"Yeah…at least that's what we call them…called them."

"What are they?"

"They're big, twice the size of a man. There are three species that I've been able to find. They eat metal—"

"Oh yes. *Los Comelones*." He nodded vigorously. "I know them."

Jeff understood enough Spanish to get it. The Eaters. It was apt.

"What about them?" Tomás asked.

"They're coming. I thought they were just in my string. But they're here too now. I don't know how or where they come from. We called them Prox because they came from the direction of Procyon, but—"

"They can come from any direction," Tomás said. "They can go anywhere they are sent."

"They're moving on Sol Station. I saw it when I was searching for you."

Tomás nodded. "Then there is no time to lose. Drink up."

Jeff sipped from his coffee obediently. He had no idea what the little man meant. What were they going to do, just the two of them?

"I saw all of the Authority ships...there were a lot of ships... getting ready for battle. The largest of them were forming a line, trying to stop the Prox before they reach Earth."

"They will fail," Tomás said.

"In my world, nothing we tried really stopped them," Jeff said. "I've never faced an enemy that strong."

"They are not the enemy," Tomás said.

"What?" Jeff asked. "What are you talking about?"

"If I took this pot and swung it at your head," he pointed to the pot containing the rest of the coffee, resting precariously on two logs, "who would your enemy be? Me or this pot?"

"You, of course. That's just a pot."

"Just so. *Los Comelones* are not your enemy. They are just a pot, a tool."

Jeff squinted at him. "So...who wields the tool?"

"*Los Durmientes*."

Jeff shook his head. "Wait, the Ulim? How...?" It was unsettling how all of their conversations kept coming back to the Ulim. The information was just not fitting together. "Okay, wait, back up." Jeff made the military field mudra for "hold still" with his free hand. "Tell me how all of this is related."

"Everything is a story," Tomás said, sitting down. He sipped at his coffee. He pointed to another large log, inviting Jeff to sit. He did. "So I will tell you a story. My people were subdued by the United Kingdom. The histories of your world and mine turn out quite differently, I imagine, as we are a couple of strings apart. The British were ruthless, organized, unstoppable. *Sudamerica* was…disorganized. We didn't stand a chance. They used us as slave labor, essentially. Oh, they paid us…but just enough to soothe their consciences, just enough to skirt the law. When their scientists learned how to go inside, we learned it too." He smiled sadly. "Servants…hear things, you know."

Jeff sipped at his coffee, now finally cool enough to drink. It was the bitterest thing he had ever tasted. He wasn't sure it was really coffee. And yet amazingly, it was the most delicious thing he could imagine at that time.

"They had the technology to create a whole interior world for themselves. Eventually they lived completely within their minds. Their bodies were…"

"Sleeping," Jeff said. "*Los Durmientes*."

"Yes. At first, we tended to them. Until some of them ended up dead, of course."

"That was bound to happen," Jeff grimaced.

"It was. By that time, they had mastered robotics to a point where we were…expendable. My people fled into the Andes." He glanced up and Jeff could see for the first time the centuries of accumulated pain in the wrinkles on Tomás' face. "They are still there. We learned enough of their mental techniques to shield ourselves, but not enough to *see*…or to travel. I am the first to be able to move between the worlds."

"And the Prox—er…*Los Comelones*?"

"Biological machines. They consume metal and forge it, all within their bodies. They are beautifully made, brilliant constructions. But they have no soul, no will of their own. They are *títeres*, marionettes…puppets."

"And the Ulim are the puppeteers…" Jeff breathed.

Emma stumbled out of the classroom, her arms dangling limply at her side. Her feet, back and shoulders were throbbing and her mind felt like it had been charbroiled. It didn't help that she had been wrong about being stuck in kindergarten; it would be far more accurate to call it *pre-school.* Some of the Alverian "children" had hatched only four days ago and were already outpacing her in learning their native language.

She had been confident going in. She was a fast learner and already knew three Earth languages. How hard could it be to pick up another? *Very hard,* it turned out. Being a gestural language made class a more intense upper body workout than the most advanced yoga she'd ever tried. The fact that two of her four arms were mechanical should have been cheating. But on the contrary, the mental exertion of learning to control the neural-driven prosthesis was exhausting: a distraction on top of learning a new language based upon an entirely alien mapping of ideas to symbols. She'd begged them for textbooks, instructional videos—anything more in line with how she was used to learning rather than the calisthenics-like drills she and the hatchlings were being put through—but the instructor insisted this was the only way the language was taught. At least that's what Emma thought she said.

The classes were all the same. An image was brought up on the large video screen at the head of the class. The instructor struck the pose for that particular word. The class, all standing in rows, then matched the pose. Students assuming the correct pose were praised, those that did it incorrectly were called out and corrected. If they were slow in getting it right, they risked getting a smack from the thin, flexible rod the teacher used as a pointer. The backs of Emma's legs were already bruised and stinging, which she thought wildly unfair considering how much softer her skin was than the Alverians'. Her complaints were ignored, if they were even understood.

She limped into the communal eating area. She hadn't learned the Alverian word for it yet, so she just thought of it as the *cafeteria.* She stood in line until she was given a square plate containing the only two dishes the Alverians seemed to eat: a paste made of some kind of grain not unlike Hawaiian *poi,* and thin slices of boiled gray meat, a thin broth sloshed over both. Neither dish tasted bad per se, but after a week of a completely unvarying diet, eating was becoming something of an ordeal. She forced herself to lift the plate, and shuffled it to the nearest table with an open place.

Here there was none of the drama about who you would sit with that you might find in an Earth school or prison. All Alverians were considered equal, if not completely interchangeable. And with a gestural language, eating and talking at the same time was nearly impossible. Everyone sat on the bicycle seats and ate, barely interacting with the beings around them.

Emma set her plate down and settled on her seat as gingerly as she could, attempting to minimize the pressure on her poor bruised perineum. But since her feet were just as bad, there was no compromise that didn't hurt. She dreamed about some human pain killers as she began to eat, also wishing for some hot sauce or something to make the bland food different.

A familiar face appeared next to her, dangling from an Alverian neck. "Hello, Emma."

"Hi, Amberline."

"How are your studies progressing?"

She put down the small plank-like eating implement and signed "Good."

Amberline nodded satisfaction and signed "That is excellent." Then the mask said, "You look tired."

"Oh my God. I have never been so tired in all my life. If I survive this, I will be strong enough to lift a house."

"It occurred to me that the difference in our anatomies might be a factor for you, so I brought you something." She produced a small vial of tablets and set it down in front of Emma.

"What is it?"

"Pendontoline."

Emma gasped and snatched up the bottle. Pendontoline was a powerful painkiller and muscle stimulant, a favorite of dockworkers and other laborers. She shook out a tablet and dry swallowed it, chasing it with a bite of *poi*. "Thank you. You may have just saved my life. I don't suppose you have a bottle of Tabasco for me too?"

"What is that?"

"A traditional pepper sauce made on Earth. Don't worry about it, I'm kidding."

"Ah," Amberline said. "You find the food bland."

"It's okay, but it's the only thing you guys eat! I don't even know what it is!"

She pointed at the paste and made the sign of its name. Emma automatically matched it, and Amberline nodded approval. "It's made from the seeds of a bush that grows on our homeworld, ground into paste and mixed with water.

"That's about what I thought. And the meat?"

Amberline made the appropriate sign.

Emma mimicked it, then paused. "Wait, we learned this sign earlier today. Damn, what was it, we've learned so many they all start to blur together. No, I remember, that was the sign for *male*."

"That is correct." Amberline pointed away from the eating area, across the common chamber.

Emma looked in that direction and saw the livestock pens and the strange pig/dog/bugs milling about and eating from troughs. "Oh! It's those! It's not bad considering it's meat from an insect…" She threw her eating stick to the table.

Her head began to spin. Several unconnected ideas suddenly slotted together into a horrifying truth. "No…" she sputtered, looking at the meat on her plate.

"Is something wrong?"

"I think I'm going to be sick."

"Are you ill?"

"You called them *males*."

"Yes."

"*Your* males! *Alverian* males!"

"Yes. You appear offended."

"Not offended, shocked! You… you're cannibals!"

Amberline thought about that for a moment. "No. If I ate another female, then I would be a cannibal."

"But they are the same species as you!"

"Technically, I suppose." Amberline shrugged. "But they aren't the same creature. You've seen them. They have no intellect at all. They are strong enough to easily leap out of their pens but it doesn't even occur to them. They are good for only two things—harvesting their semen and eating."

Emma thought she might faint. "Harvesting their…"

"Semen," Amberline completed helpfully. "Yes. And they are our only dependable source of protein."

Emma held her hands up. "Well, I'm not eating them."

Amberline nodded. "Yes, you will, or you will grow weak and die."

Emma crossed her arms, both sets of them. "I'll find something else."

"Where?"

"There's gotta be… I mean… you could bring me…"

Amberline shook her head.

"Oh, Goddammit…"

A tone sounded through the gigantic cavern. Amberline tilted her head. "You must return to class."

Emma frowned defiantly.

After a moment, Amberline said gently, "If you do not attend to your studies, you will be assigned other work. If you think learning our language is hard labor, wait until you work a twelve-hour shift in our laundry works."

Without another word, Emma stood and walked away, leaving the unfinished plate of food on the table.

ADMIRAL TAL HELD his breath as he watched the monitors. Although there were hundreds of people in the Command Center, no one spoke. If he had time for reflection, he would have found the silence eerie, but his focus, like everyone's, was riveted on their five largest Dreadnaught-class warships, now moving in formation to engage the Prox in battle little more than a parsec away—which was far too close for his liking.

"I want all the support you can give them," Tal broke the silence, speaking to everyone and no one in particular. "If they need high-level computations, let's run them here. If they need power, let's beam it to them. Be prepared to anticipate their needs and be there with the fix before they even ask. Move it, people!"

That broke the spell. He knew there was little they could do on this end of things, but people certainly wanted to look busy to avoid his ire. That was all right. Maybe it would do some good.

"It's going to be fine, sir," Rear Admiral Evans said, leaning in. "We've never encountered anything that could get past even one of those ships."

Tal did not respond. The rear admiral was quite correct. The Dreadnaught-class ships were large, slow, and not the least bit nimble in battle. It was one of the reasons the newly-christened ships had not yet been employed against the rebels. It was hard to get them where they needed to be in a timely fashion. The best speed they could manage was C5.

But what they lacked in maneuverability they made up for in sheer firepower. Each one of them was stocked with a full complement of weapons, which included more than a thousand fission warheads, two hundred particle cannons, and sniper lasers that were much more powerful than the standard issue. They had redundant hulls of reinforced iconel that could take fifty times the beating the next class of warship could endure. They had automatic containment cells. If one portion of the ship blew up, the others would be sealed off and protected.

These five were the best they had. They were lucky that all five were within recall range when they'd discovered the threat. He hoped they wouldn't need them all, but if they did…they were there.

Tal wrapped his fingers around a guard rail that separated the upper platform of the Command Center from the floor, where hundreds of officers were at their stations—monitoring, measuring, correcting, supplying, supporting. The Command Center was the brain of their effort. Every byte of information flowed into this place, just as every top-level order issued from it.

Tal studied the formation as the Dreadnaught approached the Prox ships. They were arranged in a flying V, with the lead ship at the top, two other ships forming wings descending to either side. The symmetry was perfect, and would need to be if they were going to act as a single unit—the deadliest military force the human race had ever managed to assemble. If this formation had been summoned against a planet, he reminded himself, that planet would be a desolate collection of rubble floating in cold space. One Dreadnaught was unstoppable. Five would be apocalyptic.

Once again quiet settled over the room as the Dreadnaughts closed the distance between themselves and the Prox vessels. Tal saw shimmers emerge from the alien ships, but couldn't make out what they were. He certainly had a theory.

"Magnification!" he called. "Zoom in! I want to see what those flashes are."

One of the monitors flickered as the optics feed was disrupted. What took its place was blurry at first, but quickly snapped into sharp resolution. Now they could see the hulls of the Prox ships, and the hulls themselves were shimmering.

"Closer!" Tal shouted.

The picture adjusted again, and Tal swore. At first, he could not figure out what he was seeing. Others around him began to voice the questions going through his own head.

"How can that metal be…moving?"

"It's like there's something metallic swarming on the hull."

"That's exactly what it is," Tal said, remembering Captain Bowers' report. "They ride on the outside of their ships, not the inside. That shimmering isn't the hull—it's the bodies of the ships' passengers clinging to the hull. And they are not immobile. Swarming is the right word."

"That's impossible," Rear Admiral Evans whispered.

"Obviously not," Tal said. "Just because a species doesn't do something as we do doesn't mean it can't be done."

Evans scowled at this, but his eyes never left the monitors.

Tal watched as a tiny dot of light drifted from the lead Prox ship, floating into space. This was followed by another, then another. Before he had drawn three breaths, entire streams of shimmers had detached themselves from the ship and were floating toward the Dreadnaughts.

"How many?" Tal asked.

No one said anything.

"Goddammit, I want to know how many of those motherfuckers are launching themselves toward our ships!" Tal yelled.

"What are they?" someone asked.

One voice caught his attention. It was from one of the engineers on the floor. "I estimate 12,000 of the aliens are spaceborne as of…now. 13,300 of the aliens are spaceborne as of…now. 18,700 are spaceborne...now."

Tal gripped the guard rail in front of him until his hands ached. The numbers were staggering. *But remember*, he told himself, *those are just soldiers. They're vulnerable. They have no protection.*

"Dreadnaught formation, target approaching Prox soldiers with particle cannons, full array. Fire at will."

The aliens had drifted close enough for them to get a good look at them. Metallic, crablike, they were cold and efficient killing machines. Tal shuddered as he saw them up close—the folded merus sections, the spiked tips of the long metal legs, the inhuman eyes, the fulminating mandibles. The legs were extended before them, preparing to make contact with the Dreadnaught hulls. Tal thought he could see the pointed tips quivering, but that could have just been the tricky resolution at this distance.

He wiped the sweat out of his eyes, despite the fact that he felt cold all over. This uniform suddenly felt too big for him, as if he were shrinking from the stress. It was a sensation he didn't understand and couldn't bother to contemplate. Not now.

"180,000 Prox now spaceborne," Tal heard in his ear.

"Gods," he swore.

But the firing had commenced. Tal noted with guarded satisfaction that the blasts from the particle array dispatched the Prox soldiers handily. The problem wasn't insufficient firepower; it was going to be too few guns.

For every Prox soldier they took out, two hundred more sped toward their targets, their prey. Tal realized that they could fire all day and all night for a week and still not hit all of them. And they were coming fast.

"We need to clear a swath of them with every shot," Tal shouted. "One at a time isn't going to do it. I need solutions, now!"

The particle cannons were effective, thank god, but they derived their power from a very focused, targeted burst of energy. The more you spread it out, the less effective it became. The particle cannons were not going to be the answer to this particular problem.

Likewise, the fission missiles were localized—Tal estimated that one could take out a cluster of Prox, but proximity would be everything. With a sinking stomach he realized that even if they launched every fission missile in their arsenal, it wouldn't take out even half of them and would leave them defenseless against the Prox ships coming up behind them.

And all of a sudden it was too late. The first of the Prox reached the nearest Dreadnaught. Tal watched with his mouth open as the tips of its legs soundlessly touched the surface of the ship's hull. This was followed a moment later by its fellows. Tal had barely taken two breaths before a hundred Prox had landed on the Dreadnaught. Then a thousand. Then five thousand.

Someone in the Command Center screamed as they watched one of the soldier Prox peel back a sheet of iconel. Then, as they watched helplessly, Prox all over the ship began to roll back the hull. A few seconds later the interior hulls were dismantled as well.

In mute horror they watched as oxygen spewed into the cold vacuum of space with explosive force. Tal fought to control his panic as he watched the debris from the warship shoot across the view screen, followed by equipment, clothing, and the jerky, struggling bodies of the dying crew.

CHAPTER THREE

Nira's clothes had gotten mussed in the scuffle, so she reset them. All it took was flipping a switch in the preferences panel in her neural. *Way cheaper than dry cleaning*, she marveled. Finally looking presentable, she stepped back out onto the street and looked around. She felt the urge to get to a more populated area, where she wouldn't be jumped again. She began to walk back toward her apartment.

It was only then, with her hackles beginning to recede and a sense of normalcy returning to her step, that she suspended her constant surveillance of her surroundings long enough to look at the message waiting in her neural.

She dreaded opening it. She realized she was avoiding it. As bad as the Interworld could be, there were far worse ways to spend her sentence. She cursed herself for getting into these situations. *I should know better,* she scolded herself. Part of her knew that being able—and willing—to fight was exactly what had saved her life in the past. It was also responsible for putting her here. She glanced up and retrieved the message.

—Meet Officer Per Wollenstein at Transition Center at 20:00.

Oh, God, here it comes, she thought, returning her gaze to the street. What would they do to her? Put her back in her body for ten years of solitary? Strand her on an asteroid? Hard labor? Who knew what kind of punishment a micro-jurisdiction like this might inflict? She had lucked out, being put in the Interworld. As much as she hated being confined anywhere, she knew that. And now she had gone and fucked it up.

She glanced up again at her neural. 20:00 was in five minutes. *Oh, Christ.* She panicked, and broke into a jog. She reached a busy street and turned right, dodging people. The smell of curry wafted out of a shop window. When it became too crowded to jog, she walked as fast as she could.

The Transition Center was where they held classes with newbies. It was where she had woken up after they'd subdued her real body. It was where the government kept offices. If someone needed a public place to have an official private meeting, that was it. It was where she checked in with her warden every three days.

Per Wollenstein was her warden. He seemed a nice enough guy. *What a miserable job he must have,* she thought. It had never occurred to her to have pity on Wollenstein before, but the irony of it struck her. She was actually free to roam at will—within the confines of the Interworld, of course. She could work or not. She could play all day if she wanted. She could have a pet, have an affair, booze it up. But he—he was stuck in an office, having perfunctory, five-minute meetings with criminals all day, every day. *Sounds like hell,* she thought.

She turned in at the revolving door of the building and took the stairs two at a time. Her virtual body didn't get tired, so she wasn't winded when she got to the top. She sprinted to Wollenstein's office and, glancing up at her neural, relaxed a bit, seeing that she had a minute to spare.

She saw that the light on his door panel was green, and she held her thumb to the pad. It scanned her ID and the door slid open. She entered and stood at parade rest.

Wollenstein scowled. "You don't…you're not in the military here, Camil. You don't have to…" he sighed. "Never mind. Have a seat."

She did. "I'm sorry about the bar thing—"

His considerable eyebrows bunched. "Bar thing?"

Nira's eyes widened. "This isn't about the bar thing?"

"Do I want to know about the bar thing?" he asked.

"Uh…what can I do for you tonight, Warden?" she nervously adapted.

He raised one eyebrow but didn't pursue it. He was in his late thirties, but his hair looked like it was transplanted from a much older man—gray with patches of white, a little wild and unkempt. He kept it tied in a short bunch at the back of his head, but it made for an unruly bundle. The walrus mustache only added to the misery. Avatars were generally tidier than people's actual bodies. When thinking of what the real Wollenstein must look like, it frightened her a little.

"So…what's this about?" Nira asked.

"You're leaving."

"What? My sentence is for—"

"Yeah, I know. It's being commuted, so long as you cooperate."

She cocked her head. "Cooperate how?"

"You're being conscripted, into the Revolutionary Freedom Coalition."

Her eyebrows shot up. "I am?"

"At full rank and pay. How's that for lucky breaks?"

She blinked. "Uh…what's the catch?"

"No catch, sign here." He pushed a pad at her.

"But I thought this station was an independent jurisdiction in neutral space…"

"It is. Wild fucking west. And…this station has reciprocity with the RFC."

"That doesn't make any—"

"Yes, it does. We have treaties and agreements with the Authority and the RFC and every other micro-jurisdiction in the galaxy—got 'em comin' out of our asses!"

"Huh. And one of those agreements…"

"Is conscription. The RFC has had their eye on you, apparently. Although since you have no discernible file, I'm not sure how that's possible, but that's espionage for you." He pressed his forehead as if he had a headache. "Anyway, you're being given a provisional pardon—"

"Provisional based on what?"

"Provisional based on five years' meritorious service."

Meritorious. She fucking *did* meritorious. She leaned over and pressed her thumb to the pad.

"Eye, too." He pointed at her head.

She raised the pad to her eye and stared at the indicated portion of the screen. A blue blip informed her that it was done. She didn't think too hard about how the avatar could have her ID encoded. Perhaps some other machine was reading her actual body. Who knew?

Wollenstein took up the pad and his fingers danced as he finalized the transfer of custody. He looked up with an air of satisfaction. "It's been lovely, Camil. You are not our standard criminal around here."

"No, sir. I should hope not."

"You're respectful, for one thing."

"Yes, sir."

"And I think you're a fundamentally good person."

"Thank you, sir."

"So here's what's going to happen. I'm going to ask you to lie down, and you're going to close your eyes. And then you're going to feel a kind of a buzz—"

"I've transferred before. I got here, remember?"

"Right, of course. Re-entry into your body is going to be rough."

"It's only been a few days."

"So you're lucky. But your muscles are going to ache like a motherfucker. So…go easy on yourself. We've told the *Talon* that you'll need rest and physical therapy for a few days to get you back into form."

"Wait, the…did you say the *Talon*? Is that the ship I'll be serving on?"

"I don't know if that's the ship you'll be serving on or not. It's the ship that's picking you up."

"And the captain of that ship is…?" She held her breath.

He looked down at the pad, but apparently not seeing what he needed, he glanced up to access his neural. His eyes flitted back and forth, then he looked down again. "Captain Jo Taylor."

JEFF STARTED TO PACE. "The Ulim are human?"

"*Si.*"

"So they lied to me. They said they had transcended their bodies."

Tomás cradled his coffee, obviously relishing the warmth in his hands. He smiled up at Jeff patiently. "It was less a lie than it was…" He fished for a word. "Aspirational. It is something they hope for, but have not yet achieved."

Jeff shook his head. "Okay, but if the Ulim are human, why invent the Prox? Why all the killing? If what you're saying is true, they actually live in a different universe—308, right? Why send the Prox into my universe, or this one?"

Tomás leaned over and grabbed a stick. He smoothed the sand in front of him and started to draw several almost-parallel lines. At first, Jeff thought he was just being sloppy, but then he realized that there was a reason the lines were set at slightly different angles. "*Los Durmientes* can see into the All, as you and I can."

"Question," Jeff interrupted. "Do they see into the All all the time? Or just when they elect to?"

"It is a good question, and I do not know the answer. But I think it is only when they elect to, because I have been able to do things that they did not know about."

Jeff's eyebrows rose. "You'll have to tell me about that."

Tomás nodded. "Good campfire stories. *En fin…Los Durmientes* can see into the All, but they have also learned to see into the future...*un poco*…a little bit."

"How so?"

Tomás pointed at the lines he had drawn. "If we start from this point, there are many plans of action we could take. If we did one thing, the universe would unfold in one way, but if we did another thing it would unfold in a different way."

"Sure," Jeff agreed.

"Each of these decisions results in a different probability thread.

Los Durmientes can discern these probabilities and run them to their conclusions."

"All of them?"

"I suppose, if they wanted to."

"That's a lot of data to process."

"They have the power," Tomás shrugged. "They are, after all, a chain of biological computers."

"They told me they had ascended beyond their bodies."

"In a way, they told you the truth—they ascended into other universes, existing only in their disembodied form, facilitated by the *cristales*—"

"Those red crystalline structures," Jeff made the connection.

"Yes, they are *rojos*," Tomás nodded. "Red." His face twitched and Jeff realized he kept pulling the little man off track.

"Sorry," he said. "You were saying they can discern possibilities. So is it like running sightlines into possible futures?"

"Yes, that is it exactly." Tomás nodded vigorously, seemingly pleased to be back on subject.

Jeff felt a cold chill run down his spine. "So…what happens if they see a timeline they don't like?"

Tomás nodded gravely. "*Los Comelones*."

"Even in other universes?"

"Of course. They know the barriers are *porosas*...uh…" he fished for the word.

"Porous?" Jeff offered.

"*Si*. I knew it was similar." Tomás nodded gratefully. "They know the barriers are porous, so they defend themselves against any species that might eventually threaten them. Whenever they discern a possible timeline that might result in their extinction, they snuff it out—"

"By snuffing out anyone who might threaten them." Jeff finished his sentence.

"*Exactamente*."

"That's horrifying," Jeff said. "Risk is part of life. Everyone lives with it."

Tomás shrugged. "Only because you must. If you could eliminate risk, would you not? Is that not why people buy insurance?"

Jeff nodded. The logic was impeccable.

Tomás held up a hand. "Perhaps I am being *demasiado dramático*, too dramatic. They do not instantly kill. First, they try to manipulate events—to nudge the timeline into a non-threatening stream."

"How do they do that?" Jeff asked.

Tomás shrugged again. "Oh, lots of ways. Advertising. Feeding memes. Orchestrating diplomatic incidents."

The hair stood up on the back of Jeff's neck. "Would that manipulation include issuing false orders...orders that soldiers in the field thought were coming from Command?"

He looked up and met Tomás' eyes. The little man returned his gaze, and it was full of meaning and compassion. "*Si, amigo*. It is one of their most frequent techniques."

Jeff felt twenty years of accumulated shame and self-hatred welling up within him. He balled his fists, and his lips drew back in a sneer as his gaze drifted off into the distance.

"You know something about this technique, I see," Tomás noted.

"I do," Jeff said.

"And you are feeling...what?"

"Like I want to kick some motherfucker's teeth in."

"*Los Durmientes* do not use their teeth," Tomás said. "But they have them."

"Can you take me to them?" Jeff asked, reflexively balling his hands into fists again, testing their weight against the gravity of this planet, wishing for a bit more heft.

Tomás nodded, grim and slow. "I can."

WHEN NIRA OPENED HER EYES, the light was painful.

She jerked upright, and it felt like her limbs were on fire.

"Whoa there," a kind voice said. "You need to ease your way back into your body."

Her vision resolved and she found herself staring at an alien with light blue fur around its neck. She seemed feminine, or at least feline. She purred as she tended to various tubes sticking out of Nira's body. One by one, she removed them. Her actions were a little more ponderous than Nira would have liked, but they were mesmerizingly graceful as well. Then Nira vomited.

"That's all right, that's perfectly normal," the cat-nurse said. "Just relax."

Fuck relaxing, Nira thought. It was then that she realized there was someone else in the room.

She looked up and saw a tall woman with captain's bars. She had long dark hair, dark eyes, and a generous Roman nose. She wasn't pretty, by conventional standards, but she wasn't ugly either. She looked tough as nails, however, and that translated to sexy in Nira's book. She also looked familiar. It took Nira a couple of minutes to make the connection. "Captain Taylor, sir."

"Commander Camil Nira," Taylor said, standing at parade rest, her arms locked behind her back.

"Yes sir," Nira said. A million questions poured through Nira's mind. She hadn't known Captain Taylor, but she certainly knew of her. They had never met, but she had seen her from a distance. Nira had looked up her service record once. She knew Taylor and Captain Bowers had been involved. The notion of Bowers having an affair with anyone created some cognitive dissonance, but she could wonder about that later.

"I have need of an XO. Do you know of anyone looking for a job?"

Nira wiped the last bit of spittle from her chin and tried to look professional. "I do, sir. I would be honored to apply."

"Captain Jeff Bowers recommends you." One side of the captain's mouth curled up in a smile. "And if he recommends you, I want you."

More questions flooded her. In this universe, what would it mean fighting alongside this Captain Taylor? What political alignments was she signing up for? Would she be on the right side? Nira thought back to her time in the cramped jail cell when she and Pho were "guests" of the Authority. The Authority felt a lot like the CDF in many ways. But there was a cruel edge to it that she despised. Plus, they had tried to blow up their ship when making their escape from Sol Station—or someone had. If not the Authority, then whom?

There were too many questions, but there wasn't time to sort them out. Anything was better than languishing in a virtual prison. Serving any constructive purpose was better than wasting precious years of her life getting into bar brawls and drinking herself into numb passivity every night.

"When do I start?" Nira asked.

EMMA FINALLY FELT like she wasn't struggling to keep up with the class. They had shifted to learning numbers and simple math, and at last she had an edge. Where the hatchlings were learning the signs for numbers and operations at the same time as how math itself worked, Emma literally did advanced calculus in her dreams. All she had to pick up were the gestures, and it was going quickly.

Hooray! I'm holding my own against four-week-olds! she thought, but she knew it wouldn't be for long. The Alverian children learned *very* fast. They had practically eidetic memories and only needed to cover each topic once or twice, then use the idea practically a couple of times, and it was in there for life. As a paltry human, Emma needed a bit more repetition. She was constantly being smacked on the back of the legs for not keeping up. However, perhaps her appeals to Amberline may have finally been heard, since the teachers did seem to be hitting her less hard than before. Or maybe she was just getting tougher. Either way, it was a welcome change.

After the day's first class, she went to the cafeteria—she had finally learned the gestures for eating, food, and the room where eating happened—and ate without enthusiasm, trying hard not to think about what she was putting in her mouth. Then back to class for another four hours, and eventually she was released to shuffle back to the sleep chambers, where she flopped on her thin mattress and was generally asleep in less than five minutes. Her dreams were filled with language and mathematics practice, and after what felt like mere moments, her fellow students were prodding her out of bed for the next session.

With no sunlight, Emma was losing track of time. Even her chronometer didn't mean much anymore. Everything was a blur of learning and practice, opening a new part of the brain to handle functions that had been the domain of another, and non-stop physical exercise.

After a while, the learning took a shift. The language studies became more specialized, focusing on spatial relations and mathematical functions. They also started learning a form of computation Emma had never seen before. The students were lined up in a closely spaced grid pattern. Each student was given a set of instructions such as *add 10 to the number you have and pass it forward.* Then they held their arms up in a specific numerical value. Occasionally, the instructor would step up to a student on the periphery of the grid and indicate a new instruction, such as "Divide 300 by your current number" and tap a student. That student, already holding a number, would make the calculation, display the result, and tap the student in front of or beside her. That student would use her specific function to combine the previous number with the one they were already holding, and pass it along.

Emma thought of the ingenious scheme as *computational tai chi* and found that the class could do extremely complex computations surprisingly quickly, by organizing themselves into an organic computer.

The Alverians used a base 4 numerical system, which slowed Emma down at first, forcing her to translate to base 10 and back. But with practice, she'd begun thinking in quaternary automatically and was beginning to feel completely natural and comfortable with it.

That morning she was surprised when she reported to the classroom at the usual time, but none of the other students was there.

"Hello Emma," the teacher signed. They'd come up with an original gesture to use as her name, a combination of *missing two arms* and *not one of us.* She'd been hurt at first, but quickly realized that it wasn't meant as a slur, simply a statement of facts that were unique to her. She accepted it and mentally understood the sign only as "Emma."

"Where is everyone?" Emma asked. "I'm not late."

"You are on time. We have a new assignment for you today."

Crap. Emma thought. *I washed out.* She'd been afraid that eventually her classmates would get so far ahead of her that they would either hold her back to a younger class, or simply put her to work elsewhere. Without asking questions, she followed the beckoning teacher out into the tunnel and deeper into the hive. They walked down a long curving ramp to a lower level she'd never been to before. Alverians scampered in both directions down the tunnel, and the teacher danced between them quickly, causing Emma to work to keep up.

The next room they entered took Emma's breath away. It was huge, possibly even larger than the common chamber. They entered on a catwalk that went around the room; the floor of the chamber was around forty feet lower. Spread out across the entire floor, arranged in a close grid, were *thousands* of Alverians, all flailing their limbs in computation.

"It's a super computer!" Emma whispered in English.

Her teacher gestured, "This is a counting chamber. You are ready to put your training to use."

"Doing what?"

"Counting." The teacher motioned for Emma to follow, then clambered down a ladder to the crowded floor. She reached the edge of the arranged mass of Alverians and walked until she found a narrow separation between sections, then turned and disappeared. Emma ran after, dodging flailing arms, keeping the teacher in sight. After counting off about twenty columns, she stopped.

"A number will be passed to you from the person in front of you. Raise it exponentially by the number displayed by the person to your right, then pass it backwards. Do you understand?"

Emma nodded. It was a very simple operation, even if she didn't know what she was doing it for.

"Good. Take the number that this person is showing and take her place. *Now!*"

Startled, Emma held her arms up. The Alverian she was replacing showed 6,480. She gestured the same value and stepped into the hole that the previous counter vacated. The other Alverian retreated down the aisle, but the teacher remained, observing.

The person in front of Emma displayed 428, and indicated a pass back. Emma glanced right, where another Alverian displayed 3. She did the math in her head, and displayed 78,402,752, and passed it back.

"Correct. Faster."

Another number came. The exponent to her right had not changed. She raised the number to the power of three and passed it back.

"Correct. Faster."

Another number, another calculation, another result.

"Good. Continue." The teacher began to walk away.

"Wait!" Emma said aloud, but also signed. "For how long?"

"Twelve hours." Without further delay, she walked away.

The person in front gestured another figure. Emma quickly did the calculations, passed the result. She struggled at first, but occasionally got a brief respite when a new number did not come for several minutes. After a while, she began to find the rhythm of the thing. It became automatic, reflexive. She was a component in an organic computer, a logic gate, a register, and part of whatever program they were all running together.

After a few hours, her arms were burning, her feet throbbing, her back screaming, but she continued, trying to keep repeating her function in time with everyone around her. She glanced around the chamber on pauses and noticed a large set of windows higher up one wall, where a number of Alverians were overseeing the process. Runners darted around the outer edges of the counting array, taking numbers from key positions and carrying them forward. *Work product*, she thought, breathing hard.

A new number came up and she took it, then looked right to get the exponent, when much to her horror, that Alverian's left arm fell off.

CHAPTER FOUR

Dead silence. The air in the Command Center was as quiet as the vacuum of space. Then, as if on cue, everyone began shouting at once. Admiral Tal recognized what he was seeing: blind panic. He felt bile run up the back of this throat. Maybe he couldn't stop those goddam Prox, but he sure as hell could stop this. He looked up, accessed his neural, and connected his voice to the public address system. When he spoke, he spoke evenly, quietly. But the room thundered with his words.

"Quiet! This is a setback, not a loss. I told you this would be a hard-fought battle. Did you think it would be a walk in the arboretum? You are soldiers! Act like it!"

Silence returned. Everyone in sight looked at their shoes. *Good,* Tal thought. *They ought to be ashamed. But they also ought to be scared.* He knew that his job was to channel their fear, their panic, in a constructive direction. It could be a fatal liability or it could be fuel. *It's damn well going to be fuel.*

"This battle is just getting started. I want to see senior officers in the conference suite—any rank above captain, I want you there. The rest of you, if you have any creative ideas, you shoot them to your ranking commander. Commanders, any ideas that have any merit at all, you bring them to me personally. I don't care if I'm in the head or having dinner. Bring 'em all. It isn't firepower that is going to save us, it's creativity. Now do your fucking jobs."

He didn't need to swear, but he couldn't help it. He stepped off the platform and made a beeline for the conference suite. He saw the other ranking officers doing the same, wending their way through the hundreds of soldiers in the Command Center. Precious souls, every one of them. Every one of them representing a thousand more aboard the station, a hundred more on those ships out there. And all of them his responsibility.

He swept through the door to the conference suite. *How many have we lost already?* His head swam. A Dreadnaught-class starship carries a crew complement of 400 souls. They'd just lost 2,000 troops. "Jesus," he said aloud. He noticed that his hands were shaking. They were also cold as ice. He went to the food synthesizer panel on the wall and selected coffee in a mug. He marveled at the normalcy of the action. How many cups of coffee had he ordered, from how many synthesizer units? When the coffee arrived, he cradled it between his cold hands, pressing them together around the cup, still shaking.

When he finally sat down at the conference table, the room was mostly full. Every couple of seconds another officer would come in, but most of the people he wanted there were already seated.

He didn't waste time on formalities. "I want ideas," he said, lowering his head but meeting their eyes. He realized he was glowering. Good. "Our best idea just got chewed up and spit out. We just hit them with the biggest hammer we have. If brute force isn't going to stop these motherfuckers, what will?"

No one said anything. "Now, dammit!" Tal yelled. *Keep it together, Jason*, he told himself. He gripped the warm cup even more firmly. He was sneering now, he knew. He didn't care.

Vice Admiral Ankh raised her hand. "Vice Admiral?" Tal acknowledged.

"One of my weaponers suggests we seed the field with fusion detonators."

"Mines?" Tal scowled. "They went right through our mines before."

"These can be a lot bigger, and we can generate them quickly."

Tal nodded. They could create another minefield in time. They could pack those mines with about twenty times the firepower as the last field they sailed through, and about ten times more power than the fission torpedoes the Dreadnaughts rained down on them. It was more of the brute strength approach, which had yielded them nothing thus far, but surely even the Prox had their limit.

"It may not be *the* idea, but it's *an* idea, and unless it takes precious firepower away from another plan, it would be foolish not to try it." He nodded curtly. "Admiral Ankh, I am appointing you project manager on this. Get it done."

She stood, saluted, and ran from the room.

"Wormhole generators," Admiral Pacholok said without raising his hand. Tal was the only Fleet Admiral present, but apparently Pacholok considered himself to be of sufficient rank that deference was optional. Tal let it slide.

"Say more," he commanded.

"We know how to create wormholes. We can do it wherever and whenever we want. The technology isn't complicated. We can throw about a dozen of them together before they reach us."

"To what end?"

Pacholok scowled, as if wondering how Tal could be so stupid. Tal stood his ground. "Don't make me infer anything, Donald, tell me what you're thinking."

Pacholok rolled his eyes. "We can load the wormhole generators onto probes—it requires triangulation, but probes aren't a problem. We've got plenty of them."

Tal nodded. "Go on."

"The probes run in stealth mode. We hit all of their ships at once. It'll shunt them into another part of the galaxy."

"But wormhole generators aren't stable," Rear Admiral Vautin objected. "Nothing that has gone into an artificially generated wormhole has ever survived."

"And that's a problem why?" Pacholok cocked his head.

"It's…a great idea," Tal decided. "Pacholok, make it happen."

Pacholok gave a curt nod, rose, and rushed from the room.

"More!" Tal demanded. "I haven't heard the sure thing yet."

Rear Admiral Carfew raised his hand, his eyes still rolled up into his head, obviously reading something from his neural.

"Carfew," Tal spat.

"One of my captains suggests using Mars as a shield. The proximity is right—we're lucky that way. We can position Sol Station behind it, so that Mars is between us and the advancing enemy, sir."

"First of all, the Martians will hate that idea," Tal said, considering it. *Don't dismiss this out of hand,* he told himself. *It might be a bad option, but it might be a better bad option than any other.* "That will shield us from direct blasts, which would be useful against a conventional enemy, but the Prox do not shoot. What would prevent them from simply going around Mars?"

"It would provide a horizon, a target, as they came around," Carfew was reasoning on the fly.

"That would be strategically useful," Tal agreed. "But it wouldn't stop them."

"No sir, but it would provide a small advantage—the space equivalent of seizing the higher ground."

"That's a possibility. I'm going to set that…over here," he pretended he had a box in his hand and set it on the table to his right. "More ideas. Quickly."

Rear Admiral Lower Half Wengret raised her hand. "I have an idea for deploying our remaining ships in the most effective way possible."

"Say it."

She actually stood in place. Tal liked the formality. "If none of the other ideas work…and I hope that they do…I suggest a funnel formation as their ships approach."

"Explain."

She looked up and accessed her neural. "Graphic display mode, please."

Around the room everyone looked up and switched the mode on.

Tal did the same. When he looked back down, Wengret was drawing in patterns of light with her fingers.

She made a small circle to her right. "One end of the funnel is Sol Station." She made a much larger circle directly in front of her, as large as her arms would reach, and turned it so that she was holding the edge. "Around the periphery of the wide part of the funnel will be every remaining ship we've got."

She drew three small circles to her left. "These are the approaching Prox ships, at the other end of the funnel. The advantage of the funnel formation is that we can bring every one of our ships to bear without shooting each other. No crossfire."

"No crossfire for a good long time…enough time to…" Tal didn't finish the sentence. He nodded. The glimmer of a smile arose at one end of his mouth. "This is good work. Rear Admiral Wengret, I'm putting you in charge of battle plans—"

Someone cleared his throat. Admiral Lukas stood, his face almost glowing. "I like this plan—"

"I do too," Tal said. "Do you have something to add to it?"

"Yes," he said. "As the Prox ships approach, they're going to concentrate their shields at the tops of their ships"—he jogged over to Wengret's model—"here, to take the fire we're generating. What about the underbelly?"

"What about the underbelly?" Tal asked.

"They won't expect to be boarded," Lukas said.

Tal's eyes grew wide. A smile broke out on his face, bright as the sun. "No, Admiral. I dare say they will not."

"What is it you want?" Tomás asked him. It was a question out of nowhere. The little man knelt and began rubbing their dishes with sand.

"I want to strangle someone," Jeff said. "I want to strangle everyone." He opened and closed his fists as he stared at his hands. He had good hands, strong hands. They would be very effective at strangling.

"Aren't you responsible for enough people's lives?" Tomás did not look at him as he spoke.

Jeff scowled. "You don't think we should kill the Ulim? Isn't that the mission?"

"Must you always have a mission?" Tomás smiled.

"I'm a military man. There's always a mission."

Tomás shook his head patiently. "You don't get justice or peace by being as evil as your enemy. Real change comes when you are so kind to your enemy that it breaks his heart."

Jeff blinked, not understanding where the little man was going with this. "So…are you suggesting we bring the Ulim some roses? Maybe some candy? How about champagne, while we're at it?" He was joking, but his jests were laced with venom.

"We must not allow them to continue, but this does not mean we must seek revenge. A good parent sets limits for a child, but doesn't retaliate against a child's anger."

"The Ulim are children now?"

"Aren't we all?" Tomás stood up and brushed the last of the sand from the metal plates. He placed them back in a canvas equipment bag. "*Mi amigo*," he said, placing a hand on Jeff's arm. "You must learn some things before we do anything."

Jeff towered over him. "What things?"

"You must learn to use those talents of yours. Safely."

Jeff felt the hair on his neck stand up. He crossed his arms. He was about to refuse when Tomás turned away again.

"It was why you came here. It was why you sought me out. To refuse is to refuse your destiny."

"That's dramatic," Jeff objected.

"It is also the truth."

Jeff's stomach twisted into a hard, painful knot. His brows furrowed.

"Do not be afraid," Tomás said. "I will not let you kill anyone."

"Gee, thanks," Jeff said.

"Let us begin then." Tomás pointed to the log they had been sitting on. "Balance on that log."

Jeff scowled and did not move.

Tomás sighed. "If you will not trust me, I cannot help you…and we will not stop *Los Comelones*."

Jeff uncrossed his arms, sighed, and rolled his eyes. Then he got up on the log. He stretched his arms out to balance and held his pose. "Now what?"

"Just notice. What happens if you lean too far to your right?"

"I'll fall off."

"And to your left?"

"I'll fall off the damn log," Jeff snapped. "What's your point?"

"We are healthy when we balance extremes. If we go too far to one side, we slip into chaos, disorder, disease…even evil. If you go too far in the other direction, the same thing happens, only in different ways."

Jeff cocked his head. "Give me an example."

Tomás nodded. "Food. Think about food. If you have too much food, you become unhealthy. If you have too little food…" He didn't finish the sentence.

Jeff did. "You get sick."

Tomás nodded. "*Exactamente*. This is true of everything. Poverty and wealth. Humility and pride. Liberty and regulation…"

Jeff nodded. He was tracking with Tomás' thought. But he still didn't understand how it connected with their situation.

"This is true of community as well. Let me ask you, *mi amigo*, would you consider yourself a *social* person?"

"Uh…no, I would not say that," Jeff admitted.

"What would you say?"

"I would say that other people are a necessary evil and if I could be alone all the time, I would be."

"Is that an exaggeration?"

Jeff shrugged while still keeping his arms out for balance. "Not much of one."

"Isolation is not healthy," Tomás said.

Jeff did not contradict this.

"On the other hand, *Los Durmientes* have gone too far in the other direction. They have joined their minds. They are completely enmeshed. This makes them…unwell. And their sickness spreads whenever they make contact with others."

"Can I get off this now?" Jeff asked.

"Health requires togetherness and solitude, in similar measure," Tomás continued.

Jeff stepped down without permission. "What are you saying to me?"

"I am saying this is where we start. Would you say that you are a man who trusts others easily?"

"No," Jeff answered.

"Are you a man who accepts help willingly?"

Jeff flashed back to his childhood, to the time when he caught hypothermia in the wilds of Alaska. He remembered how angry and distraught his father had been that he did not call for help. He heard his father's voice in his head, *You've gotta let yourself be helped sometime, Jeff.* "Never," he said.

"Are you a man who relies on others when your life depends on it?"

Jeff shrugged again. "Sure. Of course. Mechanics work on my ship. Superiors give me orders. Cooks make my dinner. I rely on them."

"What enables you to do that?"

"Necessity, I suppose."

"Does it always…" he fished for a word, "irritate you?"

Jeff narrowed his eyes. "Sometimes."

"I think you will be very irritable in the next few days."

"Why?"

"Because you must learn to rely on me."

Jeff nodded gravely. "I get what you're saying."

Tomás put a hand on his elbow and squeezed it. "Good. Now first, there is no danger in looking, which I think you have discovered. You found me, nothing bad happened. This is safe. You can even look beyond the universe into another—"

"You can?"

"—and this is still safe."

Jeff's eyes grew dark. "But moving objects…"

Tomás nodded. "You can move yourself, and you can safely move things smaller than yourself. You do not need to worry about this. But…"

"Wait—" Jeff held up his hand. "I moved a house, and nothing bad happened."

Tomás shrugged. "You got lucky—that time." He looked away, toward the horizon. "Do you know why your universe was…disappeared?"

The question came like a punch to the gut. It was also worded strangely, as if it had resonance beyond the present situation, but Jeff was not aware of what that was. "No."

Tomás knelt and began rummaging in his bag. He pulled out a small poly ball—it looked like a handball, Jeff realized. Then he pulled out a tube of brightly colored woven fabric.

"What is that?" Jeff asked.

"It is a sleeve," Tomás said.

"A sleeve?"

"I am making a coat," Tomás said. "And this is the sleeve."

Jeff had heard of people making their own clothes, but it had always seemed eccentric. He reminded himself that he didn't know how things were done in Tomás' culture, let alone in his universe. "Okay, it's a sleeve."

"You have two hands," Tomás said. "Pass the ball through the sleeve without allowing it to touch the sleeve." He held up one finger. "You cannot palm the ball. That is cheating."

Jeff nodded and picked up the ball. He held up one end of the sleeve and passed the ball into it. He was able to get about half way, when he needed to let go and hold up the other end of the sleeve for the exit. But as soon as he did so, the fabric over the ball collapsed, touching the ball.

"Uh…okay, this material is lighter than I thought, so it's not very… it doesn't *stay*, so…"

"But what if you had another set of hands?" Tomás said. He pinched the fabric at the far end of the sleeve and held it up. Jeff was able to pass the ball all the way, and he dropped it out the other side.

He looked up at Tomás. "Are you saying that if there were two people making the jump from one universe to another—"

"If one tends to the entrance," Tomás nodded, "and one tends to the exit, no damage occurs."

"You can travel between universes?" Jeff nodded, getting it.

"We can do that *solo*. It's moving things larger than ourselves that requires assistance."

"And *we* can do that," Jeff said, emphasizing the "we." It wasn't a question, but a statement he was trying on for size.

"We can," Tomás said. "But we must work together to do it."

Jeff looked down at him, weighing his words, his demeanor, his veracity.

"You must walk off a cliff…and trust me to catch you." Tomás met his eye.

"That's hard," Jeff said.

"Have you ever turned down a mission because it was difficult?"

"Never."

"Then this is your mission now, isn't it?"

JO AND NIRA stared at one another. "Are you ready to do this?" Jo asked. Her face was hard, but Nira suspected it was always a little hard. There was kindness in her voice, though.

Nira nodded and stood. She was still a little wobbly from her time in the Interworld, but no more so than after a week in bed after a bad cold, she was pleased to discover. She'd been doing physical therapy aboard the *Talon* for the past few days and was feeling almost herself again. She did not miss the weird appearance of her avatar, although she did miss being tall.

"I think we should just put it all out there," Jo said. "No need for secrets. People are going to talk; let them talk about what's real. Okay?"

"Absolutely," Nira said. "Uh…Captain?"

Jo paused in the middle of her turn. "Yes?"

"Thank you."

Jo smiled. "It was the least I could do for…well, for Jeff. You better be as good as he says you are, though." She narrowed her eyes in mock-threat.

Nira laughed out loud, then brought her hand to her mouth to stifle it. "Sorry." Jo turned again.

"Captain?"

Jo paused again.

"Do you think there will be some resentment? I mean…I'm an outsider."

Jo shrugged. "Who knows? I stopped thinking I could control what other people think or feel a long time ago. They'll feel how they feel. Then they'll fucking get over it or they'll find themselves on another ship. Can you live with that?"

Nira's eyebrows rose, but she nodded.

Jo softened. "Besides, people are transferred on and off ships all the time. It's not uncommon to host a crew member from another jurisdiction. And god knows there's enough of them out there," she waved at space, apparently, or maybe at neutral space. Jo met Nira's eyes and gave her an encouraging look. "It'll be fine."

Nira clasped her hands behind her back and puffed out her chest, wishing just this once that her breasts were bigger. The new red uniform fit well, though, and it looked smart on her. She made a good appearance, and she knew it. "Let's do this."

Jo finally completed her turn and exited her ready room. Nira stepped through and heard the door slide shut behind her.

The bridge crew were hard at work, but it was quiet work. One by one, they stole a glance over to the captain…and to her.

Nira moved to stand beside the command chair to the immediate right of the captain. *Her* command chair. The traditional spot for the XO, the Number One.

Before she sat, though, Captain Taylor cleared her throat. "Can I have your attention, please? I'd like everyone to meet Commander Camil Nira, our new XO. She's not from around here…in fact, she's from String 310."

There were some gasps. Jo waited for that to sink in. "It's true. There she served with distinction under Captain Jeffrey Bowers, a trusted colleague of mine. Some of you met him recently. On their string there is no civil war, no RFC, no Authority. The Colonial Defense Fleet still exists…or existed, until recently. It's…a long story, and I'm sure Commander Nira will be glad to tell it at another time. The point is, she's here, now, and she's in command. You will treat her with the same deference and respect that you do me. Are there any questions?"

There were a couple of open mouths and lots of raised eyebrows. Yes, they had questions. They had a lot of questions. But no one was asking any of them now, which was exactly what Jo anticipated. "Good. Commander Nira will spend some time with us on the bridge today, but starting tomorrow, she'll command the B team during your off-hours."

Jo introduced her to the bridge crew. Nira had already read the files and memorized their names: Navigator Marcia Chi, whom she found irresistibly cute. Communicator Tash Liebert, who had an aw-shucks smile. Weaponer Shell Ditka, who was sexy as hell but whose hard look and spiky white hair scared her a little. But it was a good scare, and she would enjoy getting to know her. "After shift, I'll introduce you to Doctor Mbusa, Commander Ocampo in Engineering, and Security Chief Dixon."

"Thank you, sir."

Jo looked at Nira and gave her a curt nod. Nira nodded back. Jo sat. Nira did the same. Everyone else turned back to their controls, apparently eager for a return to normalcy.

Nira took the few minutes of quiet that followed to review their current mission—escorting a caravan en route to Deseret colony. Deseret was on the edge of neutral space, just inside RFC borders. It had been plagued recently by pirates. Their mission was to make sure the twenty-one ships in the caravan made it to the Mormons in one piece. Simple.

"Sir, I have an incoming report from RFC control."

"Classification?"

"Unclassified, sir. It…it's a general announcement."

"On screen." Nira watched Jo shift in her chair, leaning forward. She didn't know this captain, but she suspected that Jo was exactly the person she aspired to be. She would watch her closely.

The screen flashed and a woman's fleshy brown face filled the screen. *Who in the world is this?* Nira thought. She was wearing a red uniform, and she recognized admiral's insignia. *Whoever she is, she's important.*

"All personnel, listen up. As you've no doubt seen on the news feeds, the Authority has withdrawn every one of its ships to engage a fight at Sol Station. We now know why. The Authority is under attack from an unknown alien aggressor. We don't have much, but here's what we've been able to glean…"

Nira's mouth opened wide as she saw an all-too-familiar sight unfold on the screen—the Prox, approaching with their metallic legs extended. She watched them land and then watched the same legs tear sheets off a hull, shoving them in the direction of their mandibles. Nira shuddered.

She thought she'd left those bastards behind, that they'd been eliminated when her own string was destroyed. It was as if she had awakened from a nightmare only to discover the most terrible part of it was true. The tiny hairs on her arms stood straight up.

It was just a clip. The admiral's soft, friendly face reappeared. "We don't know much about these creatures—"

"I do," Nira said, loud enough to be heard.

"—but we know our enemy is in trouble. We do not wish our enemy evil. Our enemy is our family. Our differences are political, not personal. We have sent overtures to the Authority through official channels to offer our assistance against this threat. So far, we have heard no response. But I want you all to know that we have made them. Go about your business, but prepare for war. Do your previously assigned duties, but prepare your hearts, for if our brothers and sisters call, we will rush to their aid, whatever our differences may have been in the past." Her features softened from resolute to compassionate. "I know some of you will have feelings about that. The Authority killed my entire maternal family, so…I understand how you might feel. Nevertheless, trouble and opportunity often arrive as twins. Let us not take up only one of them and leave the other on the doorstep. Admiral Alinto out."

The screen went blank.

Every eye turned to Nira.

Jo cocked her head. "So tell us what you know."

When Captain Danny Hightower stepped on the bridge of the *Horatio Nelson*, Ernst Foulon called out, "Captain on deck!" Everyone stood, as he expected. Had there been a hesitation? Danny scowled. And was that hesitation in his XO's announcement or in his crew's reaction? It had been a fraction of a second, and memory was plastic. He couldn't say for sure. He felt slighted, he just wasn't sure why.

As was his wont, he let them all stand up completely. "As you were," he said finally. They sat. No one would look at him. *What is that all about?* he wondered. He was used to not having friends. That was a captain's lot. But there was something about the crew's response to him in the last few days that he couldn't quite put his finger on.

"Report," Danny said, taking his chair.

"Our intelligence checks out," Foulon said.

"I told you it would." Danny flashed him a roguish smile.

"Yes sir."

No smile from Commander Foulon. Danny frowned. *Be that way,* he thought. He stabbed at a button on his command chair. "Engineering," he said. He could have asked Lieutenant Lo to connect him and ordinarily would have, but his teeth were on edge from the cold shoulder he was receiving.

"Tenzin here," a voice came from the speaker in the arm of his chair.

"Raj, how is the camo coming?"

"Almost finished, sir. Fortunately we're a small vessel, as warships go, so it wasn't hard to camouflage us as a transport rig. We even put a few mock storage containers on the underbelly."

"Good work. What are they made of?"

"Foam, sir! Sheer bulk, light as air. We can jettison them any time we need."

"Colors?"

"Not a scrap of blue left, sir. No insignia. No call numbers…well, new call numbers. We dug up an expired registration from a neutral space vessel out of Trafalgar. The ship was retired for scrap, but it used to do a small circuit and its call sign is still active. We painted the call numbers on our hull and…presto! We're the *Spruce and Bonnet*."

"*Spruce and Bonnet*?"

"The Brits named their ships after pubs for a while. It was a fad."

"Good thing." Danny nodded. This was good, all very good. "Engine signature?"

"That's the one thing we can't disguise, sir," a note of weariness crept into Tenzin's voice, as if he had really been working hard on this one and still hadn't been able to crack it.

"You don't need to disguise it, Commander. I just want you to change it."

"You can't make *momos* into *kheer*, but you can make them unrecognizable as *momos*, is that what you're saying?"

Danny nodded more vigorously, then remembered that Tenzin couldn't hear a nod. "Just so, Commander."

"Hmm…I have some ideas about that."

"I'll leave you to them. Bridge out." Danny stood and strode over to Communicator Lo's station. He saw Lo stiffen. "At ease, Mr. Lo. How is that message coming?"

"I'll pull it up, sir," Lo said, his voice quavering. Danny hated that he had that effect on people. He also loved it.

It was a text message, suddenly flashing in the air above Lo's station. A position requisition to the Deseret Import and Trading Company for a location in the caravan. Danny saw that the message was from a Captain Onigi Hiraja. "I can't play Japanese in case someone wants to speak to me, Lieutenant."

"Sorry, sir. That was the name of the captain of record for the *Spruce and Bonnet.*"

"Shit. Well, ships change captains," Danny noted. "Make me a Brit."

"A Brit, sir, yes sir. How about Captain Perry Byrd?"

Hightower nodded. "Captain Byrd. I like it…"

"Yes sir."

"Make the changes and send it."

"Yes sir."

"Mr. Foulon, in my ready room."

"Yes sir." Foulon rose and waited for the captain to cross.

Once the door had slid shut, Danny motioned to a chair. "Sit."

Foulon sat.

Danny poured two whiskeys and set one of them down in front of Foulon. It was too early in the day for it, but it had become a little ritual for them. It was, Danny realized, an expression of good will. A peace offing.

"Tell me what's up, Ernst," he said, sipping at his glass. "The crew is off. *You're* off. What's going on?"

Foulon looked away. Danny waited. He took another sip. "I don't know if you've noticed this, Commander, but I'm not a particularly patient man."

Foulon glanced back at him, met his eyes for a split second, then looked away again. "No sir."

"Then tell me. What. The fuck. Is going on?"

"At Epworth, sir. Everyone who went ashore, who needed to…"

"I get it, Commander, people need to go ashore when stocking and such."

"Yes sir, and they saw the news. I saw the news. We don't know what's happening…back home, sir…but we know *something's* happening. And it's happening without us."

Danny tapped on the side of his glass with his fingers.

"So people are worried, and they're scared, and if they're like me, they feel like…well, like we're not where we're supposed to be."

"Is that how you feel?"

Foulon's eyes narrowed. He came across as edgy but cool. Danny approved. "Feeling isn't really my strong suit, sir, but your crew is human, and most of them *have* feelings. It's something we need to manage."

It wasn't untrue. It was, in fact, one of the essentials when it came to commanding a crew. It was just one of the essentials Danny knew he wasn't particularly good at. "How do you manage your feelings, Ernst?"

"I try to be logical, sir. You are the captain. Your word is law. End of story."

"Is it?" Danny swirled his whiskey and took another sip. Morning whiskey. He could get a little too used to that.

"And the rest of them?"

"I think we need a cover story."

Danny bunched his eyebrows, but he smiled. "Tell me more."

"We're on a classified mission to eliminate the Kali of Aken."

"Funnily enough, we *are* on a classified mission to eliminate the Kali of Aken."

"We just need to suggest that the mission comes straight from the Admiralty, sir."

"Without saying as much?"

"Without raising any suspicions to the contrary. We should do things…as we normally do, sir."

"We could…let them in on the mission."

"We're about to engage. That's standard procedure."

Danny nodded. "You think that will cure our…malaise?"

"Cure it, sir? I don't know. Cauterize it…?" There was a tiny curl at the edge of Foulon's lip. The man didn't like what they were doing, Danny could see that. Foulon couldn't quite bring himself to enjoy the conspiracy. "That we can do."

ADMIRAL ANKH HAD WORKED FAST. Within a half hour of their meeting in the conference lounge, the first of the scouts loaded with fission mines had launched and sped to a point midway between Sol Station and the advancing Prox ships.

Tal glanced up at his neural to check the time. It was now two hours after the meeting, and already they had succeeded in creating a minefield twenty kilometers thick and six hundred thousand kilometers wide, with mines planted every thirty-three kilometers.

He wouldn't have thought it possible to deploy them so quickly, but some far-sighted lieutenant in the armory had already fixed warheads to an army of probes. All they really needed to do was dump them at strategic points, and their internal navigation systems would move them into place. They'd also be attracted—as if magnetically—to any hull not pinging out an Authority signal.

Tal was relieved that they'd had the surplus of drones—they'd need more before the day was out. He was also relieved that there was no lack of fissionable material on station. *A couple of lucky breaks*, he thought as he stood at parade rest at his post in the Command Center. *We'll need a couple more of those.*

Tal could sit. He had a chair. But his anxiety was too great. Instead, he obsessively checked the readouts on the great screens in front of him and bounced on the balls of his feet. If he lived through this day, he might lose some weight. The thought caused a smile to curl up one side of his mouth.

It soon faded as he received a message. He glanced up and blinked, retrieving it.

—Mines set and in place. Scouts returning to port.

Tal nodded, selecting a standard "good work" response.

Tal looked at the firepower statistics one more time. The original minefield had been set with 5-megaton fission bombs. That's enough to blast a hole in the side of a Dreadnaught. The mines they'd just finished setting were 20-megaton bombs. There were no such things as 20-megaton bombs. There had never been any use or need for them before. Why use twenty when five would do just fine? It was a lesson learned from the 20th-century's Cold War. No one needed to blow up the world thirty-seven times over when one time would do.

They'd accomplished the task by stacking. They literally stacked four 5-megaton warheads on top of one another, wired them in series, and fastened them to the original warhead fixed to the probe. The result looked like an ugly science experiment, but Tal had confidence in his armory. They might look like hell, but they'd work like a dream—of that he had no doubt.

Tal had never seen a ship that could withstand a 5-megaton blast. Not until now. He bit the inside of his lip as he accessed his neural and reviewed the speculative schematics of the Prox ships assembled by the tiny but brilliant xenoengineering team. There were three columns of information, each item cross-referenced to every other related item. The first contained known facts—measurable data. The second was populated by educated guesses extrapolated from the known data. The third column was filled with sheer speculation—possibilities. All of it was useful as hell.

The Prox had three ships. The minefield contained 12,000 mines. Each ship would be met by at least six 20-megaton bombs as it crossed the minefield, no matter what point of access they chose. Tal's confidence rose a tick. He nodded.

It was a good plan, and he'd need to commend Admiral Ankh and whatever captain had suggested it. It would almost certainly eliminate the threat without loss to a single further ship. That thought caused his mood to darken again. The loss of the Dreadnaughts was a grave matter indeed—not just due to the loss of personnel, although that was all he would be able to acknowledge publicly. He also grieved the loss of the ships themselves. Their loss was almost impossible to gauge—the firepower, the strategic opportunities, the yielding of ground to the rebels, the inestimable financial cost of the great, lumbering ships…

He shook his head. Those ships were nothing but debris now. *I can't let myself dwell on it. I have living people to save here*, he reminded himself. As he read the third column filled with speculations, he flashed back on the one man who actually knew something about their enemy—Bowers, a captain in a Colonial Defense Fleet that still existed on some other reality string. He had not really believed it then, and he barely believed it now. But still, he had known. He would give anything for Bowers' presence now. *Hell, I'd make him an official advisor. I'd give him a field commission!* He cursed himself for letting himself be influenced by Hightower. The snake. The demon. The very thought of the man—his deceit, his abandonment of duty, his theft of an Authority vessel—made Tal want to spit. He had never trusted him, not in his gut. Turns out his gut was right. *Isn't it always?* he thought.

And what did his gut tell him about his minefield? Nothing good. He prayed to whatever cosmic powers might persist beyond the prevalent cynicism of his age that this time, this once, his gut would be wrong.

The PA crackled and a voice announced for the benefit of the entire Command Center, "Lead Prox ship is now approaching the minefield."

Tal gripped the handrail that separated the elevated command platform from the working floor, tightening his grip on it, threatening to twist it into scrap. The main viewer flickered and resolved on an ideal perspective, the Prox ship nearly filling the screen. The probes were too tiny to be seen, but Tal knew they were there, even now being drawn by their programming—their *telos*, their reason for being—toward the enemy hull.

"Lead Prox ship has entered the minefield."

It was only a matter of seconds now. Tal glanced at a map of the minefield, spread out over three monitors. The perspective was bird's eye, from above. He could see the three Prox ships, the first one having crossed the imaginary line where the first of the mines was placed, somewhere along the six-hundred-thousand-kilometer edge of the field. He could also see that the ship was about to bump into one, no two, of the blinking probes.

"Nukes are armed and ready." The announcer's voice cracked.

That's what's at stake, Tal thought. *That humanity, that vulnerability. We try not to show it, but it's the only thing that makes us precious.*

Tal studied the ships. He saw the teeming soldier Prox, impossibly swarming on the outside of the hull. Their inhumanity made him feel cold, made his flesh crawl. It looked as if the entire hull was in motion, a roiling, shifting substance that could not be solid. The sight of so many alien soldiers on the hull made Tal wonder just who was inside, who was pulling the strings, directing the attack? It occurred to him that it wasn't the crablike creatures swarming over the hull that was their real enemy—it was whoever was protected inside those impenetrable hulls. The soldiers were just weapons. But whoever was driving those ships—those were the brains behind the guns.

Tal began to count. He didn't know why. Perhaps it was a way to mitigate his tension as he waited for the first explosion in the minefield. But also, probably, to keep extraneous thoughts at bay. It was a centering technique, although he didn't think about it. He just did it.

He had reached seventeen when the first explosion hit. Tal narrowed his eyes as the screen lit up, going completely white. He watched the entire room flinch, turn their eyes away from the screen.

It was just a screen. It could only emit so much light, and not enough to hurt anyone, but people shielded their eyes anyway. They did it reflexively. Tal resisted the temptation, but he felt it.

He knew it would take a while for the screen to resolve again. It occurred to him that the time after a nuclear detonation and before a detectable result was a time of pregnant quantum potentiality. In those few seconds, the Prox were both dead and alive. Schrödinger's Prox. It was a paradox he was eager to resolve.

The screen flickered as the view shifted to another camera, one less affected by the blast. Tal held his breath and leaned over the railing.

The Prox ship sailed on. Tal blinked, barely believing his eyes. Another blast wiped out the screen again, then another took out all their monitors. The lieutenant controlling them cycled rapidly through his options, looking for some shot, any shot, that would give them a clue as to the fate of the enemy.

A young man from the floor stood, addressing him directly. "No visuals, sir."

"Keep trying, son," Tal said.

The young man sat and the screens resumed their flickering.

"Surely we've got more than visuals," Tal said, raising his voice.

"Radiation sonar is out," came one voice.

"Subspectrum light," Tal said.

"On screen," someone shouted.

Tal looked up. The picture was monochrome, rendered in differing shades of purple. A flicker, then it was just black and white and a variety of grays. Tal found that easier to look at, which was no doubt why the monitor controller had switched it.

At first, Tal couldn't find his orientation. Then he realized it was the camera that hadn't found its orientation. It zigzagged wildly across the star field until it found purchase on a still white-hot explosion. It locked on and zoomed in.

Tal's jaw dropped as he watched the Prox ship moving toward them, whole and unharmed.

More explosions began as the other ships entered the minefield—the ultraviolet sensors were not nearly as disrupted by the detonations, and Tal studied how the blasts seemed to burst outward, away from the ships.

The lead ship was close enough now that he could still see the swarming soldiers. Even they were unharmed.

"Goddammit," he swore. "Theories?"

But there weren't any. Not yet. They'd need to study the data, especially when their sensors were all back online. *But will we have that data in time?*

"ETA on Prox in swarming range of the station?" he asked everyone and no one in particular.

"Twelve hours," came the response.

Twelve hours to say goodbye. Twelve hours to make love one last time. Twelve hours to mourn. "Twelve hours to fight," he said aloud.

CHAPTER FIVE

"Let us start small," Tomás said. He walked toward the west. Jeff followed. After about .25 kilometers he came to a large felled tree. Its bark was black, and its branches were spindly and twisted.

That is the ugliest goddamn tree I have ever seen, Jeff thought.

"Let us move this tree from here to an equal distance on the other side of our camp." He smiled patiently.

"Why not?" Jeff shrugged. He appeared nonchalant, but he had started sweating. He felt like he was playing with fire. It was dangerous, irresponsible. He had been carrying the guilt of innocent people's lives his entire adult life. He didn't need any more.

"You stay here, I'll go over there. You have a…" He couldn't find the word. He pointed to his head.

"A neural? Yeah. No connection here, though."

"But your *reloj*…timekeeper…it still works, no?"

"Yes, no problem."

"In ten minutes, I will meet you in…" he cocked his head. "I have never had to speak of it before. Well, since you have called me *curandero*, I will meet you in the Otherworld."

With that, the little man turned and walked back the way he had come.

Jeff wrestled with how to feel about him. He was still not over the fact that, in some tenuous way, Tomás *was* him. Battling against those feelings, however, was an ominous blanket of dread. He did not want to do this, whatever they were about to do. The tree, fallen and gnarled as it was, was considerably larger than himself. He could do a lot of damage here. He gritted his teeth and steeled himself. It seemed a high price, but it needed to be paid if they were to have any hope against the Ulim.

There had always been something off about them. And as clumsily as they had inhabited Danny's form, they seemed to have no problem knowing how to act human. At least that mystery was solved.

Jeff shook his head and checked his chronometer. It was time. He sat down cross-legged about a meter away from the trunk of the tree and took a deep breath. As he exhaled, he entered into the All.

It was a familiar feeling by now. He wondered if all those stories he'd heard his whole life about out-of-body experiences had simply been this.

He went out—drawing energy from a nearby star. Then he expanded, filling everything—then contracted, searching for Tomás. He found him. It wouldn't have mattered if he were .5 kilometers away or 500 million. There he was, and Jeff went to him.

He saw him meditating cross-legged on the ground, just like himself. Then he felt a tug. He looked, and there was Tomás—another Tomás—like a pale, shimmering shadow. "This is the astral form," Tomás said. The apparition's mouth was moving, but Jeff heard the voice in his mind. He nodded.

"I want you to go back to the tree and move it. I'll hold the other side of the…" Tomás pursed his lips, thinking.

"Transport tube?" Jeff suggested.

The ghost of Tomás laughed. "That name has no beauty. But it is good enough for now."

Jeff turned and instantly found himself looking at the tree again and at the meditating form of his own body. He reached out and pinched a point in space near Tomás, but saw Tomás holding up his hand. Tomás pinched the space, then held his hand out to Jeff. Jeff grabbed hold of the space just under the tree, then reached through to grasp Tomás' hand.

What he met wasn't solid, but it was real. He closed his non-fingers around it and felt a tingle of energy. He felt Tomás' non-fingers tighten just when he thought the force of the energy would make his arm careen wildly—but their connection held. Jeff felt a rush of energy as the tree moved through.

A moment later, the energy was gone. Tomás' non-hand was gone. Jeff opened his eyes and found himself sitting cross-legged next to a bare patch of ground where a tree used to be.

He jumped up and jogged back to where Tomás was. He passed their camp and kept going. He was winded by the time he saw the little man's form.

Tomás smiled when he saw him. "You didn't have to run," he said, which Jeff took to mean he could have just transported. He wasn't comfortable with that. Not yet.

Tomás pointed. The tree was there, looking just as ugly as it had half a kilometer away. It was lying on another side, but it was obviously the same tree.

Tomás patted his arm. "How was that?"

Jeff nodded. "It was okay." It was a little weird, but he wasn't going to let on.

"Now we will try something bigger."

Jeff nodded his agreement. "How much bigger?"

Tomás looked around. "Take a look at this place. What's missing?"

Jeff put his hands on his hips and turned around completely. There were trees, but it was mostly flat plains. "I don't know. Animals? Hills?"

Tomás nodded. "Hills. This place needs a hill. Or a small mountain. Don't you think?"

"We're going to move a mountain?" Jeff narrowed one eye at him.

Tomás grinned. "*Que si tuviereis fe como un grano de mostaza, diréis a este monte: Pásate de aquí allá; y se pasará.*"

"Come again?" Jeff asked.

"Let's find our mountain," Tomás said. He patted the ground next to him. "It is easier to send than to receive."

"Easier to pitch than catch," Jeff translated.

Tomás scowled a bit, but it was an amused scowl. "So when we find our *pequeña montaña*, I want you to teleport there. Then send the mountain to me."

"If the mountain will not come to Muhammad…" Jeff smirked.

"Who is Muhammad?"

Jeff blinked. "Your universe is *definitely* different from mine," he said. He closed his eyes and moved into the All.

He felt, rather than saw, Tomás' presence. He spoke, and although he heard his own voice, once again it was in his head. "How can I be sure I won't drop the mountain on top of you?"

"I'll direct its path on this side. Not to worry."

"I worry."

"Trust me."

And that, Jeff realized—so profoundly that he experienced a moment of vertigo—was the crux of the matter. Jeff didn't trust Tomás. He didn't trust *anyone*.

Tomás seemed to sense his tension. He felt the proximity of Tomás' presence, although he was sure geographic location had little to do with it.

"Trust is not innate," Tomás' voice said in his head. "It is a choice. It is not something you *possess*, it is something you *do*."

Jeff had not thought of it that way before. A moment later, Tomás was gone. He searched for Tomás' presence again and found it. Not surprisingly, it was near a large hill.

"So, just move the whole…" Jeff began.

"You'll have to cut it off at some point." Tomás's ghostly hand made a horizontal slicing gesture near the hill's base.

"Just…cut it off."

Tomás gave him an encouraging smile. "I know you can do this." Then he was gone.

Jeff reached back and pinched the space near where his body was sitting, then pinched the space where his essence was hovering. Then the brought the two together. When he opened his eyes, he was sitting at the base of the hill.

The universe had not disappeared. Nothing and no one appeared to be dead, or to have suffered in any way. Jeff exhaled an enormous sigh of relief. Then he closed his eyes again, quickly went into the All, and found Tomás.

The little man was waiting. Jeff pinched the ground, a huge swath of it. In his mind's eye, he scooped up the earth all around the mountain. Then he reached out for Tomás.

He was there. He grabbed at his ghostly, astral arm. He clutched it as tight as he was able.

As the energy hit and the mountain rumbled and shook, Jeff held on for dear life.

We lost a battle, not the war, Tal reminded himself. Repeatedly.

He felt dizzy. He flailed one hand toward the handrail separating the levels of the Command Center, found it. But the buzzing in his head was so loud, so overpowering that he almost lost consciousness. He couldn't collapse. Not here.

I have a command chair, he thought. He never sat in it, but he had one. Who was going to blame him if he sat in it now? In a haze, he turned and stumbled in its direction.

"Sir, are you all right?" Liu caught his elbow. *Bless him,* Tal thought, as the younger man held it steady while Tal made his way to the chair. He sat, and Liu darted away. A moment later he was back with a glass of water. Tal grasped it, grateful, and drank it all.

He didn't realize he was on the brink of collapse until he was there. Then a semi-autonomous and rational part of his brain did a quick calculation. He'd been awake and on his feet for seventy-two hours. No wonder…

He waved at Liu, and the younger man bent, his ear near Tal's mouth for privacy. "I need a doctor. Nothing acute, I just need…something to keep me awake and alert until…until this is over."

Liu nodded, but he didn't dart away again. Instead, he rose to his full height and put one hand on the back of Tal's chair. Tal's brain flashed on the image of some ancient sentinel or a lioness protecting her cub. Liu had been the best goddam secretary he'd ever had. The young man was loyal, knew how to keep secrets, and took good care of him. He'd never stopped to consider that he held the younger man in esteem, and even with affection, but he did.

Tal flashed on an image from one of Earth's historic religions—now largely forgotten—of the great leader (Moses—was that right?) standing on a cliff overlooking a great battle. So long as he kept his hands in the air, his soldiers would win, but when he dropped them, his men began to lose. All would have been lost had he not had the help of another man to hold his arms up for hours upon hours… As long as he had Liu to hold his arms up, they might just win this thing.

He didn't have to look at Liu to know that his eyes were rolled upwards, sending for the admiral's surgeon. *Will other people worry when they see a physician attending me?* He wondered. But he expected Liu would navigate that discreetly. He didn't need to know how. He had never micromanaged his secretary, and he wasn't about to start now.

Just sitting down had helped. He felt less dizzy, and no doubt some water had helped his electrolyte balance, too. *It is no shame to sit*, he reminded himself. It was going to be a long battle, and he needed to take care of himself.

He turned his mind back to the art of war, to the oncoming enemy, to the protection of all he held dear. He punched at one of the buttons on his command chair. "Pacholok, I want an update on those wormhole generators."

It took a moment to get a response, which is what he would expect from Pacholok. Tal might be in command, but Pacholok was the same rank as he and wasn't about to let him forget it. "Gimme a minute, Jason."

Only another admiral would dare call him by his first name. Only another admiral would dare tell him to wait a minute. Tal sighed and began to count. At seven, the speaker crackled and Pacholok's voice emerged again. "Okay, Jason, here's what we've got. Sixty-three probes, all with stealth capability, all with a top speed of C5. We've got them wired into triangulation patterns—so they'll go out in groups of threes and operate as a single unit."

"So what we've basically got are twenty-one mobile wormhole portals," Tal said.

"That's it. The biggest problem was the amount of power it takes to generate and maintain a wormhole. So every 'team' of three has one augmented probe carrying an extra reactor."

"I assume these are dirty reactors," Tal said.

"Yeah, we didn't have time or, frankly, room on these little damn things for clean ones. So, an extra advantage if we want to detonate any of them. They won't make very powerful bombs, but they'll go boom and generate a shitload of radiation."

"I can't imagine needing that, but keeping them light and assembling them fast was the right call. How soon can we deploy?" Tal asked.

"We're uploading the last of the revised code now. Thirty seconds?"

"And how fast can they engage?"

"We came up with a number of different scenarios and simulated the best of them. The one with the best chance for success—by a long shot—has them traveling at C3.565, then entering normal space about 2,000 kilometers from the enemy ships, directly in their path. It'll take them four minutes and twenty-two seconds between our bay and their operational positions. There are three of them, so we've got seven chances at each of them."

Tal nodded. If they couldn't get them with seven tries, they *deserved* to die.

"Make it happen, Don," Tal said, intentionally using Pacholok's first name. Two could play at that game.

"Expect launch in three minutes. Pacholok out."

Tal noticed movement in his peripheral vision and looked up. Doctor Basiliedes, the admiral's surgeon, was making the rounds of those on the upper level of the Command Center. Tal saw him putting his hand on Liu's shoulder, prying open his right eye, checking the pupil, then giving him a hypo-spray injection.

It was a good show, designed by Liu, no doubt, to deflect suspicion away from the surgeon's attention to Tal. A moment later, however, he was placing his hand on Tal's own shoulder.

"Admiral, how you holding up?"

The surgeon was Nigerian, black as midnight, in contrast to the coffee color of Tal's own skin. He was a solid man, and Tal noted how his neck bulged in back as the doctor pried open his eyes—both of them, in succession—and peered into them. The doctor's eyes were bloodshot and yellow, but then they always looked that way, Tal remembered.

Those yellow eyes narrowed, and without asking permission or saying a word to warn him, the doctor snatched up Tal's hand and felt the wrist. He could have just accessed his neural for Tal's vitals, and no doubt had been, but Tal figured there must be some value in feeling for oneself the strength of the pulse, something that mere numbers could not communicate.

"You need to rest," he whispered.

"Like hell," Tal whispered back.

"I want a summary of your operational timeline in twenty seconds or less. No arguments or I'll sedate you and have you carted away."

"We have an attack starting in five minutes."

"And then?"

"If it works, I'll sleep for a week."

"And if it doesn't?"

"Plan C…which is going to take us a few hours to set up."

"Very well. I'm going to give you a shot."

"What's in it—" before he could finish the sentence, Tal heard the spray employ. "Christ sakes, doctor, what did you just do?"

"You have one hour before the sedative takes effect. Make good use of that time. Make sure your next-in-command is ready. Here's what is going to happen. You'll get very sleepy and you won't be able to resist it. So one hour from now, make sure you're in your room or you'll suffer the indignity of being carried there in front of everyone."

"I'll have your fucking job—"

Basiliedes ignored him. "Then you'll drop into a hyper-accelerated sleep state. Four hours later you'll wake up feeling like you've just had the best night's sleep of your life, and someone has given you an espresso IV drip."

"I like the sound of that."

"You won't dream, you won't waste any time falling asleep or waking up. It'll be like a light switch, off and on. And when it comes on, no one will be able to stop you."

"How come you haven't given this to me before?"

"Because if you use it three days in a row your heart explodes." Doctor Basiliedes smiled.

"Huh. Okay, good to know."

"I'm going to move on now. Got to make the show a good one."

"Of course. Uh…thank you, doc."

Basiliedes nodded and snagged the next officer he saw.

Tal stayed seated, but barked out using his best command voice. "I want all screens on those probes when they launch."

"Launch sequence in five…four…three…two…"

Tal squinted as he saw the probes, in neat formations of three, float through the port doors into space.

"Engaging cloaking protocols…"

The probes winked out of sight, as if they had been stars that had moved behind a moon.

Tal gripped at the faux leather of his command chair and leaned forward.

A schematic offered a god's eye view of the deployment. He could see the three Prox ships moving almost imperceptibly toward them. *Why don't the bastards just flip into C-space and get it over with?* he wondered. But he was instantly sorry he asked the question, because he knew the answer. It was as clear as the schematic in front of him. Their purpose wasn't simply to conquer and consume Sol Station. It was to utterly deplete their ability to resist, to defend the Earth. They knew that the humans would throw everything they had at them now and would have precious little left by the time they got here. They were counting on it.

Tal felt his heart sink within him. The truth of it dragged the one remaining scrap of hope he possessed out of his chest and beat it to a steaming bloody pulp in front of him. He blinked back tears and looked away from the screens. *Master yourself, goddammit,* he thought.

He pinched the bridge of his nose and wiped his eyes surreptitiously as he did so. He sniffed and set his teeth in grim resolve. He saw a schematic of the first of the probes, in perfect triangulated formation, approaching the lead Prox ship.

He suspected it would stay just ahead of it until the other two were likewise covered. They only had one shot at the element of surprise, and he was sure Pacholok would not waste it.

He was right. He watched as three formations positioned themselves directly in front of the Prox ships. The Command Center was dead quiet, and Tal realized he was not the only person holding his breath.

Then he saw all three Prox ships wink out, the space suddenly black where they had been mere moments before.

"Yes!" Tal shouted, standing. A roar ascended from the Command Center. Officers were jumping up and down and hugging one another. The noise erupting from the room was deafening. Liu leaned in, "Congratulations, si—"

Tal held one hand up and took another step forward, almost right up to the guard rail.

One by one, people looked up at the screens and fell silent. The Prox ships were back. They were all in slightly different positions, but they were moving inexorably onward. They were still there, and they were still coming.

"That's impossible," Tal breathed. "Nothing has survived a wormhole generator."

"That we know of, sir," Liu corrected him, albeit politely. "Things go in, but we don't know where. We lose contact with them, and we can't get them back. But…we don't actually know what happens to them."

"So how are these motherfuckers back?"

"I...don't know that, sir."

The second string of generators was in place, and once again the Prox ships were wiped from known space.

A couple of seconds later, they reappeared.

And they kept coming.

Tal watched the schematic as the third set moved into position, but this time the Prox ships disappeared before the generators employed, winking back on the other side of the disrupted space. They had simply skipped over, or around, or through—Tal wasn't sure which—the generators.

"How are they doing that?" Tal asked.

No one had an answer.

Four more generators tried to move into place, but the Prox ships evaded them all, simply by seeming to dematerialize and rematerialize out of range of the danger.

Tal sat heavily and buried his head in his hands.

"Plan C, sir," Liu said.

Tal did not feel the need to answer him. He stood. He straightened his jacket.

"Make sure we've run all the equations for Admiral Wengret's funnel idea and get the strike team moving. I want them drilling in twenty minutes, running through every scenario they're likely to encounter when they breach the hulls of the alien ships." He nodded at the screen. "I want plans for how they're going to get in and how they're going to get out. I want a weapons recommendation, and I want them to train with everything on it."

"Yes sir. You can count on me, sir."

Tal's shoulders sagged. He reached out and steadied himself on Liu's shoulder. "I know I can. I'm...I need to lay down."

"Let's go, sir. I'll make sure you get there. And I'll make sure everything is in place when you wake up."

Emma stood in the shower, letting the hot water run over her head. She had to hand it to her captors, when they saw a need for a function, they made that function happen and pronto! It was abundantly obvious that a function was desperately needed after she finished her very first shift in the counting chambers. After twelve hours of what amounted to calisthenics, her jumpsuit had been soaked with sweat, and she reeked. The Alverians had been extremely alarmed when they saw her condition. Apparently losing that much bodily fluid would be life-threatening to one of them, and they were concerned for her health. She explained that such 'leakage' was completely normal for humans when physically exerting themselves, but that she would need a facility where she could wash on demand.

She'd expected them to balk at her request, if only for the use of water. Emma still had no idea where their water came from, or how much of a reserve they had. She also didn't expect for them to expend much effort providing for her comfort. They didn't seem to value comfort much, even for themselves. But much to her surprise, they didn't even question the necessity of a shower and built one to her specification before the end of the following shift. The way she smelled at that point may have driven the point home.

She looked at her arms, barely recognizing them as her own. Her biceps were huge and ropey, her forearms bulging. They looked more like the arms of a martial artist than a scientist. Then she realized it had been weeks since she'd seen her own face. The Alverians apparently had no use for mirrors. They definitely didn't share the same sense of individualism, of self, as humans did. It would never even occur to them to contemplate their own appearance. Aside from minor variations in coloring, they were all shockingly uniform in appearance.

Emma washed her jumpsuit in the shower using the "soap" they'd provided her. It made disappointingly little lather, but seemed to get the fabric clean. She rinsed it, then turned off the water and wrung it out as best she could and hung it on a hook in the wall.

The towel they'd arranged for her was scratchy and coarse, but absorbent enough to do the job. She dried off, fluffed her hair, then laid the towel flat on the floor. Next, she took the jumpsuit, folded it up loosely, and laid it on half of the towel. Then she flipped the other half over it and began stepping on it, walking all over the towel to force as much water out as she could. When she felt she could do no more, she put on the still-damp jumpsuit and hung the towel on the hook.

The common chamber was filled with the usual buzz of activity, but Emma ignored it, willing herself to keep moving. She lined up at the cafeteria, got the same disgusting food, and shuffled toward a table. *This must be what prison is like,* she thought.

Her mood picked up slightly when she saw Amberline waving, saving a spot for her at one of the tables. Emma smiled and joined her.

"How are you?" asked the mask.

"I am so tired, I barely know what I'm doing."

"You will get used to it."

"Maybe, at least until my arm falls off."

Amberline tilted her head. "Is that likely?"

Emma groaned. "It certainly feels like it. It happened to the person next to me on the counting floor."

"That is unfortunate."

Emma ate some *poi*. "What will happen to her?"

"Which arm fell off?"

"Her left large arm."

Amberline shook her head. "That is unfortunate," she said again.

"Will they make a fake arm for her? Like mine?" She gestured to her prosthesis.

"I'm afraid not. The large arms are for lifting. If we made a prosthesis for her, it would be much weaker, not as functional."

"Can she get by with three?"

"Unlikely. We do not do well when we do not function properly. It does not allow us to serve the hive to our fullest."

Emma felt herself starting to tear up. "So what then? You'll kill her?"

Amberline shook her head. "More likely she will kill herself, then be eaten."

Emma gasped. "What? I thought you said you don't eat females, that would be cannibalism!"

"Correct. We do not eat females."

"Then who is doing the eating?"

"She would be fed to the males."

Emma felt nauseated.

"You do not approve."

"No."

"Would you prefer she go to waste, not serve the hive one last time?"

Emma shook her head. It was too much for her to deal with. She reminded herself that she was not dealing with humans, their ways were not her ways, it was not her place to judge. Still, she could not bring herself to eat any more.

"I have something that may lift your spirits," Amberline said, pulling a small parcel from her satchel and placing it on the table.

"Is it a hamburger?"

"It is not."

Emma half-heartedly picked up the package and began unwrapping it. Inside was a new tan jumpsuit. Emma's eyes went wide. "You found one!"

"It was not hard to procure. I will add the cost to the fee my client will pay when we return you."

"Thank you!" Now she could allow the outfit she washed in the shower to dry overnight and have a clean dry one to change into right away. She put her arm around Amberline and gave her a squeeze. Amberline allowed it. "This is *almost* as good as a hamburger."

"Good."

She *did* feel better, enough so to finish her *poi*. The meat could fuck right off, though.

CHAPTER SIX

When Jeff opened his eyes, he felt paralyzed. A great jagged wound marred the landscape. Where just seconds ago a large hill had dominated his vision, there were now only several square kilometers of raw soil. Jeff wondered at the destruction he—they—had just wrought. He felt a tinge of guilt at what must be hundreds of animals they had just displaced, earthworms suddenly bisected, mammals crushed beneath the undiscriminating weight of a small mountain.

"I just destroyed another universe," he said. Why had he not thought of what would happen before he did it? He felt a wave of shame roll through him once more.

Tomás was suddenly beside him, placing a hand on his shoulder. "What are you thinking?" he asked.

Jeff did not respond at first. When he did speak, his voice was thick and low. "I'm tired of destroying things."

Tomás nodded and looked down. "Today you were a force of natural evil."

"No. I was a force of moral evil. I…we…*chose* to do this."

"We intended no malice."

Jeff met his eyes. Tomás looked away. "*Si*, you are right, amigo. Shall we move it back?"

"And add damage to damage?" Jeff shook his head. "I can't see how that would help."

"*Las tuzas* will at least get their holes uncovered. They can get out."

"*Las Tuzas*?"

"Gophers…or whatever pass for gophers on this world." Tomás gave him a weak smile.

"Yeah. Okay. Save the fucking gophers."

"I need you to do it."

Jeff seemed to snap out of it. "Right. Of course." Then Tomás was gone.

It was easier the second time, almost surgical. Jeff went into the All and tapped into the sun's energy. Then holding the space where he was standing, he reached through and held Tomás' arm. He held on and felt the rush of unimaginable energy pass between them. Then when he opened his eyes, the hill was there again.

It was not exactly in the same position. He could see a slash on the landscape where raw soil was still visible, but it was a narrow ribbon. It was close. Good enough. Jeff closed his eyes, went back into the All, focused on Tomás, and was suddenly with him at their camp.

"You're getting good at that," Tomás said.

"What now?" Jeff asked.

"*Almuerzo*," Tomás said. "Lunch."

"How can you even think about food right now?" Jeff snapped. "The Prox are about to dismantle and eat Sol Station, we can do something about it, and you want to sit down for lunch?"

Tomás pulled tamales out of a small cooler. "We'll heat these up with some *pimientos*."

"I don't like being ignored." There was a growl in Jeff's voice.

"I am not ignoring you," Tomás said, setting out a small jar of jalapeños. "You are *enojon*. Grumpy. I plan to wait until you are kind again."

"We don't have time to…" Jeff's anger rose to the point where he wanted to break something. The little man's neck would do for a start. He clenched and unclenched his fists. "I'll be right back."

Jeff closed his eyes and went into the All. A few moments later, he was back.

Tomás raised one eyebrow at him. Jeff shrugged. "I had to do something."

"At least you did it quickly." Tomás pushed a metal plate at him. "Eat. You won't be any good to your people if you do not sustain yourself. You must eat. You must sleep. You must *tomar un descanso*…take a break now and then."

He was right, Jeff knew, which only made him madder. Grudgingly, Jeff sat cross-legged on the dusty ground and picked up the plate. Cold as they were, the tamales were excellent. The corn meal was sweet and nutty. The filling was…unusual.

He screwed up his face into a questioning look and pointed at the tamales.

"Butternut squash," Tomás said, through a mouthful of food.

Jeff's eyebrows rose. He took another bite. "Here's what I don't understand," he said.

Tomás grunted, taking a bite of tamale.

"If the Ulim are running sightlines on possible futures, why aren't they here now, trying to stop us?"

Tomás chewed slowly, and it was clear that he was thinking. He put his plate down and looked Jeff in the eye. "Because you and I…we are no threat to them. What we are going to do…it is impossible. They can see no timelines in which we do them any harm at all."

Jeff put his plate down and swallowed. He struggled to sort out his feelings. At first he felt defeated. Then he felt his anger rush back, nearly drowning his reason. When that subsided, he was left with resolve. "We're going to kick their asses," he said. His voice was quiet but solid. Resolute. It was not an aspiration, it was a fact.

Tomás smiled. "*Muy bien*! We are certainly going to try."

"So what's next?" Jeff asked. "After lunch, that is?" It was an apology of sorts.

"Now, I will take you to see them."

"To see who?"

"We will cross the barrier, into another string. We will go to my universe. We will visit *Los Durmientes*."

"Tell me about our traveling companions," Captain Daniel Hightower inquired. He unrolled his utensils from his napkin. The last of his senior staff were just now sitting down at the table. He had called the B Team in an hour early to man the bridge, and "invited" his A team for a working dinner. Everyone looked a little edgy and nervous—just the way he liked.

They had joined up with the caravan without incident. Lo had done a bang-up job with the credentials. No one had given them a second glance. Danny had to wonder just how stupid pirates in neutral space could be, if caravans could be so easily infiltrated. He reminded himself that this was not his problem.

Foulon had been right. After they'd announced their "mission" to the crew, morale had improved markedly. They had a purpose, they were doing something important. And most importantly, they weren't outlaws. It was a shame that they actually were, but Danny wasn't losing any sleep over that. Admiral Tal would have scolded him to plan long-range, to think further out, but fortunately he didn't have to deal with that toad anymore. He had one objective, and she was so close he could taste her.

Navigator Galli swept her hair back and cleared her throat. "There are twenty-seven ships in the caravan, including us—not including the *Talon*. Twelve of them are class six transport ships. I can break them down by make, if you like..." Her voice rose at the end, waiting for Danny's pleasure.

He waved at her. "Too much detail. Tell me who they are and what they're carrying."

Galli looked up to access her neural. "There's the *Sneaky Bison*. As you might expect, they transport bison meat."

"Why is the bison sneaky?"

"I...I don't know that, sir."

"Go on."

"Class six, crew complement of eight. Six hundred forty tons of meat."

"That's a lot of steak," Danny nodded, tucking into his own. As he put the meat into his mouth, he realized he had just given everyone else tacit permission to begin eating themselves. He didn't realize they'd been waiting for him, but he was glad they did. Danny enjoyed deference.

"Then there's the *Craft Angel*."

"Who names these goddam things?" Danny nudged Foulon's elbow.

Foulon raised his eyebrows and shook his head, his mouth full and chewing.

"What, for God's sake, is the goddam *Craft Angel* carrying?" Danny realized he was enjoying himself. He always ate alone. It was a rushed affair, usually, a matter of biological necessity, like shaving or shitting. But he realized he was feeling pleasure here, in the presence of his crew. It was an odd feeling. He'd have to think about it later.

"They….are….carrying…." Galli's eyes were rolled up in her head, searching for the information. "Beer, sir."

"Beer?"

"Yes sir. 920,000 liters of it."

"Are all these ships culinary transport?"

"Uh…no sir. I grouped them by cargo. I could start with machine parts or maybe with textiles."

Danny waved the suggestion away. "No, just curious. Continue with the food. Seems appropriate." He speared a Brussels sprout—the necessary evil of cruciferous vegetables.

By the time they'd finished eating, they were only halfway through Galli's list. Danny shut her down. "That's enough, I think. We get the idea. Send me that list, will you?"

"Of course, sir."

"Okay, then. Our mission is to get close to the *Talon*, study her, figure out her weaknesses. Foulon, I want engineering on this. I want to know about every weak spot. Look, but don't let them know you're looking."

"We'll make like we're at the beach with sunglasses on."

"That's my boy." Danny waved for the galley steward. The young man looked nervous as he leaned down to address the captain.

"Yes sir?"

"Bring dessert. Enough for everyone."

"What would you like, sir?"

"I don't give a fuck, just bring enough for everyone."

"But sir, we have over three hundred desserts on file—"

"Cake, goddammit! Bring some fucking cake."

"Yes sir." He started to scamper away. He stopped. "We have twenty-eight kinds—"

Danny threw a fork at him and glowered. He continued with his scampering. Danny turned his attention back to his bridge crew.

"It would be easier to observe the *Talon* if she were doing something," Foulon said. "Depending on what she was doing, we could observe and measure different systems. That would help us find a weakness." He lowered his head conspiratorially. "And we can choose what systems we want to test by dictating what she does."

"I like the sound of that!" Danny clapped his hands and grinned. "And just how do we dictate what she does, Ernst?"

"Well, for instance, if the *Craft Angel* were to…I don't know…lose propulsion, the *Talon* would have to bring her along with a tractor beam until she could be repaired. That would allow us to test—"

"High power output, voltage fluctuation patterns, energy distribution…" Danny's eyes brightened. "That's good. Very good."

"By the time we reach Deseret, several of the ships could meet with…little accidents…that would allow us to test every one of the *Talon*'s essential systems—most of them by passive reception. They won't even know we're looking."

"And how do we instigate these…little accidents?" Chief Engineer Tenzin asked.

"Well, that would depend on what we want to go wrong. I'll draw up a chart of actions that will test every major system, the…incidentals...that will allow us to test for them, the caravan ship best suited to such...incidentals...and the means of causing them."

"Spectacular, Number One," Danny felt something like real awe for another human being. It was a novel feeling and he did not like it.

"In the meantime, off the top of my head, assuming that we began with the *Craft Angel*—"

"Just because we hate the name," Danny interjected.

"Exactly. Assuming we start with her, I've been looking at her schematics, and she has—and this boggles the mind—she has fuel transport hoses that are exterior to the hull, in two places, for half a meter each. Worst goddam design I've ever seen."

"Dark lasers," Tenzin interjected.

"That's it, right there," Foulon pointed at the chief engineer.

"Come again?" Danny asked.

Tenzin was on the other side of the table, so for Galli and Lo the exchange was a bit like watching a tennis match from mid-court.

"Tiny high-power laser bursts. Monitors run at 4700 Hertz, so we time the bursts to sync with that, which will make them undetectable. Dark."

"It's not much use in a combat situation, where you need a lot of power focused in a single spot all at once," Foulon explained. "But this is more chipping away, burst by burst, until the poly gives."

"Like water dropping on a stone eats through the stone."

"Yeah. Very Lao-fucking-Tzu, Tenzin, but that's good thinking. That's exactly the kind of shit we're after here," Danny nodded.

"I'll have a detailed plan for every...well, sabotage"—Tenzin shrugged as he said it—"that we need to get a full workup of the *Talon*'s capabilities...and vulnerabilities."

"This is enough to make a man die fat and happy," Danny said, just as the cake arrived. He turned to the steward, who was nervously placing slices of cake in front of the bridge crew.

"Chocolate cake? Really? Are you an idiot? I fucking *hate* chocolate cake."

SLUMPED IN HER COMMAND CHAIR, Jo stared into space. The star field in the main viewer rotated imperceptibly as the *Talon* moved through space, but she didn't notice. In her head, she was playing Admiral Alinto's words over and over: *We do not wish our enemy evil. Our enemy is our family*. "My enemy is my family…" she said out loud, but not so anyone could hear. She was having a hard time wrapping her head around that one.

"Sir, the *Craft Angel* has dropped out of C-space," Tash Liebert said. "I'm receiving a distress call from them now."

That snapped her out of it. She sat up straight and shook the cobwebs from her brain. "Send a message to the whole caravan to reduce speed. Standard propulsion, 1500k."

"Yes sir." Liebert touched a few nodes on his panel. A moment later, he said, "Done."

"Mr. Chi, I want you to take us to the *Craft Angel*'s current location, with all possible speed."

"Yes sir."

Jo turned to Ditka. "Weaponer, any sign of threat agents?"

Ditka didn't respond immediately. Her fingers were flying, and Jo knew she wanted to be sure of her answer before she responded. "None, sir. Just a bunch of gas and empty space."

Jo turned to her left, to Liebert again. "Open a channel to the *Craft Angel*."

"Aye sir."

While she waited for the captain of the client vessel to respond, Jo asked no one in particular. "What the fuck kind of name is *Craft Angel*, anyway?"

"It's owned by a brewery," Ditka said. "They make beer."

"Why is a beer ship headed to a Mormon colony?" Jo asked.

"There was a vice carve-out for 'gentiles' in the original colony charter, sir," Liebert responded. "New Deseret didn't want it, but the Colonial Union made it a condition of their approval of the charter."

"How do you know that?" Jo asked.

Liebert shrugged. "Poli sci minor."

"Well…it's a stupid fucking name," Jo announced.

"Yes sir," Ditka agreed.

A moment later the main viewer flickered and the *Craft Angel*'s captain appeared. The woman looked distraught. She had a bohemian sensibility, and wore her hair in an old fashioned bun, a style not unpopular among those types. But the bun had become undone, and many strands of mousy brown hair splayed out in different directions from her head.

"Captain Eliza Tanner," Liebert announced.

She looks like she just woke up, Jo thought. "Captain Tanner, this is RFC Captain Jo Taylor, caravan escort, responding to your distress call. What's the problem, Captain?"

"We're not sure yet," Captain Tanner responded. "We know we're leaking fuel into space and can't sustain C-speeds."

"How fast can you diagnose it?"

"Uh…three hours?"

The look on her face showed Jo that this was an optimistic guess. The woman had no idea.

"Captain, I can't ask the whole caravan to run in circles while you sort this out. We have a schedule to keep, and I intend to keep it."

The woman's eyes darted back and forth, and Jo saw something like panic arise in them.

"You're just going to abandon us here?"

"Don't be stupid, Captain," Jo snapped. Instantly she regretted it. This cornflake might captain a glorified food transport shuttle, but she was still a captain and worthy of Jo's courtesy, if not respect. "Give me a minute, please."

"Off screen," she said to Liebert. A moment later, Jo was looking at the star field again. It whirled as they came about and dropped out of C-space. Jo punched at a button on the arm of her command chair. "Chief Engineer Ocampo," she called.

"Ocampo here, Captain."

"We've got a…situation, Chief."

"I live for situations, Captain."

Jo smiled. "We've got a light transport vessel streaming fuel into space. The caravan is proceeding on standard propulsion for the time being, but we need to get back into C-space if we're going to get back on schedule."

"Understood, Captain. Did the ship give you an estimate for repairs?"

"She's talking out of her colonic-traumatized ass, I'm afraid."

Ocampo laughed. "One of *those*."

"I was thinking a tractor beam…" Jo floated the idea.

"We could do that," Ocampo said. "Although if there are any exterior repairs to make, we'd have to wait until we entered normal space to make them."

"Could we carry them the whole way?" Jo asked.

"Sure," Ocampo said, in the equivalent of a vocal shrug. "Although…it's not efficient, fuel-wise. We'll burn twice what we otherwise would just keeping us balanced in C-space. It'll be awkward as fuck…if you pardon my use of color, sir."

Jo bit her lip. She had to get this caravan moving again, that was certain. "Chief, how quickly can you do a diagnostic?"

"I could tell you what's wrong with her in fifteen minutes, but I can't promise I can fix her that fast."

Fifteen minutes vs. 150,000 chits worth of fuel. That was an easy decision to make. "Okay, then, you've got your fifteen minutes. Does it matter if we're moving at standard propulsion?"

"Nope, not a bit."

"Then give me that tractor beam and let's at least be able to say we're moving in the right direction. And give me a full report in fifteen minutes. I'll be watching the clock."

"No problem, Captain. I'll get my number one on the tractor beam. You'll have it in under a minute. You'll hear from me before the fifteen is up. Ocampo out."

Jo nodded. Ocampo had the personality sparkle of an assembly-line robot, but he had never failed her. She knew she'd hear something soon. First she'd need to report back to that civilian captain and her bed hair…

Exactly thirteen minutes later, Jo was savaging a fingernail with her teeth when Liebert interrupted her. She realized what she had been doing and sat on her hand. “Tell me some good news, Chief.”

They’d gotten both ships up and moving at maximum speed for standard propulsion. It would take them four weeks to catch up to the rest of the caravan at this speed, but Jo didn’t expect to stay at this speed for long.

“The good news is the *Craft Angel* is fixable. Begging your pardon, Captain, but this ship has the most ludicrous design I’ve ever seen. It has two poly fuel hoses exterior to the hull.”

Jo scowled. “You’ve got to be shitting me.”

“No sir. If it was us, we’d be replacing those damned hoses every week or so. They are thick bastards, though—the hoses I mean.”

“That’s insane.”

“It’s a shortcut, that’s for sure. Anyway, we can repair those in about a half hour, but not from C-space. We’d need to do it at standard propulsion. Any speed is fine.”

“A half hour…” Jo gritted her teeth. She did not like the sound of that. “The other ships are not going to like playing patty-cake and leapfrog while we—” Jo stopped and cocked her head.

“Sir?” Ocampo’s voice asked.

“Leapfrog,” Jo said. “Chief, how fast can we go with the *Craft Angel* in tow?”

“C6, no problem.”

“Most of the caravan can’t do more than C4 or 5.”

“That’s right,” Ocampo’s voice came through the speaker.

“Chief, let’s get the caravan up to speed again, then let’s drag the *Craft Angel* out in front of them at maximum C. We’ll drop into conventional space while we make repairs. We’ll be done by the time the rest of the ships catch up to us. Any problems with that plan?”

She could almost hear Ocampo nodding. “That should work, Captain.”

“Get on it, then. Taylor out.”

She swung her chair to the left to face Liebert again. “Mr. Liebert, get those ships moving, C4, all of them.”

“Yes sir,” Liebert’s hands began dancing over his panel.

"And open a channel to Captain Cornflake."

DOCTOR BASILIEDES HAD BEEN RIGHT. One moment Tal was awake. The next moment he wasn't. It was a very good thing he'd lain down in time.

When his eyes opened, he nearly sprang out of bed. He felt panicked, but didn't know why. It took a moment or two to remember who he was, where he was, what was going on. Then it all came rushing back—a fact that both comforted him and filled him with anxiety and dread.

The Prox were coming. And they were coming fast.

He rushed to the sonic and realized he had not felt this hale or energetic in twenty years or more. He felt like he could run a 10k race without breaking a sweat. The feel of the sonic on his skin was even more invigorating.

As he dressed, he paid special attention to every detail, making sure no creases marred his uniform, and that every pip was exactly in place, facing the right direction. If this was going to be the fight that defined his career, he wanted to shine.

He was just about to leave his quarters when something in his peripheral vision caught his eye. He turned back, and there, on the bed, was a piece of white paper.

He scowled and picked it up. *Was this here a minute ago?* he wondered. *Had it been on the bed while I was sleeping? Or did someone enter and lay this on my bed while I was in the sonic?* How could he know?

He knew he'd smoothed out the bedclothes after rising. It hadn't been there then, had it?

Even more disturbing, however, was what was on the paper. He felt a shudder go up his spine as he read.

Admiral Tal, I bring you greetings from exile. I have seen what you are up against, and I don't wish it on you. In my world, Captain Jo Taylor devised a method of protection against the Prox. 150,000 volts through the hull whenever they try to land. It won't stop them, and it will be less effective with every burst, but it will slow them down and will make them think twice about landing on your ships. Try it or not. I just offer it in the spirit of "the enemy of my enemy is my friend." From one soldier to another, I wish you well in your fight. —Captain Jeff Bowers

---

Tal felt a seizure of conscience, and his hand went instinctively to his chest. He had wronged that man Bowers. He knew it, and he suspected Bowers knew it too. He had let Hightower sway him, had allowed himself to be poisoned by that snake. He wasn't sure of much, but he knew one thing: once upon a time, he had chosen between those two men, and he had chosen wrong. He had chosen Hightower, and Bowers had died. And then, little more than a month ago, fate had improbably given him another chance, a do-over he had never anticipated. He had chosen again, and once more he had backed the wrong horse. *If I had to choose between them right now, I'd want Bowers on my team rather than Danny, even a Bowers from another universe. Instead, I handed him over to the Butcher.*

But here was evidence that Bowers had escaped fate once again. *Lucky bastard,* Tal thought, smiling. And not only was he alive, but he was putting himself at some risk to send them a message. A message that would help them.

He froze and wondered if perhaps it was a ruse. Maybe the voltage will actually attract the Prox, and Bowers is simply exacting his revenge. It was possible. *Don't make the same mistake a third time*, he told himself. *For once in your life, trust the right man.*

He straightened his coat and walked to his door. He paused as it slid open. With the energy of a thirty-year-old, he strode the corridors toward the Command Center, giving curt, affirming nods to every officer he passed.

Basiliedes is a fucking genius, Tal thought. *This was the right move. I hate to admit it, but it was.* If he had twenty-four hours of fighting ahead of him, he needed to be rested. And goddammit if he wasn't. He stepped onto the bridge of the Command Center and four hundred people rose to salute him.

"As you were," he said, and mounted the stairs with the energy of a bucking baby goat.

"How do you feel, Admiral?" Liu asked him. Liu had held everything together while he'd been gone, and the strain of it was showing. There were hollow circles under the man's eyes, and he looked shaken and gaunt.

"I feel like a billion chits. But you need some sleep, Lieutenant," Tal said. "Trust me, it'll do you good."

"It seemed to do you good," Liu affirmed.

"Update?"

"The Prox haven't wavered. They're still coming, their speed is constant."

"And Plan C?"

"Ready to deploy in…" Liu looked up to note the time. He looked back down. "Thirty minutes."

Tal nodded.

"Full operational notes are ready for you. They're linked to your neural."

"Good. I'll review them. But…I've got something else I want to try."

Liu's eyebrows rose. "Did you have an idea while you were sleeping?"

"I had a…call it a revelation. A message from beyond."

Liu looked skeptical.

Tal ignored him and sat in his command chair. "Get me someone from engineering, and get them yesterday," he instructed. "We're not sending another ship to confront those bastards without some protection."

CHAPTER SEVEN

"I've met the Ulim," Jeff said, his lip curling up in distaste. "I don't care to meet them again."

"We will not be speaking to them," Tomás assured him. "We will simply observe them."

"Will they know we're observing them?" Jeff asked, one eyebrow rising.

The rotation on this particular planet was a fast one. Jeff estimated they'd had about eight hours of sunlight, and twilight was already teasing an unfamiliar color palate from the sky.

"They certainly could," Tomás rocked his head back and forth on his neck. "I think it depends on whether they are paying attention. My guess? There is a war on. They will be plenty busy."

Jeff nodded. "And…what if they do notice us?"

"I imagine they will try to swat us away, like a pesky mosquito."

"And would that be fatal?" Jeff asked.

"Would it matter if it was?" Tomás asked him.

Jeff swallowed. "No, I don't suppose it would."

Tomás nodded and stood, clapping the dust off his hands. "Then let us get started." Tomás stretched his arms forward and did a few deep knee bends, as if he was preparing to run a race.

“What are you doing?” Jeff asked.

“Making sure I’m well circulated. We may be sitting for a while.”

“Ah,” Jeff said. Feeling a little foolish, he did the same.

When Tomás sat, he sat next to him. Tomás closed his eyes and placed his hands on his knees. Jeff did the same. To any casual observers, had there been any other sentient life nearby, it would have looked like they were meditating.

“Meet me…out there,” Tomás instructed.

Jeff relaxed and entered the All. His consciousness instantly became diffuse, and he had to concentrate to focus on his own body. He reached out for energy to the star the planet was circling, then he refocused on Tomás, now a disembodied presence in space. It was unsettling to think that he was the same. He felt so much like himself.

Tomás acknowledged his arrival and continued his instructions. “Good,” said the voice in his head. “Now go beyond.”

“Beyond what?” Jeff asked. He could hear his own voice, also in his head, but it sounded strange.

“Beyond everything you understand or know.”

“I’m not sure how to do that,” Jeff confessed. “I am at the edge of all things.”

It was not hubris, nor was it an exaggeration. His consciousness was at the center of every point in the universe. What was it Jo had said? It seemed like years ago now. “Its center is everywhere and its circumference is nowhere.” It was exactly like that.

“*Beyond* is a metaphor,” Tomás said. “There is no further out that you can go. You must not go out, but through.”

Ordinarily, Jeff would have simply looked puzzled, but he doubted Tomás could see his facial expressions just now. “You’ll have to explain that.”

“If you want to travel from one string to another, you cannot get there by going out, but by going in, or through. Language does not serve us when talking about such things.”

Jeff could hear the weariness in his voice. His heart went out to him. For the first time he thought of Tomás as his friend. The realization warmed him a little. “I don’t understand.”

"It will not be like jumping from one very large rope to another," Tomás explained, his voice even and patient. "The strings are metaphors, too."

"All right. What *is* it like, then?"

"It is like finding a door behind your door."

"That makes no sense at all," Jeff said.

"Did you ever try to explain how you moved through space to someone?"

"Yes," Jeff said.

"How well did you do?" Tomás asked.

"Okay. You get a pass!" It wasn't possible to actually laugh, disembodied in the vacuum of space, but he hoped some humor came through in the tone of his voice.

"I would take you with me if I could," Tomás said. "But I would just slip out, and you would just be here by yourself."

A memory surfaced for Jeff. "I was in Tokyo, on a large pedestrian speedway. The belt was moving pretty fast, but there were these little roundabouts that slowed your velocity just enough so that you could jump off and start walking normally again. Is it like that?"

"No, but…that is the right direction."

"Should I be worried about this?"

"You should be worried that there are 758 reality strings, and you can pass into any of them as easily as another. I want to be sure we end up in the right one."

"Oh Jesus. I hadn't even thought about that," Jeff said. He was getting used to his interior voice. One wrong move and he could be stranded somewhere very different from his home, or even from this string. Perhaps so different it was uninhabitable. Had there been strings where humankind had not survived its nuclear wars? Surely there were. He shuddered. *Why am I doing this again?* he asked himself. *Oh yeah, because these demonic monsters are hell-bent on destroying the human race. Good enough reason.* "I'm open to suggestions," he said to Tomás.

Tomás was silent, but Jeff imagined he could hear the man think, body or no body.

"I do have one, but you're not going to like it," Tomás began.

"With a setup like that, how can I resist?" Jeff quipped.

"You learned to move by watching *Los Durmientes* move you, *sí*?"

"*Sí*...yes."

"Then you must learn to shift strings by watching me do it." Tomás's voice was logical and resolute.

"Okay." That sounded reasonable.

"Allow me to inhabit you," Tomás said. "And then allow me to pilot you."

Jeff was unsure how to respond. It meant giving up control. It meant a level of intimacy with this man that he was not comfortable with—as he wouldn't be comfortable with any person. It was also the only path he could see toward victory over those motherfuckers.

"What do I do?"

"What did we find out?" Danny asked, emerging from his ready room.

All heads turned in his direction, but no one spoke.

"What, are you all idiots? What did we find out about the *Talon* from our little experiment with the *Craft Angel*?"

"You've got a report waiting for you on your neural now, Captain. From Chief Tenzin." Communicator Lo's voice quavered, but at least the man spoke up.

Danny cursed himself for not seeing it, but Lo was right. When he looked up he saw the blinking blue light of an unopened message. He strode to his command chair and Foulon stood to surrender it with due ceremony. Danny nodded and Foulon stepped down to his own post. Danny sat and looked up, opening the message.

"What did we learn?" Foulon asked.

Danny looked down and saw him leaning over, his voice almost a whisper. *He might be on board yet*, Danny thought. There was nothing in the report he deemed secret. Indeed, there was much to be said for the whole team knowing what they'd learned. They were turning out to be more creative and resourceful than Danny had initially given them credit for. They'd be able to see things in the data he wouldn't. He knew that and it didn't bother him a bit. *If you can't be smart, command smart*, he reminded himself, recalling a maxim from one of his professors at the academy.

The thought made him feel old. It seemed like a lifetime ago. It was, in fact, a revolution ago, a war ago, and in the intervening time he had lost his innocence, his best friend, and his fear of authority. He shook his head to clear it. Then he turned to Foulon.

"The *Talon* has more juice than I would have guessed for such a small ship," he said. "They latched onto the *Craft*...shit, the beer ship...they latched onto it with a twelve billion stroh tractor beam."

Foulon whistled. "Do all their ships have those?"

"God help us if they do. The best we'd be able to manage is eight billion stroh."

"It would get the job done." Foulon cocked his head.

"Yeah, but with twelve billion stroh, you'd be able to not just tow the damn thing, but wave it around in front of you if you wanted to. Solid as a fucking rock."

"Why do they need that?"

"We've already got our answer to that," Danny said, looking up to check the statistics again. "Our tractor beam would only be able to tow under conventional propulsion—"

"They're towing in C-space?" Foulon's face fell in disbelief.

"Yep. Leaped into C-space about two hours ago, looks like." Danny saw Navigator Galli looking at them over her shoulder, listening. He spoke a little more loudly, for her benefit. "It's Tenzin's guess that they're getting a bit ahead of the caravan to make repairs on the... the beer ship."

"You just can't bring yourself to say it, can you?" Foulon grinned.

"God help me," Danny agreed. "Stupidest fucking name I ever heard."

"Worse than the *Spruce and Bonnet*?"

"Don't remind me." Danny sighed. "Lo, get me Chief Tenzin."

"Right away, sir," Lo said.

"Tenzin here," a voice emitted from the overhead speakers.

"Chief, good work on your report on the *Talon* and that beer ship."

"Thank you, sir."

"What's next?"

"I've made a list of seven primary systems I'd like to test, and fourteen secondary systems I'd love to get to if we have time."

"Can we double up on any of those?"

"Great question, sir. I'm sending over a grid now of possible…sabotages—"

"Let's call them 'experiments,'" Danny suggested.

"Excellent….a grid, then, of possible experiments and the systems each…experiment…will allow us to test. We can cover most of the territory on the grid with four experiments…but I'd love a fifth if we can get to it."

"And what do you suggest for the next one?"

"Well, if you'll note on the chart, we've got eight primary systems: military, power, societal, maintenance, emergency, communications, sensors, and shielding. The secondary systems—"

"I've taken note of all the systems, Chief. Move along."

"Er…right, sir. The *Talon* is an Inaffeffew class warship—"

"I've never heard of that," Danny scowled.

"Infaffeffew is an Igberiti word, meaning 'fierce,' appropriately," Tenzin said. "And it's an Igberiti design. It's a fairly new class, built especially for the rebels. We captured one about two years ago and reverse-engineered its schematics. So we know a lot about its capabilities as a class, but not much about the *Talon* specifically. It's no doubt been modified in any number of ways."

"I've never met an off-the-shelf warship yet," Danny grunted his agreement.

"Exactly, sir. Every ship shares certain qualities with other ships in her class, but every ship is…tweaked to ready it for its specific mission."

"And the mission of the *Talon* is—"

"Well, don't let its current occupation as caravan escort fool you.

Under Captain Telouse, it was one of the deadliest light crafts in the RD…that the rebels had…have, sir."

"So it isn't just Captain Taylor who's a badass."

"It's a pretty badass ship, sir," Tenzin agreed.

"But we need to find out just *how* badass it is."

"And its weaknesses, hopefully."

"Tell me about these two experiments."

"It depends if you want to test societal or military systems. Or communications."

Danny could almost hear the shrug in his voice.

"We know a lot about her military systems," Danny noted.

"Yes, we can extrapolate from previous encounters with the ship. In fact, I've already begun to compile a speculative summary."

"Good work. Let's find some holes in life support, then."

"I was about to suggest the same. For that, we just need to tax their systems and watch carefully. It would help if we could access some of their monitoring—"

"Leave that to me. We've got a mole on board."

"Great! Inform him we need the daily societal threadline summary. The good news is those are small, generally, just a few hundred k daily. It would make a barely perceptible data packet."

"I'll have the first one for you within twenty-four hours."

"That will provide a handy baseline, so that's great. Then we'll fuck with it."

"And how will we do that?"

"Tax the shit out of their life support and watch the numbers."

"And how will we do that?" Danny asked again.

"Easy. We add more bodies than the *Talon* was built to sustain. Four of our fellow ships are carrying pilgrims, are they not?"

Foulon leaned over. "About two hundred people on each, all of them headed for Deseret with New Zion temple recommends. They do a crazy-ass ritual and then go home, feeling holy and smug and superior."

Danny felt himself recoil. "Where the hell did you pick that shit up?"

Foulon looked away. "I was raised Mormon. I've done this pilgrimage."

"No shit. What happened to you?"

Foulon looked him dead in the eye. "Part of being a good soldier is knowing what duties you're cut out for, and what you're not. I wasn't meant to be a holy joe."

"Did you wear the magic underwear, too?"

Foulon held his gaze and did not blink. "Still wearing it, sir."

Danny started laughing then. Then he laughed harder. He slunk in his chair and filled the bridge with deep belly-shaking guffaws that felt better than a good fuck. "Oh my god," he said, covering his face with one hand. When he recovered, he sat up and turned back to Foulon.

"So what we need is a life support crisis aboard one of these pilgrim transports."

"The *Liahona* has the most people on it, but the *Carthage* is the oldest and creakiest," Tenzin said. "If something were to go wrong, that's the ship that everyone would expect. I took the liberty of doing some quiet scans on it, and it looks like we've got about a hundred and sixty life signs aboard. Some of those might be dogs or cats or tendarii. Mormons love their pets."

"That's true," Foulon agreed. "But that's irrelevant, because the Latter Day Saints aren't going to let themselves be rescued without their animals, either. A large dog takes up as many life-support resources as a human child."

"I love the idea of overrunning the *Talon* with animals. Mormons and animals!" he grinned. "You'd think Captain Taylor was our enemy or something."

Foulon's face jerked in an attempted failed smile.

"Okay, how do we 86 the *Carthage*, then?"

"I've got an idea," Tenzin said. "Not one thing, but three. None of these system failures alone would necessitate an evacuation, but the confluence of them—"

"It's just rotten fucking luck, isn't it, XO?" Danny grinned.

Foulon managed an actual smile.

"Rotten fucking luck, sir."

Lieutenant Commander Avery Harrak stood at attention as Admiral Tal stepped into the room. So did everyone under his command.

"As you were," Tal said.

The Admiral was clear-eyed and grave. He also exuded strength and compassion in equal measure, a quality that confused Harrak. He aspired to be a good leader—no, a great leader. In the moment, he recognized that the balance he saw in Tal was unusual and had made him who he was. He instantly wanted to claim that quality for himself, but didn't know how. Was it something you could turn on, like a light? Or was it something you had to cultivate by arcane means? He hoped it was the former, but feared it was the latter.

Then it occurred to him that it might be innate—something Tal was born with, like his kinky gray hair, or the dark brown of his skin, none of which Harrak possessed, nor ever would.

He saw his crew relax, stand at parade rest. "Permission to sit, sir," Harrak asked.

"Granted, Lieutenant Commander."

"All right, sit, you grunts." Harrak was relieved to see the curl of a smile on Tal's lips.

"You're no doubt wondering why I called for this briefing with you," Tal said. Instantly, he began to pace, his hands behind his back, his head low. Harrak could see he was choosing his words carefully. "There are forty-seven specialized units aboard Sol Station at present, from various branches of the armed forces. I haven't asked for a briefing with forty-six of them…only with you."

Tal paused, and Harrak could see he was letting this sink in. Harrak looked at his soldiers. There were eight of them. A couple were wide-eyed, but most were serious and resolute.

"I'm not going to sugar-coat this. I'm sending you on as dangerous a mission as I have ever ordered. I cherish and value every one of your lives. You are my responsibility, you are my charges, and because we are navy, you are my brothers and sisters. I would trade my own life for any one of yours, and I would not hesitate, not even for a second."

Tal had stopped pacing and was looking each of them in the eye now. Harrak did not doubt his words.

"You've trained for service above and beyond. You've practiced and prepared and studied so that when we need people we can trust in the most dangerous situations to face humankind, you are there to rush in and do the fucking work."

Harrak saw his people nod. Tal understood them. He *got* them—their reason for being.

"We need you now." Tal paused and once more made eye contact with every soldier in the room. "I don't know how your immediate superiors are presenting the facts, but the media is spinning positive to keep people from panicking…too much. But here's the unvarnished truth. We're getting our asses handed to us. And nothing we've tried has worked. And we're running out of options. We need a miracle, and you're it."

Tal started pacing again. Harrak's team seemed frozen in their camo uniforms—a solid block of blue and gray, unmoving and unmovable.

Tal looked up, accessing his neural, and a moment later a 3D hologram of a Prox transport vessel floated in the air to one side of him. "This is the lead Prox ship. As far as we can tell, the other two are identical. As you may or may not know, the Prox do not travel on the inside of their ships. They cling to the outside…somehow."

Harrak's mouth dropped open. This was new information for him and for his crew. He heard the buzzing of surprised comments, and he barked, "Silence!" He turned to Tal. "Sorry, sir."

Tal nodded. "We make allowances for astonishment, Lieutenant Commander."

"Yes sir. Thank you, sir." Harrak turned and glared at his team.

No one made another sound. All eyes were on the Admiral. Harrak turned slowly to his commander. "Please, sir, continue."

Tal nodded. "Each ship is…massive. They carry about 500,000 Prox soldiers. Each one."

Harrak himself would have whistled at this in a less formal environment. He was grateful that his soldiers controlled the urge.

"But the ships *do have* an inside," Tal said. "We can't see past their shields, so we can't get a reading on life signs. We don't know how many of them there are, or of what species. The Prox are metallic, so we don't know if they're organic or manufactured, or…some combination of the two. We only know that nothing we have can kill them in sufficient numbers to make any difference at all. We also know that their ships are so well armored and shielded that nothing we've thrown at them—including 50-megaton fission torpedoes—seems to have given them so much as a scratch."

"What do you need from us, sir?" Harrak asked.

"We're defenseless against their limbs, so we need to cut off their heads."

Harrak didn't understand, and he could see that his men didn't, either. But instead of asking for an explanation, he bit his tongue and waited for Tal to elaborate.

"We need you to board their ships. Then we need you to take out whatever or whoever is commanding these demons."

Harrak saw his team nodding. Tal reached for a chair and placed it in front of them. He straddled it, resting his arms on its back. Tal's voice softened. "I'm not going to pretend this isn't a suicide mission." Suddenly, he was not the firm, invincible commander, but a vulnerable fellow soldier. Harrak resisted the urge to take notes. "It probably is. We don't know what you'll find once you board those ships. We don't know what kind of internal defenses they'll have. We don't know what kind of firepower you'll face. We only know we're sending three of you into each ship with absolutely no idea what you're up against. We don't have any intel whatsoever as to the biology of their commanders. We don't know anything about their weaponry. Hell, we don't even have a floor plan for you to study. We've only got this." He held up a small black box with a neural interface logo on it.

No one asked what it was. They would wait. Harrak felt pride for his team welling up in his chest.

"Every ship has an airlock. Every airlock is the same. Airlocks are simple, they're reliable, and they're remarkably uniform from one species to another. This"—he turned the black box in his fingers—"will jam every signal going to and from an airlock and will override any command related to them. There is no airlock known to the Authority that this little gizmo won't open. Think of it as a master key."

Harrak cleared his throat. "Question, Admiral."

"Yes?"

"You don't know for sure that this will open the airlock on the Prox ships, do you?"

Tal shook his head, but his expression did not change. "No, son. No, we don't. But it's the best shot we can give you." He looked them all in the eye again. "And *you*...you're the best shot we've got."

CHAPTER EIGHT

Jeff didn't know what to expect. The dread lurking in the back of his mind was that it would be emasculating. Instead, it was more like shoving twice as much stuff into a suitcase as ought to fit.

He calmed and centered himself, and then he consented. That was all Tomás needed, apparently, because suddenly there were another set of memories, another thinking, feeling sentience filling his interior space.

It was an odd feeling, Jeff acknowledged, but not painful or uncomfortable, or even particularly violating. Just…crowded. *I feel like I'm going to step on your feet*, Jeff thought. *I have no personal space*.

That is very true indeed, Tomás acknowledged. *But allow me to get you there, and I'll rectify the situation quickly*.

Jeff didn't answer, as he supposed Tomás could read his assent the same way Tomás' intentions were laid bare before him. If he harbored any doubts about the little man's motivations or history or account of things, they had all dissipated in an instant once his memories and thoughts were as available as Jeff's own. Jeff relaxed. This was going to be okay. Maybe not the human race, maybe not the universe, but this little experiment, this invasion of his space…it was okay.

He felt Tomás navigate to what felt like the forefront, to his volition. His brain substituted the symbolic image of him handing over the reins of a horse to the little man for whatever was really happening. He understood enough psychology not to question this or wonder at it too much, but he did notice it, and it seemed marvelously apt.

Then they were rushing into the All, at a much more magnificent velocity than Jeff was accustomed to. He reminded himself to pay attention. He watched as Tomás slipped between. He saw what seemed like limitless ribbons of reality, each indistinguishable from the others at their height. No, not indistinguishable, he realized. They had feeling tones. The one they were in felt familiar but cold. And there was a dead space where, he realized, his own universe should have been.

A rush of shame and recrimination rolled over him, and he fought to master himself and not let it carry him away. *Stay present,* he told himself, and felt the calm, reassuring presence of Tomás supporting him.

He struggled with vertigo as they were suspended, it seemed, above all possible worlds—seemingly worlds without end. Then, he felt a sudden rush as they plunged down once more, and he felt the clingy enmeshment with matter tug at him. It occurred to him that this sensation would be much stronger if they had been moving their bodies, but the effect was still perceptible.

And then he and Tomás, two natures united in one mind, were moving through a jungle much like Jeff had experienced on his own planet in his own universe. They were traveling fast, faster than embodied humans can travel, unimpeded by obstacles or entropy.

Before long, he felt Tomás hesitate, then stop. They were still in the thick of the jungle, but as Jeff looked around, he could make out flashes of gray concrete peeking through the green in one direction.

Ulim? he asked in his mind.

Si, Tomás answered, just as silently. *Los Dumientes have slept in this place for a thousand years.*

Moving around the structure, Jeff noted how unremarkable it was. In his own world, the architecture would have been labeled "brutalist." It was low, squat, wide, built for minimalist endurance. It yielded not an inch to aesthetic concerns or beauty. Although he did not consider himself an expert in such things, Jeff suspected it may easily have been the ugliest building he had ever laid eyes on.

Are we going in? Jeff asked.

The answer came from Tomás in a rush of images and reasoning, but not in words so much. He just knew that going inside now would be pushing their luck. Right now, they were probably flying beneath the Ulim's radar. An inside breach would change all of that. Instead, he saw something else—what must have been Tomás' memories of the place, from an earlier venture inside.

A cascade of images rushed past him. Jeff caught the general layout of the building's interior. He was shocked at how quickly he could assimilate the information. It occurred to him that after experiencing this rush of memories, if he had to navigate inside the building, he could.

But it was the rest of the memories that truly arrested him. Projected on his mind's eye was an ethereal scene: thousands of human bodies dangling in free space, each suspended from the high ceiling by black bio-transport lines that must have been carrying electricity, blood, data, waste, and vital fluids. A soft blue light suffused the whole scene with an eerie balance of power and weakness in equal measure. A sense of dread rose up in Jeff's brain, threatening to paralyze him, to smother his will.

It is enough, Tomás' voice said in his head. *Time to return*. A beat later, Tomás added, *You steer*.

If Jeff could have smiled, he would have, despite the horror still resonating in his memory. With a final look around at the jungle and the concrete, he willed himself into the All, made contact with the sun, then went through. Suspended above the worlds, he felt for the one they had just come from. Intellectually, he knew it was String 311, but that was an arbitrary designation, like street names or the imaginary borders of nations. The feeling of it, however, was real. It told him something true about the kind of place it was—something that could not be easily articulated. *Like emotions*, he realized.

He entered it, and his eyes snapped open in his own body.

He saw Tomás' round, brown face turn up in a smile, saw his eyes open.

"Now you know how to go *between*," Tomás said.

"Yes," Jeff said.

"Do you think you could do it again?"

"No problem."

"Do you think you can do it alone?"

"No problem."

"What do you think we should do now?"

"Kick some Ulim ass."

EMMA WAS grateful that she'd been sent back to school. Her arms had gotten a lot stronger with practice, but the long shifts on the counting floor were still brutally painful, and she was still haunted by the image of the Alverian arm lying on the ground.

Even better, she was now learning Alverian written notation for both language and mathematics. Instead of standing the entire time she was allowed to sit on one of their narrow seats at a low desk with a touch screen built into it. She'd gotten used to the bicycle style seats, after developing what she thought of as *a taint of steel.*

Once again, she struggled with the language. There seemed to be no logical correlation between the gesture for any given idea and the ideograms used to convey the same idea in print. Most of them were an arrangement of four thin triangles, sometimes vaguely reminiscent of the corresponding four-armed gesture. But more often than not, they appeared to be just a random geometrical scattering.

Mathematical notation was coming much more easily; math was universal. Each base four digit was arranged in familiar columns, with specialized marks for operators. The teacher seemed to be impressed when Emma solved a geometric proof almost as fast as it was presented. The teacher paused when she did the same thing with a differential calculus equation. Emma smiled when the teacher presented the class with a linear multidimensional state-space model.

The other students reacted with surprise and confusion. Emma just put her head down for a moment, and after a bit of calculation, returned the solution.

"[Only two arms, not one of us], I am aware you are fitted with a neural interface device. I'm sure you are aware that its use is forbidden in this classroom."

Emma stood. "Of course I am aware, and I would never cheat at something as important as this," she signed frantically, betraying her frustration. "I have told you people a million times, I am a scientist. This math," she tapped the touch screen on her desk, "is my…" The language gulf failed her. She thought *bread and butter,* but there was no Alverian equivalent. "It's what I do. And this…" again she tapped the screen, "this is easy."

The teacher stood very erect, and Emma couldn't tell if she was angry, offended, or impressed. "Please come with me" was all she signed. Then, to the rest of the class, "Continue with your studies."

"I hope I didn't offend…" Emma signed as she followed the teacher down the tunnel, but the teacher had her back turned—yet another problem with a gestural language.

They seemed to be walking toward the counting chamber, but at the last moment, they made a left turn and went up a steep staircase. The teacher led Emma into the high room with the huge windows that she had seen from the floor of the counting chambers. The teacher stood silently, waiting to be acknowledged by the dozen or so Alverians in the room. All were wearing a red band of fabric around their upper leg segments. As they waited, Emma looked out the window. The counting chamber was even larger than she thought it was when she was on the floor. She watched the calculations flowing and shimmering as the counters waved their arms, passing numbers, performing operations, weaving math like a living tapestry. She could see patterns; each position on the floor was a component of a larger equation.

Finally, one of the red-banded Alverians waved the teacher over. They began to talk, but Emma wasn't able to follow much of it, they were talking very fast and using vocabulary that she didn't know. At one point, the red-banded one got the attention of several of her counterparts, and drew them into the conversation as well. Emma saw her "name" used several times, and the words for language, mathematics, and science, but little else made sense.

One of the red bands broke out of the group and left the room in a hurry. The teacher stepped to Emma. "You will wait here. They will speak with you soon." She started towards the door.

"Wait!" Emma said aloud, startling everyone in the room. Then she signed, "Where are you going? What is happening?"

"We will have a new task for you," she replied. "You will understand soon. Please wait." Then she left the room.

None of the others were paying attention to her, but were talking frantically among themselves. Emma returned to her vigil at the window. Below her, the calculation continued, and she started piecing together the equations. The shifting numbers were difficult to follow, but their relationships remained constant. One number was being multiplied by the number next to it. The product was being divided by another number which was squared. That number was being multiplied by another number which never changed, a constant. She suddenly recognized the equation, which she knew intimately.

"Gravity! It's Newton's law!" she whispered to herself. But they were plugging negative numbers into it, and the result was being fed into another part of the overall equation.

She turned to face the red bands and shouted in English, "What the hell are you guys working on?"

Jo FELT a squish underneath her boot. She stopped and looked down, but the smell hit her before the sight of it did. "Why is there dog shit in the corridor?" she yelled. But it was rhetorical, and despite the fact that there were plenty of crew around, no one answered her.

Not only were there plenty of crew, but they were in the minority. Every section of her ship was packed with slim, healthy, cheerful people. So much so that it made Jo want to punch one of them. It didn't matter who.

Not only were they overrun by wholesome, happy people, but with animals as well. Dogs mostly, but cats and tendarii, too. Jo had seen a ferret, a sulaman, and an alpaca on the deck below.

"Sorry about that," one of the civilians said as he dove for her boot with a poly bag. "I'll get some cleaner to tend to that."

"See that you do," Jo said, but regretted her testiness as soon as she'd said it. Jo removed her boots and carried them so as not to track the shit further through the halls.

The *Carthage* was a pilgrim transport ship, on its regular run bringing Latter-Day Saints to the New Deseret Temple complex and resort. It had suffered multiple systems failures all at the same time. Jo had been in crisis mode for the past twelve hours, just trying to get all the sentient creatures off the *Carthage* in time. Her staff were now trying to relocate them on other ships to lessen the overcrowded conditions aboard the *Talon*.

She finally made it to the bridge and her shoulders sank as the door slid shut behind her. "Sanctuary," she said out loud. Marcia Chi turned and covered her mouth to stifle a laugh and Commander Nira smiled slightly, vacating the command chair.

Jo felt like running for the isolation of her ready room, but she resisted that urge. Instead, she deposited her boots beside the door and tossed her chin in Tash Liebert's direction. "Mr. Liebert, get someone up here to launder my boots and to bring me a fresh pair, size 10D."

"Right away sir."

"I can take those to the laundry on my way out, Captain," Nira offered.

"Oh. That's very kind of you, Commander. Thank you."

"Not a problem." Nira seemed to have been in the middle of running a report or something because she didn't immediately leave the bridge, but instead moved to the XO's station.

Jo went straight to the wall replicator and ordered a Mayan hot chocolate. Then she went to her command chair. She blew on the cocoa and sighed. "This has been one hell of a run."

"It's been a little *too* eventful, if you ask me, sir," Nira said.

Jo cocked her head at her number one. "What do you mean?"

Nira checked one more figure on a data pad, then pushed it away. She met the captain's eyes. "I mean I'm suspicious about the confluence of accidents."

"You mean too many of them in too short a time?" Jo asked.

"Exactly."

It wasn't like Jo hadn't had a similar thought. She had dismissed it, though, partly due to triage, and partly because she simply didn't have enough evidence to support such a theory. She wasn't the sort to chase after ghosts.

"There's something to be said for that," Shell Ditka added. Jo turned toward her spiky-haired security chief. "We've had three 'emergency' incidents thus far on this run, and they've all happened at astonishingly regular chronological intervals."

Jo scowled and took a sip of her cocoa. "Lay it out for me."

Ditka got up and started pacing, eyes rolling back in her head gathering data as she spoke. "Thirty-six hours ago, the fuel tubing on the *Craft Angel* started pumping oxetene hydrochloride into space, forcing us to tow her into port." She quickly changed the angle of her chin and turned.

"Twenty-four hours ago," Ditka continued, "the *Carthage* had a series of mishaps that caused its life-support system to fail."

Jo noticed that Nira was looking a little too intensely at Ditka. Would she have to give them the whole workplace romance talk? She hoped not.

"Twelve hours ago, *Industrial Steel and Fiber Conglomerate Transport Number 92* mysteriously lost their micrometeoroid protection, resulting in fifteen pinprick breaches in both primary and secondary hulls, forcing us to extend our shields to envelop them."

"It's been a shitty couple of days," Jo nodded.

"Too shitty," Nira said.

"I concur," Ditka added.

"Sir, begging your pardon," Liebert's voice interjected, high-pitched and talking fast. "Engineering reports they've noticed a visual distress signal off our port stern."

"On screen," Jo said, returning her bare feet to the floor.

The screen flickered and revealed a brilliant field of stars, one of which was blinking.

"It's standard Morse Code. SOS, sir," Liebert noted.

Jo nodded. Three short bursts of light and three long, followed again by three short. A moment later, the cycle started again. "What ship is closest to the position of that signal?" Jo asked.

Chi had the flight plan closest to hand. "That would be the *Augmented Bovine*, sir."

"Hail her," Jo said.

"Not responding to hails, sir."

Jo pursed her lips and stared at the signal. Three short, three long, three short.

"Tell me about her," Jo commanded.

Nira already had the manifest up on her neural. "Commercial vessel, enhanced dairy products, although they auction off their unused capacity to other vendors. This run they're carrying 26,000 liters of vita-milk in fourteen flavors, and six varieties of advanced probiotic yogurt cultures for the local dairies. Fully half of their stock is gourmet cheeses from all over. Pricy stuff. But they're also carrying electronics, tanning chemicals, hydroponic supplies, and toys."

"Crew complement?"

"Seven, including the captain's noncommissioned spouse."

"And what does that person do?"

"Sound collage artist, according to the manifest."

"God, I hate that noise," Jo said, shuddering. "What do our scans show?"

Ditka was on it. "Initial scans are inconclusive, but…"

"But what?"

"There's a pocket of CO2 near them, sir. And there's no reason for that to be there."

"That can't be good." Jo said. "So, they're probably leaking from their air reclamation units, and at the same time their communications facilities are mysteriously offline. All of them."

"Yes sir," Ditka said. Jo turned toward communications. "Mr.

Liebert, brief Ocampa and Dixon. Let's get a shuttle over there to assess the situation."

"Yes sir."

"I'm beginning to distrust the whole coincidence thing," Jo said.

"Yes sir," Ditka said again.

"These things aren't just happening," Jo reasoned out loud. "Someone is *making* these things happen. So who and why?"

"Ah…I might have something, sir," Nira said. Her eyes rolled up and rushed back and forth as she read.

"Make me proud, Number One," Jo said.

"If these…incidents…began thirty-six hours ago, what happened thirty-six hours ago that changed?"

Jo narrowed one eye, waiting for the answer. She set her empty cup into the holder on her command chair.

"Checking thirty-seven hours, checking thirty-eight, checking thirty-nine, checking…bingo."

"What?" Jo asked, almost leaping out of her chair.

"Forty hours ago, a ship joined up with us, the *Spruce and Bonnet*. She's a crown-registered supply transport vessel, according to her manifest."

"Crown? That's a British Colony ship then?"

"Yes sir—under contract with the East Anglia Company."

"Scan her," Jo said.

"Wait," Ditka held her hand up.

Jo didn't take offense. Instead, she inclined her head. "What is it, Mr. Ditka?"

"If we scan them, they'll know we're scanning them. If it's them, best if they don't know we suspect them."

Jo nodded. "So how do we test this little theory of ours?"

Nira stood and stepped toward the main view screen. "Computer, show relative positions for all caravan ships for the past forty hours, one thousand times normal speed."

Everyone's eyes flitted back and forth as they watched the computer sketch of the ships' positions in rapid replay. When the replay was finished, Nira turned back to her captain. She appeared to be chewing on her lip.

"There's no proximity," Chi noted.

"There don't appear to be any interactions between the new ship and the others," Ditka growled, clearly not liking the turn their investigation was taking.

Jo wondered if they were chasing the wrong rabbit.

"Line of sight," Nira said.

Everyone looked at her. "Say more," Jo commanded.

"The *Spruce and Bonnet* was within line of sight of every ship that developed problems. Watch it again." She replayed the recreation, pausing every now and then to point out the direct path through space between the *Spruce and Bonnet* and every affected ship. "It's not proximity, or even interaction. It's line-of-sight attack."

"But no one reported—or even noticed—an attack," Jo said.

"And that accounts for the length of time between attacks," Nira said. "My guess is that they're using low-power, low impact means, probably below detectable scan thresholds."

"Holy crap," Jo said aloud. Jeff was right about Nira. She was gold.

"Which leaves us with one question—what do we do about it?"

"Here's my plan…" Nira said, smiling. She was clearly relishing the moment.

THE BOTTOM of the Prox ship loomed above them like a black hole. The light of stars seemed to disappear within it, and Harrak felt as if they were ascending into the Void, into nothingness, into non-being.

And perhaps we are, he thought. His fingers tightened around his blaster as he considered the danger of the mission. He glanced over at his men; his responsibility for them, his affection for them nearly overwhelmed him.

They were coming in 3X dark—no light, no propulsion, no electronics. A field dampener cloaked their life signs and any ambient radiation from the tiny ship's navigational processor. Unless the Prox were to make direct visual contact with them—unlikely, since the bulk of their ship eclipsed all the available light—no one would see them.

There was the problem of shields, of course. Most ships had navigational shielding and weapons shielding—two completely different systems used to ward off different kinds of threats. The Prox were not in C-space, so second-order navigational shields were not in play. First-order, sure, but those were not as sensitive. Their weapons shielding would be at full strength, but they reacted only to energy.

You're assuming that the Prox shield system is like ours, Harrak reminded himself. He shoved the thought aside, however, because such speculations weren't his job. Other, smarter brains aboard Sol Station had assessed this very problem and had judged it no problem. Who was he to second-guess that?

What he knew, and the only thing he knew, was that he was speeding toward the unknown, toward the dark.

Montalbano and Pastore were checking their equipment—no searching reflections for these two. That made Harrak smile. His mind flashed on their other two units, even now ascending from beneath up toward the second and third Prox ships.

Helmets, Harrak signed. He wasn't about to speak here. They were careful not even to step too hard, not to let a helmet scrape against a bulkhead. Any sound could betray them. Who knew what kind of eyes and ears these monsters had?

Pastore nodded and fitted on his helmet. He was a hulking giant of a man. Not an ounce of fat on him, though. Just tall and thick and mean—the kind of man he wanted on *his* side in a fight.

Montalbano donned his helmet last. The man was slightly smaller than Harrak himself. But he was quick and smart.

Carefully, Harrak moved to the airlock. The others followed. After the door slid shut behind them, Harrak used his neural to instigate depressurization. Then he made a cut-throat motion, indicating that they should take their neurals off-line.

It was time. Harrak slung his blaster over his shoulder and crouched, ready to spring toward the alien ship. They wouldn't be using the navigation jets built into their space suits, not if they could help it. They'd be using the old-fashioned energy of coiled muscle, sinew, and tendon to propel them to their destination.

Out of the corner of his helmet, he watched Montalbano get into position. It was not exactly the same pose as a runner preparing for a race—they'd be sprinting up, after all, but it was reminiscent of that just the same. Pastore crouched, but as he did so, his blaster caught the edge of the airlock wall, causing a resounding *dungggg* that made every muscle in Harrak's body tense. He moved his head to glare at Pastore and saw him shrink in shame, as much as a man that huge and hulking could shrink.

Then the airlock door burst open, and they took advantage of the rushing air to help propel them toward the alien ship. They pushed off with their legs. Harrak gave it all he could give without throwing himself off course.

It felt exactly as if he were floating into nothing. There were no lights, no stars, no visible structures. Just black, black, black. Harrak closed his eyes. What did it matter?

At first, as they were clearing the airlock, he had felt motion, but now, swallowed up as they were by nothing, he felt like he was floating, motionless, still. He looked down and was comforted by the blanket of stars beneath his feet, so vivid and bright he almost felt like he could walk on them.

But there was metal rushing toward his head. He knew that. He fixed his face once more toward the midnight void and waited for his eyes to adjust.

The ambient light from the stars beneath would serve as their lamps now. It would be enough. Already, Harrak was able to make out their destination—the alien airlock. It wasn't directly above them—they were flying blind, so that kind of accuracy was impossible. But it wasn't far.

Harrak put his hands above his head to absorb the shock of contact. He tensed, not against the inevitable impact, but against whatever possible shielding they didn't know about. They'd been fitted in suits made entirely of poly, specially made to avoid detection. Whatever circuitry they possessed was made of poly superconductors. Harrak braced as he anticipated his collision with the ship—a little too fast, it seemed to him.

But when his gloved hands made contact with the ship, there was no jolt of electricity, no repelling force field. His arms gave, careful not to push back so as not to send him spinning back into space. He rolled, allowing his velocity to be absorbed by the whole surface of his body, and in the meantime, his hand was ready with a carabiner. He found a surface to hook it into and squatted on the hull. Magnetic boots might be detected, so the engineers had adapted mountain climbing gear to keep them in place or maneuver on the ship's surface.

Harrak stood, feeling his line go taught. It would read his motions, even anticipate his intentions, giving and taking up slack as he'd need it until he positioned the next 'biner. He was terrified his men wouldn't find a place to hook in, but they both had. Within seconds, both of his men were standing, awkwardly walking, looking to him for direction.

He pointed at the airlock, and they all turned in that direction. Harrak visually scanned the hull for hook points and discovered, to his great satisfaction, that there were many. In fact, the ship was ridged with tiny ledges, giving the effect of siding or even shingles. *Of course. The Prox need to hold on somehow*, Harrak thought. They hook their little metallic legs underneath these…

The Prox. Surely there were still some clinging to this hull. Harrak glanced around wildly, but he didn't see any. He allowed himself to relax—a bit. They were further off target than he'd hoped.

They all set new carabiners and resumed their trek. One more length of line and they'd be there. Harrak saw motion through the right side of his helmet and jerked in response. Turning his head, he saw a port blast open, releasing a cloud of vapor or smoke or something, then close quickly. *Relax*, he told himself. *It's not a Prox. It's just venting. It's not a Prox.* He repeated this as a mantra until he felt his pulse resume a normal pace. By that time, they were there.

They hooked in again at the airlock, and Harrak crouched, withdrawing the airlock key from his space suit pocket in slow motion. He couldn't access it with his neural, but there were manual controls along one side. The problem was that the fingers of his space suit were large and clumsy and the buttons were subtle and small. It took him a few tries to enter the correct code. But to his great relief, the proper light flashes informed him that it was in the correct mode, and if it was like any other airlock in known space, it would soon be gushing whatever passed for air in that ship and opening a way for them to board.

With rising tension, Harrak watched the light sequence play out from beginning to end. A red light began to flash. *Damn*, he thought. He clumsily started the sequence again. Again, nothing. The doors remained closed.

Harrak looked up at Pastore and Montalbano. Through their helmets he saw their eyes, wide with alarm. And of course, they were looking to him for answers, for orders.

He didn't have a clue. He felt panic leap into his throat and start to twist. He couldn't breathe. He stood and forced himself to take deep, slow breaths. He cleared his mind of everything except that breath—going in, going out. He waited until he felt some semblance of a center return to him.

He felt a tap on his shoulder. He looked up and saw Pastore pointing back the way they had come. *Prox!* he thought, but no. He couldn't see any of the crab-like creatures. Pastore was striding away from them, and Harrak felt he had little choice but to follow. *It's not like I have any ideas*, he thought.

Pastore made a beeline for the vapor vents. *Of course,* Harrak thought. They had to re-hook twice to get there, but soon enough they were crowded around the vent, studying its rhythm. Harrak counted fifteen seconds while the vent remained closed. When it sprang open with a great whoosh of vapor, he counted four seconds until it sealed up again.

Four seconds. It was enough. Just enough. But who knows what they'd find on the other side? What was the vapor? Was it an acid that would disintegrate the poly of their suits? Was it radioactive discharge that would poison them?

So long as it doesn't kill us immediately, I'll take it, he thought. He was, after all, a soldier. Dying was what soldiers did.

The vent was an oval, about three meters across lengthwise and two meters wide. At the far end of its long side it was hinged with a gear a meter tall. It looked solid and formidable. They might be able to mess with the gear, but it would take time and tools they didn't have. They'd do better to try a clean jump when the monster ship's jaws were open.

Harrak was about to signal an order when he saw Pastore crouch, carabiner in hand. Harrak began to wave the abort sign, but it was too late. Pastore launched himself toward the opening, just as a great billow of vapor shot out of it. For a moment, Harrak could not see his man. Harrak thought a quick prayer to whatever cosmic forces might smile on them, but his hopes were quickly dashed.

As the vapor cleared, Harrak saw that Pastore had misjudged his timing. The vent had closed on him, trapping him, especially his legs, near the geared hinge. Vapor continued to spill out, though, because the vent could not seal—it was stuck on Pastore's helmet.

Harrak's mind raced. Pastore was larger than both Montalbano and himself. Even their helmets were smaller. Looking up, Harrak saw that Pastore's helmet had begun to crack. He also saw his man's face contorted with pain.

Harrak bit the side of his cheek and tensed, knowing action was required, but not knowing what to do. Then he caught a flicker of motion beyond Pastore's writhing, trapped body. A Prox soldier scuttled over the horizon of the ship and was coming at them full tilt. Behind it, Harrak saw a host of its brothers, all scuttling toward them on quick, soundless, metal legs. They wielded their pincers, their deadly blades flashing in the distant starlight.

Who knew how many more seconds they had before Pastore's helmet would be crushed and the great jaws of the vent closed again? Harrak knew Montalbano couldn't hear him, but it didn't stop him from shouting, "Jump! Jump!"

CHAPTER NINE

When Jeff opened his eyes, he was back in his body, and more importantly, alone in his body. Tomás instantly stood up and began rummaging in his pack.

"What are you doing?" Jeff asked.

"Making dinner."

"Of course you are." Jeff stepped around behind him, and looking over his shoulder, spied a canteen. "May I?"

Tomás nodded and Jeff screwed the top off, taking a liberal swig.

"What's your plan?" Jeff asked.

Tomás shrugged. "We go in. We find a way to stop them."

"That's not much of a plan."

"I am not a soldier." Tomás smiled sadly. "That's why I need you."

Jeff felt momentarily frozen. Up until that moment, all of his experience with Tomás had been awash with a sheen of mysticism. In his imagination, Tomás was a shaman, hinting at mysteries unseen, teasing him with revelation.

When he'd actually met Tomás, the relationship had changed. Tomás had become a mentor, training him in the use of his gift. That training had itself been a gift—he had traded the sheen of mysticism for the sheen of destiny. There was some great deed that he must perform, and Tomás was the prophet and guide for that gift.

It did not occur to him until this moment that Tomás wanted something—needed something—from him. Jeff felt a sour taste gather in his mouth.

He sat and took another swig. *He needs my military experience,* he thought. *Of course he does. That's why he sought me out. That doesn't make him weak, it makes him smart.* He glanced over at Tomás, as if seeing the little man for the first time.

Tomás appeared to notice. The sad smile returned. "You look *desilusionado*…disappointed," he noted.

"No," Jeff lied, "just…coming to grips with what we're really doing here."

"I am sorry if I am not what you thought I was," Tomás said. "I'll tell you who I think I am. I think I am trying to find a way to save my people. I want them to be able to come out of their caves, to stop hiding, to stop living in fear. I want them to plant and harvest and have *niños* and love their lives again. I want to stop the reign of terror that *Los Durmientes* have held over my people for hundreds of years." He put down a poly bag full of tortillas and wiped his nose on his sleeve. "Of all my people, I am the only one with this gift. I must do something. I know how to do many things, but…I do not know how to fight." He nodded at the sound of his own words. He looked up and met Jeff's eye. "Does that make me *malo*? A bad person?"

Jeff handed the canteen back to him. He shook his head. "No. It just makes me an idiot. I just…I'm still piecing it all together." He stood up and started pacing. "Look, Tomás, I'm not good at people skills. I'm a good commander, and I take orders well, but I'm not so good at…let us say *reciprocal* relationships."

Tomás cocked his head.

"Never mind. I guess what I'm saying is, I'll do better with a division of labor, where I know what I'm in charge of and I know what you're in charge of."

"Nobody is in charge of anything," Tomás said, shrugging.

"They are if we say they are," Jeff countered.

"Like what?"

He started to fit things into categories that made sense to him. "You're intelligence. You know more about the Ulim than I do. I'll look to you for information. Same with research and development around our little…talent. You're my science officer."

"I am not much of a scientist…" Tomás sounded unsure.

"Play along, okay?"

Tomás shrugged.

"I'll be in charge of military strategy. We'll consult, then I'll make a plan. How does that sound?"

"It sounds like a lot of unnecessary nonsense." Tomás gave him a mock-serious look.

Jeff laughed. "Oh my God," he said. "You're right. I'm overthinking this."

"No, I think I understand what you are doing," Tomás said, turning to dinner preparations again. "I think you are putting this into a context where you feel competent so you can grasp it and feel effective. No?"

"I guess I am," Jeff said, putting his hands on his hips.

"That isn't a bad thing. You had to go there, but now you can come back with a new perspective. Something has changed, hasn't it?"

It had. Jeff felt less lost at sea, more able and ready to tackle this problem. "Yeah."

"Good. We must tell ourselves stories to understand the world. This is why we gather around the fire and listen to the adventures of the gods. It tells us who we are. It prepares us for what we have to do. You had to tell yourself a story about yourself and about me. Now you are ready."

Jeff nodded. "You know, you're a wise little shit."

Tomás smirked. "I suspect that even though we went to the same place and saw the same things we noticed very different things. One of the reasons I need you is I need your eyes. I want to know what you saw that I did not."

Jeff nodded.

"So what did you see?"

Jeff kicked at a rock. "I saw a fortress. I'd need to get closer to see what kind of immediate defenses they've got—how do you get the doors to open, for one thing?"

"I can tell you about that."

"Good, because it didn't look to me like we could blast our way in…unless…" His eyes drifted off into the distance. "You know, it would be really good to have that option."

"What option?" Tomás asked.

Jeff looked back down, but ignored the question. "And even though we didn't see any Prox, the place is crawling with them."

"Yes. We know them. But how did you know?"

"There was damage to the foliage consistent with the bodies of their soldier species, for one. Then there were tracks—they were fresh and clearly indicated lateral hexapodal movement. I don't know how many Prox are patrolling the place, but they're there—no doubt providing security. So whatever we do, we'll need to be ready for them."

"I have some ideas about that," Tomás said.

"Good. Hold that thought." Jeff chewed on his lip and continued his pacing. "We'll need to create a diversion large enough that we can slip in without really registering."

Tomás' eyebrows went up. "*Bueno*," he muttered, eyes flashing back and forth as he thought. "That is just what I was hoping for. How do we do that?"

"Easy. We need a starship."

"You have a starship," Tomás pointed out.

"Yes, but if we're both on the ground, there won't be anyone *in* my starship. Besides, my ship has no firepower to speak of. No, we need a warship and a crew. He straightened up and met Tomás' eyes. "We need a captain."

"Where will we get all of that?" Tomás asked.

"You picked me for a reason, right? So leave this to me."

"MR. LEIBERT, please summon the captain of the *Carthage.* Have him meet me in Conference Room Two as soon as he arrives. Mr. Nira, with me."

Jo strode to her ready room with a bounce in her step. She hated playing defense. She hated reacting to things. It made her feel out of control. But now they had just turned the corner. They were playing offense. They were taking control of the situation, and it made her want to slit someone's throat and bathe in their blood, laughing hysterically. Or, she could just have a celebratory beer, maybe compliments of the *Craft Angel*. Still, a girl could dream…

The door slid shut behind Commander Nira, and Jo ordered up that beer. *Who cares where it comes from?* she thought. "Beer, Commander?"

"I'll pass, thank you sir. Uh…" Nira cocked her head. "Should you be drinking on duty, sir?"

"It's just a beer. I won't be sliding under the table, I promise. But you should have seen Captain Telouse. Oh my God. That man would drink his lunch and would return to the bridge as loose as a clown's pockets. And he was still the best battle captain I've ever seen, *especially* after lunch!"

Jo set the beer on the table and sat. Nira was frowning, not looking at her. "Camil, what's wrong?"

"I've been reading the feeds."

"From Sol Station?"

Nira nodded. "Whatever we're doing here…" she waved around. "We're just biding time. If we're not in that fight now, we'll be in it as soon as they've finished wiping the Authority out."

"Are you so sure the Authority isn't going to hand them their asses?"

"The Prox don't have asses, sir. Not that I can tell."

"Everybody has an ass. It's the great equalizer." Jo sipped at her beer. Nira's fear was infectious, though. The Authority's war had been like a pin pricking at the edge of her brain for days now, threatening to unravel her peace of mind—and probably would have, had they not been so distracted lately. "But here's the thing—the Authority has not asked us to help. It would be different if they had. And until they do…"

"We should be preparing. We should be planning…"

"Do you think we aren't?" Jo asked. "Do you honestly think that Admiral Alinto and the RFC brass aren't studying every scrap of feed they can get their hands on, trying to figure out how to beat this enemy, should the Authority fail? Do you think we won't learn from their mistakes?"

Nira looked up at her, then at the floor. "I'm sorry to be so…solipsistic, sir. Of course they are. I'm just…here, so I'm not seeing it."

"Do you think you could do more good there? Advising the brass?"

"I…kind of. Yes sir."

Jo nodded. "I'll talk to the Admiral about it. How's that?"

Nira's mouth fell open. She seemed frozen.

"Commander?" Jo waved her hand at Nira's eyes.

She snapped out of it. "I…that's incredibly gracious of you, sir."

"Like hell." Jo took a swig. "We're military. We're all about putting the right people in the right places to do the most damage. Am I right?"

"I hope you are, sir."

Just then the door slid open. A small man with greasy hair and a rumpled uniform entered. It was a civilian flying corps uniform, but not a corps that Jo recognized. Probably one with its central offices in neutral space. It was the civilian corps that licensed non-military starship officers, and it was exactly what Jo was expecting. What surprised her was not the uniform, but the man.

"I'm, uh…Captain Honig."

"You're a Mormon?"

"Uh…no sir. I just fly the route to Deseret."

"Oh, 'cause—" Jo stopped herself. She was about to say something snide, but thought better of it. She scowled at her beer and pushed it away. "Please take a seat, Captain."

"Of course. Uh…you said this was urgent?"

"It is. Your ship didn't suffer a series of accidents. It was sabotaged. As were a couple of other ships on this run."

"I did have my doubts…" The man had tiny little eyes that creeped Jo out a bit. Those eyes looked away from her as the man thought.

"We have a theory—actually we're pretty certain—about who is responsible for these…attacks. Let's just call them what they are." Jo got up and began to pace, her hands behind her back. It was unconscious, but she felt the shift of power nevertheless. "We have a plan to turn the rats out of their nest, but to do it, we need to impugn your honor. I just thought it was politic to get your permission before we did it."

"Impugn my honor?" The man's eyebrows rose. He looked like he'd been slapped. Well, that was appropriate. He soon would be.

"Yes," Jo said. "We need to board the…suspect ship. To do that we need a cover story. We need to tell the caravan that when the *Carthage*'s cargo was transferred to the *Talon*, we discovered…contraband."

Now the man looked like Jo had just stabbed his sister.

"Contraband? What kind of contraband?"

"I have no idea. It's a fiction. We don't have to say more than that."

"But people will think—"

"Exactly. We want them to think you were up to something illegal. It's just for a day or so. We'll set the record straight. What's more, we'll give you an RFC commendation for your assistance."

"That…I can do without."

The man was right. If he were trying to keep peace with both sides, he did not want a commendation from the RFC in his personal file. He might as well put on a rebel uniform.

"What about a small…reward?" Jo asked, narrowing one eye.

"A reward?" The man's eyebrows shot up and his face brightened. Now she was talking his language.

"Sure. Let's say…10,000 chits."

"Oh...uh…" his eyes were moving back and forth and she could tell he was trying to figure out whether he could hold out for more.

"Don't try my patience, Captain," Jo said, an edge creeping into her voice. "I don't need your permission. I can just wipe your name in shit and toss you to the winds. And when your process server arrives

I'll put a blaster hole in his chest so large you could pass a kitten back and forth."

The brightness fell out of his face, but his eyebrows stayed aloft. Then recognition dawned. "You're Captain Joleen Taylor. *The* Joleen Taylor."

Jo enjoyed watching the penny drop.

"You're the Kali of Aken."

How had he not known who she was? It wasn't like her name was a secret. Suddenly it occurred to her that she was a celebrity now. And nobody expects to meet a celebrity. The captain had assumed it must be a different Jo Taylor, because what are the odds? Jo leaned over the table, loving every moment of this unexpected turn. "I am. And you know what? I eat greasy little captains for breakfast and shit their eyeballs into space."

Captain Honig looked for all the world like a wax replica of himself. He was completely immobile. Jo wasn't sure the man was breathing. She put one hand on the table and leaned down so her nose almost touched his. "So what'll it be, Captain? Shall we treat you as a friend or an enemy?"

It took a few moments for the man to find his tongue. "I…I would like to be your friend."

"I'd like that too," Jo said, straightening up and smiling. It was not an insincere smile, either. After all, they were friends now. "Can I offer you a beer?"

Honig shook his head.

"Too bad. Okay, then, I'm going to say some terrible things about you. But you're not going to take it personally, and you're not going to refute it. You're going to say…what?"

Honig looked at the table top, his tiny black eyes moving back and forth quickly as he thought. "I'm going to say the *Carthage* crew is cooperating fully."

"Excellent!" Jo said. "Text me your account information so we can arrange that reward."

The man brightened. "Yes sir. Right away." He got up, then froze. "Uh, may I go?"

"I wish you would," Jo said, waving toward the door. "We've got a shitload of work to do here."

EMMA LOOKED up as Amberline came into the room. "Thank God you're here!" she shouted and ran to embrace her.

Amberline awkwardly returned the embrace. The mask said, "I was told I was needed as translator."

"That's an understatement! First off, who are these people?"

Amberline tapped her thigh and made the gesture for *science.*

"They are scientists, like me?"

"Exactly."

One of the red-banded scientists approached and began gesturing. Amberline translated for her. "She says that your teacher brought to her attention that you are an Earth scientist of great distinction."

Emma brushed the bangs out of her eyes. "Well, that's relative, of course. But let's just say I know my shit." She waited to see how Amberline translated it.

She just gestured, "Correct."

The scientist gestured her to follow and brought her over to the largest video table she'd seen in the hive. It was completely filled from edge to edge with complex equations that continued past the edges of the table. "Does this make sense to you?"

"Wow," Emma said, taking it in. "This is some serious…" she trailed off as she got lost in the numbers. She tapped one set of equations. "This is a multidimensional transfer function, looks like, uh, eight dimensions… This is a time-dependent Schrödinger equation, uh… stability coefficient, cosmological constant… whoa." She looked up. "You are calculating the distance between two strings."

Amberline translated, and the scientists talked among themselves excitedly.

One of them stepped forward and actually bowed towards Emma. "We are pleased to meet you," she signed. "We knew that there were formidable scientists among the humans, but we never thought we'd get to meet one."

Emma signed back, "The honor is mine."

A second scientist pushed forward. "Your understanding of our work is remarkable, but incomplete."

Emma laughed. "Considering I've been looking at it for two minutes, I'm not surprised!"

Amberline translated, and they all made a quivering gesture with their right claw.

"Is that laughing?" Emma asked.

"Essentially, yes."

Emma smiled and made the same gesture. "Good to know. So, what's the rest of the picture? Is this just theoretical work?"

"Not theoretical."

Emma scratched her head and momentarily wished again for conditioner. "In everything I've ever read, the space between strings should be zero." She made the sign for zero.

The one that appeared to be the lead scientist shook her head and signed "not zero." There was something about her bald head and round eyes that reminded Emma of an old Earth philosopher named Buckminster Fuller. She decided to think of her as Bucky.

Bucky pointed to a region of the equation set, highlighting a couple of key functions.

Emma looked them over.

"Interesting. You've added provisions for uh...a kind of pressure between the strings."

Amberline signed frantically. Bucky signed back, "Correct."

"And if that pressure is strong enough, it fills the space between the strings, pushing them apart."

"Exactly."

Emma looked up, imagining the phenomena. "You'd get a sort of bubble sub-universe. But you'd get some strange interactions where it pressed upon the adjacent strings." She perused the equations; they had indeed noted the interaction in their calculations.

"Yes," Bucky signed, as Amberline vocalized. "And you would

expect the pressure on the two adjacent strings to be equal and symmetrical."

Emma nodded. "Yeah, that makes sense."

"So what do you think it would mean if that were not, in fact, the case?"

"I would think that it would indicate the density of matter in the adjacent strings was not equal."

"Correct. Now what if your observations indicated that the density of matter in one of the adjacent strings was zero?"

She shook her head. "That's not possible. The only way you could have a zero matter string would be..." She stopped suddenly, unable to breathe. "This *isn't* theoretical, is it? You've measured this."

"We have."

"And this bubble universe you've described. It's real."

"It is."

"Show me."

The Alverians huddled up and began signing frenetically. They clearly didn't agree about something. One of them just signed "No!" over and over, and then stormed out of the room. They glanced over at Emma. They apparently thought she didn't know their language at all, because they made no effort to conceal their words.

"How can we trust her? She's not one of us."

"She *is* one of us, she's a being of science."

"There is too much at stake."

"We have to do something."

"Even if she can be trusted, what could she do about it?"

"Maybe nothing, but we have to try.

"The council should decide."

On that point they seemed to agree. Bucky broke from the huddle and came forward again.

"We must discuss this with our leaders," she signed, and again Amberline translated. "We are dealing with matters too important for mistakes."

Emma nodded. "I understand."

"We will send for you when we have an answer." Bucky gestured a farewell.

Amberline gestured for Emma to follow and left the room. "Are you hungry?" Emma asked as they walked down the stairs.

"I had just arrived when they sent for me and I am very hungry."

"Uh, I'll sit with you, but I don't know if I can eat right now." Her head was spinning. "Did you understand any of that?"

"I understood the words, but not many of the ideas. I am not a scientist or a mathematician. I serve the hive differently."

"Of course."

"Whatever it is," Amberline said as they entered the common chamber and moved towards the cafeteria, "they were very concerned about it all. It must be very important."

"Yeah," Emma said solemnly, then fell silent. *Maybe to me as well.*

THE LID of the venting port was wedged open like a clamshell, threatening to crush the pearl of Pastore's helmet at any moment. Montalbano launched himself at the tiny wedge of an opening. Harrak watched as if it were in slow motion as the smaller man acrobatically positioned his body to slide through with the minimum amount of contact. Only his helmet scraped the lip of the vent.

Once he saw that Montalbano was going to make it, Harrak followed. He jumped, felt the nauseating vertigo of weightlessness, then promptly banged his knee on the lip of the vent. He allowed himself a yell—after all, who would hear it? But as soon as the red flash of pain subsided, he was subsumed in steam or smoke or something. He could see nothing.

In his mind's eye, though, he watched the Prox soldier coming closer. *Damned if they're going to get Pastore, whether he's dead or not,* he thought. He searched for a purchase point and then felt around for Pastore's suit. He found the big man's arm and pulled. He put both feet against the side of the vent, his buttocks hugging a small lip about 20 centimeters wide. He pulled with everything in him. He couldn't see

Montalbano, and had no idea what had happened to him. He needed the help right now. *Dammit, where is he?*

There was a catch, and suddenly Pastore was tumbling inward. Harrak almost lost his balance and clutched at the little lip he was sitting on. Pastore fell inward just as the smoke cleared.

Harrak's stomach lurched as the vapor cleared beneath him, revealing giant rotating blades, spinning at high velocity. Duct fans and blood spatter were all he could see. He leaned forward, hoping against hope to see that Montalbano had found a way to save himself. Harrak almost lost his balance again and hugged the wall of the vent for safety.

His heart was pounding in his chest, in his head, in his ears. The vent had sealed now that Pastore's body was no longer propping it open, but the vapor was beginning to accumulate again, too. Suddenly the lid of the vent flew open, and precariously balancing on a ledge too small to hold him, poised above the certain death of the vent fans, Harrak found himself staring into the stalked eyes of the soldier Prox.

He remembered that his blaster was hanging from his shoulder, but he wasn't quick enough. The alien jabbed its claw into the vent and the sharp metallic tip of it pierced Harrak's suit. He felt an ache in his chest, followed by a cold that seemed to creep downward toward his gut. He pushed the tip out with his hands, and nearly tumbled. Then the vent door was closing again and the Prox snatched its claw back just in time to avoid being crushed.

Fifteen seconds, Harrak thought. I've got fifteen seconds before that vent opens again. The only light he could see was coming from behind the fans. He tried not to look down at them, not only to stop the vertigo, but so his eyes could adjust and, hopefully, see another way out.

He saw another lip of sorts, although it was perhaps simply a design element…or almost anything else. In the dark, and from his angle, it was hard to tell what it was. But it was *something*. Whatever it was, it lay halfway between himself and the fans.

He estimated it was about six meters down to the fans. He tried not to look at the macabre pattern made by his friends' blood on the walls.

He edged himself around to get a better look at the…whatever it was. And then he ran out of time.

From the shudder of the metal that held him he realized the vent was opening a split second before the gap appeared. He breathed a quick prayer, and launched himself toward whatever it was on the far wall side that broke the monotony of the cylindrical walls, just barely ducking the frenzied stabs of the Prox's claw.

Free falling, so slow it seemed to tease him, he beat back the image of the great circling blades snapping through his space suit, rendering his life support pack a useless scrap of mangled poly and shredding his body's meat into tiny slivers of gore.

He realized with horror he had misjudged the leap. He twisted in free space, reaching for the…whatever it was…but he saw with a sinking feeling in his gut that he was going to miss it. He screamed into his helmet and punched out with his gloved hand.

CHAPTER TEN

"Sir, I've got a message from the *Talon* in the queue—general broadcast announcement to the whole caravan."

"Let's hear it," Danny said. He narrowed his eyes and looked over at his XO. Foulon smiled weakly, but nodded firmly. Danny nodded back and turned his attention to the screen.

His stomach gurgled. They'd been so busy with their sabotages that he'd forgotten to eat. The first rule of combat was to take care of your body, and he'd let it go. *Ah well,* he thought. *I've never been as disciplined as some.* He instantly thought of Jeff. He instantly regretted it.

The image of Captain Joleen Taylor filled the screen, looking as hot in her forties as she ever had in her twenties. The uniform fit her frame snugly, expertly, accentuating every enticing curve. Despite himself, his loins stirred, and his eyes looked momentarily sad.

"Attention all Captains traveling in this Deseret-bound caravan. This is Captain Joleen Taylor. As you are probably well aware, this particular passage has had more than its share of...inconveniences." Danny watched her shoulders sag and a sad smile form at one side of her mouth. She shook her head. "I'd say there's never a dull moment in space, but I'm sure you all know differently." Danny heard a couple of chuckles around the bridge. She had gained some leadership skills since he'd seen her last, he had to give her that.

"Unfortunately, there have been some troubling developments that will require your attention and cooperation. I'm sorry to say that this cooperation is necessary, not optional. I hate to invoke your transport contract, but...well, that's how serious it is."

She looked down, apparently regretting the news, or perhaps dreading her next statement.

"She can't see us—right, Mr. Lo?" Danny asked.

"Oh, no sir. I'd never activate the camera without your permission. This is a view-only broadcast. One way."

"Just checking." Danny turned back to the screen.

Jo cleared her throat and looked back at the camera. "I don't want the rumor mill to spin wild tales, so I'm just going to tell it to you all straight. We are all captains, after all, and worthy of our rank and respect. Sixteen hours ago, the *Carthage* suffered multiple systems failures. Unlike many of our other ships, it was not repairable or salvageable, and we had to evacuate her crew, passengers...*pets*"—she made a face—"...and cargo to the *Talon*. Everyone is safe, but...I am sorry to report that we discovered contraband among her cargo. Serious contraband that we suspect was intended for one of the Fundamentalist LDS separatist terrorist organizations on Deseret."

"Holy shit," Navigator Galli said aloud.

"Just our luck," Foulon breathed. "Damn."

"Why, what does it matter?" Lo asked him.

"Wait for it," Foulon said.

Ernst was right, Danny knew. He felt a sinking in his empty stomach, and it wasn't for lack of food.

"I will require a private, face-to-face meeting with the captain of each ship. You'll be hearing from our communicator, Mr. Leibert, soon to arrange shuttle transport and a schedule. After our interview, prepare to be boarded and searched. When you come, make sure you bring all cargo and passenger manifests. If you like, you may send those by data packet anytime between now and your interview."

She looked down again, her face grave. "I'm sorry for the inconvenience, and we'll try to be as expeditious as possible. Thank you for your cooperation and support."

The screen flickered and was replaced with the RFC insignia.

"Well, shit," Danny said. "What were the odds of that contraband? I mean…jeez. Mormons, right?" He looked at Foulon.

"Orders, Captain?" Foulon did not react to the insult.

"Incoming message from the *Talon*, sir," Lo said.

"That was fast," Foulon said.

"Well, it's just a scheduling grid. Two of them, actually. One for the interview, and…." his fingers tapped at his pad, "…one for the search. They have suggested times for both. Captain Taylor would like to see you at 1400 hours."

"Today?"

"Yes, today."

That was only two hours hence.

"Begging your pardon, sir, but Captain Taylor doesn't know my face," Foulon said. "She only knows the name Captain Perry Byrd. It doesn't have to be you who goes over."

Danny held one finger up in Foulon's direction. He nodded. "That's good thinking, Number One." He swung his chair back toward Lo. "When do they want to board us?"

"Uh…tomorrow, 0800."

"That can't happen," Galli said.

She was right, of course. They could disguise the outside of the ship, but one step past the airlock and it would be screamingly obvious that this was a war vessel, not a culinary transport. Danny wanted to say, "No shit," but bit his tongue. He didn't need to alienate his A-crew right now.

Danny stood, a plan forming in his mind. "Mr. Foulon, from now on, you are Captain Perry Byrd."

Foulon nodded once. "Yes sir."

"You are also acting captain of this vessel in my absence."

"Absence, sir?" Foulon's eyebrows rose. He looked concerned.

"Yes, Number One. You're going to meet with Captain Taylor. You're going to assure her of our full cooperation. Then, at 0750, you're going to jump into C-space and head back toward Authority space. You're finally going to get your wish. You're going to rejoin the fight against…whatever is threatening Sol Station and Earth."

"And where will you be, sir?" Foulon asked.

"I…well, I still have a score to settle." He smiled grimly. "Don't I?"

HARRAK CAUGHT the lip of something with one finger of his gloved space suit. Whatever it was, it was set into the smooth wall of the venting tube. In the dim light he couldn't make out what he had caught. He pulled with his finger and was grateful that in the relative weightlessness of his environment, it wasn't hard to counteract inertia. He began to float toward…it. With overwhelming relief he saw that the break in the wall was, in fact, a hatch. A standard, no-nonsense industrial service hatch, no doubt placed here to access and repair the blades and perhaps even the vent itself.

From this angle, Harrak could see tiny ridges all the way up, invisible from the other direction. Ridges no doubt used by the Prox as footholds on the otherwise smooth surface of the tube. They were too small to be of any use to him—not even the finger of his space suit would fit into one. He might be able to wedge a single-axle climbing cam in one…but that was an experiment for another time.

He clutched at a recessed disk set into the hatch. *How does this work?* he thought. At least he could hold on to the damn thing and not fall while he figured it out. He wished there were enough lip for him to sit on, or at least gain purchase for his feet, but that was perhaps asking too much. He hung from the disk, exploring its contours with the numb fingers of his gloved hand.

He wished he had the advantage of his nerves, his skin, the tips of his fingers. He had never truly appreciated his skin as an organ of perception—not until this moment. He pulled at the disk but nothing happened. He tried to twist it, but to no avail. He tried to push it one way, then the other. Nothing.

Breathe, he told himself. He stopped and paid attention to the oxygen rushing into his lungs, then to the carbon dioxide he let out slowly, intentionally. *Okay, how would this work if you had pincers?* The thought reminded him of his suit, of the fact that he was probably leaking air, that he was probably wounded and simply pumping out so many endorphins at the moment that he couldn't feel it.

He summoned an image of the pincer that had stabbed him. It had happened so fast that he hadn't seen it clearly, hadn't even thought to study it. He had a vague notion of its shape, however, and it was like nothing he could make his own hand do.

But what about *hands*? He had two of them after all. And even in the space suit, they were posable, movable, pliant. He conjured an image of the pincer, according to his best memory of it. Using one hand to hold onto the disk, he inserted the other hand as close to it as he was able and pushed forward. He felt a plate beyond it give. Then the whole hatch lurched inward, and once again there was a lip to put his knee onto. Still holding fast to the disk with one hand he pushed the door open with the other, and pushing with one knee, he fell forward into it, gibbering with relief.

He rested on the horizontal surface of the service tube, just grateful to feel something solid beneath him. He gave thanks to whatever cosmic powers had rescued him from certain death. His chest heaved with sobs as stress and grief wracked him. It also started to hurt.

After several minutes of just lying there, prone, he felt his breathing return to normal, felt the tension seep out of his limbs, felt an overwhelming fatigue roll through him. He could sleep. Right here, in the tiny, cramped confines of the service tube, he could sleep, and wanted to.

But I've got a fleet to save, he thought. *A people. A planet. It's all on me, and the clock is ticking. If I sleep, all of this will be for nothing.*

He kicked against the edge of the hatch and wormed his shoulders forward. The blaster was between his shoulder blades now and tremendously uncomfortable. With every twist of his torso, pain stabbed in his chest. He forced himself not to think about it. It couldn't be too bad, or he wouldn't be alive, after all.

After a few feet, the hatch widened, and he found he could crawl. That, too, was a relief, as he was beginning to feel claustrophobic. *Should I turn my neural on to check my suit's condition?* he wondered. *No. Knowing won't change anything.* He would either run out of air or he wouldn't, and turning his neural on wouldn't change that. It would only alert whoever was driving this death machine to his exact position.

Instead, he set his face toward the oncoming tube and crawled as quickly as he was able. He moved like a soldier, regulating his breathing, timing his movements for maximum speed and efficiency. He also quieted his flailing emotions, demanding their submission, and getting it. *Pastore and Montalbano will not have died in vain, goddammit*, he swore to himself. He briefly flashed on the other two ships, the other two missions, and wondered what was happening to them.

But he didn't dwell on it. He just kept moving. Eventually, he came to the end of the service tube. It concluded in a T. He could continue to the left or to the right, or he could exit the hatch directly in front of him. The idea of moving about on his feet appealed to him. It would hurt less, for one thing, if he was not using his arms for locomotion. He moved his gloved hand before him into an approximation of the shape of a Prox's pincer, snatched at the disk with one hand, and pushed with the other. The hatch fell away from him with smooth precision. *Damn, I'm getting good at this,* he thought. He crawled through and tumbled onto the floor of a corridor. Only then did he realize that he had experienced no increase in gravity. On an Authority ship he would have felt the artificial gravity at some point as he got closer to an inhabited deck.

There was gravity, but it was slight, so he tumbled to the floor without damage. He stood and unslung his blaster. Despite the fact that its electronics might be detected, he powered it up and cradled it in one arm. Then he pushed off against the wall, weighing how quickly he would be able to walk without launching himself toward the low ceiling.

Not very, he grumbled to himself. Still, it was better than crawling.

He discovered that he could move more quickly by holding one hand above his head, jumping off with his feet, and pushing down with his hand. Hopping like this, he traversed the corridor, towards...he didn't know. He stopped and felt himself fall back to the floor. *Where the hell am I going?* he wondered. At any moment, he knew, a Prox could come around the corner and spear him to the wall. He would not be so lucky as to receive another flesh wound again.

He summoned up his memory of the approximate schematics—Sol Station's engineers' best guesses as to what the Prox ships might look like on the inside. He located himself as to where they had landed, where the vent had been, how far he must have crawled and in what direction. At the end of all that, he had a vague notion of where he was on the map in his head, but of course, it was all speculative. And he had probably gotten turned around somewhere.

Then he laughed. He laughed at all the guesswork and the danger and the corpses of the men under his command. He laughed at the cosmic justice of the Authority being subdued by a superior force—they who were accustomed to doing the subduing. He doubled over as the hilarity poured out of him, purging from his guts all the stress and fear and grief that had been building up, needing to blow like the vent on the skin of the ship above him.

Spent, he crouched, resting his arms on his knees. *If someone came around the corner, they'd think I was taking a shit in their hallway,* he thought, and that set him off again. Once that wave of laughter subsided, he stood up, feeling light-headed and a little sick. He reminded himself that he was wounded. He reminded himself he had a job to do. Walking in one direction was as good as walking in another. The thing to do was just to walk, to explore, to find...whatever was here. And then to destroy it.

At any moment he expected to round a corner and be attacked by solider Prox. But at every corner, he found just another empty corridor. He ventured into some of the doorways and found nothing but empty rooms. Empty of Prox, empty of equipment, empty of anything.

This is a fucking ghost ship, he thought.

The hair on the back of his neck stood on end. He had been frightened of boarding an enemy vessel—who wouldn't be? But that was his job, and it was his job to be courageous and to act despite the fear. But this wasn't just scary, this was surreal.

He quickened his step. *If there are any Prox inside this ship, I'm going to damn well find them. And kill them.*

The corridors seemed labyrinthine, but eventually something changed. He came to a large room. He stopped and blinked in the dim emergency lighting. He turned on his helmet light and stepped into the room.

Tables and chairs. There were tables. And chairs.

Harrak caught at one of the chairs and steadied himself on the back of it. He almost sat down. Instead, he pressed ahead. *A mess deck,* he thought. *This is a mess deck. A human mess deck.*

On the other side of the mess were showers and a head. Then the berthing area, and even a few cabins, presumably for officers. Inside each was a bed, long unslept in. Across from each bed was a small utility sink.

The thought of lying down on one of the beds and sleeping was overwhelming. *It would be dereliction of duty,* he reminded himself. He pressed on.

The ramifications of what he was seeing overwhelmed him. He did not know how to make sense of it. The Prox were as alien a species as they had ever encountered. They were utterly inhuman. How could their ship possibly be made for humans?

He stopped and straightened up. Perhaps the interior was not for a crew, but for prisoners? Was this a slave transport ship? That didn't make sense, either. These weren't prison cells, these were accommodations much like those he had lived in his entire adult life. And where were the jailers?

He skirted what must have been the periphery, if the portholes were any indication. Then he climbed down, into the belly of the beast. If there were a bridge, it would not be topside—it would be in the heart of the thing, as far away from the hull as possible, with as many layers of sealed decks between it and the vacuum of space as its designers could manage.

He found a rounded wall and followed its curve. It ended at a massive set of doors. Like doors aboard Sol Station, these slid shut. He pushed awkwardly at the doors, trying to wedge his glove in between them.

He succeeded, and he shifted his body to prise them apart, ignoring the pain in his chest as he did so. After some effort, he succeeded in pushing them far enough apart to fit his helmet through. He walked onto the bridge and saw an arrangement that would not have been out of place on an Authority ship.

In the captain's chair was a figure. He froze. Aiming his blaster, he carefully picked his way around the circumference of the room, keeping his eyes trained on the figure in command. As he came about to face him, he saw the eye sockets were empty, its uniform long faded and slack on its deteriorating frame.

"So, what happened to you?" he asked out loud.

The slack jawbone of the captain offered no answers, but the questions multiplied in the silence. Harrak slung the blaster over his shoulder and sighed. He turned on his neural and checked the time. A new urgency leaped within him. There was only one place he needed to find now.

Engineering.

DANNY ENTERED the hangar deck with a swagger that was larger than he felt. He hated spacewalking. Despite the fact that he'd had to do it numerous times in his career, it always made him nauseated.

As he drew near the shuttle, Chief Engineer Raj Tenzin looked over his shoulder and stood, saluting.

"As you were," Danny said.

Tenzin knelt again and finished fixing a clamp.

"I take it I'm riding in the undercarriage?" Danny asked.

"That's the only place that will be out of sight," Tenzin nodded. "You'll need to go dark with the suit—life support only, on quiet mode—and you'll need to turn off your neural, too."

Danny's lips pressed together in a grim line. *Fear is just something to be faced,* he remembered from his academy days. Who had said that to him? Palamar? Yes, it was Palamar. The irony was rich, since Palamar was the most cowardly person he had ever known.

He couldn't let on that this whole crazy notion made him nervous. The only thing to do was to bluster through. *I can do that,* he thought. *I have to do that.* "It's going to be hard to maneuver under there in the space suit," he noted.

"Well, the design is misleading, because of this apron and the lip." Raj pointed to the flare near the bottom of the shuttle's hull. "Actually, there's about .75 meter's clearance between the skis and the undercarriage. Even with your helmet, that's plenty of room. I've been under there for the past hour and a half getting you a transport carriage set up that won't tax your arms and legs."

He threw himself on the ground and turned over, pointing to the undercarriage. "Take a look, sir—I mean, begging the captain's pardon—if you'd like to take a look, I can show you what we've done."

Danny grunted and went down on one knee. The space suit was bulky and made it hard to bend. Once down, he pivoted and allowed himself to fall onto his back. He wormed his way under the shuttlecraft, smarting from the indignity of it.

"There, and there, we've got X-clamps that will fasten to the biopack on the back of the suit. It's the most rigid part of the suit, and the heaviest, which means it was designed to distribute its weight across your hips and torso. This is good for us—"

"Because it goes both ways. If I'm the weight…" Danny began.

"Exactly. It's well distributed to the pack. You'll essentially be hanging from the pack, face down."

"What about release?"

"We've rigged up a tiny remote that you can reach with your glove, right there." Tenzin pointed to a small box with one red button on it. Simple. "It's actually wired, since any kind of remote signal could give you away."

Danny nodded, though he knew Tenzin couldn't see it. "That'll take care of my torso. What about my feet?"

"Two E-clamps, right there. They'll function like stirrups. We'll get you into them. Just don't pull your feet out until you're ready to...disembark."

"Will they slip out mid-flight?"

"Not unless you intend it. Once we get you harnessed up, you can practice getting out of them. You'll see...it won't happen accidentally. It'll take some mild gymnastics."

"But the suit—"

"Sir. It will be fine. I know we haven't been serving together for very long, but...have I let you down yet?"

Danny turned and looked at Tenzin, as if seeing the chief engineer for the first time. "No, you haven't. I'm..." Danny was momentarily at a loss for words. He'd never considered Tenzin's loyalty or competency before. It was just a fact—like the tensile strength of wire or the refraction of light. For the first time it struck him that he was saying goodbye to this crew and this ship...and his career.

Something wet caught in Danny's chest. He swallowed it. "Thank you for your stellar service since I've been aboard, Tenzin."

"It's been an honor, sir."

Danny reached up and, grabbing a strut, slid himself out from under the shuttle.

The doors slid open and he saw Foulon coming toward them, dressed in a civilian captain's uniform. Foulon saluted, and Danny returned it.

Foulon circumnavigated the shuttle, inspecting the camo job. "This still looks like a military shuttle," he said. "The paint is good," he pointed to the graphic of the spruce branch crossed with a Victorian Easter bonnet, along with their new call designation, "but civilian transport shuttles often have racks on the top for extra cargo."

"Those are coming," Tenzin said. "I'll have them in place by launch—five minutes from now. I'm just waiting—ah! Here they are."

Two ensigns with engineering insignia approached, carrying a bundle of rails on their shoulders.

"Those look pretty light," Foulon said.

"They won't be functional," Tenzin said. "They're just poly—note the sag in the middle between them. But they'll look right, and that's the important thing."

The ensigns put the rails on the floor.

"Quick epoxy those to the topside hull, running bow to stern, parallel, each with a meter between them. I thought there were supposed to be five of them?"

"We checked, sir. The most popular brand only has four."

Tenzin nodded. "Good for us. Faster." He jerked his head toward the top of the shuttlecraft. "We could have put you up there, but for two things—the rails would have had to be functional and they'd have been more likely to inspect them."

"Good thinking," Danny said, although in truth he'd much rather be under a tarp up top than clamped to the bottom of the damn thing.

The bay door slid open again and two men with civilian security insignia came toward them. "That's my crew," Foulon said. "Captain, let's get you stowed away."

ALL OF THE muscles in Danny's body tensed as he saw the floor below him start to move. It was surreal, being so close. He could reach out a hand and touch the floor, if he chose to, but he wasn't stupid. He crossed his arms and even hooked his gloves on little spikes near his shoulder patches. Those were designed for sleeping in the suit, upright, under weightless conditions, but they worked fine for him now. Hugging his chest, he closed his eyes as the floor started moving faster and faster.

He wanted to check in with Foulon, but his suit was dark and his neural was off. He was alone, strapped to the bottom of a shuttlecraft, with nothing between him and the certain death of the vacuum of space but the thin curve of his helmet. *God, I hate this*, he thought.

To take his mind off of it, he thought about Jo. He thought about their lovemaking, all those many years ago—the animal roughness of it. He remembered his hands around her neck, and the bruises she'd left on his lower back the next day. He relaxed. *They should make a way to jerk off in these suits*, he thought, but it would be like trying to tickle someone rolled up in a carpet, gangster-style. Not happening. *Ah well*, he sighed, and returned to the fond memories of hair-pulling, blood-letting, and the shrill cursing of various gods.

"SIR, the envoys from the *Spruce and Bonnet* have just landed in the main landing bay. Security are on hand to escort them to the conference room."

"Thank you, Tash," Jo said.

She saw motion and swiveled the command chair to face her XO. Nira had been pulling double shifts and it was beginning to show. She was a determined cuss, and reminded Jo of herself, more every day. "Do you have something, Mr. Nira?"

"Yes sir. I've completed my analysis. From everything I've been able to glean via passive scans, it is my opinion that the *Spruce and Bonnet* looks more like a light-class warship than a culinary transport."

"That explains a lot…" Jo nodded slowly.

"You could be walking into a trap," Nira said.

"On my own ship?" Jo scowled.

Nira stood, as if preparing for an oration. "First, captain, we don't know the provenance of that ship. It's most certainly not from the UK colony and it sure isn't carrying bangers and mash. We don't know what their endgame is, what technology they have, or what they're capable of. To allow you into a sealed meeting room, alone with them—"

"I'll have security with me—"

"And they'll have theirs. It'll be an even match in that room. And before any help could get to you…" She did not finish the sentence. She did not have to.

"Well, I have a captain waiting in a meeting room and the clock is ticking," Jo said. "We have a plan. So just what do you suggest?"

"I suggest you leave the small stuff alone and face up to the real threat."

Jo froze. It was a man's voice, coming from behind her. It was Jeff's voice. She stood and spun around. Everyone else turned as well.

And there he was, standing behind her, unshaven and looking like he'd slept in his clothes for a week. Beside him was a smaller man, much smaller. He looked Mesoamerican, and the clothes he wore were definitely traditional Latin American.

Nira launched herself toward the upper riser, but it wasn't an attack. It was a bear hug. The relief and real affection pouring out of her XO made Jo blush, despite her own pleasure at seeing Jeff. Was her XO sweet on her… her what? Boyfriend? What was Jeff to Jo, anyway? It was too complicated to parse. But no, this hug wasn't infatuation. It was something good, something wholesome. Something the universe needed a whole lot more of.

Jeff laughed and hugged Nira back. Nira then stiffly separated herself and turned to Jo. "Begging the captain's pardon, sir."

"No pardon required, XO." Jo smiled. "I'm glad to see him too."

If she had any doubts whatsoever, they vanished in the next moment as Jeff stepped down the riser toward her, caught her up in his arms and kissed her.

The kiss seemed suspended in time, and Jo wished it would go on forever. When their lips finally parted, Jo stepped back and straightened her uniform jacket, trying to reclaim some of her dignity. The eyes of her crew were like saucers as they stared at her and at Jeff, as if they were some roadside attraction or a machinery accident.

"You smell like you've been sleeping in a grizzly bear's anus," Jo said, pushing him to arm's length. She shook her hair and raised her chin.

"I do my best work rank," he said. He snatched at her hand, pulled her in, and kissed her again.

This time she just melted into him and let him kiss her.

Like all kisses, it ended. When they finally separated again, she found her crew very, very busy doing something, anything. She saw that they were also trying very hard not to smile. All except for Nira, who was watching them with her hands on her hips, grinning like an idiot.

"So, you two…"

"It's a long story, Mr. Nira," Jo said.

Jo put her hand on Jeff's chest. "Um…not that I'm not glad that you're here, but…we're kind of in the middle of something."

"Forget it," Jeff said.

"What's that?" Jo asked, her eyebrows rising and her jaw tightening.

"Don't get like that. Can we talk?" He pointed to her ready room.

"Sure. Privately?"

"Maybe Nira and Tomás could join us."

Jo didn't know who Tomás was, but assumed Jeff was referring to the little man with him. She nodded and led the way. The door slid open, and she found her spot, sitting as the others found chairs. Once they were all seated, she turned to Jeff. "So what's this about?"

"Sol Station is under attack," Jeff said.

"I know," Jo said, her shoulders slumping. "We offered the Authority our help, but they refused it."

"They're idiots, but it wouldn't have helped." Jeff folded his hands in front of him on the table.

Tomás sat beside him. Was the little man mute?

"The creatures they're fighting…well, we were fighting them in our universe. It's why we're even here. We were trying to develop a way to beat them."

"And it didn't work out so well," Jo said tentatively.

"No," Jeff agreed. "I…I didn't know what I was doing." He turned to Tomás. "But he does."

Tomás smiled.

"You found him. Your shaman," Jo said.

"Yes. Tomás has been mentoring me in how to…use this gift of ours."

"You have it too?" Jo hoped that by addressing the little man directly, she'd hear his voice.

Jeff answered for him. "We know how to…move, and move things…without putting the reality string at risk."

Jo nodded, still not quite believing it all. But she'd just seen Jeff appear on her bridge, hadn't she?

"Jo, the Authority doesn't have a chance. I know they're your enemy, but if they're destroyed, it doesn't help you, because the Prox will just come after you next—after they destroy the Earth, that is. And you won't stand a chance, either."

She didn't dispute it. She didn't know what to think.

"Whatever you're dealing with here, it might be nefarious, but it's small potatoes. If you want to subdue the real enemy, here's your chance." He jerked his head toward Tomás. "We need you. You can either help us now, or you can wait until billions more people have died."

He paused and looked her in the eye. "What will it be?" he asked.

"I'm just supposed to drop everything and put myself, my ship, and my crew at your disposal?" Jo asked.

"I'm asking you to save the universe."

Jo blinked. "Well, when you put it like that…" She looked down at her hands. She saw a hangnail. She desperately wanted to chew it into submission. It mocked her. She looked back up at Jeff. "How can I just abandon my orders?"

"Contact your admiral. Explain the situation. From everything you've said, you have her trust. Surely she'll see the advantage to dealing with this now before the colonies are devoured by metal-eating monsters, one by one."

He was probably right. Admiral Alinto would listen to her. She was sure of it. "What am I supposed to do about this caravan? I can't just abandon it here."

They sat in silence for a long minute.

Nira stood. "Sir. You should go with him. I can bring our mission to completion here, with your permission."

Jo scowled. "Mr. Nira, how will you accomplish this? We only have the one starship, and it's full of Mormons at the moment."

"Begging your pardon, sir, but we have two."

Jo cocked her head.

"We have the *Spruce and Bonnet,* sir. We don't know whose

warship it is, but it's a warship, without a doubt. We have their captain isolated now. How hard could it be to commandeer it…for a good cause?" She smiled. "We could bring over a skeleton crew and then move the Mormons."

"And what will we do with the *Spruce and Bonnet*'s crew, Mr. Nira? They won't fit in the brig."

"We could transport them to their homeworld," Jeff said. "How long will it take you to make preparations?"

Nira looked surprised that her idea was being considered. "Uh…at yellow alert, thirty minutes."

Jeff and Tomás looked at each other and nodded. "We can empty a starship by then."

CHAPTER ELEVEN

Danny was beginning to sweat. He was used to hangar decks being cold as hell, but once the blast doors had closed, the heat had pumped in quickly. His space suit was still running quiet, which meant he had no temperature regulation. In space it had gotten very cold, but since docking, Danny had begun to sweat. He watched as a bead of perspiration gathered on the end of his nose and dropped into the bowl of his helmet.

He was beginning to collect a pool.

He couldn't be sure how long he'd been suspended there. It felt like hours but was probably less than one. *Be patient,* he told himself. *The right moment will come. Timing is everything here.* But he was terrified that the meeting would conclude and Foulon and the others would get back aboard and take off—with him still riding the undercarriage. *Like hell.* He decided a little more risk was probably going to be necessary.

And then the moment arrived. The lights went out, which meant the last human had exited the deck. It might be momentary, it might be for hours. That was impossible to know, but what Danny did know was that, for the time being, he was alone.

He retracted his boots from the E-clamps one at a time and then felt for the button that would release the X-clamps on his pack. He fell the

.75 meters to the floor, breaking his fall with his gloved hands, emitting an audible "Oof."

He felt a bit like a turtle, struggling to turn over, and then tore at the zipper of his suit.

It was no small feat, getting out of a space suit on one's own. For the whole of his career, Danny had had someone to help him—other grunts, and later, men under his command—to tug and pull and fasten it in the places he couldn't quite reach.

Finally, however, after a good deal of thrashing and pulling, the suit lay in a heap beside him, and he took a deep breath, enjoying the cool air against his wet skin.

It quickly turned cold.

Working with haste, he stowed the boots and gloves inside the suit and reattached it to the X-clamps. The suit would go out the same way it had come in. Then, beginning to shiver, he crawled out from under the shuttlecraft.

Instantly, the lights blazed. He shielded his eyes with his arm and fought back panic. He was about to dive back under the shuttle when he realized what was happening. In all likelihood, no one had entered the bay—now that he was no longer shielded by the shuttle, he had simply triggered the motion-detector and the lights had come on. *The only danger is me*, he thought. He smiled at that.

Before leaving, the *Horatio Nelson* had sent a message to their mole, so a fresh uniform should be waiting for him underneath the concave poly bottom of a waste can. There were probably several of them around the bay, but he jogged to the one nearest him. He knew he'd make quite a sight sprinting across the landing bay in his underwear. He could have brought a change of clothes, but it would have been the wrong clothes.

He snatched at the large trash receptacle and got lucky on the first try—beneath it was a short stack of neatly-folded clothes.

He dressed quickly, wishing he'd had a pair of dry underwear, too. But there was no time for that, or even for wishing. Just as soon as he'd finished with the last fastener, he heard voices. He froze.

He cast around for a hiding place. There was a space under a workbench, but it looked greasy. He didn't want to soil his new uniform so quickly. There was another shuttle in the bay, nearer to him now. He dove under it just as two mechanics entered the bay from a connecting corridor.

"Oh my god," one said. "That's not the way I heard it."

"How did you hear it?" This was a woman's voice.

"I heard she launched herself at him and wouldn't stop kissing him."

"That is not the way it happened. I talked to two people who were there."

"How do you know the A-crew on the bridge?" he asked.

"I don't. I was in the mess. They came in. I listened," she answered, a note of mock hurt in her voice. "Where did you get your information?"

"From the cook."

"And she heard it from…?"

He didn't answer. Danny assumed he had shrugged or something.

"Look, you can believe your fifth-hand information if you want, but I heard it directly from people who were there," she said.

"Here, hold this," he said. "Okay, so what *really* happened, then?"

"He just appeared out of thin air."

"Is that some kind of transporter technology? Because if so…"

"No, I don't think so. I think he just…appeared. Him and another man. Little guy. From Peru or something."

Danny scowled. What the hell were they talking about?

"And then he ran to the captain's chair and kissed Captain Taylor."

Danny's eyebrows jumped. This was getting interesting.

"And she kissed him back. And then he did it again."

"No shit. I guess that's a little more dignified."

"You better not diss the captain," she warned.

"I do *not* want to get on the wrong side of the captain," he agreed.

"So now what?"

"I have no idea. Top secret shit. They're interviewing the other captains, right? That's going to take a while."

"No, no, no. I heard we've got new orders coming," she said.

Danny cocked his head. New orders?

"Yeah, but there's always new orders coming, and you can never second-guess them. So, until they get here…what's on our checklist?"

Danny heard the clatter of someone dropping a data pad, then the woman cursing.

"Okay, here it is. Three items, so we're doing pretty good. First up, quarterly check of the atmospheric filters."

"Doesn't Environmental do that?"

"It's on *our* checklist, so…I would guess no."

"Shit."

"You know what makes me all wet and trembly?"

"No…and I don't want to," he answered. Danny could almost hear the eye-rolling.

"The idea that Captain Bowers would travel all the way across the universe—or even from *another* universe—to kiss me…her. That's… that's a fucking kiss, right there."

Danny's head jerked up. Bowers? Bowers was *here*? Now? *Two birds,* he thought. *One stone. Oh, this is going to be a good day…*

It took more than thirty minutes for Jeff and Tomás to empty the starship—but not much more. Jeff commandeered a uniform from one of the *Spruce and Bonnet*'s visiting security men and teleported aboard the ship. It only took a moment to ascertain where the ship was really from. He strode into the mess like he owned the place and took a seat at one of the tables, hanging his head over a discarded cup of coffee. Then he went into the All.

He found Tomás there. *They're not from a UK colony,* he thought, knowing Tomás could "hear" him. *And the* Spruce and Bonnet *is not the name of this ship. This is an Authority warship.*

He heard Tomás' voice in his mind. *Then we will take them to Earth.*

To Earth, Jeff agreed. In the All, he felt Tomás teleport away, found him again, distant yet near, available. He reached through and grabbed

Tomás' arm. Jeff flashed back on Tomás' explanation of the sleeve. Tomás was holding his end of the sleeve aloft. And then the portal was open.

As if in two worlds at once, Jeff rose and began to circumambulate the mess hall. There weren't many people in it, and no one seemed to be paying attention to anyone else. *All for the better*, he thought.

At first it was hard to navigate. Jeff was seeing the universe from the perspective of the All, but superimposed over it were the images his eyes were registering from the Authority vessel. It was disorienting, and Jeff stumbled once, striking his thigh against a table. "Ouch," he said out loud.

"Hey, are you all right?" a woman asked him. She was putting a tray down on a table. "And what's with that uniform, are you—"

With a flourish of his arm that was completely unnecessary, Jeff sent her tumbling toward Tomás, toward Earth. He saw her with his physical eyes first, sucked into nothing. One minute she was standing there, the next minute she wasn't. Then he sensed her traveling through the All.

Got her, Tomás said. *We must hurry.*

Hurry he did. Jeff surveyed the room, then began to walk in the direction in which he'd be able to approach the most people from behind. He didn't need any drama. He certainly didn't need anyone to raise an alarm. The best way to empty this ship was *quietly*.

He walked up behind a man hunkered over a bowl of soup and sent him spinning into the All. Next was a woman standing at the food synthesizer panel. Gone. He turned and approached a table where four people were eating and talking with some animation. *Do I need to send them individually or can I send them in groups?* he asked.

We are pleased to accommodate parties of any size, Tomás answered.

Jeff grinned. He approached the table and leaned over it, placing his hands on its edge.

The conversation stopped and everyone turned to look at him, their eyebrows raised in surprise. Then the four of them were gone.

"Hey, what just happened there?" a man asked.

Jeff turned and gave him a disarming grin. "Oh, it's the coolest thing. Take a look at this." He offered his hand as if he were going to shake it. The man reached for his hand, and the next moment was tumbling into the All.

Jeff looked around at the empty mess. He put his hands on his hips and sighed.

Enough self-congratulation, Tomás' voice resonated in his head. *We have a starship to empty.*

Jeff nodded and headed toward the door. None of his subordinates would have said something like that to him. And none of his superiors would have been in a situation like this. Jeff wondered at how odd it was to be working as a team with someone. Jeff was used to taking orders or giving them. But to work *with* someone…he found that he enjoyed it.

He imagined the layout of a typical warship of this size. He couldn't be sure the Authority would design their ships the same way as the CDF, but thus far things seemed pretty familiar. He got his bearings and began a systematic sweep of the ship, sending its crew tumbling one by one into the All, toward Tomás, toward Earth.

EMMA HAD BEEN LYING on her mattress in the sleep chamber for hours, with no word from anyone. She hadn't been summoned to work in the counting chambers, nor had she been directed to go to class. It was the first real downtime she'd had since she arrived at the hive. She should be relishing it, but instead, she was fretting.

The implications of the Alverian scientists' calculations were staggering. It was clear that whatever they had been observing, the balance of forces involved had been disturbed when String 310—*her* string—had been destroyed. If there was something pressed between two strings, and then suddenly one of them *went away*…

What? Would it suddenly expand to fill the newly vacant space? Would it be flung away from the remaining string like a child bouncing on a trampoline? This was unmapped territory, Emma had never even read speculation about such things. She had to know more. If only the Alverians could find the courage to trust her.

She heard a commotion in the tunnel outside the sleeping chamber. Any Alverians who had been sleeping stirred to look. Emma felt certain that whatever it was probably concerned her, so she leapt to her feet and ran out to try to restore the peace.

"People are sleeping," she signed to the crowd in the tunnel. Bucky and Amberline were there, along with four of the red-banded scientists and a taller Alverian. She wore a sort of gold-colored scarf draped over her shoulders and a powder blue circle painted on her forehead. It was the first personal decoration that Emma had seen in the hive. She felt that this Alverian must be important, so she bowed and signed a respectful greeting.

"Greetings and welcome, human," she replied. "I am Blue Circle, leader of the council."

Well, nothing beats a literal name! Emma thought, amused. *Certainly makes it easy to remember.*

Blue Circle continued, with Amberline vocalizing. "I am being asked to take you into our confidence, to trust you with our most dear secret. Nobody outside the hive has ever been given that level of trust before. Do you understand?"

"I do," she said, nodding. "At least in part."

"If we place this trust in you, and you betray our confidence, even without intending to, it could mean the death of the hive and the end of the Alverian people."

Emma's stomach churned. She'd already helped destroy one universe, and that knowledge stabbed at her whenever she allowed herself to think of it. She couldn't bear the responsibility for wiping out another civilization.

Blue Circle studied Emma's face, which must have been as alien to her as the Alverians were to Emma. "Normally I would not even consider a risk so great, but these are not normal times."

Bucky signed emphatic agreement.

"Our scientists tell me that you possess very advanced knowledge in the matters concerning us, that you and you alone may be the key to understanding them." She then stood silently.

Emma glanced to Amberline for guidance. "She wants you to confirm that," Amberline whispered.

"Although I do not fully understand the matter at hand, I offer my full expertise and will serve the hive in any capacity I can."

Amberline's mask smiled as she signed the translation.

Blue Circle nodded contemplatively. "Very well. We will open the hive to you fully. I beg you to care for it as we would." She made a few gestures toward the scientists that Amberline did not translate, turned and walked regally away.

The scientists suddenly appeared nervous, or perhaps just excited. Bucky signed to follow, and led the party down the tunnel. They walked in silence until they arrived at a bank of elevators Emma had never seen before. One of them stood open, and Bucky stepped inside. None of the others joined her. "Come," she motioned to Emma.

"Uh, where are we going?" Emma muttered, suddenly apprehensive.

"To the heart of the hive."

Emma took a deep breath and stepped into the lift. To her great relief, Amberline followed close behind. The doors closed and the elevator began to descend.

ADMIRAL TAL SAT. He was beginning to feel weary again. He saw Liu pass and reached out to snag his sleeve.

"Are you alright, sir?" Liu asked.

"Just winded, Lieutenant. Bring me caffeine in any form, please."

"Yes sir. Right away sir."

Lieutenant Liu was not a glorified waiter. He knew that. Liu was a highly skilled military secretary. But if Tal had a friend aboard Sol Station, Liu came closest to that category.

Tal had been obsessively checking the board for information about their strike teams. All three were dead silent. The Prox ships just kept coming. Tal said a silent prayer for the teams' success and wondered for the thousandth time what was happening to them.

In the meantime, there were preparations to make. Tal rolled his eyes up to check for reports on the funnel formation. There it was—a report from Admiral Wengret herself. He blinked to open it and dove in. His eyes flashed from side to side as he read. She had done a very thorough job. Her assessment of the funnel formation's strengths and weaknesses left no stone unturned, so far as he could see. He found himself nodding as he skimmed through the relevant sections, skipping ahead to find the tables for ship deployment. A ring of sheer firepower, with Sol Station on one side and the approaching Prox ships on the other. He liked it. He didn't know if it would work, of course, but if they had any chance at all with conventional weaponry, this would give it to them.

He made a few notes and sent it back. He expected Wengret would turn it around in minutes. The next draft would go out with orders. He glanced at his chronometer. Just enough time to get everyone in formation.

If only we had the rebels with us, he thought. *We should be fighting this war together.* He felt suddenly sad. The rebels were not, after all, without justification for their rebellion. They had legitimate grievances, and any thinking person would say so. It was how they chose to protest those grievances that made them outlaws and enemies. Every now and then, though, at three in the morning, when Tal considered where he would be if he had been among those who had been wronged, he wondered what side he would have come down on. In his secret heart he knew the answer to that, and for that reason he did not judge them too harshly.

"Here you are, sir," Liu said, handing him a cup of coffee.

His secretary had been thoughtful—he'd put cream in it, even though he knew Tal didn't ordinarily use cream. But it would cool it off for faster drinking. Liu thought of everything. "Thank you, Liu." Tal took a large swig and placed the cup in his chair's holder.

A communications operator down on the floor stood and turned toward him. "Sir," he yelled over the din, "I have a transmission from Commander Harrak."

"General PA," Tal yelled back, "Back it up to the beginning."

Everyone froze and stopped what they were doing. The operator threw himself into his seat and started tapping at his console. A moment later, Tal heard Harrak's ragged voice through the PA.

"Commander Sean Harrak to Sol Station."

Why was the commander breaking radio silence? Tal stood, his tiredness forgotten.

"This is Admiral Tal, son. How is your team?"

"Sir, my team is…dead, sir. I'm the only survivor."

"I'm sorry to hear that, commander. Tell me what you've got there."

"Sir, I'm in."

Tal nodded. He waited. He knew in his gut that what came next would be important. "What did you find?"

"It's a…you're not going to believe this, sir. But…it's a human vessel. Parts of it seem to have been adopted for use by the Prox, but the basic vessel is outfitted for humans."

Tal scowled, and a general gasp arose from the Command Center. People began to talk until the hubbub threatened to drown out Harrak's voice. "Silence!" Tal shouted, holding his hand up. The room froze.

"Human, commander?"

"At least humanoid. But…it looks weirdly familiar. There are tables and chairs, and showers in the head with corporate logos on them. There are sleeping berths and officers' quarters almost identical to our own. There's a bridge, too, with a human cadaver in the captain's chair."

Tal sat back down again, reeling from the shock of the information.

"I wouldn't have believed it if I hadn't seen it with my own eyes. I'm transmitting a data packet with everything I've captured on my neural since I turned it back on, sir."

"You turned on your neural?" Tal said. "Aren't you worried about being located?"

"Uh…begging the Admiral's pardon, but there's no one here.

Except for the cadaver…I appear to be the only inhabitant. There's literally *no one* aboard. And it doesn't look like anyone has been aboard in a very, very long time."

"How is that possible?" Tal breathed. "Who's flying the thing? Who's navigating? Who's giving orders?"

"I don't know the answer to that, sir. I only know that they're not *here*."

Tal's head spun with the dissonance of the information. He looked around at all the astonished faces, the slack jaws, the wide eyes. "Does anyone have a clue?" he called to the room at large.

No one spoke.

Tal rubbed his jaw and shook his head slowly. "Where are you now, Commander?" he asked, finally.

"I'm in engineering, sir. The engine room, specifically. It's the only place where…where I can be sure." The voice quavered and faltered.

"Commander?"

"Admiral, will you tell my parents…and my girlfriend…will you tell them I love them?"

"Commander?" Tal stood and raised his voice.

He waited. His eyes travelled to the central monitor. He expected to see an explosion as the commander activated his nuke. But there was nothing.

"Commander!" Tal demanded.

"Nothing, sir," the communicator called over his shoulder.

"Get him back!" Tal commanded.

Silence. After several minutes of frantic attempts, the communicator stood and turned to look at him. "We've lost him, sir. His neural signal is gone, too."

"Gone? Gone where?" Tal thundered.

Every eye in the room was on him. But not one of them had any answers.

"Goddammit!" Tal roared.

He glanced up at the schematic on the right-hand monitor. The Prox ships were still in formation. They were still moving. They were still coming.

CHAPTER TWELVE

Tal rose, his fatigue forgotten. On one monitor he saw the whole array of his forces, in ring formation. Sol Station was also depicted, hovering in the center of the ring, but about 20,000 kilometers above it. Also in the center of the ring, but about 40,000 kilometers below it, were the approaching Prox.

Tal still could not shake the eerie stillness that had pervaded the Command Center after Harrak's voice had simply…stopped. Where had he gone? What had happened to that brave young man? And the other strike teams, were they all dead, too? He realized these were questions he may never find the answer to, if only because he may not live long enough to investigate them.

Tal waved and got a communicator's attention, a wiry-haired red-headed young woman. She inclined her chin. "Yes sir?"

"Open a channel to all ships. Make sure the news feeds on Earth can hear me, too."

"I'll need a few seconds, sir," she said, putting her head down and tapping away furiously.

He nodded his assent, even though she wasn't looking at him. A few moments later she looked up again and held his eye. "Channels open, sir."

"Authority fleet, this is Admiral Jason Tal. Our enemy is coming…." He paused. What in the world should he say? He hadn't given this speech a moment's preparation. But they were on the cusp of the deadliest battle humankind had ever faced. Surely something needed to be said. "Our enemy is coming," he repeated, "and we are ready. Thus far the Prox have resisted our attacks, but they are now faced with the full might of our fleet." *None of which add up to much more than the firepower of one of the Dreadnaughts*, he thought, but he pushed the objection away. "Our ships are arranged in a ring of pure, deadly firepower. I'm going to call this the Wengret formation." *More like the Wengret gambit…our chances are not good. But it's the only thing standing between us and oblivion.* "Cadets a hundred years from now are going to study it. They are going to study what you do here today."

He paused and took a deep breath. "Those three ships are coming to kill you. They are coming to dismantle and destroy this station. And if you let them, they surely will. But they will not stop here. Once they have shredded our ships and our station into scrap metal, they will head toward Earth. Earth has defenses…but not half as many as are arrayed here. We are the defense of the Earth. The only thing standing between these alien killers and the murder of every man, woman, and child on Earth is you." He let that sink in a moment. "There has never been a battle with higher stakes than this one. There has never been a greater force assembled in the history of warfare. We have never faced an enemy so deadly."

He was on a roll now. He paused for effect. "There has never been a more glorious cause than this one. There has never been a night so dark and cold and long as the one we will tumble into if we do not…" his voice caught. He cleared it. "…if we do not prevail." He waited for his emotions to settle. Master of them once more, he said, "We *must* prevail. Every laser, every mine, every particle cannon, every torpedo, every nuke in our arsenal is powered up and loaded and locked onto those ships. Hell itself could not withstand the fury we are about to unleash." He looked up and watched as the Prox ships crossed the

20,000-kilometer threshold, exactly mirroring Sol Station's position on the other side of the ring. "Captains, fire at will."

JEFF STUMBLED into Jo's bed, not even bothering to undress.

"No," Jo said. "I don't care how tired you are, you are not sleeping in my bed with your clothes on."

Jeff had known bone-crushing weariness before, but nothing like this. The energy it took to teleport a ship's complement, a crew of nearly two hundred, was more than he had expected. He had not noticed before that each teleport drained his energy. But then again, he had never teleported this many people or objects, nor over such a long period of time. It registered in his brain—somewhere far off, it seemed—that Tomás must be equally tired. *Good*, Jeff thought. *Serves him right.*

Jeff turned over and undid his belt. He raised his hips and shoved his pants over them. Then he just lay there.

"Oh, that's a good picture," Jo said. "Goddammit, let me help you." She started with his boots.

"That's a good idea," Jeff mumbled.

"Do you need a doctor?" Jo asked.

"Maybe," Jeff said.

"I'm serious."

"I think I just need some sleep." He heard one boot fall to the deck. Then another. He felt Jo grab the ends of his pant legs and pull. A shock of cold air met his legs. It felt good.

"Jacket. Off."

Jeff turned slightly onto his side, raising one shoulder, and froze there.

"You are fucking pathetic."

Jeff moaned.

She grabbed his sleeve and started to pull his arm out of it.

"I want to see Emma—" Jeff started.

"You're about to get into my bed, and you're asking me about your girlfriend?" Jo snapped.

"Is she okay? And the others…"

He heard Jo sigh. She stopped working on his jacket. Instead, she sat cross-legged on her bed beside him. "Maybe we should talk about this once you've had a good sleep."

Jeff forced his eyes open. Then he forced himself onto one elbow. *This does not sound good*, he thought. "What? Nira's here. I thought…"

"Whoo boy. Where to start?" Jo wasn't looking at him.

"What, goddammit?"

"Now you've got energy?"

"Jo. Tell me."

She was nodding. "Martin Pho is dead. Killed in a brawl or something. In a food court on Epworth."

Jeff's mouth dropped open. "No…" he said.

"Nira was there when it happened. She killed the bastard that did it. She went to jail. We sprang her. You're welcome."

Jeff looked down at the bed. He shook his head slowly, trying to take it in. "Pho…Pho was…well, he was goofy but capable."

"So I hear. It's not the kind of epitaph a family wants to read on your columbarium tube, though, is it?"

Jeff's head snapped up and he looked Jo in the eye. "And Emma?"

Jo shook her head. Then she put her hand up. "She's not dead. Not that I know of. But she's missing. Kidnapped, as far as we can tell. Nira hasn't given up on her, but all of our leads have gone nowhere. Her neural signal just…stopped. She's no doubt somewhere, but we're damned if we know where."

Jeff struggled to a sitting position. "That's not…" He didn't finish the sentence.

Jo didn't press him.

"I have to find her," he said.

"You need to sleep. Wherever she is, she'll still be there when you wake up."

"I should have checked in on her."

"The fact that you didn't says a lot," Jo said.

Jeff gave her a wounded look.

"I'm sorry," Jo said, softening. "But it's still true."

Jeff reached out and grabbed her hand. He didn't know why. Intuitively, he supposed, he was looking for support, maybe even for energy. He closed his eyes and projected himself into the All.

"Where are you goi—ope, there he goes..." he heard Jo's voice, becoming rapidly distant.

He felt his consciousness expand into every point in the universe. The battle with the Prox was raging near earth...but there were countless other battles, too, many among species humans had never encountered.

But he didn't care about any of that. He reached out for Emma's presence, but there was...nothing. A part of him began to quail. His hands began to shake as his desperation escalated. He felt around for her corpse—something residual. But there was nothing.

She was not in this universe. And there were 756 more universes to search. He could not do that now. He could barely balance on one elbow. He sank back down on the bed as his consciousness resumed its customary seat.

"She's not here," he said.

"No shit," Jo said.

"No, I mean, she's not in this universe."

"Wow. You just searched the whole universe? You couldn't even take your pants off."

"Her corpse isn't here, either."

Jo didn't say anything to that.

He closed his eyes. His will felt pulled in different directions. He bit his lip.

Jo reached out and held his hand. She squeezed it. He squeezed back.

"I'm sorry," Jo said.

A long silence passed between them.

"I have to find her."

"In another universe? Like you did me?"

"No." *Damn*, he thought. *I'm too beat for this*. If he wasn't careful, he'd say something stupid and ruin it with Jo. "I don't mean find her analog—"

"Oh. I'm just an analog. That's swell."

Goddammit, he thought. "Jo, listen to me. If…if whoever took her brought her to a different universe, I have to find her."

"I get that. Leave no man behind. But listen to me, soldier, you have priorities. Save the universe from the Prox. *Then* find your girlfriend. You ever hear of triage?"

Despite himself, Jeff smiled. "I love you," he said. He hadn't meant to say it. But there it was, out in the open. He felt a moment of panic, wishing he could take it back, bracing himself for whatever stupid repercussions were to follow.

Then he felt her lips on his, tender and even trembling a bit.

"Don't be mad at me."

"I'm not. But if you don't let yourself sleep, I'm going to get a doctor in here to drug you into oblivion. I'm *not* joking."

"Okay, okay."

"Take your goddam coat off. You're not fucking sleeping in my bed in your coat."

"Yes sir."

DANNY FINISHED HIS SANDWICH, noting what a good idea it was to put food synthesizers in engineering—it enabled those on active duty access to some refreshment without going too far from their posts. He made a mental note of it.

He rose and nodded curtly at those he passed in the halls. No one stopped him. No one questioned him. So long as he did not venture into those areas of the ship where he was likely to see someone he knew—which was basically Jo or Jeff—he found he could move about fairly freely.

The uniform left for him had the red engineering patch on the shoulder, so that helped. It gave him a place to "be," and so long as he didn't draw the attention of the chief engineer or one of the other commanders, he should be all right.

He had to hand it to the rebels. The myth prevalent in the Authority was that the rebels were disorganized, even feral. But what he saw here was a well-oiled military machine, one that he'd be proud to command. Perhaps that was the way the rebels really were…or maybe that was just Jo running a tight ship. It was hard to tell, but he suspected the former.

He made his way to a computer terminal near a port isolation hatch. He assumed it was there in case a hull breach necessitated interior segmentation—so that those trapped in an isolated segment would not lose access to the mainframe. Neural connections were unreliable in emergency situations, after all. If the neural transponder goes down, it's down. But a mainframe connection was hard-wired and reliable so long as emergency and backup power were running.

No one would question his presence here—his patch saw to that. But no one was likely to even notice that he *was* here, which pleased him greatly. It was a quiet place to work, where no one would be likely to ask why he was working at that particular work station. He had spent four shifts down there, and had slept there once. Not a soul had disturbed him.

Sure enough, once he passed through the port isolation hatch, he saw no one. It wasn't easy to find a completely deserted place on a starship. Every inch was precious, and engineering liked to pack as much into every square meter as it could. But every ship had odd corners, too. You just needed to know how to find them.

Danny grinned once more, recalling his good luck. He was here to kill Jo, "the Kali of Aken," and that goal was so close his fingers itched. He remembered how they felt around her neck in the days of their youthful love play. He felt them pressing in on her slender windpipe again.

But the fact that he had another shot at Jeff, too? Well, that was pure gold. When Jeff and his crew had "escaped" Sol Station, he had expected to destroy both him and Jo. He had packed enough explosive into the hull of their ship to peel back the hulls of ten war-class starships. And somehow, impossibly, it seemed, they had eluded death… and eluded *him*. But now, it seemed, fate had given him another shot.

He flashed back to the academy, where his rivalry with Jeff had begun. Their friendship had begun there, too, but it had been one based largely on competition. They were always trying to outdo one another, always trying to best each other.

"Just like old times," Danny said aloud.

He saw the computer terminal and stepped toward it, but doing so, he almost ran into a cadet. He had not expected to see anyone down here, and the cadet's presence shocked him.

"Cadet," he said, pivoting to move past her.

She was a dark, short, young woman. Pakistani? Hard to tell.

"Lieutenant," she acknowledged. Her face looked troubled. "Uh…" she hesitated.

He cocked his head. "Something wrong, Cadet?"

"Uh, no sir, except…I think someone is sleeping down here."

"That would be me, Cadet." Danny squinted. He was thinking fast.

"Sir?"

"I have an H-317 medical dispensation." He gave her an apologetic smile. "It's…well, it's kind of embarrassing."

She looked away, reflexively moving her hand to her chest. "Oh… I'm sorry."

"No, it's nothing secret or anything. I just…I need frequent short catnaps. Ten minutes every hour or so. It's a chronic fatigue injury I got from exposure to chemicals during an Authority attack." He appeared to wince at the thought of it.

"I'm sorry," she repeated.

He shrugged. "You live with it. You do the best you can."

"Of course."

"So, I don't actually sleep down here, you know, when I'm off-shift. It's just impractical to climb up to my berth every hour. Besides, when the fatigue hits…well, I just gotta lie down."

She held her hand up and gave him a pained, apologetic look. She opened her mouth, but before she could protest, he offered the *pièce de résistance*.

"That's why I work down here...I don't want to disturb anyone, and I don't want anyone tripping over me. Chief thought it best to set me up, you know, out of the way."

"I totally understand," she said.

"Did you need something, though?" His eyebrows shot up. He gave her the open, curious face of someone who wanted to be helpful.

She blushed. "Sometimes, I just...I need to be alone."

He nodded sympathetically. "There aren't very many places where that's possible on a ship like this."

"That's it," she said. "Thanks for understanding."

"No, your secret is safe with me. You come down here anytime, except that...well, when I'm on shift, it kind of defeats the purpose, doesn't it?"

"It's not a necessity. I won't bother you again." She pushed past him and shot him a sad, grateful smile over her shoulder.

He waved at her. Once she was out of sight, he let out the breath he had been holding. *Whew*, he thought. *Almost had to kill her.*

He strode to the workstation he had made his own and saw that he had stupidly left a pile of blankets and a pillow beside it. He cursed himself for his carelessness and cast about for a place to stow them. He found one—a half-empty storage cabinet only a few steps away. He quickly folded the blanket and put it on top of boxes filled with god-knew-what. He put the pillow on top of it and closed the door.

He walked back to the workstation and began tapping. He'd gotten a login code from his contact, and it was working perfectly. He pulled up a schematic of the weapons system, and began to study it. He nodded as his eyes flashed over the images. *Yes...* he thought. It would need some minor modifications, most of which he could do from his workstation, but the most important change would require a climb through the service tube to the aft gunnels. *No problem,* he thought. *I'm up for a climb.*

"We need a plan," Jeff said. They were in Jo's ready room—he and Tomás and Jo and Nira. Jo was sitting with a steaming cup of Mayan hot cocoa in front of her.

Jeff's poison was black coffee. Tomás had the same. Nira had declined. *All business*, Jeff thought. *Well, that's all right. It suits her.* He'd hoped for a chance to take her aside, to say how sorry he was about Pho. But this was not the time. After the…operation, perhaps.

He hated that word. Operation. It always reminded him of Catskill, the place where everything had gone awry, where his life had started to spin on the wrong trajectory, where Danny…*his* Danny…had lost his life. That reminded him of Emma, how he didn't know whether she was alive or dead. He shook his head to clear it. It was time to focus on the matter at hand.

"Tomás and I have done some reconnaissance on the Ulim," Jeff said. He looked up, accessed his neural, and a moment later scenes of the concrete bunker in the forest were on display, courtesy of his neural's image capture feature. "We've surveyed the outside."

"But you haven't been *inside*?" Jo asked.

"No."

"I have…on a previous occasion," Tomás said.

All eyes turned to the little man. Jo seemed surprised that he could speak. "Uh…welcome to the party, Tomás."

Tomás smiled at her as if he did not get the joke. But Jeff knew better. Tomás was as cunning a bastard as he'd ever encountered, and then some. He knew how to play on people's erroneous estimation of him, and it seems he did it for fun.

But the time for fun was over, and Tomás was stepping up. Good.

"Why didn't you destroy the Ulim when you were there before?" Jo asked. "What prevented you?"

"I was six, and I was looking for a frog," Tomás said. "I had been training him for a jumping contest, and he got away from me."

"Oh…" Jo pursed her lips, obviously amused. "So…you grew up on this planet."

"Earth. Yes."

"I mean…in this universe, the universe the Ulim come from?"

"Yes. I believe you would call it String 308. The Ulim are native to it and continue to reside there. Here," he waved around the room, "they are just interlopers."

Jeff nodded. That's what they were, all right. Enemy interlopers. "The first thing we'll do is transfer the *Talon* to String 308."

"How do we do that?" Jo asked.

"Leave that to us," Jeff said. He blinked and the forest display faded out. "It will happen very quickly. What worries me is what will happen when we get there." He turned to Tomás. "Does Earth have a moon in String 308?"

Tomás shrugged. "Of course. But it actually is made of green cheese there."

Jo seemed delighted to be seeing more of Tomás' personality. Jeff raised one eyebrow and ignored the joke. "I suggest that when we teleport, we appear on the far side of the moon. It will shield us from detection until we're ready to strike. Then we can do a brief acceleration and be in firing position in less than a second and a half. I'm estimating, but it's close enough."

"Then what?" Nira asked. Her eyes were wide, and Jeff was beginning to suspect that she was sorry she wasn't going to be on this mission.

"Jo has enough firepower to reduce the entire Ulim compound to rubble and ash."

Jo and Nira were nodding.

Tomás cocked his head. "There is only one thing wrong with this plan."

Jeff scowled across the table at him. "And what's that?" There was an edge of irritation to his voice that he did not intend, but Tomás had recruited him to handle the military planning, had he not?

Jo's eyebrows rose and she sipped her cocoa silently, her eyes flashing back and forth between the two men.

"Because *Los Durmientes* are people. We cannot just kill them."

Jeff blinked. "The Ulim are our enemy. They are wiping out every human soldier the Authority has as we speak. Killing the enemy is kind of the purpose of the military."

"I hope we do not need to go into a debate about just war theory," Tomás said patiently, "but the purpose of the military is not to kill the enemy, but to protect the vulnerable."

"And the Ulim are the vulnerable all of the sudden?" Jeff could not believe what he was hearing.

"I am saying that, if we can, we should accomplish our goal without becoming as monstrous as *Los Durmientes*."

"They are enemy combatants. They have forfeited their right to life by attacking us."

"They showed you mercy, *mi amigo*. You must show them mercy in return."

It was clear Nira was not following the nuances of the conversation. Her brows bunched up like knotted cords. Jeff noticed but did not feel like explaining. He put his head in his hands and moved it back and forth slowly. Then he moaned. "Then for god's sake, what are we doing here?"

"Why did the Ulim have mercy on you?" Jo asked, although it was not clear whom she was asking.

Tomás turned toward her and smiled. "Everyone has a flaw, a moment of weakness. *Los Durmientes* are human, after all."

"Why is it a flaw when they do it, but a moral necessity when I do it?" Jeff asked.

"It?" Nira asked.

"Not killing," Jeff clarified. She really had lost the trail of the conversation, hadn't she?

"It is, as Augustine called it, *felix culpa*," Tomás explained. "A happy fault. A sin to rejoice in. A fortuitous mistake, even. You are alive, are you not?"

"Hip hip hooray," Jeff growled.

"Let us rejoice in the mercy we will show them, as well."

Jeff's teeth were grinding. He felt ready to bite the head off a rodent. Tomás would do, in a pinch.

"Killing them is an option," Tomás conceded. "But should we not examine *all* our options, to discern which is the best, most moral way ahead?"

"What are our other options?" Jo asked in a conciliatory tone. Jeff glanced at her and saw how very, very much she was enjoying seeing him ready to spit nails. *Goddam her,* he thought.

"We could simply stop them," Tomás said. "We could wake them, disconnect them from their life support, so that they will need to return to the fold of human community in order to survive."

"Wait, I was in the Interworld for a few days and felt like hell coming out," Nira noted. "How long have these fuckers been on life-support?"

"Two hundred and thirty-seven years," Tomás said.

Nira whistled. "*That* will kill them, too."

"They might wish themselves dead," Tomás nodded. "But they will *not* be dead. They will, however, cease to be a threat to your world, or any other."

"What will stop them from just going back into the All once we're gone?" Jeff asked.

"Shame," Tomás said. "My people will come out of hiding and tell them our stories."

"Don't they know your stories?" Jo asked.

"Knowing a story and meeting a person who is hurting are very different things," Tomás said. "In this world, I believe this process is called 'Truth and Reconciliation.' It is a worthy goal."

"It's easier to blast them into oblivion," Jeff noted.

"It is easier," Tomás conceded. "But easier is not always better."

"So you're saying our goal should be to infiltrate their compound and disconnect them from their life support—"

"And from their computers," Tomás added. "That is very important."

"Why?" Jeff asked.

"Because it augments their brains, connects them."

"Are you telling me that what you and I can do organically, they require a computer to accomplish?" Jeff asked.

"I am."

Jeff took a moment to let that sink it. His brain was racing.

"I think we just witnessed an 'Oh shit' moment," Jo whispered to Nira.

Nira grinned.

"We can destroy their computers," Jeff said.

"Oh, yes. I have no problems with that," Tomás said. "You may indulge your every violent impulse against their computers."

"*May* I?" Jeff raised one eyebrow. Was Tomás calling the shots now? Jeff had been operating under the impression they were partners, equals. *Probably he just spoke imprecisely*, he reasoned. *English is not his first language, after all*. He set the offense aside.

"Okay, boys, if you're done growling at each other," Jo put her cup on the table and leaned on her elbows. "Let's talk this through. It sounds like stopping the Ulim is preferable to killing them. That's good military logic."

Jeff's brows darkened, but he didn't interrupt.

"We're materializing on the far side of the moon. Then what?"

"Then Tomás and I transport into the Ulim compound," Jeff said, a grudging note still coloring his voice.

"And then what?" Jo asked.

"If the shaman here has no objections," Jeff scowled in Tomás' direction, "the *Talon* provides cover for us by creating a diversion."

"If the two of you can move the *Talon* to that universe so quickly," Jo reasoned, "why won't the Ulim just zap it to another universe as soon as they notice it?"

"They may well do that," Tomás said, "but I do not think they will notice it until her part is played."

"Anyone ever tell you that you talk funny?" Jo asked.

"I am not from here," Tomás smiled patiently. He took a swig from his coffee, now probably as cold as Jeff's own. "*Los Durmientes* are engaged elsewhere. All of their attention will be focused on the battle against the Authority. Remember that they are controlling about 1,500,000 *Comelones*—"

"Prox," Jeff translated.

"—and that is no small task. *Los Comelones* are machines—with some biological components, *si*, but with no will of their own. There are no other spacefaring races in my reality string. *Los Durmientes* know of no race that can cross from one universe to another. They will not be paying attention to whatever may emerge from behind the moon in 1.5 seconds."

"It'll give us what we need," Jeff said.

"What's to keep the Ulim from flinging us into the sun once they *do* notice us?" Jo asked.

Jeff and Tomás looked at each other. "Nothing," Tomás said. "We must hope that they do not think of it, or that mercy will prevail. The best we can hope for is that they…fling you…" he seemed to enjoy wrapping his mouth around the new word, "elsewhere, where you will not be in danger."

Jo shrugged. "Well, every military action has risks."

"Wherever that is, we can find you," Jeff said, "and we will retrieve you."

"So long as you're not dead," Jo said.

"So long as we're not dead," Jeff agreed.

"Well, what are we waiting for, then?" Jo asked. She shot a look at Nira. "Don't you wish *you* were coming?" The sarcasm was thick, and Nira did not answer.

"Let's go," Jeff said.

"One thing," Tomás said. "I have a gift for you."

He disappeared from sight. Nira jumped in her seat, her eyes wide.

Jeff held his hand up. "You get used to it."

A moment later, Tomás was back, holding the carapace Jeff had found.

Tomás turned it over and placed the plate of Prox armor on the table, its rounded edge down like an upside-down turtle shell. He slid it over to Jeff.

Jeff scowled as he picked it up. Inside the shell, Tomás had somehow fashioned anchors. He might even have filed them directly into the carapace, judging from the marks inside the shell. Onto these anchors he had woven leather strands, which secured a single gauntlet, a perfect fit for Jeff's own forearm.

"It is a shield," Tomás said. "Guaranteed to withstand the attacks of *Los Comelones*, because it *is un Comelón*."

Whatever irritation he had been feeling toward the little man evaporated. Jeff chewed on his lip as he turned the carapace over, then fitted his left arm into the gauntlet. Perfect.

"I'm…that was very kind, Tomás," Jeff said. "Thank you."

"It was not kindness, not really," Tomás said. "You will need it."

"And how about you?" Jo asked.

"Every military action has risks," Tomás said.

CHAPTER THIRTEEN

[String 308]

Jeff stood behind Jo's chair on the bridge, watching the preparations. Weapons were operational, and Jo had her best weaponer at them. Jeff glanced over at the young woman with spiky white hair. *Shell,* he recalled her first name. *Weird fucking name.* But she looked capable enough. Hell, she was fierce.

The jump to String 308 had been far easier than Jeff had imagined. Tomás had gone first, holding open the sleeve, while Jeff gathered the space directly around the *Talon* and reached through. It had required a tremendous amount of energy, but Jeff could tell he was getting better at it. The moon in the new universe was shielding them well, providing time to rest and prepare. Jo's chief engineer had everything running at 100%. Shields were fluctuating between 95 and 98%, which was optimal. Jo had made sure her A-team was well-rested as well.

"Battle stations," Jo said. A yellow alert icon appeared in the corner of every visible monitor. She stood and turned back to Jeff and Tomás. "What are you two still doing here? You've got a mission to perform, haven't you?"

"A word with the captain before we embark?" Jeff asked.

Jo's eyes narrowed, and he saw the small curl of a smile at the edge of her mouth. "In my ready room, Captain."

Jeff put his hand out, a signal to Tomás to stay put. The little man's eyebrows raised, but he didn't follow as Jeff and Jo walked to the door.

They stepped in and the door slid shut behind them. Jo turned and grabbed the lapels of Jeff's uniform, pulling him in, kissing him. His mouth met hers hungrily and for a few precious moments, nothing existed but the sensation of her wet, lovely mouth on his. He felt intoxicated by the smell of her, the solidness of her. She, whom he had betrayed, now restored to him, and miraculously, loving him. He felt desperate, sad, anxious—an emotional mass that he did not have the facility to untangle or the vocabulary to articulate.

"You be careful, soldier," she said. "I want you back on this ship and in my bed by 1800 hours. You can even wear your jacket…" she kissed him again, "…but *only* your jacket."

"Yes, sir," Jeff agreed.

Then she gently pushed him away, shook her hair, and straightened her jacket. It occurred to Jeff that Jo didn't wear lipstick, so at least they didn't have to worry about smears. *Unlike Emma,* Jeff thought. *Emma is a lipstick kind-of-woman.* He pushed the thought away and focused on the task at hand.

The door slid open and, all business, Jo walked straight to her chair, ignoring the slight smiles and raised eyebrows of her crew. Jeff walked over to Tomás, stooping momentarily to pick up his carapace shield. "Let's go."

"Weapons, Captain?" Jo swiveled her chair and shot Jeff a look over her shoulder.

"They should be ready in the armory now," he said. "We'll leave from there."

"Make it so," Jo said.

Jeff smiled at her presumption of operational command. He knew she was teasing him, but did not take the bait. He turned on his heel and paused at the door of the bridge, waited for it to slide open, and stepped through, Tomás on his heels.

He reminded himself to walk slower than he ordinarily would.

Tomás' legs were shorter, and he'd have to work harder to match Jeff's typically broad stride. He matched himself to Tomás' speed, watching his friend in his peripheral vision.

Soon they were entering the armory. When Jeff and Tomás approached the desk, the lieutenant on duty looked nervous. "Uh… Captain, I'm sorry, but we didn't have the gun you requested, so I had to send a message to supply. They're synthesizing it n—"

The door opened behind them, and a large, older man swept in, instantly filling the room with the force of his grin. "Jeff Bowers, you rat-in-a-hole!"

"Palamar?" Jeff was confused. "But you're…" he was going to say *dead*, but he stopped himself. Whatever might have happened to Palamar in his own universe—and there was a great deal of speculation about that—it had not happened here, or at least it had not done him in.

He shook the older man's hand vigorously, not objecting to the low-ranking man's familiarity. He was too much in shock to take offense. "Uh, Palamar, this is Tomás, my…" he paused. Analog? Mentor? Shaman? Who or what the hell *was* Tomás to him anyway? He didn't know. "…friend," he said at last.

"What the fuck is that?" Palamar pointed to the shield hanging from the gauntlet on Jeff's forearm.

"It's the dorsal plate off one of the creatures that is currently eating Sol Station," Jeff said. It came out sounding more callous than he'd expected.

Palamar reeled a bit. "Whoa. For real? That's…disturbing."

"We'll be facing them down there, too," Jeff said, referring to the planet. *Earth*, he reminded himself. *In this universe, that planet is Earth*. "Tomás made it for me. Our guess is that nothing will protect us from the Prox better than the Prox."

"Huh," Palamar grunted. He handed Jeff an Echo 47M Blaster. "So this is for you?" The old man seemed surprised.

"It is. Best damn blaster in history," Jeff said.

"Uh…it *does* belong in a museum." Palamar cocked his head.

"Is it full?"

"It's got a full charge, if that's what you mean," Palamar said. "I just topped it off myself."

"You look good," Jeff said…*for a dead man*.

"You're looking pretty damn good yourself, for a dead man."

Jeff froze.

The old man put his hands on his hips. "Well, you be careful down there."

"Always."

Palamar offered his hand again, then he left.

"That man is *muy grande*," Tomás said.

"He can suck the air out of any place he's in faster than an open airlock, that's for sure," Jeff agreed.

He fastened the blaster holster to his belt, inserting its tab into his combat trousers, mid-thigh, to keep it from flopping about. It felt solid. He withdrew the weapon and checked its settings. Palamar had been right—it had a full charge. He holstered it again and turned to Tomás.

"You'll need a weapon," he said.

"I do not think so," Tomás said.

"Have you ever…shot a weapon?" Jeff asked.

"Well, no. Not as such," Tomás said. "Do bows count?"

"As in bows-and-arrows?" Jeff asked, his voice rising in disbelief. "You're shitting me, right?"

Tomás shrugged.

"Oh God. I just assumed…we should have been practicing at the range here."

"It is too late now."

"Uh…" Jeff cast around, giving the armory officer a panicked look. "What do you have that's powerful, small, and simple—a TX5?"

The young man scowled. "TX5?" he repeated. He obviously had no idea what a TX5 was. *So, no TX5s in String 311*, Jeff thought. *Good to know*. He snapped his fingers. "Powerful, small, simple," he repeated.

The young man's forehead bunched as he thought. He put one finger into the air silently, waited until Jeff nodded, and disappeared through a door behind his desk. When he returned, he was holding a little black blaster that looked exactly like a TX5.

"This should do it," the young man said. "A Gibbon 7."

"Gibbon?" Jeff asked. "Isn't that a small, furry marsupial or something?" It didn't sound deadly.

The young man shrugged. "I don't know, sir. That's just the name of the gun. Maybe it was named after the inventor."

Jeff nodded, suddenly aware of the time. If they didn't hurry, Jo would be giving them a nudge. "How many tar can it deliver?"

"42,000 tars per burst."

"Shit," Jeff said. "I'm tempted to trade in the Echo."

"It's comparable, but…the amperage is greater on the Echo. I checked out the schematics while Mr. Palamar was synthesizing it." He shrugged. "It's an unusual gun and I'm…kind of *into* guns."

"It seems, sir, you have found your niche," Jeff said. "Rig my friend up with a holster, please. How complicated is the Gibbon?"

"Point and shoot, sir. There is a power adjustment, but you can only turn it down. It's a battlefield weapon, so it always defaults to full power. There *is* a safety, here," he pointed it out to them. "Slide it back with your thumb and it's ready to shoot. The safety does not automatically engage, so you need to be sure to slide it up when you're out of danger."

"Got that?" Jeff asked Tomás.

Tomás gave him a moon-faced look that he was beginning to hate. It seemed to express both disagreement and non-cooperation without actually saying "no" to anything. Inside, Jeff growled.

He knelt and fixed the holster to Tomás' belt.

"There's no tab receptor in his pant leg," Jeff said to the man.

"Try this." The young man rummaged in a drawer. He pulled out a length of leather. It might have been a boot lace. "Old school," he said. "Tie it to the bottom of the holster—there's an eye there for it—and then tie it around his leg. Not too tight."

"What is this, the wild fucking west?" Jeff said. He worked quickly, and in less than a minute he stood up and surveyed his work.

"I feel absurd," Tomás confessed.

"You look badass," Jeff countered. It was an outright lie. Tomás looked ridiculous.

"We should go," Tomás said.

"Thanks for the help," Jeff said.

And then they were gone.

[STRING 311]

SINCE THERE WAS no traditional floor indicator like those found in human elevators, Emma couldn't tell if the lift was going incredibly slow or travelling a very long way. She stared at her feet, occasionally glancing at Bucky and Amberline for clues as to whether they were getting close or not, but their faces were as blank and unmoving as ever.

She began to detect a high-pitched ringing sound, but she couldn't tell where it was coming from. It was growing louder, as though they were approaching it. And then she started to feel queasy.

"Something's wrong," she said, reaching out to steady herself on the wall. "I feel sick."

"You will be fine, it's just disorienting."

"No," Emma insisted. "I feel really weird." Her head was spinning and her stomach was clenched in knots. Her feet looked very far away and seemed to be receding. "I think I've been drugged. Did you drug me again?" She stared accusingly at Amberline.

"No, I assure you. There are no drugs involved," Amberline said, raising a claw in oath.

"Then… what's happening?" Her feet detached from the floor. She looked at the two Alverians, who were now floating in the cab, stretched into surreal, elongated versions of themselves. The high-pitched sound was now deafening, threatening to split her skull open. Emma was terrified and closed her eyes, trying to hold on to her sanity. That only made her nausea worse, so she opened them again. The elevator cab appeared to be fifty feet tall, the floor—and her feet—disappearing into the distance, as was the ceiling above them. Emma curled up into a fetal position, trembling. She felt Amberline's steadying touch, turning her over until her feet were aimed at the ceiling. But were they? She opened her eyes and couldn't see any difference, the elevator was almost perfectly symmetrical vertically, and if she had turned, so had the Alverians.

The floor and ceiling were slowly moving back towards each other. She was compressing like a stretched rubber band being slowly released, the others returning to more normal proportions. Gravity was also slowly returning, and she settled gently to the floor on her side. Emma tried to clamber to her knees, but her stomach could take no more. She began vomiting uncontrollably, and when her stomach was empty, she was wracked with dry heaves. Crying, she tried to get up to her feet, but was too shaky. Amberline reached down and helped her up.

Everything appeared normal again, and the ringing sound was receding below them. Yes, it felt like the elevator was going up now, but at the same slow, trundling pace. Emma glanced at the puddle on the floor; the cab was filled with the smell of her sick. She glanced at Amberline. "I'm sorry."

Amberline made the sign of dismissal. "I am the one who should be sorry. We did not take your physiology into account. We should have prepared you better."

"Prepared me for what? *What was that?*"

"The heart of the hive," Bucky signed. It didn't explain much.

Ashamed, Emma stood in silence until the elevator finally stopped and the doors opened, letting in a breath of blessed clean air.

They stepped out into a large lobby of sorts, or maybe a waiting room. A row of Alverian chairs was set up along one wall, a large archway opened through the opposite wall. Bucky gestured to follow and walked into the dark chamber beyond.

"Where are we going? What is..." Emma trailed off as her eyes adjusted to the darkness.

They were in an observation gallery, a long building on the surface of the asteroid. Enormous windows opened out onto a breathtaking vista of space. A field of stars brighter and more crowded than anything she had ever seen before wrapped around and above the rocky landscape. A reddish planet dominated the sky, illuminated by a small red dwarf sun.

"Not an asteroid, a moon…" she whispered, reluctant to break the silence.

"Yes," Amberline's mask said. "This is our homeworld, and the hive is its moon."

The planet didn't look hospitable by human standards, but then it wasn't meant for humans. It was relatively dry-looking compared to Earth, with very little standing water and sparse, rugged-looking vegetation. But it *was* clearly inhabited. Complex cities spread out across mesas and plains, all arranged radially around a central hub, all connected by highways or maybe travel tubes. On the dark side, intricate webs of lights twinkled and danced. In the distance, she could see small spacecraft rising up from the planet's surface and drifting toward the hive.

"Wait," Emma said, confused. "I saw the hive from the outside when we first approached it. It wasn't orbiting a planet. There was no planet."

"Incorrect," Bucky signed. "This is the outside of the hive. What you saw before was the inside of the hive."

[STRING 308]

Jo chewed on her fingernail. It was at the point where if she chewed any more it might bleed. She put her hand under her thigh.

Waiting was the worst part of command. And there was so damned much of it. Jo looked around at her team. She couldn't honestly say that any of them were the best she had ever worked with, but they were all, in their way, talented and competent—occasionally exceptional.

That was fine. Jo was a believer in the "good enough" crew. That was, after all, the only kind she had ever known. She suspected that, outside of fiction or the vids, it was the only kind there really was.

"I'm reading two human life forms on the ground," Mr. Liebert said.

Two human life forms in danger, she thought. *If only I didn't love one of them.*

Tomás was a strange little man. Jo didn't know quite what to make of him. He seemed trustworthy. He even seemed…strangely familiar. She supposed they were lucky to have someone from this reality string on their team.

That thought made her close her eyes and shake her head. *Too weird*, she thought. *It's just too weird.*

She thought back to Jeff's kiss, just a few minutes ago, just before he and Tomás had disappeared. She breathed deep, reliving it, feeling the emotion and the chemicals surge through her brain and body. It felt heady, intoxicating. She wanted more of it. Which meant that, somehow, she needed to keep Jeff alive. *Well, I've got a starship with enough firepower to take out a large city,* she thought. *That'll have to do.*

The idea had been Jeff's. The Ulim compound would be crawling with Prox—standing guard outside, certainly, but that wasn't a problem. Jeff and Tomás would simply teleport to the inside of the facility. But that's where most of the Prox would be, according to Tomás—tending to their masters. The *Talon* would create a diversion that would send the Prox scrambling to meet the threat, leaving Jeff and Tomás free to approach the Sleepers and sabotage their computers.

Jo didn't understand why they didn't just take out their power source. All they needed was its location, and a well-aimed particle cannon would take it out, cleanly and simply. But Tomás had nixed the idea with some bullshit about life support and keeping the Ulim alive until they could breathe and eat and poop for themselves again. *Bullshit*, she thought. But they had agreed on a plan. She glanced up at her neural's chronometer. Time to execute it.

She stood and straightened her jacket. "Mr. Ditka, power aft particle cannons. As soon as we're in position, I want you to lock onto the mission target and prepare to fire on my mark."

"Aye, sir." Shell Ditka's fingers began to fly over her console.

"Mr. Chi, I assume you have that course locked in and ready?"

"Locked in and ready, aye sir."

"Then take us in, Lieutenant."

The *Talon* shuddered as the sub-light drive kicked in, shoving the ship out from behind the moon.

"In position, sir," Chi called over her shoulder.

"Fire," Jo said.

In her peripheral vision, Jo saw Ditka's fingers enter the command. Then the impact hit the bridge.

Everything happened quickly, but in Jo's memory, in slow motion. The lurch came first, throwing her off her feet, pitching her headfirst into Marcia Chi's navigational panel. Jo heard the crack of her own skull, felt her neck jerk out of alignment with a sickening snap. Blood gushed from her forehead as she struggled to regain her feet.

The bridge was a cacophony of warning lights and sirens. It shuddered beneath her like the most dramatic earthquake she had ever experienced enhanced by several magnitudes. Gravity was askew, making the bridge seem like it was at an impossible slope. The ship around her shuddered with some unknown, unseen impact, and she heard the screams and groans of twisting metal deep in the guts of the ship.

Jo crawled toward her command chair, and with a cry of exertion she did not bother to moderate, she swung herself into the seat and strapped herself in. "What the fuck was that?" she called out to her crew. She was relieved to see that they were all strapped in and alive. Not waiting for their answer, she wiped the blood out of her eyes and looked up, hoping to find some real-time data about the state of her ship online.

"Explosion in section 27D," Liebert said.

"The aft weapons system…" Ditka's voice sounded desperate. "… it exploded when we tried to fire."

"What happened?" Jo spat.

"No idea, sir," Ditka answered. "Weapons were checked and double-checked. They were in perfect condition. I…don't have any explanation, sir."

One more sabotage, Jo thought. Was there a connection? She didn't have the time to wonder about it.

"Damage report," Jo yelled, although she could already see some of it filtering into her neural interface. The data was sporadic and feeding from only about half of the sensors. She gave up and looked down, deciding to trust her people to mediate what was important.

Liebert's head was moving back and forth as he tried to synthesize the information he was seeing from different sources. "Hull breaches in four places," he called. "We got active vacuums on decks 21, 22, 26, and 30. Structural integrity at 22%...and dropping, sir."

"This ship is going to fold up like a tin can," Jo said out loud. Instantly she regretted it, but she didn't have the leisure to soften her remarks or second-guess them. "Signal abandon ship. Let's get everyone to the pods. Now!"

The red alert was blaring, but on top of that the evacuation siren began screaming.

"Move out, all of you," Jo yelled above the din. "Go straight to the pods and don't look back!"

"What about you, sir?" Chi asked.

"That's an order!" Jo answered. "Now move!"

She watched as they struggled to unbuckle themselves without falling.

"Faster!" Jo demanded.

They struggled uphill toward the bridge door. Once they were out of sight, she put them out of her thoughts. She transferred helm control to her command chair and called up an image of the planet on the only remaining monitor. It was coming closer. It was coming fast.

Then the lights went out, and in the few seconds of absolute dark before the gentle glow of the emergency lighting kicked in, she heard her own breath, the pounding of blood in her head, and the twisting groan of metal as her ship folded in on itself.

CHAPTER FOURTEEN

When Jeff opened his eyes, he was surrounded by the same lush jungle he had seen before. It was relentlessly green. He glanced to his left and saw Tomás crouched like a tiger, vigilant.

"What?" Jeff asked.

Tomás pointed. "Don't move," he whispered.

Slowly, Jeff turned his head in the direction Tomás had pointed. A Prox soldier was scuttling through the trees about twenty meters away. Reflexively, both Jeff and Tomás started to lower themselves, very slowly, to the ground.

"Shit," Jeff whispered. "Do you think it saw?"

"I think if it saw us, it would run toward us," Tomás said.

From where they were, Jeff could see the Ulim bunker. At least, that was how he thought of it. He knew it was probably massive inside. He had seen that, after all. It didn't look that big from his current perspective, however. He noted that the building abutted a large hill, and guessed that it extended into it for some distance.

"As soon as the *Talon* starts its battery, we'll jump inside," Jeff said, repeating aloud the details they'd both gone over many times.

"*Si.*"

"Tell me about the location we'll be jumping to," Jeff requested.

Tomás shrugged. "It has been a long time, and I was very little. There were lots of places to hide, and when I was there before, it was largely dormant." He grinned. "That word is the same in your language and mine."

Jeff ignored the linguistic diversion.

"I'm guessing that once the explosions start, any Prox that have their pincers in a tub are going to scramble to protect the Ulim, so the laundry room will be empty."

"That is a logical assumption, I think."

Jeff scowled. *The little guy really does irritate the shit out of me*, he thought. He looked back over to where they had seen the Prox and rose up slightly to see over the tangle of vegetation that shielded them. It was moving away, not swiftly, but steadily.

"I think we're in the clear," he said.

"They are not terribly perceptive," Tomás said. "They are built for strength, not sensitivity."

He could be describing me, Jeff thought. It had never occurred to him that he and the Prox had much in common. He did not like the idea.

He studied the bunker. There were windows, but they were as narrow as prison windows—too narrow to allow passage. *Are they trying to keep people in or out?* he wondered. It occurred to him that the building might have been originally constructed for another purpose. Had it been a prison at one time? If so, where was the wall? Perhaps it had dissolved into the jungle over the centuries.

"How many of those patrols are there?" Jeff asked.

"When I was a boy, I counted six, each with overlapping *territorios*," Tomás replied.

"You were either one brave motherfucking kid or a stupid one," Jeff said.

Tomás shrugged.

Irritating as fuck, Jeff thought.

"Any time now, Jo," Jeff said through his teeth. He glanced up into his neural to check the time. "Five seconds," he said.

"We should be on the ground," Tomás said.

They both crouched as low as they could, steeling themselves for the shaking earth that would soon result from the particle barrage.

"…2, and 1," Jeff counted, his hand instinctively going to the blaster on his thigh. Every muscle in his body tensed against the coming assault.

His breath drew in, it went out. It came in, it went out. His tensed muscles ached.

He glanced at Tomás. Tomás glanced at him. Nothing.

"What the fuck, Jo?" he whispered. She was a professional. He was counting on her. What the hell was she up to?

Tomás slapped at his arm and pointed up. "*Observar*," he whispered.

Jeff looked up.

The sun was bright, but the sky was clear. There wasn't a cloud anywhere to break the solid curtain of powder blue. The sky was only interrupted by a tiny flare of light blooming in the middle of the air.

[STRING 311]

TAL HAD SEEN plenty of warfare in his time. He had never seen anything like this. The Wengret ring, as he'd come to think of it, contained, at last count, 2,927 ships—all of them armed, all of them with weapons trained on the Prox ships. And then all of them were firing.

Nearly three thousand ships arrayed against three. The odds would seem to be in their favor. For a moment, Tal allowed himself a flicker of hope at the thought of this.

But the problem, he reminded himself, *isn't the three ships—it's the hundreds of thousands of Prox soldiers, each of them spaceborne, each of them deadly, each of them so small they're almost impossible to hit at a distance—that's the problem.*

They'd worked on a solution to that—rapid-fire, computer-controlled particle cannons that could pinpoint the Prox soldiers and hit them where it hurt most, to the tune of 27 shots per second. But there were a lot of "ifs" involved before that system would deploy—*if* they got past the Wengret ring, if the distance didn't too badly erode the particle burst, if the targeting algorithm was sufficiently accurate. The good news was that the closer the Prox got, the more problems were solved with the system. The bad news was that the closer the Prox got, the closer they were to the Prox.

Tal shook his head to clear it. That was another battle. One he hoped he did not have to fight. He hoped the Wengret ring would do the trick.

Tal looked up at the ashen, drawn face of Lieutenant Liu. He was standing by Tal's chair, ready for anything the Admiral might need, but the man couldn't take his eyes off the monitors. Tal's gaze travelled down, sweeping over the Command Center. Liu wasn't alone. Everyone's gaze was frozen on the monitors. They didn't even seem to be blinking. It occurred to Tal that if they lived through this, there were going to be a lot of sore necks in the morning. He almost smiled at the thought.

He couldn't avoid it any more—he looked up at the monitors himself.

The Prox ships were steadily advancing, 10,000 kilometers and closing. The funnel formation on the schematic monitor was beginning to be blunted on one side, the neat symmetry of the formation eroding now as the Prox side of the funnel became shorter.

Tal glanced at the display from the exterior camera, zoomed in to provide an adjacent perspective to the Wengret ring. Their ships were wedged so thickly into the ring that Tal could imagine a giant hopping from one ship to another, all the way around. But the scene still seemed serene.

The real action was on the infrared and ultraviolet monitor, since the energy signatures of most weapons were not visible to the human eye. It was on this monitor that Tal saw every ship firing at full capacity. He could still make out the ships, but they were obscured by a tangled fog of light—manifested on the screen in either red or purple, depending on weapons signatures.

He could see that some ships were blasting wide, hoping to catch as many of the Prox soldiers as possible. "Liu, contact the captains of the ships that are blasting wide, inform them that they are just wasting their shots. The energy from the blasts is too dissipated to do any damage to the enemy. Tell them that narrow, targeted bursts will be more effective."

"Aye sir," Liu put his hand to his earpiece and began issuing orders.

In seconds, Tal saw his adjustment take hold. He also saw the tally of Prox kills increase dramatically. He nodded his satisfaction, but the tally would still not be enough.

"Prox ships are at 5,000 kilometers and closing," one of the engineers called.

One glance up told Tal what he feared most—the furthest Prox soldier was considerably closer than that. 1,000 kilometers, then quickly into the hundreds.

Tal gripped the arms of his chair.

Three thousand ships were in open fire, sending the most deadly array of energy humans had ever mustered against an enemy, and yet the Prox floated on serenely, as if nothing were happening. It chilled Tal to the bone.

At least the Prox soldiers were dying—the death count increased as their proximity closed and targeting became more precise. Tal watched with a thrill of pleasure as the count soared into the thousands. *That's good,* he thought. *But it's not enough and not fast enough.*

"The first of the Prox soldiers is approaching the ring, sir," called one of the people on the floor.

This is it, Tal thought. His fingers dug into the arms of his command chair. "I want all ships in that quadrant of the ring redirecting their firepower from the ships to picking off individual Prox," he ordered.

"Aye, sir," Liu said, communicating his orders immediately.

With one eye, Tal watched the blur of energy detonations on the

IR/UV monitor, with the other he watched the death count. They were making headway…but…

"The first Prox soldier is about to land, sir. Twenty seconds…nineteen…"

"Oh, Christ," Tal said out loud. "Employ the DPB." The DPB was what Tal had called the intelligence Captain Bowers had left him, a deterrent power burst wired into the hulls of the ships. They'd gotten the devices wired up in nearly half of their ships, but Tal had no clue about their effectiveness. For one thing, they'd had no time to test them and no opportunity to test them on Prox. For another, there was no uniformity—they had sent the plans by data packet to every ship in the formation, with orders to construct them as seemed best for each individual ship design. They had a hodge-podge assembly of three thousand very different ships, and each one was interpreting the schematics in its own way—some of them eccentrically, he was sure. Half had completed the deterrent in time, half had not. None of them had been tested.

He was about to find out how well the engineers of the *Spearhead* had interpreted the plans. It was a class five warship, assigned to the Deep Space Marines. It was a good test case. The DSM were highly efficient. If anyone could adapt the plans quickly and effectively, it would be their engineers.

"Zoom in on the *Spearhead*," Tal barked. "I want to see this thing in action. And get an IF/UV monitor on it, too."

It had been such a simple idea—a high-voltage burst along the surface of the outer hull. But Tal had no idea if it would work, or how effective it would be. He only knew that he trusted the man who had brought it—a man from another universe; a man he had exiled; a man who had outmaneuvered him.

"Let's hope you are right, Captain Bowers," Tal breathed.

"Sir?" Liu asked.

Tal waved him away and focused on the monitors. He held his breath as he saw the first of the Prox approach the *Spearhead*, its spindly legs held out in front of it, ready to absorb the impact with the ship's hull. Tal nearly tore the fabric of his chair as the Prox landed, then hopped and skittered with the force of its contact—it had been really moving. But now it had extended all of its legs—and all seemed to be working. Tal watched as it raised one great pincer, ready to pierce the iconel sheets of the hull.

And then he saw a flash of electromagnetic energy on the IF/UV monitor, showing up as yellow. He bit his lip as he saw the Prox soldier freeze, then drift away from the hull, motionless.

"Yes!" Tal shouted. But a moment later he regretted it.

The soldier must have rebooted itself, because within seconds its limbs were working again, and it was moving toward the hull once again. It landed, and once again the electrical burst lit up the screens. This time, however, the Prox was ready. It still needed to reboot, but it wasn't going anywhere. Tal squinted to see why, but couldn't. Had it magnetically attached itself? Or had it hooked whatever passed for a Prox toe onto a structural feature of the ship? He couldn't tell from this distance.

The voltage hit again, but with each blast, the Prox soldier seemed less fazed by it. An abyss formed in Tal's belly as he watched the pincer rear back, strike, and pierce the skin of the hull. His mouth dropped open as he saw the creature roll back the plates of iconel. He shook with rage and frustration as the atmospheric seal was breached. He saw a great gush of oxygen and heat and scrap metal blow out past the Prox soldier. He felt numb as he watched the writhing bodies of marines shoot out into the vacuum of space, gasping, twitching, dying.

[STRING 308]

THE EXPLOSION FILLED THE PORTHOLES, and everyone in the escape pod jerked to cover their eyes. Danny grimaced, trying to tough it out, but even he had to move his hand in front of his face. Even with his eyes screwed shut tight, the light coming through his eyelids was painfully bright.

The light was intermittent, however, because the pod was tumbling end over end. Danny felt his lunch lurching for his throat. He clenched his fists and bore down to keep his food where it was. At least with his eyes closed there was little sensation of motion, so he kept them that way.

He had just barely made it to the pod in time. *I misjudged that*, he thought. *That was stupid.*

But it was a near thing. He couldn't be seen hanging out near the pods. People would have wondered how he knew he'd need to board it. Then they would have concluded that he had caused it, after all.

Instead, he had searched for a food synthesizer nearby and ordered up a snack. Who knew how long it would be before he had another meal?

He hadn't known exactly when Taylor would use the particle cannon. It could have been minutes or days. He didn't know what she was planning. He only trusted that she had a trigger finger that wouldn't quit.

He had tumbled into the escape pod just before the door had slid shut and sealed behind him. *I am one lucky bastard*, he thought. And he was not the only one. The pod was already full. Twelve people were strapped in. Danny and four others were holding tightly to straps and poles as their bodies were drawn into the middle of the weightless room, like cantilevers at odd angles to one another.

"Hey, it's you," a voice said. It was a high voice, female, familiar. Danny twisted around to see the speaker. It was the Pakistani cadet he'd met in the corridor.

"Hey there, cadet," Danny said, swallowing the bile that was threatening the back of his teeth again.

"I'm glad you made it," she said.

It was a kind thing to say. Maybe it was even sincere. Too bad he couldn't return the sentiment. In his heart, Danny cursed everyone in the pod but himself. Every survivor was a failure, after all. Every escape pod, every living human body still breathing was a potential kill that he hadn't been able to notch onto his blaster.

He grimaced, showing her enough teeth to pass for a smile. "Good to see you too, cadet."

JEFF AND TOMÁS didn't even need to speak. Nor did Jeff think. Acting on pure instinct, he closed his eyes and projected himself into the All. His consciousness surrounded the *Talon* like a cloud of presence, taking in every aspect of its situation, every detail.

It wasn't pretty. Jeff could see the escape pods drifting away helplessly, little aimless pockets of breathable air scurrying away from the listing beast that had been home. He could see where the explosion had taken place—in the aft weapons array. There was nothing left of that, nor indeed of the portside C-drive accelerator. There were hull breaches on almost every deck. There was nothing left of engineering, save for the first couple decks, and those were badly damaged.

The fore of the ship fared better, and Jeff found several people still alive who hadn't made it to the escape pods. And Jo? There she was, her presence strong and defiant, in her captain's chair, ready and willing to go down with her ship.

"Not today," Jeff said.

He squashed space and teleported to the *Talon*, materializing just in time to send four of the crew spinning into the All toward Tomás. Jeff sensed the little man's will, his intention, just as he knew Tomás was reading his own. They acted as two halves of a single brain, coordinating their own set of skills toward a common purpose—saving as many lives as possible.

Jeff snatched people up as he jogged through the corridors, pacing himself so that he wouldn't tire and have to stop. He dispatched them into the in-between place; he sensed their safe reception. He had no idea what Tomás was doing with them, only that he was doing something, only that they were safe.

As he ran, he sent his consciousness out ahead of him. He played with his field of vision, now in a mess hall, now encompassing the ship, now radiating out to two decks above and below, now three. He wasn't systematic, but he wasn't chaotic, either. He was making it up as he went along, trusting his gut, and every time he went wide, encircling the ship, he assessed his progress. And it was good.

An explosion rocked the deck under his feet and he stumbled. Pain shot through his ankle. "Shit!" Jeff said aloud. He put his hands out to break his fall, and rolled to absorb the impact. Once in a sitting position, he felt at his ankle. Not broken. Sprained maybe. He stood and, limping, continued his survey of the ship.

The center of gravity was off, making it seem as if he were running uphill. The only way that was possible was if the hull were buckling and the deck was out of skew with the sight horizon. If that was the case, there was no saving the *Talon*. Its less damaged decks might allow it to serve as a lifeboat to get them home, but that was all it would be able to do at this point. And Jeff was not even sure of that. There was no way life support would be sustainable with engineering out.

Jeff heard an echoing scream of metal that made his flesh crawl. *That's not just the hull, that's the lateral ballast struts*, he thought. He had never heard of a ship losing those.

His pulse pounded in his ears as he limped around a corner. There was a door up ahead, and two people huddled within it. He didn't need to touch them. He didn't even need to open the door at this point. He reached out with his mind, found them, propelled them into the All, toward Tomás, toward an unknown safety.

Jeff had made a circuit around the surviving portions of the ship. Now he headed for the center. There was only one person left. *I don't need to hobble there,* he reminded himself. He closed his eyes and projected himself into the midmost section of the ship, to its most protected kernel—the bridge.

He opened his eyes and saw Jo, her hands gripping the arms of her command chair, as if holding on to her purpose, her identity, until her dying breath. Were her eyes wide at the terror of oblivion, or at his sudden appearance out of thin air? He didn't know, and it didn't matter.

He rushed to her and caught her up, embracing her fragile frame and fumbling at the straps that held her.

"No—I—there are people—"

"No there aren't. I got them all. And now I've got you."

"Jeff, I've got—"

"You will not go down with the ship, goddammit. Not today."

He got her free, took her hand and pulled her out of the seat, then closed his eyes and propelled himself toward Tomás. As he did, he felt the bridge erupt behind him as the oxygen in life support exploded, bathing the remaining decks in fire.

CHAPTER FIFTEEN

Jeff clutched at Jo's writhing body, pressing her to himself as they traversed the void. In his mind, he reached out, seeking Tomás' energy, his presence. He found him. He willed himself there, and in moments he was setting Jo down on the floor of a cave. He was surrounded by people, destitute people, small people. He glanced about to get his bearings. Harsh sunlight illuminated one side of the cave—the entrance, no doubt. Fire flickered deeper in. Tomás was arguing in Spanish—so quickly and ferociously that Jeff couldn't catch any of what was being said. He gathered only that they were not entirely welcome.

Jo pushed him away and jumped to her feet. Then she fell. Jeff caught her. Pain shot through his ankle again and they both almost fell. He lowered her to the floor of the cave and sat beside her. He saw an item of clothing near by—a bright strip of cloth that might have been a scarf. He leaned over and snatched it up. "Jo…" he knew giving her orders was not going to fly. He struggled to mediate his response in a way that she could hear. "The teleportation is…disorienting. It's best to sit for a bit before standing up." He took off his boot and examined his ankle. As he suspected, it wasn't broken. He tore the scarf lengthwise and began to wind it tightly around his ankle.

When he looked up, Jo's face was a confusing mixture of rage and fear and incomprehension. She looked as helpless as he had ever seen her. Even when they had been making love, she was entirely in control. His heart twisted a bit at the thought of how uncomfortable she must be. He reached for her hand. He was grateful that she did not jerk it away.

Instead, she clutched it, and using it as leverage, she hoisted herself to a sitting position. Then she kept holding it, nodding at some interior dialogue, and beginning to take in their surroundings.

All around them were what remained of the crew of the *Talon*. Many were still on the floor, but some were trying their legs out again, a couple were walking around the circumference of the cave.

Tomás' people let them be. Jeff noted with surprise that among his people, Tomás was tall. He smiled at that.

"What?" Jo asked. "What are you smiling at?"

Jeff looked back at her. He didn't feel like explaining. "Tomás seems to be in a bit of a pickle," he said instead.

She looked over at where the supposed shaman was arguing, gesturing wildly with his hands with a small gaggle of old men and women. Jo cocked her head.

"He's been exiled," Jo said. "They're angry that he's back."

"I didn't know you speak Spanish," Jeff said.

"They're even angrier that he's brought all these gringos," she said.

"They did not say 'gringo,'" Jeff said. "I would have picked that out."

"No, they're saying *los ingleses*," Jo said. "Same thing."

"Huh. None of us are English that I know of."

"Just shut up, please." Jo was listening.

Jeff squeezed her hand and let it go. He stood to his full height and tested his ankle. It hurt, but the new support helped. He walked and was able to do so without an obvious limp. *Walk it off,* he thought, and headed over to Tomás. Tomás was engaged in conversation and didn't seem to notice him. Jeff sensed a presence behind him and turned to see the hard, determined features of Shell Ditka.

"Mr. Ditka," he nodded.

"Captain," she said.

He turned back to Tomás. There seemed to be a stalemate.

"Care to explain what this is all about?" he asked.

The elders glanced up at him, as if noticing him for the first time. He forced a smile and waved awkwardly at them, even though they were close enough to shake his hand.

Their eyes travelled down from his face to his uniform, to his captain's bars. Their eyes widened.

"Uh…do they like the military, or not so much?" he asked Tomás.

"They don't like power or servitude," Tomás said. "They are afraid you have come to enslave them."

"What?" Jeff jerked his head back, blinking.

"When every stranger you have ever known is a tyrant, every stranger looks like a tyrant," Tomás said. The sadness in his voice seemed infinite.

"Uh…have they noticed that we're refugees?" Jeff asked. "We have wounded people here. We're vulnerable—"

"You have weapons. Therefore, you are there to exploit and enslave them." He sighed. "It is a simple equation, really."

"Too bad it's wrong." Jeff put his hands on his hips.

"It is," Tomás said.

"Did you tell them why we're here?"

"I tried."

Jeff realized it was rude for them to be talking in English in front of the elders, but it was a tricky time for propriety. "What did they say?"

"They say that we are here to destroy them. They are afraid we will wake *los Durmientes*, that we will somehow lead them back here. They accuse us of bringing their doom upon them."

"That's a little dramatic, don't you think?" Jeff scowled.

Tomás shrugged. "It is what they believe. It is not unreasonable."

"You know, your habit of seeing all sides is really irritating."

This elicited a smile. Jeff was glad to see it. "It is good to know that you care," Tomás said.

Jeff met the eyes of the elders. "So let me get this straight," he said, speaking to Tomás. "They are not going to help us destroy their oppressors."

"That is correct."

"Will they give us food or shelter?"

"They will not. They want us out of their caves."

"Are there more caves?"

"There are twelve hundred of them, roughly."

"And *los Durmientes* don't know you're all here?"

"We learned enough of their art to shield ourselves. We have a temple. The priests have one job—concealing our village."

Jeff shook his head. "Twelve hundred caves? This is more like a city, Tomás."

"They cannot rest for a second."

"I was able to find you," Jeff said.

"That was because you know *me*," he said, emphasizing the last word. "*Los Durmientes* do not know any of us. They do not care to know any of us. Therefore…we are invisible to them, because they do not have a *someone* to look for."

"They can't just go into the All and see all of you?"

"The shield is not observable if you do not know it is there. And if you are not looking for a particular presence…" he shrugged. "It seems precarious, I agree. We are, I think, hiding in plain sight. But we have done it for a long time. It is how we have survived."

"And you were exiled because…?" Jeff cocked his head.

"Because I have learned to do more. And that frightens them."

"Don't rock the boat," Jeff said.

"I do not know that idiom, but I understand. It is apt."

"Well, I guess we'll have to go it alone," Jeff said. "Can you translate for me?"

Tomás froze.

"Look, Tomás, these are your people, I get it. Their rejection hurts. Everything they say triggers some kind of painful childhood memory. But I don't give a damn about them or what they think about me. So just…translate what I say—accurately."

Tomás' eyes widened. He nodded.

"We mean you no harm," Jeff said. "But my people's enemies are your people's enemies. And we have come to do battle."

Jeff halted and waited for Tomás to translate. So far as he could tell, Tomás was executing his duty with fidelity.

"We do not seek your approval. We do not need your permission to attack our enemies. They have killed many of our people, and our blood is in their mouths."

Tomás spoke quickly. The elders' eyes were nearly popping now, and they started arguing among themselves.

"*Silencio*!" Jeff shouted. They stopped. Jeff continued. "You will give our people hospitality. You will tend their wounds and feed them. You will keep them safe until we can bring them home. If you do not do this, then when we are finished with our enemies, we will turn our wrath upon you."

Jeff enjoyed employing the stilted, mythological language. Even more, he liked seeing its effect. But when the elders hung their heads in resignation, his delight turned sour. *I don't want to defeat these people*, Jeff thought. *They've been beat up enough.* "Care for them well and we will reward you. First with your freedom, and then with supplies, with food."

The elders blinked. Their faces were impossible to read.

Apparently, Tomás could read them. "They do not believe you."

"About what part?"

Tomás shrugged. Jeff hated that shrug. "About any of it."

"Well, then, we'll just have to prove them wrong."

JEFF NODDED AT TOMÁS. Tomás nodded at Jeff. They closed their eyes.

"Hey, hey, hey! Wait just a minute," Jo said. She picked her way around the crew members sitting on the floor of the cave. Weaponer Ditka was right behind her. "Where do you think you're going?"

"To battle," Jeff said.

"Not without me you're not," Jo said, checking the blaster in her holster.

"Jo, I…" Jeff didn't know where to start. Should he say, *I don't want to lose you?* He had lost Danny in a battle situation—his Danny, the real Danny…real to him, anyway. He wasn't about to lose Jo. But he knew it would insult her if he said it. Jeff fumbled for words. It seemed an impossible situation.

"Out with it," Jo put her hands on her hips.

"Jo, I…"

"You said that."

Jeff blinked. Then he had an idea. "Look, I know these are Tomás' people, but they're not happy that we're here. I need someone I can trust to make sure they don't try anything. I need someone strong to stay here and protect your crew."

"Mr. Ditka can do that," Jo said.

Ditka's mouth opened to protest. She was determined to come with them as well, apparently.

Jeff felt more confident now. He held his hand up. "I need you here. Your crew needs you."

"You just want all the macho glory for yourself." Jo's eyes narrowed.

It was such a ridiculous statement that Jeff almost laughed out loud. He wanted to say, *Sure, you just go on thinking that. I've got a universe to save*, but he restrained himself.

With one hand he patted the carapace slung across his back; with the other, he confirmed his blaster was in place. Then he nodded at Tomás again and they were gone.

He knew that he had left her spluttering, mad as a wounded hornet. But that was Jo's problem.

The problem before him now was infinitely more complex…and dangerous. When he opened his eyes, he was in a room. The walls were unpainted concrete. Rivulets of water-stained rust ran down them at irregular intervals, their only adornment. The place looked impossibly old.

Jeff pulled his blaster from his holster and slid the safety off. He doubted it would do much against a Prox soldier, but it was what he had. The futility of the task before him washed over him like a wave. He felt defeated already, and they hadn't yet begun.

"Hey Tomás, do you think we have a chance?"

"If I didn't think we had a chance, would I have brought you here?"

"How much of a chance?"

Tomás looked up and met his eyes. "Not *much* of a chance."

Jeff nodded. It was the answer he had expected. "Well, let's die trying."

"*Si, amigo*," Tomás agreed. He stepped toward an archway that opened into a hall. Jeff raced to get in front of him and signaled for him to wait. Jeff unslung the carapace and fitted his forearm into the gauntlet, holding it against his chest. Then he flattened his back against the wall along one side of the arch. He peered into the hall, first one way, then the next.

"Clear," he whispered. "Which way?"

Tomás pointed to the right.

"How do you know?" Jeff asked.

Tomás shrugged.

"Great...." Jeff growled. "Do you think maybe we should think this through a little more?"

"I don't have a complete map in my head," Tomás said. "I just know that *los Durmientes* are that way."

"Okay, okay." Jeff held his blaster in front of him next to his shield as he entered the hall. He only lacked a battle helmet. He wished he had one for Tomás even more. That was standard gear, so why hadn't he thought of it?

Jeff stepped with long, catlike strides, ignoring the pain in his ankle. Tomás trotted behind him as if he were on an afternoon stroll. There was a lot about the little guy that Jeff simply did not understand. *And that needs to be okay right now*, he told himself. *Focus*.

He reviewed the plan in his mind. Find the sleepers. Find their computer. Blast the shit out of it. Don't get killed.

Simple.

They came to a T in the corridor. Jeff looked at Tomás. Tomás pointed to the left. Jeff flattened himself once again against the wall and peered around the corner into the new hallway. "Clear," he whispered.

He was amazed at the lack of security. But then again, these were a people with no natural predators. What were they to be scared of? Who would dare enter here? Except for Tomás' people, who even knew where they were? And Tomás' people were no threat…except, it seemed, for Tomás.

Jeff froze. What did he really know about Tomás? He'd come out of nowhere. He'd left Jeff clues to follow. And he'd brought him… here. Jeff's brain buzzed with suspicion. The Ulim knew he was a threat to them. All they needed to do was to send someone to lure him to them so they could eliminate him.

He jerked his head around and looked at Tomás. He stopped short of pointing his blaster at him. He stared at the little man.

Tomás cocked his head, looking confused. "*¿Que pasó?*" His eyes looked like the eyes of a puppy. He exuded innocence. If Tomás had been enlisted by the Ulim, it would explain his estrangement from his people. But then why would he have trained Jeff? The Ulim would not have wanted him to know *more* about how they did things, would they? It made no sense.

He had to make a call. He knew that. He could shoot Tomás dead on the spot and carry on with the plan. Or he could choose to trust him. Jeff felt paralyzed.

There's no one calling the shots but you, he told himself. *There are no superiors to blame if this goes sideways. It's all on you. You can't even blame the Ulim for this one. No one is sending false orders. There aren't any fucking orders. There's you and the enemy and this… unknown factor.*

The unknown factor's eyes shifted back and forth, and Jeff saw a splinter of fear in them now.

"Jeff," Tomás said. "What are you thinking?"

He wasn't good at trusting people. He knew that. It was why he had taken nothing but solo jobs for the past several years. He wasn't even sure he trusted himself, but he trusted himself more than anyone else. He raised the weapon and pointed it at Tomás.

"Jeff, what—"

"Are you one of them?"

"One of…who?"

"The Ulim?"

"No. I…" Tomás looked around. He seemed desperate. "How could you think it? *Los odio!* I hate them! They destroyed by people. They hunted us. We have barely survived."

"Then why don't you want to kill them?"

Tomás shook his head, almost as if he pitied Jeff. "Because, *amigo*, I will not let them turn me into *un monstruo*...a monster. I will not let them make me like them."

Jeff's brain buzzed. Tomás was displaying a level of self-awareness far higher than that possessed by the pseudo-Danny that the Ulim had concocted back in String 310. He retracted the blaster, holding it parallel with his own chest. If he squeezed the trigger, he'd blow off his own chin.

"Okay. Sorry…I…"

"*Muy bueno*," Tomás' eyes showed both understanding and compassion. "It is hard to know who to trust."

Jeff nodded. Then he sensed movement behind him. They were at another archway. Beyond it he saw the Ulim suspended from wires…or was it rods…from the ceiling, dreaming their dreams of domination and empire.

And coming straight at them, scrambling on six legs moving so fast that they blurred together, was a soldier Prox.

[STRING 311]

"IT'S A WORMHOLE!" Emma shouted excitedly. "What you call the 'heart of the hive' is a wormhole, connecting this, uh, bubble universe, with the one we know as String 311." She was frantically putting it all together in her head, twisting imaginary geometry through multiple dimensions until it fit what she was experiencing. "The hive, as you call it, is like a Klein bottle, with two apparent surfaces, but twisting through four-space into one continuous manifold…"

Amberline had stopped signing. Her mask spoke. "You are beginning to use terminology I do not know how to translate."

Emma did not seem to hear her. "Did you build it? The wormhole, I mean. Did the Alverians create it?"

"No, the heart of the hive has always been here. Though we did not always know about it," Bucky signed, with Amberline vocalizing. "We first crossed the distance of space and began settling our moon fifteen generations ago. We began digging tunnels both for shelter and to explore the structure of the moon. As we tunneled deeper we discovered anomalies in gravity, in the curvature of space-time. We investigated. At the center we discovered the heart, and the universe beyond it."

Emma nodded. "Okay, yeah, that makes sense. At some time in the distant past, millions of years ago, maybe thousands of millions of years, something caused a portion of String 311 to twist, forming a bubble separated from the whole. She began pacing. "This region of space-time, including your star, your home world and its moon, were drawn into the bubble and trapped. I can't even imagine forces strong enough to make that happen, but, well…" She gestured at the windows. "Here it is. The opening between the two domains would twist closed, kind of like making a balloon animal, resulting in the wormhole."

"Balloon…?" Amberline sounded confused.

"I'll explain later. Hell, I'll show you! But not now." Emma waved it away with her hand. "Over time, this end of the wormhole would be attracted by gravity, eventually settling into a stable spot at the core of the moon. It might have rested there for millions of years. You would never have found it if you hadn't dug…" She suddenly looked down. "Wait, did you dig all the way through the wormhole? You'd have to, to come out the other side of the manifold…"

Bucky was nodding. "It took many generations. Many Alverians were sacrificed. The digging was most difficult at the center of the hive."

"I can imagine!"

Amberline interjected, "Keep in mind, the heart of the hive does not affect us as adversely as it does you."

She nodded. "Of course. But you'd still be floating in zero G, disoriented, and boring through solid rock."

"We are accomplished tunnelers," Bucky signed, then gestured towards the planet. "What you can see of our cities from here is just the surface. The portion below ground is vastly larger."

"I would like to see that someday, if it's allowed."

Bucky made the sign best translated as *the future is uncertain,* or as Emma preferred to think of it, *we shall see.*

"Oh my god, when they finally reached the other surface…"

Bucky tilted her head. "It was the birth of our fascination with multi-dimensional science. We'd theorized about other universes before that, but it was mere speculation, mathematical curiosities. Of course, now we understand that we hadn't actually found a new universe, but the original universe that our region of space had been separated from."

Emma was impressed. "And you had your own personal, secret doorway between them!"

Amberline nodded. "That secrecy was fortunate. We were not aware of any other sentient people in our region of space. As soon as we began to explore this side of the heart, we encountered humans, and it was not always… amicable."

"I bet," Emma agreed.

"We saw many worlds held by humans," Bucky signed, "and the way they fought over them. Such brutality we had never seen before. We felt that if humans knew of our homeworld, they would likely take it from us."

Emma nodded. "Yeah, that's entirely possible."

Amberline's mask frowned. "That is why we keep our secret so carefully, and why you are the only human who has ever been here."

Emma found herself tearing up. "I…I am humbled by the trust

you've placed in me. And I swear to you, I will never betray that trust, even if it means dying."

"You can thank Amberline for that," Bucky signed. "If she had not testified to your character, your trustworthiness, and your scientific expertise, we would never have allowed you to see even the hive, much less our homeworld."

"Thank you, Amberline." Emma bowed deeply.

Amberline nodded back. "In dealing with humans for so many years, I have learned that not all are savages, and that in many areas, your science has progressed much farther than ours. When I was contacted by my client to detain you and I learned of your credentials, I hoped it might be destiny."

Emma was astonished, "What destiny? It looks to me like you have this all figured out, and have had for some time."

"Not all of it," Bucky signed. She made a huge sweeping gesture across the gigantic windows.

"I don't understand," Emma said.

"The stars," Bucky signed.

"What about them? They look normal to me."

Bucky stared at her native sky like she'd never seen it before.

"Until about one Earth month ago, only 18.7% of them were here."

[STRING 308]

THE PROX SOLDIER was coming fast. Jeff's blood began pounding in his head and time started to slow down as his adrenaline peaked. He didn't even feel the pain in his ankle as he leaped across the archway and pushed Tomás back, out of the soldier's line of sight. Then he dropped to the ground, crouched behind the carapace and raised his blaster.

The scrambling Prox was almost upon him when he heard Tomás shout, "Aim for the legs! Just above the second joint!"

The information was noise. Jeff squeezed off three shots in rapid succession into the middle of the Prox's body. He double checked the setting—maximum. It hadn't even slowed the beast down for a second. "Aww...shit," Jeff breathed.

"Legs!" Tomás shouted. He kept shouting it.

The Prox was almost upon them. It halted just shy of the archway and reared up, flaring out its legs and claws as wide as they would spread. *What is it hoping to accomplish with such a display?* Jeff wondered. *Is it trying to inspire fear and awe?* It was working.

He glanced back at the little man and saw him fumbling with the blaster Jeff had given him. "Oh, Christ," Jeff whispered under his breath. "That was a bad idea." Tomás would probably shoot him in an effort to shoot the legs off that thing—

The legs. Why was he screaming about the legs? To aim for an appendage went against all of Jeff's training. If you are going to shoot, you shoot to kill. And that means a chest or head shot, period. You don't want to wound your enemy. You want to fucking *end* him.

But this enemy was not going down. *What was I thinking?* flashed through his brain, quickly followed by, *A blaster is no match for a particle cannon.* But the particle cannons had taken these suckers out —one-by-one, anyway. Why not a blaster?

He shook his head to clear it and turned back to the Prox, which had, it seemed, finished its victory dance, and rearing back its barbed tail, stabbed toward Jeff with a lightning movement.

Jeff curled onto his side, letting the carapace take the full impact of the stab. It held, but even so, it felt like someone had just hit his spine with a wrecking ball. He nearly blacked out from the impact, and then watched with wide, horrified eyes as Tomás rose and confronted the beast.

The little man fumbled at the blaster, trying to work the safety, trying to find the trigger. He almost dropped the gun, and in catching it, activated the trigger, which sent an errant bolt of destructive energy zinging by Jeff's ear. *Holy Christ,* he thought. *Holy fucking Christ...*

But then Tomás caught the gun and pointed it in the general direction of the Prox, who began its threatening dance for Tomás. Jeff could see the gun shaking wildly. *I do not want to be in his line of fire*, he thought, and rolled toward Tomás' feet. He jerked himself upright and raised his blaster again, aiming for the tiny head of the creature. He squeezed off three more shots, and the little head disintegrated, resulting in an arcing shower of sparks.

But it did not stop its dance. The head, apparently, was not where its motherboard was located. No, if its designers had any sense at all, it would be in the thick of the chest, the most heavily-armored section of the creature, just as the bridge of any reasonable starship was deep in its bowels.

Tomás got two shots off, but they were wide of their mark. Plus, the little man was aiming for the legs. Jeff's eyes narrowed as he considered that. But what the fuck did Tomás know about Prox or blasters or war, for Christ's sake?

"What the hell?" Jeff said, raising his blaster and targeting the Prox's forwardmost legs. He aimed as Tomás had instructed, just above the second joint.

But before he could squeeze off a shot, the Prox's claw stabbed out again, straight at Tomás.

Tomás twisted, just in time to avoid being skewered through the heart, but it still caught him in the chest. Jeff's blaster roared, and so did he. Two shots, and the two front legs of the Prox soldier folded up beneath it. Off balance now, the claws began gyrating wildly, but to no avail. The Prox tumbled to the cement floor, almost rolling straight into Jeff, its barbed tail thrashing.

Jeff leaped up and snatched the collar of Tomás' shirt, pulling and running as far from the Prox as he could manage, as fast as he could. He looked back at the Prox soldier, on its back now like an upside-down turtle, all of its legs turning helpless circles in the air. A tail of bright red blood pointed from the Prox all the way to Tomás' dripping feet.

Jeff dragged Tomás through another archway into what appeared to be a supply room. Jeff didn't have time to divine the nature of the supplies. He dragged Tomás against the wall, shoved him into a seated position, and put his blaster on the ground beside him. "Tomás, Tomás!" Jeff shouted.

The chest wound was massive. The blood trailing from Tomás' mouth told Jeff his lung had been punctured. The realization struck Jeff in the head like a bolt from a blaster—Tomás was not coming back from this. Tomás had seconds, maybe minutes, but that was it.

The little man's eyes were already glassy. He turned his head. "The legs," he said in a raspy voice that sounded obstructed and wet.

"Yeah, I got it, the fucking legs," Jeff said.

His past came rushing back to him—the moment he had lost Danny at Catskill, the moment he had killed Jo when he jumped the *Bohr*, the moment he had destroyed every living soul in the universe he called home. And here he was again, responsible for the death of his partner, his accomplice, his friend.

Jeff howled, not knowing what to do with the feelings pummeling him, nor even what they were. He just felt the animal intensity of them, and it made him want to kick, lash out, stab, kill.

"Jeff, I do not think I'm going to…*sobrevivir*," Tomás said.

Jeff had no idea what the word meant, yet he understood.

He clutched Tomás to his chest and held him close. Jeff's teeth ground furiously and his face darkened into a mask of frustration and rage.

"This is not something you can do alone," Tomás said. His voice was growing thin, his breath raspy.

"I'm not letting anyone else die," Jeff said.

"Then you will…*we* will…fail." Tomás coughed. Bright red blood appeared on the floor beside him in perfect, symmetrical drops.

"You must bring Captain Jo," Tomás said.

Jeff wasn't going to argue with him. He just needed to hold him until Tomás died. It wouldn't be long. "I'm not going to fail, goddammit. *You* are not going to fail. But I'm not going to let anyone else die." There he was arguing. What was he doing? He squeezed his eyes shut and rocked back and forth on the cement floor.

Images flooded his brain. He saw the way Catskill had affected him, how the trauma of it had twisted him. He saw how he had cut himself off from Jo, from his family, from everyone who mattered to him. He saw how his isolation had made him into less of a man, not more. Emma had tried to tell him, and he had rebuffed her, abandoned her. And now she too was lost.

"*Estar solo no te ayuda,*" Tomás said.

"What?" Jeff asked. "What does that mean?"

"Being alone…it does not serve you, *mi amigo*."

Tears squeezed out of Jeff's eyes, but he was not aware of them.

"*Pero para mi…*to die…it is to be gathered to my people." Tomás' breathing had become ragged. "But I have no people."

Jeff tried to understand what that meant. He flashed back on the cave, the grim elders. There must be something there that Tomás loved. He knew that other cultures were far more communal than his own. It was a concept, not something he had seen. It was like speculative astrophysics—a mind experiment, nothing more. And yet…

He listened to Tomás' breathing. He could hear the obstruction in his chest. There was an unnatural gurgling that just sounded wrong.

"We can teleport back," Jeff said, "back to the cave."

"No." Tomás spoke the word emphatically. There was the force of shame behind it. Tomás did not want to be nursed by the people he had failed. He did not want to die under their disapproving scowls. Jeff didn't blame him.

And then Tomás' limbs went slack.

CHAPTER SIXTEEN

Jeff lowered Tomás' body to the floor. He checked for a pulse, but it was as he suspected. "You were not a little man after all," Jeff said out loud.

He stood and felt suddenly weak, drained, dizzy. He reached his hand out to steady himself against the wall. He bit his lip and breathed deep, steeling his resolve.

A part of his brain was lashing out, screaming at him about letting another comrade die. About surviving. "There are already about 600 trillion notches on my gun," he whispered to that voice, coldly, evenly, "that I know of. What's one more?"

It was a tough line. And right now, he wished he believed it. He needed to be hard. He needed to be focused. He didn't need the distractions of guilt or shame or despair or anything else vulnerable or human.

I need to be a killing machine and nothing else, he thought. But he knew that was wrong, too.

For a moment, Jeff felt lost. A vertigo washed over him and threatened to bring him down. He did not know how to balance the military needs of the moment with the frailty of his soul. He realized what he needed was a chaplain…or a shaman. And what he had was a corpse and a roiling mass of interior conflict.

"Use it for fuel," he told himself.

He snapped a new battery unit into the hilt of his blaster and locked it into place. He listened for the whine of the gun charging up to full power. He slung the carapace over his back. Then with a final glance at the shell of his friend, he stepped into the corridor.

He did it without looking. *That was stupid*, he told himself. But except for the Prox soldier on its back, pinwheeling its legs at the far end of the hall, it was empty.

He strode toward the struggling Prox soldier, and unslung the carapace. Holding the shield between himself and the fallen Prox, he hugged the wall until he cleared the archway that led to the room where the Ulim were sleeping.

Just beyond the archway, he paused and took in the Sleepers. The Ulim were human, just as Tomás had said. They hung suspended from the ceiling, their torsos flat, their thin, atrophied arms hanging limply from their sides. *There must be a plank or something beneath them to support their bodies,* Jeff thought. *Otherwise they'd bend at the waist.*

However it was they were suspended, the effect was eerie. The natural sunlight coming through the high, narrow windows was fading, and Jeff blinked as his eyes adjusted to a ghostly blue glowing emitted by the machinery below the sleepers. Jeff hadn't noticed that before. Below every one of the Ulim was a little black box about a meter across and half a meter wide. Tubes ascended from it, snaking into the orifices of the sleepers.

Jeff shuddered.

He stepped to one side and saw that there was a passageway of sorts between two hanging Ulim. He stepped into it and gasped. To his right, stretched out into what seemed like infinity, were hundreds, maybe thousands of Ulim. To his left was another bank of Ulim stretching out just as far. The little blue lights formed a pattern as they grew smaller at the far side of the cavernous room, like a runway with guidance lights to pilot by. Little blue lights… "Fireflies," he said out loud. He flashed back on the memory of his rescue, of the first time he had met the Ulim, the little blue lights that had seemed real and unreal at the same time. "Well here they fucking are—the Ulim fireflies."

He shook his head to clear it and adjusted his blaster, readying it to fire at the smallest movement—but there was no movement. He shook his head at the magnitude of the task before him. Even if he wanted to kill every Ulim in the building, the slaughter would take days, maybe weeks. He wasn't sure if Tomás had been right about the morality of the genocide of the Ulim, but his alternative plan was, quite simply, much more practical.

"Find the mainframe," he said through his teeth.

It was tempting to just start shooting. It would feel good. He could blast the desiccated flesh off of every one of the hanging mother-fuckers in sight, and it would feel *so good.* He would blast them for Danny, for he was sure it was they who had sent the false orders all those years ago at Catskill. He would blast them for Jo…his Jo, killed in a mangled lump of metal when ships from two different universes fused together. He would blast them for every living soul in his universe that had been snuffed out…or had they? Tomás had implied that his universe was still there…somewhere. But goddammit, he would blast them for Tomás, and for every human on String 311 where the Prox were killing right this very moment.

But he didn't.

He kept moving. His strides, initially slowed by wonder and rage, picked up again. He was almost jogging when he caught movement out of the corner of one eye. He jerked his head to one side and crouched, aiming his blaster in that direction.

No matter how busy the Ulim were with their war against the Authority, someone had been controlling that Prox soldier, he reasoned. Someone would sound the alarm. It was just a matter of time before every Prox in this facility would be raining down shit on him. *This must be the first of them*, he thought.

But when the movement came, it was not a Prox soldier. It was small. It was human.

It was Danny.

Jeff stood as the figure came closer. Danny's steps were halting, his hands up, as if he were being arrested. His face was soft, friendly, even a little sad.

"You found us," he said.

It was not the Danny he had left behind in Authority space. Nor was it the Danny of String 310, the one who had died at Catskill. This was the Ulim Danny, the analog he had first met on the moon of New Manila.

"Hello, Danny," Jeff said. *I'll play along,* he thought. *Why not?* He knew they were using Danny's form to manipulate his emotions. He was under no illusions that these bastards played fair.

"What do you intend to do?"

Jeff cocked his head. Was there really any reason to talk to these assholes? No. There was nothing they could say that would divert him from his path. And talking to this Danny-puppet would only slow him down. He realized with a grunt that this is exactly what they wanted.

"What do I intend to do? This," he said, and blasted a hole through Danny's chest.

[STRING 311]

ADMIRAL TAL FELT SICK. He felt helpless. He felt like a failure.

In mute desperation, he watched the last wave of Prox soldiers detach themselves from their ships and launch into space. He watched them swarm toward every ship in the Wengret ring.

There were no more orders to give. It was open, mad, furious warfare. Tal struggled to keep up with it all—but there were too many ships, too much territory, too much death.

One by one, Tal watched the Prox soldiers land, feet extended like spears, barbed tails slicing, piercing the hulls. He felt every attack as a stab at his own heart.

There was no stopping them now. Any hope Tal had nurtured that they might prevail turned sour once he saw the sheets of iconel being stripped off all over the ring.

He saw Liu falter. He reached out and grabbed the forearm of his secretary, squeezing an unspoken entreaty for courage.

Tal saw that smaller Prox—with eight legs, not six—were landing as well, many of them riding on the backs of the larger soldiers. He remembered that Bowers had called these "Workers" in his report. Tal saw that these were more systematic and ruthless about the project of dismantling their ships. Another kind of creature whizzed by. *This must the be third species Bowers wrote about,* he thought. *An Expediter*. It reminded him of a squid or a jellyfish, touching the soldiers and the worker with one of the tendrils tailing after its body. Tal had no idea what function this being served.

It would all have been intellectually fascinating had he not been witnessing the genocide of his people. Instead, he simply watched in mute horror as ship after ship after ship was breached, their hulls peeled back like a tin of rations, their crew suffocated by the ruthless void of space.

"We failed, Adrian," Tal said. His voice was weary. He was still clutching at his secretary's arm.

Liu looked down at him. He was biting his lower lip, and his eyes were brimming. He jerked free of Tal's grip and grasped his hand instead. He shook it, held it, and held Tal's eyes as well. "It's been an honor serving with you, sir."

"We're still going to pummel the hell out of them with our particle array when they start coming for us," Tal said. "We can pick off twenty-seven of them a second with every gun we've got."

"It isn't going to be enough," Liu said.

"No. No it won't."

"We're going to die today."

"Yes." Tal didn't say the next part, and he hoped Liu wouldn't either. The Prox's next stop would be Earth. Tal shuddered.

"The doctors want permission to distribute the Happy Ending tablets—especially to the children and noncommissioned adults aboard, including the tourists."

Tal nodded. He'd hoped it wouldn't come to that. The pills would provide a minute and a half of euphoria, then sleep, then the heart would stop. It would be over in three minutes. "But the seals will remain locked until I give the order." They could hand them out, but no one would be able to open them. Not until…

It was the order Tal hoped he would never have to give.

It took four hours for the Prox to board every ship in the Wengret ring. It felt like four years. Tal felt the pang of every death, took it personally, bore the moral weight of it in his bones. He was responsible for every death. If there had been a plan that might have succeeded, he did not find it. It was all on him. He sighed, and it was a despairing sigh that revealed an agony too deep for words.

Everyone in the Command Center continued to watch the screens. Tal knew what would happen next. It was like a play or a vid he'd seen several times before. Inside, he'd say, *Oh yes, this bit*. When the last of the ships had been defeated, the worker Prox stayed to finish the job while the soldiers launched themselves once more into space, their legs leading, pointed straight at Sol Station. *Oh yes, this bit*—the final act, his own death, and the death of everyone who toiled and lived and loved under his command and protection. *Oh yes, this bit.*

"Estimated time before those fuckers arrive?" Tal asked no one in particular.

"Forty-two minutes," a voice replied. Tal didn't notice whom.

"Forty-two minutes," he repeated.

He stood. He straightened his jacket. "Weaponers, at your stations. I want every particle cannon we've got trained on the enemy. Pick your shots carefully while they're at a distance. Open up and make the most of their proximity as they get closer. Leverage every advantage you can find to kill as many of them as you can before they get here. The rest of you…take thirty minutes to say goodbye to the people you love. Then I want you back at your posts."

Tal looked down from the screens and saw that everyone in the room was standing, facing him, staring, not moving. "Go!" Tal shouted.

The room erupted into motion. The weaponers looked busier than ever, but everyone else trailed toward an exit.

"You too, Adrian."

"I have no family aboard, sir."

"No one…special?"

"Uh…no sir."

"Friends?"

"I have some friends, sir, but…my place is here."

Only then did Tal realize that he was still gripping his secretary's hand. He squeezed it. "Good man." He let it go.

The joints in his fingers ached. He wondered at that, at how good and wonderful it was that his joints ached, that he had joints, that they could ache. An hour from now, he would not have them.

"Adrian?"

"Yes sir."

"You know that I can't eat salt or butter…"

"Yes sir."

"I'm hungry."

Impossibly, he saw his secretary smile. "Yes sir. What would you like, sir."

"Bombay butter chicken, I think. Extra spicy. What do you think of that?"

"I think I would like to join you, with your permission, sir."

"Nan and saffron rice."

"Muttar paneer on the side," Liu said.

"Why the hell not?" Tal agreed.

"Anything to drink, sir?"

"Scotch," Tal said without thinking. "And you'll join me in that, too."

"Gladly, sir."

Tal enjoyed the meal, but he enjoyed the scotch more. Liu had snagged the oldest, most expensive single malt on station. It seemed even more buttery than the chicken. Tal felt a warm sentimental glow flood his brain as he finished his first glass. He wiped his mouth on his sleeve and pointed to the glass. Liu filled it.

Tal had never seen Liu smile this much. He'd always taken his secretary for an efficiency machine, but never so much as a person. Not that Adrian had ever showed much personality in the performance of his duties. But he seemed to have let his professional guard down now, and Tal decided that he liked the man more than he thought he did.

Maybe that's just the whisky talking, he thought. Maybe it was. But who the fuck cared now?

Minutes later, the chicken was finished, as was the nan. Liu carried away a tray bearing the last of the rice. A moment later he added another finger to Tal's scotch.

Tal set it in the cup holder built into his command chair. Then he forgot about it. The communicators and navigators and astrophysicists and brass were filtering back in again. Their faces looked broken, crumpled, puffy. Tal wondered if some of them had gotten into fist fights. But no…it was grief, not pugilism that disfigured them. Some wiped at their eyes, some assumed an air of detached dispassion that fooled no one. Some of them did not return. Tal sipped at his whisky. He could hardly blame them, and he didn't. The Command Center did not need to be fully manned for them to die, after all.

Like most people in the room, he watched the schematics monitor, watching the enemy death count soar as the particle cannons did their worst—their worst, but not enough. The death count was 346,000 Prox dead and climbing. The numbers changed faster than Tal could easily make out.

But it would not be enough. 1,150,000 more of them were on their way.

Tal shifted his eyes to gauge their proximity—500 kilometers…450…400…

There were no speeches left in him. None were needed.

"Incoming Prox, sir. Contact in 5, 4, 3…"

Tal watched the monitor as the first of the Prox soldiers landed. Its barbed tail reared back over its tiny head, then speared forward, puncturing the space station's hull.

[STRING 308]

JEFF STEPPED over the pseudo-Danny's body. *I need to move more quickly*, he told himself. Fortunately, his boots felt strangely light beneath him. His adrenaline was pumping. He could feel it rising with the danger.

They definitely knew he was here. They were probably freaking out. *Good*, he thought. *Hopefully that will distract them from killing humans back at Sol Station.* That was another universe away, his brain reminded him. *So what?* he answered. Distance meant less and less to him now.

Except for the distance beneath his feet. He could just project himself into the All and materialize at the mainframe…if he knew where it was. But there was nothing to feel for. *But I can search more quickly that way*, he reasoned. But, countered his brain, you would leave your body vulnerable—blind, dumb, and helpless—until you squashed yourself into the new space.

That is not optimal, he had to agree. It was good when his brain and he agreed on something.

The Ulim went on forever. The sunlight coming through the windows had completely faded now, and his eyes had adjusted to the glow of the blue fireflies that filled the cavernous room. He tried to estimate how many football fields might fit within this space. Twelve? It was massive. *Most of this must be built into the hillside,* Jeff thought. That was when he noticed that the windows were only on one side. He kicked himself. That was the kind of thing he should have noticed before.

Instinctively, he unslung the carapace and held it before him, sliding his forearm into the gauntlet. His blaster was powered up and ready in his dominant hand, his finger light on the trigger.

He passed row after row of Ulim, sleeping but not asleep. Dead, but not dead. Vulnerable, yet dangerous. It was hard to connect all the events of his past—all the hardship and failure and guilt and self-loathing, all the death and destruction and bone-breaking toil—with these seemingly serene figures, floating in their reverie, still and dormant for centuries, basking in the soft, ghostly light of their machines. They were several universe strings away. They were peaceful monks, surely. They were hibernating scientists.

"They are killers," Jeff said aloud through gritted teeth.

He saw an opening to his right and stopped. A corridor led into dim space where he saw a bank of blinking lights. He turned toward the lights and nodded. Lights equal machinery…and maybe computers.

He started down the hallway to investigate. The hallway opened into a larger, windowless space, surrounded by a glass enclosure. Behind the glass, about a hundred meters in front of him, was what could only be a mainframe.

It would take quite a computer to link the minds of all the Ulim, to calculate their movement, their society, their communications and interactions, their entire life in whatever Interworld they had assembled for themselves. It struck him as ironic that what his people considered a punishment, a form of prison—as Nira had been sentenced to—these creatures had chosen as preferable to the sensual life of the body.

The bitterness of it struck Jeff in that moment in a way that had not occurred to him before. In rejecting the physical world, the Ulim were rejecting everything that made life dear—the touch of skin, the preciousness of time, the ecstasy of lovemaking, even the poignant frailty of the body. It was the Gnostic rejection of the gift of creation, removed from myth, discarnate through binary code. The irony of transcending dualism through the fundamental duality of the distinction between zeros and ones suddenly seemed sweet and apt.

But this was the stuff of late-night college conversations over drinks and cannabis. He shook his head to clear it of such heady thoughts. Then he noticed motion in his peripheral vision. He jerked his head to the left to see a Prox soldier scrambling on its six legs to intercept him, to block his access to the mainframe.

Jeff raised his blaster and aimed for the creature's legs. But he was too late—skittering behind the soldier was another, then another, then another. In rapid succession, a whole platoon of Prox soldiers spilled into the passageway, forming a line to block his advance.

In mere seconds the hallway had gone from being empty to being a writhing mass of pincers and legs. Jeff estimated there were fifteen, maybe twenty Prox in a line ahead of him. How many of their legs could he shoot before the others rushed him?

"Not enough," he breathed.

Jeff heard something behind him, and spinning around, he saw another ten, twelve, fourteen Prox blocking his retreat.

They had found him, all right. And now they were advancing from both directions. Jeff turned back to the Prox guarding the mainframe. Their pincers scissored the air in front of them, snapping and slipping and flashing, even in the dim light…all but one.

This one remained where it was, scooting forward only after its fellows had entered the hall in Jeff's direction. Jeff knew he needed to squash space and jump out of here, and quickly. But at least he knew where the mainframe was. Now he could get back here.

As the Prox grew closer, his eye travelled to the one that lagged behind the others. It stopped altogether. Then it waved. Then, holding one great pincer over another, it gestured toward itself, mimicking a motion that was all too familiar to Jeff.

Jeff flashed back on the time Tomás had showed him the sleeve from the shirt he was making, when he had explained how they could safely move objects through space. Could it be? Could it be that this Prox soldier was pretending to hold aloft a sleeve?

JEFF PROJECTED himself into the All. He knew he would have to be quick, because until he actually teleported, his body would be vulnerable, and he had Prox rushing him from both sides. It occurred to him that it wouldn't be a bad way to go, if you had to go—projecting your consciousness away from your body as whatever happened to it… happened. But then what would happen to your consciousness? Tomás had just raised that question in a way that Jeff could not answer.

He quickly located the cavern, found Jo's presence and gripped it between two fingers. He squashed space, bringing the Ulim compound and the cavern together, then letting space snap back, trusting its elasticity. He opened his eyes and found himself looking at Jo nursing a wounded member of her crew. She jumped when she saw him.

"Jesus! Do you have to do that?"

"I guess I could materialize out of your field of vision and then walk into it," Jeff conceded. "But that seems a little silly, given the circumstances."

"And just what are the circumstances?" Jo asked. "Where is Tomás?"

Jeff looked down.

"Oh shit," Jo said. She patted her crewman and stood up. She reached out and touched Jeff on the arm. "I'm sorry."

"So am I. But—" But what? What could he say? *It's okay because Tomás' consciousness is now living inside a Prox soldier's body*? Well, why not? "It's okay because Tomás' consciousness is now living inside a Prox soldier's body," Jeff said, wincing.

Jo blinked. "You're shitting me, right?"

He shook his head. "It's how we're going to get you there without destroying this reality string."

"Get me where?"

"Into the compound."

"Hold on. Back up. What the fuck are you talking about? Did you destroy the Ulim computer or not?"

"No. They killed Tomás, and then I was attacked by Prox. But I found the mainframe. I know where it is. I can take us directly there." Jeff realized he was wasting time. Every moment they stood here talking was a moment closer to the Ulim contriving a way to stop them. It was comforting to know they were not omniscient or omnipotent. And he wanted very much to take advantage of the fact that their attention was divided.

Jo put her hands on her hips. "Wait just a goddam minute. Are you saying you need my help? *My* help? You don't just need my starship—which is a steaming pile of twisted metal right now, thanks to you."

Urgency filled Jeff's limbs and made him impatient. He didn't have time for Jo to gloat. "We need to go—"

"No, goddam it. I want to hear you say it."

"Jo, I—"

"Say it, fuckhead. Say it now or you're on your own."

He could probably enlist Shell Ditka instead, but she would need Jo's permission, since she was under her authority. Jeff's captaincy had no real relevance beyond his now nonexistent world. He was stuck. He looked at his boots and closed and opened his hands, feeling the tightness of his fists.

"All right. Fuck. Jo, I fucking need you. You. Not your ship. You. I can't do this without you."

A smile curled at the edge of Jo's lip. "Damn straight." She withdrew her blaster and checked its charge. "Was that really so hard?"

Jeff continued making fists but didn't answer.

"Mr. Ditka, you have the conn—"

"The conn, sir?" Ditka stood up from where she had been tending another of the wounded crew members. There was no conn—the *Talon* was a smoking piece of space detritus in orbit around this planet.

"You know what I mean," Jo said, rolling her eyes.

"Yes sir."

Jo nodded, turning back to Jeff. "What are you waiting for, soldier?"

[STRING 311]

Admiral Tal glanced at the monitor fixed on what was left of his fleet—scrap metal floating in random, chaotic patterns. The only order he could detect was the systematic dismantling of anything connected to anything else by the Prox. It occurred to him that he was looking at a living icon depicting the state of his own heart—chaos punctuated by destruction.

He forced himself to look away, staring this time at the incoming Prox troops sailing toward them through space—a vast host descending on them like rain, moving fast yet eerily still. He marveled at the serenity of the images compared to the aggression of their intent.

More were landing now, twelve, twenty-eight, seventy-two… They hit the outer rings of Sol Station first and immediately began digging in. They ripped up the iconel plates and pulled insulation and wiring out, setting them free from their intended servitude to float into space, forming webs of detritus that rippled and flowed like underwater fauna.

The station had rotated from its standard position in order to put the largest array of particle cannons between the Prox and the rest of the station. Those cannons had done their worst—and now they were food. Tal watched as the alien soldiers ripped their guns up with their mandibles, fewer of them firing now. Soon, none would be operational.

Tal had ordered all civilians into the section of the station furthest away from the enemy, but he could see how hopeless that was. Tens of thousands of Prox were landing now, and tens of thousands more were simply sailing past the batteries, past the engineering decks, straight toward the gymnasiums and theaters where the civilians—the children and businesspeople and tourists—were huddled together and taking instruction in the use of their Happy Ending pills.

Overcome with grief, Liu had become faint. Against his will, Tal ordered him to sit. He had not objected. Tal felt the distance between them acutely. So much so that he rose and walked behind Liu's chair, putting both hands on his secretary's shoulders. "We failed, Adrian."

"We tried, sir. We gave it our best."

"Our best…was not enough."

There was no answer to that. The words caught at Tal's conscience, however. *We did not give our best, goddammit,* he thought. *Our best would have been to reach out to the rebels, to call a cease fire until we defeated our common enemy.*

That was out of his hands, but he still felt the moral weight of it hanging from his neck like a noose.

"Here they come, sir." One of the weaponers stood and looked at him.

There was nothing to do but watch them come. They had no weapons left, no defenses, no prayers…no hope.

"Here they come," Tal repeated.

The Command Center, like the bridge of the space station, was not nestled safe into the guts of the place, as it would be on a ship. The station was a series of concentric rings, with no part of it any more or less safe from attack. It was not, after all, a fortress or a warship. It was a way-station, a habitat, a merchant center. It launched ships to protect itself, ships that were now nothing more than floating scraps.

"The Prox are approaching the Command Center, sir."

The lights suddenly went out, leaving the room in complete darkness. Tal counted five seconds before emergency power came on. The monitors flickered and resumed their dreadful reports, but only some of them had working cameras now.

Tal could have ordered Happy Endings for the people under his command, but he had decided against it. It seemed unmilitary. If they could not go down fighting, at least they could go down staring the enemy in the eye. They would not yield the moment of moral confrontation. But as he saw all the young men and women in front of him, when he thought of how, mere moments from now, they would die, and die horribly, he questioned his decision.

But it was too late now. He heard a booming clank as a large, heavy object made contact with the hull around them.

"They're here," one of the weaponers said. No one was working now. There was nothing to work on. There was nothing to do. Nothing to do but die.

Yet it seemed someone was still watching the monitors. "The Prox are approaching the recreational ring, sir." The recreational ring, where the civilians were huddled.

"Adrian..."

"Yes sir?"

"It's time."

Adrian looked up, accessing his neural, sending the order for the civilians to swallow their pills. In mere moments, fourteen thousand women, men, and children would peel back the plastic top of the tiny bottles and swallow the euphoric poison. Babies would be injected.

Tal's eyes welled up and he cursed his own finitude—not the fact that his life would soon end, but the fact that he had not done enough, had not been creative enough, strong enough, brutal enough to save his people. He hated himself, and he roiled in that loathing. He hated himself more than he hated the Prox—the Prox, who seemed to have no actual animosity toward them. To them, humans seemed to simply be irrelevant. They seemed to be interested only in the metal. They were like great whales feeding on plankton. There was metal to be eaten, and now the eaters were here.

CHAPTER SEVENTEEN

[String 308]

Jeff projected himself into the All. Then he reached out for Tomás. It felt like a stab in the dark. After all, Tomás was dead. How would his essence manifest? And he realized he might have been imagining the whole sleeve thing. Maybe the Prox soldier was just experiencing a malfunction. It was possible.

But in his heart he knew. He knew that somehow, Tomás had once again beaten the Ulim at their own game. They somehow controlled the Prox by the imposition of their will on the monsters' circuitry. Tomás, in the moments before he died, must have figured out how to do the same.

If Jeff was wrong, he would know in seconds. He cast around for Tomás—first he cast wide, as he normally did, but then narrowed in on where he expected Tomás to be. But Tomás was not there. Jeff fought a moment of panic. *Relax,* he told himself.

From a long way off, he heard Jo's voice, as if underwater. "Are you just going to stand there, or what?"

He sent a call into the All. It was not something he had thought of before, and he was not sure where the idea had come from. But he sent it just the same. And a moment later, he heard a familiar voice in his brain. *I am here, amigo.*

Jeff relaxed, relief flooding his body. *Oh my God, I'm so glad to hear your annoying little voice.*

Hmm...tell me how you really feel, amigo.

Jeff's body smiled. He heard Jo's voice afar off. "What's so goddam funny?"

Are you ready with the sleeve?

Ready, mi amigo.

Here we come.

Jeff...

Jeff hesitated. *Yes?*

This is a good move. I am glad you are bringing Captain Jo.

Yeah. Uh...let's just get this done.

Jeff snagged the space around himself and Jo. Then he reached through and felt for Tomás' arm. He had a moment of panic as he realized that Tomás no longer had an arm. Would he feel a cold, metallic pincer, instead? But no, there was an arm, or at least the suggestion of an arm, as real and solid as anything was in the All. He clutched at it and brought himself and Jo through.

When Jeff opened his eyes, he saw that Tomás had navigated them past the bank of windowed walls, directly into the room containing the mainframe. Jo wobbled on her feet; Jeff reached out instinctively, hands on her waist, steadying her. It only took a moment. As quickly as Jeff could blink, Jo had assumed a solid, wide stance, bringing her blaster into position—whining up to full power, ready to fire.

Jeff was slower to assume a pose. He turned around, taking in the room. Like everything in the Ulim compound, the place was massive. Jeff estimated it to be nearly 25 meters deep, maybe half that wide. The mainframe took up the bulk of it, its towers two meters tall, stretching to the uttermost limits of the room.

Unlike the outside chamber, where the Ulim hung, this room was well lit. Soft, yellowish, light-emitting orbs were suspended from a high ceiling, much as the Ulim were. And light radiated from the mainframe itself—thousands of towers, each casting a warm orange glow from the code in constant, rapid display across what looked like stacked metal casings that were also monitors.

Jeff wondered at the sight—it was the container for a world a people inhabited. *It's an electronic planet*, Jeff thought. Hundreds of thousands—hell, maybe millions—of souls were residing in those stacks. Or were they residing in the bodies floating in the massive room adjacent to this one? Or were they, somehow, both? They did, after all, need their bodies or they would not have kept them alive. And they needed this virtual world, or they would not have the mainframe.

Suddenly, the Ulim seemed far less omnipotent. The precarity of their situation pricked at him. He almost felt sorry for them. Because he was here. And Jo was here. And they weren't here to make friends.

Neither were the Prox. As Jeff finished turning around, his focus returned to his more immediate surroundings. About twenty meters lay between him and the mainframe. But standing in a line, from one side of the room to the other, were a hundred Prox soldiers...or more.

They were inordinately still. It was as if they had been moved into position and then powered down. Only the fact that a couple of them were opening and closing their pincers reflexively alerted him to the fact that they were online and ready to attack the moment their masters so directed them.

Then, almost as one, the line advanced.

Even though there was plenty of distance between them, both Jeff and Jo instinctively took a step backward. Jeff quickly assessed their firepower. It was woefully inadequate. Even knowing that they should disable their legs, even with Jo and him firing non-stop, they would not be able to bring enough of the fuckers down before they were overwhelmed. It was the same strategy the Prox employed when attacking larger targets. Individually, they were stoppable. Together, however, they were overwhelming. And that was their secret.

"I love you, too," Jo said.

"What?" Jeff asked, momentarily shocked out of his thoughts.

"Look…if we're about to die…I want you to know. I've always loved you…whatever you there was. I loved the you that died here. I love the new you too. That's all I'm saying. Don't get weird on me."

Jeff blinked and turned back to the line of advancing Prox. Their legs skittled on the hard floor beneath them. They could rush them, but they weren't. The Ulim were enjoying their kill.

But then one of them suddenly broke ranks and scrambled toward them with lightning speed. Jo aimed and fired—projecting a pocket of disruptive energy. It caught the Prox soldier square in the chest, a direct hit, but as Jeff anticipated, the Prox's defensive shields dissipated the blast, rendering it harmless.

"Two things," Jeff said. "First, if you want to stop these fuckers, aim for their legs—second joint from the bottom. Second, that particular Prox? I don't think he's the enemy."

Of course Jeff couldn't be certain. But while the Prox seemed to be operating in unison, this one was not. And he knew that there was at least one Prox soldier hosting the soul—or the consciousness or the essence or whatever damn thing it was—of his friend.

"It's the little man," Jeff said.

"What?" Jo asked, aiming for the legs.

As the Prox skittered dangerously close, Jeff caught Jo's blaster and forced it down so that it pointed to the floor. "It's Tomás."

Jeff didn't need to look at her to know that her eyes were wide with alarm. And…he could be wrong, of course. But in his gut, he knew he wasn't.

Almost upon them, the Prox's legs began to skitter backwards, trying to halt its momentum. It tipped forward, bashing the edge of its carapace on the stone floor.

It was close enough to touch now, halting no more than a meter in front of them. Its legs gyrated before them, as if pedaling unseen bicycles. Jeff reached out and patted its carapace. "Hang in there, buddy. You'll get the hang of how to operate that thing."

The Prox righted itself and made a quick, jerky bow to Jeff and Jo. Glancing at Jo, Jeff suspected that if he poked her, she'd fall over. Instead, he clutched at her elbow and squeezed. "No, really. It's Tomás.

Somehow, when he died, he was able to…I don't know, take one of them over."

The Prox-who-was-Tomás towered over them. It skittered its legs, turning to face its fellows. It took a step forward, interjecting itself between Jeff and Jo and the gauntlet of Prox.

"He's not a little man anymore," Jo whispered.

"No."

"He's neither little…nor a man."

"Are you through?"

"I'm….nervous as fuck."

"Me, too." He glanced over at her. She smiled. He smiled back. "I'm glad you're here."

"Not threatening your manhood, then?"

"Fuck you, Taylor."

"That's a date, Captain." She winked.

The line of Prox had momentarily halted, assessing the new situation. If they were confused about the fact that one of their own had just taken up with the enemy, their crablike demeanor did not betray it. A moment later, they began advancing again.

"You know, Tomás, it's great that you're here and all, but we still can't stop them."

"Who needs to stop them?" Jo asked.

"What do you mean?"

"We don't need to stop them," she said. "We just need to finish the fucking job."

She took aim again. She fired.

Jeff scowled. She had not hit any of the advancing Prox—and Jo had always been an ace marksman. She damned well hit what she aimed at. She was aiming at the computer towers.

Jeff suspected they were shielded, and a split second later his suspicion was confirmed—the blast slammed into a rippling wall of blue energy, behind which the computer stacks remained whole and unharmed.

"We could do that all day," Jeff said. "We'd deplete our blasters before we wore down those shields."

Jo didn't respond but fired in what looked like a random pattern—left and right, high and low. Every now and then she hit a Prox soldier, but Jeff suspected that was by accident.

The Prox were getting close. Jeff saw Tomás hunker down, raising his deadly pincers, digging in his legs for traction as he prepared to spring forward.

Jeff started firing at legs.

"What are you doing?" Jo asked.

"The legs, goddammit. Fire at the legs."

He took down one, two, three…five. Deep inside he felt a wet flipper of joy twitch every time one of them rolled onto its back, legs pinwheeling helplessly in the air.

Gotta love design flaws, Jeff thought.

But it would not be enough. He knew that. It would be their last stand. He knew that, too, and he hated it. He glanced over at Jo and loved her. He glanced up at the Prox-who-was-Tomás and loved him. And suddenly, despite the certainty of his death—and theirs—he realized that there was no place in this universe or any other that he wanted to be. To die on this battlefield, with these friends, that was as much as any soldier could hope for.

"Incoming," Jo said, jerking her head behind her.

Jeff looked over his shoulder and saw another swarm of Prox skittering their way through the archway, into the corridor that led from the Ulim to the mainframe.

The Prox from the gauntlet, however, were already upon them. Tomás reared up, doing the angry dance he and Jeff had witnessed before, brandishing his pincers, making himself as large as possible. But the Prox ignored him, attempting to move past him directly to Jeff and Jo.

Tomás slashed down with his right pincer, the large one, tearing a split into the metal hide of the foremost Prox. Only then did they seem to notice his presence. Suddenly there was an eruption of Prox legs, as the attacking Prox met Tomás' dance with its own—and then immediately engaged.

Jeff heard the metallic crunch as their bodies pounded into one another, their claws and legs a roiling blur in the air almost directly above him. He jumped and rolled as a projectile came at him—just missing his skull by mere centimeters. It was a discarded leg, sheared off in their clash.

The attacking Prox was nearly crawling over Tomás now, its pincers reaching for Jeff, quivering in the air, eager but frustrated that it was not able to reach its prey when it was so, so close. Tomás looked like he was about to be crushed by the sheer determination of his enemy, when other Prox began to swarm past him. He stuck out whatever legs were not immediately engaged, but they did nothing.

"We need to get out of here before Tomás goes down," Jeff shouted to Jo, "because if that happens, we can't *both* get out of here."

He saw the look of fear in Jo's eyes and knew that she understood him.

"We're trapped," Jeff said. "We need to teleport out. Now."

"We have not completed our mission, soldier," Jo said.

"And we're not going to," he said. As romantic and glorious as the idea of dying with Jo and Tomás beside him would be, he couldn't let it happen to them. Not them.

It required both of them to take Jo with them without endangering the fabric of space. And Tomás was going down fast.

Jeff closed his eyes, but Jo yelled, "Like hell."

Jeff felt his blaster being ripped out of his grip.

Jo had grabbed it. She had transferred her weapon to her non-dominant hand and reared back. Then, with a graceful motion that seemed out of place, Jo lobbed his blaster into the air, over the heads of the approaching Prox, into the thick of the mainframe stacks.

Faster than Jeff could track, she took up her blaster in her right hand again, took aim, and fired. Jeff expected the blaster to hit a force field and clatter to the floor, but it kept going, falling now into the midst of the computer stacks. At the last possible moment before it disappeared from view, an energy pocket from Jo's blaster caught up with it, connected with it, ignited it.

Jeff's field of vision erupted into a wall of fire.

[STRING 311]

TAL HEARD the booming sound of the hull being pummeled and punctured. The booms were scattershot at first, and then they were legion—a hundred dread hammers beating down upon them. He knew that all up and down the hull, the atmospheric seals were being breached. People were dying as the air rushed out into the void, leaving their lungs heaving, then collapsed.

And then, as if someone had just severed a power cord, the beating just…stopped.

A dreadful silence followed. Tal saw everyone around him with their shoulders hunched up to their ears, anticipating one final blow before the air was sucked from the room, from their lungs. But the blow did not come. The silence was louder than the hammering had been.

Tal jerked his head up to whatever monitors were still giving a picture, and his mouth dropped open. The Prox had ceased their warlike crusade. They did not move. They did not cling to the hull, nor did they attack it. If there was any life in them, he could not see it. Instead, he saw their bodies floating aimlessly away from the hulls of the station, once more lost in their mindless serenity, only now it was an unconscious serenity.

Are they really unconscious? Tal wondered. *Are they dead? Or are they simply void of will? Has the connection with whatever power directs them been momentarily severed? Would they, moments from now, power up and resume their slaughter?*

Tal did not know. He only knew that he was grateful for the reprieve, for even another minute of life.

Terror struck him. "Adrian!" he shouted. "Belay that order!"

He had given the order to the civilians to take their pills. How long ago had that been? It felt like hours ago, but in reality he knew that it had been less than a minute. But a minute could be too long…

"Adrian!" he shouted. He saw that Adrian's eyes were rolled up into his head. He knew his secretary was doing all that he could. He bit his lip as he saw the man's eyes drop, then look down. When Liu finally did look up again, Tal saw the saddest eyes he had ever beheld.

"Are they all…?" He could not bring himself to finish the sentence.

"Not all," Liu said. "But…many. The adults made the children go first."

"Oh Christ," Tal cradled his head in his hands. "Oh Christ."

He waited for the sound of the hammers to resume, but the only sound he could hear was the pounding of his own pulse in his ears.

[STRING 308]

THE FORCE FIELD surrounding the mainframe held steady, containing the flames from the explosion of Jeff's blaster, and concentrating the force of the explosion within it. But the force field was only three meters in height, and a cloud of flame and percussive energy erupted from the top of the force field, spilling out into the room.

Jeff raised his arm to shield his eyes from the ferocity of it, and rolled onto his back to get as low as possible, turning the carapace on his back toward the blast. Jo had stumbled from the force of the explosion. Grabbing her arm, he jerked her down to the floor beside him. A second explosion rocked the foundation, so powerful he felt the cement bucking beneath them, then a third, a fourth, a fifth—as the liquid oxygen cooling mechanisms in the mainframes began to explode, taking every working computer node with them as they went.

The explosions didn't stop, nor did they increase in intensity. The sound was oddly familiar, and it took a moment for Jeff to connect with what it sounded like. *Popcorn,* he thought. *It sounds like popcorn, if I were two centimeters tall and inside the pan as it was popping.*

The mainframe room had been massive, and Jeff curled his body around Jo's, trying to protect her from whatever falling detritus might strike them as the explosions continued, random yet constant for the next several minutes as the massive mainframe exploded, node by node, down the length and breadth of the cavernous room.

Finally, however, the explosions happened further and further away, less and less frequently, until finally they stopped altogether. The floor stopped bucking. The heat subsided. A quiet descended that seemed timeless and equally unfixed in space. Jeff felt a familiar spinning of vertigo until he opened his eyes and grounded himself in proximity to concrete things. Here was Jo, curled within the protective tangle of his arms and legs. He reached out with his awareness to check his own limbs. Yes, he could feel them. Yes, he could move them. He felt the sensation of metal scraping on the back of his hand, and received it with the force of a divine revelation. He was embodied. The one he loved was alive.

For now, his brain said. He jerked upright. And the Prox. The explosions might give them pause, but—

"Jeff," Jo began to uncurl, emerging from the fetal position nestled under his belly. "Are you all right?"

"Yeah…I think so. You?"

"I don't know. Give me a whisky and a hot bath and I'll let you know."

Jeff couldn't help grinning. This might not be *his* Jo, but it was sure as fuck Jo.

He sat up and lunged to snatch Jo's blaster from where it had fallen. He checked its settings, made sure it was powered and ready, and only then did he look around.

Smoke hung heavy in the air. The lights had been taken out with the mainframe. He could see only by the glow of the ghostly blue light seeping in from the room where the Ulim hung. Jeff fished in his pocket for a hand torch. He clicked it on and fixed it under his shoulder epaulet. Its beam produced a solid pillar of smoke wherever he turned. He fished a handkerchief from his trousers and began to tie it around Jo's mouth.

"What the fuck are you doing?"

"Smoke inhalation."

"Put your filthy hanky over your own mouth. I've got one."

Jeff did as she said. Then he started to study their surroundings. The Prox were still here. Many had rolled onto their backs—probably from the force of the countless explosions. Some were still upright, balanced on their spindly metallic legs. But they were frozen in place, as if someone had switched them off, as if they were replicas in a museum—empty suits of armor, reminders of a bygone era, discarded by time.

Then he noted motion. He swung the blaster around, aiming it at the one Prox soldier still moving. It had been blown onto its back, and its feet were scrambling to find purchase in empty air. Jeff wondered if the break in consciousness was temporary, and this was just the first Prox to recover from the shock.

But then he heard a voice in his head. *If you do not mind, amigo, I could use* un poco de ayuda...*a little help.*

A comical image flashed in his mind of a Prox soldier wearing the ridiculous little bowler hat that had been perched on Tomás' head the first time Jeff had met him. He laughed out loud.

I do not see what is so funny, Tomás' voice complained.

"Sorry, *amigo*," Jeff said, struggling to his feet.

"What are you talking about?" Jo asked.

As soon as he felt solid, he offered Jo a hand up. She took it.

"It's Tomás. He's...talking in my head."

"Oh great. The psychologists are going to love you now."

"At least Osprey is dead."

"Who?"

"Never mind...another universe, another Jo."

"I am never going to get used to that."

"Neither am I. C'mon, Tomás needs our help."

By the limited, intermittent light of the torch Jeff picked his way through wreckage and the frozen, motionless bodies of innumerable Prox soldiers. He followed the motion of Tomás' pinwheeling legs until he was able to lay a hand on his friend's carapace. "I'm here, *amigo*," Jeff said. He looked behind him and held his hand out to Jo. She took it and he guided her beside him. "How do we do this?" Jeff asked.

I believe I can find a foothold on my left side, Tomás' voice said in his head. *If the two of you can push my right side up...once we get my carapace perpendicular, gravity should do the rest.*

"Right," Jeff said.

"Okay, you're hearing things I'm not hearing," Jo said. "So if you want my help, you need to read me in."

Jeff nodded. It was a reasonable request. "Tomás has a good foothold over there—you can see where the concrete has buckled, creating a ridge. He can get his pincers and legs fixed against that, no problem. We just need to tip him up and over."

"A Prox."

"Yeah."

"You and me." She sounded incredulous. "You realize that's like us trying to flip a shuttlecraft, right?"

She was right. He knew it. Then he had an idea.

"Tomás, we don't need to move you. You can just teleport out, and then back in the right position." It took a moment for Tomás to respond, and Jeff was amused that this had not occurred to his friend.

Soy un idiota, Tomás' voice said in his head. A split second later, Tomás winked out of sight, and then rematerialized upright, with all six of his legs beneath him.

"Feel better?" Jeff asked.

I would feel better in my own body, Tomás said.

"This body might have its advantages," Jeff reasoned.

It might indeed, Tomás agreed.

Jeff turned in a circle, taking in the wreckage of the place. "We did it."

"You're welcome," Jo said.

EPILOGUE

[STRING 308]

"We need to get back," Jo said.

The Prox soldiers lay where they fell, devoid of soul, will, or, it seemed, electricity. They were nothing more than silver hills dotting the smoky, apocalyptic landscape of the bunker's interior.

"There's something I have to do first," Jeff said.

He holstered his blaster and slung the carapace over his back. Then he set out for the room where the Ulim hung. Jeff heard a scrambling of metal legs on cement and flinched, ready to draw on whatever was coming up behind him. But it was only Tomás. The Prox-who-was-his-friend skittered in front of him to block his way.

Jeff, what are you doing? What do you intend?

Jeff halted and held up his hand. "No harm, *amigo*. I just want to talk. Trust me."

Tomás hesitated for a minute, then bowed slightly and backed up. It occurred to Jeff that he had not seen a Prox retreat before. It looked like an unnatural movement.

Jo fell into step behind him as he approached the nearest of the hanging Ulim. It was a woman. Jeff hovered over her and studied her.

She looked young, yet Jeff knew that it was only the chemicals that kept her so. She was, he reasoned, impossibly old. And now she was more alone than she had been in several thousand years.

Jeff slapped her face, and her eyes snapped open, large with surprise.

"Now you know what it's like to be cut off," Jeff said. "Now you know what it's like to be isolated." *Now you know what it's like to be me,* he thought. All the years of self-loathing after Catskill, all the hiding, the self-imposed exile, all the loneliness, it rushed in on him, flooding him with rancor, with bitterness, with rage. *These people started it all. They killed Danny. They twisted my soul into a hard, dark thing, curled in on itself, festering with guilt, with shame.*

But what did he want her to say? There was nothing she could say that would undo the damage. She could give no apology, even if she were inclined to offer one, that would give him his years of exile back, or that would restore the pieces of his soul that had been cut off and discarded over three universes. There were no possible words and no possible penance that could restore his Danny or his Jo.

But there was something he wanted to say to her. "You saved the wrong motherfucker. Everything you have built is gone, and you will never get it back. And if you try, I will come back here and tear your limbs from your miserable, atrophied bodies with my own fucking hands. That's not a threat, that's a promise." He waited a moment for that to sink in. Then he leaned in so that his nose was almost touching hers. "Now you have a new project. Now you must learn to live in isolation together. Just like the rest of us." As he was saying it, he realized that this was his mission now, too.

He straightened up and stepped away from her. "Now what?" he asked his friends.

Tomás' voice rang out in his head. *Now I will go back to my people.*

"Whoa! I heard that!" Jo said, clutching her head.

It would be rude to speak only to Jeff, Tomás explained.

"Okay, true, but a little warning…"

"What will you do?" Jeff asked, putting a hand on his friend's carapace.

Well, first, I must convince them that I am me, despite my appearance.

"Uh...I wish you luck with that. Now they'll have two reasons to hate you."

True. But as Lo Tan says, "At the extreme of yang, yin begins."

"I have no idea what that means," Jeff confessed.

Tomás did not explain. Instead he placed a metal claw on Jeff's shoulder, which would have nearly crushed him if Tomás had allowed him to bear the weight of it. *And then I will lead my people back here, where we will minister to* los Durmientes. *We will feed them and work their muscles and make their bodies strong again. We will teach them...how to be human.*

"*You,*" Jeff said, a smile breaking out across his face. "Are you going to teach *them* how to be human?"

"I am."

"You are the weirdest motherfucker I have ever met," Jeff said. Then his eyes grew moist. "And I'm going to miss the hell out of you."

Well, you can visit anytime, Tomás reminded him. *Now that you know how.*

"There may be times when I need you," Jeff said. "Especially, the new you. For one thing, I need help getting some things...and people...back to their proper places.

Then let us make haste. We have much to do if we want to save los Durmientes.

Jeff wasn't at all sure that saving the Ulim was at the top of his list, but he didn't argue with his friend.

[STRING 311]

"Is THERE anything else I can get for you, sir?" Liu asked.

Tal slouched in his chair, covering his face with one hand. His study had been unmolested by the Prox attack. He had been lucky in that. There were plenty who were not. Large barracks had been set up in the recreational centers with hundreds of makeshift cots and pallets in neat rows after the destruction of so many private quarters.

"Sir?"

"Oh, uh…no, Adrian. Thank you. I'll…I'll call if I need you."

"I'll just be in the next room, sir."

"Thank you."

The door slid shut after Liu. Tal was alone.

Tomorrow the work of cleanup and rebuilding would begin. Every time Tal shut his eyes, though, all he could see were the lifeless Prox floating away. He still half expected them to roar to life again, to turn around and finish the job.

There were plenty of rumors about what had happened to the creatures, why they had just suddenly shut down, but no one knew anything. Not really. The Abrahamic Union and other religious groups were saying it was the hand of God. *Maybe it was,* he thought. But Tal had little use for a God whose help came so late.

Suddenly he heard noises he couldn't account for. Close noises. Noises in his own room. He lifted his face out of his hand and opened his bleary eyes.

Then they went wide.

"Admiral," Jeff said.

Tal stood, his weariness and grief momentarily forgotten.

Captain Jeff Bowers stood in front of him, blaster drawn. A living Prox soldier stood behind him, almost too large to fit into his study. The creature had to stoop not to bash its head against the ceiling. Kneeling in front of Bowers was Captain Daniel Hightower.

Hightower looked like he'd been on the wrong side of a bar brawl. His hands were cuffed behind his back. He looked madder than a hornet.

"What is that—that—doing here?" Tal pointed to the Prox.

"Relax. He's with me. He's my muscle. He's on our side."

"He is?" Tal's voice cracked as he spoke.

Bowers smiled. "He is. I'll tell you the whole story…soon." He nudged Hightower with his boot. "Is this one yours?"

Tal locked eyes with Hightower. Hightower sneered.

"No, he is not." Tal met Bowers' eyes. It appeared to Tal that Bowers saw the truth in them, because he nodded, apparently satisfied.

"We were able to stop them," Bowers said. "The Prox, I mean. No thanks to him. Because of him…we almost didn't."

"If you are the one that made them stop…then I owe you my life, and the life of everyone on board. Not to mention the life of everyone on Earth." Tal looked down at his desk. "It's too bad it came too late… for so many."

"I saw the wreckage on our way in. Horrible. I'm sorry. That's… what we were trying to stop."

"That's not the half of it. I had just given the order for the civilians to take the Happy Ending pills," Tal said. He looked up to meet Jeff's eyes. "That's when you stopped them, I guess. We were able to belay the order…but not before the children ..." He saw Bowers wince, the pain on his face evident. "They're calling it the Children's Massacre. People are already wearing black armbands. Even soldiers. I'm not stopping them. People need…"

"They need to grieve," Bowers said.

"Yeah."

Tal sat.

Bowers holstered his blaster. "While you were fighting them here, I was with the RFC fighting them…elsewhere. We prevailed. You don't owe your life to me…or not only to me, is what I'm saying. Captain Joleen Taylor of the Revolutionary Freedom Coalition saved you, along with her crew."

Tal nodded, feeling a momentary spin of vertigo. "If that's true, the implications of that are…substantial."

"It's true. I'm hoping that we can make good use of this moment. I'd like to suggest that you and Admiral Alinto of the RFC have a private meeting first before bringing in the civilian authorities."

"I would be…open to a clandestine meeting," Tal affirmed.

"Good. That's a start then." Jeff stepped over to where Hightower was kneeling. "Can I trust you to take care of this one?"

"He stole one of our ships and took himself and his entire crew

AWOL," Tal said. "He's not going anywhere anytime soon. I can promise you that."

"Good. From what I've heard, the Authority's penalties are a good bit more severe than the RFC, so I thought I'd let you deal with your own."

"We are obliged to you for that, too, then."

"I wasn't alone," Hightower spat.

Jeff's eyebrows furrowed. "What are you talking about?"

"I had an inside man on the *Talon*. I didn't do it alone. If I'm going down, I want to make sure he goes down with me."

"Who?" Jeff asked.

"Palamar."

"No shit." Jeff sighed and shook his head. "I'll let Jo know. It'll kill her, but she needs to know."

"You do that."

Jeff kicked Hightower over and put his boot on the man's neck. "Now there's just one more thing that I need from you before I'm through with you forever."

Tal rose and walked around his desk so that he was standing beside Bowers, staring down at Hightower. He was aware that there was a live Prox soldier breathing down his neck, but he suspected he was hallucinating half of this anyway and decided to just flow with it.

"You remember Emma, don't you, Admiral Tal?" Bowers asked without looking at him.

"Middle-aged woman, just a little younger than you. Quantum seismologist."

"That's her," Jeff acknowledged. "Not long after we left here and docked at Epworth Station, she disappeared. And there's only one person I know of in this universe shit enough to do something like that." He pressed his boot down. Hightower squirmed, turning red. "So, I want to ask you first, Admiral Tal—as a man of honor, did you have Dr. Emma Stewart kidnapped?"

"I did not, Captain. You have my word."

"Well, since no one else in this universe even knew we existed, that leaves this miserable motherfucker." He lifted his boot off Hightower's neck. Danny sputtered and wheezed, trying to gain a lungful of air. Jeff knelt near Hightower's head and spoke softly. "Danny, we were friends once. I want to know what you did with Emma. Where is she?"

EMMA SAT at a table near the back of the restaurant, though someone coming in from the front might not have seen her because of the stack of plates she'd accumulated. She ecstatically ate the last of her of Caribbean-style shrimp, chewing slowly, then licking the cayenne pepper and salt off her fingers. She was so lost in reverie that she didn't notice anyone approach until he spoke.

"Emma?"

As she looked up from the double order of escargot, her eyes grew suddenly wide with delight. "Jeff!" she squealed, leaping out of her chair, throwing her arms around him, and squeezing as hard as she could.

"Jesus," he grunted. "Have you been working out?"

After a moment she released him, then realized she'd smeared grease and spices all over Jeff's crisp, clean uniform. "Oh god! I'm sorry, let me get that…" She turned back toward the table to grab a napkin, but Jeff caught her by the wrist.

"Forget about that! Are you okay?"

She noticed the look of concern—bordering on panic—on his face. "What? I'm fine! Why?"

Now he looked angry. "Because you were kidnapped! Why do you think?"

Confusion crossed Emma's face, then she burst out laughing, which didn't seem to help Jeff at all. "Yeah, I guess I was! It's not like that though, not really."

Jeff struggled to understand. "Really? Then maybe you'd like to explain why I just had to pay your ransom!"

"You what?"

"The woman I talked to said that even though I wasn't the original client, I still had to pay the price Danny had agreed to if I wanted to get you back, and it wasn't small."

"Damn it, Amberline… I'm so sorry, Jeff. I'll pay you back…"

Jeff stared at her speechless. "I don't …"

"No! Of course you don't! Sit down, I'll explain. Would you like something to eat? I'm absolutely stuffed, but I can't stop eating. This place is amazing!"

Jeff slowly pulled out a chair and sat, surveying the carnage on the table. "Yeah, apparently…"

Emma also sat, laughing at the pile of dishes. "Sorry, it's been a while since I've had any real food. I've been living on *poi* and man-meat so long, I guess I got carried away."

Jeff stared. "Man meat...?"

Emma laughed again. "It's so good to see you! I have so much to tell you, I don't even know where to start."

"How about starting with where you've been?"

She opened her mouth, then stopped. "Actually, I can't tell you that."

Jeff's brow furled. "I looked for you, you know. I searched the entire universe for you, *literally.* And I should have been able to find you. When I go into the All, I can see everything. I can see *everyone.* And you weren't there. I was afraid you might be…" He couldn't finish the thought. "But then I got my hands on Danny."

She gasped. "Is he still alive?"

Jeff smiled darkly. "Just barely."

"It was him, wasn't it? He set me up?"

He nodded, scowling, furious. "Yes. And I still can't figure out how he hid you so well. I'm a little creeped out by it, if you want to know the truth. How could Danny know enough about my…ability…to find a way to hide you from me?"

"He didn't, he just got lucky. It was really the people he paid to take me."

"And when I get my hands on them…"

Emma shook her head slowly and gently put her hand on his. "No. They are really… *interesting* people."

Jeff stared at her, incredulous. "Is this what Stockholm syndrome looks like?"

"No!" She laughed. "I know it sounds strange, but even though what happened to me did *start* as a kidnapping, it turned into something different. Yeah, I've been working my ass off, and the food has been *terrible*. But I've stumbled onto something very interesting and important."

Jeff looked hurt—no, annoyed. "Well, I'm glad you've been having a good time while we've been out risking our lives and saving the universe!"

Her joviality melted away. "I figured you'd all be lying low. Wasn't that the plan?"

"Since when do plans ever go as…uh, planned."

"Never. At least certainly not for us!"

He looked away.

"Hey," she said, taking his hand. "You don't have to worry about that. I understand. And I'm okay, really. You lost someone you loved, and she came back from the dead. That's pretty extraordinary! You *did* find her, yes?"

He nodded. "How did you know?"

She barked a laugh. "Have you met you? You're not hard to read."

He smiled reluctantly.

"And your shaman? You found him too?"

"Yeah, I did. And good thing. We ended up fighting the Prox again."

Her eyes snapped open with fear. "Prox? Here? In this string? Oh shit!" Her eyes darted around as though looking for an escape route.

"Don't worry, we took care of it."

She paused a moment, taking in the implications, the sheer magnitude of what he'd just said. "You found a way to beat them?"

He nodded. "Just barely. But it turned out the Ulim were running them the whole time. I had to fight *them* instead. A lot has changed. A lot of good people died in the fight. We lost Suzi Wall, I'm pretty sure she was on a spaceliner that the Prox took out. And Pho was killed in an altercation with one of the locals."

She looked down. “I’m sad to hear it. They were good kids. I liked them.”

Jeff nodded solemnly, then shook his head. “Look, we can do this on the ship. There’s so much to catch up on.”

Emma shook her head. ”I’m not coming with you.”

“What? You’re going *back*?”

“Well, I have some shopping to do first…”

“The alien I paid the ransom to said you are free to go.”

She smiled, thinking of Amberline. “I am. But I have something I’m working on, something *big.* It’s going to re-write a lot of what we know about string theory.”

“And you can’t work on it with us?”

“I’m afraid not. And to be honest, I don’t want to.”

“Wow.”

She saw the hurt in his face. “It’s not like that! It has nothing to do with you, or us, or any of that. I’ve found a place, a group of people, who really need me. I can make a difference with them, and in turn, I’ll be making a difference for the whole universe. You don’t need me anymore, and I’m happy for you.”

He couldn’t argue. “Well then, if it’s what you really want, I’m happy for you too. Just be careful. Don’t destroy a universe like I did.”

She saw the pain darken his face. “Yeah, about that. What if I told you that you didn’t?”

“Of course I did. I’m not trying to shift that responsibility to…”

“You didn’t destroy String 310.”

“Who did then?”

“Nobody, you dumb oaf, listen to me! String 310 wasn’t destroyed. It was just… *moved.*”

What? Moved?”

She nodded, smiling. “And I know where it is!”

His jaw dropped. “Well let’s go home then!”

“It’s not that simple. The region of space it’s in is an isolated subset of String 311.”

“How is it isolated?”

"Somehow, it's been rotated in four-space so that it's out of phase with…" She noted his glassy expression. "It's difficult to explain."

"To a dumb soldier like me, you mean."

"To anyone. Just take it as isolated. You can't get there from here."

Jeff puffed up his chest. "You forget, I can go *anywhere.*"

She smiled. "Believe me, I haven't forgotten, I know that better than anyone. But this is an unusual situation, even by our standards!" They laughed, then just sat a moment, smiling at each other. "Trust me on this. I have some work to do first. There's a lot to learn, a lot of calculation to do. Luckily, I'll have a lot of help working the problem. And once it's sorted, I'll contact you."

"It's a lot to take in. I thought I'd killed, well, *everyone.*"

"You can let go of that guilt now. I've got our old universe in a bag on a shelf, safe and sound. And I'm fairly certain that Earth—*our Earth*—is somewhere in that bag, and I'm going to find it."

Jeff beamed at her. "You really are amazing."

She nodded. "So I've been told."

"And you're really going back to, well, wherever you were?"

"Yup."

"Okay then."

"Okay."

"This is weird."

"It really is."

"Can I have a hug before you go?"

She smiled and stood, holding her arms out wide. Internally, she reflexively tried to open her smaller sub-arms as well, but since she wasn't wearing the prosthesis, nothing happened. She laughed at herself and wrapped her arms around Jeff again, pulling him close, smelling him, his skin, his fresh uniform, his after-shave. Her heart was breaking, but it was as much with fullness as it was with loss.

Jeff felt weary as he stepped aboard the *Horatio Nelson.* How long had it been since he'd slept? Too fucking long. He felt beat up and traumatized and exhausted—up until the present moment, getting clean and rest and writing up reports were objects in the distance. He could see them, and they were true, but none could be acknowledged or addressed, not yet, not now.

But now…the image of a hot bath flashed through his head. Such a thing was impossible on a warship, but it was a nice fantasy. He stumbled once as he made his way to the bridge, the weariness finally catching up to him.

When the door to the bridge slid open, Jo swiveled her chair around to greet him with a full smile. Looking around, Jeff saw Ditka and the rest of Jo's A-team. He gave them a quick but friendly nod. Nira was there, too, in her position as XO. He winked at her.

"Come," Jo said, rising from her seat and heading for her ready room.

"Yes, sir," Jeff answered, and followed her. When the door closed, she kissed him.

"Hello, Captain," he said.

"Hello, Captain," she returned.

"Do I always have to call you that?"

"Only in front of the crew," she said. "In private, you can call me…" She looked up, thinking. When she met his eyes again, there was a girlish, playful smile on her lips.

"You're solo," she noted, changing the subject.

"I'm solo," he confirmed. It occurred to him that those two words contained many layers of meaning, all of them true.

"She's not coming with us?"

"That's what she says."

"Why the fuck not?"

Jeff shrugged. "She says she's onto something."

"You mean a suspicious-woman something or a science something?"

He held her close, enjoying the warmth of her. "The latter. Whatever it is, she said it's big. We need to leave her an ansible."

"Like hell. Do you think this pile of crap has a spare ansible aboard?"

"We just need to let command know that we're giving ours away so they don't worry. We'll get a new one installed at the next port. Besides…this ship isn't going to be your permanent post. We have to return it to the Authority, so what the fuck do you care?"

"Spoils of war."

"Or an olive branch." He kissed her nose.

"Hm. Well, when you put it like that… Funny you should mention command, though. Alinto wants to see you, so command is our next stop."

"What's she want with me?"

"Probably to give you a shiny piece of crap to hang on your uniform."

"I don't have a uniform…" That wasn't true. He was wearing one. But the thought of it, of what he had lost, of being clothed in what amounted to a field of ghosts… He shuddered. "I don't have a uniform that stands for anything…not anymore."

"Don't be too sure about that. She wants you to mediate the talks between the RFC and the Authority. Then she wants to propose a joint, elite RFC-Authority military unit, headed by you, of course."

He scowled and cocked his head. He wasn't sure how he felt about that. He was here, after all. Now that the enemy was defeated, what was he going to do, become a short order cook? He would need to do something, or he would go stir-crazy very quickly. "I don't know. This…this place is *like* home…but it *isn't* home."

"Well, where the hell else are you going to go?"

He looked away.

"Hey," Jo said, putting her hand on his chest. "Isn't there anything about this universe that you like? If you spend enough time here, you might warm up to it."

"I like the fact that your ships aren't crawling with spiders." Jeff tried not to smile but failed.

"It's also got me."

Jeff nodded, still not looking at her. "I was kind of hoping to go off by myself for a while…you know, sort through some shit." He swore more when he was around Jo. He liked that.

"Yeah, well…I figured you'd feel that way, being *you* and all. But…" she pointed at his heart with her index finger, "mature adults don't give into their base impulses and temptations. It's what makes them *mature*."

He blinked. "Well, when you put it like that—"

"Plus, you're a soldier. You wouldn't know what to do with yourself if you weren't a soldier. And a soldier goes where he's needed and does what must be done."

"Royfeld's class. Theory and Art of War."

"I still remember a thing or two from the academy. Besides all that…" she met his eyes, and looked into them, deeper than he had permitted anyone to see in a very long time, "*you* found *me*. Do you really want to let me go again so quickly?"

She was right, of course. He couldn't lose her again, not after all they had been through. And because words are inadequate, he answered her with a kiss.

A note from the authors:

THANKS so much for reading our book—we hope you enjoyed it! If you can, please post an honest review at amazon or whichever site you purchase books from. It doesn't have to be long, just a sentence or two with your feelings and opinions. It helps authors so much when you leave a review, and we'd be so grateful for yours! Thank you for taking the time, and thanks for reading!

—J.R. Mabry & B.J. West

If you enjoyed this book, please try...

"If you found God
—or if God found you—
would that be a good thing?"

Chaplaincy instructor Jun Battacharya only needs one more tour of duty to retire, and he is determined that his last semester will be quiet and uneventful. But the very day he lands on the planet Skagway a mining accident forces him to launch his students into action with zero training.

Jun is certain that if they can just get through the crisis, everything will quiet down and go back to normal. Then Jun receives a letter from the native alien species—specifically from their ranking clergy—inviting him and his students to attend their most sacred ritual.

Jun is fascinated to discover that the aliens worship Mystery—whatever is unseen or unknown is sacred to them. He considers this an intriguing but quaint theology, but when the humans arrive for the ritual, each of them—in very different ways—has an encounter with Mystery that brings the world as they know it to an end...

In the tradition of Mary Doria Russell's *The Sparrow* and Michael Faber's *The Book of Strange New Things*, J.R. Mabry's *The Worship of Mystery* goes to the farthest points of known space to explore the dark regions of the human heart.

Begin *The Worship of Mystery* today!

If you enjoyed this book, please try...

THE STOLEN SKY

And Other Strange Tales

by B.J. West

Many who wander are, in fact, quite lost...

• A gifted veterinarian discovers a way to possess the bodies of the birds he should be caring for and steal their places in the sky…

• A young man struggles to move past the trauma from an event in his childhood, until it returns to claim him once again…

• An astronaut finds himself alone on Mars, utterly cut off from the rest of humanity…

• An up-and-coming artist is confronted with the inhuman artifact that was once his wife…

• A film student stumbles upon a tragic secret in the basement of his college campus…

If you enjoyed this book, please try…

An unhinged tycoon.
A lodge of evil magicians.
A plan to steal every child
from the face of the earth.

Fr. Richard Kinney is having a crappy week. He's not at all sure he's the best leader for the demon-hunting Berkeley Blackfriars, his boyfriend has just broken up with him, and his last exorcism did *not* go well.

Kat Webber is in over her head. After discovering her brother's comatose body in the midst of a demonic ritual, her heart sinks as she realizes he was up to something sketchy…maybe even evil.

Reaching out to the Blackfriars for help, Kat and Richard uncover a lodge of evil magickians who make every avocado in the world disappear—then every dog.

It's a race against time as Kat and the Blackfriars try to stop the magickians from eliminating their next target—every child on earth.

Fans of *Buffy the Vampire Slayer, Preacher, The Dresden Files*, and the Mercy Thompson series will love this spine-tingling yet humorous supernatural suspense novel.

Enter *The Kingdom* today!